THE AUTHOR: Morio Kita was born in 1927, second son of Mokichi Saito, perhaps the greatest traditional Japanese poet of this century. (A portrait of his father is given in the character Tetsukichi, although the reader should be aware that this is no closer to real life than any character in a novel, as is also the case with the self-portrait provided by Shuji.) Kita entered medical school at Tohoku University in 1948, but attended few classes since he had already decided to become a writer, concentrating instead on the novels of Thomas Mann, who was to become a lasting influence on his literature. During his student days he began taking notes for a novel, which he hoped eventually to write along the lines of *Buddenbrooks*; this was to be *The House of Nire*. In 1953, the year his father died, he passed the state qualifying medical exam, and in the following year published his first novel, *Ghosts*, a lyrical autobiography concerned mainly with the deaths of his parents, sister and friends. In November of 1958 he became ship's doctor on a six-month voyage to Europe, recorded in his humorous novel *Dr. Manbo at Sea*, which appeared in 1960 and became a bestseller. In 1960 he also received his M.D. for a study of schizophrenics. The first draft of *The House of Nire* was written in 1961 and the novel completed in 1963, receiving the Mainichi Prize in the following year and establishing him as a leading writer. It is his first novel to be translated into English.

THE HOUSE OF NIRE

Morio Kita

Translated by Dennis Keene

KODANSHA INTERNATIONAL
Tokyo and New York

Jacket illustration by Kazuyoshi Iino.

Publication of this translation was assisted by a grant from the Japan Foundation.

Originally published by Shinchosha, Tokyo, under the title *Nireke no hitobito*. Kodansha International's hardcover edition of the work was in two volumes: *The House of Nire* (1984) and *The Fall of the House of Nire* (1985). These have been combined in this paperback edition.

Distributed in the United States by Kodansha International/USA Ltd., 114 Fifth Avenue, New York, New York 10011. Published by Kodansha International Ltd., 17-14 Otowa 1-chome, Bunkyo-ku, Tokyo 112 and Kodansha International/USA Ltd. Copyright © 1984, 1985 by Kodansha International Ltd. All rights reserved. Printed in Japan.
LCC 83-48876
ISBN 0-87011-859-5 (U.S.)
ISBN 4-7700-1506-2 (Japan)
First edition, 1984, 1985
First paperback edition, 1990

I

WELL DONE

Chapter

1

The kitchen or, more properly, the cookhouse at the rear of the Nire Hospital was in a state of hectic activity, for the midday meal was being prepared. Four monster pots were steaming on the kitchen range, each capable of holding a bushel of rice, which was hardly surprising since the family, staff and other dependents of the hospital numbered almost a hundred, and there were three hundred and thirty-eight patients, all of whom had to be fed.

The fire in the range had been raked out some time before, and water sprinkled on the ashes and remnants of firewood, which still lay scattered here and there on the concrete floor, smoldering halfheartedly. This mess was a tribute to the industry of those who were preparing the food. Obviously they did not have time to concern themselves with that sort of thing, and also, a more important reason, it was the old man's job, the old man being one Isuke, who had been preparing the food at the hospital for a good fifteen years, and was, as is normally the case with such people, an awkward-minded cuss who refused to let others poke their nose into his business.

After keeping everyone in suspense for some moments, Isuke slowly and majestically raised the heavy lid from the first giant pot. Into the already sultry air of the cookhouse entered thick clouds of scalding steam, with its clammy and familiar odor. Isuke raised the great wooden spoon with both hands and, as if wielding a paddle, plunged it into a bucket of hot water, and then began stirring the hot, swollen rice, which was done to a turn. In order to thrust his spoon down to the bottom of the pot, the diminutive Isuke was obliged to stand on a wooden stool, and as he stirred the rice about, the great hunch on his back became prominent, protruding further the further he leaned forward.

His clothing was also of a kind to arouse little but distaste. Since he was in charge of the feeding, one might have expected some suggestion of hygiene, if not of style, about his person, but his shabby kimono was so begrimed it was difficult to work out if it had originally been striped or not, and the same doubt applied to the coarse apron he wore. This overall black motif extended to his face and hands, which had become so ingrained over the years with the various soots of his trade that they created a startling contrast to the white of the freshly boiled rice. The overtly professional manner in which he whirled the rice about emphasized the weirdness, even absurdity, of his presence, and tended also to give an exaggerated impression of his years; for Isuke was in fact at that sad age when one should not yet be referred to as an old man.

Various attempts had been made to improve his appearance, but they had all ended in failure. As he said, he had his own ways of doing things, and when they made him put on some smock or other which did not feel right, he was unable to get the rice cooked the way it should be. It was just like the doctor's moustache (and here he was referring to the Director of the Nire Hospital himself): he had to have it all twirled and sticking out—if he didn't, he couldn't work out what was wrong with the people who were sick. It was no different in Isuke's case, and, anyway, his obstinacy was inherited from his father, and there was obviously nothing he could do about that. His brother, who had passed away some time ago, had been just like him, too.

Isuke also caused problems over his injections. The nature of his employment made it essential that he be inoculated against things like typhoid and cholera, but he had no intention of submitting tamely to ordeals of so suspect a nature. He maintained that he trusted in the protection of His Holiness Saint Kobo Daishi, and that he was immune to these diseases, even if the rest of the hospital came down with them. One last resort had been to leap on him as he took his afternoon nap, but he managed to struggle and kick his way free, escaping into a bamboo grove in an obscure part of the hospital grounds, naked except for a loincloth, and adamantly refusing to come out. Further attempts had similar results, and this was why the official cook and rice boiler of the hospital had managed to avoid having even one injection during all his many years of service.

But everyone admitted that the rice he used was of high quality and tasted excellent as well. Ever since the Rice Riots in the summer of this year of 1918, it had been difficult for him to maintain his previous high standard, for he was occasionally obliged to mix imported rice with the native product; but this did not prevent the Director of the hospital, Dr. Kiichiro Nire, from maintaining that the rice eaten in his hospital was the finest in Japan (though it must be admitted that the doctor was in the habit of referring to a great many things as being "the finest in Japan").

Shrouded in the billowing steam from the pots, Isuke completed his assured and professional stirrings and then uttered the unnaturally long, guttural howl that marked the end of this ceremony: "R-E-A-D-Y." At this signal, all the scattered members of staff assembled and began transferring the rice from the pots into the bowls. Something resembling gravy was then ladled onto each bowl of rice from another large pot. The aluminum bowls were lined up on trolleys and wheeled away, making a great clatter as they went. This lively scene was repeated three times a day, a ritual that could (rightly, perhaps) be considered the center of daily life at the hospital.

But recently events had occurred that seemed to threaten changes in the usual tenor of the place. In September the Terauchi cabinet had fallen, and the fact that his successor, Takashi Hara, was the first commoner to become Prime Minister was a constant topic of discussion at mealtimes in the Nire Hospital. The reason for this was that the head and Director of the hospital, Kiichiro himself, had become an elected Diet member at the same time and belonged to Hara's Seiyukai Party. To mark the occasion, he had provided all the members of his staff with a feast of sea bream, though the bream offered to the young interns were so small they swallowed them down like sardines, bones and all. Then, a little after that, Germany, a country full of hardworking, dedicated people, was eventually defeated. Even the remarkable Kaiser—though for the Japanese that impressive title meant principally a moustache, and for the people of the Nire Hospital the moustache was their Director's—had been worn down by the whole exhausting business.

The ordinary citizens of Tokyo had shown something close to total indifference to this war, and were therefore all the more disposed to enjoy the festive atmosphere that appeared suddenly from nowhere. In Hibiya Park in the center of Tokyo a triumphal arch was set up, colorfully decorated with the flags of the victorious Allies, and a number of people were injured in the resulting crush as crowds jostled to get a good look at it. The enthusiasm was scarcely surprising for it was decorated with many fascinating things. There was a large, broken beer barrel apparently representing the failure of German militarism, since it was labeled "The Militant Cup"; and a mock-up of a weasel about twenty feet long, with "Cease-Fire and Peace Restored" written on

5

it in characters that were clearly meant to be amusing since they alluded indelicately to the weasel's habit of loosing a huge fart as the culmination of its death pangs. Unfortunately, the wit was so obscure that almost no one seemed to grasp the joke. There was also a hanged effigy of the Kaiser himself. At night there were lantern processions, and streetcars with floral decorations ran during the day.

As a result, there was always somebody or other from the hospital who had been into town and returned with the news, so that even the lowliest cleaner, or patients who never once set foot outside the hospital, had the feeling that they too had observed these memorable events. For example, one of the decorated streetcars caught fire somewhere in the Shiba district, and this was witnessed by a young male nurse who had only recently been taken on at the hospital, and who was slightly weak in the head. It had been the first time he had ever gone sightseeing in Tokyo, so he had been extremely fortunate.

"Well, there I was, and, suddenly, there it was, all sparks and things and flames licking out, over the drapes and the flags—the whole lot went up. And then the steam pump came right off. Pop it went, the steam pump—came flying right off."

On hearing this, the lady who ran the small store in the hospital and who belonged to the cranky Tenri sect exclaimed that those decorated streetcars were very dangerous things, indeed they were, and she added a few mild imprecations designed to ward off evil.

But, to return to the actual affairs of the hospital: even though the formation of the Hara cabinet and the German defeat were godsends to the life of the place, a more pressing concern was that Prize-Giving Day would soon be upon them, an event of particular importance this year since it would also mark the fifteenth anniversary of the setting up of the hospital in the Aoyama district of Tokyo. The fact that this ceremony would shortly be followed by the pounding of *mochi*, or rice cakes, at the end of the year, and then by the New Year celebrations themselves, was something that appealed not only to those interns and nurses whose main concern in life was with stuffing themselves.

The coldness of winter already dominated the world outside the sultry warmth of the cookhouse. Two or three mangy hounds fought over the remains of food in the rusting tin drums that served as refuse containers. These stray dogs had taken up residence in the empty field next to the hospital, and no matter how often they were driven away they would patiently insist on coming back. The branches of the great ginkgo tree by the side of the bathhouse were now quite bare, and seemed to be looking north as if awaiting the winds of winter. The bath-house was an aspect of the hospital on which the Director particularly prided himself. It was true that it was not much to look at, the inade-quate heap of coal piled against the side wall only adding to an impres-sion of chilly gloom. But the bath inside was tiled and of generous size, and had a mysterious whirlpool pattern of lead piping at the bottom. It was claimed to possess remarkable curative powers, since it was a real radium bath, although even the Director was unable to give a precise explanation as to why a radium bath should be of any use whatsoever. Nevertheless, in the hospital's printed publicity great emphasis was placed on this radium bath, in language of pretentious elegance.

At a slight remove from the bathhouse was a row of cramped houses of indeterminate nature. Their size and age were not immediately ap-parent, but it was clear that the cluttered buildings offered no kind of superior accommodation. These were the quarters for the hospital staff, and here five or six, sometimes as many as fifteen or sixteen, interns lived. These interns had a lower status than their present-day counterparts, being more like glorified houseboys. Ever since the ear-ly days of the hospital, when it was a mere clinic in the Hongo district of Tokyo, the Director, Kiichiro, had been in the habit of choosing such people either because they were from his home town or because of some personal connection, however slight. There had been a con-siderable number of these unsalaried members of his staff, who were household dependents rather than actual employees. They helped around the hospital, studied medicine, took their examinations, and finally became doctors. Most of the doctors and pharmacists in the hospital had begun their careers in this way. Certainly there were some who had never passed their exams and had never seemed likely to, but the Director managed to find them some kind of suitable work. There were even some who spent years simply lazing around the hospital, doing nothing except eating, and others who disappeared one day and never came back; but this reprehensible behavior never disturbed the Director, since educating these young men was something he en-joyed.

Kiichiro was never angry, or at least he never showed his anger. He always had a friendly word and a smile for everyone. His sincerity was perhaps suspect, and no doubt his words sounded like empty flat-tery much of the time. Yet he was affable to all, even to those who were as useless as the proverbial cat. There was, for example, the par-ticularly idle student who, for some unspecified reason, happened to have got up early one morning and was standing about in the corridor by the main entrance hall. He was in the constant habit of assuring people that he had come to Tokyo to study medicine and not merely to sweep corridors. But, for all the impressiveness of this statement, he studied very little, and was the object of certain grudging remarks from his colleagues of which he was aware and which had not served to mellow his disposition. So he stood this morning in the corridor looking particularly determined not to sweep it, when he realized that, despite the early hour, the Director was approaching. Kiichiro bestowed a friendly smile upon him, and the affable greeting of "Well done." This was said in a gentle tone and in the Director's usual manner, his head tilted slightly upward as if he were talking with his chin rather than his mouth. The result was that the intern felt not only slightly put out but half resentful as well. So he replied:

"But sir, I'm doing nothing, so how can I be doing well?"

"Not at all, my boy. Your mere presence here so early in the morning creates an active, expectant air in the hospital. The place seems full of life, positively thriving. Well done. Carry on the good work."

Incidents like this were by no means rare, but one should not suspect Kiichiro of sarcasm, or even of gentle irony, since it seems undeniable that he genuinely meant exactly what he said.

The jumble of houses near the bathhouse were the residences not only of the excessive number of people who were attached to the hospital in some capacity, but also of the sons and daughters of the place and the real servants. These dwellings had sprung up more as a result of contingency than of reason, so the chaotic appearance they presented was inevitable. How great a difference when compared with the imposing facade of the main hospital, that view from the front gate for which the epithet "majestic" seemed not inappropriate. These rear quarters, from the cookhouse via the great bathhouse to the higgledy-piggledy houses, possessed the same organic confusion as the shabby back streets of any large city and presented a sad contrast to that outward magnificence.

One of these houses, a two-storied affair, was slightly better than the others, and this housed the Director's family, but not the Director himself, nor his wife. Where, then, were they living? The answer is that they lived "within." The building that greeted the newcomer on his arrival at the main gate of the hospital was one of palatial splendor, built (or so it seemed at the first casual glance) of marble. Its right wing consisted of private rooms for well-to-do patients, while its left wing housed the office, a waiting room and clinic for outpatients, and (its principal feature) those special rooms where the Director and his wife lived. These were at the end of a long corridor, and it was this inner status that had led to the whole complex of their living quarters being referred to briefly as "within." Few of the numerous employees of the hospital were actually acquainted with these rooms. A heavy black door sealed them off, and a private maid attended to the needs of the two "within," no unauthorized person being permitted beyond the door. The lower members of staff would often gossip about the rooms, maintaining that there was a really "super" Western-style lavatory, that the double bed there had been brought all the way from Germany by the learned Director himself, and that the pink walls were decorated in such a way as to excite the imaginations of both sexes. This admiration was not entirely uncritical, for nearly every newcomer to the hospital would remark, at least to himself, that if the rooms were as luxurious and numerous as gossip said, he could not see why the children of the house did not live there but were stuck away in the housing round the back.

The voices of what seemed to be two of these children (or perhaps only one) could now be heard coming from the downstairs of the unimpressive two-storied house at the back. They were singing one of those children's round-like chants in the flat monotone usual for such songs. One of the voices was the high-pitched squeak of a small child, but the other, judging from the weary way it kept going off key, seemed to belong to someone considerably older.

"Out from Aoyama Cemetery
Three white ghosts come gliding, three.
Three red ghosts come following after.
Last of all a student boy
With big, floppy breeches on:
Flippety, floppety, flap."

The little girl who was playing in this way was Kiichiro's third daughter. Today was Sunday, so Momoko did not have to go to school. The woman with her was known as Nanny Shimoda; plump and kindly-looking, she was the image of the old nurse who would sacrifice her own child to care for her master's offspring, an image which even at this time was already a generation out of date.

Her full name was Nao Shimoda, and in her youth she had graduated from the Nursing School of Tokyo Imperial University Hospital with honors. She had then been employed at the Red Cross Hospital, and if she had persisted in her career she would no doubt have become a fully-fledged matron by now. But she had made a bad marriage; the useless man had run away, and the little boy he had left her with had died of malnutrition. So Kiichiro had invited her to come to his hospital. It is true that she came from the same district as himself, but a more important reason was that he had realized some time before what a treasure she was. So she worked as a nurse while the hospital was still only a clinic in Hongo, and after the move to Aoyama she became chief sister and was in charge of all the nurses. But she was more a member of the family than a member of the staff, indeed almost more important than a mere member of the family, for her status was that of a nurse to all the children, though she had suckled none of them. When Kiichiro's wife had become ''indisposed,'' Nao had looked after the eldest daughter, Ryuko, and brought up the four children that followed. So Nanny Shimoda had become an indispensable servant of the household, and she gave such an impression of belonging that one might imagine she had been there a hundred years, although she was, in fact, younger than the head of the house. She was fifty years old. Still, the common wisdom of the time believed that the normal span of human life was two (rather than three) score and ten, so she could have been considered elderly. Perhaps there was some significance in the fact that she was the same age as the lady of the house, for the doctor's wife, Hisa, was also fifty.

The child, Momoko, was in the fifth grade at the local Seinan Primary School, so it was too early to be sure what she would look like when she was grown up, although it was already apparent that she would lack the elegant features of her two elder sisters. She had a snub nose, her forehead protruded above her eyebrows, and although her eyes rolled about in a friendly way, they were a little too animated for the cool standards of classical beauty. Still, that was not her fault, and she was well aware that she was much better liked by everyone in the hospital than either of her two sisters. She was a bright, forward child, but was still able to succumb to the kind of childish play in which she was absorbed now, so absorbed that the sweat ran down the runnels at the side of her tiny nose.

She clapped her hands smartly as a signal to start all over again, and then began patting the palms of her companion in the intervals between clapping her own, all in time with the rhythm of the song she sang:

> "Out from Aoyama Cemetery
> Three white ghosts come gliding. . ."

The climax of the game was that both should link forearms on the words "flippety, floppety," and then, on the word "flap," flash out their hands in the shape of either "paper," "scissors" or "stone." Momoko went on persistently winning, while Nanny Shimoda went on indifferently losing, though never once suggesting that the game should be brought to an end.

The saucepan on the small charcoal fire in the earthenware pot, or *hibachi*, beside Nanny Shimoda began to boil. This contained rice gruel for Momoko's brother, who was two years younger than her and in bed in the next room with flu. Momoko and her brother ate the same cookhouse food as the people in the hospital, though when the fare was unusually plain they were allowed some compensatory extras. In fact, except for those "within," all the members of the Nire family ate the common food, with the added disadvantage that they got it much later than everyone else since they were served after the patients. Momoko was still absorbed in her game, unaware that it was past lunchtime and that she had not yet eaten and should be very hungry.

But her younger brother, Yonekuni, knew that he, at least, was hungry, and his moans could be heard through the thick paper sliding door that separated his room from this one.

"Who cares about your flippety, floppety, flap? I want my food. Isn't my gruel ready yet? I'm hungry. I'm starving. . ."

This was the way he would grumble if he thought one of his sisters might overhear, but it was followed by an authentic-sounding series of coughs and wheezes, like a dog howling far off. This year there had been an epidemic of a particularly virulent form of Spanish influenza, and the baby of the family had inevitably succumbed, since he was prone to illness and would regularly catch colds when nobody else had them.

His name was also a misfortune, a result of Kiichiro's liking for the bogus exotic. "Yonekuni" was written with two characters which, in their normal reading of "Beikoku," are the Japanese for "America." His elder brother, who was six years older than Momoko and thus eight above Yonekuni, was called Oshu, which is the Japanese for "Europe," and in his case the obvious geographical meaning had not been disguised by any alternative reading of the two characters used. This elder brother had been born the year before Kiichiro went to Europe to further his scholastic researches, and Yonekuni in the year the doctor undertook a trip to the United States. Luckily, informed opinion, in the shape of the priest in Kiichiro's home town, had insisted that "Beikoku" would be too much of a burden for anybody, and Kiichiro had consented that the two characters of the name should be read as "Yonekuni." And these were not the only linguistic oddities in the family: the older girls' names, Ryuko ("Dragon child") and Seiko ("Holy child"), were certainly in advance of their times, and the doctor's surname was a fake made up to satisfy his pretensions as to what a really smart name should be. "Nire" is the Japanese for "elm tree," and it is doubtful that anyone before Kiichiro had ever borne such an extraordinary surname. It was very different from the name handed down to him by his father, which had patently bucolic implications.

Momoko, who of all the family had the most commonplace name, merely "Peach" plus "child," such as any girl might have had, sat listening to her brother's moans in the neighboring room and decided she would think of something objectionable to say just to teach him a lesson. In fact, her relationship with her brother was not bad, except insofar as Nanny Shimoda was concerned, where they were rivals if not actual enemies. The other children were all much older than these two, who now alone competed for their nanny's attention. They both slept in the same room with the old lady between them, each clinging to an arm. One would have thought that Nanny Shimoda would have suffered, since she was the object over which this battle was being so grimly waged, but no matter how much her arms were pulled in contrary directions she snored through it all without even noticing.

Momoko finally decided that she would not make a tart remark to her little brother. Instead, she took up the song again in her high, piercing voice. Nanny Shimoda had clearly had enough. She was worried about the sick Yonekuni, but also aware that if she ceased to pay sufficient attention to Momoko's wishes, that young lady could quite easily decide to burst into tears. Momoko was renowned as a crybaby, and she cried readily for the most trivial reasons. She made little noise when she did so, but huge tears, so huge as to seem false, would appear in her eyes and roll slowly down her cheeks. But at that moment the sliding front door rattled open.

"Mrs. Shimoda, would you permit me another look at the newspapers?"

"Oh, it's Mr. Billiken," shouted Momoko, so pleased that she quite forgot about the game she had been playing.

Mr. Billiken was a great reader of the newspapers. He read them out loud as if he were reciting: no straightforward recital of the facts, but one with interesting stresses and emphases. Momoko seldom had any grasp of what was being read, but this was one of the pleasures of her life, one of the pleasures that a large and varied environment like the Nire Hospital provides.

"Billiken" was the name of a kind of doll that had been dreamed up in the United States a decade earlier and had become very popular in Japan in the past few years. The doll had a pointed, gnome-like head and slanting eyebrows, and was said to bring good luck. It was also the nickname given to the former Prime Minister, Terauchi, leader of the recently dissolved cabinet, since he shared those physical characteristics; and not only to him, but to almost anyone with a slightly pointed head. The shaved skull of the Nire Hospital Billiken showed an almost classical pointing of the vertex. He had been a patient at the hospital for years now, attempting to recover from some mental disorder. It was no longer certain what the disorder was, but it was clear that he was wrong in the head somewhere.

Dr. Kiichiro Nire had started his career in ordinary general practice, but in Germany he had begun to specialize in mental illness. On his return to Japan, he began to treat people who suffered from disturbances of the mind. When the new hospital was built in Aoyama he had two signs set up at the gate. One of these was the old "Nire Hospital," but the other was a new sign, "The Imperial Mental Hospital," and although the hospital still catered for all forms of sickness, most of its patients suffered from psychological disorders.

Momoko herself had no idea what had originally been wrong with Billiken's head since even Nanny Shimoda did not know. He seemed always to have been wandering about the hospital, helping to distribute meals, helping in the garden, and there seemed nothing at all strange in what he said or did. Perhaps it was the way he chanted when he read the newspaper; he seemed to need some kind of tune when he read out loud. Momoko decided that this was probably the illness that had not yet been cured.

The hospital took a variety of newspapers which found their way to the recreation room and then, usually when they had become very old, to Nanny Shimoda. The "young master" upstairs, who in marrying the eldest daughter, Ryuko, had married into the family and so taken its name, also took a newspaper, and his, like all the others, was destined to end in Nanny Shimoda's hands. She tied the newspapers

carefully into bundles, filled the cupboards with them and, at long intervals, sold them to a wastepaper merchant. So Billiken had not come
to scrutinize the latest news, for often he would be offered something
months old and even when very lucky the newspaper would still be
a few days old. But what he enjoyed doing was reading the printed
page out loud. He entered the room brusquely, thrust open the door
of the cupboard, and took out a bundle of papers. As the papers had
been put away in no sort of order his random seizure of a bundle merely
emphasized the haphazardness of his choice.

"Hello, hello," he muttered. "Here's a find. This one looks new."

While this was going on, the gruel had boiled and Nanny Shimoda
had taken the saucepan and left the room. This did not put Billiken
out of his stride. As soon as he had the paper in his hand he began
to read it, at first in a slightly trembling voice.

He read the article entitled: "*Yokohama Celebrates—Amazing Procession of a Kind As Yet Unseen Anywhere in the World.*" This was about the
celebrations held in Yokohama, mainly dominated by foreign residents,
to welcome the victory and the coming of peace. The article described
the various floats, decorated vehicles and carriages in a procession
which, it was claimed, had extended for two miles and in which nearly all the peoples of the earth (with the natural exception of the defeated
nations) had been represented.

Billiken took up another sheet of news and read:

"*It seems there will be no cheap rice for the time being. Both white and black
rice remain expensive. Next year's prices are expected to double or treble. Still,
we can make do without rice if it is going to cost that much and yet go on enjoying
our present way of life. There will be no hardship involved in establishing one
or two days each month as days on which no rice will be eaten.*"

"I don't like that," snorted Momoko. "It's boring. Read something
else."

"All right, then. Wouldn't want to go without my rice any day,
though," Billiken replied easily, and started searching through a pile
of old papers which were liberally stained with soy sauce. "*Japan Proudly Faces the World. Great Scientific Invention. The Inventor Kocho Iida Triumphs
over Chronic Poverty to Perfect the Natural Color Photograph.*" He now read
in a splendid singsong, and Momoko was enthralled. She sat hugging
her knees like a boy, careless of the fact that the hem of her kimono
was in disarray and showed her naked skin.

At this point a gentle patter of footsteps was heard in the passageway,
the sliding door was opened in the same refined manner, and Kiichi-

ro's second daughter, Seiko, entered the room. She was perhaps almost envious of the slovenly, daring way Momoko had chosen to sit; it made a profound contrast with her own impeccable appearance, a silk crepe kimono in deep purple, brilliantly brought out by the fine scarlet of the sash knotted firmly about it, so strongly emphasizing the bloodless pallor of her skin that she looked more like a doll than a human being. As she knelt and faced about to close the sliding door correctly behind her, one noticed the long, broad ribbon that held the plaits of her hair coiled up above the nape of her neck. Seiko still clung to the Margaret fashion of doing her hair, now firmly out of date, and it suited her.

Momoko looked as if she were about to make some boyish exclamation of admiration, but instead she looked away in the direction of Billiken. She no longer wondered if she would ever be able to dress herself with the same assurance, for she had decided it was quite impossible; her sister seemed to belong to a quite different species and Momoko felt it was pointless to be envious of her or to want to be like her.

Seiko was a very striking girl, with a slim, oval face and pure white skin, and was at that critical age when changes are about to occur, but though she was due to graduate from the Gakushuin Girls' School next year, her lips and cheeks still had the gentle contours of a young girl. In comparison with her, the eldest daughter, Ryuko, certainly had an irreproachable gentility no doubt inherited from her mother, but her face was too long and her high nose was hooked, giving her a cold, stern expression. Seiko could be considered a delicate compromise between her two sisters, for if she had been a little more like Ryuko she would have appeared aloof, and any tendency toward Momoko would have given her that air of familiarity which tends to breed contempt. Consequently, Seiko was the one of the three who was most talked about in the hospital. Everyone agreed that she was the real beauty of the family.

Seiko observed Billiken with the newspaper and her eyebrows twitched imperceptibly. She then observed Momoko at some length, surveying the inelegant posture that young lady had taken up, and her eyebrows twitched again, but perceptibly this time. All she said, however, was:

"Has Mistress Ryu not come down yet?"

"Mistress Ryu? Upstairs, isn't she?"

Momoko was about to ask, half enviously, half complainingly, if they were going out again somewhere, but decided not to since she knew she was bound to be corrected for some impropriety in the language she would use. Seiko had not always been like that, and Momoko resented the change that had come over her. In Ryuko's case, Momoko had grown up expecting to be scolded since there were thirteen years between them, and Ryuko had always seemed more in the position of a mother than a sister, particularly since her actual mother was a distant being hidden away "within." But she found it irritating that Seiko, who used to be someone she played with, should also have become peculiar and started to gang up with Ryuko against her. Of course, it was all the fault of Gakushuin, although Momoko had no very clear idea why.

Once General Nogi, the hero of the Russo-Japanese War, had been made Principal of Gakushuin (the Peers School, designed for the education of Tokyo's elite), its doors were opened to the children of commoners, and Kiichiro had immediately made up his mind that his daughters should go there. Consequently, Ryuko had introduced the language habits she picked up at school into the hospital, and Kiichiro welcomed the refinements that these terms and phrases lent to daily life. No doubt there was something forced, even crude about this, the vulgar longing of the provincial for the cultured life of the city, but Kiichiro considered it absolutely essential for the Nire family. The Nire family had no traditions, not surprisingly since the family tree began with Kiichiro himself. It was a new creation, something still in the process of being created, and some sort of tradition was required—any tradition, so long as it was sufficiently out of the ordinary. The children at Gakushuin often used honorific forms when talking to or about their friends, unlike ordinary people who only used them for persons in a temporary or permanent position of superiority. The habit reflected the way the nobility used to refer to each other. Hence the "Mistress Ryu" and "Mistress Sei" usages for his elder daughters.

Even Billiken had been somewhat put out of his stride by the entrance of Seiko. Momoko was simply a girl, but Seiko was a young lady, someone close, if not in fact at least in atmosphere, to the powers "within." This was even more the case with Ryuko, who was the "young mistress" of the house and in direct line to the main seat of privilege, so it seemed hardly the time or place to be fooling around reading newspapers. But once Billiken had launched himself into a reading he found it difficult to stop; he became so involved that his surroundings faded in importance. So he continued:

"An astounding contribution to the world of photography has been made by

16

a compatriot of ours, a world-shaking invention whereby the technique of an absolutely natural color photograph has been perfected. . ."

At first he read in a slightly wavering, indecisive voice, but he soon became oblivious once more to everything else, and employed those peculiar modulations, now excitingly high, now solemnly low, that Momoko enjoyed most of all.

"Her Royal Highness Nashimoto no Miya graciously condescended to view the exhibits, and it has been announced that she was graciously pleased to offer words of praise and encouragement. . ."

The added dignity of the repeated "graciously" was noted by Billiken as he read, the story being a moral tale about a son of the capitalist class triumphing over adversities. Some major failure on the part of his father had led to the bankruptcy and rapid decline of the house, from which desperate depths the son had risen again, finally creating the complete and natural photograph, the 32,000 tints of nature apparently reproduced by various adjustments and permutations of the three primary colors. So remarkable had been his success that one Western artist had exclaimed that all the portrait painters in existence would be put out of business. Billiken was also surprised to learn that there should be as many as 32,000 tints in nature, but his voice had reached such a high pitch at this point that it did not affect his reading.

Seiko knelt down in an elegant manner beside the *hibachi* and began to turn over the pages of the *Ladies Illustrated.* She was waiting for her sister, since they had both been invited out, and was feeling very conscious that she belonged to a different world from that inhabited by her hapless, hopeless younger sister and the even younger brother who was coughing next door. But she also knew that her different world had been imposed on her from above, or rather from "within" by way of Ryuko's mediation, and that she had once been in the same situation as Momoko was in now. As she listened to Billiken's eccentric reading, she felt a strange nostalgia for the past, for this house and this room when it had been a place in which she could play untidily and without care. This sudden enslavement by memories of the grubby past disturbed her, and just as suddenly she threw them off, adjusting her kneeling position in the way she had learned from her sister, the neck held so straight as to give the impression almost of leaning backward. As she did so, she became aware once more of how different she was from Momoko, who was lying there on her stomach with her legs sticking up in the air, like some vulgar child from the back streets

17

looking at a trashy picture book. So Seiko sat displaying her own mental refinement, reading the list of contents of the *Ladies Illustrated*: "A Lunchtime Meeting of the Omote Senke Tea Ceremony Association"; "Behavior on Visiting a House Built in Semi-Foreign Style"; "Calligraphy for Young Ladies"; "Prince Kujo's Youngest Daughter on the Duke's Country Estate."

Meanwhile Billiken's reading was becoming even more animated. The intrepid inventor, struggling manfully through a series of misfortunes, had now accidentally broken a sheet of glass necessary to his researches, and wept manly tears over it; which he proceeded to do again on several other occasions.

"His wife, Kikuko, although heavy with child and her time near, spared no efforts to succor him, hardly allowing one morsel of food to pass her lips."

Momoko did not understand all of this that well, but she was caught up in the excitement of Billiken's voice and began rocking her knees to and fro in a very inelegant way.

"Thus a child was born on the 9th of February, a successful experiment completed on the following day, the tenth, and a patent finally taken out on the 23rd of July, a patent for the celluloid carbon chip."

Billiken mispronounced his way through the last three foreign words, wondering what a celluloid carbon chip or tip might be, and then went on:

"Among those photographs on display today and tomorrow is a snap taken of one of the country's rarest beauties, Miss Ohan of the Hisamatsuba being the fortunate girl to receive the honor. This natural color photograph was created by the use of three cameras, the skillful superimposition of the three images thereby obtained permitting a photograph to be formed, in a process using carbon paper and another element which is still being kept secret."

Seiko realized that at some point her interest had wandered from the *Ladies Illustrated* to Billiken's reading, which wasn't surprising since the contents were of more interest than the Omote Senke tea ceremony. But as Billiken's reading became more sober again after those passionate moments, footsteps could be heard coming down the staircase at the end of the passageway, the unmistakable, measured tread of Kiichiro's eldest daughter, Ryuko. This elder sister, eight years older than Seiko and already a mother, was the sole repository of the faith and hopes of her parents, the embodiment of all that was orthodox and central in the Nire family, and Seiko stood up to greet her. Billiken, however, was now a total slave to his obsession and seemed wholly unaware of Ryuko's approach. He had already started on another article in a different newspaper: "*Ten Years of Amorous Delights with Momokichi Goden are Now, Alas, but as an Empty, Evil Dream. Tomoharu Iwakura, All Passion Spent.*" This was the kind of purple prose he particularly liked. Here was a real opportunity for him to display his histrionic powers:

"*Fashionable young man about town, Tomoharu Iwakura, may well rue the day he first gazed upon the alluring figure of the voluptuous Momokichi, Shinbashi geisha. Unwary was he of the evil fate awaiting him, careless indeed of such, and little did he care for the demands of mother, wife and child, all cast from him unheeded and unwanted. But now those ten years spent in love's mad, sweet delights have passed and faded with the dawn. . .*"

These words awakened an echo in Seiko's breast, tightly restrained though it was by the cloth firmly wound about it, and she would dearly have liked to hear more, but she was aware of Ryuko waiting for her in the entrance hall. Her resolute sister remained totally unmoved by the antics of minor servants, half-cured lunatics or whatever, preferring to ignore the places where these raised their ugly but, to her, quite innocuous heads. How, then, would she respond to Seiko, the junior in whom she pleased to confide as in one similar to herself, if Seiko listened in all seriousness to, and was even moved by, a phrase as ludicrous as "ten years spent in love's mad, sweet delights"? How coldly she would look at her, with what contempt in her eyes.

So Seiko stood up, carefully arranged her sleeves, then cast a glance of Ryuko-like haughtiness at Momoko, who was still absorbed in Billiken's performance, and left the room. The two older sisters, representatives of the front the Nire family chose to show to the world, left the house together.

"I don't want this. It's too hot. I told you I didn't want it too hot."

Yonekuni was sulking in the other room, for the youngest offspring of the house was well aware of the rights illness had bestowed on him as he supped the gruel Nanny Shimoda had prepared. His voice at last released Momoko from the enchantment Billiken had cast over her, and she suddenly became conscious of the fact that she was hungry.

"Nanny, what's happened to my food? Don't tell me it's not ready yet," she howled in a penetrating shriek, but luckily it was not overheard by her sisters, for they had already passed out of earshot.

The two pillars of the main gateway into the Nire Hospital were made of stone, imposing, good solid granite, solid to the core. It may sound superfluous to insist on stone being solid to the core, since stone is inevitably solid, but the reason for doing so will become apparent later.

Two signs, made of solid wood, were affixed to these two pillars, one on each, and both of them slightly larger than was required. Since they were Japanese signs, with characters written from top to bottom, one would expect them to be long, but these were as tall as a man of average height. This was no doubt admirable for the purpose of catching the eye, but, aesthetically speaking, it was a definite drawback. Still, they must have reflected Kiichiro's taste in these matters, and there they were. One had the three characters for the Nire Hospital on it, and the other bore the five characters for the Imperial Mental Hospital, burned thick, black and bold into the wood.

The heavy wrought-iron gates, too, which caused the porter considerable pains to open and close, had obviously been chosen principally to impress the eye. Their tops were uneven when open, and when closed, each being higher toward one end, they formed an interesting shape that peaked at the center. Nor was this all, for the whole upper half was a complex mass of scrolls and whirls, all of which gave off a dull glitter and bore witness to the desire to impress that had brought them into being. Extending from these columns were railings, much lower than the gates, ending in each case in another granite pillar, and from there onward a long wall of red brick. These walls had endured the wind and rain of fifteen years and the brickwork had darkened, assuming the softened tone that time confers on all man-made things. But this was only true of the wall at the left-hand side of the gate, for the wall to the right was a surprisingly, indeed offensively new, bright red; not a genuine newness, but the blatant vulgarity that results from the cosmetic treatment of an old structure, startling in its artificiality and total lack of propriety.

The wall had clearly not been rebuilt with some amazing new brick, but simply manifested Kiichiro's taste. It was in the process of being done up, of being completely recoated with iron dioxide. The right-hand wall had just been completed, and it was, of course, planned to treat the wall on the left in the same style. Kiichiro found it impossible to let any occasion pass without some kind of ceremony, assembly or happening of as imposing a kind as possible, and the fifteenth anniversary of the Nire Hospital and the Imperial Mental Hospital was fast approaching. His natural inclination was to put up a building, a new annex perhaps, but the hospital buildings were as complete as they could be, nor was there any space left to put up anything else. Another reason for the modest scale of his operations on this important occasion was, if the truth be told, that his campaigning in the election in his home district of Yamagata last year had caused him to burrow very deep into his pockets. Certainly he had been able to satisfy some of his craving for honors; he now received double the amount of respect from his employees, and he was able to add some luster to his extra-large visiting card by having the title of Member of the House of Representatives printed in one corner of it. But the election had cost him a lot of money, so much, in fact, that Hisa, his frugal wife, who was normally as sparing in the use of her tongue as her money, had complained about the expense on very much more than one occasion. For that reason he had to content himself with having the whole hospital made spick and span, touching up the paintwork here and there, and coating the wall.

Just inside the wall, where the grass and shrubberies gave way to a gravel courtyard, five or six men were squatting on the ground, with buckets of red coating material and brushes at their sides. They were employees of the hospital, and they had been at work all morning. They had just eaten their share of the hospital lunch, and were now diligently loafing about, showing little inclination to return to their labors. It was a very long wall, and although the work had been ordered by the Director himself their enthusiasm was minimal.

They also knew that the Director had left the hospital some time ago. The box-like Model T Ford, a recent acquisition, had turned up in front of the entrance hall well before noon, and finally the Director had appeared attired in a frock coat, twirling his stick, and stepping smartly into the car as a number of people respectfully saw him off. As the Ford crunched over the gravel and passed out through the main gate, the men, who just happened to be recoating the wall with frenetic energy, caught a fleeting glimpse of the Director lounging grandly in the back seat and looking in their direction. His face was moving up and down, and this did not seem simply due to the remarkable vibrations of the vehicle, but was an indication that the customary words, "Well done, men, well done," were issuing from his mouth on this occasion too.

Once he had gone they felt free to sit down for as long as they liked, remaining seated even when the Assistant Director passed, although he should by rights have been in charge during Kiichiro's absence, which would extend late into the night. But the post of Assistant Director was only a temporary one, and Dr. Takada was essentially only an employee like themselves, not someone in line to succeed to real power in the hospital; it was the "young master," Ryuko's husband, who would become the real Assistant Director, and finally Director. The Nire Hospital was a family affair and Dr. Takada was no member of the family. Already a number of the medical staff were relatives of some kind; Kiichiro's sons were bound to become doctors, the daughters would take doctors as husbands, and everyone was sure that it was the Director's ambition to have all the staff related to him by ties of blood: one big, happy family.

Still, as things stood now, Dr. Takada, a medical man of high caliber and very popular with people, had to be accepted as such and was consequently the Assistant Director. The respect in which he was held could be seen from the words of one of the workmen, who thoughtfully tapped out his old-fashioned, long, thin pipe on his heel, and spat generously before saying:

"I'll say this for Dr. Takada, he's a very good one for a diagnosis. That's what being a real M.D. means. When he taps you on the chest it sounds quite different. You know, you can really hear the difference."

"Well, be that as it may, he can't match the Doctor Professor. Now, *he* taps a patient on the head and he knows straight away where he's wrong and why he's wrong, just like that."

"All right then, but he's got no M.D."

"Not a Japanese M.D., no: but he is a 'Doktor Medicine,' as they say."

"Which one's best, then?"

"Pretty obvious, I should think, seeing a 'Doktor Medicine' is an M.D. in foreign parts, and they don't exactly give them away over there now, do they? Pretty rare in this country, anyway."

"Well, better get going again," said the foreman.

So they all dragged themselves to their feet and started on the inside of the wall, washing it down first and then applying the coating. They had just started on the coating when an empty two-seater ricksha entered through the main gate. It stopped before the entrance hall, and before long two young ladies stepped into it. The rickshaman smartly tucked the traveling rug about them, then took his place between the shafts.

"Ah, there's Miss Seiko," said the man who had just been lauding the institution of Doktor Medicine, and he rested briefly in his task, ducking his head fervently toward the ricksha as it passed. Seiko glanced in their direction and made a slight acknowledgment of this loyal greeting. It was only an embarrassed, almost imperceptible movement of the lips, but the bloodless pallor of her skin and the fleeting smile with the gray clouds of winter as background had a powerful effect on the men, particularly since her attitude contrasted so greatly with that of her sister. Ryuko, a boa wrapped about her neck, was sitting bolt upright, and gave not the slightest indication that she had noticed any obeisance on the part of the workmen; whether because she had ignored it or because her response had been so frigid as to be genuinely imperceptible, it would be difficult to say. Whichever it was, Seiko soon became sensitive to the attitude her sister had taken, or seemed to, for she turned swiftly away and looked rigidly in the direction in which they were going. So the two sisters, assuming identical expressions and postures, gradually disappeared from sight.

"Ah, now, there's a real nice-looking young lady, that is," said the workman whose gaze had lingered longest. His tone expressed an even more heartfelt admiration than when he had been praising the Director's academic accomplishments.

"Which one're you talking about? The young master's wife?"

"No, of course not, the young one. She's really something."

"You know," another put in, "in this family it's the women who've got real class. Look at those two, both Gakushuin. You can't say the same about the boys now, can you? And why? Because the boys aren't up to much, that's why."

"But there's only one of them, and he's still only a kid going to primary school."

"No there's not. There's another one. He's in high school up north, up there in Sendai. They say he's failed his exams twice already."

"Well, maybe you're right. That little one doesn't look too bright, at least judging by his face."

"That's it, you see. The two young ladies are the ones with quality. Look at the young master's wife, now. She's got a real head on her shoulders, she has. After all, that's why they're called Mistress Ryu and Mistress Sei."

They all burst out laughing at that, since they found it hard to get used to the Gakushuin forms of address. Even the maidservants, who were obliged by their station in life to be surprised at nothing, were taken aback when they first heard these elevated titles, finding it hard to connect the figure of the young master's wife with the "Mistress Ryu" they had to call her. They were made easier in their minds when they found she had a "-ko" decently attached to her name just like anybody else. One of the workmen added:

23

"Still, I reckon it takes a lot of courage to call someone 'Mistress Ryu,' and that's a fact."

"Quiet, you lot. Here comes the Deputy."

They all suddenly became extremely busy, for out through the front doors had stepped a very thin man, thin as a crane or some other wading bird, who seemed, from his dark suit, to be the kind of man who must be deputizing for someone or other. Lest the crane image give the impression of some long, gangling figure, it should be added that he was of very modest height, almost a dwarf, with very little air of authority about him, although this did not prevent his being the person who wielded most power in the hospital. He was the Deputy Director, responsible for the whole clerical administration.

The title of Deputy Director, or "Deputy" as he was usually called, was one of Kiichiro's brainwaves. As his function was quite different from that of the Assistant Director, it would have been wiser to call him something like Bursar or Secretary, but because the title of Deputy Director sounded more dignified, not to say portentous, Kiichiro infinitely preferred it, as did the possessor of the title himself. This man, Hidekichi Katsumata, had originally been one of the student dependents of the hospital and, like the others, had intended to become a doctor. He had studied in the normal way, and passed the first part of the qualifying exam with no difficulty. But, for some mystifying reason, he was never able to pass the second and final stage, which was of a practical nature. He failed at his first attempt, and again at his second. When another year had almost passed and he was due for his third try, his face gradually became paler and paler as the fateful day approached, and a twitch developed in his already slightly neurotic eyelids. The doctors of the Nire Hospital began to worry about him, and produced a number of mock examination questions to prepare him for his ordeal. Hidekichi replied in a trance-like manner to all their questions, giving nothing but correct answers. Presumably this was a result of all-night study sessions, which resulted from nervous insomnia rather than from any calculated zeal. The doctors were convinced that, with this fund of information at his command, he would surely pass this time, and they told him so. But Hidekichi felt unable to believe their comforting words, and it turned out that he was right not to do so. He failed once more, and no matter how many times he took the exam he always failed.

All the while, his juniors were passing victoriously, and he began to feel that he was becoming an object of open ridicule. In fact he was mistaken, since all the interns had been through various trials of their own, and they felt sympathy rather than any desire to make fun of him; but that was the way he thought things were, and this neurotic feeling began to build up within him so that he finally lost any inclination to take the qualifying exam again. His only consolations during this melancholy period were a volume of gloomy reflections on the transience and harshness of life, written by one of the lesser intellectual lights of the day, and occasional visits to the wailful recitations given in Asakusa by women accompanying themselves on the samisen. Their soul-stirring pluckings, compounded by the emotional tales they told, were calculated to bring a comforting tear even to a hardened and despairing eye.

Kiichiro, however, skilled as he was at drawing out the hidden talents of even desperate cases, was hardly likely to cast this man aside. He had him help with the preparation of drugs, and then with the clerical work. By the time the Nire Hospital had developed from its humble beginnings into a major hospital, Hidekichi had proved to be someone who could be relied upon to handle all the tricky administrative problems of the place, and had become the trustworthy right hand of the Director. Not only had the Nire Hospital expanded in a way almost unparalleled for a private institution of this kind, as witness the numerous annexes appended at various times, but its Director had made a powerful name for himself in both medical and political circles. Consequently, the year before, when Kiichiro was elected to the House of Representatives, he called Hidekichi into his presence and said, in a voice of such warmth and intimacy it would have encouraged anyone to offer his body at the stake for this man, or so it seemed to imply:

"Katsumata, you know, from now on I am going to be busy, really busy. My hands are going to be full, you know that. You also know I won't be able to spare too much time for the running of the hospital. Now, I want to ask you to do something for me. Run this place for me. Run it as my deputy, my deputy director. Now there it is, that's it. Deputy Director. That's what you'll be. And we'll have a new seal made for you right away. A good, big seal: big and square, just like mine."

These were no empty words. The Director did all he could to thrust Hidekichi into prominence, entrusting all the hospital business to him, except for the diagnoses. If Kiichiro were pressured for some decision and appeals were made to him, he would reply calmly, his jaw thrust slightly upward, and recommend that the matter be taken up with the

25

Deputy, Dr. Katsumata, making no commitment himself.

This was, of course, a very acceptable way for the highest authority in the hospital to act, for he could avoid all public decision making; but it also meant a sudden and considerable increase in the power of the Deputy. Since the Director referred to the Deputy as Dr. Katsumata, everybody else came to do so as well, at least in public. Hidekichi was given a private room of his own next door to the main administrative office, and among the various stamps and seals that littered his desk was the one he had been promised, large and square: "Deputy Director of the Nire Hospital and Imperial Mental Hospital." Any undertaking that was not given the impress of this seal was invalid, and every aspect of hospital life was dependent on it. The title of Deputy gradually ceased to indicate only a function and began to take on the aspects of a proper name, imprecise in meaning but irrevocably linked to its possessor.

As already mentioned, the Deputy was a thin, almost emaciated person, so small as to be virtually a dwarf. His suit was without crease or wrinkle, his high collar, even more unwrinkled and creaseless, stood out starched and stiff about his neck. His forehead and cheeks retained the pallor his youthful ordeal had given him, and his eyelids still twitched and trembled nervously behind his rimless glasses. A small, well-trimmed, Chaplinesque moustache adorned his upper lip. He had always tended toward a trot or even a scamper when he walked, but recently he had managed to slow this down to a more dignified amble, a reflection, no doubt, of his awareness of the major role he played in the affairs of the hospital. But since this was a conscious attempt on his part, it resulted in no real reversal of his natural walking habits. The artificiality of his stumbling, slow-motion gait showed in the fact that he now appeared to walk like a crane, hesitating, as such a bird will do when it moves slowly searching at each step for some hidden thing on the bed of a river or lake, its claws awkwardly pausing with each new pace. Adding to this bird-like effect was a misguided desire on his part, also of recent origin, to increase the impressiveness of his mode of walking by clasping his hands together behind his back. He linked the forefingers only in the region of the fourth lumbar vertebra, thus ensuring that the other unlinked fingers pointed loosely upward. The unhappy result was no increase in dignity but an uncanny resemblance to a wading bird's tail feathers, and a consequent reinforcement of the already strong crane image.

When the Director departed in the box-like Ford, the Deputy Director had seen him off in a debonair manner, at once courteous and casual, suited to a man who knows he has total responsibility in his superior's absence, indeed even in his presence. Before returning to his office, he took a quick glance at the administrative office, which was, it being Sunday, quite deserted—except, that is, for the Chief Accountant, Mr. Oishi, who was fiddling about with the door of the safe, apparently closing it.

It was the Deputy Director who had put this not very reliable-looking person in charge of the accounts. Oishi, a man apparently in his early sixties with grizzled hair, had an extremely nervous temperament, and his neurotic obsession with minor details reflected a congenital small-mindedness. He spent the whole working year grimacing at or merely contemplating his account ledgers, or making mostly unnecessary flourishes and rattlings of his abacus, or pausing to peer once more into his accounts, then looking in almost agonized fashion at the ceiling, a general distrust of men and their calculations scrawled across his neurotic face, and so back to the abacus again, click clack click clack, until finally it would be too much and he would lurch waveringly to his feet, wander across to the safe, and crouch down before it. This act was the ceremonial center of his days. He would nervously creak the knob of the combination into its various positions, swing the heavy door open, peer inside while muttering unintelligibly to himself, then heave the door to. That done, he would return to his desk, open his ledger again, then sigh and mutter over his accounts once more. This routine would usually be repeated within the hour, his desire to check the contents of the safe being as persistent as it was unnecessary.

The Deputy Director had not been mistaken in appointing a person of this character as Chief Accountant. No matter how deficient he might be in some things, such as a certain speedy efficiency required perhaps by the new age, at least he would always make absolutely certain that none of the hospital's cash went missing. It was also indisputable that the Deputy derived some pleasure from observing another person who had failed his qualifying examinations for psychological reasons, namely acute exam phobia, an experience that had left even deeper scars in this case, for Oishi tended to become more dithery and flustered than did the Deputy, even if for the same reasons. In Oishi's presence Hidekichi felt positively solid, unswayed by irrational fantasies or unconscious fears, the stable, commonsensical anchor that held the good ship Nire firm.

When Oishi looked up and saw the face of the Deputy, he began grumblingly to address him, sounding like a man whose burden is too great for any mortal to bear, his head bent quizzically to one side as if in astonishment at the way existence itself was arranged.

"Dr. Katsumata, are you aware that the Director has again withdrawn a large sum from the petty cash to take with him on to-day's excursion, namely forty yen? And it is the same every day, or getting worse if I may respectfully say so: twenty yen, thirty yen, and today forty. I ask you, Doctor, does a Diet member really need sums of that size?"

The Deputy did not reply immediately, his silence suggesting that such deep and complex matters could hardly be explained to a member of the vulgar populace such as he was confronted with now. Instead of replying, he gazed at the wall opposite the window, which had an ancient blackboard affixed to it. On this some lines, and the days of the week, had been painted in white, though they were now faded with age; beneath, the actual dates had been chalked in with the names of the doctors on duty. But the most ostentatious information the blackboard provided was the schedule of the Director, the meetings he was to attend and the places he was to visit, so many that one received the impression that Kiichiro had no time to spare for hospital affairs. The Deputy Director looked thoughtfully at all this, nodding his approval at various points as if he were the Director himself, and finally replying in magnanimous tones:

"My good man, you must realize that a Diet member is responsible for the government and good order of the whole country. The membership fees for the various groups the Director is involved with would alone be no small figure."

The Deputy, however, knew otherwise. He was well aware that the Director had a fondness for the ladies—which was, indeed, appropriate to a person in his exalted position—and that a considerable portion of the cash he removed from the hospital safe was no doubt expended on them. Naturally the Deputy never commented on such matters, but talked instead of things that everyone in the hospital knew perfectly well since they had heard about them so often, such as the Director's tremendously busy schedule and his unique and incomparable character, for Katsumata was second to none in his efforts to bolster the image of the head of the hospital and member of the Diet. He had been appointed by the Director and was relied upon by him, and he knew how to repay that concern and trust.

So he had his Chief Accountant, who was now in an even greater state of respectful, nervous confusion, carry the accounts to his private office, where he inspected them, crinkling his nose critically as he did so. The accounts were, as always, impeccable, despite the slightly wavering, neurotic characters in which they were written, so there was nothing for him to do but apply a liberal amount of ink to his rubber seal and press it firmly onto the final page. The Deputy stamped everything, anything, and everywhere, from the day's menu to the ricksha company's bill. Nothing in the Nire Hospital could function without his stamp of approval, or all would come to a paralytic halt. And the actual operation of stamping gave him inordinate pleasure and pride.

Since there was now nothing remaining to be stamped, he folded his pale, thin hands behind his back and wandered out of the main door again. It was cold outside, and he would have been better off in his room, but the desire to gaze once more on a sight of which he never tired, the row of columns on the facade of the main building, led him to the vantage point in front of the main gate.

The emotional experience the thin, dwarfish Katsumata gained from the sight was peculiar to himself, and not all that readily intelligible to other people, nor easily available elsewhere. Even so, the casual viewer would have undoubtedly responded in some fashion to the sight that now greeted the Deputy's eyes; whether with admiration or with some more negative emotion is a question that need not detain us. Suffice it to say that a person of the Meiji era (which at this time, 1918, had ended some six years before) would have gaped in pure astonishment, whereas someone of our own Showa era (due to begin in about eight years' time) would have been puzzled by it, and would perhaps have smiled awkwardly with ambiguous feelings of incomprehension and mistrust, his confusion tending toward embarrassment, with perhaps an added trace of pure contempt.

In the 37th year of Meiji, or 1904, when the front of the main edifice was completed, the neighbors gaped at it in disbelief, as completely taken aback as they would have been if they had witnessed the sudden appearance of those black foreign ships that had ushered in the new age. Well, they were simple citizens and the building itself hardly merited such a degree of wonder, but one must realize that it was here, in Aoyama, that it had appeared—a place with only a graveyard, the occasional cluster of houses, and a great deal of open space and vacant lots, with not even the streetcar line that was to be built some years later. In those days, the valley in front of the hospital still consisted only of farmland, paddy fields and wheat fields from which arose a great croaking of frogs in summer, and even at the time with which we are now concerned, in December, 1918, half of the fields remained. It was hardly surprising that the appearance of this suspiciously impressive building should have widened people's eyes and set tongues and heads wagging, both in admiration and distrust. What seemed particularly out of the ordinary was that it should be a private rather than a public institution, and that it should also be a place that housed numbers of the mentally unwell or, more crudely, loonies and nut cases. It was not surprising that there should have been some sharp opposition from some of the neighboring people, though it should be added that eventually there was not a single trader in the area who did not benefit from the hospital's presence. At that time the one really famous place nearby, the Meiji Shrine, had not been built, and for the inhabitants of this part of Aoyama the hospital became a landmark, something that other places were seen in relation to.

"Just go a little past the Nire Hospital, then turn right," "It's just in front of the Mental Hospital," or, more simply, "near the hospital," became the means of directing people to houses in the neighborhood.

The Deputy Director, Hidekichi Katsumata, leaned his tiny body back appreciatively as he viewed the row of columns that adorned the front of the hospital, well aware of the significant part the building had played in the cultural history of the area and in local mores. The columns were, to put the matter briefly, in the Corinthian style, or something near it, with a garish and complex ornamental patterning on their upper portions. The first and second floors were thus dominated (or rather their facade was dominated) by these columns, which seemed to be aiming at some kind of cloistral effect, although above that level they were suddenly transformed into what had to be called a balcony, since a pretentious and, in practical terms, wholly useless stone balustrade had been set on top of them. And further architectural surprises lay in store on taking a few paces away from the building, when the roof came into view. Here was a true spectacle: seven great towers, built in splendid disregard of rigid concepts of uniformity or harmony and authoritatively towering, as towers are expected to do. The one on the extreme left appeared to be in the Byzantine style, for it came to an abruptly pointed end, and the lightning conductor attached to it created a striking general likeness to the staff carried by His Holiness the Pope. The one next to it was much fatter and rounder and appeared to be complacently absorbed in its own existence rather than mindful of its neighbors, a characteristic that was, in one way or another, shared by all seven, since they lacked any unifying design or purpose. They existed stolidly in their own right, looking coldly down on the race of mortals below, stirring mysterious feelings of wonder at this awful sight. But the clock tower above the central entrance should be singled out as of peculiar interest, since it was so totally out of harmony, not only with the other towers and columns but with the building itself. It was in the Chinese style, although not so much genuine Chinese as the sort of thing that appears in a child's picture book representing the Dragon God's Palace under the Sea, or some other exotic fantasy. And there it stood, smack in the center of the building, lofty, immovable, aloof.

The Deputy unclasped his hands from behind his back, removed his watch from his waistcoat pocket, and scrutinized it. He was concerned about the time given by the great clock on the clock tower, since that clock tended to be either fast or slow and never gave any time that could pretend to be correct. He knew that the Director hated the clock to be slow, and would grimace with displeasure when it was, but seemed to have no objection to its being fast. In fact, he even seemed pleased when it was, bestowing smiles on those around him and cheerily remarking that "our clock is fifteen minutes fast." It would have been quite satisfactory if the clock were one or even two hours ahead of the real time, so long as it stayed fast, but it could not be relied upon to do so. The Deputy Director checked it against his own watch and found it was five minutes fast, at which he nodded in recognition that it was behaving comparatively well today, and reclasped his hands behind his back. He raised his minute frame to its largest extent and continued his survey of this building which could still fill him with admiration, this palace from the world of fancy, this amazing monument to the genius of Kiichiro Nire. What a spectacle it was, with its white columns standing in a stately row under the dull winter sky! What refinement, what taste! How astonishing the pointed towers were! And how well this amazement was tempered by the soft, withdrawn impression given by the blunt circular ones next to them, an effect modeled on various places abroad, seen by the Deputy only in photographs. Then there were the skylights in the roof, which, in a more commonplace building, would have served as windows for attics, but in this case had no function whatsoever beyond that of providing ornamentation. Each was as splendidly independent of the others in the way it thrust forth from the roof as were the towers. Of course, if one considered the building as a whole, the most significant feature was the row of columns which, someone had once explained, was in the Spanish Renaissance style. And yet, if one changed one's point of view only very slightly, then what a peculiar excrescence the whole row was, a weird projection that destroyed the balance of this indescribable and epoch-making conglomeration, a monument to the confusion in established norms of architectural and artistic taste. Above all, there was that Chinese clock tower, so reminiscent of Neptune's halls, the Dragon God's dark lair, an invitation, a challenge to the mind to. . .

Nevertheless, the building remained a witness to the assimilative genius of Kiichiro, his ability to be creative with whatever came accidentally to hand. He had drawn up the plans all by himself. During his travels abroad, numerous buildings had created in him a silent and solitary excitement, and these impressions had sunk deep within him, had become mingled and confused with other impressions until they formed one monstrous, synthetic image, one conglomerate mélange. So once that basic desire of his to astound others with effortless displays of his accomplishments had been aroused, this form had lumbered forth from the recesses of his mind, a dubious tribute to the unfettered play of the creative imagination. Kiichiro was only an amateur in architectural matters, but his passion for the art was intense, abnormal and of long standing. He drew up the plans, then spent long hours with the master carpenter assuring him that the thing could be done and spurring him on to greater efforts. He himself went to the woodyards at Fukagawa to buy the timber; he scrutinized all the building materials himself, much to the disgust of his carpenter. And so this great hospital had been brought into being (and remained in being) through the labors of countless people who, like the Deputy himself, believed that Kiichiro belonged to a special order of human existence.

Naturally many changes and additions had taken place since then, particularly as the Director would draw up new plans or add ideas to the old ones whenever he had the leisure to do so. The left wing, with its quarters "within" and the "Coral Room" upstairs, was a creation of the last years of the century's first decade, and the rebuilding that went on at the rear of the hospital as more wards were added had been almost continuous. Certainly anyone acquainted with the total structure of the hospital would feel that the cheap inadequacy of the shambles at the back was in sad contrast to the front presented to the outside world. But the truth of the matter was that those noble columns in the Corinthian style, or something near it, were in fact not made of marble at all, but of an artificial substance invented by the versatile Kiichiro himself. This substance was basically concrete and yet, when polished carefully, it gave off a luster almost identical with that of marble. And even that is not the whole story, for (a fact perhaps difficult to credit) this false stone concealed yet another falsity: the pillars that formed the centers of these columns were made of nothing more than good old-fashioned wood, Kiichiro's patent artificial stone being only a thin layer laid over them. Nor was this the case only with the massive columns: the whole impressive edifice was built in the same way, an artificial layer over simple wood, a monument to a mind whose adherence to the principle of the superiority of trumpery shadow over dull substance showed something of the extreme workings of genius.

Naturally the Deputy Director was aware of all this, but the knowledge had not the slightest effect on his sense of the grandeur of the hospital. The false marble walls glittered bold and white, the mystic tall towers soared toward heaven. The discord and confusion that a naive attempt at pretentious magnificence must bring about was something he was congenitally insensitive to, and therefore oblivious of. So he could look at the building with untroubled admiration and breathe deep sighs of satisfaction. As he stood lost in contemplation of this masterwork, the figures of the workmen coating the hospital wall were almost nothing to him, a few ants scurrying here and there about their trivial tasks.

Yet it was toward these ant-like beings that he now directed his steps and, with his jaw thrust out in the manner of the Director, he addressed a few words to the back of the man in the blue workcoat, he whom we have already encountered as the admirer of Kiichiro's academic status, and who was now wielding his brush with some show of energy.

"Well, coming along quite nicely, I see. Still, don't forget the whitewash. We must have whitewash, you know."

The idea of painting the mortar between the brick white was presumably another of Kiichiro's irrational but eye-catching brainwaves.

The man avoided giving vent to that exasperated mixture of vexation and boredom which such amateur solicitousness naturally arouses in any worker, and instead replied with fairly good grace:

"Well, Doctor, it has to dry out properly first, otherwise we'd have the coating getting all mixed up with the wash, and red and white running into each other."

The Deputy nodded slowly in agreement and, although he did not go so far as to offer the Director's customary comment, "Well done, men, well done," the proprietary way he stood observing their work, a slight frown on his face, suggested that at any moment he might do so. After a while, he retraced his steps slowly toward the main entrance, walking with his hands clasped behind his back in his hesitant, questing crane manner, and finally vanished through the doors, giving the workmen the opportunity to utter those disparaging grunts and comments they had been yearning to make throughout the past few minutes.

All was quiet and peaceful now. Even the howls of excitable mental patients were unheard. The only sound was the occasional twittering of sparrows in the pine branches. No outpatients or other visitors came on Sunday, so nobody passed to and fro, and the whole hospital seemed to be enjoying a day of rest. But one person attracted the attention of the men as they went through the motions of performing their unwelcome task, a small person who suddenly appeared in front of the main entrance.

It was Kiichiro's youngest daughter, Momoko. She had been forbidden to go outside because she might catch the influenza now raging through the land, but she had found it unbearable to remain cooped up in that small room any longer. She had ignored the remonstrations of Nanny Shimoda, picked up her ball, and gone around the side of the hospital to the paved area in front of the entrance hall, which was the best place for bouncing a ball. She soon discarded the gauze mask Nanny Shimoda had forced her to wear across her mouth and nose, and stuck it somewhere up her sleeve. Now she skillfully bounced her ball, indifferent to the cold outside air, and chanted in her high-pitched, squeaky voice:

> "Go to the shrine across the road,
> Penny in the box and say your prayers.
> Then to the little shop next door,
> Sit you down, and drink your tea.
> Drink it slowly, drink it dry,
> While you spy
> From the corner of your eye
> A big fat dumpling—made of rice
> Or made of mud like an old mud pie?
> Which it is I do not care
> For I shall give it to my dog.
> Or shall I give it to my cat?

Ah, a big black kite flies down
And snatches it away, away.''

The song was sung at great speed and demanded complex and swift skills in the ball-bouncing art. On the words "penny in the box" the thumb and forefinger formed a circle, and at "say your prayers" the hands were folded in prayer, both gestures being performed hurriedly in the short interval between each bounce. At "sit you down" the closed fist was struck against the buttocks. All this became even more hectic as the song progressed, for the speed of the bouncing was gradually increased, and Momoko performed remarkable feats, such as raising both hands in the air or flashing her free hand beneath the ball before the other hand patted it down again, the finale being some elaborate play with her legs, stepping over and under the ball, which meant that her kimono fluttered open at the front from time to time showing her drawers for all to see. The workmen gave her cries of encouragement, some innocent but some ribald in intent, which spurred her on to greater heights.

Now she was really enjoying herself, and this showed in the satisfaction written on her face. The sweat stood out on her tiny, snub nose, and she sang her chant and bounced her ball even faster, just like any little girl in one of the back streets downtown, totally absorbed in her performance, kicking her legs in the air and showing the dilapidated wooden *geta* she had slipped onto her feet when she darted out of the house. Finally she performed the extremely complex and difficult climax of her act, a staccato series of pitter-patters with both mouth and ball, her expression that enthralled, uncritical delight shared by all true performers, a magnificently vulgar look of self-adoration.

The workman who had praised the academic achievements of the Director and the loveliness of his daughter Seiko stared at Momoko with an enthrallment similar to her own. His amazement was of an ambiguous kind, however, as ambiguous as the emotion that a view of the hospital building would arouse in objective spectators.

"Well," he muttered to himself. "They can talk about class and quality, but that little one doesn't seem to have much of it, not very much at all."

Chapter

2

"Prize-Giving Day" at the Nire Hospital was on the 14th of December each year, for this was the date of the opening of the new hospital at Aoyama in the 37th year of Meiji, 1904. The ceremony usually began early in the afternoon, and normally took a very long time to complete. Prizes were awarded not only to those who had worked particularly meritoriously during the year, but to the whole staff of the hospital and, indeed, to those who had been only casually employed at some time during that period. There were certainly some prizes worthy of the name, but as one gradually went down the list they became things that people could hardly have cared less about. Most of the prizes were in fact of the latter sort, although this did not affect the condescending and lordly manner with which Kiichiro would proffer even the hand towel for the lowliest maidservant, which was as conspicuously labeled "prize" as other more worthwhile objects. A considerable number of hand towels were given out on Prize-Giving Day, and since the whole staff would again receive hand towels during the ceremonials on New Year's Day, and again at the outdoor, evening party held at the time of the Bon Festival in the hot days of summer, no one connected with the hospital suffered from a shortage of these things.

The prize giving was held in the upstairs recreation room above the long corridor that extended from the entrance hall past several wards. It was a large room of 120 mats (about thirty feet wide by seventy feet long), and was used mainly for the various performances given each year to entertain the patients; the room had witnessed some quick-draw swordplay presented by that old maestro of the art, Raifu Hibino, and had resounded to the perpetual clacking open and shut of fans which accompanies a comic turn performed by a male-female vaudeville pair. It was also used for theatrical events put on by the staff and a few volunteer patients, and the staff party that would follow today's prize giving would be held here also. The busiest occasion during recent years

36

had been when it was used as an office for Kiichiro's election campaign, when countless circulars had been dispatched. All the staff and interns had been dragooned into the chore of addressing envelopes and slipping the printed matter inside, and even the great man's youngest son had been seen, if not helping at least wandering about, and Momoko had licked stamps with that air of absorption she showed when anything interested her. The two elder daughters, however, did not put in an appearance. This was to be Momoko's first and last taste of the election, for the real campaigning was done far off in the mountains of Yamagata. But outside these occasions the room remained unused and deserted, an empty, profitless space with some tables piled up in one corner.

Today, however, it was jammed full of folk; more than a hundred men and women were neatly lined up in six rows, facing quietly and properly to their front. The nurses were all dressed in freshly laundered uniforms and were all looking more or less at their feet. The male nurses and the clerical staff had all made efforts to dress themselves up. Even the interns had put on traditional Japanese male dress (*montsuki hakama,* a dark jacket with wide sleeves decorated with a family crest, and wide, almost skirt-like trousers) to dignify the occasion. These normally slovenly, facetious young men seemed quite different beings; it was as if they felt that this ceremonial garb reflected what they really were.

Among the interns there were some who were directly related to Kiichiro and his wife Hisa, including two, Seisaku Kanazawa and Katsujiro Nirasawa, who were expected to join the hospital elite in the future. The former had just graduated from the Medical School of Tokyo University, and the latter was still attending Chiba Medical University. Despite the fact that both were blood relations they were included among the interns and led the same kind of life as the others. Kiichiro's policy was that relations should be treated in exactly the same way as total strangers, a way of thinking natural for someone who had raised himself to his present eminence by his own strenuous efforts. He felt that treating people as members of the family from the start would only subvert the will to succeed. In fact, if any student showed himself to be of the proper mettle and studied hard and successfully, he would be accepted into the family whether he was an actual relation or not. For example, the present heir to the directorship, Tetsukichi Nire, although certainly from the next village to Kiichiro's, was no blood relation, though some such link could perhaps have been established if one went back far enough. Tetsukichi had first been adopted, and then married to Kiichiro's eldest daughter, Ryuko, some four years ago.

So they were all assembled together in the recreation room, blood relations who would soon have their M.D.'s, interns who were just interns, the porter of the main gate, a male nurse who was said to be queerer in the head than his actual patients, all seated bolt upright (or rather kneeling bolt upright) on the mats. The maids and nurses were not so bolt upright, for they were standing at the sides of the room and spent a great deal of the time fiddling with their fingers. All of them, whether sitting, kneeling or standing, were obliged to endure these uncomfortable formal postures throughout a ceremony that would be by no means short.

The actual giver of the prizes stood facing the assembled staff on the dais that was used for dramatic performances. There was a desk placed in the center of this dais and there he stood, the head and representative of the first generation of the Nire family, the man who had created the hospital, the fifty-five-year-old Member of the House of Representatives, Kiichiro Nire, maintaining an affable smile on his face and wearing a black *habutae* silk *montsuki* jacket below it. In fact, he would have much preferred to be dressed in Western clothes, since he knew how to wear his thick, dark, double-breasted suit impeccably and the suit showed off a gold watch and chain to advantage. He had a number of gold watches and chains, ranging from super-deluxe articles to pieces of trumpery, and he wore whichever seemed suited to the time and place.

Kiichiro Nire's original name had been Jinsaku Kanazawa. He was born in a small village in the northeast, one of a string of indeterminate villages along the miserably dusty road that runs below Mt. Zao, one of Japan's most famous beauty spots, from the prefecture's main town of Yamagata to the smaller town of Kaminoyama. The Kanazawas had been the leading family of the village for generations, perhaps centuries, but were already in total decline by the time Kiichiro's father, Monzaemon, was in charge. So when a fourth son was born, Monzaemon had him sent, as soon as he was out of primary school, to be adopted by another farmer in a neighboring village. Jinsaku ran away from there before the year was out, an unpardonable act that incurred Monzaemon's displeasure, and thereafter he was brought up by his elder sister, Okame, who was living in the same village. But Jinsaku did not remain there long either, simply disappearing one day. It was said that he must be in the city of Sendai, some thirty miles to the east, then it was rumored that he had gone to Tokyo, and so the years passed and he was quite forgotten.

Then suddenly one day he reappeared, wearing not only what was obviously a brand new kimono and a stylish straw boater, but also bearing, to everyone's amazement, a stamped certificate proving him to be a bona fide doctor. Having set all mouths agape, he went from house to house giving out those presents that are customary on such occasions. The presents themselves were not up to much, but at least he was doing the right thing by the village and restoring his reputation there. As soon as this distribution was over he disappeared again, and once more stayed away for a number of years. The next time he reappeared, he seemed so resplendent a gentleman that the villagers momentarily lost their powers of speech, particularly since it transpired that he was now married, had his own hospital (or, at least, surgery), and was remarkably prosperous; and when he showed them his extra-large visiting card they were quite unable to make any sense of what was written on it. When Jinsaku had lived in the village he had always despised the farmer's life, and he had also despised his own name with its rural connotations, proclaiming that he was not going to put up with a name like that for the rest of his life. Not only was his new name of Kiichiro (as a result of having the character *ichi,* meaning "one," in it) totally inappropriate for a fourth son, the fourth son being normally a candidate for the role of village idiot, but for some unimaginable reason he had taken the shattering decision to change his surname as well, not by the respectable method of being adopted into a household with the name of Nire but simply by taking the name—and, indeed, creating it. The name was more than just extraordinary, it had never existed, and so rare was the character with which it was written that practically nobody was able to read his visiting card. This gave Jinsaku or Kiichiro the opportunity to recite the wording on the card with great portentousness at most of the households he visited, a ritual accompanied once more by the distribution of presents, which were certainly superior to those he had brought previously but were, even so, more remarkable for the splendor of their wrappings than for their contents. After this he returned straight to Tokyo and once more stayed away a long time: he was now a success, and appeared to have no need for this village at the back of beyond.

Nevertheless, he did not break off all connections with the place of his birth. He adopted, by a peculiar method of his own, two boys from villages in the area, and a number of young men from thereabouts went up to Tokyo with his assistance. News was sent home about his journey to Europe and also about the building of the great hospital in Aoyama, though not too much should be made of this, perhaps, since the information Kiichiro had printed was hugely elaborate and was sent principally to places and people who could hardly be thought of as being in any way interested. Apart from these two bulletins and the occasional rumor of his doings, Kiichiro disappeared once again from the consciousness of the inhabitants of his old home, so his third reappearance the year before the one in which our story opens, complete with Kaiser moustache and walking stick, was again an unusual event, though one with a definite purpose this time: Kiichiro intended to stand as local candidate for the Diet. Not satisfied with his "Doktor Medicine" acquired in foreign parts, nor with his palatial hospital, he now wished to sit in the House of Representatives. Swaying awkwardly in a ricksha, he descended first upon the men of influence in the village, and then upon anyone who had a vote. Although, unlike today, door-to-door canvassing was permitted, the giving of presents was not, so the distribution that had occurred on the previous two occasions did not take place. Instead, appropriate amounts of money found their way from hand to hand, directed from the temporary campaign headquarters Kiichiro had set up at the best hotel in Kaminoyama; and thus he was elected.

Now here he was, in the 120-mat room, facing his assembled staff from the slightly superior eminence provided by the platform. Given his striking career, one might imagine a large, burly and imposing figure standing nonchalantly there. In fact Kiichiro was very short. He was certainly not what one would call weedy, but small he was. In compensation for this, his well-groomed hair was still jet black with a youthful sheen, as was his moustache, which was thick and upturned in a sprightly manner, consorting well with the confident line of his eyebrows. Since his eyes were rather small, narrow and mild and his nose perhaps a little overrefined, a trifle too thin at its bridge, the bristling growth on the hirsute areas of his head and face gave to the whole a welcome sense of strength, and also a repose that had a certain proud confidence about it, bordering on the condescending, even, perhaps, on the insolent.

This outward appearance was no effect of chance, but the result of a care that few people knew about. Great efforts were lavished on his proud moustache: it was liberally smothered in pomade, and its idiosyncratic upward curling was achieved by constant manipulation with the fingers. Kiichiro even powdered his face to achieve a more pleasing pallor, and made great use of the deodorant spray in one final flourish. In this way, your friendly but dignified Director was made ready for public consumption.

Kiichiro stood before the desk, which was piled high with prizes, and by his side stood the Deputy, Hidekichi Katsumata, looking almost as full of himself as his chief. The impression of smugness was accentuated in his case by the fact that his eyes were hidden behind rimless spectacles and one could not tell in which direction he was looking. Next to him was one M. Takada, the proprietor of a local shop called the Seiundo, who was wearing a loose, baggy frock coat, and who was also strikingly small. An objective viewer of the Prize-Giving Ceremony might well have wondered why the three principals on the dais should all have been so small, and might well have asked himself whether this was pure coincidence or an attempt, perhaps, on the Director's part to maintain a dignified presence by appearing with two virtual dwarfs.

Takada of the Seiundo was another of those who had originally intended to be a doctor. Things did not work out, however, and after abortive attempts to get on at two or three hospitals he had ended up in the dispensary of the Nire Hospital. As the hospital increased in size, he also began to lend a hand with the clerical work, and then, a few years ago, he had opened a small stationery store on the new main road along which the new streetcars were now running. He was always asked to take part in the Nire Hospital functions not simply because he was a former employee, nor because of his cheerful character, his constant concern for others, the smile that never left his face, but mainly because of his voice: it had a clarity and grace of modulation that resulted from a lung capacity which would not have disgraced a giant.

Seiundo (recently people had tended to call him by the name of his shop rather than by his actual surname) was indispensable at an important function like today's prize giving because of this clear, penetrating voice, for it was he who called out the names of the people who were to receive the prizes, which meant the names of the whole hospital staff. As each name was called, the recipient would move to the center of the room, where a pathway through the throng had been cleared, advance to the dais, mount the steps, and stand before the Director. The Deputy would then hand over the box or lesser bundle containing the prize (or merely a hand towel) to the Director. Kiichiro, in turn, would bestow it, calmly and courteously, upon its destined recipient, who would bow deferentially and retire. Seiundo would then call out the next name and the ritual would repeat itself, and so on *ad infinitum*.

Behind the Director was a row of chairs, and here the Nire family were seated. They were all obliged to be here, young and old, male and female, and remain right to the end of this lengthy ceremony that accorded Kiichiro such undiluted pleasure. The prizes had to be presented before the whole family as this increased the brilliance and significance of the occasion, adding that sense of pomp and circumstance appropriate to ceremonies in court circles.

The reactions of the members of the family varied, as was clear from their expressions. Momoko, who was seated toward the end of the row, was fidgeting about in her chair as if in the throes of some almost unbearable suspense. This was, in fact, the case, since she found each year's prize giving as enjoyable as did her father. What could be more amusing than to hear, on this one day of the year, Seiundo call out the real names of the staff, polite prefixes, suffixes and all, in sincere and serious tones? It was fascinating to hear the name "Katsusaburo Yoshida, Esquire," and see that it belonged to none other than a male nurse commonly known as "Mallet Head" because of his square skull. He would gape about him two or three times in apparent amazement at hearing this name, and then edge nervously toward the dais. "Miss Tazuru Takurada" turned out to be that nurse with a face like a pekinese whose shrieks of laughter were forever enlivening mealtimes. Her face turned an alarmed and alarming red, and she was unnervingly silent as she came forward gingerly to receive her due. Momoko found the pleasures these performances offered inexhaustible. Today she was properly and neatly dressed and did not look like some child from the back streets, and she was probably one of the only two among the hundred and twenty or so people present who sincerely felt that the longer the occasion continued the more it would be to her liking; the other, of course, was her father.

At the beginning of the prize giving it was customary for the Director to deliver a few words thanking everyone for their labors during the past year, and requesting similar or superior efforts in the future. This year, however, was the fifteenth anniversary of the founding of the new hospital in Aoyama (it had, in fact, been founded only fourteen years before, but Japanese people are in the habit of calling the first anniversary of anything the second, and thus always seem a year advanced in such calculations); for this reason something beyond the normal few words was to be expected, and those standing and kneeling there endured aching legs and feet in the hope that the longer speech might also mean superior prizes.

The Director was now delivering a series of remarks about the political situation. We were at the dawning of a new age. It had dawned. The old, bureaucratic, militarist government had fallen. We now had a new cabinet formed from a political party. And who were the leading figures in this new cabinet? All of them, he had the impudence to maintain—the Prime Minister, Takashi Hara, the Finance Minister, Korekiyo Takahashi, and many more—were staunch friends and supporters of his; a baseless claim, but impressive. He then touched upon world affairs. Our Empire was now one of the world's leading nations. On his earlier travels abroad this claim could not properly have been made. But now it could, and, if made, it would be found to be true. Japan had joined the major powers of the world. He then switched to a frontal attack on *nouveaux riches* shipowners, which seemed of only slight relevance to his preceding words. Perhaps he found it annoying that they should, so many of them, be making umpteen times more profit than he, and he predicted that these millionaires had a bad year coming to them—let them be sure of that. On the contrary, our hospital's prosperity, being on a firm, broad base, would continue on its upward course. He then concluded with an announcement of particular importance for the hospital and staff. The Nire Hospital and the Imperial Mental Hospital were undoubtedly the same hospital, and yet their main concern had for some time been with mental health. There had been certain criticisms of the use of the word "Imperial" on the grounds that such a word was inappropriate, even presumptuous, for a private institution. Consequently, to mark this fifteenth anniversary, the two hospitals would be given one, new, joint name with effect from the first day of the New Year. That name would be— and at this point Kiichiro's gaze wandered tantalizingly over his audience who were now pricking up their ears for the first time, as determined as he was to savor each drop of this delicious moment—that name would be the "Nire Hospital of Mental Pathology." The phraseology "Hospital of Mental Pathology" rather than mere "Mental Hospital" had been chosen advisedly, for it possessed a wider range of meaning than the simpler title, and would also help to counteract the misunderstandings and prejudices that ordinary people had about a hospital which provided asylum for lunatics.

The logic of this statement was fairly impenetrable, and the fact that no one could follow it probably accounted for the grunts and nods of acknowledgment and understanding that arose among his audience.

Kiichiro continued in the stilted style he had chosen for this address. In everyday life he used a much easier style, almost excessively easy in fact, although there was nothing odd about that: it merely indicated a desire to be less formal which reflected the supposedly modern cast of his mind. However, these lax speech habits now persisted in the rhythms and intonations of this more formal address, which was delivered in the slack nasal drawl that was the hallmark of his normal mode of conversation, producing a very peculiar effect.

But the speaker himself remained oblivious, or at least careless, of this mannerism, and continued. Ever since his return to these shores from studying psychology at the universities of Berlin and Halle, he had spared no effort to further his researches in this area. Efforts in this field were still not generally recognized at their true value in this country. However, while life and breath remained in his body, he would continue to strive, just as all those assembled here today would continue to strive with him, treading this stony, thorny path. And one day the results of all this would be recognized, and then his achievements would be seen at their true value, and he would receive his reward: a baronetcy no doubt.

"A baronetcy no doubt"—the phrase was tossed lightly and confidently to the crowd, but it was, of course, a totally baseless assumption and in this way typical of Kiichiro. It certainly had as astonishing an effect on his audience as he could have hoped for, though the few people there of some intelligence may have felt a proper skepticism, as was apparently the case with those who, no doubt unconsciously, twitched slightly about the face on hearing these braggart words. Immediately behind the Director was seated the young master, Ryuko's husband Tetsukichi, and he knit his eyebrows slightly in fairly obvious displeasure, as if to say that his adoptive father was no doubt a man of great importance, but that he found this irresponsible looking on a non-existent bright side something with which he himself had little sympathy. His wife, on the other hand, her three-year-old child balanced on her knee, remained seated just as before, looking straight ahead of her, each hair on her head impeccably in place. Her smug, unchanging expression implied quite clearly that if her father said he was going to receive a baronetcy, then a baronetcy he would receive. It was as simple as that, and this judgment seemed to be shared by most of those present, the only difference being that they did not express their faith by remaining coldly expressionless as she did, but rather by gazing solemnly and open-eyed, as if words genuinely had failed them. They showed amazement, they were overawed, they looked nervously up toward the dais, toward the presence itself. And there he stood, the baronet of the future, puffing out his chest, smiling genially at his own words, bringing his address to a close. At that moment it is doubtful that Kiichiro looked a little man at all to his employees.

However, back in the family seats the baby of the family, Yonekuni, his throat still swathed in a compress, was beginning to look very fretful, as if the dullness of the proceedings was no longer to be endured.

"Oh, I wish they'd get on with it and get it started," he muttered as if in pain, rolling his goggle eyes in furious fashion.

"Now you be quiet. It's started already, can't you see?" replied his sister Momoko, sitting next to him. She, too, was bored to tears waiting for the real entertainment to begin, but, as his big sister, she felt entitled to offer these mild words of rebuke.

Fortunately the actual prize giving did soon begin. Prizes were first awarded to those who had labored through the whole period that the hospital had been at Aoyama, and there were more than a few of such people, certainly more than could be counted on the fingers of both hands. The proprietor of the Seiundo unrolled the scroll on which their names were listed, and first read out in deep, penetrating tones the name of Hidekichi Katsumata, Esquire.

Here an odd situation arose, since the Deputy was obliged to hand his prize over to the Director, that being his role on this occasion, and then receive it back again, bowing low as he did so. But this slight absurdity was soon forgotten and normal dignity restored with the next name called: "Tasuke Kakurai, Esquire," and with respectful restraint Tasuke made his way to the central passageway and advanced to the dais; as did they all, one by one, all of them providing Momoko with the same passionate amusement as she leaned forward in her seat, unable to decide which one walked in the funniest way, which made the most amusing ascent to the dais, or which received the prize in the most ludicrous manner.

Let it be said here that the real power behind this entertaining Prize-Giving Day was none other than the wife of the Director, Hisa, although she did not perhaps give that impression. There she sat, motionless as a statue, her face seeming almost non-existent below the overlarge chignon in which her hair was arranged, a topknot which had unofficially been nicknamed 203 Meter Hill, that battleground of glorious memory just outside Port Arthur. Fortunately she had her head slightly raised at this moment and was looking straight ahead so that the face could be observed, although what was most immediately noticeable about her was the black brocade sash bound firmly about her gray, striped kimono, and the gold chain that hung low over her breast. She was exactly fifty years old, yet looked considerably older than her husband, who was five years her senior and was now contentedly handing out prizes. Since her face was even longer than that of her eldest daughter, and her cheeks hollow with age, it gave a peculiarly empty impression, an effect that was enhanced by her extremely refined and prominent nose, which hooked swiftly back at the end with twice the abruptness her daughter's did. It was a face that did not encourage intimacy, the face of an old woman in which it was hard to see the young woman's it had been. Still, when young, it had obviously been no run-of-the-mill face but one with definite individuality, though the ancient dignity of its forebears had come to dominate with the passing of the years. Hisa came from an old established family in Chichibu, the mountainous area immediately to the north of Tokyo's Kanto Plain. Unlike Kiichiro's her family had not at any time fallen into decline, and the black pillars of the ancestral home shone as heavily and prosperously as ever, as befitted the manor house of the region. One of the hospital tradesmen had once said that her face reminded him of that of a feudal lord, and it was true that its vacancy and immobility had nothing of the untutored boorishness and untamed energy that supposedly marked the rising generation. Indeed her face revealed nothing of what was going on inside her, and it was hard to tell whether she was annoyed with something or pleased with it. She had never been in the habit of talking much, either.

Nevertheless, it would be a mistake to assume that she was simply the result of generations of aristocratic inbreeding, weighed down with that dead refinement which indicates a loss of vital spirits. She was, in fact, the prime mover behind the success of the Nire Hospital. No one in the hospital had any idea by what devious roads Hisa and Kiichiro, alias Jinsaku, had come to plight their troth, but it was well known that the money required to set Kiichiro up initially in business in Hongo had come from Hisa's family. One could certainly maintain that the fashionable success which had been made of that original venture was due to Kiichiro's talents; but that Kiichiro had been able to advance from being the brightest doctor in Hongo to being the Director of a large hospital in Aoyama was very much due to the unobtrusive, tight-fisted management Hisa had practiced over the years. It had been very hard for her at first, for Kiichiro's love of ostentation ensured that his first tiny hospital (no more, in fact, than a mere general practitioner's surgery) was jammed full of alleged interns who were little more than non-paying guests. With her small household budget, she was obliged to be careful about everything. Even the soy sauce that the interns sprinkled liberally over their pickles was something to be worried about; she watered it down and added salt to disguise its enfeebled taste.

Everything was a source of anxiety, and when Kiichiro was away at his researches in Germany it was she who kept the practice going, watching over the locum Kiichiro had appointed in his place, and ensuring that her husband would find things exactly as he had left them on his return. Proof of long years of dedication to his cause could be seen in her face. Though the whiteness of her skin helped to conceal her wrinkles, countless wrinkles were still there, etched into a face which at first seemed so calm as to provide no record of any life or passion that might have worked upon it.

The Nire Hospital was firmly established now, its future assured to a degree that even Kiichiro had never imagined in his most ambitious dreams, so that the main reasons for Hisa's anxieties had mostly disappeared. Even so, it was she, inconspicuously hidden away "within," who still supported the whole great edifice. Kiichiro was by temperament a man who trusted his wildest intuitions in all things, and who made his plans accordingly. These plans were all put into effect, but it was Hisa who organized the financial side and ensured that the large dreams of her husband were firmly connected with reality. The Deputy was, of course, aware of all that went on, and for this reason trod more warily in the presence of the Director's wife than in that of the Director himself. Every week he would take the account ledgers, written in Oishi's spidery, neurotic script, to the rooms of the source of power, but Kiichiro never paid any attention to them whatsoever, and it was Hisa who would, at some time, pass her professional and careful eye over them.

Few people in the hospital had any idea of the real situation, for Hisa remained always unobtrusive, expressionless and silent, secluded "within." But one of the maids who worked "within" had once overheard that rarest of things, a quarrel between the Director and his wife. The cause of the trouble seemed to be the Director's involvements with other women, and the Director had, it appeared, fallen into a rare state of panic, replying to her accusations in a soft, coaxing tone of voice: "I know, Hisa, I know. Of course I owe everything to you. How could I forget it was you who scraped and saved and got all the money together for the hospital. You built the hospital; it was all your doing, I know. Everything I have I owe to you. It's all your doing, everything. I know."

Even Prize-Giving Day, this troublesome annual event, was all stage-managed, not by Kiichiro, but by his wife. Kiichiro simply stood on the stage with a smug expression on his face handing out prizes, but the work of choosing over a hundred prizes, and deciding who ought to receive what, was undertaken by Hisa. Since this year was the fifteenth anniversary, some special token of gratitude needed to be given to those who had worked at the hospital throughout the whole period, and although money had been very tight at home because of the outlays on the election campaign last year, Hisa had made up her mind that the dozen or so people who had been with them all the time would have to be given a kimono. The rising costs of the past year had certainly given her cause for worry, since rice and most other things had just about doubled in price. Still, the hospital was on a firm enough basis financially for that to be taken in its stride. No, what really bothered her, although she did not show it to outsiders, was Kiichiro's political involvement, which made her genuinely angry. What was the point of it? Why did her husband suddenly have to decide he must get mixed up with that kind of thing? As she saw it, politics meant nothing but a perpetual wasting of money.

Kiichiro would reply to these accusations in that careless tone of voice he always used when determined to convince somebody of something:

"Well, of course, there must be some initial outlay. But the returns will be greater than the expenses, don't you worry. The money will come back, in some form or other."

Hisa, however, who believed in straight rather than circuitous dealings, found this optimism impossible to accept. For example, at this very moment, Kiichiro was setting up a Development Corporation back in his home district, which was to apply the large-scale farming methods employed in the virgin lands of Hokkaido. This had served as excellent publicity material during his election campaign, but Hisa was unable to believe that it would work. Her cold, professional eye told her that the corporation was simply a machine that swallowed up banknotes and spewed out mud, just like one of the new tractors it used for plowing up the soil.

"Isuke Matsubara, Esquire." Seiundo's voice echoed through the room. Hisa, who, despite her secluded life, knew the names of every single member of the staff, sat wondering if it had been necessary to give a brand-new set of clothes (Japanese-style *haori* and *hakama*) to that filthy old man as well, but her expression showed no indication of this doubt, and she remained with her eyes fixed straight ahead.

Momoko and Yonekuni, however, could hardly restrain their delight. That old man who normally looked as if he had just crawled out of a chimney was now dressed in *haori* and *hakama*, which he must have borrowed from somebody although it was impossible to guess who; clothes with a slightly shabby, faded air it was true, but still very proper, as was the upright way in which he was sitting. And there was not one trace of soot on his hands or face. Forward he came, a suspicious, almost furious look on his face, and he seized hold of his large parcel much as an eagle snatches up its prey. He was not used to the baggy, trouser-like *hakama*, which seemed to hamper his normal way of walking, and he stumbled as he descended the steps from the dais.

"Miss Nao Shimoda." Seiundo's voice echoed again, and Momoko and Yonekuni very nearly started clapping as their beloved nanny made her appearance. She was dearer to them than their own mother (although it must be admitted that by normal standards they had a peculiarly distant and unapproachable mother), and they would have loved to be absorbed into her warm, gentle and very fat person; but there she stood among the crowd of lesser beings, for this one day a mere employee of the hospital. Really, she should not have been there at all but up on the platform looking after those children she had reared. But Prize-Giving Day occurred only once a year, and Kiichiro loved this formal handing-over of prizes to all and sundry; no doubt he would have been happy to do the same for his parents, if only they had still been around to let him do so.

Nanny Shimoda bowed awkwardly and received with appropriate modesty the kimono Hisa had chosen for her. As she did so, a smile hovered on the cheeks of Seiko, who was sitting with eyes lowered, looked tired and listless, a smile that represented the affection she still retained for her former nanny and a simple gratitude that overcame her ideas of what was proper behavior. The mother and sister at her side, however, remained apparently as indifferent as ever, still gazing out expressionlessly into space. Yet it is doubtful that Ryuko's feelings about Nanny Shimoda were all that different from her sister's, or had undergone any sort of change. It was merely that such emotions took second place to the more important concerns of her father, his plans for her, his principles, his ideals. In Kiichiro himself, these things were simply a part of his nature, and they had a certain redeeming comicality about them; but in Ryuko's case her father's mainly bogus spirit, his misguided and misguiding grasp of the world, had become abstracted, hardened into ideas that lacked any of the life they still had in him. She saw so much of life in terms of form, its accidental shape having taken on for her an essential quality, that it never crossed her mind to question her father's decision that the prize giving should be a pompous occasion; since he had decided so, a pompous occasion it was, to be carried out with all possible solemnity.

On Ryuko's lap sat her three-year-old son, Shun'ichi. The fact that she was holding a little boy who was at an age when children find it almost impossible to remain still for a moment, and the fact that this child was her father's first grandson, no doubt contributed to the tight-lipped hardness of Ryuko's expression. Shun'ichi had already begun to sulk and was kicking his legs about in a clearly pettish mood. Since he had been obliged to put on a formal boy's dress, which was very uncomfortable, and was also being forcibly restrained by his stern mother, this was not surprising. Obviously the child should never have been there, but Kiichiro expected everyone, particularly an eldest child of the family even if that child were almost fresh from the womb, to be present on this ceremonial occasion, and to behave impeccably in accordance with his tastes and inclinations. Since her father's inclinations were as holy writ for her, Ryuko muttered menacing threats into the child's unresponsive ear. The result was that the child struggled even more and began sliding from his mother's lap, so, while apparently still paying full and serious attention to the proceedings, she gave him an extremely nasty pinch on the thigh. Shun'ichi screwed his face up as if he were about to start howling; but he stopped, aware, no doubt, that this mother of his was capable of far more terrible things than pinching him if sufficiently roused.

Shun'ichi's father and Ryuko's husband, Tetsukichi, seemed unaware of the pinch administered to his son and heir, although this was not because he was absorbed in the ceremony. He appeared to have declined the view of his adoptive father's posterior, which was what filled his direct line of vision, and instead glared up at the ceiling with a hard, bored expression on his face. Despite the fact that he was the heir to the Nire fortune, and despite the upbringing he had undergone at the hands of his adoptive parents since he was a boy, there was still an inextinguishable aura of simplicity about him, which could be seen as honest forthrightness, or as a boorish peasant's half-witted bluntness if one chose to be critical. This impression of forthrightness was highlighted by his sitting next to his wife, who was obviously a very different character, although Ryuko's tendency to treat anything not connected with the Nire family's fortunes with cold contempt and Tetsukichi's absorption in scholarship were similarly obsessive, which suggested that their natures had something essentially in common. Despite this, they did not get on all that well with each other.

Although even a three-year-old child had been dragged to this function, there were, in fact, two members of the family who were not in attendance. One of these was Kiichiro's eldest son, Oshu, who was still at school in Sendai and so could not be here. The other one hesitates to call a member of the family since he was only an adopted son, but Kiichiro was his adoptive father and his absence calls for some comment because he was actually in the hospital. Just before the ceremony began, a number of people had combined efforts to bring him along, but he had used his ferocious strength to burst free of them and run away; and he was now probably hiding in the hospital's bedding cupboard or somewhere similar.

This child was, and had been since his birth, a sort of wonder boy, one of those rare jests performed by the hand of Creation, a freak called Tatsuji who had already reached, while in sixth grade at primary school, the amazing height of six feet one inch. He was the son of a charcoal burner from Kiichiro's home district, who lived in an even more remote part of the mountains than that in which Kiichiro's own village was situated. The wonder boy's freak body consumed a wondrous amount of rice, and his father was finding it impossible to raise him. Kiichiro heard of this and had the boy officially adopted into the household of one of his relatives back home, saying he would take the boy in himself and look after him. The charcoal burner and his monstrous son descended on Tokyo soon after that; and the father spent three days sight-seeing, then slipped off quietly back to Yamagata while his embarrassingly large son was asleep. When Tatsuji awoke and discovered his loss, he bawled so loudly that his voice not only resounded throughout the grounds of the Nire Hospital but could be heard all over the surrounding countryside. This was the basis of a rumor which persisted long after: that a lion had been heard roaring in the area.

Kiichiro had decided that the boy was excellent material for a Sumo wrestler. Dewanoumi, who ran a stable for Sumo wrestlers and was a friend of Kiichiro's, paid a visit and gave the wonder boy a toy. After that he took him to the practice room, showed him the wrestlers at work, and liberally plied him with adequate amounts of food. This happened a number of times, and finally Kiichiro asked the boy what he thought of becoming a Sumo wrestler, since it was a good life for a growing lad like him; but Tatsuji only shook his podgy, bloated face stupidly from side to side. He was not sent to the same primary school as Momoko and Yonekuni, but to the Aoyama Primary School, where he entered the fifth grade. From his slow, disjointed answers, it seemed that his aim in life was to become a doctor. This ambition was not likely to be fulfilled, for he was as timid as his body was large, and the amazing development of his physique was not reflected in his words and actions, although one thing he did respond to quickly enough was any attempt to wheedle him into becoming a Sumo wrestler: he would obstinately refuse to nod his head when questioned about that. It was difficult to work out what was going on inside that head, but it was obvious that he was ashamed of his monstrous body.

At first Kiichiro had been inordinately proud of the wonder boy, and very eager to show him off to people. One of his constant claims to his guests was:

"You know, the fact is, I've adopted two sons. One of them has the finest mind in Japan. The other has the finest physique."

But his attempts to show off the wonder boy became progressively less successful. Today's prize giving was a case in point, for Tatsuji never appeared at it. Of course, no real attempt had been made to force him to come, for the boy was very strong, and despite the low, incomprehensible mutter which was his everyday form of speech, he did, if provoked, produce that astonishing roar which would again fill the surrounding countryside.

The prize giving proceeded on its lethargic course. The long-term employees had received their rewards, special prizes had been given to those who for some trumped-up reason were said to deserve them, and now the rank and file had been reached, those who in a normal year could expect to receive a hand towel. This year, though, they were each getting a cardboard box with rather superior *geta* made of paulownia wood inside it. There seemed to be no end to these people.

Seiundo had to call out all the names, polite titles still prefixed or suffixed to each one, and even his voice became somewhat patchy and capricious at times, a slight crack here, a little hoarseness there. But the Deputy remained unruffled, handing over the prizes to the Director with the same coolness and aplomb. As for the Director himself, there was no sign of exhaustion or listlessness or strain, but rather an increase in vitality as time went on. This was combined with a greater composure, which appeared in the more deliberate and time-consuming gesture with which he handed each box over, and the more controlled dignity of the way he leaned stiffly forward to acknowledge the obeisance of each employee. A cheerful smile suffusing his satisfied face, and all the while twiddling his well-groomed Kaiser moustache as if to indicate how great a role the idea of perfection played in his life, Kiichiro never once took his eyes off the back of each recipient until he or she had walked stiffly all the way to the place he or she had come from. Only then would he nod briefly to indicate that the next name should be called. And the next was called, after Seiundo had swallowed a number of times to ensure that his throat was still in adequate shape for the task. But at last it seemed that this interminable affair was approaching something like an end.

Those standing on the 120 mats had sore feet, those kneeling had aching legs, and the cold that filled the whole room, inadequately heated as it was by the feeble glow of charcoal in the large *hibachi* in each corner, now seeped up through the mats into those exhausted legs and feet. The faces of the seated members of the family showed unmistakable signs of weariness as well. Even the person who had showed the most positive attitude to Kiichiro's ceremony, the earnest Ryuko, who had been until recently looking resolutely to her front, was obviously sleepy. Only the indefatigable Momoko showed no sign whatsoever of tiredness. She was still enjoying Seiundo's voice and thinking what a good idea it would be if Billiken could take over his role should he become sick, and maintaining a profound interest in the odd variety of approaches to the dais and the individuality of each bow. Between each performance she would turn speaking looks on the younger brother at her side, who was squirming about in the throes of acute boredom and producing the occasional cough in memory of his influenza, now just about cured.

But suddenly Yonekuni began to produce a peculiar wheeze in his throat as if he were about to have a real paroxysm of coughing. At the same time, an odd sniffling sound started to circulate in the room. It was an infectious snigger.

"Now what's wrong with you?" asked Momoko, giving her little brother a good jog, but when she looked back to her front again the following sight greeted her eyes.

Right in the middle of the room, in the pathway cleared for the ascent to the dais, stood the porter of the main gate, a person who, in his own unique way, was just as frightful a specimen as Isuke of the cookhouse. This porter, one Toyobei, was not, however, just standing there: despite his age, he was positively rushing about in that narrow space. His name had been called, not just once or twice but three times, and on the third occasion it had finally got through to him that it was indeed his name that was being called. Now a fearful panic began. Since he was right at the end of a row he had to struggle the furthest possible distance in order to emerge, thrusting and stamping his way energetically past a number of unwilling victims. On account of the impetus with which he finally arrived at the open ground, he seemed to lose sight of his objective and gaped about him in an attempt to regain his bearings. That done, he was about to set off in what would have been a beeline away from the dais, when he realized his error and moved forward in the right direction, this time at an even more furious pace to make up for lost time.

Toyobei had legs that had long ago earned him the nickname "Bandy," but the unusual speed with which he propelled himself forward meant that his legs went beyond mere human conceptions of bandiness, and he now resembled a crab that had decided to give up its normal sideways gait and was scuttling precipitately forward to the attack. The sight was enough to make anyone momentarily forget that he was taking part in a solemn Prize-Giving Ceremony. The subdued snigger spread like an infection, and Momoko was immediately overtaken by the giggles, although she resolutely pinched herself on the thighs and the back of her hands to prevent this from bursting forth in a real howl of laughter.

Still out there, Toyobei, quite dazzled by the occasion, dashed eccentrically up the steps and savagely attempted to snatch his prize before the Deputy had managed to hand it to the Director. Kiichiro, however, remained unruffled. He intended to maintain the dignity of this occasion no matter what happened. He nodded two or three times to convey the habitual sentiment that things had been, and were being, "well done," and then tried to hand over the prize in an even slower, more refined manner than usual. But Toyobei was not to be denied. He wrested his prize from the Director's grasp and made off with it, forgetting to bow and giving another dazzling display of acute bandiness as he zoomed down the steps.

This was the last straw for Momoko. Her easy capacity for tears was equaled only by her capacity for laughter. When she produced, as if by magic, her large bogus-looking tears, they were rarely, if ever, accompanied by any sound. But it was the reverse when she laughed: she produced no girlish giggle but a full-bodied bellow, a side-holding, rolling-in-the-aisles kind of letting go. Miraculously, she was able to hold it back on this occasion, but the terrible strain of doing so appeared in the contortions that now gripped her face, and then in her throat, which started to tremble. This trembling was soon transformed into deeper spasms, and from that area weird gurgling sounds broke forth, as if she were being tortured and was now at her last gasp.

"Mistress Momo," her neighbor, Seiko, admonished her. Yet even this most ladylike member of the family, as she watched the convulsions that shook Momoko, began herself to be affected. Her chin gradually sank downward and minor tremors agitated her shoulders. But she suddenly managed to pull herself together, for at her side sat Ryuko with her baby on her lap, the object and conscious representative of the widely held belief that it was the women of the Nire family who had real quality and class. Ryuko was determined that Kiichiro's pompous, self-congratulatory ceremony should end in the same vein as it had begun, and she had made a slight movement. It was so slight as to be almost imperceptible, but Seiko perceived it clearly enough. It was a warning, an attempt to save Seiko from that degeneracy with which the majority of the people in the hospital could so easily infect her, an admonition to follow the example of her sister.

Ryuko raised herself bolt upright in her chair, and the rather weary expression that had been upon her face vanished. This sacred ceremony, which only took place once a year, was in danger of being desecrated by grubby, impious hands, or rather feet. The porter's bandy legs were of no import. It was not a matter of whether a silly, childish Momoko should laugh or not. The real question was whether Kiichiro's pompous ceremony was to be conducted with the pomposity due to it, and obviously it should and must. Nothing should be allowed to prevent that. It was a mark of the narrowness of this determination that she would allow nothing to stand in its way. It was this determination which now gave that conspicuous coldness to her face, and which made her tighten her grip on the child on her lap, although the child had already

55

been rendered perfectly quiet as he sensed the unflinching resolve of his mother. Her haughty, defiant gaze took in the whole room, as if daring anyone to misbehave himself, for traces of a snicker still remained sporadically here and there.

"No, I'm afraid I never touch it. But don't let me hold you back. Drink up, Kuroda; you too, Mihira. Enjoy yourselves. You see, this is what I drink; my favorite poison, you might say. It's called Bordeaux. Now, that's a very fine name, Bordeaux."

And Kiichiro filled his glass once more with Bordeaux, a drink that was related in no way to the French wine of that name, being a completely non-alcoholic beverage, a red-tinted, sweet soft drink that had only recently come on the market. The red liquid hissed into the glass, bubbles rising cheerfully to the surface, and Kiichiro downed the stuff with apparent relish, half in one pleasurable gulp and the rest more gradually, with the fine enjoyment of a connoisseur. The unknowing spectator would have found it hard to believe that Kiichiro was only drinking some colored, fizzy lemonade.

The scene had now changed from the recreation room to the Coral Room, which was upstairs in the quarters "within," next door to the VIP Reception Parlor. The titles of these rooms were all Kiichiro's creations and were not all that precise, the VIP Reception Parlor, for example, being merely a modest Western-style living room. Whenever Kiichiro had a visitor belonging to the world of politics—although since Kiichiro represented only a minor rural constituency nobody who was politically important ever turned up—he would receive him in the VIP Reception Parlor. It was, however, an age when even an unimportant Diet member such as Kiichiro could have a district governor replaced by whispering the appropriate words in the ear of the Minister for Home Affairs, so he was constantly being visited by petitioners. Whenever he had visitors from his district of Yamagata, he would entertain them in the Coral Room (the VIP Reception Parlor being a little too grand for them), since the elegance of these traditional surroundings would knock the bumpkins all of a heap, thus softening them up for any negotiations to come. That was the idea, anyway.

The Coral Room was a Japanese-style room of twelve mats, some eighteen by twelve feet in size. Kiichiro's passion for display could be seen in the tessellated wooden ceiling, the openwork phoenix pattern on the transoms, the elaborate cloud-and-chrysanthemum pattern with which the edges of the mats were lined, and also in the incongruity created by the sliding paper windows opening onto a Western-style terrace. It was called the Coral Room because the wall of the *tokonoma* alcove in one corner of the room was not decorated, as is normally the case, with a hanging picture scroll, but was inlaid with various bits of coral. The ''coral'' was not what it seemed, being imitation, but this did not prevent Kiichiro from brazenly explaining to all his visitors:

''Well, it's always been a minor hobby of mine, collecting coral, you know. Thought I might see what it looked like inlaid on the wall like that. Didn't work out too badly, either. So it's called the Coral Room. Not a bad name for it really. . .''

Another thing in this alcove that caught the eye was a number of display cases, which filled the two shelves and were stacked below them as well, and in which a variety of unrelated objects that Kiichiro had acquired during his travels abroad were set out. There was chinaware from Holland, silverware from France; but most of the collection was of German manufacture, for that was where Kiichiro had spent most of his two years abroad, and it was a country for which he felt a strong partiality. A characteristic of some of the objects was the doubt they inspired as to whether they should be given such special treatment: for example, the steelware from Solingen, which included knives, forks, spoons, scissors, nail scissors and even hair tweezers. It is rare, surely, to come across households where nail scissors and hair tweezers serve as ornaments.

A visit to the other rooms ''within'' would have disclosed the same prevalence of German things. The double bed that Kiichiro and his lady shared was of German manufacture, as was the superior chamber pot, which was only for VIP usage (and so labeled), not for ordinary beings; both objects belonged to that motley assemblage of things that Kiichiro had brought back on his return from that country. Indeed, such was the quantity of things he had acquired there that one might well wonder whether his aim in visiting Germany had been to undertake pure research or to engage in the import trade.

Hanging above these cases was the Imperial Portrait he had received when first taking his seat in the Diet chamber, and although Kiichiro was not in the habit of bowing to it every day as he should have done (in fact he took no notice of it whatsoever), he would still point out its existence, modestly but with a certain restrained pride, to any visitor from rural parts:

"Oh, that portrait I received personally from the Emperor himself."

This would arouse such fear and trembling in the guest that he would be unable to sleep soundly during his night in the Coral Room.

Still, the Coral Room was not used very often as a guest room, and to actually dine in it was even rarer, family get-togethers here being restricted to the prize giving and New Year's Day. As today's prize giving had been abnormally long, Kiichiro had only put in a token appearance at the party for his employees that was going on in the same recreation room, and had turned up, just a few minutes before, to join his family for dinner in the Coral Room. This was essentially a family gathering, with no one who could properly be given the title of "honored guest," but there were still three faces that would not normally have been there.

One of these belonged to a professor at Keio University called Kuroda, an old acquaintance of Kiichiro's with whom he had shared lodgings while in Berlin. His name was listed among the specialists at the Nire Hospital, but in fact he had never looked at even one patient. Kiichiro had a great passion for appearances and was happy just to have the honor of using this name, though it was a privilege for which he was obliged to pay a considerable amount of hard cash. The next was a balding gentleman the children used to refer to as "our uncle from Chichibu"; he was Hisa's elder brother, Tokutaro Aoki. The last and least was a certain Shirokichi Mihira from Yamagata, who had arrived yesterday in Tokyo for the very first time in his life. His round, sunburned face proclaimed his rural origins, as did his thick eyebrows and a blunt manner of speaking that indicated a splendidly pigheaded, no-nonsense view of the social world. He was helping himself lavishly to drink, and would occasionally produce a high-pitched howl, which provided Momoko and Yonekuni with some amusement. He was here because he was Tetsukichi's younger brother, which made him, despite the lack of any blood tie, one of their brothers, too.

His face had already turned bright red with drink, and the thick Yamagata dialect in which he spoke was therefore even harder for Momoko to grasp when the young man directed the following cheerful remarks at her:

"Now then, young lady, they say as how you're a real crybaby, that they do. You know, where I come from, someone who wets the bed

59

is called a little old piss pot. So I reckon we'll have to call you a little old cry pot, hah, hah, hah, that we will.''

Since Momoko was sitting some distance away from him he had been obliged to raise his voice considerably, and the howling laugh that followed set the small dishes on the table atremble. But he had been remarkably quiet up to this point, and not surprisingly, for ever since arriving at Ueno Station in the north of Tokyo he had been overwhelmed by his surroundings. Here was his brother's new home, a hospital huge enough to make one's eyes grow round in wonder, and he had been in attendance at the solemn Prize-Giving Ceremony; and then brought to this room, which he couldn't make head or tail of, as if he had been invited to some royal occasion in a palace.

It was Kiichiro's idea to have him brought here. Some years ago, after Tetsukichi had come to Tokyo, Shirokichi had been adopted by the master of the Takamatsuya, a Japanese-style hotel, or *ryokan,* in the town of Kaminoyama in Kiichiro's home district; but the master had recently died and Shirokichi was to take over. As the new master he would be someone of importance in that small town, and, since he was also the brother of Kiichiro's own heir, he could well play an important role in the next election campaign. This was not bad thinking on Kiichiro's part although, confronted as he now was by this strikingly drunken object, perhaps he was beginning to have second thoughts. Once Shirokichi had consumed a few drinks, nothing remained of his earlier attitude of respectful restraint, and he now seemed prepared to let himself go. The fact is that he was an honest, pleasant, easygoing and vulgar person, and the way he saw it was that, since he was in this grand room in this grand hospital eating this grand food, it would be a great mistake not to put away a good quantity of this drink that was so generously provided.

When asked how much drink he could hold, he licked his thick lips and replied:

"Well, now then, let's see; if it's *sake* like now, and on an empty stomach—nothing with it, you know—well, I reckon about three or four pints. But with this good food to go with it, oh, anything from seven to ten pints. Just to start with, that is, hah, hah, hah.''

Whereupon he drained the minute, porcelain wine cup, and clicked his tongue as if in frustration because he wasn't being allowed to down the stuff in large mugfuls.

"Only one thing I can beat Tetsukichi at. That's drinking. That don't mean I'm no good at other things. Trouble is, he's too good at everything. That's his trouble. Too good for me, anyway. Always has been. Since we were kids. Amazing head he has. Genius. Damn genius. No good at drinking, though. Couldn't never take it.''

Once Shirokichi got going, he became the focus of everyone's eyes, except for those of Ryuko, who behaved as if he were not there. She simply could not understand why this person had been allowed into, of all places, the Coral Room in the Nire Hospital, since he could hardly contribute to the dignity of the surroundings. It was totally beyond her understanding—although she had not, in fact, made any attempt to understand anything, since she found the situation beneath contempt. The silent Hisa, too, although not so deliberately aloof as Ryuko, showed no change of expression, so that it was difficult to say whether she could actually hear this drunken voice or not. She merely went on searching with her chopsticks for tender things to eat, slipping them gracefully into her mouth when she found them.

Tetsukichi had a different emotional response to what was going on, a sense of unhappy isolation. Here he was, far removed from that simple, honest farming life which his younger brother represented so well, the future Director of the Nire Hospital, and the husband of the aristocratic—as he was obliged to believe—eldest daughter of the house. It had been better before, when his son Shun'ichi had still been there at the table, but now there seemed to be no one in this family he cared for. Kiichiro was someone to whom he was profoundly obligated, and that obligation would remain unchanged throughout his life, but with the passage of time it had become clear to him that the two of them had nothing in common and, to be quite honest, he could not stand the man. And he could stand the general atmosphere of the Nire Hospital even less. When his three-year-old son burst out crying, or tore one of the paper screens, or scribbled something nonsensical on a scrap of paper, then, and only then, did Tetsukichi feel an indefinable sense of relief, as if some concealed emotion of his own were being given expression. Even his wife, if he were to be frank with himself, was not "his" in any real sense of the word. It is true that he could remember his own excitement when, four years ago, he had been able to refer to his benefactor's eldest daughter as his wife, because he had felt then that Ryuko was someone superior to himself, of a different order of existence, a young lady brought up in the cultured world of the capital and of the most prestigious private school in the country. But when he looked at her now and saw the frigid indifference with which she treated his brother, who, though blabbering away in his yokel dialect, was after all his brother, and the dialect was his own and he felt homesick to hear it, then he wondered if he knew anything about her at all. Was this the woman he shared his bed with? Wasn't she, rather, a complete stranger to him, someone he had never once truly met? She was a product of the Nire view of life, someone who responded solely to the combined dictates of Kiichiro's obsession with the super-swindle and Hisa's more complex legacy of ancient, aristocratic blood. He no longer believed or trusted in any of it, but while Shun'ichi had been there in the room, he could feel that something reflected him, since at least half of that child's blood was his own. But how did Kiichiro behave toward his grandson? All he could do was dandle him and talk to him in his smooth, friendly voice as if he were cajoling some person of influence in that constituency of his.

"Yes, you are heavy, aren't you? What a weight you are. Marvelous weight; absolutely wonderful."

And that was all. Kiichiro obviously found the child a nuisance and was only too glad to dispose of him into the care of Nanny Shimoda. Did he feel any love for Shun'ichi? It seemed doubtful. The only definite thing was that he never forgot his friendly manner and cheerful smile, and was always ready to dole out a pennyworth of flattery—even to his own innocent grandchild.

In the case of Hisa, one could not even begin to imagine what she felt about Shun'ichi. She made no attempt to approach the child. Grand-parents are generally supposed to dote uncritically, even on a monster grandchild with three eyes in its head; but that was hardly the case in this household. Grandfather offered a few empty compliments to the child when accident brought them together, and grandmother re-mained shut away behind the expressionless mask of her face, as if the existence of her grandchild was no concern of hers. Was this what a family was supposed to be like? But the question meant nothing, since, as Tetsukichi had come to realize, the Nire household had not one spark of that warmth from which all definitions of the word "family" should begin. It was an empty, expanding system, forever encroaching on fur-ther emptiness. Ah well, what was the point? It was a mistake having thoughts of this kind at a time and place like this. One was supposed to be drinking. So he would drink. He stretched out his hand toward the cup in which the warm *sake* had gone quite cold.

Tetsukichi would have liked to talk to his brother, openly and free-ly. Let his brother be as drunk as he liked, he would give him more to drink so that he could hear more of that clumsy dialect which spoke of home, and finally he would reply to him in that same tongue. He had only been back home once, when his real mother had died, but that had been years ago. Still, he was in a special position and he knew it. Celebratory dinners in the Nire Hospital were more important than personal feelings. He accepted that. After all, it was many more than twenty years now since he had left his obscure village for Tokyo.

Tetsukichi had been born into a farming family in the village next to Kiichiro's. The house was not particularly poor, but it was almost a custom in the village when a second or third son was born to think seriously about having him adopted into another household. If this were not done, the family fields would have to be divided, and this could mean disaster for the main house. In Tetsukichi's case he was lucky; he was given an opportunity such as a boy in his social position could never expect. Having heard that he was the cleverest child to have appeared in that region in living memory, Kiichiro Nire, the great success story of the district and a fashionable doctor in Tokyo, suggested that he take him under his wing. So Tetsukichi was brought to Tokyo by his father and put to school there. He was fifteen years old at that time, and it was the 29th year of Meiji, 1896. This did not mean, however, that his future was assured in any way. Kiichiro's frequent, and casual, use of the term ''adoption'' merely provided one more example of his ability to persuade other people to take his baseless predictions as seriously as he seemed to take them himself. After all, a backwoods genius could be swiftly cut down to size when put among Tokyo students. Again, when Tetsukichi had first come to live in the Nire house in Hongo, Kiichiro and Hisa had as yet only one child, their eldest daughter Ryuko; but later a son, Oshu, was born, and Tetsukichi's position in the household became very sensitive. But he was not at an age when such worries loom large, and he set to work with that unyielding determination which marks the people of the North. While, in the same room, the other young men in the house, interns like himself, read popular novels, munched baked potatoes, and talked about the women in the red-light district of Yoshiwara, Tetsukichi flicked through dictionaries by the feeble glow of an oil lamp, and copied down formulas. His letters to his elder brother back home, who had just enlisted in the army and was eventually to be killed in the Russo-Japanese War, were only about study and his dreams of making a success of his life, a success that he did not see only in material terms. He wrote seriously, in a small, cramped hand:

I regret to have to inform you that the results I obtained in the

April examinations have been uniformly bad. I apologize profoundly and offer no excuses. Out of some two hundred examinees I have been placed eleventh. At first I was second, then fourth, now eleventh. It is, perhaps, at times like these that people begin to make idle complaints or blame all on the heavens or fate, but I know that to do so would only weaken my resolve, and I shall therefore abstain from so doing.

He also wrote this kind of letter:

I am in excellent health, with no physical problems to trouble me. There is but one room for us in the hospital, and there is nothing for us to do but study, and so I bless my good fortune. Yet I am unable to grasp the future, it seems so far away. This life of study beneath a solitary lamp with dreams of a life to come in the world of scholarship and books, all this perhaps is unrelated to the future that awaits us adopted children. But this is my apprenticeship now. The future no doubt holds many changes in store. I must always be grateful to my father and mother [by whom he meant Kiichiro and Hisa] for constantly reprimanding me and encouraging me in my course of study.

Ever since Tetsukichi had observed the doctor's art as practiced in the consulting room at the Nire Clinic, and seen the enormous trust the patients placed in this art, he had experienced an almost physical sense of the greatness of his calling, and had felt that a life dedicated to medicine would be one with no regrets. One night, for example, a child suffering from a convulsive fit had been brought in and Kiichiro, still in his night dress, had performed some minor act that brought the apparently dead child swiftly and noisily back to life. Tetsukichi would never forget the way the mother, who had been almost mad with distraction, had seized the doctor's hand and wept tears of gratitude.

At that time, during his early career, Kiichiro had been a general practitioner prepared to cure all possible ailments. Once, a young boy was brought in who had something stuck in his throat and had already been taken to two others doctors without result. Kiichiro produced an odd-looking instrument made of some kind of bone, hooked at one end with what looked like hair on the tip. To Tetsukichi's astonishment, he had thrust this into the suffering child's mouth, fiddled about inside his throat with it and, in less than a minute, the offending foreign body had been removed. Tetsukichi was less surprised by the boastful explanation Kiichiro gave the parent, for he had heard similar words many times before:

"You see, this is a special device of my own invention. The only one of its kind in Japan. I suppose I should not be saying this myself, but I am a first-class doctor, as perhaps you may not have known. And a well-known authority on these things. It was lucky for you you brought him here."

So Tetsukichi studied under this well-known authority with a pure, almost innocent passion for medicine. He went to the First High School in Tokyo, entered the Medical School of Tokyo Imperial University with ease, and obtained results that even a reputed genius need not be ashamed of. His adoptive father was very pleased with him and said:

"Tetsukichi, you've done well. I'm proud of you, my boy. I shall give you a gold watch."

Tetsukichi did not rejoice at these words. He had already heard the same euphoric phrase about five times before, and he still did not possess a gold watch. Not that he wanted a gold watch, anyway.

By the time Kiichiro, now the veteran of two tours abroad and Director of a major hospital, had started to think of becoming a Diet member, Tetsukichi found that the simple respect in which he had formerly held the man had turned into more complex feelings. Up to that time Tetsukichi had done as he had been told, had specialized in mental pathology at school and used his basic knowledge of medicine to help out with the treatment at the hospital. But once he had become a qualified specialist, he found that his adoptive father's methods of diagnosis occasionally made him shake his head. It was not that Kiichiro was losing his touch: his intuitive grasp of what was wrong with a patient was still first-class. No, it was the theoretical chatter with which he accompanied his diagnoses that puzzled Tetsukichi. He began to wonder if Kiichiro wasn't making it all up as he went along.

For example, Kiichiro used his stethoscope not only for examining those parts of the body for which it is normally used, but also on the patients' heads. He would listen in exactly the same way as he did when listening to a patient's heart or lungs, then confidently proclaim:

"Well, I'm afraid there's something wrong with your head. There's something gone wrong there, no doubt about it. Now, you take this medicine I'm going to give you. It's the finest medicine in Japan."

Even more surprising was the use he made of the instrument normally used for looking inside people's noses and ears. He would, in fact, still use it for looking up noses and down ears, but the ears and noses belonged not to people who were having trouble with those organs, but to people who were mentally ill.

"Ah, that's what it is. I can see it now. Your brain is inflamed. Starting to ulcerate. Starting to rot away, I shouldn't be surprised. Can see it all quite plainly. You'll have to come into the hospital, I'm afraid. Still, not to worry. Leave it all to me. I'll soon clear that up, soon stop the rot there. I'll cure you. You see, I'm a Doktor Medicine, if you know what that is. I'm a specialist, an authority on the subject."

Now, it is true that, in cases of proleptic dementia or other mental disturbances where the patient is not altogether aware of what is wrong, it is a mistake to give him a proper medical account of the situation. It is sometimes necessary to give this kind of patient, who is ruled by illusion, some kind of explanation that will enable him to gain, or regain, confidence in the doctor, even if this entails deception. But Kiichiro was completely unselective in his use of the therapeutic lie, employing it on those who were suffering from some kind of mild breakdown as well as on raving lunatics, on old countrywomen too stupid to understand anything, and on learned members of the academic profession. With the result that he gained the complete confidence of them all. Patients preferred the patter of this dwarf with a Kaiser moustache to the most correct of diagnoses, the soundest explanations of their cases, for the simple reason that they trusted him. And they also got better much faster, too. Kiichiro was a special kind of person, a mysterious person, as Tetsukichi had to admit.

But that was all he was prepared to admit now. He was no longer able to respect Kiichiro, but he did not despise him. There was a real energy, a power in the man, and his craving for the new was not necessarily a bad thing. The Nire Hospital acquired new drugs and equipment as soon as they appeared on the market, and Kiichiro's boast that they were the first to introduce diathermy into Japan was probably true. Still, what about that radium bath? Tetsukichi knew very well that there was no reason whatsoever to suppose that the whirlpool of pipes at the bottom of the bath emitted radium in any form at all, and clearly the bath could have none of the effects that the Nire Hospital's publicity claimed it had. Yet Kiichiro was always saying to patients:

"You really ought to try the radium bath at our place. It'll cure that headache of yours in no time."

Whatever Tetsukichi might think as he observed his adoptive father, Kiichiro himself had been observing Tetsukichi's progress over a longer period of time and from a much more comprehensive standpoint. Once he was satisfied that Tetsukichi was going to be a better than average doctor, perhaps head and shoulders above the rest, he made up his mind to bestow his eldest daughter on him. One reason for this was that his eldest son, Oshu, would still be too young to take over the hospital in the year Kiichiro was planning to retire, and was, besides, not all that bright. So one day, some time after Kiichiro had decided he would shortly make Tetsukichi Assistant Director (a decision made months ago yet still not put into effect), he said to his adopted son:

"Tetsukichi, your name is a bit too rustic, don't you think? Smells of the paddy fields. Better change it, I feel. No need to alter the way you write it. Just let's read it differently. You'll be called Tetsuyoshi from now on."

There was no way of going against this command, particularly since it came from a man who had shown no qualms about changing the whole of his name—surname, given name, the lot. So the directive went around by way of the Deputy that Dr. Tetsukichi was no longer to be addressed by his former name, but as Dr. Tetsuyoshi instead. Still, the habits of years are not easily broken, and people still kept referring to him inadvertently as Dr. Tetsukichi. This was a real set-back, so Kiichiro took the advice of his wife this time and send around another directive saying that Dr. Tetsuyoshi should now be referred to as the "young master," and this did seem to catch on at last. Tetsu-kichi himself hated this new title. He was, after all, not all that young. Four years ago, when he had married Ryuko, he had been thirty-three. He was now thirty-seven and still did not have his M.D. Ever since his adoptive father had become involved in matters outside the hospital, Tetsukichi had been obliged to spend more time on consultations and was deprived of the leisure he needed for research. He took scholar-ship seriously and had no desire to cook up the kind of thesis that might fool the examiners but would not deceive himself, so the thesis required for the advanced degree had not yet been written. It is true that Kiichiro, in his euphoric moments, would praise him and promise to send him abroad to complete his research, but it was much like his offers of gold watches, and before anything had come of it the First World War had broken out.

But the war was over now, and Tetsukichi intended to get away from the confusions and complexities of everyday life at the hospital and settle down to genuine research in the relative seclusion of a German university. Germany was the obvious place to go, being the birthplace of modern psychiatry. He was a married man now, married to someone twelve years younger than he, whom he had, in fact, often looked after when she was a small child; and whether or not he had been fortunate in his choice of her as a wife, the fact remained that his position at the hospital was completely settled. If he went away for two years, he need have no worries about what might happen on his return.

The question of to what extent the marriage had been a happy one was, of course, not only his problem. Ryuko herself had been far from happy when she had been told by her father whom she was to marry. Tetsukichi did not look particularly impressive, and was hardly to her taste. But her whole behavior was dominated by her own narrow, intolerant will, and since that will was in accord with her father's, she made not the slightest protest. Wasn't her father always saying that this adopted son of his had the finest mind in Japan? No doubt she would not have been so docile if the bridegroom intended had been that other unique adopted son, the one with the finest physique in Japan.

The possessor of the finest (or largest) physique in Japan was, in fact, being discussed in the Coral Room at this moment. Professor Kuroda, a Sumo enthusiast like Kiichiro, had asked how Tatsuji was getting on.

"Ah well, you see, I'm afraid he's become extremely shy of strangers, and so. . ." Kiichiro was attempting to explain the wonder boy's absence, but the explanation was not to his satisfaction, so he took another spoonful of what he called "sop."

Kiichiro ate hardly any solids, and all he did on this occasion was drink his non-alcoholic Bordeaux and sup his sop. He referred to all soups, and any dish vaguely related to soup, as "sop," and everyone else in the Nire household had come to use the word, too. Kiichiro ate three bowls of sop and touched practically none of the more substantial dishes on the table. Only a little while before he had been teaching the two small children proper European etiquette in the matter of soup, or sop, imbibing, but when he came to imbibe it himself he ignored all the rules he had so exhaustively enunciated and slurped audibly, splashing the stuff onto the ends of his carefully tended moustache. This seemed to cause him no concern, and he began on his Bordeaux again, drinking it with his customary relish.

"Well, you know, it was quite a business putting him into school. He has such a huge body, you see. Tremendous job. There was no desk or chair to fit him. Nothing suitable. So what did I do? Had to present the school with special ones made to measure."

Kiichiro spoke with no trace of a Yamagata accent. He also spoke with no trace of a Tokyo accent, either. His pronunciation and intonation seemed to be all his own. When asked by someone who knew no better where he came from, he would sometimes reply:

"Well, you see, I don't really come from anywhere. No home town, you know. As for my accent, picked it up in Berlin, I suppose. Berlin accent perhaps."

Professor Kuroda was not prepared to let the question of Tatsuji drop, and asked if he still meant him to be a Sumo wrestler.

"Now there's the trouble, you see. He's determined to be a doctor. Says so, anyway. With a build like that, too. Hopeless, of course. Couldn't have a doctor like that. Frighten the wits out of the patients if he ever showed up. They'd all run away somewhere. You'd lose the lot."

Everyone laughed at this, and Kiichiro went on:

"Still. We'll just have to see how things turn out. He'll learn. He'll come to his senses and come round. He'll realize he can't lead a normal life. Stands to reason."

Kiichiro nodded to himself at the end of these remarks, as if acknowledging that he was in complete control of everything, and that nothing ever could, or did, go wrong with any of his plans. He twiddled one sop-stained end of his moustache to emphasize this. Kuroda said jokingly:

"In that case, you'll be the proud father of a Grand Champion someday."

Kiichiro was obviously quite taken with the remark and grinned broadly, so everyone else at table more or less smiled as well. But Ryuko's smile was slightly strained. The reference to fatherhood was not pleasing. Father might have eccentric tastes, and the adoption of Tatsuji could be seen simply as the indulgence of one of his whims, but it was not very pleasant to be reminded that the monstrous boy was officially her brother. She preferred people to remain in ignorance of the purely formal connection that existed between them.

"Isuke is most kind to Tatsuji." This quiet, almost inaudible remark came from the prim mouth of Hisa, who had not said one word prior to this. It was proof that, despite her expressionless face, she was actually listening to what was being said with as much concern as the others felt, if not more.

"You wouldn't know about Isuke, would you, Mihira? He's our cook. Cooks the finest rice in Japan. Yes, that's it. That's the way.

69

Eat up. Eat your fill. That's the way."

Thus Kiichiro, who drank only Bordeaux and sop, urged more food on the red-faced Shirokichi, who was eating and drinking much more than anyone else. One might wonder what elaborate cuisine was being offered at this dinner party in the Coral Room. The truth is that there was nothing to wonder at. Most of the food in the hospital was, of course, cooked for large quantities of people, so little was to be expected from the cookhouse. The food "within" was certainly different from the cookhouse variety, for it was prepared by a cook-cum-maid, but it was a task she performed so indifferently that the results could hardly be considered proud specimens of the culinary art. There were quite a number of dishes at tonight's dinner, but all they had to recommend them was their variety, which was closer to chaos, in fact, since they failed signally to complement one another, and most of the food had simply been emptied straight out of cans onto the platter. Of course, for someone like Shirokichi, fresh from the far mountains of Kaminoyama, this was an exotic feast such as had never before gratified his palate.

"Now then, Mihira, why not try some of this? It's called corned beef. Corned beef. Never heard of it, perhaps? It comes from America, you know."

"Don't mind if I do. Just a bite, anyway."

Shirokichi transferred one round of corned beef onto his plate and then, apparently without premeditation, poured an avalanche of ketchup over it.

"Now then, Momoko. And you, Yonekuni. How about a little Bordeaux for you two, eh?"

Kiichiro was in an astoundingly good mood, even spreading his affability as far as his two small children. For Momoko, who normally had to sneak in unnoticed, it was a great occasion simply to be allowed into the Coral Room; and to be permitted to eat with the grown-ups was a particular source of pride and nervous tension. Her elder sisters had been given the right to take their meals "within" with their parents, but Momoko and Yonekuni had never once shared this experience. So far as feeding habits and overall upbringing were concerned, the older girls belonged "within," and the two young children belonged in the cookhouse. It was no wonder that Momoko should sometimes have asked herself whether there was not some good reason for the furtive obscurity in which she and her little brother were being brought up. She realized that their father was of extraordinarily high social rank and so could be seen very rarely. But when he could see them, he was all smiles, as if he had just that very instant remembered their existence, realized that he did, indeed, have other children, and he would compliment them on how big they were, so big, they'd grown so big, really big, marvelously, wonderfully big—it was an absolutely splendid thing, growing so tall as that.

Momoko was very cheerful now, though, for she was being allowed to pour her own Bordeaux into her own glass all by herself, which she did with great care, tilting the bottle slowly and watching, with enormously wide eyes, the bubbles fizz and rise as the liquid ran into the glass.

"I want to pour my own out, too," Yonekuni protested in a slightly rasping voice that still had traces of influenza in it.

"No, you can't, because you'll spill it," replied Momoko, desperately clutching the bottle as if she would refuse ever to part with it; but Seiko managed to talk her into passing it to her brother, which she did with great reluctance. Her eyes grew even larger, like saucers, as she watched Yonekuni handle the bottle; she was convinced he would do something horribly wrong, swamping the whole table and bringing disgrace upon them both.

"By the way, is Oshu still in Sendai?" It was their uncle from Chichibu, Tokutaro Aoki, who spoke, turning the back of his perfectly bald pate toward Momoko and Yonekuni, not in some peculiar reverse obeisance to them but because his face was directed toward Kiichiro.

"Yes, well . . . his exams aren't over yet, you see," the head of the Nire household replied, but without much fervor. He had no great hopes for his eldest son, despite the magnificent name, "Europe," he had bestowed on him. Oshu had grown into a big, strong lad, which was unusual for Kiichiro's children, who tended to be sickly or of modest physique, and this seemed to have given him a rather lordly attitude to life. He was not the kind to worry himself over minor matters, and so had failed to graduate from his high school on two occasions already. Kiichiro did not touch on that minor matter, however:

"He's a lad of parts, is Oshu. We can expect good things of him, I feel. Leadership, that's what he has. Good at doing things. Playing quite a role up there, I hear. In the Judo club, I believe, although. . ."

"In the Kendo club, Father," Ryuko coolly corrected him.

"Ah, that's right, the Kendo club. Very good at sword fighting, you see. He won all his contests in his last match. Marvelous really. Does his best. Lots of potential." Kiichiro seemed quite happy to flatter his eldest son in his absence. Ryuko, who was also no believer in any form of self-deprecation, was not, however, prepared to let uncritical praise of the undeserving pass unchallenged. In a tone of voice that implied scrupulous objectivity in her judgments of others, she flatly contradicted what her father had just so casually said:

"I would have thought that Oshu is a classic example of the adage that the eldest son is often the dullard of the family."

Her tone of voice left no room for doubt. Oshu, despite his imposing name, was a hopeless good-for-nothing, and for this reason, her tone implied, she, a mere woman, had to make twice, or thrice, the effort she would otherwise have made. Perhaps it should be said in Ryuko's defense that for many years her father had frequently murmured to her, not in his customary tone of wheedling flattery but in a voice full of feeling, a genuine sigh from the heart, "Ryuko, if only you had been born a boy!"

Since Ryuko had consigned the topic of Oshu so deliberately to an early grave, the uncle from Chichibu turned his attention to the second daughter, Seiko, stating that no doubt in the not too distant future she would be a lovely blushing bride, so beautiful in her wedding dress that even an old baldpate like himself (and here he stroked that glittering dome) would fall head over heels in love with her. As Seiko blushed, the blood rising suddenly to her pale cheeks, the adults around her all smiled their agreement with these fine sentiments. Seiko would obviously be a lovely bride, and there was no harm in teasing her a little about it.

The uncle from Chichibu had made the preceding remarks in a very loud voice. As he had previously explained at some length, there was a saying, "the high voice of Chichibu" (a saying apparently restricted to the area of Chichibu itself), and he was a good example of that, for he had a very loud voice. But an even louder voice responded, a sonorous, crude bellow that expressed heartfelt agreement with the sentiments just voiced. From the beginning, Shirokichi had shown a respectful reserve toward his brother's bride, but he had not concealed his fervent admiration for her younger sister. So far, this had appeared only in his looks, for he lacked the courage to express it in words. Now that he had downed his three or four pints, however, he had sufficient Dutch courage to seize the opportunity to say a few relevant words, his stuttering oratory being delivered at such a roaring pitch it could well have shattered glasses, even rocks. Fortunately his ardor was expressed in so thick a dialect that most of it was unintelligible to his listeners, though the import was clear enough, and Seiko sat there in a state of embarrassment and shame that made her look, of course, more charming and ethereal, as if she might fade into the air at any moment—as, no doubt, she sincerely wished to do.

Kiichiro glanced at Seiko, but curiously he had nothing to say, no flattery to offer this praiseworthy possession of his, this pearl of price. But, in what appeared to be mute acknowledgment of the sentiments that had, presumably, been just expressed, he raised a hand and twiddled one end of his moustache. Soon he let go, and the end of the moustache sprang upward again. He twiddled it a second and third time, with the same result. Whenever he did this, he was either planning some masterstroke, which, in its novelty of conception and clarity of vision, was well beyond the powers of others to even contemplate yet alone emulate; or he was rescrutinizing some plan that he had already set in operation, the occasional slight smile indicating satisfaction with himself and the products of his vaulting imagination. At present, it was a case of the latter, and over his discreetly powdered face a broad smile slowly unfolded. He smiled because, unknown to anyone else there, the successful candidate for his second daughter's hand (and thus also for a certain role in the Nire Hospital) had already been decided upon; by Kiichiro himself.

The prospective husband was of good family, a good medical family with a history of some centuries, always as doctors. Even now, there were a number of well-known doctors in the family, although none of them was actually in practice. Obviously it would do the Nire Hospital no harm to establish close relations with a household that dominated one of the more powerful academic cliques in the country. The young man in question was still a medical student, but the academic results he had so far achieved were of very high standard. If he had not been from such a distinguished family, Kiichiro would have wanted to adopt him. In this case, it was obviously out of the question.

The prospective bride and groom were both still at school, so it was arguably a little premature to be thinking in terms of marriage. But this argument would not have been acceptable to Kiichiro; not at all acceptable. If clocks were doomed to keep the wrong time, then it was better that they be fast rather than slow. Indeed, the faster anything was, the better. Even if the marriage had to be put off for a while, there was no good reason why they should not become engaged now. Naturally, all this had been worked out between the parents of both sides (or, rather, the fathers), and all that remained was to introduce the young couple to each other. The question of what this young couple might actually think about the situation had never crossed Kiichiro's mind.

He smiled once more with satisfaction, then turned toward Tetsu-kichi, who was watching his cheerfully and totally drunken brother with mixed affection and detached interest, an expression of deepening seriousness on his face.

"Tetsuyoshi, since you'll be going abroad to study some day, why don't you talk to Professor Kuroda about Germany?"

Kuroda's knowledge of Germany was as limited to the prewar situation as that of Kiichiro, who could have given his adopted son as much outdated information as he might require, so the remark could only be interpreted as an attempt to flatter his guest.

A similar concern for his guests was apparent in his next action. He ordered the maid to go into the VIP Reception Parlor next door and bring back a book. The book in question was *The Medical Cure and Prevention of Mental Asthenia,* and its author was Kiichiro Nire, Director of the Nire Hospital and Imperial Mental Hospital, Doktor Medicine. Dozens of copies of this book were arranged in a glass bookcase in the VIP Reception Parlor. Kiichiro took the book in hand and turned toward the young master of the Takamatsuya.

"Mihira, this is a book I wrote. A book I wrote it. This is a copy especially for you."

Shirokichi, struggling to focus and just about managing to read the title on the cover, finally answered with a roar:

"Looks like a real hard book to me. Wouldn't do me no good. No good at all. Don't have no mental asthma, anyway. Don't want it."

But his elder brother hurriedly interposed some well-chosen words, and before long Shirokichi bobbed his head in a rustic nod of acknowledgment and thanks.

"In that case, much obliged I'm sure. Don't suppose I'll be able to read it though."

While watching these goings-on, Kuroda was obliged to simulate a cough to cover his stifled laughter. He too had received a number of these special copies on various occasions.

Yet it was a perfectly sound book, as a glance over its pages would have shown. It began, for example, with an Introduction:

The soul exists only with the body, and the body with the soul. Body and soul are one. Can one truly say that the soul is unquestionably without shape, or the body inevitably with form?

That was its impressive, perhaps slightly too impressive, opening. On turning a few pages one found this:

> Most truly of this wondrous mystery of the nervous system did the great philosopher Schopenhauer say that it was an organ of absolute mystery, and did He, the Supremely Enlightened One, speak of painting in black and white the sound of the wind in the pine trees

—a quotation that nicely demonstrates the author's easy and familiar handling of Western and Eastern wisdom, a main characteristic of the book. It then proceeded with this impassioned cry:

> Is it that progress must always be accompanied by some regression? Lo, the ages of superstition, of religious belief, are already past, and truly we now live in an age of science. Many doors into many a mystic treasure trove have been unlocked with this new key, such as wireless communication and the aeroplane. Radium has been discovered, the spirochete has been revealed, as if truly we had now reached that stage at which a total understanding of the whole material world lay easily within our grasp. Yet, what is man? What is he that his heart should know of nothing but unrest, his body's daily progress being but toward infirmity?

The last two questions presumably explained why the author had felt the need not only to exhaust the treasures of European and American psychiatric research, leaping with agility from one branch of learning to another, but also, at intervals, to avail himself of the Wisdom of the East as he found it in his own culture. Thus there were quotations from the seventeenth-century Confucian moralist, Kaibara Ekiken, on the proper cultivation of the spirit; from the Zen Masters, from Hakuin's *Orategama,* that eighteenth-century masterpiece whose title still defies explication even if it is known to have been the name of the sage's favorite tea kettle, and from more up-to-date treatises on Zen methods of purifying the mind; from the early nineteenth-century Shintoist, Hirata Atsutane, concerning his methods of discipline; and many others. Given the richness and variety of the work, its all-inclusive scope, one might ask how a good book should be defined if this book were not to be considered one.

Kuroda was thinking about Kiichiro and coming to the conclusion that he truly was the "wondrous mystery" his Introduction had mentioned, perhaps even Schopenhauer's "absolute mystery." He then recalled the events surrounding Kiichiro's departure on his second trip abroad, to America, and this time a mere cough failed to conceal his mirth, so he simply leaned back and grinned broadly at the ceiling.

Kuroda had received notification of the time of the departure, and despite the fact that he had ample work on his hands and no time for ceremonies of this kind, he turned up at Shinbashi Station in central Tokyo to see him off. The large missive had expressly stated that Dr. Kiichiro Nire, Doktor Medicine, was due to leave for America from Yokohama on the *Kanada Maru* at such and such a time, and that one was (in the unlikely event of one's having that much leisure, although that was not written there) invited to see him off from the quayside itself. But it also added the hope that those who were unable to go that far would honor Dr. Nire with their presence at Shinbashi Station at such and such a time. The oppressive elegance of the style was such as to allow a grasp of the meaning only after much time and labor, but this also ensured the arousal of powerful feelings of guilt in those who could not stomach the prospect of going all the way to Yokohama, so that it seemed imperative to drag one's unworthy self as far as Shinbashi Station. That was how Kuroda had responded, anyway.

Kuroda feared he was going to be late, so he had hurriedly taken a ricksha to the station, arriving even later than he had expected. Despite the fact that it was past the appointed time, there was no sign of Kiichiro. Kuroda did not know it then, but Kiichiro had allowed a considerable amount of "time to spare" when giving the projected time of his arrival at the station, so the innocent Kuroda had been roundly deceived. Ignorant of Kiichiro's belief in the principle that clocks should be fast, Kuroda, after hanging about for some time, telephoned the Nire Hospital from a shop in front of the station, to be told that the Director's party had left about two hours before (Aoyama is some two miles from Shinbashi) and would no doubt shortly arrive at the station. There was nothing for him to do but wait, and he became more and more irritated as he did so. Eventually, he began to get cramp in his legs from standing about so long, and he decided to stretch them in the main road outside the station. Thus it was that he noticed the "procession" when it was still some distance away.

At first he wondered what on earth it could be, but he was soon able to read the writing on the huge vertical banner that a man in a dark blue *happi* coat, some kind of standard-bearer, was carrying at its head. This banner had written on it, in thick black characters running from

76

top to bottom, "Congratulations to Dr. Nire on His Voyage to America." The mysterious thing about all this was that there was no feeling of farce; absurdity had been pushed to such an extreme that it appeared as its opposite: as slow, solemn dignity.

So the procession proudly advanced, several men in *happi* coats following the standard-bearer, and then a number of Sumo wrestlers. These were only of the lowest grade, of course, but their unkempt hair, as yet lacking the wrestler's characteristic topknot, certainly added an exotic air to the proceedings. After these came a number of rickshas, in the first of which sat the hero of the hour, Kiichiro Nire, in a tasteful frock coat. He leaned back with a nonchalant, aristocratic calm that suggested he was in the habit of doing things like this most days of the week, absentmindedly raising his hand in a regal gesture to twiddle his moustache. Another twenty or so people were in the rickshas behind him, all dressed, Japanese style, in *haori* and *hakama,* and looking pretty well done in into the bargain. But their obvious state of fatigue and discomfort had no effect on the procession, which maintained its steady, dignified pace forward. Three men in *happi* coats were walking alongside the rickshas, and they were also carrying banners, although somewhat smaller than the one at the front. The whole procession was followed by another, unofficial one. Scores of small children, the majority of those living in the neighborhood apparently, were trailing along behind, entranced by this parade whose object remained a mystery to them all. . .

The man was an absolute mystery all right, Kuroda reflected again, clenching his teeth to swallow back the laughter that had once more risen inside him.

Tea and light refreshments had appeared on the table, indicating that the banquet was approaching its end. Kiichiro, who still ate nothing, was urging Shirokichi to help himself again.

"Now, Mihira, try a slice of this. It's a sponge cake from Nagasaki called Castella."

"You don't say. Well, I shall have a bit, that I shall. Don't mind if I do."

This remark, in that blatant dialect, gave the two children another fit of the giggles, and Momoko had a particularly bad attack, screwing her face up in agony in her attempt to hold the monstrous laugh down.

Luckily, at this moment there was a distraction, for the sliding door into the room opened a fraction and Nanny Shimoda's face appeared low down. It appeared like this since she was kneeling outside and was not attempting to enter herself, but was variously bullying and cajoling someone outside in the corridor with her to do so. Finally, the reluctant object of her efforts crawled abjectly into the Coral Room on all fours (a normal mode of entry, although the hangdog style in which it was performed was not). And there in person was the king-size, overeating wonder boy of Yamagata, Kiichiro's other adopted son.

Seen for the first time, his exceptional size gave no impression of a fine (let alone the finest) physique, of a blessing bestowed on him by nature; it seemed more an aberration, a deformity indeed, an unnatural, ludicrous swelling brought about by some imbalance in the secretions of his pituitary gland. Since he was still only in sixth grade at primary school, he would obviously get even larger than this, the snowballing effects of age and growth turning him into some kind of mobile snowman.

"Well, look who's here. It's Tatsuji," said Kiichiro with pride reverberating in his slightly fuzzy voice, as if one more of the treasures he had in store had been brought out to be viewed. "Come on, come over here."

The wonder boy did not move. He had knelt down as near the entrance as it was possible to be without actually being outside the room, and was staring dejectedly down at his ill-formed knees. His specially-made school uniform had already been outgrown and was much too small for him. His fat, round cheeks would have given him an air of artlessness, if only they had not been quite so fat and round. That, however, was the only indication that he was a twelve-year-old schoolboy, and it was easy to see how that face would lengthen and widen, for the jawbone was already obviously overdistended.

"Tatsuji, come over here and say how do you do to everybody." Hisa moved her lips a mere fraction and mumbled these few words. Her voice was low and difficult to follow, but possessed a secret dignity that had greater powers of persuasion than the mellifluous tones of her husband. But the monster stayed unmoving. In contrast to his great body, his soul was small and timid, and life had taught him, by means of the curious stares and the jeers to which he was always subjected, that it was best to reveal his true height to others as little as possible. This boy, who had been the greedy-guts and blockhead of his village, could hardly have worked out for himself that he was here at the Nire Hospital merely to satisfy Kiichiro's empty vanity, but there must have been some instinctive awareness of this somewhere within him which told him not to move, not to move because he was too big.

So Kiichiro lifted the plate with the Castella sponge cake on it and showed it to him.

"Tatsuji, look. Come on, I'll give you some."

Tatsuji's skull was of normal human size, for the top half of his head had not yet shown any unnatural development. Presumably it was the child still residing in him there that made him stand up, oblivious of people's eyes, and make unceremoniously straight for the Castella. When he stood up, those who were seeing him for the first time were taken aback, since he was much larger than it was possible to imagine while he was kneeling down. Kuroda folded his arms and nodded to himself as he gravely observed the phenomenon, but our uncle from Chichibu and the master of the Takamatsuya were dumbfounded, and gazed up in awe at this unnerving schoolboy who towered above them. Only Ryuko stared pointedly away as if loath to look on this hideous and disgusting spectacle.

Tatsuji took the whole plate of Castella and then sat heavily down again. It appeared he was not quite sure what to do with a treat of this kind.

Then his adoptive father spoke again:

"Well, Tatsuji, are you working hard at school?. . . . .
Very well, then, you can go now."

Tatsuji reacted with alacrity and disappeared, taking his plate of cake with him. He lodged in the tiny, cramped, smoke-begrimed cookhouse with old man Isuke.

"All I can say is, if he does become a wrestler he'll make Grand Champion." This was the uncle from Chichibu's comment on the matter, given as if he were merely talking to himself, but in so loud a voice one could not be sure if that were so or not.

Kiichiro made no reply. He was sitting nodding to himself, fiddling with his moustache, as if he were once again secretly enjoying the contemplation of one of those remarkable plans of his, seeing it launched and successfully entering into orbit.

It was time for the guests to begin smoking. In fact, both Tokutaro and Shirokichi had started some time before, Shirokichi enlivening the proceedings by puffing on a tiny, thin, old-fashioned and very bucolic pipe. Kuroda now produced his cigarette case for the first time and, as if responding to some cue, Kiichiro drew out a silver cigarette case. He flicked it open, and there was a neat line of gold-tipped cigarettes, one of which he placed in his mouth and lit.

Even Kiichiro's way of smoking was peculiar. He did not actually suck the cigarette but pursed his lips and briskly blew through it two or three times, not inhaling the smoke but merely keeping the cigarette alight. Once he had got it burning merrily and had created a satisfactory cloud of smoke about him, he removed it from his mouth, assumed his former dignified but relaxed expression, and let the thing dangle in his fingers, careless of whether the ash fell on the table or the floor. After some time had passed, he returned it to his mouth and busily puffed the fire back into life again, raising another large cloud of smoke.

Kiichiro did not have a taste for alcohol, nor, as a rule, did he smoke. It was merely out of courtesy to his guests that he placed one of those gold-tipped cigarettes in his mouth.

4

The year of the Armistice, of Spanish influenza and inflation was coming to an end. The Nire Hospital held its traditional rice-pounding and *mochi*-making party on the 28th of December that year. Seven or eight of the not very distinguished wrestlers from Dewanoumi's stable came to the hospital, a great bonfire was lit behind the cookhouse, and the naked wrestlers pounded away with wooden mallets at the rice in its huge mortar, raising valiant cries from noon until dusk, and great quantities of rice cakes were produced. The wrestlers were presented with casks of *sake* for their labors before they went home. During that whole period of time, the enormous figure of one of the two adopted sons was nowhere to be seen, for he had hidden himself away again.

On New Year's Eve the hospital was scrubbed, rubbed, dusted and polished. This normally took until around midnight, since Kiichiro liked the place to be spotless from floor to ceiling, and this year was no exception. Every light in the hospital, electric and gas, was turned on, and beneath that trenchant glare every member of staff was set to work cleaning. By the time the last area to be done, the long, wide corridor, was spick and span and the cleaners could relax, the midnight bells had begun slowly and solemnly tolling in the New Year.

New Year's Day of 1919 began quietly with the fitful light of the sun seeping through a layer of thin cloud, but that night there was a sudden rainstorm, rare for that time of year, with winds gusting over 35 mph, prophetic perhaps of the depression that was about to overtake a nation that had been enjoying the economic benefits of the Great War throughout the past few years.

But the morning, at least, gave no indication of what was to come. Looking from the main gate of the Nire Hospital—on which the new sign ''Nire Hospital of Mental Pathology'' had just been affixed— toward the entrance hall, one would have seen a gaiety that belied the quiet gray of the morning. Before those extravagant columns huge numbers of people were assembled, from specialist doctors down to the lowliest nurse, and even patients. They were lined up in impressive ranks, for this was the day on which the Director, Member of the House of Representatives, was to proceed to the Palace to present his respects or credentials or whatever.

The Model T Ford, its engine running, was waiting for the Director to make his entry in frock coat and glittering silk top hat. But Kiichiro made no move to do so. He was still exchanging pleasantries with one and all of his guard of honor, one hand holding gleaming white gloves and the other twiddling his moustache. He was clearly determined to savor this irreplaceable moment to the utmost, and he gave the impression of having been transformed, perhaps, into the Special Imperial Japanese Envoy about to depart for the Peace Conference in Versailles (as Prince Saionji was to do later that month).

In contrast to the calm of our hero, the young Yasusaburo Sugano was standing to one side in terrible agitation of mind. He was a distant relation of Kiichiro's, a young graduate of the Yamagata Agricultural School who had been called to Tokyo some six months before in accordance with Kiichiro's policy that the more useful young men he assembled about him the better. Just two days ago the Director had suddenly said, to Yasusaburo's stunned amazement, that he had to go to the Palace to pay his respects and Yasusaburo was to accompany him. Words such as "Palace" and "respects" were sufficient to weaken the knees of this gangling country boy, and also to impress on him the remarkable status of his chief and benefactor, who was, he had decided, not as other mortals were. Consequently, Yasusaburo had been virtually unable to sleep a wink the night before. His lack of composure, contrasting conspicuously with the Director's fullness of it, showed in the way he kept nervously trying to pull down the sleeves of his *montsuki* jacket, which had been borrowed from somewhere and was far too small for him.

At last Kiichiro climbed into the car in leisurely fashion, and Yasusaburo followed stiffly and awkwardly after him. As the car was about to lumber into gradual motion, the Deputy, Hidekichi Katsumata, straining his tiny body to full height, raised both arms even more strenuously above his head and, in a high-pitched nasal squeak, called for three cheers for the Director.

This really required the voice of the proprietor of the Seiundo, who would have performed the office with a verve the Deputy could not hope to emulate. To make matters worse, it seemed not to have crossed the minds of most of those assembled that they might be called upon to cheer, so no real chorus of voices was raised at first, only a few sporadic shouts of "*Banzai!*" As these attained some kind of volume and concord, the Director could be seen smiling cheerfully behind the glass, nodding out his normal "Well done, well done" message so energetically that his glittering top hat seemed in imminent danger of falling off.

The car began to rumble away, when a truly incredible thing happened. It was so remarkable that the already nervous Yasusaburo gave out a fearful scream that very nearly ruptured certain vital organs. A heavy object thudded onto the roof of the car, a dull, ripping sound ensued and, before Yasusaburo's very eyes, two human legs appeared through the canvas.

A man had jumped from the upstairs balcony. Normally only very special patients were allowed to use the balcony, but today, since the Director wanted to depart before as many well-wishers as possible, it had been opened to all, except the chronically ill and unbalanced. Of that large number enjoying the freedom of the balcony, one had been so excited by the sudden semi-chorus of cheers that he had climbed up onto the balustrade and, as a result of overeagerness perhaps, had found himself precipitately in midair, descending, in the manner of the silent movies, with marvelous, accidental precision onto the center of the roof of the vehicle that had just set out on its mission to the Palace.

The resulting consternation was considerable. At first everyone merely gaped in horror, but a swarm of men soon surrounded the car, which had immediately come to a confused and grinding halt, and strove to extricate the patient from the roof. The nurses screamed and raced off in all directions to find first-aid boxes. The doctors—and luckily there was no shortage of doctors on this occasion—got hold of the man after he had finally been dragged from the car, arms and legs threshing in agitation. They laid him firmly on the ground and began feeling him all over to see if there were any broken bones. The faces of the Deputy and other notables were contorted with anxiety at the thought that their Director might have suffered some misfortune, and they muttered things at one another that even the speakers, let alone the auditors, must have found unintelligible. No one behaved in a rational or coherent way.

Or, rather, only one did: the Director, Kiichiro, who remained calm and impassive inside the car as if nothing untoward had happened. He called in steady tones for another car to be produced, and one was certainly required, for the Ford had a gaping hole in its roof and could hardly be considered suitable for a visit to the Palace. The Deputy gasped this order to one of the students, who ran off to telephone the nearest car-hire firm. Then an announcement was made: by amazing good fortune the man who had so suddenly descended in that extraordinary way had received not the slightest injury, not even a scratch. He had been tranquilized with an injection and was being taken away to a more suitable place. On hearing this, Kiichiro nodded his quiet acceptance and got out of the car.

Kiichiro maintained a remarkable composure, but surely even he must have lost some of his good spirits and must have been frowning, at least slightly, over the disaster that had ruined his great occasion, and which could also be seen as a bad omen for the coming year? But Kiichiro was not the kind of person to click his tongue in displeasure at a blunder that boded so ill for the hospital, or reprove those who had failed to foresee it. That would only increase the sense of guilt from which the whole staff was already, no doubt, suffering. Instead, once the hubbub had subsided and people were at last aware of the weirdness of what had happened, Kiichiro seemed to become even more affable and smiling, to an almost ridiculous extent.

His renewed high spirits persisted well after the new car, which had arrived with commendable speed, had made its way through the gate accompanied, if not with cries of "*Banzai!*" this time, at least without mishap. Kiichiro kept saying over and over again to Yasusaburo, who was still suffering from palpitations:

"This is a good day for us, Sugano. I mean, a patient falls from the roof, and suffers no injury whatsoever. Absolute miracle. Amazing. A hole in the roof of a car is nothing whatsoever by comparison. No importance at all. Yes, I can see this is going to be a very good year."

Which only increased the young man's admiration for this remarkable person. What a wonder he was! How truly great! That's what it takes to make a Director of a Great Hospital and a Member of the House of Representatives. And as the car began to approach the end of its journey, he became so acutely aware of the honor of being able to accompany this splendid human being on his journey to the Palace to Present his Respects that he began shaking inside and outside as well.

This nervous excitement, however, proved hardly justified after they had entered the extensive Palace grounds. Yasusaburo had assumed he would be made to wait somewhere while Kiichiro paid his respects and kowtowed, at some distant remove perhaps, to His Imperial Majesty himself. But this was not to be. The car certainly passed over the main bridge across the Imperial Moat, but it then went on to a sequestered and inconspicuous building in front of which a marquee had been set up with numerous tables. Kiichiro walked up to one of the tables, signed his name, and that was that. All that was left now was to go home, and Yasusaburo, who had hardly had a moment's sleep the previous night and had gone through agonies of apprehension that morning, felt understandably let down, perhaps even the victim of some deception.

The "*banzai*" incident, or the affair of the falling patient, left a small mark on the hospital since it provided a topic of conversation for some time, but there were no end of incidents that left similar marks, though their capacity to do so bore little relation to their real importance. For example, considerable drama was aroused when the male nurse known as Mallet Head helped himself to a fishhead that someone else had left one morning, and got a large fishbone stuck in his throat. News of this incident was not restricted to the cookhouse and its environs, for after the run-of-the-mill attempts to remove it, such as back-slapping, forced feeding of rice, and invocations of a vaguely religious nature, all of which had no effect whatsoever, the victim was taken to the surgery where three doctors worked in relay on the problem but without result, either. If only the Director had been there, he might have been able to demonstrate his skill with that remarkable instrument he had invented some twenty years before, but unfortunately he was away attending several gatherings that day. The Nire Hospital of Mental Pathology had to admit itself beaten, and the tearful Mallet Head was taken to a specialist hospital. Thus the fishbone remained in his throat for more than eight hours.

There was also the incident of the influenza vaccine. Kiichiro, with his passion for the new, insisted that everyone should be vaccinated as soon as the box of vaccine, its label ominously misspelled, had arrived at the hospital. The result was that even the very healthy suffered for some days from red, inflamed arms, and a number of people ran high temperatures. The only person to be unaffected was old man Isuke, the cook, for he had followed his normal practice of being unavailable while the vaccinating was going on.

And, naturally, incidents occurred in the world beyond the hospital. Most of these raised surprisingly little interest within the hospital and were hardly talked about, but there was no way of avoiding Billiken's recital of newspaper reports days or weeks after the events had occurred. The New Year had been only a few days old when, on the 5th of January, the actress Sumako Matsui committed suicide. Sumako, famous for her portrayals of Ibsen's Nora and Sudermann's Magda, had reached a larger audience as a singer of songs related to the European dramas in which she appeared, and also as the archetype, in real life, of the "new woman" she played on the stage, her scandalous relationship with the married director of her company, Hogetsu Shimamura, having provided gossip columnists with material for years. Shimamura had died suddenly from pneumonia on the 5th of November, 1918, a victim of the Spanish influenza that was sweeping the country, and Sumako had chosen to follow him exactly two months after his death, hanging herself in her dressing room after a performance of *Carmen*.

"Not one hair of her head disheveled or in disarray, her makeup perfect in its artifice and beauty, she hung there by the neck from the scarlet silk crepe sash she had tied about the crossbeam of her room."

Billiken read this in a specially high-pitched voice, and Momoko wrinkled her tiny nose and listened entranced; as did Seiko who, by chance, was in the next room having her sash tied about her by Nanny Shimoda. Seiko turned to Nanny and raised her eyebrows a fraction as if to show distaste at the sordid affair. And yet, when she had heard someone from the hospital telling Nanny about Sumako's funeral, which had been held in the nearby Aoyama Cemetery, she showed some inclination to listen to what was being said. Otherwise she pretended indifference.

Then the first Sumo tournament of the year began. Soon people were discussing the latest news about it, and learning from that devoted fan, Kiichiro himself, that Tochigiyama had injured his left ankle in practice and other pieces of arcane knowledge. The principal members of the hospital all went to see the tournament at some time or other, which was then still held outdoors in a tented enclosure. On the seventh day, when Seiko went with her father to see it, the last contest of the day between Onishiki and Otohira was so disputed that the referee's decision was overruled and a lengthy adjudication was held by the judges who sit around the ring, rising in a lordly manner to go to the center of it and perform an inquest whenever one is required.

The inquest went on so long that Seiko went home before the final judgment was made, but her father remained behind, remarking casually to his neighbor that quite obviously Onishiki had won. However, after an hour and forty minutes of deliberation, it was announced that

Onishiki himself had confessed to putting one foot outside the ring, and was consequently the loser. This did not ruffle Kiichiro's composure. Blowing through one of his gold-tipped cigarettes, he remarked to the same neighbor:

"Well, of course. It was obvious enough from the start that Onishiki had stepped outside. Obvious to me, anyway. Didn't think he'd admit it just like that, though. Not really the thing to do, you know. Bit late in the day, after all that."

In the space of a few days many things would happen, both inside and outside the hospital; and people would be astonished, or amused, or become very straight-faced and serious. But days, weeks, months would pass, and one would cease to know what had happened. This had happened, that had happened, but the life that had informed these things had gone, just as the emotions that attend all happenings disappear when they are written up for the dead face of the printed page.

More things happened. The Director distributed tickets for the public gallery at the Diet, for he was due to give his maiden address there. A number of people, among them Yasusaburo Sugano, went to the Diet building, which was then a wooden structure in Hibiya some distance from its present site. Yasusaburo craned forward in his seat and squinted, and there, at the distant speaker's dais, was Kiichiro. His lack of height was a drawback perhaps, but he stood there impressively with his chest puffed out, twiddling his moustache frequently in his usual nonchalant manner. It was almost impossible to catch a word he said, for his voice failed to reach the seats where the public were gathered. Yasusaburo cupped his hand behind his ear, but it made no difference. So all he could do when he got back to the hospital was compliment the Director on the excellence of his speech. Kiichiro smiled in response and replied that his speech today had been a model of the way speeches ought to be made. It was only much later that Yasusaburo found out what the speech had actually been about. Kiichiro had been supporting a motion to the effect that the Aoyama Cemetery should be moved elsewhere. It was extraordinarily wasteful, he had said, that so large a site in the center of this great metropolis should be used for virtually nothing, and it behoved the government to move the cemetery into the suburbs forthwith.

But who cares about the Director's speech? Surely things of greater interest than that occurred? They did. Tatsuji, the wonder boy, now six feet three inches in height, finally agreed to become a Sumo wrestler. This year he had entered junior high school and must have been subjected to even more curious stares and jeers than he had so far endured. As a result, he had despaired of his earlier ambition to become a doctor, realizing that a freak like himself could live nowhere but in the monstrous world of Sumo. Kiichiro was delighted:

"Tatsuji, well done, well done, my boy. A fine decision. A decision well made. I congratulate you. I'll buy you anything you want."

But old man Isuke, who had looked after the bulky boy, silently and unostentatiously gave him a lucky charm of His Holiness Saint Kobo Daishi to protect him when in need.

So Tatsuji left the hospital, taking with him his few bits and pieces of possessions, and went to join the stable of Dewanoumi.

More things occurred, one of the more important being something that had been planned by the powers "within" without anyone else in the hospital knowing. Seiko was brought together with the young man her father had marked out for her. Neither of them objected to the match, and it would not have made the slightest difference if they had. No formal announcement was yet made by the two families but, in effect, the young couple were considered engaged. Of course, the two young people discussed nothing of the matter between themselves, since all the negotiations were carried out by their respective families.

Then Hisa had a fabulous dress, a *robe décolletée*, made for a chrysanthemum-viewing party. Being a conservative sort of person, she had always gone to such functions in Japanese-style court dress, and doubtless she had been prevailed upon by her forward-looking, always up-to-the-minute husband to accept this monstrous transformation, a long, thin dress which revealed the lower portions of the neck in a reckless way and seemed to be composed almost entirely of a preposterous number of pleats, tucks, gathers, puckers and creases. Some of this was concealed by a satin stole trimmed with fur, and the whole was topped off with an extravagantly wide-brimmed hat. Nobody in the hospital had ever seen anything like it. The grande dame of the hospital had been transformed into a European crone, an ancient, midnight witch. It was difficult to gather from her expression what she felt about the matter, since her face was concealed behind a copious veil, but once she had actually got the dress on, she seemed to lose whatever doubts she might have had, achieving a calmness close to resigned apathy by the time she edged herself cautiously into the car. Kiichiro himself looked wholly delighted as he stepped in briskly after her, his walking stick under his arm.

Various things had certainly occurred, but it would be difficult to say if anything had really happened, for what real changes had any of these things led to? The extraordinary events of the New Year simply slipped into the past, as the end of the year came around again bringing yet another New Year's Day. The prize giving took place again, the rice pounding and cake making, the great year-end cleaning; and so what images had the old year left, but grubby Isuke stirring the rice in the monster pots, the porter Toyobei urging on his bandy legs, the Deputy still wandering slowly about like a wading bird? Or the young mistress, her boa wrapped about her, making yet another grand departure, or Miss Momoko bursting into raucous laughter and then subsiding into large, bogus-looking tears, or Yonekuni catching cold again. Perhaps this year had not really existed at all, since nothing had happened in it. No one had changed, and neither had the hospital. Even the fine new name, the fruit of long deliberation on the part of Kiichiro, failed to become current, for no one could be bothered to call it the Nire Hospital of Mental Pathology. In people's mouths it was the Nire Hospital still, or just the Mental Hospital. No one, nothing had changed. The hands in the clock tower were almost never slow, and if they were the office staff would hurriedly put that right. Usually, the clock stayed five minutes fast. The great columns remained as heavy and imposing as ever, still shining like marble, and the lightning conductor on the tall, pointed tower continued to glint dully in the sky.

Naturally things had happened elsewhere. Korea had had its own "*banzai*" incident, but these cries were for independence, and the disturbances lasted for six months. China had the Fourth of May Movement, a protest against Japanese interference in its affairs. And the Treaty of Versailles was signed. But what did all this matter? The year came to an end and no one in the Nire Hospital had died. Life went on as ever, and the hospital was prospering to such a degree that it seemed it must always do so. The massy columns and the seven towers seemed eternal.

Of course, all that was just illusion. Things always change with time, even if no one is aware of what is happening. There is an eddying back in the stream of what seems normal, some constant force of entropy that works away hour by hour, minute by minute, impeding and wearing away, altering a life, a family, a whole country even, although we neither see nor understand. So what had happened this year? Nothing. And the prize giving came and people wondered what they would receive, since it would obviously be much inferior to last year's gift. And that was all. One year is of little account in a man's life. In one year he hardly ages at all. Nothing had happened, or it was at least exactly as if nothing had happened. The hospital and its various inmates stayed the same.

Nineteen twenty, however, did see a sudden, and unforeseen, change in circumstances. In the General Election on the 10th of May, Kiichiro failed to be reelected.

The election itself had been unexpected. Kiichiro had certainly not expected it. Early that year, the newly constructed National Sumo Hall had been opened in Tokyo, so contests would no longer have to be postponed because of rain. Kiichiro had his own box in that resplendent hall, and his own adopted son embarked on a career that would doubtless end in his becoming Grand Champion; so he cheerfully invited distinguished guests to join him in his box. But people saw more than Sumo wrestling in the early days of that year, for other struggles and grapplings were going on. Popular demands for universal suffrage took on a new virulence, and public meetings were held that led to demonstrations, even to invasions of the Diet building and the Prime Minister's official residence. The Hara cabinet found it hard to resist the pressure and, in a spectacular volte-face, the demands were acceded to and the House of Representatives was dissolved toward the end of February.

As far as Hisa was concerned, here was yet another of those wretched elections, though she managed, as one would expect, to refrain from any open expression of her feelings, except a slight knitting of her eyebrows. Kiichiro, who did not share her antipathy toward politics, was overweeningly confident of a happy result. The number of visitors from Yamagata increased all of a sudden, the recreation room was again filled with desks, and numerous circulars were dispatched. But the real election fever seemed to bypass the hospital, except for Hisa with her financial anxieties. The battlefield was elsewhere, in Yamagata, and shortly Kiichiro's forces were transferred there, including the Model T Ford, which was transported all the way to the mountains by train. And so, equipped with a full-scale model of the Nire Hospital of Mental Pathology made, at his own express instructions, out of seashells, and with twice the amount of pomade on his moustache, Kiichiro made a triumphal entry into his home town, confidently assuming that the opposition would simply melt away. His dreams were untroubled except by the luckiest of omens, and his election workers seemed to share his confidence. But the unbelievable occurred, and he was solidly defeated.

Obviously he had been too confident, and his casual methods of campaigning had been the principal reason for the fiasco. The candidate himself had seemed overly relaxed, lacking in the zeal required in these contests, that *"wild, impassioned battering on each door to wring out yet one more reluctant vote; that feverish trudging, lame and footsore, of long, weary roads,"* to borrow some phrases that Billiken read from the newspaper. Kiichiro had got into his automobile and been driven all over the place, followed by adults and children who had never seen a car in their lives, and had twiddled his moustache at them, gloating complacently as if he knew he had already won. Consequently he, and those about him, became dangerously unaware of what was really going on. It was, for example, some time after the campaign headquarters had been set up in the finest hotel in Kaminoyama that a mistake on the signboard outside was discovered. This was an error of sufficient importance to send one of the campaign workers rushing breathlessly to the office, calling out in his uncouth dialect that Kiichiro was not being proclaimed a Member of the House of Representatives but a Member of the House of Elephants. The character for "representative" differs in only minor ways from that for "elephant," and the ignorant signwriter had chosen the wrong one.

There were also more specific reasons for the defeat. Kiichiro's Development Corporation, with its Hokkaido Wide Open Spaces farming methods, was not doing very well, for example. But the main thing in a rural election, in any election for that matter, is money. In the previous election Kiichiro had been evaluated as the candidate who was rolling in it. Perhaps that reputation was his undoing, since people expected money but found there was not as much coming their way as they had assumed there would be. The money certainly flowed, enough to cause Hisa to struggle for breath, but much of it ended up in the wrong pockets. The various go-betweens, perhaps out of mistaken optimism or even a desire to economize, would pocket half the amount of the bribe they were supposed to hand over. Since each go-between took a fifty-percent cut, the bribe, by the time it reached the intended recipient, was sometimes so small as to be virtually nonexistent. But there is no end to the number of possible causes that can be submitted at this kind of inquest. The important fact is that Kiichiro had expected to be reelected but had failed.

The shock did not appear to affect the Director all that much; or, if it had affected him, he chose not to show it. He still maintained his affable mode of speech:

"Well, you know, this is not a matter of personalities. No limited question of individuals. You have to take a broader view of things. The Seiyukai Party has done badly in the cities. Right. But in the country it's been a landslide. Two hundred and seventy seats, why, that's an outright majority. So, you see, the dissolution of the Diet has been vindicated. They have gone to the country, and they now have the popular will right behind them. The Seiyukai is still there, right on top."

This was surely an odd explanation: since the Seiyukai had this massive victory in the rural areas, and since Kiichiro was a Seiyukai candidate in a rural area, why had he not been carried along in the landslide as well? Surely to fail to be reelected at such a time was particularly shameful? But Kiichiro did not see it that way.

"The fact that I personally was defeated is beside the point. You know, in politics we talk about riding the crest of the wave. Well, I suppose I just tend to do the opposite of that."

One of the former interns came to pay his respects. He had left the hospital some years ago, but had recently received his M.D. and was going into general practice.

"Well, well, so you're an M.D. now. Well done, my boy, very well done indeed. I'm proud of you. I shall give you a gold watch as a memento of the occasion."

Whereupon Kiichiro surprisingly pulled his own gold watch up by its chain and showed it to him. Perhaps he was really going to give him a gold watch.

"Look closely, my boy. Now, this is dirt cheap, a piece of mere trumpery. I'll give you something much better—one I used when I was in Germany. It's away being repaired at the moment, but I'll send it on to you as soon as it comes back. Still, it's not just the watch that counts. It's the person who wears it. It's got to suit you, and you have to suit it. You've got to become the kind of person who suits a gold watch. If you're not, then you can wear the finest watch ever made and it will look like a piece of imitation rubbish on you. When you're like me, it's different. Now I can wear a watch that is merely gold plate, but it will look like solid gold."

Kiichiro then very kindly went on to give his former student much detailed advice concerning the problems of running one's own practice.

"When you're in general practice, the main thing is to be the kind of doctor that patients constantly feel grateful toward. Take me, for instance. You know, people are always showing me marks of gratitude. I wouldn't like to say how many patients I cured as long as ten years ago who still write to me. People who stay in this hospital, any number of them, make a point of leaving a photograph when they go.''

Kiichiro stood up and went and fetched a large dispatch box in which he kept these photographs. He opened the box and it was, indeed, jampacked with them. They were of various shapes and sizes but startlingly similar in content. Most of them showed a patient leaning either against one of the columns next to the entrance hall or on the balustrade of the balcony above. All stood in almost the same posture, arms resolutely folded with the half-impudent self-consciousness of someone who knows he is being photographed for posterity. They looked for all the world like the bully-boy bodyguards of some politician. On the back of each photo was written the name of the patient, the date on which the photograph was taken, and conventional words of respect directed to ''His Excellency the Director of the Nire Hospital.'' Perhaps it was because he naively enjoyed being referred to as ''His Excellency'' that Kiichiro kept these mementos; and perhaps the desire to show them to someone was a small instance of the first signs of wavering, of decline, even of degeneration.

Degeneration is no doubt too strong a word, but the remarkable psychological energy and verve Kiichiro had shown for thirty years, that will to press always forward (leaving the mess for Hisa to clear up behind him), surely that had now reached some sort of peak, a point of inertia and repose before the slow but gradually accelerating descent began? Didn't this new dwelling, if only momentarily and lightly, on the past indicate something of that kind? Whatever the case, Kiichiro spent some time looking at these photographs, emblems of a past in which he had urged on his builders to give shape to this unparalleled hospital; in which patients with strained, unnatural faces would stand to be photographed with Kiichiro's monument behind them; in which people had once called him ''Excellency.''

So intensely did he scrutinize the pictures that his face took on the same strained and solemn expression that those faces photographed so many years ago bore. The way he looked at these yellowing, faded images seemed different from the innocent vanity, the natural air of self-sufficiency and self-congratulation, that he normally displayed. Was it evidence of some deep-rooted change? Perhaps he had at last grown serious and lost his innocence.

But Kiichiro still showed no obvious signs of slowing down. His great political setback had not persuaded him to give up politics, for he still attended those meetings of his political party for people who were not actual Diet members. Obviously, however, the time spent on such political duties was considerably less than it had been, and once more he applied some of his energies to the running of the hospital and to diagnoses. His bedside manner remained as lively as ever, and although his words lacked, by objective standards, any kind of logic, he certainly had an affable way of talking people into agreement with him. He would listen with passionate interest to what the patient had to say and, with the same passion, explain what a tremendous authority he was. He would then smartly clap his stethoscope to the patient's head, or peer up his nose or down his ear with the instrument that served this purpose.

"Ah, look there, now. Nothing wrong with your cerebral nerve at all. Things are nothing like as bad as you seem to think they are. You're just suffering from slight nervous prostration, what Baird refers to as neurasthenia. No more than that. Try this medicine I'm going to give you. It's K.N. pills. You'll only find them in this hospital."

That was certainly true. These pills, which made use of his own initials, were only made in the pharmacy of the Nire Hospital.

To another patient he would say:

"Hello, your neck's stiff, is it? Well, it's no use getting upset about something like that, you know. 'Anger raises the spirit. Joy softens the spirit. Sorrow makes the spirit fade away.' The words of Kaibara Ekiken. What we call illness is all in the mind. Or, to use the phraseology of Bleuler, a sentient notional complex—that's what we've got here. If you're still worried about it, try our special massage. It's not just any old massage we have here, you know. The machine is the only one of its kind in Japan. Look, just go over into that room there and see our principal massage expert, and he'll arrange everything for you."

The patient would then go into a separate room and sit down in an extremely comfortable armchair, and wait until the so-called massage expert appeared. He, too, was a very small man. He had a pair of thin-rimmed silver spectacles perched on his nose, and was dressed formally in one of the Director's cast-off frock coats; this was his dress whenever he performed his art. He carried a curious instrument such as was not to be seen elsewhere in these islands. In one hand he held a shaft, attached to the end of which were two cogwheels surmounted by a thin metal disk. Beyond this extended a bent metal rod, and on the tip of that was a rubber ball. When the small crank attached to the lower cogwheel was revolved with the other, free hand, a complex, linked motion was set up between the two cogwheels, producing a trembling in the metal disk that created even subtler vibrations in the rubber ball. The vibrating rubber ball was applied directly to the patient's neck and the treatment lasted for twenty minutes, one hand constantly revolving the small crank throughout. This device had been brought back from America by Kiichiro, who was always on the lookout for something new. Its operation required no special expertise, and the "expert" now making it revolve was a former intern who had clearly not been cut out for a doctor. So he had become a masseur whose role in life was to turn a small crank. Despite Kiichiro's designating him "our principal massage expert" he was not in charge of any subordinates; he was the only masseur there was. Even so, the massage he gave was highly thought of by a number of patients, some of whom sent him boxes of cakes as a small token of their gratitude. These boxes would be addressed to "The Doctor in Charge of the Massage Unit," for, like many great artists, he liked to remain anonymous.

After dealing with the outpatients, Kiichiro would make his round of the wards, followed by numerous retainers. The indefatigable Director would keep up a very brisk pace, and the young doctors and nurses accompanying him would gradually be worn into the ground with the effort of keeping up.

But all this was not because Kiichiro was genuinely tireless. To be fifty-seven years old in Japan in 1920 was truly to be an old man, and Kiichiro was an exception only in that he did not look his age when he knew that other people's eyes were on him. When he was busy with patients or speaking affably to his staff, his face glowed with health, his brain was incisive, his lips were fluent. But when he woke up in the morning his body was heavy and his waist and hips felt stiff. His mind, too, seemed to be covered with thick curtains of mist, and he would have no idea where he was. Each morning, he felt an undefined anxiety at being unable immediately to grasp his whereabouts. However, once his wife, who rose before he did, was aware that he was stirring restlessly, she would swiftly and silently bring him a hot cup of bitter green tea. Kiichiro would not attempt to drink it right away, since very hot liquids did not appeal to his palate; but Hisa made no attempt to cool the tea, nor did Kiichiro ask her to do so. He waited for the tea to cool, and during that time he also waited, with patience and resignation, to come to himself. By the time he had finally sipped down his tea he had become about one-quarter of the man he normally was.

Kiichiro would get out of the German-made double bed and put on a dressing gown over his pajamas. Then he went to take his bath, not in any private bath but in the large radium bath at the rear of the hospital. He left his quarters "within" and walked along the main corridor past the wards, where the corridor narrowed, finally becoming very cramped before leading on to the cookhouse. Halfway along the narrowest part was a small door, and Kiichiro went through it, slipping on a pair of *geta* and walking across to the separate building that housed the bath. There, the huge bath was filled to the brim with water, and it was all for the Director, for himself alone. It was surely very wasteful to heat that huge quantity of water for one very small man (the bath was larger than those in most public bathhouses), but the Director insisted on his early morning bath and also claimed that to have hot water steaming away at such an hour gave an air of affluence and vitality to the hospital which was all to the good. Luckily, in the same way that he preferred his tea lukewarm, he liked his bath water tepid; so that the expense was less than might be imagined.

Kiichiro stood naked in the wide, empty bathroom. Unlike the normal Japanese person, who will wash or at least splash himself with water first, Kiichiro plunged straight into the bath without any prior ablutions, much like a religious believer entering a holy river. The image is just: Kiichiro's belief in the efficacy of his radium bath was wholly irrational, not to say unfounded. This bath was his fount of energy, his source of life. He soaked himself in the water, his eyes closed. He remained like that for a long time, making no attempt to wash himself, unmoving, as in a trance. So, in one corner of a wide expanse of clear water, only a slight mist of steam rising from it, this little old man sat alone, like a figure from a comic cartoon. He had all the sadness of a clown in repose, and the scene was almost desolating in its gloom. Not that Kiichiro was feeling gloomy in any way, of course; thoughts of that kind would never even have crossed his mind. He just sat there, quietly, taking his time, letting the lukewarm water permeate his body. At the same time the mystic rays of the radium, or some other ghostly influence, would pass through his skin, burrow along his veins, and awaken the sleeping cells within his brain. He would slowly open his eyes, and spend another five minutes in the bath. He did not wipe his face with his cloth, he did not stretch his limbs; but his brain had started to tick over again, and before long it had swung fully into action. Ideas began to visit him, plans for today, plans for this month, plans for prognostications for the more distant future, plans coming thick and fast now, swarming and disappearing in droves, then swarming back again. Now he would select one from out of that multitude; would scrutinize it, concentrate on it; and as he thought and thought again, that torpid, stagnant feeling engendered by the night and the various exhaustions imposed on him by old age left his limbs and vanished, leaving not a trace behind. . . At least, that is the way he felt about it, for he was convinced that the radium bath really worked.

He leaped from the water a different man. Scarcely bothering to dry himself, he threw on pajamas and dressing gown and returned the way he had come to his bedroom. Now his toilet began, an activity that bore a striking resemblance to the actor's art of makeup. He rubbed ointment into his skin, which remained oddly bloodless despite the fact that he had just got out of the bath, and on top of that he smeared and smoothed a whitening cream. He next spent a great deal of time on his hair and moustache, time that had become longer as the number of his white hairs had increased. Facing the mirror, he meticulously applied a black pomade, after which he brushed, moving his hand with delicate concentration and making many a sensitive alteration of the posture of his head.

"Moustache brush," he would say briskly, and Hisa would hand it to him.

"Moustache pomade," he would say again, and his taciturn wife would pass that to him too.

With an almost pathological care Kiichiro applied the finishing touches to his moustache. Then, with an air of something like relief, he sprayed himself with scent. Now it was done, and the confident, bustling Director of the Nire Hospital was ready to face the world, unperturbed by whatever the busy day might have in store.

In the afternoons the radium bath was used by the patients. Some of these were fairly serious cases who needed constant supervision and were only allowed there in groups. This would be over by dusk, and from then until quite late the bath was used by the staff and such patients who were not all that ill. The Director now occasionally showed his face among these people, even though the water, being at a temperature that most people enjoyed, was too hot for his taste. Although always working for changes in public opinion ("Don't you find it a bit too hot? You don't? Well, you surprise me. Amazed you can stand it. You must be very tough. Extraordinary thing. . ."), he would get into the bath with the others.

Was it that the one immersion in the morning no longer sufficed, his age being what it was? Perhaps, but the main reason for choosing to have another bath at this time of day, when the bath water was by no means clean, was to be at one with his staff as they relaxed after the labors of the day; it gave him the opportunity to flatter and thank them as they enjoyed the water together. He offered words of encouragement and praise not only to his staff but to patients as well. Such was his zeal, his desire to serve the hospital, that on occasion he would go so far as to demand payments from patients who had fallen behind in that respect (something he had never done before), although they were, of course, patients who were suffering only from some mild mental breakdown and were capable of making a rational response to requests of that kind.

Besides those patients who were supported by the City Council, there were others who had entered as private patients. A considerable number of these were behind in their payments, and some of them seemed never to have paid anything at all, although this was a matter in which the Director had shown scant interest up to now, leaving that side of the business to the Deputy. How was it that a man who had always ignored material things, a former member of the Diet, should now approach patients about money in such a direct, even brazen way?

"Ah, it's you. You'll be leaving us soon I see. Not to worry, though. You'll be all right. I can vouch for your health, as an authority, you know. You can put yourself at ease on that score. However, on another score, there is the small matter of your bill. You see, it really has to be paid, and paid promptly. Take it up with your relations next time they come. Remember. Can't go on like this. Not the way things should be done at all."

Once, on a late night visit, Kiichiro entered the bathroom to find only one other person there. The lighting was dim, and there was a lot of steam about, so he could not work out who the other person was. He dipped his towel into the water, which was fairly dirty by now, and found to his satisfaction that it was not very hot. He slipped slowly into the water, then turned to the other person, who was some distance away and whose face Kiichiro had no clear recollection of having seen before, and said:

"Well, getting on all right, are you?"

The other replied politely that he was.

"Marvelous thing, this radium bath. Look how healthy I am. Still a match for you young fellows. Life in the old dog yet."

The other muttered a few awkward words of ambiguous assent.

"Water's just right now. The way it should be. By the way, you are paying your bills regularly, aren't you?"

The other maintained an uneasy silence, obviously not knowing how to reply. Observing this, Kiichiro did not hesitate:

"Look, if you can't pay then you don't have to. Doesn't matter. Can't be helped. But if you actually can pay, then that's different. We can't just have you being idle about it, can we?"

The other person now rose slightly in the water and his face showed more clearly, and even the Director was not prepared to press his demands any further. He was a doctor who had just recently been taken on the staff.

Whatever the results, Kiichiro continued to do his best, continued to strive. He fought against his old age by means of the curative powers of the radium bath. He redoubled his efforts, both mental and psychological, to increase the prosperity of the hospital, and his subtle brain was certainly needed in these hard times, for the country was facing a recession, as frequent bankruptcies made all too clear. He also had to try to recover the considerable sum of money he had wasted during the election, if only to dispel the apprehensions of his faithful old helpmate, his wife.

And his labors seemed not to be in vain. The hospital remained as solid and stable as ever; the columns, the towers, the railings, the gate, all firm, substantial, safe. So how could any of his plans be upset? Tatsuji had become a Sumo wrestler just as he had hoped. Seiko would soon be marrying the husband of his choice. He would be able to arrange things for his other children. Then there was the next election. . .

Kiichiro knew only certainties. And certainty, belief in himself, was what had brought him success. With the exception of that last election he had always been proved right in trusting himself and his intuitions. And that had only been a temporary setback, anyway. There would be no more setbacks like it. Things would turn out as he had planned and knew they would. There would be no more disappointments, no more betrayals, for such things did not happen, or would not happen any more. Surely they would not, could not? Surely they were not there just beside him, waiting to spring suddenly out of the dark?

"Mistress Sei. Answer me please. Have you no tongue in your head? And look in this direction, if you don't mind. Look up and look at

99

me. Do you still not understand? Are you unable to grasp the shameful, the disgraceful nature of what you have done?''

The voice continued, telling her that she would not look in that direction because she could not, because she was in fact aware of the disgrace she had brought upon them all; and the voice belonged to Ryuko, who sat rigidly upright, staring with cold anger at her younger sister, who sat before her, head lowered, able to say nothing.

The language she used was more formal than is customary between sisters, but these were no ordinary sisters. Ryuko felt more like a mother, indeed not so much a mother as the representative of the Nire household itself, the embodiment of the amalgamated souls of Kiichiro and Hisa, and as such she interrogated and abused her sister; for she was attempting to break her will or, to put it more tamely, trying to make her change her mind. This was her duty, the sacred task that had been imposed on her—though mostly by herself rather than by anything or anybody in the world outside her ego.

We are now in that two-storied house we visited before, where the younger children lived downstairs and the older above; but this time we are upstairs in the living room of Ryuko and Tetsukichi. It was that time of the year when the late afternoons and early mornings grow colder, so the charcoal *hibachi* in the corner was alight—not a large, round, porcelain pot but a small, square, wooden box, creating no perceptible warmth although it made the iron kettle placed on top of it sing pleasantly enough. This clear sound was augmented by a cricket stridulating in another corner of the room. There was plenty of shrubbery at the rear of the hospital, and a bamboo grove covering the cliff beyond, so no shortage of visiting insects.

Seiko sat in the silence that was broken only by these two sounds, beaten into despair but clinging firmly to the one idea she had to keep uppermost in her mind if she was to be saved. As she stared at the mat floor she heard the cricket's voice endlessly singing from a different, far-off world. . . Hardly a voice that Ryuko was likely to hear, it was so thin and plaintive; and she did not listen.

''I wonder if you fully appreciate what you have done? Do you appreciate the atrociousness, the heinousness of it? I have been grossly mistaken in you. I have totally misjudged you. Don't you realize you are not alone, that you cannot think simply of yourself. You are a member of a family, the Nire family. Have you ever once seriously thought about what that means, what that implies? Do you really think Father and Mother have forgiven you, or ever will? Well, let me assure you, they most certainly have not. They have not forgiven you. They are not permitting you to do exactly what you like, with their fond approval. They have simply resigned themselves. They have decided to ask no more of you. They have given you up, cast you off, thrown you away. Do you understand? You have gone against your father's wishes and desires, rebelled against him, betrayed him. Yes, betrayed him in the most disgraceful and disgusting way imaginable, with some nobody, some man, some person of a most dubious kind. . . No, that I cannot forgive. I shall never forgive this betrayal. It is unforgivable. A vile disgrace.''

What had happened to arouse such wrath in Ryuko and stimulate this flood of theatrical invective? Ryuko would have replied by relating a squalid tale involving unbelievable humiliation, shamelessness and effrontery, for her younger sister, a graduate of Gakushuin like herself, had, in spite of everything, in spite of the fact that she was engaged to a worthy and suitable young man, exchanged pledges of love with a person whom nobody knew anything about, a mere teacher of English. This would not have occasioned much surprise had it been a matter involving her much younger sister, the hopeless Momoko. But she had always believed that the Nire family could be proud of Seiko and trust her to bring no disgrace upon it. Seiko was to have been Ryuko's colleague, her sister in arms, in providing the main—though modestly retiring—support for the hospital in the years of progress to come. And what had happened? She had behaved like some little slut from the back streets, falling in love with a man and wanting to marry him. Not that falling in love and wanting to marry was necessarily a bad thing. But with what kind of man? That was the point. Who was this man for whom she had broken off a perfectly worthwhile engagement? A nobody, a nothing. What contribution would her marriage make to the Nire family? None at all; the opposite, in fact. The family would be jeered at, sneered at, whispered about. Her father's reputation would be jeopardized, both in the eyes of the family of the young man with whom the engagement had been broken off, and in the eyes of society. And how could the family reply to these jeers and insinuations? There was no way of replying, none whatsoever. Seiko's action was a mark of total degeneracy, the kind of thing that could only be condoned in a family that had gone completely to pieces. It was unthinkable in a family proud of its unique name. It could not, it must not, be allowed to happen.

Ryuko was now carried away by something close to religious fervor, and the language with which she flailed away at her wretched sister (who could only sit there with her head lowered and gnaw her nether lip) became even more incantatory, so grossly theatrical as to seem quite hollow.

Ever since Seiko had confessed, some days ago, to her mother, admitting an emotion about which she could do nothing and begging for her understanding, the dumbfounded Kiichiro and his wife had tried every possible method to shake her resolve. They had put her under the equivalent of house arrest, interrogated her, cajoled her, threatened her. They would make purely utilitarian appeals to her, then switch their attack so as to appear as parents who were simply worried about their child and only wanted the best for her. Allies in the form of her uncle from Chichibu and one of Seiko's former teachers were called in. An immediate investigation into the man in question was made. His name was Sasaki, and a year before he had returned to Japan after several years in America. He was twelve years older than Seiko and taught at some technical college, and the two had met at one of the dance halls in vogue at the time. Kiichiro had secretly hoped that this might be some gigolo back from the States who was leaving a trail of broken hearts enamored of his city-slicker ways behind him, for that would permit various solutions. But this was not the case. Seiko was not a mere passing fancy, it seemed, for he had asked that she be given to him in marriage, publicly and formally. Kiichiro was, of course, not much interested in whether the two loved each other or not, nor much concerned about the matter that had so excited Ryuko's wrath: of the man's being a nobody. What had really shaken him had been Seiko's reaction: her obstinate refusal to budge an inch. He had always assumed that Seiko was as gentle and compliant as the sweetness of her expression suggested, and he had found her passionate obstinacy incredible; she seemed to be the original immovable object.

Would Kiichiro, then, become the irresistible force? Now that he had realized his daughter's affections were so abnormally strong, what measures would he take? Would he dream up some remarkable plan to keep the two lovers apart? Well, no; he would not and did not because Kiichiro was not that kind of man. In fact, he resigned himself more quickly and readily than the average parent would have done. This was how things were and nothing could be done about it. Seiko could marry the man she loved. He had done all he could for the girl herself and for the hospital. Since all his care had been repaid in this way, since his labors had come to nothing and his concern been thrown back in his face, it must be the will of heaven or fate or whatever; things must simply be allowed to take their course.

But last night Kiichiro had called Ryuko to his room "within" and said:

"Ryuko, what's happened has happened. I blame no one but myself. When a child goes wrong the fault lies with the parents. I shall simply have to bow my head and humbly apologize. Well, that's no great trial. It does no harm to grovel occasionally, depending on the time and place, of course. Still, I'll tell you this, Ryuko, and I'll tell only you: this is the first really serious disappointment I've had in the whole of my life."

He went on:

"I've never approved of dancing, Ryuko. It's bad for people. No doubt you'll have more children, Ryuko, but there's one thing you don't want them to do. Don't let them dance. I don't want to think of my children dancing, nor my grandchildren, nor my great grand-children. . ."

If we ignore the contents of these remarks, the manner in which they were delivered was remarkably similar to the tone of heartfelt sadness with which Kiichiro had told his eldest daughter on various occasions in the past, "Ryuko, if only you had been born a boy"; and this tone created a similar response in Ryuko, who sat there even more bolt upright than usual, her neck straight and unflinching.

Although her father had abandoned Seiko and her mother was resigned, the eldest daughter of the house was determined to pursue the matter. Her younger sister had been brought up as her successor, the person to whom the torch could safely be handed on. For that reason Ryuko had given Seiko a special place in her affections, so her anger and dismay at what had happened were proportionately greater.

Ryuko continued her assault, alternating abuse with painstaking explication. Seiko said nothing in her defense, so Ryuko's peroration became more a laying bare of her own beliefs than an attempt at persuasion. It was because Father had worn his fingers to the bone slaving day and night for the hospital that it had been possible to celebrate its fifteenth anniversary the year before last. Everybody knew that. But that was only the fifteen years at Aoyama. The hospital had really been in business for thirty years if one counted the clinic in Hongo. Look how their mother had slaved and suffered, watering down the soy sauce for the interns their father was doing his best to turn into wonderful doctors, and staving off her own pangs of hunger with odd bits of pickled radish in order to keep the clinic going until Father could create the present Nire Hospital. Father and Mother had striven for this, and it was their labor and suffering on which the hospital had been built. And now that it was created it had to be maintained. It was no child's play keeping a hospital of this size going. Only the genius of Kiichiro could guarantee its continuing prosperity. No ordinary director would have managed—not even a board of directors. It was hopeless to rely on strangers; only relations would serve, and those had to be doctors of genuine ability. That is what Father had been working for, what he had hoped for, the aspiration he had vested in *her* for so many years; and she was prepared to ignore all this out of pure selfishness and trample on her father's dreams. And for what was she prepared to do this? For some vulgar affair, for something so disgraceful and immodest that retribution must surely be visited swiftly on her, something which in proper households would arouse such horror that people would refuse even to admit its existence. Ryuko continued:

"Now, you listen to me. Is there one person, even one person, who approves of what you're doing? Of course not, because they all have a superior understanding of the world to yours. Suppose, for example, Tetsuyoshi were here. Do you think he would agree? His is, of course, a very different character to Father's, but he wouldn't accept what you are doing. Obviously he wouldn't.''

As Ryuko had said, loyally following her father's directive in the matter of pronunciation, Tetsuyoshi, alias Tetsukichi, was not there. Early that summer he had left for Europe to undertake the research he had been waiting patiently so many years to do. Leaving behind his wife and child, he had set out on a quest for knowledge, crossing "ten thousand leagues of briny wave," to use the cliché that had issued from Kiichiro's mouth that day at Yokohama harbor when they had all gone to see him off. The cliché had not satisfied Kiichiro:

"Well, of course, in my time, when I went overseas, you know, it really did seem like ten thousand leagues. Bit more like three thousand now, I should say. What with the way things are going, we'll soon be able to get on an airplane and make it to Europe in ten days or so, I shouldn't wonder. . ."

A gong sounded and the visitors were obliged to leave the ship. Then paper streamers were thrown from the ship to shore, some falling vainly into the oily water, others being successfully caught by those on shore and fluttering upward in the stiff sea breeze. Kiichiro appeared wonderfully pleased with it all; he looked as if he were congratulating not only himself but everyone else as well on the marvelous way everything was going, not bad at all, well done, well done. But he made no attempt to grab any of the paper streamers.

"You know, I let other people do that sort of thing. You get hold of one of those things and then, before you know where you are, you can be dragged into the sea. Dangerous practice. Not for me."

Ryuko, meanwhile, was standing there with a severe expression on her face, having just given her six-year-old son a ticking-off, for the little boy had been so overwhelmed by the smell of paint and salt sea air and the unusual experience of saying farewell in this way, that he insisted on saying he wanted to lower his trousers somewhere. But the main reason for her solemn dignity of expression was not the wayward demands of her son, nor grief at parting with her husband, but a combination of pride and hope at the thought of the future Director of the Nire Hospital going abroad and eventually returning an even more distinguished man. . .

However, now as she observed her younger sister, her head bowed and yet still apparently shut away inside some hard, obstinate shell, Ryuko decided she would change her tone of voice, and she suddenly softened the cold formality of her approach. She stopped gazing down on her victim, and spoke with something like that hail-fellow-well-met tone used in cracking jokes with an amiable crony.

"Mistress Sei, you really are rather young, you know. And a little too ignorant about things, I must say. Who doesn't want to marry the man she loves? Of course everybody does, not just you. But marriage isn't quite as simple as that, you see. It's not just a small, exciting part of your life, but the whole of it. And it's not just the two of you; it's the family, the world about you; it's a long journey with all these things. Now, do you really think I was delighted to marry Tetsuyoshi? Well, I'll tell you a little secret. I didn't want to become his wife. I hated the idea. I've never told anybody about this, but I'm telling you now. Still, I did marry him, and I didn't say a word of protest, either."

Ryuko never took her eyes off Seiko as she spoke; she seemed to be expecting some kind of change. But Seiko never took her eyes off the floor; she simply sat with the same unchanging, hard expression on her face.

"I've always been rather envious of you. In my case, there was never any question of choice. It had been decided years beforehand that I was to marry Tetsuyoshi. I was obliged to take a husband who would succeed to the command of the Nire Hospital. If Oshu had been born a little earlier perhaps . . . but that would hardly have made any difference, I suppose. All the fool can do is fail his examinations. Quite hopeless, I'm sure you'll agree. Even so, although Tetsuyoshi was certainly not my type, I wasn't averse to marrying him. Why do you think that was? Because Father said he had adopted the man with the finest brain in Japan. Of course, Father does tend to have a bee in his bonnet about things being the finest in Japan. I doubt if Tetsuyoshi's mind would really qualify as that. Perhaps he would rank around the thousand mark, or even ten thousand, with lots of cleverer people above him. Even so, he is talented and he is intelligent. Even if he never manages to lose that boorish air of his, he is still well qualified to take over the running of the hospital; the only person truly qualified to do so, perhaps. In my case . . . well, I suppose I'm not the person to say so, but I'm not exactly a fright, am I? I'm not all that awful to look at, and when I was younger there were, quite honestly, enough admirers and more, I can assure you, but when Father told me what I had to do I didn't hesitate. In fact I *was* delighted to marry Tetsuyoshi. I was proud to do so. Why? Because I'm a daughter of the House of Nire, and I know my duty. Compared with me, you've always been in a much easier position. I really don't understand you. I can't think why you should have got involved with someone with so vulgar a name as Sasaki, someone of whose family nothing whatsoever is known. . .''

Seiko moved for the first time. She suddenly raised her head as if she had been struck a blow deep inside and looked her sister straight in the face. Her complexion was even more bloodless than usual, and her thin, drawn appearance emphasized the shining blackness of her eyes. Although her lips trembled and her voice was low, she spoke distinctly:

''I should be grateful if you would not mention his name here. He is not the kind of person you assume him to be.''

For a moment Ryuko could only stare back at her, unable to make any kind of response. She had never seen Seiko's eyes so glittering and black before, never seen them so obstinate and challenging. She had never even considered that Seiko might be capable of such an expression. But her rage soon returned, more powerful this time. She straightened her posture and launched once more into the attack, her voice becoming shriller as she did so:

''After all that, do you still refuse to understand?''

For one or two seconds the sisters glared at each other, one hard and impassive, the other almost painfully biting her lower lip. But it did not last, for Seiko's resistance soon crumbled. Her head hung down again as if her neck had been broken, and above it echoed her sister's merciless onslaught.

"Mistress Sei, you are not making even the slightest effort to understand the situation. Have you any idea what this marriage you contemplate is going to be like? You will have no parents or relations to rely on—they will all have cast you off. You have been brought up in the lap of luxury. Do you imagine for one moment that you will be able to live on the salary of an English master? Have you ever cooked anything in your life? Love in a cottage is all very well in romantic songs, but it is hardly reality. Have you any idea of how wretched such a . . . are you listening? I suggest you listen now because it will be no use claiming later that nobody ever told you. It will be too late to start crying over spilled milk then."

Ryuko did not have any experience of cooking either, but she put that matter aside as she looked down on her rigid, silent sister, reflecting how unready she was to face the world. She kept up her verbal assault, determined to find some way to make her change her mind and save her from herself. But it was hopeless. The only result of her efforts was this rocklike silence.

Ryuko briefly frowned and made her final appeal:

"Very well. This is the last thing I shall have to say to you. I hope you are not taking any light, frivolously optimistic view of the matter. You are, I trust, not embracing the fond illusion that Father will eventually forgive you? Well, let me assure you, you will never be allowed inside this house and hospital again, not once in your whole life. It's out of the question. How could you possibly be? Even if this marriage is permitted, I hope you will not have the impudence and effrontery to show your face here again. Of course, if Father should meet you somewhere by chance, he might recognize you, even smile at you. But Father smiles at everyone. He will smile at a stray cat. He is that sort of person. But that is all it would be, a mere smile. It would mean nothing. And that is all you would get. Mother, of course, would not even look at you, even if you were right under her nose. If you dared to speak to her she would most likely cut you dead. You understand all this? And you accept the consequences? Very well then, if that's the case, do exactly as you please. So long as you really know what you are doing. Go on, enjoy yourself, throw mud in your parents' faces . . . Mistress Sei, is that what you really want to do? I suggest you give the matter your serious consideration once again.''

But Seiko sat in exactly the same position as she had from the very beginning, her lips sealed as before.

A fresh access of rage rose in Ryuko, and she brought out her final question:

"Simply answer me one thing. Will you or will you not change your mind?''

Ryuko looked down on her younger sister. Some small response, the slightest indication that somewhere within that motionless frame remorse was stirring, would have been enough for Ryuko to change her tone of voice, to find different words. But not one hair moved on that still head. Ryuko suddenly shook herself, and made her final declaration in a voice so full of rage and contempt that no hope of any concession remained:

"Very well. In that case I have also made up my own mind. You are no longer my sister. You are, from this day hence, a total stranger to me.''

She stood up and appeared to be going into the next room, but suddenly changed course, opened the sliding door, and went into the corridor. The stairs creaked sharply beneath her tread as she swiftly descended.

Her sister's footsteps died away and Seiko sat unmoving for a long time, aware only of a vacancy that seemed as if it could never be filled. Then her slim body, which had been kneeling there for so long, suddenly slumped forward onto the floor. A whole complex of emotions and thoughts took hold of her, causing slight convulsions in her shoulders and the occasional sob to escape from her throat. The humiliation she had endured for so long, the dreadful cold unrest within her that she could neither place nor understand, rebelliousness that bordered on despair, and then the single sense of rapture that she clung to as the one real thing she had, all these swayed and entwined and weighed on one another, and there was nothing she could do or say to give expression to them.

She clawed her fingernails on the matting, but then her hands went still. Her body seemed dead—right to the fingertips—from exhaustion, and she remained face downward for a long time.

While she was lying there, she seemed to be remembering something, and suddenly she worked out what it was. It circled slowly in the center of her misery, like the slow, irresistible hands of a clock. It was the voice of Billiken, and he was saying:

"His wife, Kikuko, although heavy with child and her time near, spared no efforts to succor him. . ."

"Fashionable young man about town, Tomoharu Iwakura . . . the demands of mother, wife and child, all cast from him unheeded and unwanted. . ."

"Hung from the scarlet silk crepe sash she had tied about the crossbeam of her room. . . Not one hair of her head disheveled or in disarray, her makeup perfect in its artifice and beauty. . ."

For a moment Seiko forgot her own plight, absorbed in this irrelevant trick played on her by her memory, and she raised her tear-stained face a little. But she soon lowered it again, laying her cheek flat on the cold matting, conscious of the slight sound made as it moved involuntarily there; for she was weeping again, her shoulders and back convulsing, and that gentle rubbing upon the straw matting sounded deep in her ear.

One day, at the beginning of winter that year, a month before prize giving was due to come round again, Yasusaburo Sugano was called to attend his master "within."

The Director had one of his rare colds, though only a very slight one, and had been in bed since noon. He was not, however, in the bedroom with the double bed but in an eight-mat Japanese-style room, which was normally unlived in for most of the year. The Director maintained that, in cases of minor illness, one was better off not sleeping on springs but on the harder *tatami* mats with just a thin mattress laid on top of them. This provided a stimulus to one's psychological backbone, and gave sufficient spiritual resistance to combat the illness successfully. Heaven only knows whether this was true or not, but when Kiichiro said so it certainly sounded like the truth.

Kiichiro was lying down on his thin mattress in the eight-mat room, and when Yasusaburo made his appearance the Director gave him his normal affable smile.

"Ah, Sugano. Come in. Perfectly all right now. Quite recovered. Not ill really. Just felt a bit tired and thought I'd have a lie-down. Look, the thing is, would you go and get me some oil?"

"Oil, sir? What kind of oil, sir?" Two and a half years had passed since Yasusaburo's arrival at the hospital, and he now spoke fairly standard Japanese. The Director's wife had a particular distaste for the dialect of the northeast, so Yasusaburo had striven to learn the Tokyo one. Of course, he never quite got rid of his natural way of speaking, which persisted especially in his intonation.

"Oh, any oil you like. Just oil. Ah, wait a moment. We've just had the wards repainted, haven't we? The oil we used for dissolving the paint will do. Fish oil, wasn't it?"

"What will you do with this oil, sir?"

"Slap it on the ceiling. I've been waiting to have this ceiling done for ages."

"On the ceiling?"

"That's right. All over the ceiling, lintels and all. It's depressing the way it is, don't you think?"

Yasusaburo may not have thought so, but the Director's word was law. So he brought the oil, got up on a stool, and began smearing the oil over the ceiling with a brush. The ceiling in an eight-mat room is only slightly more than twelve feet by twelve, so the work would not take very long. Kiichiro remained lying on his mattress, which had been pushed to one side so as not to interfere with the operation, and watched what Yasusaburo was doing with interest. He suddenly decided that he wanted to talk.

"Sugano, do you think they'll be over again tonight?"

"Hah?"

"The airplanes. The Western Army's air force. I suppose they'll be dropping flares again as well."

Some spectacular military exercises were being carried out at the time under the imperial leadership of the Crown Prince. Swarms of airplanes belonging to the Western Army—in fact there were only about ten of them—would attack the night skies over Yoyogi just to the west of Aoyama, and last night the "miraculous" F-16 had turned up, its huge shape caught in the searchlight beams.

"Terrifying things, airplanes. Suddenly creep up on you in the dark like that. Do you think there's any way of stopping them?"

"Yes, well. . ." Yasusaburo gave this inadequate answer because he was perched on top of a stool and doing his best to spread the oil on the ceiling with his brush, and so was neither in the position nor in the mood to give his full attention to the problem that troubled Kiichiro.

"Now, the Zeppelin," Kiichiro went on, following his train of thought and virtually talking to himself. "That's a good name, Zeppelin. I really like it. Sugano, Japan will certainly have to build some of those, won't she?"

"Hah." Yasusaburo's reply was noncommittal, not only because

110

he was busy with his brush but also out of respect for the Director's opinions. He worshiped Kiichiro in his own simple way, and he had done so for a long time now. It was true that he sometimes felt he had been deceived by him, and there were even occasions when he gasped in surprise at what Kiichiro did, but he still considered the Director a genuinely rare human being. He believed that Kiichiro was entitled to show off; in fact, Yasusaburo felt it would be perfectly in order for the Director to sprout an extra Kaiser moustache in order to preen himself the better. This was because apparently casual remarks let slip by the Director almost always came true.

One good example was something that had happened only a couple of weeks ago. It had shaken even the people in the hospital who were normally indifferent to happenings in the outside world, and, because of his affiliations with the Seiyukai, the Director had been most upset: Prime Minister Hara had been assassinated on the platform at Tokyo Station.

"There're a few damned idiots about in this world, I must say," Kiichiro had said to Yasusaburo as he hurriedly made himself ready to go out. "Still, that's politics. We politicians have to live with danger—it's an everyday part of our lives. Hara often used to say he didn't expect to die in his bed."

Kiichiro had twiddled his moustache as if to indicate that he, too, was in the same boat, although it hardly seemed likely that some desperate assassin was about to force his way in.

"Mark my words, Sugano, the next one will be Korekiyo."

And he was right. Prince Saionji was unwilling to take the reins, so the former Finance Minister, Korekiyo Takahashi, was made the next Prime Minister.

Yasusaburo had already taken written missives from Kiichiro to the Takahashi residence. It was a house of considerable splendor. He was made to wait in a drawing room full of imposing screens and busts before being taken by a servant into a garden with spacious lawns. The ancient Takahashi was there in one corner of the garden, seated in a rattan chair, wearing Japanese dress and reading an English-language newspaper, looking for all the world like a *Daruma,* or Bodhidharma, the armless, legless Buddhist saint of menacing aspect and facial hair who brought the Word from the west and whose image turns up in some unlikely corners of Japanese popular culture. As Yasusaburo approached, Korekiyo did not once look up, yet Yasusaburo had realized that this little potbellied man with the drooping moustache was the intended recipient of Kiichiro's missive, and he approached him with great trepidation and respect. When the old man finally lowered his newspaper, Yasusaburo passed him the letter with a trembling hand. Korekiyo slit the envelope open, cast an eye rapidly over the notepaper, which was packed with minute characters written in Kiichiro's crabbed hand, and then called for his writing equipment. It was brought him by his servant, and Korekiyo scrawled one or two lines in reply. Yasusaburo took this letter back, handling it with great respect until it was safely in the possession of his master, who read it, sagely nodding as if in considerable agreement with the contents, and as if they had also come as no surprise to him:

"Well done, Sugano, well done; and many thanks."

Absorbed in these recollections, arms and shoulders stiff and tired, Yasusaburo finally accomplished his task. He had covered the ceiling with shiny fish oil and the whole room was filled with an evil stench. Yasusaburo could hardly breathe because of it; but Kiichiro from his vantage point in bed grinned broadly and with great satisfaction, showing a number of glowing, gold-capped teeth.

"Ah, Sugano, that really looks nice. This room has always been too dull and humdrum for my taste. Now it certainly looks quite different."

"But what about the smell, sir? Should I open a few windows?"

"Smell? No, the smell doesn't bother me. Quite unimportant. It's amazing what a little inventiveness can do, isn't it? Looks quite different. That gloss on the ceiling gives a real quality to the place, an imposing, dignified air, don't you agree? Yes, that looks much better now; very nice."

The one thing that Yasusaburo had been feeling dubious about, the filthy stench resulting from his work, appeared not to trouble the Director at all. He seemed completely unaware of it as he lay there on his back, narrowing his eyes to look up at all this suspect renovation. He gazed at it for a long time with smiling eyes that had, nevertheless, a certain weariness.

Chapter

5

Momoko's childhood was free and unclouded, like that of a little princess, a rather unrefined little princess, perhaps, who was permitted to do exactly as she liked. This evaluation, it should be pointed out, was not that of others but of the heroine of this carefree childhood, Momoko herself.

With her sweating snub nose and her smiling chubby face, the youngest daughter of the house showed no interest in the decorous manners proper to her station in life, but enjoyed herself like a vulgar child of the back streets, eagerly absorbing the lively, inferior modes of speech that the various employees of the hospital used among themselves. One moment she would be howling with laughter as she shared her midday meal with the nurses; the next would find her being severely scratched by a cat over whose head she had insisted on placing a paper bag; and she possessed the expressive language appropriate to both occasions.

She was, of course, rebuked by her Gakushuin-graduate sisters if they ever caught her using such language. But she didn't care, because they belonged to a different social rank. Ever since she could remember there had always been in one corner of her mind a realization that they were "within" people whereas she was a mere "cookhouse" child. Fortunately, these sisters tended to ignore her, so she enjoyed a very free and easy existence under the care of Nanny Shimoda. Her parents seemed miles away.

On the rare occasions when she was invited "within" to dine with them she was always conscious of Hisa's watchful eye on her table manners, and unable to enjoy any of the food.

Kiichiro, however, on those very few occasions when they met, was always the good and loving father to her:

"Well, well, haven't we grown? Only have to take my eyes off you a moment, Momoko, and you soon spring up. Now, what are you going to be when you're really big?"

"I want to be a pianist."

"Well, well, do you really? All right, then, all right; we'll have piano lessons for you."

If Momoko replied that she wanted to be a painter she would receive very much the same answer.

"Yes, well, that's a good idea, that's fine. We'll have to get you a teacher, though, won't we?"

Not surprisingly, given the rarity of these meetings, no further discussion of these projects took place, and nothing came of any of them.

Her mother was the exact opposite; stern, unsmiling, hardly ever uttering a word except to admonish Momoko for some unfortunate phrase she had used, and then putting on her expressionless mask of silence again. Momoko didn't like to be in the same room as her mother. She didn't even feel she was her mother, but simply some oppressive presence, the spirit of that world "within" which had nothing to do with the wide world outside to which Momoko belonged. That other world was hers, where she could do as she pleased and breathe at will once more; except, that is, for those upstairs rooms in her house which belonged to her two sisters and partook of the atmosphere "within."

The outside world had everything. It was full of interesting people whose attitudes you never had to worry about, and they were all pleased to be friendly with this rather slovenly little child, and mostly overlooked the things she said and the way she said them. "Within" was stifling and oppressive, but outside she could do exactly as she pleased for there she was certain her word was law. Even outside the hospital this seemed to be the case. Most of the shops in the immediate neighborhood would give her preferential treatment once they knew she was the young lady from the Nire Hospital. Because of this, Momoko got the idea that, although in social terms she was definitely inferior to her elder sisters, she was still someone whose name was widely known and she could expect to be welcomed wherever she went. And when she first went to primary school she received a minor shock on being asked by her form mistress where she lived; she found it hard to believe that anyone should not know, and she said so.

She would go everywhere and anywhere. Now she would be in the nurses' dormitory playing cards with them, then with the interns being given a baked potato. After that she might go to the hospital pharmacy, falsely claiming that she had a headache, and the white-coated pharmacist would give her a glass of water with a drop of red wine and a spoonful of sugar in it, which she would drink with pleasure, reflecting that the color was just like the Bordeaux her father was always drinking.

When a school friend came to play she would proudly lead her on a tour of inspection of the most imposing rooms in the hospital, the VIP Reception Parlor and the Coral Room. This was never done openly because if she were caught by the Deputy, for example, he would approach with his dignified, wading-bird gait and, rimless spectacles aglitter, advise her in his thin, ingratiating voice that madam, her mother, would rebuke her if she were aware of her presence there. If she did manage to sneak in with her companion, she had plenty of impressive things to show her. The VIP Reception Parlor was graced with a piano, inevitably of German make, whose only function was ornamental since nobody could play it. At times in the past Ryuko, then Seiko, had plonked the keys a little, and a thin piano teacher with hair like a starling's nest had come, but his visits soon ended. None of the Nire children showed any talent for music since, as soon became apparent, they were all tone deaf. Nowadays the piano served simply as another place to display things, in this case some porcelain on a piece of sable.

But this did not prevent Momoko from bragging to her friend:

"When I go to girls' school Father's going to get me a piano teacher."

After savoring the respectful silence this gave rise to, she would show her companion all the other treasures Kiichiro had brought back from abroad, including the knives, forks, hair tweezers and nail scissors, in a condescending, self-congratulatory way that could hardly have been outdone by the owner himself.

"Any idea what this is?" she would say, wrinkling her nose and pointing to a bulky, yellowing, round object. "No? Well, it's an ostrich egg. You could make dozens of omelettes from just this one egg."

"Does ostrich egg taste nice?"

"Nice? Sure it tastes nice. Father says it's so lovely it just melts on your tongue. Makes you rub your tummy."

She would then take down a number of weighty albums from the parlor bookcase.

"These are photographs taken abroad."

"Abroad where?"

"I don't know. Some foreign country. Look, this is a foreign woman. Funny sort of hat she's got on, hasn't she?"

These were, in fact, picture postcards Kiichiro had obtained during his stay in Germany, views of various cities which looked as if they had been finely drawn in ink; pictures of old Berlin, of the Kaiser

115

Wilhelm Memorial Church with spires twice as spiky as anything in the Nire Hospital, and the Schloss Bridge jammed with cabs and horse-drawn carriages. All had been stuck in the album, as also had various prettily colored cards which celebrated Christmas and other festive occasions. There were actual photographs as well, in which Kiichiro was usually prominent. Most of these were group portraits taken at the Japanese Club, and the young Kiichiro was already sporting his Kaiser moustache and puffing out his chest, his face deliberately *en profil* as he smirked ostentatiously somewhere right in the middle of the picture. There was one postcard that was a solo portrait of Kiichiro, a rose in his buttonhole and wearing a white bow tie, looking as if he felt he might easily be mistaken for some well-known actor. In the blank margin at the side he had written in his crabbed hand:

A photograph of myself in the 34th Year of Meiji taken on the 13th day of September, it being my birthday and this a record thereof from which I expressly had this postcard made. In this month I also completed my first examination thesis and considered the occasion worthy of record. In the year 1901 of the Western Calendar at the University of Halle in Germany. Kiichiro Nire.

But there were more remarkable pictures than this, as Momoko discovered as she leafed through the album. There was, for example, a postcard that Kiichiro must have bought at the small hall somewhere in Berlin where he had seen the lady: she was tattooed all over her body, from her neck to her toes, with peculiar faces and designs similar to those eccentric images found on ancient maps. And there was an even more disturbing picture of a human being with two heads, one inclined to the right and the other to the left. Kiichiro had appended one of his near-unreadable inscriptions to this:

This two-headed person is a woman, the head on the right being Elfie, the head on the left being Bianca. Whichever name is called the appropriate head will respond. She is said to be seventeen years old.

There was also one of a dwarf standing beside a very large wine bottle. This too had a footnote:

This picture seen at the Vintermüller Restaurant in Leipzig, Germany, of a waiter only three feet high and weighing just forty-three pounds, aged thirty-four years. I immediately ordered a copy to mark the occasion.

There were many more photographs, but Momoko decided she would now entertain her friend with the music box. (There was a gramophone with a large horn, but that was too noisy and was bound to attract some busybody grown-up if it were played.) The music box had a metal cylinder with numerous holes in it, and when wound up it revolved, mysteriously producing an eccentric succession of musical sounds.

"See, I've got lots of nice things here, haven't I?"

Her little girl friend would agree, with an obvious envy that was reflected in the rider:

"Still, they're not all yours, are they?"

"Not yet," Momoko replied. "But when I'm grown up Father will let me have them all."

"All of them? What about all your brothers and sisters?"

"Yes, but I'll get all these," Momoko obstinately insisted. "Including the music box and the ostrich egg. Anyway, let's go and look at something else."

She then took her friend to the Coral Room.

"That's coral, you know. Coral is terrifically expensive. All of that would cost millions and millions of yen. Around a billion billion, I should think. I'll get half of it when I grow up."

Certainly Momoko was happy so long as she escaped the restraints "within." There were no end of friends to play with—the staff children in the barrack-like houses round the back, neighborhood children, even her brother Yonekuni—and Momoko was their leader, more energetic and willful than any boy. She would climb up through the trees and bushes on the cliff, and come back with scarlet lips and her mouth stuffed with silverberries. Her favorite game was "detectives." One of the gang would have to become a criminal and the rest would be detectives. When the hapless criminal was finally caught, he or she would be tied up to a tree with a sash or some other suitable thing. Whenever Momoko felt that Nanny Shimoda had been guilty of some special favoritism toward Yonekuni, she would appoint her younger brother the villain, immediately apprehend him, and mercilessly tie him to a tree. The unhappy Yonekuni had no hope of untying the rope so tightly bound about him, and there he would remain, sniveling pathetically, until discovered by a passing maid.

Momoko often went to the Seiundo stationery store. Just beyond the hospital gates there was a field known as Moto-no-hara, and after crossing it diagonally one came to a police box, and just beyond that, a little way before coming to the main road and the streetcars, was the small Seiundo shop. The proprietor, he of the famous voice, the irreplaceable functionary on many a Prize-Giving Day, would smile all over his face whenever Momoko appeared, and the tiny woman who was his wife would immediately make her a nice cup of tea. The shop was something close to paradise for Momoko since everything could be acquired here on tick, and thus, as she saw it, for nothing. You could get red rubber balls, all sorts of drawing and writing books, as many colored pencils as you could carry, fifty even, and it all cost nothing. But if she aimed for something of really superior quality, such as a sketchbook for a genuine artist, then the lady would gently admonish her:

"Mistress Momo, you are still only a little lady, and I think that is perhaps a trifle too grown-up for you. What about this one?"

Seiundo and his wife had both been connected with the Nire Hospital in some capacity for a very long time, and they used the standard Gakushuin "Mistress" form for the daughters of the house. Momoko would scowl a little when they wouldn't let her have what she wanted, but she always did as she was told, and on such occasions she would return home with an extra-large eraser in a paper bag. Momoko must have acquired an average of ten erasers a month from the shop, but she always needed more since she had the generous habit of giving them away to her friends. It was, after all, a generosity that cost her nothing.

Momoko never received any regular pocket money. This should not have bothered her at all, as she could get most things she wanted free, but it did. She wanted to have pocket money. At New Year and at the Summer Staff Party she would receive money, as did everyone else, but hers was always much less than theirs, the derisory sum of ten sen. Another important source of income was the visitors and relations who came to see Kiichiro and who would sometimes give the children a money present. The uncle from Chichibu would normally give her as much as fifty sen, and then Momoko would love him, but his visits were not as frequent as those of his younger brother, who was mean and only brought some boring local cake. Those who came from Yamagata were invariably stingy and would bring pots of local plum jelly. The hospital was always overflowing with this jelly and the mere sight of it was enough to make Momoko feel quite miserable. So she was constantly whining about having no money, though this was mainly because she was such a spendthrift, often buying things at other shops that she could have got for nothing at the Seiundo. She was also in the habit of buying quantities of indifferent sweets and cakes, even though she got enough to eat at home.

This craving for inferior foods she did not really need manifested itself in other ways, too. There was a veteran patient nicknamed the Cremator, owing to his habit of constantly lighting fires to brew or cook various potions. He would occasionally prepare himself a meal of thinly sliced beef boiled up in a little saucepan. Like Billiken, he was one of the patients supported by the City Council. Normally there was nothing the matter with him at all, but about once a month he tended to throw an epileptic fit. When the Cremator was dissatisfied with what the cookhouse provided he would buy five sen's worth of beef and, when the cookhouse was not in use, he would boil up the meat and eat it all by himself.

Once, Momoko noticed him busy over the stove, and when she went closer to see what he was up to he picked a sliver of meat out of the saucepan and popped it into his mouth, saying as he did so:

"It tastes really lovely, young missy."

Momoko was desperate to have at least a taste of it, and her mouth was watering. She swallowed down some saliva and then her pride.

"Give me a slice, then, go on."

"That I shan't. Not something that tastes as nice as this."

"I'll buy some off you then. Just one mouthful."

Momoko had recently become interested in the idea of eating out, and she knew one paid for it. She also remembered she had only three sen left in her purse and wondered if she could afford it.

"It's pretty expensive meat, you know."

"How much?" she asked nervously. "Wouldn't three sen be enough?"

"Three sen? At a pinch I suppose I could let you have three slices for that."

Momoko dashed excitedly to her room and came racing back with three one-sen notes in her hand, then ate the three slivers of beef cooked in soy sauce. The meat was appallingly tough, but she still felt she had partaken of a rare feast.

When Momoko had saved some money she would sometimes go to the tiny store in the main corridor of the hospital which was run by the woman who belonged to the Tenri sect, and there buy a can of beef. When this woman had no customers she would retire into the tiny back room and offer prayers for her salvation, beating a drum in time with her chanting to increase its efficacy. This noise traveled a long way, and some people felt that a person with such habits should not be running a store in a hospital. Kiichiro, however, did not agree:

"No, no; it gives a lively, spirited atmosphere to the place. Also, there's no way of telling how many of our patients may not actually have been cured by those prayers, is there?"

The cans she sold certainly had "Beef cooked in soy and sugar" written on their labels, but they contained, in fact, whalemeat. Even so, once Momoko had paid her money and bought her can and was quietly eating the contents somewhere, she would wonder if there could possibly by anything in the world so delicious, although she must have eaten superior food on most days, even if she were only an inferior member of the Nire family, a cookhouse child.

There were many other sources of expenditure. Along the main road of Aoyama, between the third and fourth blocks, was a temple called Zenkoji which had a fete once a month, and a great many little stalls would be set up in and around the precincts. Momoko would be taken by Nanny Shimoda to see it. Beneath the glare of acetylene lamps, with their peculiar, bitter smell, all sorts of interesting things would be going on. Here was a man baking lovely, warm *taiyaki,* a kind of flat cake with sweet bean jam inside, shaped like a fish. Here were tiny goldfish swarming about in an enamel bowl, and little terrapins stretching out their necks as if wondering if they should come out of their shells or stay put. Here was a man energetically selling bananas, and there a clockwork toy staggering awkwardly about. There were lots of things to buy: a conjuring device that allowed you to draw multicolored handkerchiefs from between your fingers, candies with spots and candies with stripes, and beautiful picture books.

There were so many things Momoko wanted and so very little money to buy them with. If she had only just a tiny bit of that billion billion yen's worth of coral in the Coral Room, just one little fragment torn from the wall, she could exchange it for this cute little chick cheeping away in front of her. Momoko felt faint at the thought, her breast heavy with excited longing, and she became almost dizzy. So she brushed aside Nanny Shimoda's attempts to stop her and bought a cardboard cut-out doll which had paper clothes you could put on it, and all her money was gone. And then she saw a whole row of brilliantly colored drinks, and a little snotty-nosed boy drinking one of them. Momoko started to pout and fret, and when she was told to behave herself she began stamping her feet in vexation until finally those huge tears were rolling down her cheeks. When things reached this stage Nanny Shimoda had to admit defeat. Still, it would do her no good at all if it became known that she had let the child drink this sort of thing, so she gained a promise of secrecy from Momoko and bought her a bottle of colored water. Beams of joy spread over Momoko's tear-stained face and she sucked up the orange liquid through a straw, making a great noise as she approached the end. It had a slightly sweet taste. That was all, and then it was over.

Among the more renowned of the Nire patients was a middle-aged woman called Satsuki Shimada. Like Billiken and the Cremator she never went outside the hospital. She was obviously suffering from some enormous illusion about herself, for she would offer an immediate and imperious show of violence to anyone who did not prostrate himself before her. For that reason she had to be kept locked up most of the time, and while she was in her cell she would busily occupy herself making banknotes. She would draw some indifferent picture on slips of paper, and mark them as worth five, ten or a hundred yen. At the bottom of the note she would record the fact that this banknote had been made by Satsuki Shimada and was valid currency all over the world. When she was in a very good mood she would ungrudgingly bestow these upon people, even the hundred-yen notes, and a considerable quantity must have been in circulation in the Nire Hospital. Momoko had quite a number of them, but even she did not attempt to buy things with them at the stalls in the temple. She had been able to use this money only once, and that was when Yonekuni had been much smaller and she had managed to get eight sweets off him in exchange for one of Satsuki Shimada's ten-yen notes.

Eventually, however, Yonekuni gained an understanding of the money that really is valid currency, if only in Japan. He learned which coins and notes were which, he obtained gifts of money from his uncle from Chichibu, and he began to manifest an attitude toward financial matters that was the exact opposite of his sister's. By the time he had reached the age of eight and was in the third grade at primary school, he had transformed himself into a monument of economy and thrift. The money box that Nanny Shimada bought for him always made a deep jangling sound, stuffed as it was with silver and copper coins, and he would not spend even half a sen. He ignored all shops except the Seiundo, where purchases could be made for nothing.

But one temple fete day, Momoko came back with an unusual purchase. It was a kind of celluloid box with molds in the shape of a number of animals, including a tortoise and a hare, and these had been filled with pieces of colored sugar. When the celluloid cover was taken off the candy retained the animal shapes, and this you ate. Momoko tried one, but was soon bored by the taste. And then Yonekuni approached with a longing expression on his face and asked her to give him a piece.

"No, I won't. I'll sell you it all if you'll pay."

Surprisingly, the skinflint said he would pay if it were cheap enough.

"I paid ten sen for it. I'll let you have it for half price, because there's still much more than half left."

Despite his wealth, Yonekuni found the idea of parting with five sen intolerable, and offered her two.

"Certainly not. Five or no deal."

"All right. Then I don't want it."

Miser Yonekuni seemed to have no difficulty whatsoever in reconciling himself to his loss. But this was not the case with Momoko, who immediately regretted having tried to drive such a hard bargain. After all, two sen was better than nothing. She had wasted her money anyway, and would get some of it back. So she accepted her brother's proposal, only to become the victim of another example of his business acumen. Having eaten the sugar candy, Yonekuni set to work with the celluloid container, using it to make clay models of the hare, the tortoise and the other animals. Naturally the clay had been obtained free from the Seiundo, as had the painting set with which he neatly colored the animals he had made. When Momoko saw them she immediately felt an unbearable desire to possess them, and eventually she found herself in a situation where she was paying one sen for each, and since Yonekuni had industriously made all of the six possible shapes she found herself parting with six sen altogether. Her younger brother had made a clear four-sen profit.

Momoko would often visit an intern called Senaga, who was more commonly known as Four Hundred and Four after the total number of human illnesses laid down by traditional Chinese medicine, for he appeared to suffer from the lot. Senaga hoped to become a doctor, but even before he became one, his was more a case of "physician heal thyself." In fact, he was not a walking compendium of diseases; he merely had a neurotic inclination to believe that every symptom he came across in the most exotic corners of his subject could inevitably be observed in himself. Since he was lodging at the hospital he had access to any drugs he wanted from the hospital pharmacy, but he still insisted on spending his last penny on cure-alls that were obtained from not very reliable outside sources. Every time he scanned the newspaper advertisements he would come across something that would at last cure his fatigue, his headaches or his stomach disorders, and he would immediately buy it. Perhaps the most cheerful and fulfilled moments of his daily life were when he was reading, on the label of the new bottle or box he had just bought, a reassuring account of all the things the substance inside would cure and the efficiency with which it would do this. His tiny desk-cum-table was jammed tight with such boxes. "New Cure for Beriberi: Essence of Silverhide" was there, as also was something called "Bulgarin," a product of lactic acid bacilli created under the supervision of one Dr. Mechnikov, thanks to which Senaga's digestive organs were still just about managing to tick over. There was also something called "Peter: the Fount of Youth," an alimentary tonic, and also a nutritional tonic called "Iron Phytin" concerning which it was claimed that "the French savant Dr. Pasternak's preparation of iron salts of phytic acid is a special new medicine for the cure of Nervous Ailments, Physical Debilitation, Anemia, Prostration of the Sexual Organs and other complaints." There was even a bottle that bore the legend "Look in the mirror in seven days' time and notice the difference: Genso Fluid will make you whiter," which seemed to be aimed at anxieties that could not properly be called medical. On top of all this (although he did not go so far as to approach old man Isuke for one of His Holiness Saint Kobo Daishi's lucky charms), Senaga still downed great quantities of that traditional cure-all, dried bonito soup. Yet not one of the countless symptoms that constantly troubled him showed the slightest improvement at all.

Senaga possessed a great heap of cuttings about such medicines from newspapers and magazines. One of these he read out to Momoko. It was a full-page announcement in a newspaper placed there by a company that sold a medicine called "Sintan," and it concerned the measures the company was taking to foil the machinations of its numerous imitators. The writing was much too hard for Momoko to make any sense of, but Senaga of the four hundred and four read it to her with the ease and assurance that much practice gives, providing at the same time a passionate commentary on the subject.

"*Trademark Infringement: A Heartfelt Appeal to the Whole Nation,*" was the bold headline and, after giving full details of a counterfeit product, it went on:

"*The above is but one example: doubtless others exist in the country, in numbers unknown to us, which require investigation. Were we to leave the situation as it is, this would not only mean forfeiting our high reputation, but would also cast doubt upon our conception of our responsibility toward our many well-wishers and admirers, viz. our customers, throughout the land. We have therefore, after long and bitter heart-searching, decided on the following drastic and sacrificial measures, by which impeccably legal methods we shall endeavor to fulfill our responsibilities, even though this could entail the total annihilation of our company.''*

After this proclamation of intent, which sounded much like an Imperial Rescript for the declaration of war, it explained what these measures and methods were. Any person who discovered one of these imitation products was requested to send five packets to the legal adviser of the company, upon which he would receive in return the price he had paid plus a reward of not less than one and not more than one hundred yen. This prospect stirred Senaga.

"You'd get a lot of money if you could find one of those counterfeits. Then I'd be able to buy lots more Iron Phytin and become a bit more like a normal, healthy person."

"I'll keep an eye open for you," said Momoko, always eager to be of service.

Still, Momoko was more interested in the "Genso Fluid will make you whiter" variety of medication than in the harder stuff that preoccupied Senaga. She was a precocious child in one respect only, in her persistent desire for the kind of intelligence or information that is not proper for a young lady of her age. A place like the Nire Hospital cookhouse and thereabouts, frequented by crowds of people exchanging language of rich vulgarity when there was no one about to enforce restraint, was hardly a suitable environment for a young maiden to grow up in. There were all kinds of dubious conversations, ranging from the nudging type about who was carrying on with whom, to the reports which one intern brought back from a series of lectures sponsored by the Japan Association of Sexual Studies and called "Sex and Sexual Love." It would have been much better for her not to have overheard such talk. Not that she eavesdropped on these conversations: she chose to listen to them quite deliberately and with every sign of profound interest.

Momoko had noticed, for example, that after a session of newspaper recitation Billiken would often take away one or two sheets of newspaper with him, and those sheets always had photographs of some popular geisha of the day. She realized that he intended to cut the photos out for some purpose of his own, and it was that purpose she wished to know about.

"What do you do with them?" she asked. "Do you like women like that?"

"Well," he said, feeling flustered. "There's all kinds of faces, and I just sort of like to compare them. It's interesting, you see, just looking at them."

Momoko became fascinated by the subjects of sex, sexual love, passion and so on. She had found out why the porter Toyobei walked in so bow-legged a fashion. She had heard it whispered that he had suffered some hernia or rupture or other disaster in that area, and since he was of terrific size thereabouts he was obliged . . . and then the phrase "the badger's spacious pride," which she could never understand, would always recur: the Japanese badger being a mere raccoon dog of undistinguished appearance, except for its large bushy tail. This incomprehension encouraged her curiosity; and she had an overwhelming desire to see what the thereabouts of the old man were like.

In summer Toyobei would often walk about with his loins girded up, generously revealing his thighs. One day Momoko was walking along behind him with an innocent expression on her face, when Toyobei, who seemed to have a shrewd idea of what was really on her mind, suddenly swung around, placed both hands on his loincloth in readiness for action, and said:

"Well, young missy, shall I give you a good look?"

This was too much even for Momoko who turned tail and ran, although she felt awful pangs of regret as she breathlessly scampered away, having missed the opportunity she had so longed for.

So the days passed, days spent more passionately absorbed in her detective activities than any small boy would have been; hours spent trailing after the cart that belonged to the tobacco pipe mender, with its thin smoking chimney, and picking up the glittering pieces of paper he sometimes dropped; hours of puzzling over what the badger's spacious pride might be; carefree childhood days that passed quickly and were gone.

As she grew up and began to gain a more balanced understanding of the world about her, some of her cheerfulness and zest for life disappeared. The difference between the way she was treated and the way her sisters were treated was so very great and, on the other hand, she could not depend any more on the exclusive attentions of Nanny Shimoda. There was someone even worse than her arch-rival Yonekuni: her nephew, Shun'ichi, Ryuko's son, who was gradually taking up more and more of Nanny's time.

This began to sour Momoko and she felt depressed about life. Nobody was interested in her, nobody cared about her. Was she really her father's legitimate daughter? Her sisters were treated with respect, like real ladies, so why not herself? Could she have been born on the wrong side of the blanket, the offspring of some servant, some menial in the cookhouse? The way her sisters behaved you would think so, always correcting the way she spoke, because they were nasty, stuck-up princesses who had been to Gakushuin and she herself had never learned to speak proper but simply aped the vulgar drawl of the commonest workman.

Just before she was due to leave primary school, her father said to her in a tone that implied he expected little to come of the proposal:

"Momoko, would you like to try for Gakushuin?"

Momoko had never had the slightest interest in the question of what school she might go to, but when her father said this she felt a sudden desire to go to Gakushuin and see what it was like. If she managed to get in, she might begin to be treated like one of her sisters and so become a real child of the house, which she certainly did not feel herself to be at the moment. Still, it was very difficult to pass the entrance exam into Gakushuin, because the competition for places was very stiff. Competition . . . now if it had been a contest in ball bouncing or playing detectives, then she had every confidence in her ability to come out on top. But schoolwork was something she really hated—even more than plum jelly—and the thought of all the studying she would have to do to pass that exam gave her a sudden pain in the pit of her stomach as if she had swallowed a dried plum, stone and all. What's more, her sisters held out little hope for her success, and told her so. Even the relatively kind Seiko said with obvious scorn in her voice:

"Mistress Momo, I am telling nobody, nobody at all, that you, my sister, are to sit the examination for Gakushuin. Have you any idea how hard I studied for it? I almost had a nervous breakdown. There are fifty applicants for each place, you know, and yet all you do is play your childish games. . . Let me tell you quite plainly now; you have no chance at all of passing, none whatsoever."

Thank you kindly, I'm sure, my lady, and no doubt all shall come about as you most wisely relate, said Momoko to herself, mentally poking her tongue out at her sister. Thus when Kiichiro arranged for a private tutor, Momoko was never to be found whenever he came, for the youngest daughter of the Nire house would be elsewhere apprehending criminals in her capacity as a leading detective.

Momoko surprised nobody, least of all herself, when she failed the Gakushuin entrance exam. After that she tried a round of schools together with another girl of her own age called Hamako, whom Momoko thought was some distant relation; she was, in fact, Momoko's half sister, born to a woman of no official status whom Kiichiro had made pregnant. Luckily all the schools had their entrance exams on different days, and having failed in swift succession Futaba, Miwata and Seishin, all three of them prestigious girls' schools, Momoko finally managed to scrape into Jissen High School for Girls. Did this make her stuck-up and proud? No, it did not, because she absolutely loathed the school uniform. The girls wore old-fashioned, trailing *hakama* in navy blue, the hue of which varied according to whether one was taking the normal or the practical course. So it was perhaps inevitable that they should be nicknamed Monopoly Bureau workers, since the anonymity that marks people who labor in such state organizations seemed to have been imposed upon them too.

Despite the fact that she was now going to a good girls' school, there was no improvement in Momoko's status in the Nire household. Still not one fraction of the attention accorded to her sisters by those "within" was extended to her. Momoko decided it was all the fault of her school uniform, and started hating school shortly after having with such labor managed to get in.

Nanny Shimoda now had her hands full with Shun'ichi. One day, in an effort to let off steam, Momoko bought an overripe banana at one of the night stalls, ate the lighter parts herself, and then stuffed the suspect remainder down the nasty little brat's throat. But the third-generation heir to the Nire fortunes accepted it with grateful pleasure, swallowing the rotten banana with every appearance of relish.

"How pathetic," said Momoko. "The kid must be pretty near starving." So she gazed scornfully at the child in an exact imitation of the way her sisters so often looked at her, and said in a strenuous attempt to catch the refined modulations of their voices:

"Just like a little downtown brat, I do declare. I confess myself amazed that this should be Mistress Ryu's eldest."

"What do you mean by downtown brat?" said another voice, so rustic, bored and tired that it seemed a matter of indifference to that voice whether it uttered anything or not.

The voice belonged to Dr. and Mrs. Nire's eldest son, Oshu, who was down from his high school in Sendai on one of his rare visits to the hospital, and was now reclining on the floor of the same room. He dressed in the typical style of a high-school student of days gone by, which is not to suggest that he was scruffy and wore a dirty beat-up cap. Obviously there was some inheritance from his father's side, for he took some care over his appearance. His blue kimono was well worn, worn almost to a state of disintegration but also worn stylishly. His footwear (which he was not now wearing, of course) was another case in point. His tall *geta,* or *hoba,* which high-school students were always clacking about in at the time, had been made to look out of the ordinary, for he had removed the thin thongs that normally run from toe to heel, replacing them with inch-thick strips of leather that looked like part of a belt.

Almost for as long as Momoko could remember, this brother had been a high-school student, and the impression she received was that he would stay on the books (in the sense of being officially registered as a student, and not that of studying with diligence) forever. Oshu would occasionally turn up during the winter and summer vacations, but would never stay long, saying he was off to some Judo Club training camp or other. It will be recalled that Kiichiro had once claimed he was in the Judo Club and had been smartly corrected by Ryuko. She had been quite right at the time, but a little later he had been dragooned into taking part in a Judo contest because they were one contestant short. Oshu, who was well built and looked strong, had astounded everyone by showing that he really was very powerful. So he had switched to Judo and was now captain of the school team.

"What's all this about a downtown brat?" he asked again in his bored voice that verged on the bad-tempered. "Momoko, you seem to have some pretty pretentious ideas about our family."

Momoko was too surprised to say she had meant to be funny, and remained silent. She had hardly ever spoken to her brother, and she had found his great *geta* with the fat thongs particularly unnerving.

"Look here, your high-class sisters may go on as if they were to the manner born, but, believe you me, that's just a few monkey tricks they've learned. We can put on as many airs as we like, but we're just a lot of country bumpkins, that's all we are. Don't put on that stupid Gakushuin act, Momoko. It doesn't suit you or any of us. And don't talk about downtown brats. This family's got nothing to do with towns, down or up. We're just a load of peasants; yokels, that's all we are."

Momoko accepted the diatribe against Gakushuin manners, but was not happy about them all being labeled yokels.

"Still, we are a rich family, aren't we?"

"Rich? Are you kidding?" This was news for Momoko, and though from the mouth of someone who was, in many ways, more of a stranger to her than people like Billiken or the Cremator, she assumed he spoke with as much authority as they, perhaps even more.

"I suppose you think we're rich because we have this big hospital? I'll tell you something. We don't have any money. It's all a load of bluff. Even this land isn't ours; we just rent it. The old man lost a packet on the election, for one thing. If you want to know the real truth, then I guess you could say we don't have a penny to our name, not a penny, not a single penny."

Oshu was certainly not in the wonder boy Tatsuji's league, but he had plenty of fat on his body even at this early age, and perhaps this was why he looked so cheerful as he roundly proclaimed that they did not have a single penny. He became quite talkative now.

"And those stupid cows still keep going on about what they saw at the Imperial Theater and what they bought at the Mitsukoshi Department Store, and we don't have a penny. Look, Momoko, if you want proof that we're just a bunch of yokels, how about this? Is there anyone in this household who has an appreciation of the arts—is there? Nobody can play the piano. They go to the theater and can't understand a word of what's going on. Nobody ever reads a decent book. It's all sham, all bluff, the whole thing."

Momoko held her breath, so great was the shock she had received. She wrinkled her nose out of tension and asked nervously:

"Well, in that case. . . I mean, what sort of book should you read?"

Oshu replied with the confidence born of five years spent at a three-year high school:

"Yes. Well. Well, you know, something like Dr. Nishida's *The Concept of Good,* or Soseki's *Shinran and His Disciples.* That's the sort of book."

Oshu was not well acquainted with even the outsides of books, and his bestowing of the authorship of *Shukke to sono deshi* on Soseki was rather like claiming that Henry James had written the *Forsyte Saga.* The fact that he soon rolled over, turning his back on Momoko and showing that he had no wish to continue the conversation, probably indicated that he knew he was out of his depth.

Although Momoko was aware he did not wish to talk any more, there was one thing she had to ask him. She didn't mind about people not reading decent books, but she found it impossible to ignore the question of their not having a penny, so she said in a very small voice:

"But there's the coral and. . ."

"What are you on about?"

"The coral. The coral in the Coral Room. That's worth a good deal, isn't it?"

Whereupon her brother—who certainly seemed well informed about dark family secrets that she had not even dreamed of—burst into a wild peal of laughter. As the great gusts of laughter continued, Momoko clearly heard, in the small lulls in the storms, as it were, words that seemed to thrust her down into the innermost depths of hell:

"You . . . silly little . . . fool. The whole lot's . . . fake. . . It's fake . . . all of it. . ."

Momoko spent the next few days in a state of serious unhappiness. The future had suddenly clouded over. She knew she could never hope to be treated like her sisters, but she had always hoped that one day she might be able to wear pretty clothes and go for a ride in a car, and now this delightful illusion seemed to be suddenly collapsing about her. She even found herself brooding on the contents of Yonekuni's money box. Buying things at night stalls was obviously out of the question now. In her efforts to work out methods of raising money she even went so far as to visit Senaga of the four hundred and four.

"Are those Russian rubles still on sale?" she asked.

Senaga had been unable to discover any Sintan counterfeits, and had instead been buying up Russian rubles in the form of banknotes issued by the government in Omsk. These were being sold along the main road of Shinjuku (which at that time was nothing like the bustling place it has since become, but was a remote, indeterminate district), and one ruble was going for just a few sen. The same ruble had once been worth more than one yen, but the war had resulted in a spectacular drop in its value on the international money market. But the man who sold him the rubles had said that they were a real bargain: "Buy these up now and eventually you'll get fifty times your money back."

But at Momoko's question, Senaga only shook his head sadly and pathetically:

"It's no good, miss. I found out those notes were worth nothing, nothing at all, just bits of paper."

Lately the Iron Phytin and other medicines seemed to be having no effect, and there had been a marked increase in the number of illnesses whose symptoms he felt he had. It was only too obvious to him that there was something horribly abnormal about the way his vertebrae projected, and this was causing a really frightening disorganization of the nervous system, which was why he suddenly woke up so many times at night, eyes staring, bolt upright in bed, and had to belabor himself about the backbone. He was convinced that if he did not do so he would suffer paralysis of his respiratory organs, and never open his eyes again.

Senaga's despairing face made Momoko feel even worse about things. Finally she made up her mind to ask Nanny Shimoda, and whispered in her ear:

"Nanny, how much money do we have? I know the coral's all imitation and we only rent the land, but we must have about a hundred yen in the safe, haven't we?"

"Don't be absurd, Mistress Momo," said the reliable Nanny. "The Doctor, your father, certainly possesses a great deal more than that. Whatever has put such ideas into your head?"

This was all the assurance that Momoko needed. One could tell at a glance at Nanny's face that her words were trustworthy. But the portly grade-two Judo wrestler struck again one evening when Momoko was complaining about the food. He suddenly rebuked her in that thick, rustic voice of his:

"What are you moaning about? Do you know what people in Germany are going through at this moment, with nothing at all to eat? The children are suffering so badly from malnutrition they only have to fall over to break an arm or a leg or something. Even you must have heard there's an epidemic of illnesses connected with food shortages, continual craving for food, stunting and I don't know what. They call them Greedy Guts disease and Tom Thumb disease. Is that what you want? If you don't like the food provided then don't eat it. Make do with rice and pickles. Feel thankful you've got even that."

This seemed to affect Yonekuni more than Momoko, as he sat there on the other side of the table goggling from one face to the other. He asked Oshu what these Greedy Guts and Tom Thumb diseases might be, for he had never heard of them before, and Oshu replied with such a flood of lurid nonsense that Yonekuni was smitten with sympathy for those unhappy children in a far-off land.

"Then I shan't eat pickles any more," he said, and for two or three days he kept his word, causing Nanny Shimoda great anxiety; she was obliged to think of all sorts of ways to make him change his mind.

Oddly enough, the very Oshu who had so powerfully affected the eating habits of his little brother went out with two of the interns as soon as he had finished dinner that night and proceeded to put away eight bowls of beef and rice, without so much as turning a hair. Momoko learned of this from his two accomplices, but a much more interesting event, which her investigations did not lay bare, took place a few days later, when Oshu slipped into the office and managed to browbeat the timid Oishi into giving him a large sum of money.

The following scene subsequently took place in the Deputy's office, where the accounts had been brought for the weekly examination.

"Uh, yes, well this is the, er, the um entry, ah, the entry on. . ."

The prematurely graying accountant pointed to the entry in question, which had been carefully and properly made. He had already turned pale and his pointing finger was shaking slightly.

"This is uh, the er, this is. . ." he muttered, as if he had a speech defect.

"By 'this' I presume you are referring to the entry indicating the sum that Master Oshu has taken to cover the expenses of the training camp he is now attending?"

The Deputy, Hidekichi Katsumata, remained seated in his chair and craned his neck forward in a way that conformed well with his other wading-bird mannerisms. The narrow eyes behind the rimless spectacles narrowed even further as he gave serious and formal attention to the figures before him. Recently his manner of speaking had become even more like that of the Director, though he still retained his own individual and eccentric high-pitched squeak:

"Well, yes, the fee for his camp, of course. But, really, you know, it seems a rather large sum, don't you think? Too much, surely?"

"Hah," replied Oishi from in front of the Deputy's desk, his lips, his whole jaw, trembling in dismay and bewilderment, as if he were striving to endure this burden that had so unfairly alighted upon his not very resilient shoulders.

"Um, yes," the Deputy squeaked through his nose, and then, after a little while, he said the same words again, only this time he breathed them out slowly and resignedly, ending with a slight snort. He leaned back in his chair, assumed a thoughtful air, and was lost in silence for much longer than was necessary. He looked up at the ceiling. He folded his arms. He unfolded his arms. He looked sideways. He looked back to his front again as if he were going to say something at last, but merely cleared his throat and folded his arms once more.

All this time the wretched Oishi remained standing there, rigid and unmoving except for a nervous wringing of the hands. Hidekichi Katsumata, on the other hand, was savoring the situation, enjoying these precious moments to their full. He could sense the unease, the despair of his subordinate, could almost hear the other's heart beating louder and louder.

Finally, however, he nodded.

"Well, there it is. It will do."

He heard quite plainly the sigh of relief the other made, and he went on this time in a generous, we-all-make-mistakes, man-of-the-world vein:

"Master Oshu is rather what they call a 'big noise' at school. He has a number of responsibilities. Tell you what I'll do. I'll take these 'within' and straighten the matter out there."

So the thin, small Deputy stretched out his hand toward a box that was full of rubber stamps. He drew out a big, new, square one with "Nire Hospital of Mental Pathology" on it, one to which he was not all that accustomed.

He applied a liberal amount of ink and stamped it down on one corner of the accounts that Oishi had written up with so nervous a hand. How different from that hand was the Deputy's own! How different was his whole comportment as he performed this task with an air of nonchalant ease, an ease born of the strong inner conviction that this was the act of a truly fulfilled existence.

There were a lot more people to be found in and about the Nire Hospital cookhouse, and some of these had an influence, greater or smaller, on the growth of Momoko's mind, even if that mind was nothing remarkable in itself. Perhaps the unremarkable nature of her mind accounted for the way she was so easily influenced.

There was that intern, for example, known for his lethargic ways, who had been thanked by Kiichiro simply for standing about in the entrance hall doing nothing. His name was Kumagoro Sakuma, an inappropriate name since it gave a strong feeling of brisk activity for reasons hard to define, although the fact that *kuma* means "bear" may have had something to do with it. He never worked, he never studied, but was one of the most prominent of those who ate the meals provided and spent the rest of the day employed in various forms of loafing, loitering, idling, skiving, shooting the breeze or what have you.

Even in his very youthful years he had been an important figure in cookhouse circles. As the usual pointless chatter was going on, his great booming voice would overwhelm all rivals. This was particularly so when the conversation was about martial exploits, for he had a great passion at that time for the military, and his own excited spluttering at such moments seemed to have something of military valor about it:

"In accordance with the declaration of a state of war existing between our Empire and Germany with effect from noon of the twenty-third, the BLANK BLANK BLANK of our BLANK, BLANK, BLANK, BLANK and BLANK regiments of the Imperial Army's BLANK and BLANK divisions have immediately commenced their prearranged deployments."

Kumagoro's ruddy face was a mass of rashes, eruptions and efflorescences, for which he was known as the Pockmarked Bear, and these became even more florid in the sudden access of excitement that seized him as he read out this eccentric sentence. We are back in the summer of 1914 when Japan declared war on Germany, a unilateral declaration that was given banner headlines in the special editions from which the above quotation is taken.

Kumagoro then read, or howled, on:

"The Imperial Navy, having completed beforehand their BLANK BLANK at BLANK, now regrouped in BLANK BLANK BLANK of BLANK, rendez-vousing at BLANK, and the imperial warships BLANK, BLANK, BLANK and BLANK escorted by the BLANK consisting of BLANK, BLANK, BLANK and BLANK raised anchor at BLANK and set off majestically in line-ahead formation for BLANK, and are due to arrive at BLANK at BLANK, BLANK BLANK on the BLANK of the BLANK."

He was particularly aroused by the bewildering succession of blanks, reciting them energetically with great sprays of saliva blowing from his lips, something that accorded nicely with the nautical contents of what he was reading. Kumagoro always tended to get carried away, and when he did so he spoke with a nagging, missionary zeal. He had already given up the idea of becoming a doctor, and announced at various times that his ambition was to join one of the exhortatory professions, perhaps as a narrator or *benshi* at the motion pictures, an attorney, or a big politician.

"I tell you, friends, there is a depth of meaning, a profundity of import, in those blank spaces, those blanks that move the heart. This, ladies and gentlemen, is, I tell you, valor, this is bravery, this is the essence of martial courage."

Such was the depth of the emotion that the blank, blank, blank and blank had aroused in him that his whole face, to its pimples' highest peaks, glowed dark red with pride.

There was, however, a sudden reversal of Kumagoro's ideological beliefs with the ending of the war and the recession of the years immediately after, for he started to claim he was a socialist. One reason for this conversion was, it seems, the sudden disappearance of the hospital's chauffeur. The driver of the Model T Ford was a quiet, kindly person of a shy disposition, a peaceful and obviously good man, but one day a detective from the Aoyama police station arrived at the hospital and asked for him. A rumor rapidly spread that he must be one of those Koreans (a well-known race of suspect, leftist dissidents), and while the matter was being discussed at the cookhouse it became apparent that the man in question had suddenly disappeared. In fact the man was no Korean but a native of Aomori Prefecture, and was no socialist, either—nor did the police think he was. The detective had come to tell him that his brother had suddenly died and so he had gone home to Aomori.

Still, Kumagoro maintained that an innocent citizen had become a victim of the poisonous fangs of authoritarian bureaucracy, adding with sudden force that it behoved us all to destroy the capitalists.

"What's a capitalist?" Momoko asked.

"People like your father are capitalists," said Kumagoro, raising his shoulders ominously so as to give her a bit of a fright. "I tell you, comrades, the food we are receiving nowadays is a disgrace. I tell you it stinks. So what are we going to do about it? Friends, comrades, surely this is unsupportable, surely this is too much?"

Momoko was half relieved to hear her family referred to as capitalists, and half insulted as well. However, Kumagoro made an exception of Oshu, perhaps because he had been stood a bowl of beef and rice at some time, and said nothing bad of him.

"Oshu is a remarkable person in his way. There's something of the anarchist about him which I like."

But Kumagoro influenced Momoko in a more important way than filling her small head with ill-comprehended political misnomers, for it was he who took her to see the motion pictures from the time she was still at primary school. The motion-picture palace they went to was along the Aoyama main road in the direction of Shibuya: the Aoyama Hall, a building of rotting wood more like a shack than a palace. At first it had shown old-fashioned Japanese screen dramas, but by the time Momoko first went to the movies it was showing imports from America, indifferent, crude serials with a new installment each week. But Momoko loved them and thought they were marvelous. It was a totally different world which made one's heart

135

beat fast and the sweat stand out on the palms, a world in which she could be lost. As soon as the four-man band stopped playing and the narrator, in *haori* and *hakama* or in Western suit, or even in the frock coat of some more leisured age, took his place to one side of the stage, she forgot the world about her, the earthen floor, the hard, squeaking wooden seats, even the ceiling that threatened to collapse at any moment.

The *benshi,* or narrator, was a unique part of the Japanese cinema, similar to the *compère* in the very early days of the cinema in France, and much like the master of ceremonies in the old-style British music hall or vaudeville. The Japanese love of being put fully in the picture through informed explanation was satisfied by the vocal presence of this narrator, who disappeared only with the advent of the talkies. The Aoyama Hall being a backward place, there was still a long preliminary explanation provided by the *benshi,* although his main role was to comment on the action as it took place.

". . . Thus the ill-fated, beauteous Yolande, treading a dangerous path 'twixt sternest honor and fond love, when lo her footsteps err and thus she falls, down into a gulf whose depths remain unfathomed, lost in a watery grave. . . A tragedy in four acts which I shall not explain in too great detail lest your enjoyment be spoiled, so I shall save fuller comments on some finer points until after the actual film commences and at relevant times in its progress. . ."

Momoko clapped so wildly with excitement during the performances that her hands hurt. She sighed deeply down her small nose. She was moved by everything, but what she most loved was the real "Western" film, the cowboy film, where the fight between good and evil was as clear as that between night and day, and where good could be expected to triumph in the end. These dramas moved her to her very soul.

The various *benshi* who narrated at the Aoyama Hall were naturally only third- or fourth-rate, and although they would perform their preliminary explanation fluently enough they tended to get lost during the actual performance. The script in front of them was lit only by a tiny bulb, and as they struggled noisily through its pages, muttering words as lacking in confidence as in clarity, the film itself would unwind in complete indifference to the state they were in. But such confusions never troubled Momoko. In fact nothing bothered her, not even the *benshi* who only gave information that was obvious to all and required by none. This man's voice seemed to be unrelated to his vocal organs, more like a stifled emanation from the region of his kidneys.

With this special groaning sound he would explain in exhaustive detail what must have been patently apparent to every one of his customers who was not actually blind:

"And now the villain . . . ah, he has drawn a revolver. He holds it in his right hand . . . he aims . . . a puff of smoke. . . The bullet, oh, it strikes the pursuing Jack in the right shoulder. . . Jack holds his shoulder with his right hand. . . Oh, he falls down. . ."

At last the inevitable scene of the chase would come round and even the loquacious *benshi* would ring his bell at this point and leave everything to the orchestra. The four-man band would lurch confusedly into *Orpheus in the Underworld,* and the car with the villain aboard would race wildly along the top of a cliff, pursued by the skillful detective who would be living a tire's width more dangerously in his. Frenzied excitement would grip the audience, and Momoko would cry out and leap up and down in her seat, until the film faded to its unfulfilled ending and the empty appeal to look forward to next week's exciting installment.

On one occasion, when a *benshi* in Japanese-style dress was providing a commentary on a scene where the faces of a man and woman draw close to each other, there was a sudden voice from the back of the hall: "Narrator. Careful." Momoko jumped with surprise and looked around, and realized it was the voice of a constable who was sitting grandly in the overseer's seat at the back.

When the film was over Kumagoro clicked his tongue in disapproval and said:

"There you see, miss, the arrogance of our authoritarian bureaucracy. It's in that way they repress socialism."

Thus the movies became an addiction for Momoko, a drug which her soul found it impossible to do without. After entering girls' school she would go to the movies every week, either by herself or with school friends. She was no longer satisfied with what the Aoyama Hall could offer, so she went farther afield, to the Empire in Akasaka or the Musashino in Shinjuku, sometimes even trekking as far as the bright lights of Asakusa. She had to keep on devising ways to raise the necessary money; for example, getting Oishi to give her the cash to buy a season ticket for the streetcar to school and then walking both ways and spending it on her "drug." She was even forced sometimes to beg from that skinflint Yonekuni of money-box fame. When she was really desperate she would wheedle the necessary out of Nanny Shimoda.

"Mistress Momo, I gave you the same only a few days ago, surely? I'm not all that rich, you know," she would say, but having hand-reared all the Nire children she spoiled them hopelessly, and Momoko would always receive, on the sly, whatever she asked for.

So she would enter the dark realms of magic again, that shabby-gorgeous retreat from the outside world, where, to an accompaniment of popping corks from lemonade bottles and munched crackers, she would yield herself to ecstasy. This was her place, the only one that was her very own.

But now, rather than the unending pursuit of villain by detective, Momoko found herself drawn toward the tender attraction of the love story. She had been aware for some time, from the student's reports about the lecture series on "Sex and Sexual Love" and other sources, that love existed in the world, but how different from that flat report-age was the grandiloquence of the *benshi*. There, in the splendor (if compared to the Aoyama shack) of a motion-picture palace built of stone, the smooth-tongued *benshi*'s stream of words would penetrate all the receptive hearts in his audience.

One of these hearts was Momoko's. The way the words were spoken created a great, heavy lump within her, and she was borne along on the current of the voice, feeling that at any moment she would cry.

"As the poets from far Europe sing," the low voice would begin, making her palms tingle in anticipation. "Fain would I be thy mirror, love, that I might reflect thy form. Fain would I be a little bird, to come unto thy windowpane. Ah then, ah then, should a hawk fall, and choose my body for his prey, fain would I, by his talons torn, so die beside thy window, dear."

Then the voice would rise: "The wind doth mingle with the wind, the wave invite the wave. Warm sunlight doth embrace the earth, the moonlight kiss the sea. Ah, love, permit me but one kiss; if not, what recks it when all things do thus each other hold, yet you will not be mine?"

The voice set Momoko's midriff aflutter and she seemed almost to be stifling with feeling.

"Ah love, sweet love, the pure wine of our days; river of life, ah love. In one brief moment born, presiding o'er our momentary bliss. Ah, that I loved, ah, that I loved. Without sweet love what is this youth of mine?"

Momoko had recently arrived at puberty. Her round cheeks had filled out even more, making her already narrow eyes unfortunately narrower. Her arms and legs were also more rounded, slightly but perceptibly different from those of the child she had been such a little time ago.

It's true; absolutely true—the most important thing in the world is love. It's the only thing there really is. So she bought a bottle of lotion for her face which said on the label, "For passionate lovers of beauty, one drop will bring that special faintest touch of whiteness to your skin," and she rubbed it vigorously into her cheeks. She preferred it to Four Hundred and Four's "Genso Fluid will make you whiter" because of the elegance of that "faintest touch."

She still moved in cookhouse circles, inclining an eager ear to the talk of the interns and nurses, but she was now a seasoned campaigner of numerous motion-picture romances and felt herself to be well informed, indeed something of an authority, on the subject of love. As soon as she got home from school, she would immediately change out of the loathed Monopoly Bureau worker's uniform, then walk the neighborhood streets with a coolly calculating look on her face. If some young man approached who seemed a suitable object for love's darts, she would not lower her eyes meekly as befits an innocent maid. Instead she would raise her face slightly, snub nose in the air, and allow the trace of a smile to play about her rounded features as she passed him, an invitation to look over in this direction, young man, and observe an authority on love's mysteries walking by.

Another thing that spurred this interest was a startling revelation she heard from Hamako one day, when she had come to the hospital to play. Momoko was not all that shocked to hear that Hamako was her half sister, born of a different, unofficial mother, since she vaguely remembered hearing something of that kind from someone else before. What really appalled her was the realization that her father was in the habit of marrying people off to whomever he pleased, either out of pure whim or from a desire to consolidate the position of the hospital. This had been the case with Ryuko and Tetsukichi, and with a few likely interns, and it extended to arranging the marriages of nurses and even casual laborers at the hospital. Recently, for example, the maid with the fat, round face who worked "within" had given notice. Why was that? Because she had been given a secret hint about the man who had been lined up for her to marry, and once she had got wind of it she had run back home. And who was the intended? Who else but the amazing wonder boy, Tatsuji the freak, who had taken the professional Sumo name of Zaosan (Mt. Zao). Apparently Kiichiro had first thought of the match some ten years before—not a long time for him where such matters were concerned: he liked to plan well in advance. Her own case would be no exception, said Hamako in a voice that suggested she was well informed about such things, which was not surprising considering the special environment of the pleasure quarter in which she had been brought up. She was destined to become the bride of either Seisaku Kanazawa or Katsujiro Nirasawa, young men who were due to be given positions of central importance in the hospital sometime in the future.

"Well, do you like them, either of those two?"

"Not likely," said Hamako. "The man I really like is Valentino. Still, it can't be helped, can it?"

"Valentino?" said Momoko incredulously, suddenly become passionate. "What's supposed to be good about him, I'd like to know? I think Richard and Antonio Moreno are simply miles better, really lovely."

Richard and Antonio Moreno were not a famous pair of screen twins, nor did they even have the same surname. "Richard" was Richard Barthelmess, a homespun heartthrob of the time, but the Japanese found the surname difficult to pronounce and unmelodious when they did, so they solved the problem by dropping it and making him plain Richard. Antonio Moreno was one of Valentino's rivals. Hamako knew who these people were, and Momoko continued uninterrupted:

"Of course, I admit Valentino's better than Seisaku anyway. . . I know, you ought to run away; leave home. Then love the man of your choice."

"Leave home? Love?" Hamako puckered her mouth a little as if she were trying to stifle a yawn. "Don't be so silly. What can you or I do about it? Life's not like the movies, you know."

But Momoko was too serious to let things be shrugged off in this way.

"No, that's not true. Love is important. You ought to be in love when you get married. Loveless marriages shouldn't be allowed."

"All right, you'll see," and Hamako looked at Momoko with pitying eyes. "I shall marry Seisaku and you'll be made to marry Katsujiro, or the other way round perhaps. You'll see; it'll be one way or the other."

"What? Me marry Katsujiro? That little creep?" Momoko howled with laughter; briefly.

Katsujiro Nirasawa was a distant relation of the family into which Kiichiro had been born. He was like a farmer in his honesty and simplicity, and had still not lost his North-country accent, although he had gained certain polite accomplishments after becoming a medical student; he used, for example, to remove his cap whenever he came here from school and passed through the small gateway (next to the big one) into the hospital grounds. He was now on the medical staff at the prestigious Keio Hospital, helping out at the Nire Hospital on the side, and he already had a reputation as a skillful doctor, so that under normal circumstances Momoko would not have dreamed of referring to him as a "little creep."

Still, circumstances were not normal. The real problem was her father. She hardly ever met him, but had always believed implicitly that he was a great man and a good father, and now he was presented to Momoko's eyes as something quite different, the Machiavelli of the medical world, a wily master of machinations; the whole atmosphere of the hospital in which she had formerly breathed so freely seemed suddenly black with dank miasmas, lowering clouds and dark intrigues, a land of mists where swarms of evildoers lurked. Only the *benshi* at the Empire in Akasaka could have done justice to this place, and how the audience would have responded to that evil, croaking voice: with cold sweats and shivers at the horror of it all.

Momoko repeated her contemptuous remark about the little creep and, either because she cut her great howl of laughter short so quickly or because there had been some sudden, violent alteration in the way she felt, tears welled in the slightly drooping corners of her eyes. But then she spoke in solemn tones, as if she were swearing an oath to someone or something:

"I don't care who is planning what. I shall love whoever I choose. I shall love someone, and that is certain."

The incident didn't seem to dampen her spirits in any way, and she remained apparently the same cheerful person with no clouds hovering over her, no shadow across her cheerfully smiling face. Only, her deportment and general behavior became more uncouth than ever, and the number of times she went to the cinema each week increased from once to twice or even three times. Since she was afraid that her mother might be keeping a secret eye on her from "within" (a prospect she found much more terrifying than the thought of a total stranger silently supervising her every move outside), she stopped leaving the hospital by the front gate but scrambled instead through the bamboo grove on the cliff round the back, often tearing her clothes as she did so.

Meanwhile, the Pockmarked Bear was suffering similar mental turmoil. The idle Kumagoro, self-styled socialist, had gone to observe the second May Day demonstrations which, in 1921, were held at Shibaura. The rally took place, as Billiken read out, *"in an atmosphere of considerable tension, and many persons were apprehended and taken into custody."* In fact, Kumagoro had only been there to watch the procession, but it had so upset him that he came away having lost all faith in the Communist Party. It was the behavior of those walking in the protesting column that had offended him. It was perfectly all right for them to greet each passing democratic streetcar with cheers and each passing bourgeois car with howls and jeers, but he could not forgive the way they totally ignored a person like himself, walking upright on two legs just like them, and waving to them in a friendly fashion; just ignored him.

Momoko herself was not unaffected by the events that took place at this festival of labor, for among those arrested was the blind Russian poet, Vasilii Eroshenko, who had been publishing poems and children's stories in Japanese since 1916, five years before. "The blind poet, Eroshenko"—everything about the phrase appealed to Momoko, and the photograph that appeared in the newspaper had just the right dark melancholy about it, the poetic sorrow of the outcast life. Ah, if only a meeting could be arranged between herself and this man from a far-off land. . . The poet would move his slender, hesitant hands and slowly touch her face. Then, in a voice more sonorously low and filled with sad passion than the *benshi* at the cinema, he would whisper softest language in her ear. And she would answer, forehead modestly bowed low on this occasion, with that one word which almost never passed her lips, a breathless word that would soon fade away, a modest, meek, brief affirmation; for she would answer "yes." Momoko lay on her thin, hard mattress and dreamed of this with such imaginative clarity that, for the first time in her life, she passed a sleepless night. But the blind poet who had flurried her heartstrings in this way was deemed to be an undesirable person with anarchistic tendencies, and was unceremoniously expelled from the country.

A few days passed and Momoko, with a surprisingly disinterested look, asked that authority on political terminology, Kumagoro the Pockmarked Bear, what an anarchist might be.

"Anarchists are pretty remarkable people. They are opposed to all government, young lady, and they chuck bombs all over the place."

A few more days passed and Momoko was walking down the side street where the Seiundo was, when she saw Katsujiro Nirasawa coming from the opposite direction, probably returning from his work. Being a courteous individual, he would not ignore even someone as insignificant as this youngest daughter of the House of Nire, and he stopped and bowed very politely to her. Imagine his astonishment when, instead of receiving an artless grin from this girl who normally looked much more childish than her years, he was greeted by an awful hardening of her expression as she turned a deliberate cold shoulder to him, and almost ran past.

Momoko herself was overcome by a complex of emotions, mostly humiliation and rage, and, breathing heavily, she said to herself:

"The absolute impudence of it, pretending he knows nothing and making that insolent bow. They're all in it together. They're all plotting against me. They're all trying to ensnare me in their trap."

She had not particularly meant to go to the Seiundo but she dashed inside all the same, took a quick glance around, then gathered up a number of deluxe notebooks, an expensive-looking pencil sharpener, and ten excessively large erasers each in the shape of a rabbit.

"Just charge these up for me, will you?" she said aggressively to the Seiundo lady who had just appeared from the back of the shop.

"Oh, my goodness, Mistress Momo. What do you want with all those erasers? And a pencil sharpener, and you only had one the other day."

The gentle art of persuasion, which had always worked until now, had no effect this time.

"Well I just want them. All of them. I need them for my work. I don't see how anyone can complain about that. So that's ten erasers, right? Got it?"

Momoko threw the words out in rough, tomboyish style, picked up her loot in both hands, and dashed out of the shop. She walked a hundred yards or so determinedly looking straight ahead, ignoring the world around her. But then the rabbit erasers seemed on the verge of escaping from her hand, and she became aware of their peculiar resilience, their softness in her palm, and her eyes began to tingle slightly as if she were about to weep.

But she fought that impulse down. Allowing an evil glitter to come into her eyes, she shook her shoulders firmly once and walked defiantly on, whispering to her cold, rebellious heart:

"I'm an anarchist. That's what I am, an anarchist."

Chapter

6

The sea broke on the shore, on layer after layer of hard rock, broke with a long deep-throated roar. Wave after wave flowed in, bursting in white spray against the glittering, dark brown rocks, then pulling back in circles of foam. But that was to the right, and here the gently sloping beach, sand tinged dark gray, spread wide to hold a gentler sea. As each new wave drew back it left a swathe of sand grown dark, and a transitory shining. There your foot sank lightly in, and you felt as if a host of bubbles were ascending around it—like numerous tiny crabs quitting their secret holes. In places, tangled seaweed had been cast up on the shore, and hermit crabs were busily carrying seashells about on their backs, suddenly hiding within them in panic at the sound of another wave approaching.

A light breeze blew, seeming to wrap the odors of the beach around the body. Far out, beneath that distant portion of the sky where a few clouds had gathered, unreal as if they had been painted there, the color of the sea was subtly different.

Momoko was not much interested in the various sights and sensations the sea so liberally provided. She was absorbing something more abstract, the general sense of joy that the sea can give, the feeling that all stifling restraints have been cast aside, and so she played and rejoiced in a completely childish manner. She splashed about idly at the water's edge, dashed forward to chase the retreating waves and then dashed back again, raising meaningless shouts and screams.

It was the summer of 1922. Momoko had been invited with two or three others to spend a fortnight in a house by the seaside which the family of one of her school friends was renting for the summer. It was in a still rural area of the Miura Peninsula, which is twenty-five miles or so to the south of Tokyo, a resort that had nothing but its beach. The grown-ups in the house were pleasant people who did not bother the girls in any way, so the latter could do as they pleased, and since it was summer and they were by the sea, all in their third year at school

144

and more or less friends, they shouted and screamed whenever they felt like it, which was quite often.

Here, surely, were days that could be spent far from care and trouble, but Momoko's heart was not completely free of those shadows that seemed to have become her lot in life. This year Kiichiro had decided to have a cottage built in Gora, a hot-spring resort in Hakone, the mountain resort area nearest to Tokyo to the west, this side of Mt. Fuji, and still the most popular place for escaping the humidity and heat of the Tokyo summer. The cottage itself was a good thing; the bad thing was that when Momoko returned home after her two weeks by the sea she was not to be allowed to go there. They said it was because there would be so many guests for the housewarming; but if that was so, why was Shun'ichi being allowed to go? He would surely be much more of a nuisance than she would ever be. The little brat and his terribly refined mother were going to be there all summer.

"I can't say I'm surprised, though. That's how it always is," and Momoko unconsciously scooped up a handful of sand and threw it idly at a small crab that had the misfortune to be passing in front of her. "I know what's going on. There's no mystery about any of it. I know."

But she had suffered a more profound upset than this, and had a sense of misgiving that was difficult to pin down and was not one she had had before. It concerned marriage, and had to do with the marriage of her sister Seiko at the end of last year. As Momoko looked toward the horizon, which seemed misted often now, it was to this problem that her mind kept returning.

The whole marriage had been veiled in secrecy. It was true that a formal ceremony had been publicly gone through, but the number of invited guests had been very limited. Except for Kiichiro and his wife, and Ryuko, Oshu (who happened to be at home at the time), and Momoko herself, no other relatives had attended, not even the two small children, Yonekuni and Shun'ichi. Momoko, who was used to the bustling atmosphere of daily hospital life, found this quietness unnerving, even ominous. On top of that Seiko had, since the day she got married, simply disappeared, never once returning to the hospital.

Momoko had in fact seen Seiko since then, because she had been taken by Nanny Shimoda to visit this sister who had married a man about whom Momoko knew almost nothing. It was a long journey, first by streetcar and then down narrow streets until finally one reached a street where all the houses seemed to be on top of each other, and there Seiko lived in a tiny house with a broken fence in front of it. When Nanny Shimoda went to visit Seiko she always carried a huge bundle, remarkable for its bulk rather than for the value of its contents, which were mainly vegetables in season, onions and carrots with the earth still on them, or fruit that appeared to have been picked straight off the tree and was not placed in the clean, neat little box in which fruit would normally be presented as a polite gift when paying a visit. Sometimes she even took some rice. These were things that Nanny Shimoda had managed to obtain by stealth from the cookhouse stores, and what they lacked in value was amply compensated for by the genuineness of feeling with which they were given.

As Seiko carried them through into her small, grubby apology for a kitchen, Momoko heard her whisper:

"Nanny, thank you so much. I'm sorry to always put you to such. . ."

"Now please, Mistress Sei, you know it's no trouble for me. It's no trouble at all, you know."

Nanny and Seiko went on with their whispered conversation, but Momoko paid little attention to them since she was much more interested in her surprising surroundings. The house was dustier and more cramped than the accommodation the interns had round the back of the Nire Hospital. Even so, the small six-mat room (about twelve feet by nine) was remarkable for its brand-new cuckoo clock and a glass-fronted bookcase with foreign books inside it. Then Seiko herself was quite different, with no trace of the person one associated with Gakushuin and her sister Ryuko's nature. The Seiko who poured out her tea and brought cakes for her gave only an impression of kindness, of a rare gentleness of spirit.

Momoko cheerfully stuffed herself with cheap cakes and spoke at great speed, at first not quite sure what she should talk about, but soon giving a breathless recital of what went on at school, of what a miser Yonekuni was, of the nastiness of Shun'ichi. As she got carried away, she would unconsciously produce some resounding vulgarism at which she herself would gasp inwardly with horror, but Seiko seemed to remain unaffected by it and certainly did not scold her. Indeed she said very little, listening with gentle interest and occasional surprise, her pale, slightly unhealthy face smiling a little from time to time. Momoko had never seriously disliked Seiko before, and now that she had married into another household and smiled at her with an affection Momoko had not seen before, she felt at ease, free to be her natural self.

She talked too much, and laughed too much, and ate too much, and as she crammed the last cake into her mouth she mumbled almost incoherently:

"Mistress Sei, why don't you come to see us ever?"

Seiko smiled with an indescribable sweetness, and said perhaps she would at some later time; and Nanny Shimoda said they had already overstayed their welcome and it was time to be saying good-bye.

As they went home Nanny told her that she must keep today's visit secret, using very much the same tone of voice as when she had let Momoko buy bananas from a night stall when that activity, too, had been strictly forbidden.

After a number of such visits Momoko had been able to draw on the rich store of knowledge she had gained from the world of the American motion picture, and train the sharp light of her intellect on the problem. She quickly arrived at the conclusion that Seiko had married against her parents' wishes. For this reason she had been cut off without a penny and was never allowed to darken the door again. She had become that ill-fated woman the *benshi* was always talking about. Oh, those vile, disgusting villains at home! And the cause of all this was love, what else but that love which fain would die beside thy window, dear.

Momoko looked out across the wide expanse of glittering, deep blue sea and gave a deep sigh as she listened to the melancholy sound of breaking waves. It was then she made a tearful resolution, one that was not to be forgotten easily:

"I shall simply have to fall in love. I can't leave Seiko all alone like that, all unhappy by herself. Mistress Sei, I won't leave you alone, I promise."

Beneath the bathing costume, which though it covered her body completely was considered daring and smart enough at the time, she was conscious of her trembling breasts, which had grown quite large now. Love, she felt, could surely not be all that rare; the world must be filled with it, just as the seashore where she stood had seashells scattered all over it. Even this beach where almost no one came should present some object worthy of love's fires.

And she was right. Young, sunburned men with flashing teeth were not lacking even here. The members of some club at a private university had a training camp of sorts here, and had rented the house of a fisherman for the purpose. There were not many of them, and the first day they had appeared Momoko had chosen one of that energetic handful, by some high, mysterious intuition, and fixed her heart on him. He stood out because of his exceptionally sunburned skin and the red loincloth he always wore. He swam with a brilliant overarm stroke, slicing his way through the water. Far out in the water floated a wooden diving platform, its white paint flaking off, moored to a buoy. The young man in the red loincloth would swim comfortably out to it, pull himself up onto the platform, and then rest there awhile, his well-formed naked body basking in the sun.

If Momoko could only swim out that far, she could clamber up onto the platform and spend some moments being rocked alongside him, even if at some remove. . . And as soon as she became conscious of this wish Momoko realized that she had fallen in love.

But one immovable, enormous object stood in love's way: Momoko could not swim. Not only did she not have a hope of swimming as far as that platform, but her body obstinately refused even to float. Another annoying matter was that all her friends seemed to have been affected by the young man in the same way, even though this sacred feeling should have been hers alone. They all gossiped about him, calling him "Red Pants" after the brief loincloth he wore. But these misfortunes were balanced by one piece of really good luck: none of the girls could swim out to the raft. So they all lay on the sand and chattered about him to their hearts' content.

"Hey, what did I tell you? Red Pants is looking over in this direction."

"I think it's a shame to call him Red Pants. There must be a nicer name than that."

"He who in crimson garb doth gird his loins," suggested one girl whose father was a poet of the modern sentimental school, and had perhaps taught her a trick or two. "How about 'Crimson Garb' for short?"

"Crimson Garb" was the last straw for Momoko, and she rose from the hot sand in a rage and ran into the sea, jumping vigorously into a fairly shallow part near the shore, plunging her head courageously into the water and thrashing about wildly with her arms and legs. But it was no use; her plump body was like a stone and soon sank. She swallowed a large mouthful of salt water and stood up to her waist in the sea, coughing and spluttering.

"It's enough to drive you mad," she said to herself, trying to rub the salt out of her eyes. "Why on earth can't I swim? If I could only get to that raft, for heaven's sake. And love lies waiting, beckoning to me!''

Yet fate, or perhaps the magnanimous spirit of the seashore, soon brought the university students and the schoolgirls together, not as individuals, of course, but as two groups; and just as minute organisms on the floor of the sea will group together and transform themselves into some single, new configuration, so even the striking individuality of Red Pants seemed somehow to have been absorbed into an almost inconspicuous conformity. As if in accordance with some unwritten and unspoken promise, they associated with each other only as two groups and played only commonplace and innocently childish games.

In this respect Momoko was no different from the others. She squealed and shrieked like they all did, and her shrill screams were aimed at no one in particular, or did not seem to be. Still, as the day approached when they would have to leave, Momoko resorted to a little piece of cunning. There was a group photograph of the girls which had been taken almost as soon as they arrived, and on the back of it they had all written their names and addresses. Momoko handed this over to a student nicknamed Hippo, since he was the most easily approachable of the group.

''Here are our addresses,'' she said. ''Drop us a line sometime, won't you?''

She then turned casually toward Red Pants and extended a similarly offhand invitation to him, although in this case it was backed by all the mystic powers that prayer could summon up:

''You, as well. Don't forget, will you?''

The plot bore fruit. Momoko returned to Tokyo and sweated out the remaining days of the long, hot summer, amusing herself as best she could with Yonekuni for lack of anyone else, and then a picture postcard arrived from the students. It was a conventional enough missive, and no doubt the same sort of thing had been sent to the other girls as well. Red Pants' real name turned out to be the commonplace one of Yasuda.

Momoko had confidence in herself and waited for something better. She was not under the illusion that she was the most beautiful girl in the world, but felt she was attractive enough to make people like her, as proof of which there had been the letter from an unknown man she had received that spring.

The letter came from a thin, gloomy-looking individual who had sidled up to her one day as she was coming home from school and handed over a white envelope without saying a word. Momoko's intuition told her it was a love letter even before she had opened it. The contents were to the effect that he sought an opportunity for a good, long talk with her, and he named the time and place. The letter ended with three *waka,* short poems in a traditional form and using ancient literary language which she was unable to make head or tail of. Eventually she copied the three poems out on a separate piece of paper and tried them on the interns, but they couldn't work them out either. Momoko had been excited by the incident, but because of the unintelligible poems and the fact that the man himself had a gruesome appearance that gave her the creeps, she decided not to go to the appointed place. The man never showed his face again, but he had served the function of giving a large boost to Momoko's self-esteem.

But still no letter came from Red Pants. Autumn was near; already the large cicadas of summer seemed weary and produced only tired cries, while the smaller ones which sing through autumn were now shrieking busily away. They were summer's parting knell.

Yonekuni, with his goggle eyes, was searching all over the place for the hapless insects, a lime stick in his hand with which to knock them down. Noticing Momoko's melancholy face as she looked out over the garden, he called up to her:

"I've just about worked out the kind of noise they make. Shall I teach you how it goes?"

"Oh, can't you shut up for a moment! Who cares how it goes?"

She was clearly in a very bad mood, and was thinking about other things, such as whether Red Pants were not perhaps a trifle insensitive, and assuring herself that he surely could not have been immune to her attractions.

With so little of the summer holidays remaining, even the overweening Momoko was beginning to lose a little of her self-confidence, when a letter finally arrived with the name Yasuda written in large, black letters on the back. The size of the Nire Hospital and the swarms of people who worked there probably ensured that this letter to Momoko, written in a masculine hand, got through to her with no problem at all. She was not, however, as excited on receiving it as she had thought she would be. She had been waiting impatiently for so long that she had exhausted her sense of expectation.

But she managed to coax a sense of satisfaction out of it:

"You see. It's all turned out as I thought it would. If I really put my mind to something then things always turn out as I know they will."

Luckily there appeared to be no poems attached to this one. It said that he often recalled the happy days they had spent at the seaside. He himself lived in Shibuya, but he occasionally visited a friend in Aoyama, and he had happened to pass by the hospital one day and had remembered that was where she lived. The contents were all very proper, and written in a precise hand.

"So he came all this way to investigate," Momoko decided, even though Shibuya itself was not much of a distance away. "Lucky we live in this impressive place and are pretty obviously capitalists. If this were some barrack of a building then I really would have to reconcile myself to being ill-fated."

The letter went on to say that he would shortly be visiting his friend again and that he intended to walk a little in Moto-no-hara (the field near the hospital) some time toward evening, and how happy he would be if he were to unexpectedly bump into her near the large pine tree in the far corner of the field. There were no romantic phrases in praise of her beauty.

"Men. They're all the same. Heartless deceivers ever," thought Momoko, rubbing the skin beneath her small nose with her finger. "The kind of letter anybody might write, and I suppose he thinks a woman will just trip along for an assignation in a place like that. Hasn't he any sense at all? It's right next to the hospital for a start."

This coolness soon disappeared, however. She started to remember the deep lines of his face burned dark by the wind off the sea, and the accents of his fine, clear voice. She took out the letter, which she had put back into its envelope, and read it now as if she were fearful of it. She read it three times, then a fourth time. As she did so, the child with two plaits of hair hanging down her back, the self-styled authority on affairs of the heart, was transformed into a love-stricken maiden, unsure of herself and of others, afraid of herself and of her own feelings, unreliable and weak. Her firm aims seemed as confused as the objects in a half-remembered dream.

So, late in the afternoon of the appointed day, wearing a casual *yukata* or light kimono, she slipped secretly out of the house. She had been unwilling to change into anything else for fear of drawing attention to herself. There were a few children in Moto-no-hara chasing dragonflies. She crossed the field at a speed of which she was unaware, arriving at the primary school, which was now quite deserted, and then passing the police box. The policeman on duty, saber dangling authoritatively from his belt, stared in what seemed a very questioning manner in his capacity as custodian of public morals. So she hurried on, dashing past the Seiundo with almost no idea of where she was going, until she reached the main road, where she slowed down and, after making a considerable detour, arrived back again at Moto-no-hara.

The summer evenings were still long. From some distance away she noticed a young man standing under the pine tree. He, too, was wearing a *yukata,* only his was white. He had his back toward her and was looking in the direction of the hospital. The realization that the young man was actually waiting for her restored her confidence. She felt a kind of conceited awareness of herself, as if she were taking part in the film version of her own life, and by the time she had come within hailing distance of him she was back to her normal, relaxed self. She made the conventional cry of surprise, and was able to recite the fluent lie, by way of greeting, that she was just on her way home from an errand.

She had not at first looked him in the face, not only because she was telling a small lie but because it is not customary to do so when greeting someone. When she did, however, she received a shock and felt an unexpected embarrassment that showed in the way her sentence trailed away.

This was not because she had made a mistake and picked on the wrong person. This was indeed Yasuda, the Red Pants of the beach. The trouble was he looked so different from the strapping figure who had bounded about half-naked under the sun. Was it perhaps because his face had lost so much of its sunburn?

Yasuda muttered a casual, monosyllabic greeting, and grinned awkwardly at her with his white teeth. Everything seemed incoherent and confused. The uninhibited world of the seashore had gone, and they had also ceased to be university student and schoolgirl and become simply Momoko and Yasuda, two people who were meeting each other for the first time in their lives. That carefree, naked dignity with which Red Pants had gained the awed respect of the watching girls had disappeared, and not one trace of it remained. There was no easy confidence here, simply a young man who stammered a few polite, empty words. Momoko's response was to reply in kind, in a voice that seemed to belong to someone else.

But Momoko had not been totally transformed. Somewhere lurking within her was the old Momoko, clicking her tongue in vexation and wondering what was going wrong, and hoping that whatever it was would get back to normal soon, "normal" being what she had dreamed things would be like.

As they continued a series of awkward, pointless, and usually brief conversations, the two set off walking, away from the hospital and past the primary school, in the direction of the streetcar stop at Minamimachi. It was almost twilight. The blue of the sky was fading, and small bats were flying about. Momoko wanted to say, "Oh, look, there's a bat," very much in the way the heroine of a film she had seen had drawn the hero's attention to a swallow flying by. But even a simple phrase of that kind seemed unable to make the passage up her throat, and she felt like stamping her foot out of sheer annoyance with herself.

In order to break an embarrassing silence, Yasuda started to say a few words, but they came out as the most dreary clichés imaginable, to the effect that he hoped her friends were all well, very well, and that the summer in Tokyo was hot, very hot, particularly the end of the summer, which was hot, very hot, although after the sun had set it was not so hot, so very hot, as during the day, and so a little bit more bearable. . .

The real Momoko was critical of this, very critical. Is that all the fool can say? I was taken in by those red pants, that's for sure. Put him alone with a girl and what is he? A boring, pathetic, fumbling creature who can't say anything. But there was another Momoko who felt differently, and this one started to predominate as they walked, and she felt an irresistible joy soaring within her. This was something other than self-conceit or pride. It went beyond her ego, her small idea of her self; a passionate intuition in which there was no arrogance, no self-deception, no mistake. This feeling was real. Or at least she felt it was real, so she decided that the boy really loved her, and that was why he was so dull and awkward. This was the truth then; the young man was madly in love with her. And she may well have been right.

Clearly, something should be done about it. She brought all her extensive knowledge of other affairs of the heart to bear on the problem, and realized that she should walk closer to Yasuda, not immodestly close of course, but with a certain restrained passion. So she did just that, which was not all that easy since at times they seemed likely to stumble over each other's feet. And it was all to no effect. Yasuda's language and behavior remained exactly as they were. She was beginning to find this genuinely annoying.

What a clumsy dolt he is. Surely he knows when you can take hold of a girl's hand? He must be very, very ignorant. I expect he's never been to the cinema once in his life. That would explain it. That's why he doesn't have a clue as to how to behave.

So the Momoko who was not the normal Momoko asked him very politely if he ever happened to attend showings of motion pictures. He replied haltingly:

"The motion pictures? Well, I can't say I go very often. I hardly go at all, in fact. I did see *The Cabinet of Dr. Caligari*. That was very interesting. It's the new art form, Expressionism, isn't it?"

Momoko was taken aback by the "new art form, Expressionism," but she had heard of the film, and her own horribly repressed desire for expression suddenly burst forth:

"Dr. Caligari? Oh, I missed that; or, I mean, I gave it a miss, rather. I mean, I saw a photo in the newspaper. That Dr. Caligari looked really terrifying, really creepy."

"Yes, well, there was something slightly. . ."

"I can't stand those horror films. There's that one where a man comes and kills women when they're asleep. I hate that. I don't want to see things like that, not at all, believe me. . . Still, in some ways I really wish I had seen Dr. Caligari, I wish I had. I know all about it, you see, because Werner Krauss took the lead role, and he's gorgeous."

"Well, I don't remember," said Yasuda, who seemed a trifle surprised by this sudden torrent of words. But once the floodgates were opened Momoko would not stop.

"The fact is no one in our family has any interest in the arts at all, none whatsoever. My brother said that. Of course he's just as bad as the rest of them, talking a lot of nonsense all the time about things he knows nothing about. Look at Soseki's *Shinran and His Disciples*. I went to the bookstore to buy it and what happens? The assistant tells me it doesn't exist, although there's a book of the same title by a different author. I ask you. . ."

Yasuda could grasp less than half of what she was saying, but felt obliged to chuckle a little.

"Still, there are lots of interesting movies even if they aren't the new art form. Have you heard of *The Dark Star*?"

He shook his head.

"Marion Davies is in that. She's a famous film star. She's beautiful.

You'd really like her if you saw her, I'm sure you would. I like Antonio Moreno best, but that's because I'm a girl so I'm bound to like men more than women, aren't I? There're so many things in the movies that are such fun. How about Hurricane Hutch? What a name! And you ought to see Harold Lloyd, he's really wild. Oh, I almost forgot. You know Fatty is coming to Japan? You don't? You know Fatty, don't you? Fatty Arbuckle? No? Well, he's coming here. I don't just mean a movie. He's really coming himself. He's going to make a personal appearance at the big comedy show in Asakusa. Now I really must go and see that.''

There seemed to be no way of stopping her now. On she went, pouring out words with wild disregard for what went before or what came after, and even "love" seemed to have taken second place to her present passion. But Yasuda made no complaint as he walked along the narrow streets with her, listening with passionate interest to her fluent talk, which demonstrated so wide a knowledge of the cinematic art. At least, that is how Momoko interpreted his response.

Momoko suddenly realized it was growing dark. She stopped talking in apparent surprise, and commented on the lateness of the hour. She was aware that, having made this remark, the crucial moment had come, that moment when even a girl of good family could be expected to forget her customary modesty.

"Yes, it's late, isn't it?" said Yasuda, not taking the hint. "I hadn't realized. I was so interested in what we were saying. May I see you home?"

Momoko modestly declined but, after a nominal altercation, agreed to be seen as far as the field in front of the hospital. The children hunting dragonflies had already gone home, and the only living things to be seen were occasional bats flitting in a sky in which only a trace of twilight remained. The two said good-bye at the edge of the field without so much as shaking hands.

"Well, that was really fun. I honestly enjoyed that," said Momoko in a voice that was full of feeling. "Let's walk together again sometime."

"I'll write," said the other with an extremely serious expression on his face.

"Well, when you do, there's one thing," said Momoko in a wheedling, sugary voice. "Couldn't you write in a sort of feminine hand? On the envelope, I mean. You know, perhaps you'd better use a girl's name too; something like Toshiko Yasuda, something like that. . .''

She decided, as he smiled and agreed, that he must be an absolute amateur in these things, and she would have to teach him every little thing.

When she got home her face was hot with something mysteriously like fatigue, although her body felt light all over, almost as if it belonged to someone else. Nanny Shimoda scolded her for being late for supper, but Momoko said nothing, merely eating with a hearty appetite and leaving nothing on her plate.

On thinking over what had happened, she at first felt that she might have spoken about the motion pictures too much, but after a while she decided it had probably been for the best. He was so ignorant of the subject and he really should go to the movies more often. They ought to go together.

The new term started at school, but the two occasionally met near the hospital and walked together talking about innocent matters of no importance. Yasuda's behavior never altered in the slightest. Momoko found this frustrating, but one should never judge by appearances, and although she found his attitude vexing and tantalizing it was probably due to his introspective nature—or, more likely, to a lack of knowledge, which going to the motion pictures would have rectified. For this reason their conversations mostly consisted in Momoko holding forth about what she had seen in movie palaces. She would be completely carried away by her own descriptions, sighing, throwing out her arms, wrinkling her nose, until she suddenly recalled that she had put none of her knowledge to any use, that she had not performed what she, as an authority on love's mysteries, should have done; and that it was already time to part.

On one occasion, however, she asked him what he was studying at college. He replied that it was economics. She repeated the word wisely, but she was not clear exactly what kind of thing economics was, although she was aware it had nothing to do with hospitals and curing people. She had been made to realize during the past year that her father would not readily let her marry someone who was not a doctor. Still, she knew that economics had something to do with money, so she asked, in a sudden burst of enthusiasm:

"Then that must mean you have a lot to do with accounts."

"Accounts? Accounts of what?"

"Not accounts of anything. Just accounts. You know, adding up lots of money, bills and things like that. Accounts."

Yasuda laughed out loud, which was rare for him, and said that obviously accounting had some connection with economics, but why had she asked him?

Momoko didn't reply, but she was thinking that it would be a good idea to get rid of that grizzled old Oishi, who looked hopeless for the job anyway, and replace him with this fine young economist. She could just see him sitting at the accountant's desk with the hospital safe behind him.

Considering the vast numbers of people who had some sort of connection with the hospital it was unlikely that Momoko's carryings-on would pass unnoticed. Before long a message was transmitted "within," and the following incident took place.

One day, one of those letters which, up to now, had reached her without difficulty was not delivered. Momoko, of course, knew nothing of this, but the consequence was that late one afternoon the figure of the Deputy was to be seen moving in the direction of the impressive iron gates at the entrance to the hospital. It could have been observed that he had not chosen on this occasion to link his hands behind his back and to stalk slowly along. Instead, he was moving at a brisk pace and he went through those gates at something approaching a trot. He crossed the field at the same speed, passed the primary school, and arrived at Minamimachi. At this point he slowed down and began peering through his rimless spectacles as he walked in a questing manner. There was a mailbox some distance from the school, and next to it was a young man in the uniform of a university student, obviously waiting for someone.

Hidekichi Katsumata nodded to himself in satisfaction and began to approach the student in his customary wading-bird style. Having got within striking distance, the thin, dwarfish figure suddenly sped over the remaining few yards and abruptly addressed the student. The tall young man looked down suspiciously and made some kind of reply. The Deputy clasped his hands behind his back, stretched himself up to his full height, and began to expound something in considerable earnest. The encounter went on for a long time and Hidekichi did most of the talking. The young man spent most of the time gazing down at his feet, which he shuffled about occasionally. He appeared to be angry about something. Eventually some conclusion was reached, for the young man turned abruptly away and set off with long strides, gradually disappearing down the street, over which evening had just begun to fall. Hidekichi stood motionless by the mailbox, still straining and erect in the attempt to give himself as great an air of authority as possible, until the student had turned the far corner at the end of the street and was no longer to be seen. Then he nodded slightly. That was all right, then; that was done.

After that no more communications came for Momoko. She wrote a letter. She wrote a second letter; then a third. Yet still the letter she was waiting for did not come. If it did, it certainly did not find its way into her hands.

Momoko was besieged by a variety of emotions. She felt, in turn, confused, suspicious, desperate and angry. Once she went to try to find the house where he lived, and she searched the area for some time, looking at the names written on the gateposts of each house. But as she walked from door to door an unbearable sense of anxiety and fear suddenly came over her, and she ran back home.

At night she still slept in the same room as Nanny Shimoda and Yonekuni. Nanny's loud snores, which had never troubled her before, added to her feelings of anger and irritation.

"He's got himself another woman," she decided to herself as she lay there staring into the darkness, imagining things that should not properly pass through the mind of a young lady of good family. "You can't trust men. They're all the same."

She thought the matter over again: "Perhaps it was because I talked about the movies too much. He doesn't like them. I should have realized that."

Finally the unfairness of it all overcame her, and she bit her lip hard with mortification: "I don't care. I'm not interested in that show-off in his stupid red pants. There're plenty of other men in the world. I'll find someone else. I'll fall in love with lots of men. I'll show him."

But things did not go the way she had decided they would. A disaster she had not foreseen settled everything with an absolute finality, and it all happened surprisingly quickly.

It was late autumn of the same year. The leaves of the ginkgo tree next to Kiichiro's pride, the radium bath, had turned a deep yellow. The nights had grown cold: you felt the chill in the late evenings and early mornings. The stray dogs that lived in the neighboring field and ate the waste food from the cookhouse were often dirty and bedraggled, sometimes with their fur still wet from a drenching in the previous night's cold rain.

The change in the season had no effect on Momoko. She had

recovered from the dreadful blow she had suffered from that evil man—for that was her view of Yasuda's character now—and she no longer plaited her hair like a child but wore it long down the back with the sides swept up and done in a bun on top, in the manner of the senior girls. Her hair was fortunately a rich, deep black. She was in competition with her friends to see who could grow their hair the longest, and she was determined not to be beaten. "At least my hair is inferior to no one's," she thought as she gazed at a toy barometer she had just had bought for her.

The scientific toy was of German origin, and consisted of a beautifully made little summer house from which, when good weather was forecast, a schoolgirl carrying her books would appear and, when rain was due, a gentleman carrying an umbrella. Because of the way the machine was made, the girl and the gentleman were fated never to meet.

"I know it will all work out somehow. I shall manage," thought Momoko. "If the worst comes to the worst I can become a woman boy."

At that time the weird title of "woman boy" was in fairly wide circulation. The English word "boy" had been taken into the Japanese language much earlier, indicating someone who works in a hotel and, by extension, a variety of jobs in restaurants, bars and so on, which would probably be covered by the word "waiter" in real English. Since a word was required for females who worked in up-to-date Western-style establishments, the Japanese word for "woman" (*onna*) was simply tagged onto the English loanword, producing *onna boi* which could be translated as "woman boy," "female boy," "girl boy," "lady boy," or perhaps even "boyess," although "bar girl" or "waitress" would be more correct. Still, for someone of Momoko's age, a woman boy seemed exotic and independent, being modern, Westernized, and rather shady, and she would scan the advertisement columns in the newspaper, noting that a largish salary of more than eighty yen a month was promised and thinking of the number of motion-picture performances she would be able to see with all that money. It was also a time when emigrants to South America, the majority of them ex-soldiers, were seeking brides by placing ads in newspapers, and Momoko would read these as well with great interest for hours on end. The important thing was that one should firmly reject the bridegroom one's parents chose for you, and go looking for your own man.

Then, one Saturday, around lunchtime, Momoko came home from school her normal cheerful, radiant, energetic self, all ready to go out and have fun, and, as it turned out, living in a fool's paradise, for she was immediately summoned "within."

What awaited her there was something so wholly unexpected that it could properly, and without exaggeration, be described as a bolt from the blue. The terrible thing was that, though one could not imagine this happening even in one of those foreign movies that made her weep such fountains of tears, it was definitely happening in the real world. Here was Momoko in her third year at girls' school, and they were going to make her go through a temporary form of marriage, since she was too young to be married in the legal sense (although that would presumably come later). And this marriage was to take place today, immediately.

Here was yet another of Kiichiro's schemes, from his point of view no doubt a perfectly reasonable one, dictated by his remarkable ability to foretell what the future held in store. He had no intention of letting Momoko travel the same road as Seiko. His youngest daughter appeared to be extremely precocious in at least one respect and, since she already had one or two dubious incidents to her credit, it was not unnatural that he should have had anxieties about her turning into a woman with an abnormal interest in the opposite sex. There was nothing surprising in his playing a trump card infinitely more promptly than any normal person would have done, for Kiichiro prided himself on the speed with which he put any tactical scheme into operation. It was much the same when he played *shogi,* or Japanese chess, for such was the fertility of his mind that he would, on occasion, and when his opponent was not looking, move two pawns at once; an amazing feat to which many people could bear witness.

But despite the fact that the decision was, in the light of Kiichiro's character, obviously unsurprising, Momoko received so huge a shock that she seemed to lose all powers of resistance. She responded to what she was told to do in a state of trance, like a puppet on a string. The only respect in which she differed from a puppet was that she wept: an unceasing flood of those large, counterfeit-looking tears of hers, tears after tears after tears filling her eyes, pouring down her cheeks, then dripping from her chin to the floor.

It was some time before she could ask the not unreasonable, though to someone unaware of the situation no doubt laughable, question as to whom she was about to marry. She was told it was to be Dr. Takayanagi, a very splendid person indeed. This information was provided by an old woman whom Momoko knew as their "granny from Kanda," an intimate of Kiichiro's since his days in Hongo (Kanda being an area of Tokyo next to Hongo). He seemed to look upon her as some kind of mother figure, for he always referred to her as "Mom." She spoke in a peculiar croaking voice, and her words were obviously meant to be comforting.

At least it wasn't to be Kanazawa or Nirasawa, as Hamako had foretold. At first the name Takayanagi meant nothing to Momoko, but then she suddenly brought him to mind.

It was in June of that year. Momoko had got a large boil on the back of her hand and had gone to the Keio Hospital to have it lanced. The doctor who performed this minor operation had been Takayanagi. She had been back a number of times to have some ointment dabbed on it, and at the end of her last appointment he had said casually:

"Well, that's the last time you'll have to come here. I think you deserve some kind of treat, so I'll take you out somewhere."

Naturally Momoko had been delighted. Since Takayanagi was an acquaintance of her father's, which was why Momoko had come to him for treatment in the first place, there could be no objection, and Nanny Shimoda, who had accompanied Momoko to the hospital, immediately gave her consent. So Takayanagi and Momoko went to see a foreign film at the Empire, and then to have something to eat at a place called the Asakusa Paulista. Momoko was in high spirits and made schoolgirlish jokes and puns about the fact that "cafe" in Japanese pronunciation could, to a generous mind, sound like *kahei,* or "currency," a rather grown-up word for a girl like Momoko to know, and she wittily concluded that he must have spent all of his. Takayanagi had seemed amused by this, even appearing to be impressed by her knowledge and wit, and he chimed in with a few witless puns of his own, a game in which Momoko had been only too glad to join.

Takayanagi escorted her home and, despite the fact that his forehead was too large and his ears stuck out at almost ninety-degree angles from his head, he seemed a nice, kind man, and that was the way Momoko thought of him. But now that this nice man had chosen suddenly to appear before her in the aspect of an unavoidable adjunct to her life, she began to view that apparently innocent meeting some months back with suspicion. No doubt the scheme had been worked out in advance, and that meeting was the first move in the game. Perhaps even Nanny Shimoda had been a party to it.

Although she was not absolutely right in these assumptions, she was not far wrong either. Shiro Takayanagi had been born near Sendai, at no great distance from Kiichiro's own birthplace. The family were traditionally makers of *sake*. Like Kiichiro, he came from a family that was by no means wealthy and, as a doctor, had attracted the attention of the medical world. Kiichiro was very conscious of this similarity, even though Takayanagi was fourteen years his junior. Kiichiro wanted a surgeon in his group because he was confident that the time would come when mental disorders would be curable by surgery; and so, as usual, he did no beating about the bush but frankly asked Takayanagi to become his adopted son, promising him his youngest daughter and also a trip abroad for study.

Even Kiichiro had not, of course, been thinking of acting with the haste that he now felt was forced on him. The lightning decision to go through with this temporary marriage which, no matter how admirable it might be, would certainly look bad in anybody else's eyes, had been brought on by the fact that he had been extremely worried by Momoko's carryings-on and by what they seemed to imply about her future.

But his worries could hardly be compared with what Momoko was going through now. She had finally realized what all this meant, and her whole body was trembling with humiliation and hatred. When she thought of the cunning with which she had been lured into this trap, she not only wept but produced drawn-out moans and sobs. Everyone attempted to comfort her; even her mother came to her side and offered the odd kind word. Nanny Shimoda was fidgeting about in the background not knowing what to do. And while these preparations were going on, Kiichiro put in a brief appearance and told them they could do anything so long as they got her ready in time.

The maid who served "within" came to do Momoko's hair in the plain style across the ears. They hadn't even called in a proper hairdresser; instead the crone from Kanda croaked out a few brisk words of instruction. Momoko went on weeping, her tears washing away the thick makeup almost as soon as it was applied.

Even if Momoko had rejected the conventional view of marriage in favor of a more romantic ideal, she had still been looking forward to her wedding day in the way most girls do. She had imagined it taking place in smart surroundings with herself in the most wonderful wedding garments, and was now horrified to find that none of the careful preparation normally allowed a bride was to be hers since there was simply no time for it. She was bundled into a black kimono with some crane motif which she was fairly certain she had seen before; no doubt some cast-off belonging of the disgraced Seiko's. The sash she was tied up in, however, was of a gorgeous crimson with a brilliant gold pattern worked into it.

Thus adorned, she was taken to the recreation room, in the center of whose 120-mat vastness two rows of small tables had been set up. In front of them a dozen people were squatting. It seemed a symbolic demonstration of the emptiness and futility that life now had in store for her.

Not that Momoko saw the room in these terms, for she hardly noticed the room at all. She sat at the head of the tables, the granny from Kanda on her left and Takayanagi in a dark brown suit on her right. The actual wedding ceremony was a very abbreviated version of the real thing. Momoko sat in a state of total despondency, receiving the betrothal cup and setting it down as if she did not know whether this was taking place or she was dreaming. She spent the whole time staring down at the crimson tassel of the small, purse-like ornament that had been pushed halfway inside her sash, and continued to weep, large tears rolling steadily down her cheeks.

The party over, she was dressed in a different set of clothes and taken to the entrance hall. In the courtyard, twilight had already given place to night, and two rickshas were waiting.

As she swayed in the ricksha, shaken as if by nightmares, her confused, half-vacant mind decided that all the blame for this should be laid squarely on her father and his devilish schemes, and that Dr. Takayanagi was not a bad man and he would understand her once she had explained things to him.

Eventually they arrived at an inn-cum-restaurant, although she could not work out what part of Tokyo this was, and finally she was aware that all that had happened so far to her today was no dream but reality, as also were the consequences still to come, which were as clear as they were unavoidable. There would be no going back now. In the room next to the one in which she was sitting she glimpsed, through the sliding doors, the garish colors of the bedding, which had already been laid out. She noticed that there was only one bed for the two of them.

At this point she lost control of herself, becoming reckless of what she did or said. She attacked Takayanagi, who could be considered just as much a victim as herself, as if she had gone mad, raining blows on his chest with clenched fists, sobbing and fervently pleading in fragmentary, incoherent words. She told him he was not to touch her; she was still a schoolgirl and she wanted to stay pure and intact at least until she graduated. She maintained a constant stream of pleas and execrations, her body rigid with accumulated fears of the sexual act.

Nothing the man tried served to quieten her down. For a girl pledged to him in marriage by Dr. Nire himself, her behavior was preposterous, and it was probably embarrassment that finally made him take firm hold of both her hands, which she was still aiming wildly at his chest, and tell her that he understood and would not force her to do anything she did not want to do. He was obliged to repeat these words a number of times before she calmed down.

With a sullen, angry look on his face—for he was, not surprisingly, in a very bad temper—he called the maid and had her put down another set of bedding. But even then his child bride refused to go to bed. Takayanagi was obliged to get between his separate sheets first and reiterate his promise a number of times, explaining to her that she would catch cold if she did not go to bed.

Momoko rubbed her swollen eyes and undressed in the other room. She then put her knowledge of the movies to good effect by taking her sash and winding it tightly around the lower half of her nightdress. Having cocooned herself in this way she crept into her separate bed.

For a while she was nervously on her guard, waiting tensely for something to happen. The man sleeping in the same room did not seem to find it all that easy to drop off, and she could sense him twisting and turning there in the dark. A very long time seemed to pass before she heard the sound of regular breathing, which seemed to indicate that he was asleep at last. Still, perhaps he was only pretending, so she lay cautiously awake for much longer yet. His breathing grew louder and he finally began giving the occasional snore.

Momoko felt a slight sense of relief, of safety, at last, and this made her aware once more of the grief and humiliation that her wild protests had almost driven from her mind. She was overpowered by the sense of being drained dry, of a body and soul reduced to nothing. All that passed through her mind was how she had not at first disliked this man, but now . . . and her hatred for her father—how had he been able to do this to her?

So the tears, which had ceased for a while, began to flow again, a full flood of them, soaking her pillow.

Tetsukichi was dreaming.

The images in his dreams were mostly vague and blurred, but occasionally there would be a series that achieved an extraordinary clarity before fading away. At such times he would be conscious that he was dreaming, but that awareness would sink out of sight and he would entrust himself once more to the enticing flow of scenes that seemed to drift past and away from him into obscurity, then darkness.

The long lines of spiky buds on the sallows were swollen to an impossible size. They shone a voluptuous silver, at once sensually attractive and alien and remote. A brilliant sun shone down. For this village lost in the snows of winter for so many months the long-awaited shining of the sun was like an act of grace; the rays of light seemed scented and generous. The village streets had been turned into a quagmire by the thaw. In the early morning cold the mud had still been frozen, but it had melted and his feet squelched right down into it, and it became more and more difficult to walk. His straw sandals were starting to wear out, and they slid about his feet. He was on his way to school and still had a long two miles to go. . .

At this point Tetsukichi seemed to wake up, but in fact he remained half in his dream, contemplating a repetition of the images he had just seen.

For some time now he had been dreaming every night, and each night the dreams went further back into his past. At first he had occasionally seen his wife and child. Ryuko would watch him with contempt while she argued about something which was of only minor importance, but she spoke at great speed and without a pause. He would spend the dream waiting for his turn to speak, preparing to say this, preparing to say that, and then wake up. Shun'ichi had appeared less frequently. When Tetsukichi had left home his son had been six years old. But one image occurred a number of times, that of the child's contorted, howling face as he refused, stamping, screaming and crying, to go to kindergarten. Kiichiro appeared, too, strutting toward him in his superior way and starting to say something to him, but then abruptly turning his back on him and walking away toward a shadowy building like a palace.

Then, about six months ago, the dreams had ceased to be about his more immediate past. Now they went back, much further back. He was sitting in the interns' room in the Nire Clinic in Hongo beneath the gloomy light of the oil lamp hanging from the ceiling. One of the interns, whose name he could not recall, had borrowed some books from the old man who came around, a kind of walking lending library, with a great bundle of magazines and books on his back. The books were the popular reading of the time, entertainments concerning the loves of unhappy geisha with honest gangsters in harbor towns, or detective stories set in the more exotic West—mostly garbled versions of works that had previously appeared in other distant tongues. The dreams had become so vivid that they even seemed to involve the sense of smell. He recalled the pictures of various beautiful women and of soldiers from all the nations of the world that had been in his box when he had first come up to Tokyo, and this image was strongly associated with the aroma produced by an imported tobacco called Pirate. It was a smell that had possessed a peculiar attraction for him when he had been a small boy, a fragrant, bittersweet odor. There was also an image of Nanny Shimoda, not as a nanny but as a young nurse in white uniform raising her arm and giving some kind of advice or direction to one of the interns. When he woke from this dream, Tetsukichi recalled how she had often given him advice, in a rather smug tone of voice, about his use of language when he had first arrived in Tokyo as a nervous, awkward country boy. Thus his dreams provided him with occasions to embark on a conscious quest of what had once seemed the forgotten past.

Recently his dreams had been about his childhood and earliest memories. The peak of Mt. Zao appeared half-hidden in thick, freezing cloud. Snow remained in the hollows on the mountainside still deep in shadow. He could see the storehouse by his home, its white walls scored with cracks. Then there was the tiny stream, a mere trickle that ran right by the house, where he used to wash his face. And he saw the local temple, remote, and hidden in long grass. These images now grew hazy, seeming at the same time to swell and take on a significance that soon eluded him, parts of a disconnected sequence that made no final sense. Then there were strange, childish things that seemed to be a dream within a dream, as if one had awoken and were trying to recall lost images of the night before, which suddenly came back at last. There was a hairy baboon holding a young woman, and the front of her kimono had been pulled open in disarray. Before them stood a samurai, sword upraised, barring the way. Or a brigand was jeering threateningly at some loyal wife. These must have been images from a puppet show that had come to the village when he was very small.

His father sometimes appeared, his real father. Horribly small and emaciated, he was always coughing and spitting up phlegm. He had been afflicted with this cough for as long as Tetsukichi could remember. Seven months ago he had learned that his father had died. At the time of his death he had not once featured in Tetsukichi's dreams, so why should he now appear so constantly, always alive, perpetually coughing up phlegm, and never once looking in Tetsukichi's direction, but always with his back toward him, a small, shadowy figure whose image wavered as if the focus was uncertain? He remembered how his father had made offerings to the gods of the three mountains of Dewa and of Mt. Zao, and had given up eating all the things he liked, such as fish, cereals, even salt. Why, when he should long since have joined the ranks of the silent dead, did he always appear to Tetsukichi as if he were still living, only smaller and more shriveled than any living person would be, constantly doubled over, racked with pain as he tried to cough up the phlegm accumulating in his throat? When Tetsukichi awoke from these dreams he was overwhelmed with a sense of loss and sadness. He had no idea when he might be able to visit his father's grave.

Once he had been adopted into the Nire household at the age of fifteen, Tetsukichi had made a conscious effort to distance himself from his home village. He had turned his back on the superstitious North, where not only gods and buddhas but even foxes and badgers were objects of religious veneration, and had devoted himself to the study of the scientific laws that govern the natural world. But what had in fact obsessed him at the time was his resolve to learn the way they spoke and behaved in Tokyo, so that he could be accepted into the Nire household and hold his own against the Tokyo schoolboys who chuckled with glee every time he opened his mouth. Now, after so many dreams and the memories they had awakened, he began to have doubts about the rightness of the way of life he had chosen. Certainly that way of life had been to a large extent imposed on him, for his area of choice had been obviously restricted. Perhaps it was his village that had left him rather than the other way around. Even so, he felt too far away now. He was the heir to the Nire Hospital, but he was also a countryman from the North, a villager. He wondered how his brother, Shirokichi, was getting on. His sister would be busy with the haymaking now. He ought to write to them. Thinking thus, he fell back into restless sleep and dreamed again.

He was alone in what seemed to be a dark laboratory. He was dissecting something gray and flabby to the touch, probably a human brain. He was not doing it very well. The thin sections were to be used for demonstration slides, and each had to be placed precisely on a small, fragile sheet of glass. He could feel his frustration slowly turning into panic as he became more and more unable to perform the task, and the brain dissolved into a disgusting, mucous slime. The dream then faded to another where a similar psychic pattern was at work, that of not being able to find one's way.

He was walking along an unknown mountain road that passed through what appeared to be dense forest. The sky still held the darkness of dawn and his footsteps were uncertain. He seemed to be carrying a lighted lantern in his hand. Then he was walking in what must have been water, and his feet became unable to take another step forward. Far below he caught a glimpse of a river through the trees. But there was someone else walking ahead of him, and that person turned back and scolded him. It was his father. He saw the face clearly approaching. . .

Tetsukichi awoke. The world of dreams was soon dispersed. The face that had so clearly been his father's blurred and faded, dissolving into an abstraction, a pain about the heart that seemed to lack an object. He turned on his bed and sighed. The bed groaned back beneath him. He was trying to recollect the place, and realized that it was the pass leading through the mountains from his home. When Tetsukichi had left for Tokyo there had been no railway to Yamagata, so his father had walked with him the thirty miles or so to the hot spring at Sakunami where they had spent the night, traveling the remaining ten miles to Sendai on the following day.

These dreams were reviving memories that were dear to him and had long lain buried, but Tetsukichi realized they also indicated how emotionally and mentally worn out he was.

Day seemed to have already dawned. A white, cloudy light came in through the windowpanes. But there was still no sound to be heard, no sign that the streetcars had started running yet, nor that the great dray horses were trundling the carts laden with beer barrels through the streets. Even the song of the *Amsel,* the blackbird, could not be heard yet. In the thin light of dawn and dusk this bird would sing its wonderfully full-throated, melancholy song. Although he knew the season had passed in which the blackbird could be heard, he still felt it was strange to hear nothing. A doubt arose as to where he was, so he looked intently at his surroundings in the pallid light.

There were the walls with peeling paint, on one of which an embroidered cloth had been hung to hide the worst of time's ravages. No, this was not his home, not even the continent on which he had been born, and it gave him nothing of that former life. This was Europe, one room in southern Germany, in the Bavarian capital of Munich. Tetsukichi was no longer a young man full of dreams about the future, but a student studying abroad, a student in his forties, easily fatigued, unhealthy-looking, and no longer young in any sense of the word. He had come to Munich four months ago, and it was more than two years since he had left Japan.

Tetsukichi had gone first to Berlin and then to Vienna where, at the Neurological Institute, he had completed a paper on the cerebra of paralytic imbeciles. He had found a number of Japanese like himself in Vienna studying the same field of medicine. But in reality they had little in common: they were either a dozen years junior to him, young men full of ambition and high spirits, or they were real scholars with work already to their credit, who were enjoying a stay abroad as one of the pleasant perquisites resulting from services previously rendered. Tetsukichi was in a very different position. Since he had been obliged to spend so much of his career helping with the work at his adoptive father's hospital, he had had neither the time nor the energy to produce even one short research paper. He was past his prime and what awaited him on his return to Japan was the same drudgery that he had known before.

Massive inflation had affected the German mark and Austrian kroner. The atmosphere of social unrest caused by rocketing prices and continual strikes was hardly conducive to peaceful academic research, although students from abroad found that the constant devaluation of the local currency meant that they were comparatively well off and could act accordingly. Some of those on Japanese Ministry of Education grants led a life of considerable luxury. In a town where pallid housewives would look wistfully after each heavy cartload of coal as it lumbered through the streets, these students would drink the finest wines and amuse themselves with the girls. Tetsukichi had nothing to do with such people, but attended classes and worked in the laboratory regularly. During his early days in Hongo there had been interns at the Nire Clinic who dressed in some attempt at style, constantly talked about women, and whose only gestures in the direction of study had been to memorize those parts of the physiological dictionary that concerned sexual matters. Tetsukichi was strongly reminded of these people by the Japanese medical students who frequented the night spots of Berlin and Vienna.

It was not that he had any strong moral urge to lead a pure and upright life, but he certainly did so, remaining stolidly chaste. It was more that he could simply not accustom himself to life abroad. He could never manage the language properly, he was the wrong age to be a student, and so he felt a constant nervous unrest, a sense of being left behind very similar to the feelings he had suffered when he had first arrived in Tokyo a quarter of a century ago. Sometimes he would see a girl in the street with bright hair and large eyes, and he would experience a strange excitement, much like the emotion he had felt as a boy when he caught the aroma of imported tobacco, or when in the market held in the grounds of the Asakusa Kannon Temple he had bought a picture of a young geisha called Ponta who was washing her hair. He was so strongly attracted by this picture he could hardly bear to look at it. In the same way he felt unable to look at these girls, and would turn his eyes from them as if he were dazzled. This was behavior suited to a shy adolescent, hardly to someone of his age, as was the way he would hasten away from such encounters, walking energetically along the fragrant tree-lined streets, or wandering about in the slowly fading light with no particular aim in mind. He would stand a long time watching the jackdaws settle, rise, then settle again on the roof of the gray, ancient cathedral. In winter he would go down to the riverside and watch the Danube pass. The ice that covered parts of it made a harsh, astringent sound, as if coarse cloth were being rubbed over the frozen surface.

Not surprisingly, the other Japanese students found this dreary way of life of his a justifiable cause for amused, contemptuous comment. Some even appeared to be genuinely concerned about him.

"If you go on like that you'll become a nut yourself. Why don't you have a bit of fun occasionally?"

Tetsukichi would smile back, indicating his beer glass to show that he was doing just that. Since this was always a mere half liter it was not a very convincing demonstration, and the small amount he drank did little to dispel the melancholy either from his face or from his mind.

In class he worked with real persistence. It was a long time since he had been able to enjoy the experience of real research and here was an atmosphere, born from a long tradition and fostered by the intellects of distinguished teachers, that was ideal for study. It was a dark, musty world, a world ruled over by an obstinate passion for the definitive in all things for which it was hard to feel any affection; and yet it was a world of endless possibilities and Tetsukichi accepted it with a desire that was close to greed, with something like the trembling expectancy of sexual passion.

One late afternoon Tetsukichi was seated in a corner of the laboratory dissecting the brain of a paralytic imbecile. His aim was to discover what cell changes could be seen in the various parts of the cerebrum, and he was obliged to take fifty sections of different structure from that one brain. The really frustrating chore, however, was taking dozens of brain segments and putting them all in different bottles and labeling them. Tetsukichi had his own method of doing this, which was to mark the various segments with *sumi* (traditional Japanese ink), neatly applied with a fine writing brush he had brought with him from Japan. *Sumi* was much better for this purpose than European ink.

He became aware that someone was behind him and he turned around to see the stooping figure of an old distinguished professor emeritus, retired some time ago, who almost never appeared in any of the laboratories and certainly not at as late an hour as this. Tetsukichi jumped up in surprise, and since his grubby hands precluded the European form of greeting, he simply bowed stiffly and returned to his work, feeling even more tense about it than before. The old professor watched him working for a while, and then said, as if speaking to himself:

"The Japanese are certainly very clever with their hands."

Then he spoke directly to Tetsukichi:

"Exhausting work, no doubt. But no work completed in a month is worth anything. So you must try to endure it as well as you can."

Whenever really fiddly work, such as dyeing the specimens, was not going well or was taking an inordinately long time, Tetsukichi would remember what the old professor had said, and that would spur him on to renewed efforts. There was no one he could talk to, so even very minor pieces of friendly encouragement meant an absurd amount to him. There was, for example, the tall, freckled, usually uncommunicative girl who worked in the specimens room; once, when Tetsukichi's eyes were exhausted by staring through the microscope and he was looking out of the window to rest them, she had, as she walked briskly by, asked him if he were tired. It was a totally conventional phrase and her face retained its usual hard, angular expression, but the cadence of her voice was gentle, as if she actually meant what she said. Occasional words such as these gave an indefinable sense of warmth to his life, no doubt because of their rarity.

Tetsukichi spent a year and a half like this, moving between his lodgings and the laboratory and lecture rooms, and, while in Vienna, he completed a thesis of some hundred and forty pages. This meant that he had achieved his main objective in coming to Europe, the purpose for which Kiichiro had sent him; it would be sufficient for him to gain his M.D. and be fully qualified to take over the directorship of the Nire Hospital. But Tetsukichi was not yet satisfied. He felt that now, after all those years of expectation, he stood at last on the shore of the great ocean of knowledge, its waves lapping his feet. He would never have another chance to devote himself entirely to scholarship and research. And so, though Kiichiro had advised him in a letter to travel widely in order to broaden his mind and then return to Tokyo, Tetsukichi decided he would push himself as far as possible and go to Munich, which had the most advanced psychiatric research center in Germany, the Kaiser Wilhelm Institute.

One thing he particularly noticed in this elegant city was the number of military uniforms in the streets. Another thing was that people would sometimes stare at him and whisper the word "Jap" in such a way that he could clearly hear. One evening, as he was returning from the Institute, he entered a small restaurant and, since there were no empty tables, he was obliged to sit at the same table as an old man. He said "Excuse me" and sat down, whereupon the old man, without saying a word, immediately stood up and went to sit elsewhere.

Tetsukichi simply lowered his eyes and decided he should ignore this, but it wasn't easy. To be called a Jap was not very disturbing, neither were the cries of "Chinese" that groups of small children occasionally hurled at him. But this was the apparently considered action of a grownup, indeed an elderly person, and it genuinely wounded him. When this kind of thing happened, it was not surprising that his thoughts should turn to the question of the Jews, since they were undoubted objects of contempt and ostracism both in Vienna and Munich. Once when Tetsukichi was amusing himself with a group of children at play, asking the names of the schools they went to and listening to the various answers they shouted back, one of the children pointed his finger to the rear and said, "That one's a Jew," whereupon all the others winked and burst out laughing. It was the same tone of sniggering contempt with which a Japanese student might draw attention to a woman and say, "She's one of those."

At first Tetsukichi had tended to sympathize with the Jews, out of that generosity which comes from seeing people treated as inferior even to oneself. But after hearing rumors of how, while the German people were suffering from the sudden collapse of the international exchange market after the war, the Jews were on the contrary becoming wealthier, taking control of many things including one of the leading newspapers in Vienna, even taking over whole courses in colleges by ensuring that the student attendance was one hundred percent Jewish; and after he had witnessed what went on in a synagogue, the exclusive, racialist nature of the ceremonies of solidarity performed there, he had gradually come to be wary of them, even to hate them.

He often went looking for medical works in secondhand bookshops, and whenever he leafed casually through a popular magazine he found evidence of this intense anti-Semitism, directed from any number of angles. But he also found cartoons against the Japanese, in magazines published during the war. The Japanese had been so drawn as to resemble, even to Tetsukichi's eyes, either extremely cunning monkeys or lean, hungry, evil-eyed stray cats prowling around the outskirts of Tsingtao. And, gazing at these drawings, he would notice that he was frowning, that his brows were drawn together in a mixture of displeasure, anxiety and shame.

But soon after he had arrived in Munich, Tetsukichi had met with a much worse shock than that, something that shook him to the core of his being. Why the experience should have affected him in such a way was something he found virtually impossible to explain to anyone, and when he thought about it afterward it seemed no more than a minor incident which he really ought to have felt ashamed of mentioning to his friends.

The name of Emil Kraepelin had been a familiar one to Tetsukichi since his student days, an object of reverence and aspiration, as one of the founding fathers of modern psychiatry. He had possessed a copy of one of the later editions of the *Kompendium der Psychiatrie* for years, and had lately been able to lay his hands on the original first edition, published in 1883, when the author had been thirty-seven. This first edition, which Tetsukichi treated with great care, was a small book of around 380 pages, a collection of essays concerning various phobias in which one could see, as yet, no sign of the system of classification that was to be the author's great contribution to the subject. This was gradually to appear in successive later editions with the constant addition of remarkable new concepts that still, in 1923, seemed unshakable in their validity. It was a monument of classificatory method that appeared to be as solid as a Gothic cathedral. One of the reasons, perhaps the main reason, for Tetsukichi's coming to Munich was the strong desire to see the great man in the flesh, a desire that he had never made public.

On the day of the incident he had finished his lunch in a cheap eating house near the Institute and was returning to the laboratory. These were still early days in Munich and he was not accustomed to the routine and had not yet got down to serious research. He was lounging about when a red-faced doctor who had come down from Hamburg University to work here, and who seemed to derive great pleasure from involving himself in other people's business, came up and told him that there was to be a film-showing in the main lecture hall. He asked Tetsukichi if he would like to come along and added that he had heard Professor Kraepelin would be there.

This news aroused Tetsukichi from his lethargy, and he felt an excited sense of reverence and humility, much as one might feel prostrating oneself before an image of the Buddha in a temple. He saw himself as a mere student from a far country who had crossed oceans to look upon the savant's face. And in this sentimental frame of mind he even composed a few schoolgirlish phrases in case an introduction ever took place.

When he arrived at the lecture hall it was still fairly empty, but after he had sat down a few graduate assistants arrived, and then the Director of the Institute, whom Tetsukichi knew by sight. He was talking to an old man, and Tetsukichi realized that this must be Kraepelin. He felt the physical excitement of a person who has fallen in love. The doctor from Hamburg University, who had been sitting by his side, walked down the steps to where the great man was, shook hands politely with him, and spent some moments in conversation. Then the Director advanced on Kraepelin leading a young, Oriental-looking man, whom he introduced. The man had a slightly ruddy, yellow complexion. Kraepelin shook his hand as well.

The red-faced doctor from Hamburg came back and in his usual clear and cheerful voice asked Tetsukichi if he should introduce him. Tetsukichi hesitated, then asked:

"Where does that man, that Oriental, come from?"

"Ah, he's a doctor from Java. He's just come to have a look around the Institute today."

Hearing the word "Java" gave Tetsukichi courage, no doubt because he was unconsciously comparing the status of that country with his own. Then the man was a mere visitor, unlike Tetsukichi, who actually belonged to the Institute and was engaged in research here. Obviously Kraepelin would treat him with greater consideration than he had shown to the other Oriental, to whom he had been properly courteous. So Tetsukichi accepted the invitation, stood up, and walked down the steps side by side with the red-faced doctor. As they approached, the old professor glanced briefly in their direction. Kraepelin's hair was white, but his eyebrows still retained some color. His long, untidy beard looked rather like an old-fashioned broom. He had glittering gray eyes, and despite his age there was something stern, almost heroic, about him. He had the sort of face one imagined a wandering samurai might have. This, at least, was the impression Tetsukichi received in that brief moment.

He gave his name and emphasized that he was doing microscopic work in the specialist laboratory, politely producing his name card. Kraepelin took the card but made no attempt to look at it, nor did he say a word. Instead he turned away from Tetsukichi and addressed the others in a voice which, although deep and mellow, was loud and clear enough:

"Gentlemen, would you kindly take your seats."

Tetsukichi felt lost for the moment. His bewilderment was colored with shame and disbelief, and he made his way back to his seat. Kraepelin was sitting just below him to his left and as Tetsukichi glanced at the old man, who was talking to the Director in a perfectly friendly fashion, he began to have doubts about the insult he thought he had just received. After all, the film was just about to start, so it was hardly the most convenient of times. Even so, surely he could at least have shaken his hand.

The windows were closed and curtained over, the lights put out, and the film began. It showed a variety of psychiatric patients and the different ways in which they behaved. Tetsukichi opened his notebook,

175

as he had done on many similar occasions before, and began to take notes in the semi-darkness, writing in a mixture of German and Japanese: "Five or six *Schüttelzittern*. *Choreatisch* trembling—*stereotypisch* tremors some cases. After while seems like *Stereotypie* of *Katatonie*. Shoulders, arms, then heads shake same way."

But his attention began to wander from the film toward the dark shape sitting below him to his left, for the aged Kraepelin sometimes gave directions to the projectionist concerning the speed at which the film was to be shown.

The film took about an hour and then the lights came on again. The doctor from Hamburg University stood up smartly and paid his respects to Professor Kraepelin. The old man with the samurai expression thrust out his arm and they shook hands. For some reason Tetsukichi was also eager to get into the act and he offered a similarly speedy few words of thanks. Once more Kraepelin said not a word in reply, and was quite studiedly ignoring him when the doctor from Java turned up to pay his own respects. The professor shook his hand in a simple, casual manner. Yet Tetsukichi had still not grasped what was going on. He believed it would be his turn next to shake hands, because he particularly wanted to shake the hand of the great man, the scholar for whom, over so many years, he had felt such respect and affection. So just before the handshake between the professor and the Javanese was over Tetsukichi thrust out his own hand in readiness, with the result that Kraepelin withdrew his as soon as its previous office had been performed, leaving Tetsukichi's dangling limply in midair; he then turned his back smartly and went down the steps toward the exit.

Tetsukichi stood rooted to the spot, first in dumbfounded surprise, then with a feeling of humiliation and rage. The tense way in which he stood was reminiscent of the cataleptic postures of some of the patients in the film just shown, for his forearms were slightly raised, his fists tightly clenched, and he was aware that his hands and wrists were trembling. His round, unattractive and shortsighted eyes were open almost painfully wide behind his thick-lensed spectacles, and with unblinking gaze he followed the black-suited figure of Emil Kraepelin as he made his way over to the farthest exit and disappeared. His lips were trembling, but not because he was trying to say anything. Nevertheless, deep within himself he was searching for some verbal outlet for this rising passion which seemed beyond expression. Unhappily, all he could find was a sad and ugly piece of abuse, a jeer worthy of some frenzied yokel, which he repeated inwardly to himself a number of times:

"Hairy foreign swine. Hairy damn foreign swine."

While Tetsukichi had been at high school, the Russo-Japanese War had broken out. On the day when the Imperial Rescript proclaiming the outbreak of hostilities had been announced the whole school had assembled in the hall to listen to the headmaster's address. When this had ended one of the senior boys had ascended the dais and given a speech to the effect that a war might be going on but their main duty as students was to study, because study was something independent of the war effort. Whereupon one of the teachers had barged onto the platform and pulled the student away from the rostrum before he had finished what he had to say. This teacher then made a violent address, spitting out the words with passionate energy. Our country, he said, had now entered a period of trial and danger. People were risking their lives in this great struggle. Was this a time to mouth pretentious phrases about our duty as students? Was this a time to sit quietly and pore over one's books? Was this a time to sit listening to lectures? No, classes should be canceled, canceled and then canceled again. We should go down to Shinbashi Station and cheer our brave soldier lads on their way to the front.

The master kept up this harangue with a fluency that had an effect like fire. Tetsukichi listened with growing excitement, with the same mindless passion he was experiencing now, two decades later, as he clenched his teeth and held back those oaths about hairy foreign devils.

He returned to his lodgings physically and emotionally exhausted. His landlady was in the small room that served as both kitchen and dining room, seated before the table on which a birdcage stood with a canary in it. But today the bird was out, perched on the landlady's finger, and she was singing a song to it, an ancient song which the students had no doubt sung when she was young, a song about love being ever changeable and new for the carefree student lad, today for Johanna, tomorrow for Susanna. . .

The Japanese students in Munich referred to her as their Japanese granny. When she was a young girl, her mother and she had opened a boardinghouse which, over the years, had come to cater exclusively to the Japanese students who came to Munich, stayed a while, then left to be replaced by others. She was now nearly sixty and for all that time, with the exception of the war years, she had lodged Japanese students in her house. On the white wall, as well as the ancient, blackened crucifix and the equally old stone engraving of the Virgin Mary, were displayed a silk Japanese fan and a framed lacquer painting of snow-covered Mt. Fuji. Her album had numerous photographs of Japanese students pasted in it, and some of herself surrounded by such students when she was still young. She cooked well, boiling Italian rice on her gas stove and sometimes giving them *sukiyaki* as a special treat. Tetsukichi was only a temporary lodger, spending his first days in Munich in the room of someone who was away traveling.

The old lady turned toward Tetsukichi, who was still looking extremely sullen, and as she played with the bird with one hand, she smiled at him, wrinkling her already wrinkled face even more, with an expression of simple goodness.

"This bird is an old woman just like me. Look at her poor leg there. It's all rheumatic, so she's like that, poor thing."

Tetsukichi felt some of the tension in him dissolve at these words. He began to feel somewhat ashamed of the passion the incident had aroused in him. He realized that his rage had been like a child's—and that the great scholar's behavior had been similarly childish.

One thing the incident did was to make him devote himself even more rigorously to the work he had come to do. He regretted every moment he did not use for that purpose. He became even more thrifty, eating the cheapest of meals, and spent long hours searching through the secondhand bookshops, buying up works of psychology and back numbers of psychiatric journals which had hitherto not been related directly to his research. He now had a secret ambition, which had not existed when he first left Japan. He was aware that he would have to return to clinical practice when he went home, and he would have almost no spare time. But he was not prepared to allow things to end there. At some time in the future he could expect to regain some of the time he would at first lose. In a corner of the Nire Hospital he would have a laboratory, no matter how primitive, in which he could work, and once every three years, say, he would produce a proper research paper. He was now determined to collect the materials that would allow him to do that research.

For some people dry-as-dust scholarship can operate in much the same addictive way as hard drugs. Also, that innocent infatuation which marks the person who has taken only a few paces toward a distant goal no doubt moved Tetsukichi to make this resolution of his. But more complex motives were probably at work too, and it would be unwise to ignore the stimulus he had received from the old white-haired scholar who had refused to shake his hand.

Early that summer Tetsukichi was obliged to leave his lodgings with the Japanese granny, and he found the quest for new quarters much more of a business than he had imagined. He put an advertisement in the newspaper, but the various replies he received from a number of poor, slum-like houses in the town only led to disappointment, and he was unable to find anything satisfactory. At one house, for example, the apparently plain-dealing *Hausfrau* had assured him he need only pay a price equivalent to that of three rolls of bread (at that time a bread roll cost, in fact, fifteen thousand marks), so he took the room for a while, but she had a wheedling technique of raising the rent, constantly adding extras to the bill, asking if the *Herr Doktor* knew that a glass of beer cost twenty-five thousand marks and surely he would not wish to deprive a poor widow of her sole comfort of a little something to drink each day, and so wouldn't he kindly add a. . . In another house a bald-headed, fat, round man demanded, in unpleasantly cheerful and brusque fashion, three million marks a month, and Tetsukichi could not see the point of trying to beat him down from that exalted level. At another he was obliged to pay a million marks as deposit, and found on the first night that he was attacked by what seemed to be a corresponding number of bed bugs. He finally managed to find something suitable not all that far from his original lodgings, but only after he had tried more than a dozen places.

In summer the laboratory was practically deserted. Munich, being in the mountains, was often visited by thunderstorms, particularly that summer, making one feel that there was unrest in society which might break out in similar disturbances. Even a large beer hall like the Hoffbräu suddenly seemed to lose a great many of its customers. But Tetsukichi noticed little of this and was unaware of the signs of what was to come. He went each day to the hot, airless laboratory, and continued the fastidious series of experiments he was carrying out on the brain of a rabbit.

Toward the end of that summer, on the evening of the 3rd of September, 1923, Tetsukichi was sitting at a corner table in the restaurant he always went to, blinking his eyes in an attempt to get rid of the tiredness caused by hours of peering through a microscope. It had been drizzling since morning and was a raw, damp day. Prices were continuing to soar, and a fairly simple meal nowadays cost something in the region of 1.3 million marks. Since one could hardly keep such vast quantities of notes about one's person it had become obligatory to make constant journeys to the bank, and this was another reason for the growing nervous prostration he felt.

He ordered a glass of beer and drew some letters out of his inside pocket, all of them from Japan. Most had arrived some time before, but it was his habit, once the day's work was done, to sit in front of a glass of beer and read or reread the letters sent to him by family and friends, the Japanese script and the associations it aroused providing him with the only occasions on which he felt relaxed and free from the tensions that dominated his daily life.

There was a letter from his wife. Ryuko wrote in a style that gave a remarkable impression of haste, as if the whole thing had been dashed off in the intervals of an incredibly busy day. She leaped confusedly from one subject to another:

I hope you are in health and progressing with your studies. Everybody is well here, although we are still having a great deal of trouble with Momoko. As I mentioned in my last, she is married to Shiro Takayanagi—I suppose I should call him Shiro Nire, since he *is* a member of the family—but she still insists that she does not like him and is continually causing trouble about this. Shiro has been offered a post in China as chief surgeon at the Benevolence Hospital in Hankow. He has received permission from Father to spend two or three years there, and it was decided that as soon as Momoko graduates from school I should take her there to join him. Now, in spite of all that, Momoko still goes on objecting to being married saying really quite vulgar things in front of people claiming that she is still a virgin and things like that and I must say, although she may be my own sister, I really have quite despaired of her. It makes me quite angry to think how hopeless and useless a person she has become.

Shun'ichi is very well, only he seems unable to make any friends at school and always objects to going and even when he gets there he is so very difficult, always complaining and hiding away in a corner. This habit of shutting himself away from everyone must be something he picked up from you, don't you think? Father is certainly getting no younger. His taste in food is becoming even more grandfatherly. He is now in the habit of mixing Bordeaux with his oatmeal in order not only to dilute it but to cool it down before he eats it.

I am certainly looking forward to the day you decide your

research is complete and you can return to Japan. Father says that, all things permitting, there is no reason why I should not travel to Europe to meet you. I am already much looking forward to it. Mother is very well. Recently, at Father's suggestion of course, she has joined a number of charitable organizations and spends much of her time away from home. I usually go with her, to the League of Patriotic Women and things like that. I have, in addition to all this, a large circle of acquaintances and am kept extremely occupied every day. You know it really is very irritating the vulgar way in which Momoko looks so pleased because Shiro will soon be leaving for Hankow and so she will be rid of him for a while. She is quite impossible and I wish you would write to her and tell her you are not at all satisfied with the way she is behaving. Oshu has finally managed to get into the medical faculty in Sendai, but the great fool seems to do nothing but his stupid Judo and I wish you would write to him as well telling him he should try to straighten himself out a little. I have not seen Seiko. Yonekuni has now got into the habit of keeping loathsome insects in his room. I must say the children of the Nire family are a pretty awful crowd, causing trouble and contributing absolutely nothing. If I were not perpetually doing much more than my fair share of the work I imagine Father's hospital would simply fall into ruins. Father says there was no necessity for you to go to Munich so I can only say that the earlier you finish your research the better as far as we are all concerned, especially myself, and hope there is some speedy method by which you will be able to do so.

Tetsukichi read through this old letter again, resting his elbows on the grimy table, and thought about his family and the hospital and other things. Even allowing for her being "occupied" as she said, her letter was surely written in rather too slovenly a way, the contents were a bit too meager, and the whole thing seemed concerned with things only insofar as they affected herself. There was no sign of the prim and proper Ryuko here, simply a petty and total egotism. Tetsukichi, as her husband, had been aware for a long time now that this egotism represented, more than anything else, the real Ryuko, and he could only feel a slightly bitter amusement at the inflated idea she had of herself in relation to her father and the hospital. "Father's hospital would simply fall into ruins"—the Nire Hospital was hardly likely to collapse as easily as that. And she seemed totally unconcerned about the struggle that he, her husband, was having to face every day of his life abroad; it needed little insight to work out from her letter that her own daily life consisted mostly in dressing up and going out on the social round. No doubt Ryuko would maintain that all this was done not for herself but "for the sake of the hospital," but one could hardly take that seriously. In this context her remarks about there being no necessity for his going to Munich were particularly galling, and each time he read that final section of the letter he could not help feeling a petty, spiteful anger toward her.

Tetsukichi derived a certain comfort from the thought of his son, Shun'ichi. She had only written three or four lines about him, so he could well imagine how, with her various occupations, she had no time for the child and had simply dumped him on Nanny Shimoda. He would have to ask her to send more details of the boy next time. So he sat thinking of these things and, in contrast to the local inhabitants, downed his beer extremely slowly, taking very occasional sips.

A small boy, pathetic, hollow-faced and wretchedly clothed, came around selling the evening papers. Tetsukichi bought two papers off him and glanced casually over the front page of one of them. There were headlines about increasing tension between Greece and Italy and then, just below that, another headline which suddenly caught his attention: "*Die Erdbeben-katastrophe in Japan*"—Earthquake Disaster in Japan.

Tetsukichi raised one hand to the rim of his glasses as if attempting to see better, and read a small portion of the article with genuinely bated breath.

> *Telegraphed report from Shanghai. . . The earthquake occurred early in the morning of the 1st of September. . . One hundred thousand people died in Tokyo-Yokohama. . . The Arsenal exploded killing thousands of workers. . . The towns of Atami and Ito some fifty miles west of Tokyo simply vanished. . . Mt. Fuji erupted losing half its cone. . . The large island of Oshima sixty miles southwest of Tokyo has sunk beneath the waves.*

It seemed completely unreal. He ordered another glass of beer and this time drank half of it in one gulp. He then placed his hand against the rim of his spectacles again and read the article through carefully, word by word. A terrible fear gradually grew in him, becoming an irresistible terror that surged through him and made it impossible to remain seated there any longer. The eruption of Mt. Fuji and Oshima disappearing into the sea indicated a natural disaster of huge proportions, one that would have caused much more than the hundred thousand deaths mentioned in the Tokyo area. It was the kind of catastrophe that only occurs once in hundreds of years. What should he do? Should he go straight to his old boardinghouse, where there were two or three compatriots of his? But what was the point? They could hardly be expected to know any more than he did. Even if they did, what could he do all these thousands of miles away? The hospital? The Nire Hospital must have been completely destroyed. As for his family, how many of them would still be alive? And which of them? And if they were alive, what then?

Once his confused thoughts and feelings had reached this stage they had nowhere else to go. All he could sense was darkness, a darkness in which the present and the future were both equally beyond his grasp and comprehension. Tetsukichi just managed to raise his hand to his spectacles once more, and he read the newspaper for a third time.

Chapter

8

Kiichiro Nire had spent most of the summer of 1923 in his cottage near the hot-spring resort of Gora in the mountains of Hakone. Gora is the terminus of the mountain railway that climbs up from Odawara some ten miles away, Odawara being another fifty miles or so from Tokyo. After leaving the station you go up past the park and eventually arrive at Mukoyama. Mukoyama means "facing the mountains" and, as the name implies, two large peaks, part of the mountain chain that encircles the Kanto Plain, overlook the area, Mt. Myojin to the north and Mt. Myojo to the east. The Nire cottage was here, in a place still undeveloped at the time, an expanse of cedar forest which had probably been untouched for centuries. There were only three other cottages to be seen in the area.

At morning and evening the *higurashi,* the clear-toned cicada that sings of cool weather, would sound in piercing chorus. At night great gusts of wind would sweep down from the peak of Mt. Soun, which was close to the west, swaying the branches of the cedar trees and making a roar as if a tidal wave were flooding down the mountainside. This was the first summer either Momoko or Yonekuni had spent in the summer cottage. It had its own hot spring, a sulfur bath detached from the main building, and after dark, when they walked the raised, half-open wooden passageway to the bath, the black shadow of one awesomely towering cedar tree would arouse in them the occasional ice-cold shiver. For a little boy like Shun'ichi who had only just started going to primary school that year, the atmosphere of the cottage was somber and lonely, particularly as Nanny Shimoda had been unable to come with him, and every other day he would sulk and demand to be taken back to Tokyo.

Kiichiro, however, was in particularly good spirits. The political situation was very grave and unsettled, for Korekiyo Takahashi's successor,

Prime Minister Kato, was seriously, perhaps critically, ill. The opposition Kenseikai was determined to form a government next time, which meant that the Seiyukai (Kiichiro's party and the one now in office) would have to struggle even more manfully than before, although Kiichiro was naturally affecting an air of complete indifference to all this. In the past he might well have felt worried at any news implying that the Seiyukai was declining in popularity, but now he was delighted to have an increase in the number of his visitors because of the political situation, and delighted also since it appeared to be turning into a real crisis. Next year would be an election year. This feigned air of unconcern came from a nervous awareness of the possible reactions of his wife to the smallest sign of interest on his part, for she had pleaded with him after the failure of the last election to give up politics because she was sick to death of it and the dreadful amount of money it wasted. But, in fact, he was as swollen with political ambition as ever, and was already planning various first moves for the forthcoming campaign.

Today Kiichiro was loosely dressed in a *yukata* (in this case a casual bathrobe). He was sitting in a cane chair on the veranda and entertaining a guest from Yamagata.

"Well, looks like Germany's about to go bankrupt, I must say. And what about this new Chancellor they've got, Stresemann? All this talk about an assassination plot. I wonder. Do you believe that?"

Presumably it was because his wife Hisa was lurking nearby that Kiichiro, twiddling his Kaiser moustache all the while, launched into this irrelevant topic, which was of no possible interest to his rural guest. There was no indication that he might be worried about his adopted son Tetsukichi, who was still over there in that perilous country.

"No doubt about it, sir, either way as they say, in a manner of speaking. I don't know nothing, I mean I'm not all that well in, I mean up, on Germany. I mean the situation there as it may be."

His guest was making great efforts to keep this high-powered intellectual conversation going in as polite and cultured a manner as he knew, nodding seriously all the while but wisely deciding before long to bring the subject nearer home:

"Zaosan will soon make *juryo,* anyway."

"You're quite right there. Bit odd if he wasn't up to it with a physique like that, I must say. I wager he makes it further than that in no time. Just you wait and see."

Tatsuji, the gluttonous wonder boy who had once disliked Sumo wrestling so much that he had seemed desperate to avoid any connection with it, had now taken as his professional name the name of the mountain in whose shadow he had grown up, Mt. Zao or *Zaosan,* and was gradually working his way up through the various grades and divisions. *Juryo* is the second division, which a promising new wrestler needs to make fairly quickly if he hopes to be taken seriously. The first division, or *maku-uchi,* was what Kiichiro was thinking in terms of, and his guest felt obliged to go one further:

"They say back home he'll make *ozeki* and no mistake. They're backing him real strong, anyway."

Ozeki is the second-highest rank in Sumo, coming after *yokozuna* or Grand Champion. These are the only two ranks that, once achieved, cannot be lost, unlike all the ranks below, which are subject to the same ups and downs that occur in most competitive sports with leagues or divisions.

"Only trouble is he's a bad mover," said Kiichiro, frowning as if he were determined to restrain his own justifiable jubilation by means of a little modesty. "You know, you get some little fellow leaping in at him low down, and he's all over the place, goes to pieces, just like jelly. It's his thighs, you see: all unbalanced, no power there, no drive. Only the other day that skinny streak Masagoishi, of all people, just picked him up and flipped him out of the ring. Of course, Masagoishi has just married into the teahouse business so he wants to make a good impression. Still, hah, hah, once he'd put Zaosan out he was properly sat on for his pains. Got the whole weight of the lad on top of him. Crushed him flat. Weighs a ton, you see."

The guest laughed loudly for a brief spell, then suddenly adopted a serious, reverent facial expression.

"Incidentally, if I may make bold to say so, what a wonderful sight that is, your hospital in Aoyama. The view from the front gate is, well, my word, just tremendous. That's all I can say. Stupendous."

Now that he had been touched on a really soft spot Kiichiro was unable to resist a sudden surge of self-satisfaction, and his face was wreathed in smirks.

"Well, yes, you know, well, I really had a great deal of trouble with that. Racked my brains over it. It's modeled on the Vatican in Rome, of course."

With Kiichiro at his most beaming and self-confident one might have expected a stunning remark of that kind, and his guest, who hadn't the remotest idea what sort of animal a vatican might be, was further stricken with admiration, as was obvious from his face, and this spurred him on to even greater heights of flattery:

"I was honored to be transported to Shinbashi Station in your automobile, and I was wondering what kind of vehicle it might be?"

"Got a new one quite recently," replied Kiichiro the non-smoker, drawing a gold-tipped cigarette from his silver cigarette case. "Using two cars at present. One's a Fiat. Italian job. Very economical. Doesn't eat up gasoline, you know. Now the other. . . Now what is the other one?. . ."

Kiichiro seemed to have a sudden lapse of memory. In fact he had genuinely forgotten, something he tended to do lately for he was now sixty years old. But he was not the sort of person to sit thinking about anything for very long.

"Ah yes. It's a Beach. That's right, Beach is the name. I think that's probably the one you rode in."

The small Shun'ichi, who was listening to this conversation from the passageway near the veranda, started giggling because he knew the car was a Buick. He peeped in to see what kind of expression Kiichiro wore after making this blunder, but his grandfather seemed remarkably relaxed, lighting his cigarette, puffing energetically through it once or twice, and then gracefully allowing the small fire to smolder away all on its own.

Kiichiro's teacher of *shogi,* the Japanese form of chess, was a man called Yokoi, a master of the game and holder of the sixth rank. He too spent a long weekend here this summer. Kiichiro had his own special method of playing the game, which requires some explanation. *Shogi* is similar to chess, and in most cases it is not difficult to find chess equivalents for *shogi* pieces. The main difference is that there is no queen in the Japanese game, its functions being performed by two pieces called *kin* ("gold"), which are next to the king on either side of it and normally used for defense, and by another two pieces called *gin* ("silver"), which are next to the *kin*. The *gin* move forward, straight or diagonally, one square at a time and can also move backward diagonally, and these are normally used in attack. But Kiichiro, of course, had his own, very original, technique. He used his two *gin* for defense, always neatly hiding his king behind them regardless of anything his opponent might be doing, and then moving his two powerful *kin* forward in a direct assault on the enemy. No matter how severe a battering the other pieces in his defensive system might receive, the *gin* stayed tucked up tight alongside their king and took some shifting. There was also the special mode of attack alluded to already, whereby he would use both hands, when his opponent was not looking, to move two pawns forward at the same time.

This special ploy would, of course, work if he were playing one of his employees, but there were problems involved in using it against the man who was his teacher of the game, for Yokoi would certainly be aware of it. This opponent was an expert, and no matter how indifferently he might seem to be moving his pieces about, he was a master at reorganization and could retrieve the most awkward-looking situations. Obviously it was unlikely that a man with so good a grasp of the pattern of the game would be unaware of a pawn appearing where it could not properly be; and although Kiichiro knew this very well it did not stop him from making frequent use of this dubious move. Usually it got him nowhere, and it also put an additional burden on his teacher, for Kiichiro had a great dislike of losing the pawns he moved forward so rashly. Even when playing with his teacher he particularly hated losing a game if it were the result of a mass slaughter of his pawns, and during the inquest that followed, when Yokoi explained the various skills by which an opponent's pawns could be disposed of (as Kiichiro's had just been), he would listen with an expression of sulky inattention on his face. Yokoi had grown to understand this predilection and would tread warily in that area. He had also realized that Kiichiro definitely preferred to win rather than to improve by profiting from his own mistakes, so he would make deliberate errors in order to give his opponent more than a sporting chance.

One day, Yokoi was in a very benevolent mood and had already lost two games. For their third game they were to play without the usual handicap (the teacher normally gave his pupil one or two pieces before the game started), and although it would have pleased Kiichiro enormously to win under these conditions, Yokoi had his position as teacher to consider: he felt obliged to make a genuine game of it and stormed into the attack. By the time they had arrived at the middle game it was clear that this had gone too far, so Yokoi made two or three feeble moves in order to let Kiichiro back in with a chance. Unhappily Kiichiro failed to notice and took no advantage of them so that, despite the honorable intentions of his teacher, his position went from bad to worse. Yokoi had by now come to the conclusion that no swindling on Kiichiro's part could get him out of this hopeless situation, and he was reconciled to the idea of having to defeat him. At this point, however, Kiichiro became peculiarly hesitant in his game, chattering away about this and that and making no attempt to move any of his pieces despite the fact that it was his turn. Yokoi took the hint and went off to wash his hands.

When he returned, though, there were real surprises in store for him. Kiichiro's bishop, which had been in a position where it must have been taken, was now transferred to a square from which it could dominate the game, and the pawn at the side, which Yokoi had carefully placed so as to provide an escape route for his king, was now on a square where it positively blocked the king's way. To add insult to injury Kiichiro was gazing calmly out into the garden, and innocently remarked:

"We get a lovely breeze here. Now, sir, I believe it was my turn, wasn't it?"

Toward the end of that summer, however, Kiichiro became extremely busy, traveling between Tokyo and Hakone a number of times. Prime Minister Kato, whose instant recovery or imminent decease had been causing varying joy and gloom in the two main political parties for some weeks now, finally passed away on the 24th of August, and the cabinet was dissolved. The Kenseikai felt their luck was in and were confident of victory, whilst the Seiyukai took a more negative stance, attempting to block the opposition's progress.

After all this excitement Kiichiro had returned to Gora, where he smilingly welcomed Tetsukichi's brother, Shirokichi Mihira, who had come all the way from Kaminoyama in Yamagata, and was accompanied this far by Yasusaburo Sugano. Kiichiro was delighted to see him, not only as a relation but as a person of influence in Kaminoyama, and he arranged that he should be shown the sights of Hakone. That was not, of course, the main purpose of the visit, as Shirokichi himself knew only too well. A close friend of Mihira's was about to stand in the prefectural elections in Yamagata. It would be to Kiichiro's advantage as a Diet candidate in that area to have a local politician among his acquaintances, and it was to discuss this matter that Shirokichi had been brought all the way to Tokyo and then to Hakone.

Kiichiro was aware that Shirokichi was terrified of his wife Hisa, and that he would be unable to broach the subject of politics in the cottage, so he invited him out to a restaurant to try some exotic Western cuisine. No such restaurant existed in Gora, although only a short distance down the mountain railway was the Fujiya Hotel at Miyanoshita which could have provided something of the kind. Kiichiro, however, had no intention of going there, and wouldn't even settle for the shabby cafe in front of Gora Station, but took Shirokichi instead to an old-fashioned, rustic teahouse just in front of Gora Park, and there, as they drank nothing more exotically Western than iced water, they became engrossed in conversation about matters of state and the secret methods by which Shirokichi's friend might be elected.

The main question was money. If Kiichiro provided the money, Shirokichi reckoned he could fix things back home, and Kiichiro nodded magnanimously in assent. Tomorrow they would both go to Tokyo, and Kiichiro would draw the money out of the bank and hand it over to Shirokichi. It was also decided that Kiichiro would donate the money for a bridge to be built between Kaminoyama and the village in which both Tetsukichi and Shirokichi had been born. The bridge would be named "Kiichiro Bridge."

It was the 31st of August. After dinner that evening Kiichiro had another look at the newspaper and said cheerfully:

"Mihira, they've got a typhoon down in Kyushu, but once that has passed through into the Japan Sea there's nothing else to worry about. It looks as if the 210th day will pass without anything untoward happening."

The 210th day as counted from the beginning of spring according to the old lunar calendar usually falls on the 1st of September. It has traditionally been a day on which people are particularly worried about typhoons damaging crops; a natural disaster day.

Because the new school term was due to begin, Shun'ichi, his mother and Yonekuni had already gone back to Tokyo. Only Momoko was left to enjoy Shirokichi's broad, unrestrained northern dialect, which she did, pinching herself not to burst out laughing. Hisa sat unmoved as ever, muttering occasional words to Shirokichi in a flat, expressionless voice as her part of the conversation.

On the following morning, Kiichiro and Shirokichi took the ten o'clock train from Gora. They had been caught in a sudden downpour as they walked to the station and Shirokichi had been soaked to the skin. Kiichiro had been wise enough to take an umbrella and had even invited Shirokichi to shelter under it with him, but it was obvious from the way he marched on ahead with the umbrella held directly above his own head that he had no intention of allowing Shirokichi to accept this polite, if empty, invitation. Shirokichi was still dripping wet when they boarded the electric train that would take them slowly down to Odawara, and Kiichiro pointed to a seat on the opposite side of the compartment some distance from his own and ordered him to sit there.

At Odawara, where they arrived some minutes before noon, the weather was cloudless with a hot sun burning down, and there they waited for the steam train that would take them on to Tokyo. Kiichiro bought two jars of pickled plums, generously giving one to Shirokichi and explaining that it was a well-known local delicacy and would make a nice present to take home. Shirokichi did not feel particularly impressed. He left his jar on the waiting-room table and went for a stroll in the small square in front of the station. He noticed that the roofs of the houses seemed to get gradually lower in one direction, and then realized that the sea must be over there and that the land sloped down toward it. The sun shone fiercely on those low roofs.

It was then that the earth shook. There was a great, deep roaring in the earth like thunder, something so beyond Shirokichi's experience that he was seized with terror. At the same time his body was jerked upward with the movement of the earth, and then shaken violently up and down and from side to side as well. He found it difficult to stand, so he half lay and half fell down. The earth was roaring, writhing, swaying like some living thing. People came tumbling and staggering out of the station waiting room behind him.

As Shirokichi lay on the still swaying earth he observed a two-storied house on the other side of the station square. It swayed heavily from side to side, then leaned over and collapsed. At the right-hand corner of the square was another house with a van belonging to the Fujiya Hotel parked next to it. The house twisted in a strange contortion so that its paper-screen windows all snapped and sprang away from it as if beaten out by an invisible hand; then the whole building slipped sideways and fell. Screams and cries were coming from a number of places.

The convulsion seemed to end almost as soon as it had begun, but this was because Shirokichi had been so shaken he had lost all sense of time. Since everything seemed to have quietened down, Shirokichi picked himself up from the ground, only to be greeted by another shock. This had followed the first by a minute or two and was almost as bad, causing more houses to collapse. Cracks opened in the ground and mud spurted up through them. More shocks followed, but they were not as severe as the first two and gave people some assurance that no more damage was to follow. Shirokichi joined a small group wandering toward the houses that had collapsed. People were dragging tiles off the roofs and helping the unlucky victims to escape that way. Shirokichi saw a middle-aged woman whose hair had come loose being carried away. Her face and hands were covered with blood.

The sight of fresh blood seemed to shake Shirokichi from his stupor and made him wonder at what had happened. This could have been no ordinary earthquake. Mt. Hakone must have erupted. That would explain it. He came to this conclusion because he had been to the tourist spot of Owakudani (Great Boiling Valley), which is not far from Gora, and had been impressed by the hellish nature of this desolate place, with its bare, red earth from which clouds of sulfurous fumes poured forth; and he had trembled with awe at the living nature of the volcanic earth, for even on the high point above the crater he could feel the heat of it through his straw sandals.

Shirokichi now noticed a small man in black *haori* holding a raised umbrella in one hand and walking along, looking about him as if he were making a tour of inspection. It was Kiichiro, whom Shirokichi had completely forgotten about. The gold chain hanging across his chest occasionally caught the light of the sun as the umbrella moved, and glinted sharply. The umbrella was raised in order to keep off the hot rays of the sun. This reminded Shirokichi that it was indeed a very hot day and he became aware that his face was soaked in sweat.

He called out the doctor's name, and Kiichiro turned around with an expression of almost no surprise. He looked as if he felt it was not only quite natural that Shirokichi should be there, but absolutely essential too.

"Mihira," he said in his usual calm voice. "Well, you know this is a considerable earthquake. The trains won't be running now."

Shirokichi grunted rustic agreement at this, nodding his sweat-soaked head to make the affirmation clearer, although inside he was struck with wonder at Kiichiro's great calm and presence of mind.

Before long it was clear that fires had already begun to break out in a number of places, for a low pall of smoke started to form above the ruined town. Hordes of people were passing by, escaping with possessions clutched in their arms, and because of the afterquakes no one made any attempt to put the fires out. As the shaking of the cracked and splintered road on which he was standing continued, Shirokichi began to feel a new kind of anxiety.

"No good hanging about here now, is it? We'd better clear out somewhere."

Kiichiro was still gazing about him with eyes full of curiosity, so Shirokichi spoke in rather brusque, ill-mannered tones. Kiichiro nodded. Unlike Shirokichi, however, he was not thinking of finding somewhere nearby that was really safe, but only that he must get to

Tokyo at all costs. No doubt he was acutely anxious about the fate of his hospital, although he showed nothing of that in his face.

They made their way along the railway track eastward in the direction of the Sakawa River, a mile or so from Odawara Station. There were crowds of refugees in front and behind. Kiichiro had the wit to fold his umbrella and use it as a walking stick, and although he was only able to take very short strides he nipped along surprisingly smartly over the railway sleepers. Shirokichi followed after with the skirts of his kimono tucked up over his buttocks.

When Kiichiro saw the state of the steel bridge over the Sakawa River his face showed, for the first time, signs of confusion, of something close to panic. The bridge had fallen on its side and its twisted frame was in the water. Up to this point he had been walking at a tremendous pace, but now he slowed down completely and began to look exhausted. Another tremor chose this moment to rock the area, and Kiichiro decided to squat down and support himself with his hands on the ground.

"This is dangerous, really dangerous. Mihira, you had better go ahead of me."

So they ignored the bridge and followed another railway line which went northward following the river, until they arrived at a place called Shimosoga. The area near the station had been particularly badly hit, and the station building itself was razed to the ground. The rails here lay twisted upon each other in weird patterns under the burning, unlucky sun of late summer. Kiichiro gazed at the appalling sight, then went to check the damage. He ascertained that the nine members of the station staff had indeed been crushed to death.

Because of this detour, it was already getting late by the time they arrived at Kozu, which is no great distance from Odawara, although at least on the other side of the river. Kozu was on relatively high ground, so there seemed to have been surprisingly little damage. They obtained some tepid water from a house with a well, and decided to sleep on the gravel of the railway track because Kiichiro maintained there was least danger of the earth cracking open there, so they could sleep in safety. Owing to the strain and agitation, Shirokichi had forgotten that he must be hungry, although the continuing tremors ensured that he kept waking up anyway. Some time later, whether he was actually asleep or not he couldn't be sure, he was aware of Kiichiro making him get up. It was still only midnight. They walked along the railway in the dark, and just before dawn, as they were approaching Oiso, forty-odd miles from Tokyo, they came across the derailed train.

A number of passenger cars had fallen onto their sides, and the wooden walls and roofs had split open like burst pomegranates. There were many corpses, some of them decently covered with straw matting but others simply lying exposed to the sky and the eyes of any passerby. Soiled arms stuck out rigidly from some of the bodies. The sight filled Shirokichi with nausea and he turned his eyes away as he walked by. Kiichiro followed in silence.

That morning they found a grocery store open by Oiso Station, and bought a can of beef. When they asked if there was any rice they were offered the remnants of last night's supper. Since it had been used for *sushi* it had a vinegary taste, and while Shirokichi crammed his hungrily into his mouth Kiichiro ate none of it, merely adding a little water to the juice of the canned beef and sipping it straight from the tin. He gave all his rice and the bits of beef that were not tender enough to Shirokichi, who thought this behavior eccentric but was glad enough of it. Here they also managed to get hold of some leather-soled *tabi,* something like field sneakers, of the kind that Japanese laborers sometimes wear, and they changed into them.

So they walked on through Hiratsuka, Chigasaki, Fujisawa. At Totsuka, twenty-five miles from Tokyo, it was growing dark again. They found a house whose main gate was still solid though the earthen wall about it had crumbled.

"Mihira, here's a house that's been lucky. Built in the right place, you see. Got the geomancy right, whoever did it. Lucky for us, too. Why don't you go and ask them if they'll let us stay the night?"

"But look here, Doctor, you ought to go, Doctor, really you ought."

"I am asking you to go."

"No, Doctor, honest, you ought to go."

Shirokichi had decided to be obstinate, not only because he had no confidence in the way he talked, but also because the last twenty-four hours and more had given him considerable self-respect; he felt he was a person who shone once all artificial social distinctions had vanished and the chips were really down. Dr. Nire might be a gentleman of importance as he sat smiling condescendingly in a big house with a gold chain on his chest, but confront him with a natural disaster like this and how did he measure up? He was just a weak-kneed, feeble, useless old man. Hadn't he, Shirokichi, been obliged time and time again to go back and help him along?

The upshot was that Kiichiro did go first and ask at the house.

Shirokichi heard him say that he was the Director of the Nire Hospital of Mental Pathology. He also said that he was a former Member of the House of Representatives. Nobody seemed very impressed, but they managed to borrow mosquito nets from the house and by hanging them in the bamboo grove at the rear were able to get sleep of a kind. They also received some rice balls, which were freshly cooked and warm.

They left this place, too, while it was still dark, although even then there were scores of people urgently heading for Tokyo. Rumors of Koreans rioting were spreading like wildfire and people were keeping together in groups of ten or twenty as they walked by the railway. Right from the start Kiichiro had been limping and falling behind. Shirokichi himself had blisters all over his feet from the unfamiliar footwear, and as each blister burst it caused him considerable pain. Still, the thought of a band of Koreans suddenly appearing out of nowhere was more terrible than pains in the feet. They were said to have weapons, too. The group Kiichiro and Shirokichi had been walking with had disappeared into the darkness ahead of them some time ago, and the two of them had been left on their own.

"Mihira, it's no good. I can't go on any more."

Kiichiro had suddenly stopped dead and raised this plaintive cry; he sounded like a sulky little boy.

"No use saying things like that, Doctor. This isn't the right place or time. We can't hang about here; it's dangerous. Got to be moving on."

"I can't be moving on. I told you I can't go on any more."

It was clear at a glance that the little old man in his sweaty, dirty, ragged kimono had reached the end of his tether, both physically and mentally. Shirokichi gave in, feeling at his wits' end as well. He found the surrounding darkness frightening, but it couldn't be helped so he sat down by the side of the track and took a breather, a very restless kind of rest, and thought to himself that their situation was so hopeless that if the Koreans did appear he would have to run away and leave the doctor to their tender mercies.

Just as these thoughts were passing through his mind Kiichiro whispered to him:

"Mihira, it would be dangerous for you to walk on by yourself. Hardly anyone can understand a word you say. While you're mumbling away you'll be mistaken for a Korean."

This took Shirokichi aback for it suggested to his simple mind that the Director could read his thoughts. He thought the matter over again. He decided he didn't care if he was mistaken for a Korean. Take things as they come. Never say die. While there's life there's hope. In the end, however, he did not abandon the old doctor but urged that exhausted encumbrance on as far as Hodogaya, by which time he had come to accept the wisdom of Kiichiro's words.

Day had not yet dawned but people were assembled at each crossroads, and the ominous nature of these groups was obvious to everyone who passed. People held bamboo spears; there were even some who had naked swords thrust into the ground in front of them. At the next crossroads they came to, two young men, whom Shirokichi guessed to be Koreans, had been seized by a largish crowd and were being pushed, punched and jostled to the accompaniment of jeers and oaths.

Even Shirokichi and Kiichiro were interrogated. Kiichiro pointed out that he was the Director of the Nire Hospital and a former Diet member, but the young men of the Youth League looked suspiciously at Shirokichi, who kept his thick lips tightly sealed and was set trembling inside by new and unexpected fears. This reached a peak when he came across a recent corpse by the wayside, for it was clear at a glance that this was no earthquake victim but someone who had been cut down by human hands. He was glad now that he had stayed with the doctor. Indeed, as he had these thoughts, they seemed to be apprehended by the mind reader himself. Despite his wretched dress and haggard appearance, Kiichiro still managed to sound overweeningly proud of himself as he said in a tiny, hoarse voice:

"There. Look at that. Heaven knows what would have happened if you had wandered off by yourself. I told you, didn't I? And I was right."

They had been walking along roads for many miles now, and sometimes their way would be blocked by fallen telegraph poles and great tangled cobwebs of wires. In many places smoke was still rising from the embers of fires, and blackened people wandered among the smoldering ruins like wraiths.

They had finally made it as far as Tsurumi, which is just past Yokohama, and still had a good ten miles to go, when Shirokichi and Kiichiro, who looked ready to drop at any moment, were visited by a great stroke of good fortune in the shape of the car of an acquaintance of Kiichiro's who just happened to be passing that spot. This acquaintance had only a short distance to go, but when he reached home he ordered his chauffeur to drive on to Aoyama with the two safely aboard. This stroke of luck reduced Kiichiro to virtual prostration, and he had clawed his way into the car as if he had lost the use of his arms and legs, and sat there for a while gasping for breath. But now that there was no longer any need to walk, there were many interesting and astonishing sights to observe from the window, and he strove to take in as much of the disaster as possible. This, too, became tiring after a while, and he closed his eyes, the only sign of life being the occasional flicker of an eyelid, momentarily revealing a deathlike eyeball. Shirokichi began to feel worried and asked him if he was all right, but there was no reply. Kiichiro was still sitting with eyes closed or partially closed when the car entered the main road at Aoyama.

Aoyama did not appear to be all that damaged. There were no signs of any fires having broken out, and most of the houses seemed to be standing intact. They soon arrived at Moto-no-hara, but with the paradoxical feeling that they had come to the wrong place, for there was the Nire Hospital just as before, white and magnificent, its cluster of towers still soaring into the sky, with not a single one missing. Kiichiro opened his eyes slightly and spoke, not in his usual calm voice but in one that was almost harsh with triumph:

"No building I put up falls down that easily. There you are, then. Bound to be like that. Always knew it. Perfectly natural."

But as they got nearer it became clear that the hospital had not escaped damage entirely. The brick wall that Kiichiro every so often had repainted in striking fashion to make it look new had collapsed in a number of places, and in others it stood in jagged, jutting formations like incompetent examples of the small child's playbrick-building art. Broken masonry lay in scattered heaps beside it. Also half the tiles had fallen off the roof. Worst of all, the marble walls and columns were defaced with long scars and cracks. Afterward, when Shirokichi had the opportunity to inspect the damage, he was amazed to find that what he had thought to be stone throughout was nothing of the kind, for the wood was there for all to see through the scars, particularly in the case of the columns where the coating was thin. He reflected in his rustic way that he would be darned if it wasn't a case of the wolf losing the sheep's clothing, or the fried shrimp peeping out through its coat of batter, for it was lowly images like these that appealed to his mind.

But these reflections came much later. Now, as the car drew up in front of the entrance hall, the word was swiftly passed around that the Director had returned safely, and crowds of people came running out, making such a great commotion that one might think they had been startled by a ghost; or so it seemed to Shirokichi. He also saw there were a number of soldiers with fixed bayonets in the background to one side of the entrance hall. These were soldiers of the Third Regiment who had been sent to guard the hospital, and the dull glint of their bayonets together with the long cracks in the walls and the heaps of broken tiles brought home the gravity and abnormality of the situation.

Shirokichi was obliged to get out first since he was sitting by the nearside door; but nobody said a word to him, almost pushing him aside to get at Kiichiro. It was clear to all, just from the filthiness of his clothes, that the Director was in a parlous state. And though Kiichiro brushed aside those helping hands, even he could not manage his normal friendly nods and smiles and words, but simply gazed at the cracked columns of the entrance hall. It was at this moment that his eldest daughter came running out to greet him.

Ryuko was dressed in a way that expressed her own sense of responsibility, strain, and self-importance and manifested that concern with herself which the excitements of the past few days had further exaggerated. She wore a light crepe kimono with the sleeves bound up in workmanlike fashion, and what appeared to be straw sandals, though on closer inspection they turned out to be perfectly respectable slippers that had been tied tightly to her feet with string. A short sword stuck out ostentatiously from her sash. Her long face with its slightly hooked nose, which in normal circumstances always carried a hint of stern authority, had never looked so stubbornly heroic. Her long, narrow eyes seemed to slant upward, and Shirokichi, who had always kept a respectful distance from his brother's bride, literally took a few paces backward as he saw her approach, for she irresistibly brought to mind images of heroes and heroines of antiquity at that crowning moment when, after long years of trial and patient waiting, they are presented with the opportunity to strike down, in an act of perfect vengeance, the dastard who has besmirched the family's honor.

Ryuko pushed her way through the crowd and stood before her father. Her face showed no trace of any vulgar relief at his return, nor of any plebeian and sentimental welcome. That tense will, the blind faith that it was her mission to protect the hospital in her father's absence, prevented any weak relaxation of the facial muscles, which maintained all the cold severity of a No mask. She spoke with darting movements of the mouth, almost in one breath:

"You are indeed welcome home. The hospital is safe. All, including the patients, are safe. All in Hakone with Mother are safe also. News arrived yesterday that Mother had traveled to Mishima by Ten Counties Pass.''

The gardener had come all the way from Hakone to bring the information that Hisa, Momoko, Yasusaburo and the servants at the cottage had not been hurt in the disaster. He had traveled day and night to bring the news, arriving the day before Kiichiro managed to get here.

Kiichiro, on the contrary, did not acquit himself with any dignity. As he gazed at his favorite child, who was thirty years old this year, and observed her dauntless bearing as she greeted him, he responded in a way he would not normally have dreamed of doing. He lost all his usual self-control and calm objectivity and rejoiced, in an oddly disquieting fashion. This was the Kiichiro who had refused to bat an eyelid when the legs of the leaping patient had crashed so abruptly through the roof of his car; the Kiichiro whose calm became even greater and more pompous when all about him grew flustered. Little of that cool, heroic figure was apparent now. The past three days had taken their toll both physically, for he was an old man of little bodily strength, and mentally, and he seemed to have wholly lost his normal composure. All he could manage was a half cheer, half groan, and then his face relaxed into an expression of foolish blankness, and a great many wrinkles at whose existence none had guessed chose this moment to make their appearance. He failed to reply to his daughter's announcement, he paid no friendly compliments to those about him; he merely stood there, small and uncertain, like an animal at bay, and slowly turned around twice as if he were searching for something.

Finally Kiichiro seemed to find what he was looking for, some outlet for the confused emotions that had him in their spell. This was the chauffeur who had driven him here from Tsurumi. He grasped the simple man by the sleeve as if he were smartly arresting some obtuse criminal. Then he pulled out his bulging crocodile-skin wallet, which he would never normally allow to move far from the protective warmth of his body, and urged it upon the man.

''Look here, fellow, this is for you. All of it. I'm giving it to you. Take it with you. Come on. Take it. Take it.''

After some resistance the chauffeur accepted the wallet, and now Kiichiro gave another frank demonstration of a true self that was usually hidden: he staggered feebly and seemed about to collapse. Immediately the Deputy, Hidekichi Katsumata, leaped to his support, but unfortunately he was even smaller than the Director and was in danger of keeling over with his master on top of him until happily supported by the hands of another seven or eight people.

In this atmosphere of theatrical confusion Kiichiro was borne inside the hospital. His footwear was removed, causing fresh perturbation in those about him, for his white feet were covered with cuts and blisters and horribly swollen. Since they had no running water a bucket of muddy water was brought from the well round the back, and an excessive number of helping hands set to work, washing his feet and applying ointment and bandages to his wounds.

While all this was going on Shirokichi was totally ignored, as if he had not been involved in this business in any way whatsoever. He just stood there awkwardly, occasionally wiping the sweat off his uncouth face with the back of his hand. Later, he washed himself down with the bucket of water, now a deep brown color, that had been used to wash the Director's feet.

Chapter

9

The prow cut through the glorious, deep blue, tropic sea. Waves created by that motion kept up a perpetual slapping sound about the ship's long sides, their foam dissolving back through faintly glittering water toward the horizon where far clouds made thin, slow spirals. Just before noon the shapes of two or three small dark green islands appeared far ahead of them, and then another island with a mountain just like Fuji, encircled with white clouds.

There was an American child who seemed to spend all day pestering adults to play deck golf with him and then screwing up his obscenely fat red face and howling because he couldn't bear to lose. Now he was standing by the rail and bawling in his perpetually irritating voice that everybody must come and see the sight he was so energetically pointing out to them. Tetsukichi, sweat oozing from his face, walked aft, away from the noisy area, ascended to the bridge, borrowed a pair of binoculars, and looked through them. The trees of the island, which had seemed so Japanese in shape, turned out to be coconut palms, looking exactly as they look in paintings, almost absurdly so. Virgin jungle stretched away beyond them. It was just another small island in the South Seas.

To the side of it, perpetually far off, an apparent archipelago was in fact a largish continent, appearing and then disappearing in deep cloud. Finally this came nearer, became real mountains in a misted, light blue shadow.

"That's Sumatra, the main island," the ship's officer standing at his side informed him.

Tetsukichi nodded and handed back the binoculars, looking now with naked eyes at what had once again become low-lying land half hidden in light mist. As he looked, he felt an odd sense of affectionate recognition, which after a while was replaced with a sense of irritation it was difficult to account for. The land he was staring at looked to him like Japan, and he could not work out whether this was because most lands looked alike when seen at a distance from the sea, or because the three and a half years he had spent abroad had given him such a longing to see his own country that what he actually saw aroused in him an illusory sense of recognition. Since there was no way of knowing which was true he had no desire to come to any conclusion about the matter, and was left with a feeling of mild frustration.

After lunch, one quarter of the sky clouded over and curtains of rain appeared from time to time, announcing the presence of squalls. The direction in which the ship was heading hazed over and the movements of the clouds suddenly became more obvious and erratic. Then, on the ocean, which had been so flat and calm, a long approaching swell appeared, glinting grayly in the sun which still shone above the ship. The squall struck with a swift burst of wind and rain that beat horizontally against the portholes, but it was soon over. The sky appeared once more, suddenly full of dazzling particles of light. But the squall had at least made the humidity and heat a little more bearable.

Ryuko was reclining in a deck chair next to one of the American passengers. She was wearing a dress of purple georgette with a great many pleats in the skirt, which Tetsukichi felt did not suit her at all. A wide-brimmed horsehair hat decked with satin ribbon was pulled down over her face to keep the sun out of her eyes. She was pretending to be asleep. Tetsukichi, despite his long stay abroad, felt uncomfortable in the presence of foreigners, and since he had no skill in the English tongue his relationship with the Americans and others on board was restricted to passing the time of day. Ryuko, on the other hand, spent much more time with these people than with the other Japanese on board, virtually pushing her way into conversations with them. Tetsukichi had overheard some of these conversations and had noted each time that she began with her few words of broken English but would soon change casually into Japanese, regardless of the fact that her companions had no idea what she was talking about; although if one of the ship's officers passed by she would coerce him into acting as interpreter. She would even play with little foreign children, holding their hands and tickling them and, confident that she would not be understood, making remarks about them to their faces that could be taken as insults if one were so minded:

"What a cute little child you are, with your face just like a teeny-weeny monkey."

She had arrived in Europe three months before. Tetsukichi had completed his work and met her in Paris, and after a brisk tour through a number of countries they had finally left Marseilles toward the end of November, 1924, aboard the *Haruna Maru*. Before that, in the intervals of their busy tourist schedule, at hotels, in restaurants, and on trains, Ryuko had given her husband vivid details of the earthquake disaster, speaking as if the heavens had aimed this catastrophe uniquely at her. The first shock had been so enormous that the brick wall of the Nire Hospital had immediately collapsed into the road. The first night she had slept in a state of constant anxiety because of further earth tremors and news of Korean uprisings. The Deputy had simply trembled with fear and been of no use whatsoever, and she had not known if her father was alive or dead. So she had taken over the reins of the hospital and scolded the wavering staff into doing their jobs, but the hospital had only enough rice to feed its four hundred and more mouths for five days. So, girding on her trusty sword, she had hurried hither and thither, now to the ward office with the hopeless Deputy to arrange for a distribution of rice, now to the post office to send a cable to Tetsukichi. Then her father had finally turned up.

"Father was so overcome with joy at seeing me still alive that he fainted on the spot. Then he gave his wallet with all his money in it to the chauffeur. It did seem such a waste."

But Kiichiro was not the kind of man to lie in a stupor on his bed for very long, even if his feet were covered with blisters. He got together all the available money in the hospital, called Shirokichi Mihira to his bedside, and gave it to him, ordering him to return immediately to Yamagata, there to buy rice and sheets of galvanized iron, hire carpenters and coolies, and send the whole lot to Tokyo.

"Father really does think things out so quickly. Still, let's face it, he is quite old now, mixing Bordeaux with his oatmeal and becoming just a tiny bit forgetful these days. Once you're back in Tokyo he won't have to do any more dreary work, will he?"

Tetsukichi asked what had happened to Shun'ichi, since she never once mentioned their son during her recital of what had happened during the earthquake. It appeared that after the first few minutes, when people ran about seeking safety as best they could, and once the aftershocks had quietened down a little, she had urged the Deputy to see what had happened to the patients and staff, and then she remembered Shun'ichi and found him in a corner of the garden, clinging to Nanny Shimoda and crying his eyes out.

"Every time there was a little tremor after that the child was so frightened he refused to come into the house. He was like that for ages, and slept each night in the car."

Tetsukichi felt genuinely angry as he listened to this intrepid daughter of his adoptive father, a woman of such dauntless spirit that she didn't have time to think about her own child, and with such an indefatigable appetite that she never stopped eating while she recited these facts; and perhaps, in secret, he began to hate this wife of his.

Then Ryuko launched into one of her diatribes against her brothers and sisters. There was Momoko, for example, who had graduated from her girls' high school in the spring of this year, 1924, and been taken straight to Hankow—by Ryuko, of course. But the girl was so ignorant, so selfish, so completely willful and sluttish, so totally lacking in any conception, any consciousness of herself as a daughter of the Nire household, that she had spent the whole voyage crying and whimpering—it was the most appalling, the most disgraceful spectacle you could imagine. . . Ryuko's attitude suggested that only three subjects were worthy of reverence and praise—her father, herself and the hospital—and everyone else could be scorned and vilified. Since, in her nobility of soul, she seemed indifferent to what happened to her own son, she could hardly be expected to show any concern for that life devoid of comfort which her husband had been obliged to endure in a country still suffering the disorders arising from defeat in war. And she did not do so. In Germany there were no earthquakes; no Nire Hospital.

For Tetsukichi, however, the earthquake had existed in Germany in a very real sense. After seeing the newspaper article that announced the disaster, he had spent nearly a fortnight in a state of great anxiety over something that was all too real to him, but whose reality he could not grasp.

The next morning's newspapers had reported as follows. Tokyo had been put under curfew and martial law. Two hundred thousand people in Yokohama had nowhere to live and nothing to eat. According to a dispatch from New York, President Coolidge had sent a telegram of sympathy to the Japanese "Mikado" and ordered the American fleet at Port Arthur to set sail for Japan. The seismological recordings in Munich had begun to register at 4:11 on the morning of the 1st of September (German time) and reached their most violent readings just before five o'clock. That was all.

Two days later new reports came in. The death toll had already reached half a million. Many dormant volcanoes of all sizes had begun to be active again, and Tokyo, Yokohama, Atami, Gotenba (near Mt. Fuji) and Hakone had been wiped off the map. The seat of government had been moved down to the Kansai area, part in Osaka and part in Kyoto. Tokyo was still a sea of flames, and all telecommunications had been discontinued.

Even the diligent Tetsukichi lost any desire to go to his laboratory after reading that. For the next two days he remained shut up in his lodgings, making, as it were, unconscious arrangements to pack up and leave. He kept finding himself tidying up his possessions. When he managed to drag himself to the restaurant, a number of people stood up and came over to offer their sympathies, but all Tetsukichi could do was look at them with a dazed, idiotic expression on his face before pulling himself together and blurting out the word "*danke*." Eventually an article which claimed to be based on direct reports from Japan to London appeared in the newspaper, but it made the situation seem even more critical. It wrote of clashes between the civil population and the military, street fighting between Koreans and units of the army, of an assassination plot aimed at the new Prime Minister, Viscount Yamamoto, and of the deaths of a number of cabinet ministers.

Reading unreliable newspaper reports in a land thousands of miles away from the event was a wholly new experience for Tetsukichi. Even his complex, painstaking researches had given him no taste of how terrible the inability to separate the true from the false could be. One line of close print would lead to black speculations ten times as dreadful as the dubious, inflated facts actually given. Tetsukichi had almost decided there was no hope for his family. Each night he could hardly sleep and when, just before dawn, he finally managed to, he would be visited by even more dreams than ever, a constant onslaught of them. One that recurred was of a woman who looked like Ryuko and a child like Shun'ichi, but they both sat on *tatami* facing away from him so he could not be sure. No matter how many times he called their names they would not look around. The dream ended at that point, but it was so similar to those he had had of his father that he felt they must also be dead, and he tried to make himself accept the fact. One night he had a terrible dream full of flames and smoke. He was wandering in hell; and when he awoke his whole body was drenched in sweat.

Then, midway through September, a telegram came at last: "Family and hospital safe." So he went into town to drink beer, and as he listened to the laborers around him bawling out their songs he felt the pain that had racked him for so long start to ease. The next day he went out again to buy the materials he needed for his laboratory work, and while he was choosing some pigments he was suddenly overwhelmed by feelings of gratitude toward the gods and buddhas of his native land.

Tetsukichi now went to work every day with a sense of urgency. It was only the end of September but already the leaves of the wayside trees were turning yellow and falling. And there seemed to be something else, not related to the season, that drifted through the streets, an abnormal, unprecedented something that one could not quite put one's finger on. The mark continued to fall on the international exchange markets, and meetings organized by the National Socialist Party were banned, the halls and beer cellars in which these meetings had been taking place coming under the strict surveillance of the army and the police. But none of this had anything to do with Tetsukichi, so he continued his daily attendance at his laboratory and classes.

Letters from home followed the telegram, all urging him to return as soon as possible. He sat in a corner of the grubby restaurant and closed his eyes for a long time, running his fingers through his already graying hair and trying to pluck up the courage to resist these perfectly reasonable demands to which he could so easily have assented. But he had pledged himself not to throw away the one chance he would have in his whole life. Call it selfishness; he simply could not drop this task, even though it was a self-appointed one.

Winter came early that year. On the 8th of November, 1923, the first snow fell, whitening the roofs of the ancient city and settling in the streets. It was a bitterly cold day, a day on which the exchange rate reached the astonishing level of 2,793,000,000,000 marks to one pound sterling. Tetsukichi spent the morning looking at specimens in the laboratory and then attended two clinical lectures in the afternoon. After dinner he went to listen to a lecture given at the Psychiatric Society which turned into a lengthy debate, not ending until after eleven o'clock. The snow had stopped falling and fog lay over the frozen streets. As he passed the Central Station he saw that the square was full of people. He had no idea what was going on but could feel a tense, turbulent atmosphere building up there, so he hurried on home. By the time he was back in his lodgings and in bed it was already past midnight, but he could hear dogs barking, and columns of soldiers tramped down his street, singing martial songs in clear, firm voices.

The next morning, as he hurried to his laboratory wondering if it was going to snow again, he noticed a number of soldiers stationed at vantage points here and there. When he arrived he learned for the first time what had happened the previous night, although he was so obtuse about political matters he could grasp only the vaguest outlines. It seemed there had been a large meeting in the huge Hoffbräu beer cellar at which State Commissioner General Gustav von Kahr and the Bavarian Army Commander, General Otto von Lossow, had made speeches. While this was going on, Adolf Hitler entered at the head of an armed contingent, climbed onto a table, and fired one shot from his revolver into the ceiling. He then yelled: "The national revolution has begun. This hall has been occupied by six hundred fully armed men. Nobody must leave. The Bavarian and Reich governments have been removed and a provisional national government formed. The army and the police are marching on the city under the swastika banner."

The beer-cellar putsch ended in failure. The army occupied the Odeonsplatz and barricaded the two main gates into the city.

That evening, as he was eating dinner at his usual restaurant, one of the waitresses came around announcing that there would be a curfew from eight o'clock that night. He went outside and felt as if some huge store of energy in this city under martial law was waiting to erupt, and he kept unconsciously quickening his pace as he walked back to his lodgings. He came out of a side street into the Odeonsplatz and saw there a company of soldiers with machine guns, and two columns of cavalry with black tassels hanging from their naked lances. The street-cars were no longer running in Ludwichstrasse, nor were there any carriages or cars; only a light mist and a mysterious, frozen silence seemed to occupy the streets.

Two days later all classes at the university were canceled. Tetsukichi went to his old landlady's place. She was sitting in a corner of her dark kitchen watching over her equally aged, unhealthy-looking canary, and her words confirmed his misgivings:

"They say a hundred students have been killed. The army from Berlin should arrive here tonight. Then it will become very dangerous."

The curfew and the ominous atmosphere that attended it lasted for a number of days. In order to forget his own anxieties Tetsukichi absorbed himself in his work, for there was a remoteness about the laboratory that made it quite different from elsewhere, a cold world apart. Martial law came to an end, the curfew was suspended, and at his grimy table in the restaurant Tetsukichi read about the trial of

Hitler and nine others, including Ludendorff and Kriebel, for treason, as if it were happening in some distant world. The wild inflation continued until one pound sterling would buy 12,000,000,000,000 marks. This added more worries to his daily life since every time he wanted to buy some books he was obliged to run to the bank and then dash back to the bookstore with a suitcase full of banknotes—notes that would have lost half their value by the next day. . .

"Still, that's all over now," Tetsukichi thought to himself, feeling an upsurge of emotion close to pure joy pulsing through his body with the throbbing of the ship. He was on his way home, returning to Japan now with no regrets. His three and a half years of labor had provided him with all the material he needed, the books that would form the basis of his future research, and he felt like congratulating himself on having collected so much under such adverse conditions. Most of them would have arrived in Japan long ago and must now be safely lodged in the Nire Hospital storehouse. Also, just before they left Marseilles, he had heard that the thesis he had completed in Vienna and sent back to Japan had passed the examining board and that he had been awarded the M.D. his adoptive parents had always hoped he would obtain. Tetsukichi began to feel confident that his lot when he returned to Japan would be quite different from what it had been before. Obviously he would have to take over from the aging Kiichiro, and this would entail days filled with diagnoses at first; but there was no need to expand a hospital of that size, and providing he simply kept it as it was, the numerous interns whom Kiichiro had raised into doctors could take over the work, as no doubt they had already largely done. He could count on at least half the time and money that Kiichiro had spent on politics, and he would not waste it on any similar foolishness. Tetsukichi began to imagine his own, at first modest, laboratory. It would be set up somewhere in a corner of the hospital, and he felt a glow of warmth inside as a clear image of it appeared before his eyes. He had no intention of trying to compete with people in research posts at universities. He would work at his own pace, slowly, devoting the rest of his life to it. . .

So the ship glided smoothly through the Strait of Malacca after completing its long journey across the Indian Ocean, and the sense this gave of calm accomplishment after long trials was the same as that which Tetsukichi felt inside himself. The sea now had a greenness about it, and the water nearest the ship was a dull, leaden color. There was no swell, only a very fine rippling over the whole surface of the water, as though fingers were being run over an elephant's hide, as the ship went gliding forward.

Ryuko came up to him: "Isn't it lovely now the thing's stopped rolling. . . I wonder if that woman called Thompson or whatever actually speaks English. I can't understand a word she says."

"With so many Japanese on board I can't think why you always make a point of only speaking to foreigners."

"It's because I don't like listening to what other people have to say," she said carelessly. When she was not obliged to speak courteously she talked in a very blunt and slipshod manner. "Everybody's bored to death, with nothing to do, and I don't want them telling me the dreary story of their lives. If it's not that, it's someone like that so-called musician who's traveling third class going on about Captain Amakasu or whatever, some kind of socialist as far as I can make out. . ."

Captain Amakasu was a member of the military police who had made use of the social disorder at the time of the earthquake to kill off the odd anarchist, including Sakae Osugi, and had been the subject of a famous trial. Tetsukichi pointed out that it must surely be the same sort of thing when she spoke to foreigners.

"I'm sure it is, but it doesn't matter what they say because I can't understand it, you see. That's a blessing in itself."

Tetsukichi was lost for an answer and looked down over the rail, watching the foam breaking from the bow and drifting away.

"I wonder how Shun'ichi's getting on."

"Not again," said Ryuko in the weariest of tones. "He's growing, no doubt. He's grown. I don't expect he'll even recognize you. What he most likes playing at is war between Japan and America."

"War between Japan and America?"

"Oh, you know, that anti-Japanese law they passed in America this year, the whatsit, the Immigration Act. It's all about that. Everyone in the hospital got all worked up about it. Kumagoro, you know. Well, Kumagoro made a speech at the cookhouse about how we had to strike back at America . . . at least so the Deputy told me. And it's spread to Yonekuni and Shun'ichi. I suppose it really wouldn't be a joke if Yonekuni had to fight against America considering what his name means, but still. Anyway, all the kids' magazines are full of stuff about the future war, and Shun'ichi keeps on and on asking me to buy him model battleships."

Tetsukichi smiled and said at least it showed the boy was full of spirit.

"Only at home, though," replied his unsmiling wife, following her principle of praising absolutely nothing and nobody outside the charmed triangle of father, hospital and herself. "At school he just shrinks up in a corner. He really is exactly like you, although his face has perhaps a little of Father."

And Ryuko launched into another peroration about her father's virtues, indifferent to whether her husband wanted to listen or not. The main building of the hospital had been completely undamaged by the earthquake. True, a few cracks had appeared, in fact quite a lot of them, indeed so many as to astonish Ryuko herself, in the walls, the balcony and the columns; and various hidden wooden aspects of the structure had obtruded themselves on the eye. But this had provided yet another opportunity for Kiichiro to display his inexhaustible genius, and the blemishes were removed in no time. He had lots of twists of tough Japanese paper made, and these were dipped in concrete and stuffed into the cracks. Concrete was smeared on top of this and, with the help of a hone, the hospital was restored to its former palatial grandeur.

"Father's having a new house built just for us, across from the hospital on the left-hand side."

This was the first time Ryuko had mentioned anything of this, and she did so with her usual triumphant look of satisfaction.

"I was told not to say a word about it to you. They started building it just before I left. Of course I said any number of times that it was an awful waste of money, and really we didn't need anything like that. Still, I'm certainly looking forward to seeing what kind of house it is."

Ryuko then went on to relate how Kiichiro had decided not to stand for the Diet that year. There had been the earthquake, and the political groundwork in Yamagata had not gone very well, but, of course, the main thing was that he had succumbed to the stern opposition of his wife. When she reached this point Ryuko began to speak at an even more breakneck pace, as if overwhelmed with sympathy for her disappointed father.

"Naturally there was some truth in what Mother said, but I know he would have been elected if he had only been given another chance. I mean, he could hardly have lost to that awful Kenseikai person. And then he'd have been able to go to the Imperial Palace again and offer his credentials. . ."

Tetsukichi listened to this in gloomy silence, which did not prevent Ryuko from going on much more cheerfully:

"Father is really looking forward to your homecoming. He's building you a new house, and I'm quite sure he'll have had the whole of the hospital's front wall repainted for you. . ."

Her tone of voice implied that, since a person of the caliber of Kiichiro Nire was showering such honors on him, Tetsukichi would have to redouble his zeal and responsibility. Behind all she said there was the obvious demand that Tetsukichi should help her aging father make the Nire Hospital even more prosperous and magnificent.

Singapore . . . then Hong Kong. The ship did not seem to make much headway; it was the slowness of its motion that most impressed itself on Tetsukichi. Yet he knew that every minute brought them nearer Japan, nearer his homeland; and his awareness of this seemed to grow. In Singapore the signs in Chinese reminded him of home, and the occasional "Japanese Barber" or "Japanese Drugstore" appeared among them. On the streetcar, during a brief trip ashore, he had trouble because he could not understand what was being said to him, and a Malay came up and translated for him in broken Japanese: "What, what?" he said. "One man four sen, two sen change." But what he most enjoyed had been the sight, as they were leaving port, of an old Japanese man on the quayside who was seeing the ship off. He was wearing a magnificently old-fashioned outfit of bowler hat, black *montsuki,* and white *tabi* socks, and had a fan in his right hand. Tetsukichi could have gone on looking at him forever, but his nagging wife called him over to her side of the ship, where the passengers were tossing silver coins into the sea in some sort of competition with each other. The idea was that natives on a flat-bottomed boat nearby should dive in after the coins and retrieve them, which they very cleverly did.

"I suppose if it's a copper coin they wouldn't even give it a second glance. Pretty cool customers, I must say. I wouldn't throw any money to a lot of natives. Absolutely wasted on them," she said with indignation.

That was Singapore. When they steamed out from Hong Kong the year was drawing to its close, for it was noon on the 29th of December. After lunch Tetsukichi came up on deck. To the left he could see quite clearly the mountains of the Chinese mainland, and ahead were numerous small islands of red rock. On the turbid sea, black junks floated as if asleep. He looked back and already the tall hill of Hong Kong was fading away.

"It won't be long now," he thought. "We're as good as home."

One of the ship's crew, a man who had gained some popularity at the fancy dress ball the night before with his impersonation of the well-known burglar Jiraiya (the human landmine, master of a thousand and one disguises and noisy disappearing tricks) in his most famous transformation as a toad, now passed by beaming all over his face. This stocky, dwarfish man had long been notorious because he greeted all the passengers with exactly the same words, assuring them that it would not be long now, for once you were through the Suez Canal you were as good as back home in Japan. This sort of thing could definitely get on one's nerves during a long sea voyage, but Tetsukichi now found himself smiling in response to the man's well-meaning grin.

Then, just as he was thinking of going down to the saloon for a short rest, a man called Sakurai, who was working for some trading company and had joined the ship at Port Said, came up to him. Sakurai had a peculiarly grating voice and would burst into great roars of laughter (in which no one else joined) at the amusing criticisms he had to make of his fellow passengers, or at the jocular nicknames he found for the foreign girls who showed so little interest in him, and which consisted of such barbs of wit as Miss Maruko and Miss Ketsuko, or "Miss Fatty" and "Miss Fanny." His laughter was all the more noticeable because it was so extraordinarily uninfectious.

Now, however, he was looking serious for a change, and he glanced carefully about him before saying:

"Mr. Nire, there's a telegram arrived at our Hong Kong branch says there's been a fire at some private mental institution in Tokyo. People died in it, apparently."

Tetsukichi was momentarily startled, but soon decided it could not possibly have anything to do with the Nire Hospital, and left the matter at that.

After dinner, however, the ship's purser came over with a copy of a Hong Kong English-language newspaper. There was a short news report to the effect that there had been a fire in a private mental hospital in Tokyo and out of a total of 343 patients 108 were missing and 13 corpses had been recovered from the burned-out ruins. No mention was made of the place or of the name of the hospital, but the reported number of patients meant that the possibility of its being the Nire Hospital could not be ruled out. But Tetsukichi pushed the idea aside. After all, look how desperate he had been at the time of the earthquake. Surely he was overreacting again this time too.

"We're not the only private mental institution in Tokyo, you know," he said with an artless smile. He had meant to speak in a jocular tone of voice, but this seemed to have got lost somewhere by the time the words arrived at his lips.

"Well, Purser, shall we bet on it?" said Ryuko in a defiantly lighthearted way.

"Bet? What are you suggesting we bet on, Mrs. Nire?" The purser, a round-faced, honest-looking man, allowed a smile to appear on his cheeks and turned toward Ryuko.

"If this fire's at our hospital I'll let you have that wall hanging I acquired in Egypt. If not, then you'll have to give me something."

"That's hardly fair, madam. I mean, if your hospital has been burned to the ground"—here the purser hesitated slightly but went on—"it would hardly be right for me to take anything off you, would it?"

"Oh, there's no need to worry about that. I would be happy to give you the thing, anyway, for all the kindness you've shown us."

This made the reluctant purser even more reluctant, at which point the ship's doctor, who was sitting at the same table, put in a few wise words:

"Well, let's say this, if no telegram has arrived by tomorrow morning, then we can say that the lady has won her wager."

"Exactly. I shall win. And you, poor man, will have to pay up." Ryuko sounded almost flirtatious as she said this.

But Tetsukichi had had enough. "For heaven's sake!" he said in his clumsy way. "What's wrong with you? I thought you really liked that wall hanging." And he took Ryuko almost forcibly back to their cabin.

Neither of them could settle down, however, and Ryuko seemed to be in an even worse state of nerves than Tetsukichi himself. He gave her some sleeping tablets and made her go to bed early, while he went out to take a turn around the deck. There was no moon, only a black expanse of sea. The ship swayed slowly as it made its way through the pitch darkness. The phosphorescence which had been so conspicuous all through the Strait of Malacca did not seem to exist in this sea. There was only the tireless throbbing of the ship, the smell of the sea air mingled with that of the paintwork, then a breeze from off the sea that felt cold upon the skin. He saw the single light of another ship and watched it until it vanished far away on the port side. The restlessness that had beset him had still not ceased. He shook his head as if to shake himself free of his unease and returned to his cabin. He changed into his night clothes, turned off the light, and crawled into bed.

It must have been around eleven o'clock. He had still not got off properly to sleep when he heard a knock at the cabin door, and he leaped, almost fell, out of bed. At the same time he was aware that Ryuko had woken and was sitting up in bed.

When he opened the door the purser was standing there. With his face slightly lowered he said:

"Dr. Nire. In fact it was your place."

Then he handed him a telegram.

The burned-out ruins of the hospital were covered with a thick growth of weed. According to one of the interns who was interested in botany, the weed was a type imported from the North American continent, something called horseweed, a wild plant belonging to the chrysanthemum family, also known in this country as railroad weed and sometimes as Meiji weed, this last name indicating the era in which it had made its first appearance on these shores. But the weed had come to the hospital that spring, covering the whole area with its soft foliage. It had shown an extraordinary power to grow and increase, and even the most tenacious of other weeds, such as goosefoot, had eventually given up the unequal struggle. As summer approached it grew to shoulder height and more, and the formerly soft leaves became large and dry, alien growths with not the slightest sentimental appeal. The plant produced a flower with a yellow center and small, white petals, and the whole area was covered with these characterless leaves and tedious flowers, a fitting tribute to the chaos that presided over this small corner of the world.

A full half year had passed since the fire at the end of last year, which had been caused by neglecting to put out the fire used in the annual rice-cake making just before New Year. A dozen or more people had died in it. The iron gates and the brick wall remained, but they were so blackened it was hard to believe they were the same that had previously stood in front of the Nire Hospital, and they merely added to the sense of desolation. There was now a small, inadequate surgery for outpatients in a temporary building in the area where the main entrance hall had been. Beyond the wide expanse of weeds, away on the left-hand side, there was a single two-storied house, built of wood though some kind of white stone material had been applied over the exterior. This was the new house that Kiichiro had built to celebrate Tetsukichi's return, and although it had not completely escaped the fire it had fortunately been preserved and later repaired. It now served as the living quarters for the whole family. At what had originally been the back of the hospital the members of the much reduced staff were now living in hastily erected shacks.

Nothing remained of the hospital itself whose proud appearance had once enthralled the eye and taken away the breath. The sky of early summer hung over this emptiness in which the tough and ominous-looking weed held sway. Of those towers and columns that had once persuaded people that here indeed were the marble halls of far-off lands, not a trace remained; they had vanished like a dream. The 340-odd inpatients had likewise disappeared; not one of them remained. The whole hospital now consisted of one temporary building, about eighty square yards in area, which housed the outpatients surgery; this was the extent of its clinical facilities. But the fire had taken place six months ago. Surely there should have been more positive signs of reconstruction than this?

Well, the fact is that there had been not one misfortune but a whole series of them. The year before, the insurance policy on the hospital had run out and Kiichiro had decided not to renew it:

"Frankly, you know, that sort of thing, it's simply throwing money away, or just helping the insurance companies grow rich."

Certainly his policy of not crossing bridges before he came to them, in fact not crossing them at all but simply plunging wildly into the water and struggling across, had paid off handsomely on a number of occasions before. Also, had he not acquired and set up a considerable number of fire hydrants, after wisely considering the case of the recent fire at the Oji Hospital, which had been a great talking point during the year? Yes, he had, and hoses as well in strategic places. But the fire had broken out just after everyone had gone to bed and they were all too busy running for their lives to think about hydrants and hoses. The fire had spread remarkably quickly, one reason being the amount of fresh paint that the Director had splashed all over the place to welcome his adopted son home from Europe. Not only had the front of the building been newly painted but also the most unattractive wards poked away round the back. Even the cookhouse had received its share of highly inflammable decoration. Whatever the reason, the whole hospital was burned to the ground overnight; there was no insurance compensation forthcoming; and, as if to crown their woes, the present legal situation did not permit any attempt at rebuilding.

Since some of the patients had died in the blaze Kiichiro was subjected to a police investigation and the censure of the world at large.

The hospital was on rented land, and because the landlord wished to expel Kiichiro from his property there was talk of legal proceedings. The whole neighborhood began to view the hospital with coldness, open misgivings and unfriendly mutterings which would have been unthinkable in the days of its prosperity. It was said that the hospital housed lunatics, maniacs, nuts and cranks and was a very dangerous place to have around. A campaign against the rebuilding of the hospital took shape, instigated apparently by the landlord who was to be the hospital's opponent in the projected lawsuit, and this managed to get some kind of support at the Metropolitan Police Headquarters, since an order was issued refusing planning permission for any new building for the time being. Ironically Kiichiro's passion for politics, which he had always claimed would pay off one day, was now doing so in a very backhanded fashion. The days when the Seiyukai ruled the roost were over, and now it was their (and Kiichiro's) enemy, the Kenseikai, who had their fingers on the pulse of the Metropolitan Police, which was all very much to Kiichiro's disadvantage. At that time, when political power changed hands the higher positions in the police force were occupied by new people, and since the police still had strong supervisory powers over hospitals, things were looking very black for Kiichiro. The only hope was to move out of the Tokyo area, out of the jurisdiction of the Metropolitan Police, and build a new hospital in a new place. This, also, was impossible since, to the astonishment of his family, Kiichiro had no money, thanks to his extravagant spending on political pastimes and his habit of always wanting to make a great splash and show in everyday life. Thus it was proving difficult to do anything more than put up that apology for an outpatients surgery, which was built principally to make a formal declaration that the hospital intended to stay in business; although in fact Kiichiro was finding it hard even to pay the salaries of the few remaining members of his staff.

Tetsukichi, still wearing his white coat, had just left the surgery and was wandering along a pathway through the horseweed that overgrew the ruins. He was in that depressed mood which he often had when he had time to think about things; he felt that he was quite closed in now and there was no way out. When he pulled off the occasional leaf of the tall weed it gave off a rich, sappy odor that reminded him of home, although this still enabled him to feel no affection for it. Its richness seemed only destructive, as if it had been waiting all those long years for the hospital to be destroyed so that it might grow in its place. It had grown so tall it must surely be here forever. You could just about see the head of someone above it, but that was all.

Tetsukichi's eyes rested on the ruins of the hospital's storehouse, which could just be glimpsed over the tips of the weed; the roof had burned right through and fallen in. He had heard that the storehouse had apparently been intact after the main fire, but the cracks that developed at the time of the earthquake had never been repaired and it had started to blaze around dawn after the rest of the fire had died down, presumably burning from within. If only the storehouse had been spared, the books he had labored to collect during his time in Germany would have survived. As he looked at the blackened walls he felt once more the pain he had experienced six months ago, which the passage of time and various tasks those months had imposed on him had helped him to forget. When he had first stood on this spot after returning to Japan he had been too overwhelmed to experience any real suffering. That was to come a little later. He simply felt he must help his adoptive father through the consequences of this disaster and look after him.

Looking after was certainly required, for Kiichiro had lost the results of forty years of toil overnight, and he had lost his normal calmness to such an extent that those about him feared that the mental state he had fallen into might prove to be permanent. As the person responsible for a fire in which a number of patients had died, he was asked questions by newspaper reporters, and since he could not offer any real answers to their allegations he was reduced to desperate, hysterical evasion:

"Look here, you, you mind your manners. That statement of yours is totally unacceptable. All the patients were got safely away, quite out of danger. But then what happened? Some of them ran back and deliberately jumped into the flames. It is intolerable that you should ask me questions as if we were dealing with mentally normal people; an intolerable breach of manners."

Even if one takes into account Kiichiro's state of mind when he said this kind of thing, it still seemed rather extreme, both in content and in form. The representative of the landlord who was planning to take him to court, for example, was subjected to such abuse that Kiichiro could well have been summoned for libel too, and Tetsukichi had heard from the Deputy that the police were at one time thinking of doing exactly that. Fortunately Kiichiro's extreme excitability did not last long. He did not, however, return to his old serenity but to a quietness of so melancholic a nature that those who had known him in earlier days often doubted its authenticity. But it was real enough, for Kiichiro showed no signs of that decisiveness and energy which had been such notable parts of his personality before. The old Kiichiro would no doubt have had a number of smart moves up his sleeve concerning the approaching lawsuit and the question of borrowing capital to rebuild the hospital, but the present Kiichiro had lost all his former eloquence. He remained tongue-tied and silent, and his actions were performed with a slow, vacant weariness. The people about him found themselves obliged to believe that the shock of the fire had not simply aged him but had reduced him to senility. Even the Deputy who had been so absolute a worshiper at the Kiichiro shrine sometimes adopted a sharp, querulous tone of voice when he talked to him now:

"That is, of course, why I kept telling you that at least you ought to buy the land on which the hospital stood. But no, you wouldn't listen, saying, as I believe I well remember, that rented land was the only kind of land you needed, and money spent on land merely meant it was sleeping when it should be put to work in other ways."

So Kiichiro appeared to have no plans for any rebuilding of the hospital. Nor did he take any part in the, admittedly minimal, chores of running the hospital, all of which were left to Tetsukichi and his staff. He simply remained gloomily cooped up in the not very large house that alone had escaped destruction. Tetsukichi, on the contrary, had spent the whole of this day too in the outpatients surgery, although the grand total of patients during the morning session had been two, and in the afternoon there had been none, except for one person who had come to ask his advice.

He walked slowly around the back of the storehouse. Before the fire, the cookhouse had been to the right and Kiichiro's pride, the radium bath, to the left. The bath partially remained; at least the shape of the bathhouse was the same, for the burned sections had been replaced with iron sheeting and the bath itself was still in use. Since those who patronized it were now so few, it was clearly wasteful to have a bath of this size, given the expense of heating such large quantities of water, but Kiichiro had insisted and hot water was steaming away at this very moment.

The cookhouse, however, had been left to the weeds, although the area was now used as a kind of playground by Shun'ichi and Yonekuni, and also by Kumagoro, for all three were squatting down there doing something. Tetsukichi called out Shun'ichi's name, a purely reflexive action, and received a similarly mechanical response from his son, who turned toward him as if embarrassed by his presence, smiled faintly and all too dutifully, and then turned away again. This ten-year-old boy, who was tall for his age and had grown considerably while Tetsukichi was away, seemed very different from the son he had thought about so much in Germany. Though six months had elapsed he had still not grown accustomed to his father, and it seemed that perhaps he would never take to him. Tetsukichi himself now hesitated to approach the boy, who was clearly conscious of his father as he squatted on the ground and looked the other way. Although the decision made him dissatisfied and unhappy Tetsukichi left the child as he was. Even if he were to go up to him and ask him what he was doing he knew he could only do so clumsily, with no confidence in the relationship between them. The only response he could expect would be the kind that any small boy will make to a person to whom he is not yet used.

So he went away and walked past the storehouse again. He had come here last winter and dug out the burned remains of his library before having had time to experience any sense of homecoming after his three and a half years abroad. Most of the hundreds of books and magazines he had painstakingly acquired had been reduced to ashes. Some remained, however, scorched around their edges, stained with water, coated with mud, twisted into strange shapes among the ashes. So he picked out what was left, as if he were picking out the bones of a relative from the ashes at the crematory, and put them in the sun to dry. The journals of psychoneurology, which he was certain no university in the country possessed in such complete form, had been totally consumed. Certain volumes by Wundt, Bleuler and Binswanger had escaped, charred at the edges with only their centers pitiably intact. The books dried out, but the burned parts crumbled and fell away as the pages were turned. For more than three years he had gone on collecting, and when he thought back over those years now a sense of numbing futility took possession of him. What was it that had made him add to his store, that drove him to perform that mechanical act which had become so much a part of his life out there? The hospital would be rebuilt one day, but a similar collection of books would never be his again. And what would be the point, anyway, since all his energies must go now into the recreation of this hospital which had been so quickly destroyed. When he thought of the destruction that had been similarly visited on his library he knew that these two events were one event, not simply in space and time, but by virtue of having determined the future course of his life. He was never to be a scholar. That road was closed to him now. He would end his life as just another practicing doctor.

It would be strange if Tetsukichi had not felt the workings of fate in this, and he did. He felt the transience of the things of this world, although it would be untrue to say that it was a profoundly philosophical feeling or even one to which he attached any deep significance. It was the same response that the peasants in his part of the North would make to any natural disaster: a simple, intuitive reaction. This does not mean that he had any primitive religious faith or set of ideas. There was simply an innate sympathy with this kind of thinking, a sympathy which made him feel that in some way he understood what his brother Shirokichi had written to him in a letter about their father in his old age. During his final years, their father had set his heart on reciting all eighty thousand of the *nenbutsu* prayers compiled by Honen, the founder of the Buddhist Pure Land Sect, and even when his voice grew so faint and hoarse that he was unable to produce an intelligible sound he continued to chant, rosary in his hands and abacus before him, in a voice that sounded like a cicada. Tetsukichi felt he could understand that kind of obsession; the state of mind that lay behind it was by no means alien to him.

There had been that time—he was fifteen, in the same year that he came to Tokyo—when his father had taken him to visit the holy mountain of Yudono. In their village and thereabouts the mountain itself was an object of veneration, and all the boys were taken to pay their respects at the age of fifteen. Before leaving on the pilgrimage one had to bathe in cold running water morning and evening, and no killing of any living thing was permitted. Besides this spiritual preparation, one also had to polish with salt the small coins that were to be left as offerings. On the day of the pilgrimage they had to leave the village before midnight in order to walk the thirty miles and more to the Hondoji temple. The next day they again rose in the dark, reaching the village of Shizu before dawn, where they asked for a guide. When they reached the ravine that led up to the holy mountain the weather became wild, great gusts of rain sweeping down the mountainside, blowing away straw rain hats and ripping straw capes to tatters. Even so, the guide continued to make his way up, chanting his prayers for the purification of the six roots of perception and for the prosperity of the mountain.

Then they came to a gully completely filled in with ice, which they had to cross. As Tetsukichi was picking his way gingerly across, a huge gust of wind blew down with a terrifying howl and he was in great danger of being blown off his feet. His father cried out in a piercing voice behind him:

"Crawl, Tetsukichi! Get down on your belly and crawl!"

Tetsukichi dropped flat and clung to the cold ice. He could remember clearly the fear he had felt, and also the strange sense of reverence that came over him. . .

"Excuse me, Doctor," a voice called out, that of a nurse who had come looking for him among the tall weeds. "There's a patient to see you."

Tetsukichi nodded, glanced back in the direction of his son, then walked swiftly toward the surgery building.

Meanwhile, back among the weeds, Shun'ichi was briskly snapping off stems and lining them up on the ground.

"This one's the battleship *Satsuma,*" he said, putting in position a number of small thin stalks to represent guns.

"That's all wrong. How can it have guns all over it like that?" retorted Yonekuni, who spoke in this critical way because he was now at junior high school and had become bored with the game.

In fact the person most interested in this juvenile pastime was Kumagoro, the Pockmarked Bear himself. After the fire, a number of the interns had packed up and gone home; others had sought work elsewhere; yet this idler remained as ever, eating and sleeping at the hospital, although he did have some kind of function now: that of looking after the children.

"That's it. And this one's the *Tosa,* then the *Kaga,* the *Kii,* the *Owari.* . . ," he said in a fervent voice. "Then over here we have the *Amagi,* the *Akagi,* the *Takao* . . . which makes sixteen ships and our eight-eight fleet is complete."

The "eight-eight fleet" was a squadron of eight battleships and eight cruisers, but a more interesting fact was that the former socialist had, for some reason or other, been transformed into a fully-fledged patriot.

"Do you know what sacrifices we endured to create the eight-eight fleet? Listen, clerks and workers in both the public and private spheres gave up part of their salaries each month to provide the funds. And why? Because with such a fleet Japan would be invincible. And then what? The lousy Yanks started to lose their heads. You see, we're a bit too fast for their liking when it comes to building ships; a good bit too fast. So they start on about arms limitation. And, can you believe it, our politicians, the stupid fools, swallow this crazy five-five-three ratio. They're out of their minds. So we just have to put up with it.

Our people get kicked around as immigrants, and they just have to grin and bear it. And why? Because we have no eight-eight fleet. So, what are we going to do about it, I ask you? What, my boy, are we to do?''

"Make another eight-eight fleet again," said Shun'ichi.

"Right. Dead right. Good. Excellent. The exact answer." The pimples on Kumagoro's dark brown face glowed a patriotic red. "You've hit it right on the head. Why shouldn't the whole nation get together again and make another eight-eight fleet? No reason at all. Down with their stinking naval treaty. Let them stuff it up. . . So here we are then: the *Satsuma,* the *Tosa,* the *Kii,* the *Owari*. . .''

"Ah, there's Granddad," Shun'ichi said, and this time he stood up, eager and excited, a quite different response to the one he had made to his father.

It was unmistakably Kiichiro who now appeared from the back door of the house, although he was much changed from the former dandy whose condescending and energetic presence had once graced the hospital, for as little trace remained of the one as of the other. He looked no more than some old man of the back streets toddling off to the public bath, his bathrobe loosely tied about him and carrying a tin washbowl with what seemed to be a bottle in it. His originally small stature seemed to have been reduced further, as if he had actually been shrunken by the fire.

What deepened the resemblance to some common old man from around the corner was his manner of walking, for he had tucked up his robe in rustic granddaddy fashion, showing his wretched shins to all beholders. When he reached the back of the storehouse his little grandson called out to him, but Shun'ichi's voice went unheeded, most likely unheard. His back slightly stooped, Kiichiro went on shuffling toward the bath.

He was having financial problems at the moment. A trust bank he had always thought would lend him money at any time had proved unresponsive, refusing him a loan, and although he had been introduced to a money broker by a friend, the interest rates demanded had been exorbitant. On top of all this there had been another defamatory article about the Nire Hospital in yesterday's evening paper. The article claimed that, despite formal protests from more than a hundred residents in the area, the hospital still planned to override all opposition and go ahead with the rebuilding, and since the Director was short of money he had raised the rents on the houses he owned (Kiichiro did, in fact, own a number of houses for rent in the area) to an extortionate level in order to amass the necessary capital, stimulating further outcries from his incensed neighbors.

So Kiichiro approached the bathhouse deep in frowning thought, but once he had arrived in front of it, where old Isuke was at work adding wood to the fire, his haggard face creased in his old, habitual smile as he recognized who it was.

"Isuke, well done, well done."

"Ah, and is it the doctor, sir?"

Isuke was perhaps the only object in this landscape with figures that looked much the same as before. Certainly his hunchback was slightly more pronounced, perhaps because he stooped more now, but his grimy blackness remained the same—even a disaster like the great fire could not intensify that.

"Still a bit early for the bath, Doctor. The top part of it might be hot, but the bottom's still stone-cold, I'll be bound, sir."

"Not at all, no no, perfectly all right; fine, fine."

Kiichiro nodded as if in agreement with his own statement, and produced another rather tired smile on his drawn face. He slipped behind the fence that now served as the wall of the bathhouse, undressed with impetuous haste, refusing Isuke's offer of assistance, and then removed, one by one, the boards that had been placed on top of the bath to keep the heat in. He stirred the water about to mix the hot with the cold and contrive the lukewarm temperature he liked, and then, not bothering to go through the customary motions of washing himself down before entering, he plunged in.

He then did something peculiar. He stretched out his hand toward his tin washbowl and pulled it toward him. The bottle rolling about inside it proved to be none other than his favorite beverage: non-alcoholic, fizzy Bordeaux. He had also cleverly provided himself with a glass and a bottle opener, which were both rolling about in the washbowl as well. He picked up the opener and tapped the cap of the bottle smartly a number of times. The thin, metallic sound echoed awhile in the wide, desolate bathhouse. Even with such careful preparations, the fizzy red liquid still bubbled over the top of the bottle when the cap was removed, and the old man suddenly sprang into activity, making frantic efforts to catch it all in his glass. When the fierce bubbling had finally subsided, he carefully added more of the fizzy stuff to what he had already saved, filling his glass to the brim.

Now, with his glass in his hand, he sank back into the lukewarm

223

water until it covered his shoulders again. He carefully brought the glass to his lips; drank once; drank twice. His prominent Adam's apple jumped each time. Then he closed his eyes.

What kind of thoughts or reveries passed through his mind as he sat there? His hair, which had previously been so carefully groomed and shone such a lustrous black, was more than half gray now, dry, lifeless and disordered. But his Kaiser moustache remained as ever, the same shining, pomaded black: clearly he retained much of his passion for his personal appearance, and the time spent over his daily toilet was no doubt little changed. This seemed only to add to the atmosphere of pathos he exuded, this tiny, sad and comical man. There he sat, his wrinkled and unhealthy-looking face and the bony upper portion of his chest emerging above the surface of the water, his eyes closed. What thoughts and feelings were passing through this solitary head, there in the vast expanse of the bath? Did he feel that everything had ended now, that the final breakup had come? Was he resigned to his harsh fate, or overcome by despair?

The face itself showed nothing, although suddenly the eyelids flickered and the eyes opened a little, giving an unpleasant glimpse of cloudy whites and large unnatural-looking pupils that seemed to glitter with some secret desire. At the same time the skinny, bony body moved as well, as if propelled by an uncanny spiritual force. Kiichiro thrust his arm outside the tub and picked up his bottle of Bordeaux. He poured it foaming cheerfully into the glass. There was the sound of gulping, once, twice, thrice.

That was soon over. The glitter in his eyes faded; they became dull and vacant. He glanced around for some time at the galvanized iron walls, his gaze even drifting up toward the ceiling, and a look of vague confusion came over his face, perhaps one of hopelessness, even of despair, though it was too imprecise to be read clearly. Then he closed his eyes again. He still held the glass he had just drained in his hand. Now all was silence, a silence soaked in tepid water; the silence of a dull, unending vacancy.

That was one part of Kiichiro's daily routine nowadays.

The air felt strangely cold to her. It still ought not to be so very cold at night, and yet she felt as if goose pimples were standing out all over her skin. But then her forehead and cheeks, her whole body in fact, seemed hot. It was as if a source of glowing heat rose within her breast and spread throughout her body—but failed to reach the skin, which seemed abnormally cold, almost freezing.

Of course she knew it was because she had a temperature. But Seiko did not want to use the thermometer. She was afraid to watch the mercury rise coldly and heartlessly, as if trying to frighten her. A few days before she had been to the local doctor and he had told her she had pulmonary tuberculosis in a fairly advanced stage. She had kept the visit a secret from her husband, and now she lacked the courage to tell him that she had consumption and was going to die of it. For quite a long time now she had found life with Sasaki unbearable. Their marriage had not yet fallen to pieces, but it was now no more than a burden to her.

After she had rejected the suitor chosen for her by her parents, resisted all attempts to make her change her mind, and been virtually disinherited (she had not once returned to the hospital since her wedding), the early days of her marriage had been romantic and happy enough. Soon, however, cracks began to appear in the flimsy structure. Perhaps it came from the differences in their temperaments: on one side a young lady brought up with no real cares, and on the other a young man who had spent years of struggle and hardship in America. In addition, Sasaki was not a dedicated teacher so much as someone who had accepted the last thing available to him. He had not originally intended to be a teacher, but had first entered a business company, which he soon left, and had then taken several other jobs before drifting into teaching.

Seiko had been prepared for financial difficulties and was in no way surprised by them. Nor did she feel that the fact she had not been blessed with the child that Sasaki wanted so much was an important reason for things going wrong. What had beaten down her spirit until it finally broke was her husband's drinking. His character completely changed when he drank, and for the past year his drinking had become something close to actual illness. He drank because his life had not gone the way he had wanted it to go, and once he started he could not stop. He would start during the day, carry on during the night, wandering from one cheap drinking spot to another, and then crawl home around dawn. Seiko was content if he simply fell asleep in a drunken stupor, but usually he did not. He would work himself into a frenzy that made her doubt his normality. He would drag his sleeping wife out of bed and harangue her about what was wrong with her, which led to a string of insults directed at her family, and culminated in a general overturning and smashing of whatever was at hand. He would sleep right through the next day as if he were dead, and when he woke he would sincerely regret what he had done and apologize. But this reformed character did not persist for long. He would go on another bout, and recently the intervals between these drinking bouts had been growing shorter and shorter.

Seiko had been lying down but decided to get up now. She had only been resting and had not troubled to undress. Her husband would probably not be back before morning, but he could return at any time. If he came back during the night he would demand drink and she would be forced to stay up with him as he drank until morning. She shuddered as she thought of how he looked at such times, his bloodshot eyes, the way he staggered about the room, the terrible sound of his blurred, stumbling voice as he shouted and screamed at her. This was not the man for whose love she had sacrificed everything, but some other creature toward whom she felt only fear.

She coughed two or three times, then moved her tired, cold and feverish body forward and poked at the lighted charcoal in the *hibachi*. Parts of the charcoal crumbled into ash. She poked it again, for she had nothing else to do, then sat there absentmindedly with the poker in her hand. The face that had once aroused such admiration for its formal, sweet perfection was now completely lifeless. Seiko had lost all interest in her appearance long ago.

Seiko had not only received presents of rice, vegetables and other things which the generous heart of Nanny Shimoda prompted her to bring, but occasional sums of money as well. Seiko understood that these came from her mother, but her mother never once came to visit her, and Seiko's own pride would not allow her to go back to the Nire Hospital, for how could she brazenly show her face in a home she had left after so forcefully rejecting every plea to remain? But her illness demanded absolute peace and quiet, prolonged rest, and the doctor had warned her there was little chance of her getting better unless someone took very strict care of her. She herself knew that the illness was eating her away minute by minute, but she had no idea what she should do or to whom she should turn. If she told her husband everything when he was sober, she knew he would tell her to go into hospital. But where was the money to come from to pay for it? If her own family had been as it was before, she would have swallowed her pride and asked for assistance, but as things were now she couldn't. After the fire at the hospital she had gone secretly to look at what had happened, and the only thing remaining of the home she remembered was the brick wall in front, which had been rebuilt after the great earthquake. Looking at the area from Moto-no-hara she could see no trace of the building that had towered into the sky.

She had found out all she needed to know about the present state of the hospital from Nanny Shimoda, who visited her occasionally and gave her the information without having to be asked. It was quite clear how bad the situation was and she could not allow herself to add to her father's worries.

All she could do was die. The answer came suddenly and simply as the one solution available to her. She would die. She looked at the tea cupboard, inside which was a packet of sleeping pills Nanny Shimoda had brought, for recently she had found it difficult to sleep at night. There were still ten left. If she took them all in one go perhaps she would fall at last into a sleep from which she need never wake.

The idea only stayed with her for a few moments. She did not want to die. Her forehead burned, her body ached so much that she did not know what to do with herself, and yet she wanted to live. She did not care how wretched and painful living might be, for death was more terrible than that—of all things the one to be most feared and hated.

Crickets were singing outside the window, each in apparent competition with the others, reviving an almost palpable image of the past. She had been in the upstairs living room of their house at the hospital. Her sister had been trying to make her change her mind about marrying Sasaki. She could hear that nagging voice, and then another, a peculiar, chanting recitative: ". . . *from the scarlet silk crepe sash she had tied. . . Not one hair of her head disheveled or in disarray, her makeup perfect in its artifice and beauty. . .*" and she found herself involuntarily calling out Billiken's name.

Billiken, of the pointed head, the obsessed reciter of newspaper articles, was no longer in this world. He had been one of those who died in the fire. Billiken no longer existed, and neither did the hospital.

Seiko found that tears had risen to her eyes, and she wiped them away with the back of her hand. These tears were not only in memory of the late Mr. Billiken, but also for a young girl whose image then imposed itself on that of the dead man. This was her sister, Momoko, a child who had done nothing but play ball and fight her brother and talk about motion pictures, and was now a married woman living in a city in distant China, where her husband was chief surgeon at a local hospital. As Seiko remembered her, she felt a love and affection for her rather slovenly, chubby-faced little sister she had never felt before, an almost painful emotion that she had never imagined she could feel. Momoko would be returning to Japan soon.

Ever since she had been forcibly dragged off to Hankow, Momoko had kept up a correspondence with Seiko. Momoko's letters invariably took the form of emotional confessions, and she made frequent use of such expressions as: "Seiko, you are the only one who is on my side. I can only write things like this to you."

Momoko had wept all the way there when Ryuko took her out to join her husband; and she found she couldn't bear the man, no doubt because the emotional shock that came from the sudden revelation of Kiichiro's masterstroke had left a wound that would not easily heal. Since she was still not ready to endure her marriage, one day she casually bought herself a ticket and boarded a boat. The boat traveled down the Yangtze River as far as the port of Kiukiang. But at the port the Japanese police were waiting for her, alerted by her husband, so there was nothing for it but to go back. And yet, despite all this, she finally got used to life in Hankow. She seemed satisfied at least with her standard of living and the three servants she had. She became pregnant, and this was decisive since she at last accepted the fact that she was Shiro's wife. To compensate in some way for this acceptance she wrote all those secrets of which her parents knew nothing in her letters to Seiko.

But as the child grew large within her the desire to return home also grew stronger. She did not want to give birth to her first child in a foreign land. She wanted to return to the hospital where she had grown up and where there were so many people who knew her and would look after her. By what means she was finally able to persuade her parents to agree to this was something Seiko had no way of knowing. Presumably Momoko was being allowed to come home because her husband's contract would not last much longer, and once it had ended he too would be returning to Japan.

Seiko pulled herself heavily over toward the box in which she kept her correspondence, and took out a letter she had received a while ago from Momoko. It was written in a round, clumsy, not easily legible hand. Seiko read it through again.

Seiko, I shall be coming back to Japan soon. It's all been decided. I've asked Father time and time again to let me, and at last he has consented. I think you are the only one who will understand how happy, how really happy, I am.

I know I'm not wanted at the hospital and never have been. I don't care, though. I've always been useless as far as the hospital is concerned, just not in the same class as Ryuko or you. I'm sorry but, honestly, I'm not trying to be sarcastic. I was never what they wanted. It's only because things have turned out for you as they have that I can tell you the truth like this. You see, I don't like the hospital or the Nire household itself. What I like are a few people there, like Nanny Shimoda and Billiken and Senaga of the four hundred and four and the Pockmarked Bear and people like that. Then of course you; I like you. You're the only one in the family I like.

I know if I do come back I won't be particularly warmly welcomed because I'm not of any importance; I'm nobody. With the hospital in its present state I couldn't expect much anyway. Still, this time I'm not alone. I have my child inside me. I could feel him kicking just now. I hope he's a boy. If he's a boy he can grow up to be a doctor and do something for the hospital. They would like that, I know. Father may not care anything about me, but I'm sure he will smile when he looks at the face of the little grandson I shall give him.

The Chinese who comes to sell vegetables is always teaching me how to make sure it's a boy. It's all a matter of saying the right magic formulas, but they are so weird I can never say them with a straight face. Our cook said that you give birth to a boy if you eat lots of lobster and shrimps, which I am doing now all the time, and a lot of money it costs too.

I can't wait to get home and see everybody. I can't wait to see you, Seiko. Please pray for me; pray that my baby will be a boy. Please do. I'll buy you masses of presents if you do. I'll only buy them for you. Lots of different kinds. Of course this has to be a secret.

Seiko brushed her eyes with her fingertips a number of times as she read this, but then a slight smile played across her haggard face. She, too, could not wait to meet her sister. She wanted to meet her, she truly did.

The crickets kept on singing outside. There was still no sign of her husband, but she thought she would go on waiting up for him all the same. She put the letter back into the box, and then attempted to stand up still holding it.

It was then it happened. A terrible wave of sickness of a kind she had never experienced before suddenly swept over her. Something loathsome was pushing up from her breast into her throat. There was such a sense of oppressiveness there that she thrust her fingers into the back of her mouth to try to relieve it. This only made vomiting inevitable, and she doubled up in pain and spewed something out over the *tatami*. It was a huge clot of blood; then came more blood, a foam of brilliant, scarlet blood. So dazzling was the color that she had the sensation she was suffering from some kind of dizzy spell and was merely seeing red, the whole world as red. She was so overwhelmed by this sensation that she did in fact grow faint, and as she coughed again she put her hand over her mouth and doubled up. An even thicker flow of blood came out this time, oozing between the fingers of her hand.

Her consciousness grew fainter, as if she were being drawn deeper and deeper into a huge darkness. So she prayed, desperately, imploringly, in deep panic. She wanted to live; she wanted to live. It hurt so much and she didn't want to hurt. She didn't want to die. . .

Her prayers were not answered. The illness worsened surprisingly quickly and one month later, in a room in the Keio Hospital, her brief life came to an end.

She died about dawn, when the nearby rooms and the corridor were in deep silence. Three members of the Nire family, Ryuko, Yonekuni and Momoko, who had just returned from China, were in the room. Both women were equally plump in pregnancy, both clearly in the final stages. The doctor said a few words and left the room. Ryuko went over to the bedside and looked down at the dead girl's face with a hard, stiff expression on her own. Death had been kind to Seiko: it had taken away the exhaustion that life had imposed on her face. Her cheeks were sunken and there was no color of life there, but the finely shaped nose and the sweet precision of her mouth gave her what could only be called real beauty.

Ryuko's expression remained unmoved, but she stared fixedly at this sister who had rebelled against the hospital and her father, and who now breathed no more. Then she spoke, very clearly, so that those behind her might hear:

"If only you had listened to what I said. . . None of this need have happened if you had listened to me."

Momoko and Yonekuni were standing behind Ryuko. Momoko had both hands on her unwieldy stomach; her face was lowered, and she was weeping endlessly and silently. All she could do was weep, screw up her eyes and let an unending stream of huge tears flow. Yonekuni, shaven-headed and now in his fourth year at middle school, had eyes that were slightly red. He felt embarrassed by his sister weeping beside him, but also guilty because he seemed unable to weep himself.

Standing behind them, all alone, was someone else. This was Seiko's husband. He maintained a certain distance from the members of the Nire family, who were only relatives of his on paper. In fact, he was deliberately avoiding the eldest daughter of the house, who had as yet not even shown she was aware of his presence, and he stood right by the door.

Ryuko looked at Seiko's face a little longer, then raised her head again. Maintaining a decent interval of two or three paces between her own swollen body and Momoko's similarly endowed one, she made a slight movement that seemed to be meant for Sasaki. Her expression remained cuttingly cold, but the discreet movement was to indicate that they were about to leave and that he was free to acknowledge the fact in some way if he wished; also to pay his respects to his dead wife for the first time now, if he felt he had the right to do so. He could do as he liked.

Chapter

10

Spring was on its way; perhaps it was already here. The fields in the small valley beside the Aoyama Cemetery were a thick, uneven carpet of rape blossoms on which swarms of tiny drone flies gathered. The yellow petals—so bright they looked as if they had been freshly painted—swayed in a wind that was still cold, and the flies that had been shaken off hovered droning in the air before seeking their next resting place. The evergreens which had spent the winter attired in drab hues were putting forth new shoots, especially the hedgerows of spindle.

This was all in great contrast to the Nire Hospital. The land there showed no new signs of life, and the poverty-stricken air of the occasional temporary building seemed all the more conspicuous as a result. The horseweed which had grown at will last summer had now completely disappeared. While it was there the view had been shabby and desolate enough, but now it was gone one could take in the whole area at a glance, unobstructed by any vegetation, and the sense of vacancy was even more overpowering. During the winter Isuke and the few interns had cut down the withered stems of the weed and used them as fuel for heating the bath. But if you looked closely among the brown stubble, fresh shoots and small, soft green leaves were starting to appear in patches.

At the rear of the one real building, the two-storied house in which the family lived, a large number of babies' nappies had been hung out to dry. Here at least was a sign of life, since the various patterns of the cast-off *yukata* from which the nappies had been made provided a genuine riot of color. There were two babies in the house now, both around three months old, and they soiled a succession of nappies each day. They had both been born at the end of last year, with only five days between them; one was a boy, the other a girl. The first to be born had been Momoko's long-hoped-for boy, and his name was Satoru. Momoko had thought of this name herself and was inordinately pleased with it because, like the surname Nire, it was written with only one ideogram, thus providing a full name that was not only refined but convenient. She was also pleased because *satoru* means "insight" and she was sure the boy would be blessed with wisdom and learning and become a great man. The other baby was Ryuko's second child, a daughter called Aiko.

Nanny Shimoda had been walking with Aiko in her arms for a little while now, wandering about past the storehouse and in front of the radium bath, and she was singing a nursery rhyme that belonged to a time in her past she could not clearly remember:

> "Out from Aoyama Cemetery
> Three white ghosts come gliding, three;
> Three red ghosts come following after.
> Last of all a student boy
> With big, floppy breaches on:
> Flippety, floppety, flap."

Nanny Shimoda had always sung out of tune, but lately this had grown worse and she sounded as if she were chanting the sutras in the customary flat monotone. But little Aiko did not seem to mind what kind of lullaby was sung to her, or even if it were a lullaby or not, for she remained very good and quiet. Perhaps good and quiet is not really the right description, for it was more like the peace of the dead: she seemed quite lacking in any vital energy. She was wrapped up nice and warm in a new padded coat, but even this gave her no appearance of plumpness; she was a skinny little thing, excessively pale and helpless-looking. Still, she had charming, sad eyes, big, black, shining irises and the whites tinged with blue. Then her hair was beautifully soft, fluffy and straying on top, and when she cried her voice was so faint that it seemed she had been born to arouse affection in the sternest of adults. But the reason why she cried so faintly was that she lacked the energy to produce any strenuous howls. Her mother had only a poor supply of her own milk and the baby was being brought up half on cow's milk, which she seemed not to like for she would either refuse it or bring up that little she had managed to drink. When she did this she would cry in her feeble voice, though not for long. When she had finished crying her tiny little eyelids would be slightly red and swollen, and she would lie quite still looking sadly downward, which made the grown-ups who were watching say sentimental things about how helpless and lovely she looked.

233

Everybody wanted to hold this baby with the pretty nose and eyes, who was so nice and quiet.

"What a sweet little precious she is. Look at her. Look at her cute little mouth; and her lovely little hands."

When she was dandled Aiko would smile a little, but only a very little, and her look of indifferent helplessness would come back again, stimulating people to even greater sentimental heights. One of the veteran nurses, for example, said:

"Oh, isn't she lovely! I've never seen anyone so lovely. It's Miss Seiko come back to life, I do declare. Oh, but she'll be even more beautiful than Miss Seiko, that's for sure."

Nanny Shimoda's commitment to the child was absolute. She had already reared all the Nire children by hand, and here was another baby after a longish interval of years. She looked down with her own small elephant's eyes at the tiny, irreplaceable, unique and quiet little thing she held in her arms, and began her lullaby-sutra chanting again:

"Out from Aoyama Cemetery
Three white ghosts. . ."

Nanny Shimoda had no desire to pass this treasure into the keeping of any of the nurses, and certainly not into the clumsy grasp of someone like the Pockmarked Bear. Suppose they dropped her? Even if they didn't actually drop her, she was so particularly frail and fragile, such a slight little thing, like a tiny princess. Well, that was what she would call her. She would call her princess, Mistress Princess. This bright idea might meet with the mother's approval or it might not. But that was beside the point, and she puckered up her mouth and called her: "Mistress Princess!"

Momoko was not amused by any of this. She had given birth to the son she had longed for, and she loved her Satoru with as much passion as she loathed her husband, all the love she withheld from one being given to the other. Her baby was the complete opposite of Aiko. Satoru was very round and plump, so fat he had deep rings in his flesh at his wrists and ankles. In contrast to Ryuko, who frantically stuffed herself with those well-known milk-producing foods, rice cakes and sea bream, and still had not enough milk to breast-feed her baby properly, Momoko's breasts were heavy and swollen, her lacteal glands taut, and she produced plenty of milk and to spare. So Satoru was a healthy, bouncing baby boy, but also alas, if the truth be told, very ugly to go with it. He was not pale and white like Aiko but black and hairy, so hairy that the baby hair on his forehead refused to go away, seeming to be a permanent fixture. Even though he was only three months old, Momoko (perhaps only Momoko) had discovered that his ears protruded in a very abnormal and peculiar way. On top of this, Satoru was bad-tempered and gave vent to great piercing howls. When breast-feeding, Momoko's nipple would at first be too taut and Satoru found it difficult to suck, so he would work up a tremendous rage, squirming and twisting his head and body away, and setting up the most extraordinary series of bawls and plaints.

Perhaps because her child was, even at this early stage, obviously ugly when compared with her eldest sister's baby, Momoko loved him all the more; so much that she would often feel like snatching him up and hugging the life out of him.

But other people only cared about Aiko. Nobody was interested in Satoru. This was not in fact true, but Momoko had decided it was, and she would bite her nether lip with vexation. If anyone said something nice about Satoru, Momoko would assume they were merely being polite or even trying to be sarcastic, and would reply in what she considered the same vein:

"That's right, that's right, he's certainly big enough. All anything as ugly as this can do is grow bigger and bigger."

This was, of course, a public statement, but even in private she had no flattering words for her dark child. But the baby remained an obsession with her, an obsession that took the form of always providing Satoru with nourishment at the slightest whimper, regardless of time or place.

"Here we are then, here it is. Drink up, drink up. I don't need any rice cakes or sea bream, I've got enough milk as it is, haven't I? So come on then; drink it; drink as much as you like."

Just then, Momoko happened to be coming out of the back door of the house, and what should she see but Nanny Shimoda holding Aiko, and that intern Kumagoro dancing attendance in the most ridiculous manner.

"Come on, little lady. Bah, there, bah, bah. There we are, bah."

These were not insults but attempts to get the baby to smile. Still, something about his manner seemed to be troubling Nanny Shimoda, who had become even fatter recently and now had a pronounced double chin and flabby, drooping cheeks, though her expression retained the old aura of goodness and kindness. At the moment, however, she was looking so serious she seemed almost stern. She was correcting Kumagoro for some profound error:

"She's not a little lady. She's Mistress Princess."

Momoko felt piqued and mentally stuck out her tongue in response to this absurdity. Her annoyance was further increased by the Bear's subsequent remarks:

"Nanny, this wind's cold. You mustn't let her catch cold. It might lead to typhoid, you never know. There's plenty of it around at the moment."

Momoko felt that someone as pockmarked as he was had no right to talk about the possibility of spreading diseases. But it was the excessive concern he showed that really angered her, so she walked swiftly up to them, clutching her own child desperately to her breast as she said:

"Kumagoro, can babies catch typhoid?"

"Certainly they can. Babies can catch any kind of illness, adult ones and baby ones as well, so twice as many as we do."

"What about your pockmarks and spots then? Are you quite sure that's not smallpox?"

"Thanks very much. Very kind of you. What do you want me to do about it then? What do you expect me to say in reply to that kind of talk? But you'd better watch out. They've had an outbreak of smallpox in Yokohama and it'll be in Aoyama in no time, if it's not here already. Don't blame me if Satoru catches it, and don't say I didn't warn you."

Kumagoro went away in a bad mood, which Satoru seemed to catch straight away because he became very petulant. A difficult child will normally be all right if you hold it and walk about, but once you stop it will immediately revert to its former state and kick its feet and wave its hands about. But even rocking had no effect on Satoru this time, for he screwed up his face and wrenched great howls out of himself that were unbearable to listen to.

Momoko became flustered and offered the child her nipple, but the obstinate baby protested even more, bending backward and howling more horribly than ever.

"Now, Mistress Momo," said Nanny Shimoda, who was not content to remain a mere spectator and felt she must do something to remedy the situation. "His little tummy's not empty. He just wants to go to beddy-byes."

This seemed to infuriate Momoko even more, for she smartly retorted that Nanny Shimoda had no right to say things like that because it was all her fault for never looking after the baby.

"You never hold him. You don't like him one little bit, do you?"

"Now, Mistress Momo, you know that isn't true," said Nanny, feeling apprehensive in the face of Momoko's obvious seriousness. "Satoru has a good mother who looks after him all the time. I really don't know why you should say. . ."

"All right, then, all right. If you like him even just a little bit, then hold him for a minute. You're much better at holding babies than I am. Look, he's crying because he wants you to hold him. I'll take Aiko, or Mistress Princess if you like, and hold her for you. That's all right, isn't it?"

"Of course it is," agreed Nanny Shimoda, although she didn't look in the least bit happy about this.

So the exchange of babies was made. Momoko took the light, soft, passive Aiko into her arms, and thought how frail she was as she looked down into features that were certainly very small and regular when compared with those of her own child. The baby seemed a little surprised at first, looking incredulously with enormous black eyes into her aunt's face, but soon letting her gaze slip to one side to resume her apparently melancholy meditations.

Even Momoko was struck by the sweetness of the child, and found herself muttering that she really was cute and what a dear little face she had. She then gave her rival elder sister's baby a little tweak on its white cheek:

"Still, she does look miserable. No flesh on her cheeks at all. Not getting enough milk, I should think, poor thing. Would you like some of mine? Some of Auntie's? But I'd better not, had I? Your dear mama would not like it at all if a vulgar, inferior person like myself were to suckle you. She would be very angry indeed, wouldn't she? So there, there then, you poor little mite."

Momoko went on mumbling this sort of thing for some time, apparently entranced by the child, but then she happened to look to one side and see her own. Satoru had indeed stopped crying soon after he had been passed over to Nanny Shimoda, but he had turned his grubby, tear-stained face in his mother's direction and she had sensed he was looking at her. How dark his face was, not one scrap of grace or refinement about it. What a nasty, unpleasant face it was too. He seemed to have inherited everything that was wrong with her husband's face.

She was suddenly overwhelmed by a feeling of misery and oppression, and she wanted to get away.

"Give him back to me. Give my Satoru back to me."

Without waiting for any response from Nanny Shimoda, Momoko snatched her Satoru back. She gripped his plump body mercilessly to her breast, and hurried away toward the back door of the house. Behind, Nanny Shimoda was calling out to her in a worried voice, and Satoru began to complain about this rough handling and burst into howls again like a rekindled fire. But Momoko ignored both voices, and she moved even faster, half running now, her eyes filled with tears. These soon began to overflow and fall one after the other onto her plump cheeks.

Half an hour later she seemed recovered, and was cheerfully turning over the pages of a newspaper in the small six-mat room next to the kitchen. Satoru was having one of his rare quiet spells, sleeping innocently beside her with arms outstretched.

"*City Council Makes Illegal Profits by Ignoring Regulations,*" she muttered to herself. "*Maintaining that slum buildings of a temporary nature present various insoluble problems in the calculation of floor space, and by claiming there is considerable joint usage of water supply faucets, they. . .*"

How dreary can you get, she wondered, wishing that Billiken were here, for he would have found something much more interesting to read in that strange and wonderful chant of his. What a nice person he had been, she thought. How good. How much she had liked him.

So she picked up the next newspaper that came to hand: "*Pervert Arrested by Nishi Sugamo Police. Shop-Assistant and Geisha Slasher.*"

That was more like it. Her eyes sparkled with new life and she became so absorbed in what she was reading that she completely forgot about the baby sleeping at her side: "*Man with previous record . . . abnormal sexual desire. . .*"

She called out to Shige, the maid who had previously worked "within" and was now busy about something in the kitchen:

"Listen to this. It's really interesting. I'll read it out to you."

Her face was bright and cheerful again, though her expression was not what one would have expected in a young child's mother. She read out from the printed page in a loud voice, wrinkling her snub nose:

"*Whenever he saw a beautiful woman, the sudden urge to slash and cut would come over him, the lustful passion rising up. . .*"

Next to the wall in the living room was a black piano with a number of scratches on it. This was the German piano which had previously been in the VIP Reception Parlor. For some reason, in a fire in which everything else had been lost, this object had been miraculously rescued from its upstairs room by the interns. If anything were to be carried out, the very first thing should certainly have been something that was much lighter, and which ought to have been preserved even at the risk of life and limb, namely the portrait of His Imperial Majesty. The Imperial Portrait, which had been bestowed by the Imperial Hand Itself, had been quite forgotten in the heat of the moment, and destroyed in consequence. After the event the Director and the Deputy both turned pale at the enormity of the offense, and the hospital staff were told to keep their mouths shut about the matter. Luckily the question of the Imperial Portrait had not given rise to any unpleasant investigation from outside, and the miraculously preserved, if badly scratched, piano received a similar lack of attention from inside since no one could play it.

To one side of the piano was a wooden pillar on which a fat calendar hung, of the kind that records one day only on each page. This one was made of poor quality paper, the only ornamentation on the page being the number of the day itself, although there was a slight variation for Saturdays and Sundays, Saturdays being in blue and Sundays in red in place of the weekday black. National holidays were embellished with a further flourish, in that they had the national flag printed on their pages. The fat calendar needed one page torn off it each day, but this rarely happened and normally a number would be torn off every few days. Despite the likelihood that it was not showing the precise date, one could at least tell that the month of April in the fifteenth year of the Taisho era, 1926, was approaching its end.

The cherry blossoms had been over for some time when, one fine Sunday morning in the midst of spring, Yasusaburo Sugano was called into the Director's presence. Kiichiro had just finished an early breakfast and returned to his room upstairs, an unimpressive Japanese-style room that was a sad comedown from the luxurious surroundings he had previously enjoyed "within." His breakfast had consisted of the inevitable oatmeal and Bordeaux. Last year traces of sugar had been found in his urine and there had been some doubts raised about his consumption of this sweet red beverage, but the Director was not a man to change his tastes whatever the reason: he went on drinking about half a dozen bottles a day. In the morning, he would pour the liquid lavishly over his oatmeal to cool it down, stir the resultant mess with a large spoon, then slop it down in such a disgustingly noisy manner that anyone would have felt inclined to turn his eyes away, the sight was so unedifying. Recently that indifference to others and general slovenliness which old men have had become grossly apparent in his behavior, and each day after breakfast a certain quantity of a mixture of oatmeal and Bordeaux would adhere to that moustache, which was not receiving the attention of former days. He would, of course, always give his moustache a brisk wipe when he finished his meals, as one would expect of a man of his caliber and position in life, but it was always a little too brisk, a little too inadequate.

But it would be a mistake to assume that, with the disaster of the fire and the inevitable onset of old age, Kiichiro had lost all his former vitality and was now merely idling away his time drinking Bordeaux among the ruins of his radium bath. Indeed, over the past month he had shown an energy such as had not been seen in him for ten years, and although he still left all the clinical work of the hospital to Tetsukichi and the others, he was perpetually off somewhere in a state of busy eagerness. A judgment had recently been handed down in the lawsuit involving the land on which the Nire Hospital stood, and the hospital had won, providing Kiichiro with the opportunity, which he had not enjoyed for some time, to beam all over his face and declare with studied calmness:

"Well, can't say I'm surprised. Bound to happen. If only Tanabe [his lawyer] had bestirred himself a bit we'd have had the judgment six months ago."

But, for all the inevitability of this legal decision, Kiichiro was sufficiently relieved to send his wife and eldest daughter to the great Kannon Temple in Asakusa to offer thanks to the highest authorities. Despite his age, Kiichiro seemed fully recovered from his temporary afflictions, and his brain had begun to work again in its old excessively complicated way.

Just then the Deputy, Hidekichi Katsumata, came onto the scene, entering the room with rimless spectacles glinting and with that reverential yet carefree manner peculiar to him. He was carrying the draft of a letter of attorney which was to be sent to a trust company from whom Kiichiro had decided a few days ago he would borrow money.

Kiichiro glanced over it with remarkable speed.

> I, the undersigned, by the power of attorney vested in me, propose and agree to the following: The debtor, Kiichiro Nire, will borrow the sum of   yen from the Kanto Trust Company Limited in accordance with the conditions as given below, whereby both I and the said Kiichiro Nire do hereby give joint witness that

mortgage rights of the first order will be established in which the security offered is that as herewith set forth in further detail in a separate affidavit attached to this and to which we both set our hands in joint guarantee.

Conditions of Loan

1) Repayment to be completed by
2) Interest to be paid at the rate of ten percent per annum.
3) Interest to be paid on or before the fifteenth day of each month.
4) In the event of repayment remaining unfulfilled by the date as set forth above, an extra compensatory interest rate may be demanded, not to exceed   per annum.

"I suppose that will do," said Kiichiro quickly, nodding as if he found the whole thing boring and distasteful. His expression then changed to one of positive annoyance. "After all, one doesn't want anything too correct, too precise in matters like this. Something like what you've produced should do the trick. Don't want to overdo it, do we?. . . Still, well done, well done. Get this thing to Shiohara, will you?"

The Deputy bowed in acknowledgment, and his thin, wading-bird frame disappeared through the door, the figure of the incoming Yasusaburo Sugano in student uniform passing him as he went out. Kiichiro immediately glanced up at the newcomer and spoke quickly as if he had been waiting some time for him to show up:

"Ah. Now I want plenty of string. Any kind will do. What you wrap parcels up with. Anything you like. Get as much as you can."

"What would you be planning to do with it, sir?"

"Measure some land," the Director replied. "Tie all the string together and tie paper streamers to it at intervals of two yards. Make sure you tie them on properly. Want it as long as possible. Something in the region of a hundred yards should be enough."

While Yasusaburo went off to make preparations for he was not quite sure what, Kiichiro went to the kitchen and ordered a packed lunch. Eventually someone had had to tell Kiichiro that he should be careful about his eating habits if he wanted to avoid diabetes, and he now seemed to be trying to change his ways to some extent. His appetite appeared to have increased, so he now lunched each day on plain balls of rice with laver wrapped about them and with innocuous things like dried bonito and dry, bitter plums added to give some pretense of flavor. It was this kind of lunch he was now ordering.

After this, Kiichiro changed into a Western-style suit, something he rarely wore nowadays, wrapped his lunchbox in a large cloth, stuffed his briefcase with quantities of string, drawing paper, a ruler and pencils, and handed all this to Yasusaburo to carry. Then they left the house. Of the two hospital cars, one had been destroyed in the fire and the other had been disposed of, so they took the streetcar to Shibuya, a mile or so away, and changed from there onto the Tamagawa Electric Line, alighting at Sangenjaya Station from which they were to go on foot to Matsubara.

Sangenjaya Station is some two miles southwest of Shibuya, and Matsubara is in the same Setagaya ward of present-day Tokyo, another one and a half miles northwest of there. While they were walking this distance, Kiichiro told the as yet uninitiated Yasusaburo what they were going to do that day. They were going to examine a plot of land in Matsubara that was to be the site of the new hospital he intended to build.

The Director spoke with much the same fluency as when Yasusaburo had first come to Tokyo. It was not exactly eloquent, but he certainly seemed to have recaptured his ability to nip smartly from one point to another, as well as his power to stir people's emotions or deliberately confuse their minds—whichever way one chooses to look at it.

"I've already come to an understanding with the man who owns the land. The plans for the hospital have been drawn up. The contractor's decided. What do you think about that, eh? I move like greased lightning, don't I? We've won the lawsuit over the land in Aoyama, but the police still haven't given us permission to rebuild. Can't go on waiting for that forever. No idea when it will be given. And I'm not the kind of man who likes to be kept waiting, am I?"

After a significant pause he went on:

"The Deputy and the others want to stick to the land in Aoyama. It's all they can think about. Their thinking's limited; they can't see the way things are moving. Sometime in the future the whole of Aoyama will be jam-packed with houses. Tokyo will expand and go on expanding. Setagaya will eventually become part of Tokyo. A big hospital needs to be in the suburbs, and that's where mine will be. Aoyama will be mainly for outpatients. Inpatients will be sent to the hospital in the suburbs. That's the only way to do it, you know, the only possible way. You've got to look to the future. You've got to see one generation, even two generations ahead, the way I do, the way I always have done and will do."

242

As he listened to this flow of persuasive words, Yasusaburo was once more tempted to think that the Director was a remarkable man and that, no matter how senile some claimed he was, here surely was a plan for the hospital that was absolutely right. He was tempted to think this way, but he still felt a faint shadow of doubt. Even if it was a good idea to build a hospital in the suburbs, where was the capital for this project to come from? At present the very salaries of the limited number of staff were seldom forthcoming, and on top of this there was a rumor, which might or might not be true, that even the savings (which could not be much) of veteran servants, such as the maid who had served "within" and Nanny Shimoda, had been appropriated, or borrowed, by the Director.

As if he were able to read the doubt that had arisen in Yasusaburo's simple mind, the Director went on in an offhand way:

"You know, I don't have a penny of my own. But that won't stop me building a hospital. Mark my words, what really matters is using your head and getting people to trust you. So, I rent some land in Matsubara and build a hospital. I then use the hospital as security and borrow some money, thus paying for the cost of the land and the building. Just you wait and see. The hospital I build this time won't be much of a place to look at, mere temporary structure, but someday I'll put something up just like the old one in Aoyama. In fact I'll build something on twice the scale of that, something really palatial. And I'll do it before I die. I'll build a hospital and then I'll stand for the Diet again. I can't die until I've done that. Just look at me; look at my face, my complexion. Plenty of color there, plenty of life. Just like a young man. And my secret is that whatever I set out to do, I know that, sooner or later, I shall do it; do it my way in my own good time."

Yasusaburo accepted the invitation and stole a quick glance at the Director's profile as they walked along. In fact his wrinkled face had not much color or life to it, although the eyes beneath his graying eyebrows were certainly alive: they glittered with that energy of his which alone seemed always so persuasive.

The area from Sangenjaya to Matsubara was still open country at that time. The sun shone down strongly enough to make one sweat, and the road lay white and dry beneath it. Kiichiro went on talking in great good humor throughout the long walk. He had now got onto a subject that had been widely discussed a little while before, a scandal involving the Office of Reconstruction in Tokyo.

"As you can see in that case, Watanabe is one of the few really big landowners in the country, and yet he has all those problems. That's one of the interesting aspects of politics, what's really going on behind the scenes. That's what fascinates me. Of course, you're too young to understand, but politics is intriguing. You're not just dealing with one patient like you are as a doctor, but with a whole country.''

They came to Umegaoka, a place consisting wholly of cornfields with just one house in the middle of it all. This belonged to the rich farmer who owned the land. They entered the house, and it appeared that agreement must have been reached on the essentials beforehand because, after a few minutes of obligatory chatter, a map of the area was produced. It was still a little early for lunch, but as tea had been served they ate their packed lunches. Yasusaburo observed that the Director, whom he had always known as a man who hardly touched proper food, was tucking into a solid meal of rice balls with what appeared to be a voracious appetite. Even a minor accomplishment such as eating a ball of rice could strike the simple Yasusaburo with admiration for the vigor and dash of the master he was privileged to serve.

They then went out to the proposed site. Before, behind, and to both sides stretched cornfields, nothing but cornfields. There was a gently flowing stream, and on crossing that there were more fields of unripe corn with the occasional thatched roof of a farmhouse in the distance. Yasusaburo was appalled by the rural nature of the scene. How could one expect any patients to come out here? But Kiichiro seemed untroubled by doubts of that kind, and set off walking briskly, turning to look back at Yasusaburo who had halted momentarily, and urging him to come on because they were there.

So this was the place: the same prospect of flat cornfields, with nothing of interest or distinction. There was, it it true, a slight rise ahead of them and along its ridge a wood of what were probably small oaks. Yasusaburo was so disappointed he could say nothing, but Kiichiro spoke in tones of true delight.

''Look at it. Marvelous place. We build with the high ground to the rear and the low ground to the front. That's lucky. Best direction for a building. Means expansion. Wonderful place. Couldn't be better. Marvelous place this.''

Yasusaburo did not know what to say, so he asked what the extent of it was.

''Six or seven acres. Not quite sure. That's what is going to be measured forthwith with great precision.''

''Do you mean, by me, sir?'' asked the astonished Yasusaburo. How could an amateur like himself measure all those acres? "But surely the measurements are given on the map, sir?"

"Hah, you can't trust a thing like that. It's only very rough; all sorts of problems would arise later if we believed that. Now, all you have to do is follow instructions. I've done this sort of thing before. Bit of an expert, you might say. You just do what I tell you."

Kiichiro pulled the great length of string with paper streamers attached at regular intervals out of his briefcase, and Yasusaburo set to work despite his misgivings. He had to walk off into the cornfield as instructed, making constant reference to the map, and pulling the hundred-yard length of string behind him. The earth in the field was dark and soft, and with each step his shoes sank down into it.

The sky was clear. Larks were singing somewhere, unseen, probably far away above the higher ground, and their liquid notes fell through the air, descending over the whole expanse of the fields, filling the emptiness. But Yasusaburo was much too busy to stand about listening to them. Kiichiro stood at a point on the boundary of the site with one end of the string in his hand. Yasusaburo went off in the required direction pulling the string after him. When it was finally stretched out tight he would stay where he was, and Kiichiro would walk to join him and then tell him where to go next. Since the land was not rectangular it wasn't simply a question of taking a few measurements up and across. Kiichiro had made smart use of his ruler and drawn an outline of the area to be measured on a piece of drawing paper which he had spread out on the path. He divided this into segments, all of which, as he made quite clear, had to be measured. Each time the measurements were taken they would return to the path and write them down on the piece of paper.

"It's all slant lines around here," said Kiichiro, a little old man whose shoes were covered in mud and who kept wiping the sweat from his forehead, but who showed no obvious signs of fatigue. "It's no good measuring a place like this just up and down and across, you know. You need your diagonals and perpendiculars on a job like this. Working with triangles, you see. Got to grasp the area in triangular form."

The sky remained a brilliant blue. The larks still sang. The sun beat down now, inducing sleep. The expanse of corn seemed to be caught in a great silence. Some way off the figures of two or three farmers could be seen, but there was no sign of anything else moving. In this peaceful landscape, the little old man and his tall assistant worked endlessly, stretching their long piece of string, walking, stopping, returning, writing their measurements on the piece of paper.

Time passed more quickly than it seemed. The sky was still blue and clear but some of the warm light had left it, and a shadow had silently entered the landscape, unnoticed but felt all the same.

"This is the last one. This bit's square. You just have to measure over to that oak tree on the edge of the wood. A rough measurement will do. Then we'll call it a day."

Kiichiro was at last looking a little tired, and he walked slowly back through the cornfield toward the path. Yasusaburo was now used to his task and did it fairly skillfully, dragging the string along behind him between the ridges in the field, which was fairly deep in corn here, trying not to let it get too slack and at the same time ensuring that the other end did not pull away from its loose mooring.

Still, he went at a fairly smart pace toward the distant oak, and when the string had been paid out to its fullest extent he gave it a hearty jerk so that the other end was freed and could be pulled toward him. He then repeated the operation, which required concentration if it was to be done without mishap. Once he had finally arrived at the oak tree, he worked out the yards he had covered and carefully stored the number in his head. Relieved that this day's important labor was at last over, he set off back in the direction of the path.

Some distance away he could see the small figure of the Director squatting down on the pathway between the cornfields, no doubt making some eager calculations on the drawing paper. But after he had taken a few more paces, he noticed that Kiichiro was leaning forward in a peculiar way, with his forehead apparently touching the ground, like a toad with its head beaten flat by something. Yasusaburo felt a lurch of foreboding and called out to him, but there was no reply, and Kiichiro maintained the same unnatural position.

Yasusaburo started to run, but the soft earth impeded him. As he ran he called out again.

When he finally got there, Kiichiro suddenly keeled over and lay on the road. One look at his face was enough to make Yasusaburo's flesh creep. His eyes had clouded over, only the white parts staring dully, and it was impossible to be sure if he were actually looking at him and recognized him or not. Yasusaburo attempted to help him up, but Kiichiro's left arm alone responded with a twitching movement, and a thick sound escaped from his mouth.

Yasusaburo had now lost all possession of himself, and he called out the Director's name three times, but the only response was a stream of saliva from the old man's pallid lips, the kind a baby dribbles out, a purely animal reaction unrelated to the will or mind. It was clear he was trying to say something, but all that could be heard was an unintelligible, harsh sound coming from somewhere in his throat.

Yasusaburo decided he could do nothing by himself but must get help. The Director's body had gone quite stiff, but he managed to get him lying down on his back and then left him, running off along the path through the cornfields. It was a long way to the landlord's farmhouse, but in a field some distance away he could see the figure of a farmer. He shouted as he ran in an attempt to attract the man's attention, but the distant figure did not turn and look in his direction. The fields seemed to extend forever, an endless sea of green. Yasusaburo ran on, gasping for breath and howling for all he was worth, but aware, amid the passion that drove him on, of the uselessness of his cries.

By the time Kiichiro was finally carried into the landlord's farmhouse he had fallen into a deep coma. His throat gurgled occasionally, and his bloodless lips sometimes trembled with the heavy movements of his painful breathing. This condition lasted another two hours, and then he breathed his last, before any of his family or the doctors at the hospital could reach him. His final moments were watched over by total strangers. Even Yasusaburo was not there. He had gone to find the nearest telephone, which was some distance away, and did not return in time.

The funeral was attended by many people; great numbers of wreaths were offered, the wrestlers from Dewanoumi's stable stood awkwardly around, embarrassed by their huge bodies, and many former workmen at the hospital moved swiftly about the place in short *happi* coats, giving an air of liveliness to the proceedings reminiscent of the great days before the fire. In the eyes of the family, however, in particular those of Ryuko, the occasion was a poor and empty one, and lacked the magnificence it should have had.

"If only the hospital had been as it once was," thought Ryuko to herself as she maintained a stern, dignified posture, not letting even one tear fall. "Then Father's funeral needn't have been like this. How magnificent it all would have been, so splendid that even Father would have smiled in his coffin, saying 'well done' and thanking us for all our efforts."

Some of Kiichiro's favorite things were put in that coffin, although there was no great number of these owing to last year's fire. In addition, there were half a dozen bottles of the Bordeaux he had loved so much during his lifetime, all beautifully washed and nicely stacked in place. Ryuko had wanted to put in at least a dozen, but the other people involved had managed to talk her into agreeing to half that number.

So Jinsaku Kanazawa, alias Kiichiro Nire, passed away suddenly and casually at the age of sixty-three, so suddenly and casually that all those who knew him were united in finding the news unbelievable; and in December of that same year, 1926, the Emperor Taisho also died, and so the name of the era changed and the Showa period had begun.

II

WELL DONE

Chapter

1

Small, wooden, four-wheeled streetcars with safety fenders stuck out in front of them clanged by, raising an ear-piercing rattle as one-yen taxicabs nipped smartly past them on the inside. A more leisurely clatter of hooves accompanied horse-drawn carts, and the delivery boy from the noodle shop darted about on his bicycle, balancing his loads dexterously but dangerously with one hand. There were all sorts of shops—shops selling almost everything, greengrocers, wholesale paper stores, cheap eating houses with not very clean shop curtains hanging above the doorway, snug little bookstores with the inevitable banner outside advertising the *Boy's Own Weekly;* this was the main street of Aoyama Minamimachi, with the Showa era now in full swing. True, most of the buildings were still made of wood and paper, still jammed close to one another, grubby and low-roofed just as before; but now the street was overflowing with bustle and energy. This would have been unimaginable at the time the Nire Hospital had been built here, back in the 37th year of Meiji, 1904. Even in comparison with what it had been on the fifteenth anniversary of the hospital in the 7th year of Taisho, 1918, when the complacent Kiichiro had handed out prizes to so many, it was a totally different world.

Certainly, the completion of the Meiji Shrine in 1920 had made a significant contribution to the development of the Aoyama area, but then the same kind of thing had happened all over Tokyo: a sudden increase in the number of buildings, which could not be reduced to any one cause. The city itself had recently enlarged its area in one sudden leap, the number of its wards being increased from fifteen to thirty-five as various outlying, previously rural districts had been brought within its boundaries. In this way, the population rose to half a million and Tokyo had become one of the world's largest cities.

But, to return to Aoyama: if one walked away from the Meiji Shrine toward the great Aoyama Cemetery, one came across a district whose character was in great contrast to the noise and vigor of the main street.

This was an area of desirable residences inhabited by the idle rich, by the busy rich, or by senior officers of the army and navy. The dark walls enclosing these houses were long, arousing boredom in the children who walked by them. The graveled forecourts seen through the gates were always neatly raked, and the main buildings slept silently in the shadow of tall trees, arousing doubts as to whether people actually lived there or not.

When one arrived at the Nire Hospital, with its low wall of faded brick, the atmosphere again changed. The hospital, once so magnificent with its rows of columns and its towers, was now no more than a cluster of commonplace wooden buildings, such as one might find anywhere. The makeshift outpatients building which had been put up soon after the fire was tumbledown and decayed, and a few similarly characterless buildings could be seen beyond it; these were wards that had been added at later dates. The hospital's land had been more than halved, and if one inspected the sign at the entrance one found that this was the "Branch Hospital"; the "Main Hospital" was the new one that had been built in Matsubara.

Despite this reduction in size and importance, the hospital still played a peculiar role in the area. The first reason for this was the obvious one that it housed lunatics, and the second was that it provided a certain amount of open space and encouraged the existence of similarly empty areas nearby. The large field in front of the hospital, Moto-no-hara, had been reduced to half its size by the encroachment of housing, but this seemed only to emphasize the portion that remained, as well as that part of the hospital grounds which had once been occupied by wards but was now empty, the part nearest the cemetery. Although no longer hospital land, it was still surrounded by the low brick wall, being the largest open space for the neighborhood children to play in, and well known for that reason.

The field seemed to change in character according to the type and number of people in it. At times it would be a hubbub of activity and cheerful life; at others a silent vacancy. In spring and summer various undistinguished weeds flowered there, but there were also clusters of plants that provided a fragrant cushion on which to recline. There were some consisting of bunches of leaves apparently joined together at random, which produced a bitter liquid something like cuckoo-spit in appearance. Though ordinary and dull in themselves, these plants attracted grasshoppers and dragonflies which were much sought after by the children who played there. And when these various weeds had grown to maturity, and started to wither and decay, some of them —knotweed and galingale, but others, too—assumed a mysterious brilliance of color and form.

As the seasons changed so would the games the children played, and these changes also reflected the larger transformations of society, the movements of the age. Until recently, for example, the games of "soldiers" they had played in this field had had a certain innocent charm. A child holding a toy bugle, or a piece of wood that was meant to be one, would charge boldly forward and suddenly fall flat on his back, remaining motionless with the bugle or stick stuck between his lips for a long time. The game was based on an episode in the Russo-Japanese War which appeared in the school textbooks in the form of a moral tale about a hero who, though dead, "still kept his bugle clapped firmly to his lips." Recently, however, the children had thought up a new game. It consisted in entwining string between the bushes and tufts of grass to represent barbed wire. Then the children would arm themselves with bamboo poles normally used for hanging out the laundry, crawl forward, and finally, with a high-pitched howl meant to represent a bomb exploding, pretend to die near the "barbed wire." This was based on the more recent exploit of the "three human bombs" who had sacrificed themselves in this way during the Shanghai Incident of 1932.

In one corner of the field were the remains of a red brick building which now looked like an ancient ruin. It had been a ward, and the one structure of the former Nire Hospital to have actually been made of brick. Now it was mostly broken down, rubble or potential rubble, uninteresting yet still vaguely pathetic, a disfigured, cavernous shell. The children tended to avoid it, not only for the eminently rational reason that what remained might well fall down at any moment, but also because it had become a tradition among them that the remains of "a mad woman who had hanged herself" could be found there. They referred to their playground, which was precious to them even if somewhat scary (and doubtless more attractive for that reason), as the "madhouse meadow."

Grown-ups, too, enjoyed their leisure moments here, the majority of them joining in the games of the children, flying kites or playing baseball with great seriousness. Others walked about on missions of their own devising. One man, for example, who was normally attended by a nurse in white uniform, strode about purposefully. Despite the assurance with which he walked, he was undoubtedly one of the patients from the mental hospital. And almost every day a man in

Japanese dress would bring a beautifully groomed Alsatian for exercise here. Holding the wide sleeve of his right arm out of the way with his left hand, he would ostentatiously hurl a ball as far as he could. The dog would bound after it, sniffing busily and very audibly among the grass. Its master would follow its stylish antics with passionate concern, shouting instructions that added to the stylishness of the occasion since the words "right" and "left" were delivered in English. Unfortunately, this handsome sight was occasionally marred by the presence of a shabby individual, a ragpicker, who would search among the rubbish that got thrown away here for things like empty bottles; these he would pick up with a long pair of metal pincers and toss into a basket he carried on his back. He worked at great speed, as if driven by a sense of terrible urgency.

At this point in our story the "madhouse meadow" by the cemetery was a gray, chilly place. Clouds hung low over it, presaging the frosts and snows to come. A few people, both adults and children, were flying kites. It was not yet the proper season for this, so the kite fliers were obviously enthusiasts, perhaps experts, and the kites drifted up into the cloudy gray sky dangling long tails beneath them, distant, small and peaceful.

There were many more children, mostly boys, on the road just by the entrance to the field, half of them dressed in Western-style clothes, the others wearing lined kimono with shiny, grubby sleeve bands. Judging by the broken *geta* they wore on their feet and the holes in their *tabi* or socks, from which black toenails peered out, the children were of the lower orders, who had gathered here to play competitive games. In front of them were a number of old washing bowls, rusty and full of holes, which they had placed upside down and covered with ancient straw matting, creating an ideal arena for the pursuit in which they were passionately and tirelessly engaged: top spinning. Among them were two or three older boys, apparently in senior grade at primary school, who performed with all the cool aplomb of the practiced artist. One of them would quickly wind the string about his top, stand poised for a second in a strained, tense attitude, then flick the string sharply; the top would shoot onto the platform with a groaning whirr, bowling over the opponent's top. With no change in his workmanlike expression, the winner would pick up the top he'd just sent spinning off the upturned bowl onto the ground, and slip it inside the breast of his kimono. Since their kimonos were held around the hips by a sash, the appropriated top came to rest above the sash, and each boy's success could be gauged from the way his kimono bulged out around the waist.

Among the children was one little girl wearing conspicuously good clothes. Her pert little head was tilted slightly to one side and she was observing all that was going on. She wore a red, fluffy sweater, and beneath her short skirt her legs, in neat black socks, were slim and graceful. This was Aiko, the youngest daughter of the Nire household, and she had started going to primary school this year. There was no trace of the feeble, melancholy baby she had been, and it was also clear that the expectations she had once aroused had been exaggerated, for she now showed none of the charm and elegant beauty her dead aunt, Seiko, had possessed. Indeed, the willful curl of her lip gave an impression of arrogance, even nastiness, although in this company she looked sweet enough. Her clothes, her features, her upbringing seemed to give her a special place among these children, for the children from the "desirable residences" nearby never appeared in a place like this. More important, however, was the fact that Aiko had an apparently inexhaustible supply of the objects that were of such importance here. Just as her aunt Momoko had recklessly acquired erasers in the past, Aiko could get as many as she liked of these cheap, small, yet enormously satisfying toys on tick from the Seiundo.

She herself did not take part in the sport, and made no attempt to do so. Her role was different, that of a small queen who would bestow her favors arbitrarily on any subject by roughly casting one of the tops that filled her hands to the boy of her choice. Which she now did, suddenly giving one to a little boy with a runny nose who was even smaller than herself.

"Here, you have a go," she said.

The little boy was taken slightly aback and smiled in an embarrassed way, but he was overjoyed all the same, passionately winding his piece of string (which he possessed if nothing else) about the godsend, with the result that in five seconds he no longer had it.

"Not much good, are you? Still, here's another."

The result was the same, and Aiko now spoke in a positively spiteful manner:

"Right. Last chance. And don't think you're going to get any more out of me."

She was clearly annoyed that the person she had selected should have failed, and she turned icily away from him with the intention of giving a top to another boy, aware that she could choose anyone she pleased.

Another child of the Nire household was also present, the third offspring of the union of Tetsukichi and Ryuko, Aiko's younger brother, Shuji.

Recently the expression "Showa child" had come into use, and this name could properly be given to Shuji. Children born in the 1st year of Showa, 1926, were really Taisho children since that year was also the last year of the Taisho era. But Shuji had been born in the 2nd year of Showa (a month before he was expected, his mother having suddenly gone into labor while she was out driving), so there could be no argument over which age he belonged to.

The Showa era was an energetic period. The country had finally recovered from the earthquake disaster and faced an exciting future, and true Showa children were expected to have a similarly forthright character. This Shuji certainly did not possess. Indeed he seemed quite the opposite. He had a pathetic, negative appearance. Despite its not being really winter yet, he wore a padded kimono which was too long for him, and he looked as puffy as a little Chink (for the Japanese referred to the Chinese in such scornful terms at the time); the skirts of the kimono were all plastered with mud where they had dragged on the ground. The reason for the great difference in the way he and his sister were dressed was that Aiko was occasionally taken out by her mother, but Shuji never was. His appearance was solely the concern of Nanny Shimoda, and was totally uninfluenced by Ryuko's tastes.

Shuji was also quite lacking in the refinement proper to a child of good family, which Aiko had to some extent. His incompetently shaven head showed an ugly whorl of hair on the right-hand side, and his features had an air of desperation and cowardice reminiscent of an elderly, cornered mouse. He was squatting down with the other children, but was obviously not taking part in the game. In fact, he was being completely ignored both by them and by his sister. He had not yet acquired any adequate skill in top spinning, nor the confidence to go like his sister to the Seiundo and get tops for nothing. He simply gazed feebly at the other children, his mouth half open, watching their excited activity with a mixture of envy and careful observation, as if he was attempting to understand what he saw.

Except for the handful who were totally absorbed in the game, the children now suddenly turned around and looked eagerly at something behind them, those who were squatting down standing up with little gasps of satisfaction. A column of marching soldiers had appeared.

The soldiers of the Third Regiment always returned to their barracks along this road on their way back from the parade ground at Yoyogi, just to the west of Aoyama, so there was nothing special about the sight. Clattering field guns had been dragged by before now, and the children had even grown accustomed to officers riding past on well-groomed, elaborately accoutered horses. The officers were either so dignified that they sat upright in their saddles and did not even glance at the children, or they were casually confident and cheerfully waved a hand. Their assurance was nothing to be surprised at, for things were quite different from what they had been in the early 1920s when the idea of disarmament had been in favor and soldiers would wander about unobtrusively in civilian clothes. Military training had been part of the normal school curriculum for some time now, and the military no longer raised in people's minds images of distant heroics in the wars against China and Russia at the turn of the century, but were very much a part of the present. Its bold exploits during the Manchurian and Shanghai incidents had confirmed the military's role as defender of the Japanese lifelines and creator of national power and prestige.

As if to emphasize the dignity of their calling, the small column of soldiers was commanded to burst into song. So one of the NCOs marching at the head of the column drew in his breath, gazed slightly upward with solemn eyes, and led them into the first verse:

> "Hundreds of miles from home we are,
> Far from our own country,
> Parted from all that we hold dear,
> Here in Manchuria."

Whereupon the whole column opened their mouths wide and roared out the same lines. Each one of them was no doubt tired but they sang seriously, adjusting their rifles on their shoulders. Their voices gave the impression they were performing something that had become completely habitual.

The man in front went on with the next verse:

> "Bathed in the red rays of the sun
> There as it went to rest,
> I saw him lying in that field,
> My friend, behind a stone."

The chorus took up these lines as before. Though rough and unrefined, the voices were certainly manly and heroic. Their very hoarseness added interest to those sentimental old-fashioned words which made such a contrast to the brisk, martial tune.

The troops came nearer and nearer, all tough and sunburned men, their voices echoing as they marched proudly along. And now they passed right before the children's eyes, each with his rifle, ammunition pouches, bayonet, scabbard and mud-stained puttees—objects that stirred their admiration, a whole brilliant succession of them, an overwhelming flood of khaki and steel and sweat and strained, singing voices.

Aiko craned her neck to look for a familiar face among them, but the boots tramped on, the barrels of the rifles gleamed, the crude military voices sounded in her ears, and then all were gone.

"Sadaits isn't there," she muttered in a disappointed voice.

"Who's Sadaits?" asked a boy who, although older than her, was not unwilling to pay court to this girl who had so many tops by showing some interest in her affairs.

"He's one of our interns. He's a private first class now."

Sadaichi Sawara was one of the young Nire Hospital interns, a serious, honest person who had always done much more work than he was asked to do, and who was known familiarly in cookhouse circles as "Sadaits." While he had been living in the hospital Aiko had never had the opportunity to take part in top-spinning contests, because Sadaichi was always in nervous attendance on the young children of the house whenever they went outside the hospital gates. Once he had become a soldier Aiko had at last been able to indulge the desire for adventure that was so large a part of her character. But she still retained a great affection for him, and she always looked for his face whenever a squad of soldiers went by.

She repeated that he wasn't there, looking crestfallen now, even critical of his absence. But then she reflected aloud that it was no doubt because he had been promoted to lance corporal and so would be riding a horse.

"Lance corporals don't ride horses," the boy pointed out with scorn in his voice, but her attention was distracted from this by the little boy with the runny nose who had been the honored recipient of three tops from her.

"Here, look what I've got," he said, and produced from the pocket of his short trousers a small, cylindrical, metal object that glinted a dull bronze. It was a spent cartridge case he had been lucky enough to find while playing on "rifle hill," a small piece of rising ground crossed by a winding path that was almost concealed by bamboo grass. The hill was used on weekdays by the Third Regiment for firing practice.

Aiko had never touched anything like this before, and gaped at it for a brief moment as if it had been a pearl brooch; but then she turned her nose away in contempt, casually remarking that she had only to go and see Sadaits and he would give her dozens of them, as many as she wanted, just like that.

The little boy who had produced this treasure sheepishly put it back in his pocket. He had not noticed that the brother of this arrogant young lady had suddenly strained forward, his habitually slack mouth hanging open to twice its normal extent as he gaped like a cretin, eyes unblinking, agog at the vision that was so swiftly removed.

The squad of soldiers, too, had passed out of sight. They had turned the corner past the smaller cemetery, and now seemed to be marching along the valley between that and the larger Aoyama Cemetery, since snatches of song could still be heard.

> "I know that discipline is strict,
> Orders must be obeyed;
> But how could I just leave him there,
> Wounded in that field?
>
> " 'Be of good heart,' I said to him,
> Raising him from the ground.
> And as the bullets flew and sang
> I bandaged up his wounds.
>
> "I knew this kind of thing must be
> When in a bayonet charge,
> When finally he raised his head
> And then he spoke these words:
>
> " 'Go on for our dear country's sake.
> Don't trouble about me.
> You must not linger in the fight.'
> And tears were in his eyes."

The singing voices became faint as they were cut off by the trees of the cemetery, and the simple melody acquired a poignancy quite alien to a martial song.

It wasn't long after this source of entertainment had vanished that

Aiko found another. In a cheerful voice she shouted out that her mother was coming; and, sure enough, she was, in the shiny black car the hospital had recently bought, which had appeared at the distant turning in the road.

Aiko immediately began running in the direction of the car, as did a number of the other small children. Their *geta* made a dull sound as they clopped along the earthen road. Then Shuji, who had been standing about vacantly, finally grasped what was going on; and, like an obtuse parrot, he repeated his sister's message that their mother was coming, and set off eagerly after the others, the long skirts of his padded kimono getting tangled about his legs and reducing his gait to a kind of prolonged stumble.

The car stopped in front of the hospital gates. Its box-like appearance, without a hint of streamlining, would no doubt remind a later generation of a motorized hearse, but at that time it was the very latest model, a 1933 Chrysler. The fact that the Nire Hospital could afford this luxury suggested that the financial fortunes of the hospital had at last taken an upward turn, but perhaps it was more a sign that Ryuko had ceased to be the "young mistress" of the household and was now the mistress proper. Recently her visitings and leave-takings and issuings forth had become noticeably frequent.

Aiko called her mother "Mama" in the newfangled way, and this was a sufficiently unusual form of address for the deprived children who were running after her to wonder who this might be. They were certainly rewarded by the sight of "Mama" as she descended from the car, for she had an aggressively modern appearance sufficient to satisfy all of them. In fact, Ryuko was not all that dressed up since she had not been visiting. She had on everyday clothes, a slightly masculine suit of black cashmere, with a satin scarf tied at the collar. Her hair was cut short and hung neatly about the nape of her neck.

Aiko was out of breath and she bawled at her mother with a vulgarity well suited to the company she had just been keeping, asking if she had been bought a present. Shuji, who had finally come tottering up from behind, repeated the same question, though in a much dafter tone of voice:

"Mama, have you got my present?"

Ryuko glanced briefly at these two young children of hers, and then at the children surrounding them who clearly came from those poor tenement houses in front of the smaller cemetery. Her face seemed to have grown longer recently, and it now resembled her mother Hisa's face to a startling degree. This accentuated the look of displeasure that appeared as she briefly shook her head in reply. Then, without a word or the trace of a smile, she passed imperturbably in through the gates, which were very much inferior to those that had once existed here, but which still represented for Aiko's snotty-nosed troop a totally different world from their own.

"Don't seem to be no present," said one of them in so disappointed a voice one might have thought the loss was his own; and to some extent it could have been, for the young lady of the house, Aiko, would sometimes bring out a splendidly large doll for them to practice marksmanship on with their catapults.

"Not today," said Aiko. "But Mama will certainly get me something tomorrow."

One of the older boys, one of those professionals who had acquired a lot of tops that day, felt so envious he had to be nasty to her.

"Your old woman's a thief, then, is she?"

"Why should she be?"

"People who just get things are thieves. If you're not a thief you buy things properly."

This interpretation soon found the support of the other children, who were delighted to pour scorn on Aiko.

"Wow, her old woman's a thief. She's a crook."

At first Aiko stood there with a puzzled expression on her face, but then she began to look very stern. She was angry now, and with an obstinate, arrogant look, her black eyes sparkling behind long eyelashes, she glibly attempted to foil these accusations:

"Well, then, look, she doesn't buy things, and that's that. It's just like when I go to the Seiundo and get things and I don't need any money. So I don't buy things, so there. It's the same with Mama. When Mama goes to a department store she doesn't need any money either. It's all on credit, so you can't say she buys anything, Mama gets things, that's all . . . and it doesn't mean she steals things, nor she's not a thief."

This explanation certainly did not satisfy everyone; even Aiko felt her words lacked conviction. Still, the group appeared to nod its collective head as if accepting the reasonableness of what had been said, and the question of Aiko's mother being a thief was dropped. After all, if they offended the little girl in the red sweater too much, there was always a danger of losing their supply of tops.

The unreal dispute settled for the time being, the children began to drift back toward the place where they had been playing. Aiko, however, did not accompany them, for a maidservant with round, red cheeks appeared at the gates and suddenly grabbed the girl's thin arm with one hand. With the other she seized Shuji by the shoulder. But Shuji refused to come along quietly. Shuji threw his arms and legs about in an outlandish way, squirming and wriggling so much that his filthy padded kimono seemed in imminent danger of being torn to shreds.

Aiko, who had herself been desperate to escape, changed her attitude completely on observing her brother's antics and walked obediently inside the gates, reprimanding the boy in a superior tone of voice:

"Shuji, you'd better watch out. I'm warning you, Mama's going to be really cross at you. You mark my words."

But her little brother took no notice. He was totally transformed from the model of indecision he had so lately been, and with wildly contorted face he struggled with all his might to break free from the maid's hands; which he soon managed to do.

Once he had managed this, and the maid had given up and gone inside with his sister, he ran back to the top-spinning area, mingling with the children there and watching the boys at their game of taking and being taken. A long time passed. Twilight descended and the last kites were reeled in. A flock of crows flew over the field on their way home to their nests. Only about half the original number of boys remained, and still Shuji made no move.

There was no one to reprove him or urge him home. Suddenly Shuji became very fidgety, glancing up and all about him; then, as if he had finally made up his mind, he opened the fingers of one clenched hand. In it was something he had been holding firmly there for hours—one small, clammy, slightly steaming top. Now, looking as if an obscure force were driving him on, impelling him toward this remarkable act, he drew a length of string from his sleeve and began slowly and incompetently winding it about his one and only top.

A contest had just ended. The youth who was running the racket slipped one more prize inside his kimono to join the others bulging there, and said scornfully to Shuji:

"Gonna have a go, then, are you?"

Shuji nodded, and took a pace forward. His addict's abject face had become even paler with the tension of the moment, and his lips had started to tremble. He gripped the top tight and gave it two or three trial flips as he had seen the other boys do. Then, his body strained in readiness, he jerked the string with manic energy away from the top.

His top hardly rotated at all. It just managed to land on the matting-covered bowl, where it trembled dizzily. With a powerful whir, his opponent's thudded into it. Shuji's top was knocked down, and the older boy, announcing coolly that the contest was over, quickly appropriated it.

Shuji found this hard to accept. He went on staring at the matting on the bowl, making a pathetic, sub-linguistic grunt in response. He would not move from the central position he had occupied so briefly.

"Hey, you're in the way," somebody said, but Shuji made no attempt to move or alter his position, as if he had been transformed into an imbecile. This trance-like state was suddenly ended by a pair of rough arms lifting him into the air. It was one of the interns but, unlike the gentle Sadaichi, this man was famous for the speed with which he dealt with any awkward business. So the youngest child of the Nire household, still unreconciled to his fate, still complaining and kicking his legs, was carried off home.

Supper was a simple affair, usually some kind of fish broth made with slices of salmon. "Broth" gives the wrong impression since it was not thickened with stock, nor did it have the traditional garnishings of vegetable to please the eye; it merely consisted of bits of raw salmon boiled up with slices of crudely chopped onion, and was so salty that most people would have screwed up their faces eating it. But the children always seemed to enjoy it enough to ask for several extra helpings of rice. Perhaps this was because the servants seemed invariably to be from the Yamagata region, and salty dishes are the pride of the North. The food consequently was full of salt, and the children had grown accustomed to it. Today, however, of the children only Aiko and Shuji were present; the eldest son, Shun'ichi, was apparently away somewhere, and their father was at some medical staff meeting.

Ryuko got through her meals at a great pace. So long as there was nobody who had to be treated with respect, no guest of higher social rank than herself, she would get the business over with hastily and even crudely. She would also start clearing away the dishes while others were still eating, and the bits of salmon she had left would be scraped unceremoniously onto the children's plates. This lack of courtesy, reflecting a total indifference toward others, was no doubt one more aspect of her aristocratic cast of mind. She was now passing the dishes they had finished with to the maid, and telling her to serve the jelly in the other room once she had disposed of them.

Ryuko referred to the other room as "within," but this word now lacked the tremendous implications it had possessed in the old days. It simply referred to a living room of the same size as the one they were eating in, one of eight mats or about twelve feet square, the kind of living room one would find in any middle-class household. The only special thing about this room "within" was that one of the doors of the deep built-in cupboard, used in normal households for storing bedding, opened to reveal a treasure of Kiichiro's that had escaped the fire: a large, old-fashioned, mahogany wardrobe which seemed to have been made exactly to fit that space. It had rounded doors and innumerable drawers, and was very large. Ryuko referred to it as "the Western wardrobe" and, a true chip off her father's dubious block, she had wanted to have the living room designated as "the Western Wardrobe Parlor." But the length of the name prevented it from catching on, and nobody used it except Ryuko, who liked it a great deal and was always looking for opportunities to direct people to the second right-hand drawer of the Western wardrobe, or to some other part of its geography.

The jelly arrived in a bowl so large that it looked as if it would be difficult to get a good grip on it even with both arms. Into the soft, trembling, glistening substance had been inserted a number of strawberries, objects of great attraction for the children. One would have assumed that this dessert was to be eaten by the whole family, but Ryuko picked up the bowl briskly and easily and disappeared "within." This was being used as a sickroom for none other than her eldest son, Shun'ichi.

Shun'ichi had grown into a tall lad, but that was about the only respect in which he had grown, for in other areas he revealed little progress of any kind. The words Ryuko had used on one famous occasion about her brother Oshu—that the eldest son of the family was often a cretin or buffoon—tended to be used more and more by all the adult relations concerning this youth who was lying there, a little paler than usual but looking perfectly comfortable and happy, though the expression on his face proclaimed an awareness of his right to be sick.

He had suffered a rush of bleeding from the nose—no common nosebleed but one that was completely out of the ordinary and resulted from an accident almost eccentric in nature. There had been so great a discharge of blood that his family had experienced a few nervous moments in which they even thought his life might be in danger.

Shun'ichi was attending middle school in Musashi Koyama, which is some three miles south of Aoyama, and although his former timidity with other people had changed for the better, that was the only kind of improvement he showed, for his grades at school remained indifferent. He had in fact become the kind of person who only needs to be flattered a little and he will do almost anything. He had been transformed into the perfect fall guy, the one who received all the blame for the mischief his class got up to. Whenever a teacher became furious enough to seek out the ringleader of some wild prank, Shun'ichi would invariably be picked on, though it never actually was him: he was merely the dummy who took the blame. This was the background against which the incident of a few days ago had taken place.

The boys liked to buy baked potatoes to enjoy in their leisure moments, and they acquired these by lowering a basket on a string from their classroom window, making sure that it passed over the other side of the enclosing fence (which was very close to the school buildings) in order to reach the point where the baked-potato merchant plied his trade. The basket would then be hauled up with the potatoes inside. Once, however, someone in the staff room below had observed the potatoes in their slow ascent, and inevitably Shun'ichi took the rap again.

A few days passed, and the real boss, the undercover fixer, said to Shun'ichi:

"Nire. The baked potato guy's come again. You got the nerve to have another go?"

"It's hopeless from here. The staff room's right below," replied Shun'ichi, on this occasion showing a modicum of intelligence.

"Okay, then, we'll go up on the roof. We'll do it as far away from the staff room as we can get."

A number of them went up onto the roof, the fixer not forgetting to take the deputy class leader along as a precaution. This individual, called Tatsunori Shiroki, was not as serious and well behaved as his excellent grades suggested, but the boss felt that involving him in the crime would ensure more lenient treatment for them all if they were caught.

"Nire, you're best at this kind of work, so you'd better do it, all right?"

"I'll provide the ten sen, but someone else can pull up the basket," said Shun'ichi, who seemed to be growing wiser all the time.

Whereupon Shiroki volunteered his services, accepting this illegal task in a frank, manly way and impetuously casting the basket down from the roof. With the money wrapped in paper and secured inside it, the basket fell precisely outside the fence where the potato baker was waiting in readiness.

"Great stuff," two or three voices cried out, one of them being Shun'ichi, whose measure of wisdom seemed to have decreased sharply at this point, as he seemed barely able to control his feelings of admiration.

Despite the complete success of this part of the operation, disaster lay ahead. As the basket laden with piping hot potatoes made its slow ascent, the handle of an umbrella suddenly protruded from one of the windows below to impede its progress.

"Damn. It's someone on the second floor. Get going, somebody. Nire, this is a job for you."

"Okay," Shun'ichi replied, having apparently lost all the small wisdom he had recently acquired, and he was off like the wind; but as he was bounding down the stairs he encountered another student coming up. The result was a momentous clash of heads. The youth coming up was merely knocked down, but Shun'ichi started bleeding at the nose in a manner that went well beyond any simple nosebleed. Tremendous quantities of blood were discharged and it seemed the bleeding would never stop. He was carried to the first-aid room, and eventually someone had to telephone his home.

The resulting commotion can be passed over. Suffice it to say that the bleeding did stop at last, and Shun'ichi was now reclining in this temporary sickroom at home. Despite a certain paleness about the face, he seemed well pleased with the situation. Indeed, he appeared to be proud of his exploit and the serious injury he had sustained, and would often say to his young brother and sister:

"If someone loses more than a third of their blood they die. I stopped bleeding just before the one-third mark. It was a close thing."

What pleased him most, however, was that every day he was able to eat a whole bowl of jelly with strawberries in it, since jelly was well known for its efficacy in stopping bleeding. It melted deliciously on the tongue, too.

So Shun'ichi, lying on his stomach on the bed, a look of indescribable contentment on his amiable if overlong face, dug his spoon into the jelly, opened his mouth wide, allowed the full taste of this delicious food to spread over his palate, swallowed, and then repeated the process once again. All the while, Shuji was watching him from the other room, opening his own mouth just as wide. His serious eyes followed every move, from the spoon to his brother's mouth, then from his brother's mouth back to the bowl of jelly. But Shun'ichi never offered him a single spoonful. He was not unaware of his audience, and he seemed in fact to be deliberately playing to it, even the gestures he made with the spoon serving to emphasize the delightfulness of this exotic food. And why should he not play to his audience? Had he not lost nearly a third of his blood? Had he not stood on the shores of the river of death, just one pace from those drear waters? So was he not entitled to eat as much jelly as he pleased? Well aware of the obtrusive gaze of his younger brother, Shun'ichi wore an expression of fulfillment and joy that wouldn't have been out of place in the Buddhist Heaven, the Pure Land of Perfect Bliss; and he slowly dug his large spoon into the jelly again.

Later that evening, having finally shaken off his jelly trance, Shuji played for a short while with his elder sister, meekly taking part in games for girls like cat's cradle and knucklebones. Since he was very clumsy Aiko lost patience with him, and he spent most of the time gazing blankly at the superior performances of his sister.

She was now bouncing a ball on the matted floor to the accompaniment of a song, and gradually allowing Shuji to take some minor role in the activity: he had to extend his fist so that she could exhibit certain skills about it. Finally, the two children sat facing each other doing pat-a-cake with their hands, and singing the following song in chorus.

> "Li Hung-chang with his old bald head.
> It's the chink chink hats that lose and run away.
> Shaved all his head and made him cry.
> Hooray for the Empire, a great victory."

This antique song, referring back to the Sino-Japanese conflict at the end of the nineteenth century, had no doubt been taught them by Nanny Shimoda. The great thing about it was that when they sang it the words seemed to become completely circular, became a round in fact, for the final syllable of the last word "victory" (*shori*) fused with the name Li (pronounced "Ri" in Japanese). And round and round it went, the words having so little meaning that one is tempted to assume they conveyed nothing at all. But it would be wrong to deny that sheer repetition impressed certain ideas and attitudes on their little minds; namely that the Chinks in their chink chink hats were a weak, cowardly people of no importance, and the Japanese Empire was the strongest thing on earth.

It was now about time for the children to go to bed. In came Nanny Shimoda, her sagging features a mass of wrinkles each of which expressed unlimited self-denial and love, and took them away to clean their teeth. Shuji worked away at his incompetently and lengthily, with a toothbrush that was too large for him to handle properly, although this was almost entirely pointless anyway, since he had fallen into the bad habit of keeping a baby's feeding cup of red, fizzy stuff, that same Bordeaux to which Kiichiro had been so addicted, by his pillow, and he would drink it in bed.

The room the children slept in was next to the hall and of the eccentric size of seven and a half mats. The only furniture in it (except for the bedding, of course, which was put down each night and taken up and stacked away in a cupboard each morning) was a tall, narrow chest of drawers and an angular clock fixed to the wooden pillar in the corner of the room.

Aiko changed into her nightdress and crawled into her bedding, and at that moment, far off from beyond the Aoyama Cemetery, the sound of the bugler of the Third Regiment playing "lights out" could be heard faintly but distinctly.

"I don't like that bugle, it sounds so lonely," said Aiko in a very sophisticated manner interspersed with a yawn. Nanny Shimoda was tucking her in tightly. "I know I shan't be able to sleep. That song 'Comrade in Arms' is so sad, all about the battle being over and the sun setting and only the ticking of the clock; all so sad and lonely. I shan't be able to sleep."

"Now then, Mistress Ai, just you go off to sleep nicely," said Nanny Shimoda, patting the eiderdown into place in a workmanlike way; and Aiko did in fact fall almost immediately into a profound sleep, lying there like a doll carved out of wood, hardly even seeming to breathe.

Nanny then changed into her own nightdress, turned down the light and, relaxing her fleshy cheeks to such an extent that they seemed in danger of melting, she got into bed with little Shuji. Not only was Shuji the youngest, but nobody seemed to like him or care about him, and to make up for this neglect Nanny Shimoda had made him the main object of her own eccentric affections. She had brought up any number of the Nire children, one after another, and caring for Shuji was, she felt, the final duty that the powers in heaven were going to ask of her. She was now sixty-four years old, and age had clearly brought about a certain weakening of her erstwhile agile mind, for she had persuaded herself that this six-year-old child was quite exceptional, quite different from all the countless other children, a truly uncommon child, a paragon of intelligence and sweetness. When confronted with any act of his that seemed not particularly clever, if not actually cretinous, she would impose some flattering interpretation on it. For example, if Shuji should tear one of the paper sliding doors (a common enough mishap in a Japanese house) she would put this down to the unique vitality of the child; if, on the contrary, he should be in a sulk, she would see in this some ineffable but undeniable sign of subtlety of character; and if he made some messy and unintelligible scribble with his crayons she would express amazement that the child had already learned how to write at this early age. On the rare occasions when his elder brother or sister made him cry, Nanny Shimoda would feel the child's grief as if it were her own, enfolding his small frame within her much ampler one and saying:

"You mustn't cry, little Shuji. Look, now, your nanny's here to look after you."

Thus all the child's misfortunes ended in a mist of sentimentality and loving kindness, and he was horribly spoiled.

Shuji showed himself at his cowardly worst whenever the son of the charcoal burner from the North, Tatsuji, visited the house. Tatsuji now had his hair done up in the topknot of the proper Sumo wrestler and wore the black *haori* and *montsuki* which is everyday wear in that profession, for, as Zaosan, he had made the grade in some sense. These visits took place only occasionally, and each time Shuji saw the huge *zori* sandals lying at the entrance, looking like two planks and corresponding in no way to the idea of footwear current in normal society, the color would drain from his face and he would screw up his mouth ready to burst into tears. Though he had never seen Zaosan in the flesh, the image had been firmly imprinted on his young mind of some monstrous giant, six feet eight inches in height, with a weird, dangling jaw and thick, blubber lips from which husky, incomprehensible, and inhuman sounds occasionally oozed. This image was an astonishingly vivid one (and corresponded fairly well with reality), so he would never go near the living room in which Zaosan was being received; if anyone attempted to drag him along there he would contort his face horribly and resist with all his might.

269

His sanctuary was the toilet, where he would shut himself up for an hour or two. No one had any idea what he might be up to in there. If an ear were placed to the door the occasional feeble sob could be heard. At times like this it was Nanny's job to comfort the boy, the lily-livered baby of the family; there was nobody else who could have succeeded in this task. She would talk to him in tones so soothing that they would have persuaded the most apprehensive of stray cats:

"Now then, little Shuji, Zaosan has already gone home. He's quite gone now. I've been out front, even, and he's nowhere around at all."

It never once seemed to cross her mind that the boy with whom she was so infatuated might be a feeble, cowardly milksop—though it was not milk but Bordeaux that had taken his fancy. And even of Shuji's taste for this beverage, which came perilously close to a passion, she would enthusiastically assert:

"It just shows that he's got his grandfather's blood, and I don't doubt he'll grow up into a great doctor just like him."

The object of all this love and affection responded in an ambiguous fashion to the fact that his benefactress chose to sleep in the same bed as himself. It was, of course, a source of great relief to him that Nanny Shimoda should be there, but it was also a cause of discomfort because she always fell asleep before her precious boy managed to, and there she would lie in a coma so deep that it looked as if she might have died already. But this was a purely irrational fear on his part, for her body would start to tremble heavily after a while, and she would emit a continuous series of reverberating snores.

On this night, too, Nanny Shimoda fell into an innocent, untroubled sleep, which gradually changed into a symphony of heavy breathing, throat gurgles, and snortings, and mounted to a climax of snoring of unbelievable intensity that was just as unbelievably sustained, the whole of her mountainous body in the grip of an interminable shaking. Shuji lay there as usual with his eyes wide open, no trace of sleepiness coming over him. At his side lay Nanny Shimoda whom he loved, but she had been transformed into something quite different, brute matter that made no response however hard one pushed or pulled it, and produced this indescribably horrid snore. The streams of air she breathed in through her nostrils seemed to clash when they got further inside, and, after a slight pause, the air on its way out again produced a heavy rumbling in her throat that ended in an obtrusive, dull groaning and roaring which made Shuji want to get up and run away somewhere.

This was the person who would enfold him in warmth no matter what happened, the fleshy cradle in which he could bury himself and hide from the world, Nanny Shimoda of the endless affectionate smiles, but now she seemed to have changed into an eerie monster.

This was, of course, Shuji's misreading of the situation. In fact her snores never continued for long, soon quieting down as her sleep became more peaceful. But that peaceful sleep would be interrupted during the night, for Shuji was still at an age when he might wet the bed, and despite her age Nanny Shimoda would wake up out of loving care for him, shake him gently half awake, and set him, still semiconscious, on a chamber pot so that no disaster would befall him in the night. This was something that Shuji remained totally unaware of.

He still lay with his eyes wide open, feeling lonely and afraid. The five-watt bulb cast only a very dim radiance over the seven-and-a-half-mat room, making it seem horribly large, and the ceiling, which the light did not reach, seemed a frighteningly long way off. In the intervals between Nanny's monster snores he could hear the clock measuring out the progress of time with its precise, clear, heartless ticking. . .

His sister, who was sleeping just across the room, was the innocent cause of his present unrest because of her remark about the soldiers' song making you feel lonely. Shuji remembered the phrase she had quoted: "only the ticking of the clock." Then Nanny Shimoda seemed to have taken most of the bedclothes. He tried to curl himself up in the corner left him, and as the relentless snores sounded in his ears he was overcome by the desire to start sniveling.

So he raised himself onto one elbow and sought for the help that lay near at hand by his pillow. There was no form of heating in the room and he felt a cold chill on his forearm which the short, wide sleeve of his nightdress did not cover. But the sense of relief at finding his baby cup with the Bordeaux in it was more than recompense for any discomfort. He put the thin spout of the cup to his mouth and took a gulp of the sweet, cold liquid. The bubbles of gas trembled inside his mouth and throat, producing a tickling sensation on his tongue. He drank three mouthfuls and felt much better. Then he snuggled down among the bedclothes again, curled his small body up even smaller, and closed his eyes tight.

Eventually the loud snores of Nanny Shimoda became gradually quieter, and from the slightly open mouth of the little boy curled up beside her a very slight sound of breathing began to be heard.

Chapter

2

Tetsukichi's characterless room, which had no ornaments, dingy walls, and ancient, yellowing *tatami* on the floor, was ten mats in size (about fifteen feet by twelve) and directly above the seven-and-a-half-mat room in which the children slept. Rather as dust gradually accumulates in an attic room where no one lives, so books had piled up and multiplied in this, spilling out from the bookcases to be heaped in confused mounds on the floor; it looked as if the place belonged to them alone. They ranged from slim paperbacks to thick, shiny, leather-bound volumes, but all were alike in having sections underlined in red ink and bits of memo paper stuck among their pages. They gave the oppressive sense of being too many.

In the spring of 1926, when his adoptive father had suddenly died, Tetsukichi had taken over the directorship of the hospital. To put the matter bluntly, however, he was not cut out for the job. In addition to the problems that the medical side of the hospital gave rise to, there was the fact that the hospital was going through a transitional period in which it would have to be rebuilt from the ashes of that disastrous fire. The financial wizardry this required was something Tetsukichi did not have; he was not the kind of person who should ever have been saddled with such a burden. But the process had already begun when he took over. The whole plan had been worked out by Kiichiro in minute detail, and since he had not lived to see it through Tetsukichi was obliged to try and do so. As he saw it, the idea of building a new hospital in Matsubara was too much of a gamble, given the present state of the hospital, but arrangements to rent the huge area of land had been drawn up by Kiichiro some time before, and he had also promptly (or hastily) chosen a contractor. Kiichiro's earthly remains were condemned to silence now, but Tetsukichi had been in his confidence about the new hospital from its very conception and all the details were in the keeping of the Deputy, Hidekichi Katsumata. So Kiichiro, though transformed into ashes and bits of bone, still controlled the people of the Nire Hospital, urging them on down the path that led to the creation of his new hospital.

Consequently, the first two or three years of Tetsukichi's directorship, in particular the year when the business of building the new hospital was getting under way, were a nightmare. All those troublesome, everyday things that Kiichiro would have been able to handle with no loss of composure caused his successor and adopted son endless misery. Tetsukichi was totally ignorant of financial matters, and whenever a way of borrowing money from somewhere had to be contrived, the specter of debt loomed up in his mind, filling him with an extremity of despair that the situation never actually warranted.

He finally worked out how money was obtained, but managed, in doing so, only to hit upon the last resort of borrowing from a moneylender at exorbitant rates of interest. Accompanied by the Deputy, he entertained this man at a discreet, high-class restaurant and plied him with food and drink, as well as a certain amount of maladroit preparatory small talk. Finally the moneylender opened a large black bag and threw the banknotes unceremoniously on the table. Tetsukichi moistened his fingertips and counted, slowly and clumsily, the wads of hundred-yen notes of which he was in such desperate need.

There was something wrong. The sum was too small. Some of the banknotes must be missing. It was supposed to be fifty thousand yen, yet there were only forty-five thousand. Tetsukichi raised a dubious face and asked the obvious question. What? Of course that's the right amount. Nothing strange about it at all. The first installment of ten percent interest is taken off the original amount loaned. That ten percent, of course, only represents one month's interest.

So within a year one would have paid back in interest alone more than the original sum.

The moneylender explained this casually, as if he were talking about a matter of very little importance and no real concern to himself. Tetsukichi, ignorant of the ways of the world, was unable to see through his manner. Worse than that, however, was the cheerful way the man laughed, showing a fine array of gold-capped teeth, and assured him that if he was not happy with these arrangements he could always call off the deal right now. Tetsukichi felt a complex of emotions, an embittered sense of his own incompetence and uselessness, and a raw anger that made his fingertips tremble. The Deputy, who was apparently as ignorant and powerless in these matters as he, offered not one word of advice or help, but sat beside him in the same palpable confusion, with his tiny, thin, unreliable-looking frame bent forward slightly, and scratching the surface of the *tatami* matting with his fingernails. . .

Tetsukichi's diary of the time, a small notebook full of a disordered yet detailed account of things that seemed of importance to him, showed how much unnecessary worry his ignorance of these matters caused. This was one diary he was never to open and read again.

> Today the preliminary registration was completed. I produced a promissory note for the money, but was told it should be in cash. So. . .

> Yoshio Sakuma, Vice President, Tokyo Lawyers Association. Telephone number, Yotsuya 2433.

> Second mortgage to be taken out on house in Aoyama and on new hospital. Okay to delegate this to Katsumata.

> A cross-deed or bond of reference means you can cancel a loan or agreement immediately once you produce the money.

> Thirty percent of 70,000 means 21,000 yen in one year, 5,200 yen in three months (half year).

> According to Kawamoto the financier is a Mr. G. Ashiba, says he wants extra 3,000 a month interest on the 80,000 to cover additional expenses at 7 percent. This simply cannot be paid given the interest rate. . .

> Mr. Shiozaki. Send property inventory tonight.

> Ohara brought the papers for the agreement. Third of December to be last date for repayment of the 45,000. If exceeded, daily rate of 10 sen. We ought to be grateful he said. Good thing to get it over with early. Threatened to take papers away if don't accept. Nothing for it but to go along with him. Finally he told me to fork out 300 yen as registration fee. . .

> Dr. Hirazuka told me not to worry so much. The reputation of the Nire Hospital was so high that things must work out right. . .

> Nagging telephone call from Sakamoto. Kept on and on at me

talking about being forced to take final measures. . .

According to Katsumata just back from the Land Registry Office, of the 208-odd yen he paid over there 10 yen 40 sen was a tip to someone called Sakeguchi in the notary's office. He did this on Ohara's instructions, of all people. What kind of racket is this?

My mind has obviously degenerated recently. I don't seem able to sleep at night.

In order to get the Sakamoto business cleared up had Ryuko go to Sumitomo Bank and deposit 20,000 yen, then gave Katsumata a check for the 20,000 and had him go to Sakamoto's place, but he said he couldn't accept a check unless it was certified. It was then too late to do anything about it. . .

Thirty-first of December. Already dark before I went outside and put the New Year decorations on the gate. This year has been one desperate struggle—things even got so bad all the property was attached—but just managed to straighten things out before 28th of December deadline. Anyway, the year has been seen out, although I don't know how, unless through the grace of heaven. There are people to whom I have been put under the deepest obligations this year. I must never forget them and what they have done for me. . .

Thus the new hospital finally came into being, and permission was given for it to take in patients supported by the City Council. Thanks to Kiichiro's genius for planning, the hospital had a definite grandeur— if glanced at briefly and from some distance away. The main building with the entrance hall was plastered over with Kiichiro's patent stone solution and looked tolerably smart for a wooden building. The various single-storied wards attached to it looked imposing enough and had concrete fire walls at strategic points, indicating that Kiichiro had taken to heart his earlier experience. But the rest of the buildings were the most temporary-looking, shack-like structures. From the very beginning it had been intended to build these as economically as possible, but since the building contractor was not being paid his due on time, the construction was done in a slovenly way, making the buildings even more ramshackle.

The shortage of finances was the indirect cause of a number of scandals that afflicted the new hospital soon after it opened. First there was the problem of suicides among the patients. Obviously patients in mental institutions are more prone to commit suicide than most people, but the rate of occurrence was higher at the new Nire Hospital than elsewhere, and it was judged that this was due to a shortage of attendants and inadequate training. Another scandal was the number of patients who managed to escape. After a while the hospital became notorious for the apparent ease with which those patients who planned to break out from their rooms were able to put the idea immediately into practice. This seemed strange because there were bars on the windows and locks on the doors, but it was found that the patients had only to raise the *tatami* mats on the floor to discover that all that stood between them and the empty space beneath these huts was wafer-thin floorboards which were almost as easy to break through as paper.

Regular missives arrived from the Metropolitan Police:

Sanitation and Health Department: Ref. No. 1063/1

June 3, 1927

To Dr. Tetsukichi Nire in his function as proprietor of a mental institution, namely the Nire Hospital of Mental Pathology.

Sir:

With reference to the proposed renewal of the temporary permit given to the above-named hospital for the period of time as put forward in your application, permission in the main point will be found set out on the certificate herewith enclosed, yet herein we feel obliged to draw your attention to the need on your part for serious reconsideration with reference to such facilities as now exist at the above hospital for the care and treatment of such patients as are under your protection, in particular with regard to the frequency with which patients have been able to break out from your premises during recent months to the extent of creating a genuine hazard to the maintenance of civil peace and public order, and to add our fervent hope, indeed wish, that henceforth no incidents of that nature may be permitted to occur, namely relating to the care and treatment as offered by your institution to the patients in its custody, and thus we may be spared such anxieties and earnest regrets as previously we have been obliged. . .

On paper this kind of warning had some appearance of courtesy, but the treatment meted out to Tetsukichi when he was summoned to the Health Department in person was very different. He hung his head in silence as he was publicly rebuked and ordered to draw up plans for the rebuilding of the wards and submit them forthwith.

Although Tetsukichi was clearly unequal to the kind of work that the directorship of the Nire Hospital entailed, he was obliged to spend infinitely more time on the frustrating, pernickety chores that the proprietor of any business is obliged to perform than on the diagnosis and treatment of patients. He did this administrative work in an incompetent, uninspired and blundering manner which was a constant source of irritation to those about him. And despite his apparent lack of involvement in what he did, these endless tasks took their toll on him, turning him into an exhausted figure with frayed nerves and swiftly graying hair who had aged more than ten years in the past three, and whose disposition had become soured, ill-tempered and peevish.

There was, of course, the more crucial question—for a medical man—of his ability to diagnose what was wrong with his patients and successfully cure them. Even if he were incompetent in administrative matters, Tetsukichi had believed he was genuinely talented when it came to medicine proper. He knew that so far as research was concerned he could look anyone in the face. Had he not spent three and a half years in Germany, the birthplace of modern psychiatry, absorbing the latest information and research? And had he not been critical of his adoptive father, shaking his head over diagnostic methods which he knew to be absurd, albeit used by someone who had an undeniable practical talent and flair for curing patients?

This was all so, but the fact was that, once he had taken over as Director and become the principal authority in the Nire Hospital, entrusted with the task of putting the battered institution back on its feet (something that could only be achieved by curing a large number of patients as quickly as possible in order to raise the reputation of the place), Tetsukichi found that his faith in himself crumbled a little more each time he sat in the doctor's chair in his surgery. Of course, he tried his best. No matter how exhausted he was by other non-medical matters, he did not spare himself in these more important labors. Unlike Kiichiro, he wasted no time on irrelevant self-advertisement, nor did he employ any of those numerous deceptions that Kiichiro had used to conceal the truth. He gave terse, relevant explanations that were suited to the patient before him, be that patient a victim of *dementia praecox* or merely a nervous breakdown. He did not deal with them all indiscriminately in the irresponsible way his predecessor had done.

Yet Tetsukichi was surprised to find his undoubtedly correct methods did not seem to gain him the confidence of his patients. It was clear that Kiichiro's method of peering up a patient's ear and telling him that his brain was starting to rot, and that the damage was visible but that everything would be all right as long as he took these K.N. pills, the finest medicine in all Japan—this preposterous method was more effective and much more acceptable to the patient than any number of precise, truthful explanations based on scientific knowledge and evidence. Not that Tetsukichi decided to adopt Kiichiro's well-tried methods: he had no desire to do so and, even if he had, his way of speaking and behaving was so different from Kiichiro's that he could hardly have had the same remarkable effect on his patients.

Since he was unable to gain the trust of his patients, whose judgments of their own cases were, naturally enough, superficial and unreliable, it was all the more imperative to persuade the families of the patients to believe in him. At the time, however, the concept of mental illness had much narrower implications than it has now, being restricted to only the most serious cases; so actual cures were extremely rare. But Kiichiro would never admit that the chance of improvement was very slim when he talked to the patients' relatives. He told them to leave the matter entirely in his hands, for he was an expert, an authority; and sometimes it actually happened that lunatics who had not been expected to improve were cured, or at least looked as if they were cured.

Tetsukichi, on the other hand, was only too well aware of the gap between his scholarly knowledge of the problems and the inadequacy of the techniques available to him as a physician. This awareness sapped his confidence, and he found it difficult to produce the assurances that would have persuaded the families to trust him. When confronted by these anxious people, he would guiltily avoid their eyes as if he felt he was up to no good and mumble only the vaguest and most non-committal words. Obviously nobody was going to feel much confidence in a doctor like that.

The fact is that Tetsukichi's own belief in what he was doing had begun to waver. He began to think that perhaps his adoptive father had been a much better doctor than he would ever be, and he even wondered at times whether he was cut out to be a practicing physician at all. Sometimes he overheard older members of the staff whispering among themselves that the old Director had been a great doctor because he could just tap a patient on the head and find out what was wrong with him. But the new Director didn't seem able to do anything like that.

Living in the shadow of his great predecessor who had built so palatial a hospital all those years ago, Tetsukichi was fated to be the object of such criticism. The spirit of Kiichiro lived on, in the hospital at Matsubara as well as in the hospital in Aoyama, in the surgeries and in the rooms for the nursing staff, even in the rooms where the hospital families lived. People who, during Kiichiro's lifetime, had loathed and despised his ludicrous obsession with the illusory bright side of things, his irresponsible making of promises which were never kept, apparently forgot all those aspects of him once he was dead; and although he had not been dead long, he was already on the way to becoming a legend. Only his acts of supposed greatness remained in people's memories, and his many errors were distorted so that they, too, became manifestations of his unique genius.

"Well, you know, after the fire, the old doctor, he didn't look in the least bit worried. Tore up all the IOUs. Did you know that? Right under the nose of the fellow who'd come to collect the money. Official documents they were. Do you know what he said? He said he thought there must be some kind of mistake. Then, coolly and calmly, just like that, he tore them all up into little pieces. Well, those of us who are left, we couldn't do that. Can't imitate the old doctor."

The feelings of respect and admiration for the late Kiichiro were further stimulated by events in the vicinity of Matsubara. The place that had filled Yasusaburo Sugano with such misgivings when he first saw it, so empty did it seem of anything but cornfields, looked more and more promising the more it was looked at, and this promise was soon fulfilled in the development that promptly took place. The Tamagawa Line was extended from Sangenjaya northward, providing a station called Yamashita very near the hospital. Then the Odawara Express Line was built, starting from Shinjuku to the northeast of Matsubara and passing near the hospital, giving them another two stations in the area, Umegaoka and Gotokuji. This meant that the new hospital was virtually at the intersection of these two railway lines, and inevitably buildings grew up around the stations. And those doubting minds that had questioned the wisdom of building a hospital amid empty cornfields were dazzled again by Kiichiro's ability to foretell the future.

The first person to move from the Aoyama hospital and settle in the new one at Matsubara was Kiichiro's elderly widow, Hisa, although the Deputy had been resident there from the beginning. Then the two doctors, Kanazawa and Nirasawa, whom Kiichiro had intended to make members of his family, took over the medical work at the new hospital and naturally moved in there. After two or three very difficult years, the hospital at Aoyama remained as wretched as ever, but the new hospital was showing signs of real stability, and a development program was beginning to be put into effect, for the ramshackle wards were gradually being replaced with new ones.

"Well, Dr. Kiichiro was quite right. Every word he said has turned out to be true. He had a remarkable ability to see years ahead. No need to be afraid of debt, he would often say. Money comes and goes; one day you have it, one day someone else. I often heard those words on his lips. And in just four years—or rather just three. . . Why, anyone would be only too happy to lend the Nire Hospital money now. Running into debt, no matter how large the debt may be, presents no real problem—but no doubt the boldness of a concept like that is a little beyond you. . ."

This was the Deputy addressing a few well-chosen words of advice to the young Chief Accountant he had recently hired, and showing no trace of that small figure who had sat confused and lost with Tetsukichi in front of the grasping moneylender. The old Chief Accountant, the neurotic, doddering Oishi, had remained behind in Aoyama to look after financial matters there. As the Deputy recalled the air of calm indifference that the departed had always affected and his impetuous handling of affairs, he had started to feel that Kiichiro's extraordinary intuitive powers had mysteriously passed on to himself. This, no doubt, was the reason why he had stuck a large billboard advertising the hospital in the middle of a cornfield. In fact, there was method in this madness, for the Odawara Line ran along this cornfield and the sign would look most impressive from the train windows. But it was a dream that had prompted him to do this. In his dream, the passengers in a train had all looked at the sign and immediately become queer in the head, ideal mental patients, and they besieged the hospital, jostling one another in their eagerness to get in, and there was Kiichiro, his face wreathed in smiles just as if he were alive, and he was praising Katsumata, telling him that this was truly well done.

Katsumata was the most passionate builder of the Kiichiro legend. He became so caught up in the world of the fantasy figure he had created that he was led unwittingly into making more and more inflated versions of the original falsehood. His attitude had changed lately toward the new Director, who visited the hospital twice a week from Aoyama. He had decided that Drs. Kanazawa and Nirasawa were more to be relied upon, and that Tetsukichi was not worth his time and respect.

The hospital at Aoyama was no longer a matter of any concern. The real Nire Hospital was here, at Matsubara, and he was the Deputy Director, the recognized mainstay. And quite soon this became a reality. It was clear to anyone from the scale of the two hospitals that the lead had been taken over by the one at Matsubara, and the sign in front of the new hospital was repainted to proclaim in bold letters that this was the Main Hospital. The sign at Aoyama now indicated that the old place had been relegated to the status of a branch.

Then, after years of absence, someone who had shown his face only on rare occasions during the summer vacations, Kiichiro's eldest son, Oshu, finally graduated from his medical college in Sendai, returned home fatter than ever, and took up residence in the new hospital. He did not, of course, immediately take over the reins of power; nor did he start working with the medical staff or even lend them the occasional hand, for he had only just graduated and was, in terms of medical knowledge, only of intern status, a starry-eyed boy who still had all the ropes to learn. But for all those who were disappointed in the new Director, this Oshu of large, calm (and, to their eyes, dignified) appearance began to be a focus of expectations and hopes. Whatever you might say about Oshu, he was a true son of the old Director, his eldest son, and he had the doctor's own blood running in his veins. He would obviously become the Acting Director of what was now the Main Hospital in the near future. The object of this reverence was sometimes to be seen walking about the hospital grounds (although these were still little more than fallow land). No doubt he wandered about in a bored and listless way, yawning occasionally. But there was something about that yawn. What a massive yawn it was! There was something magnanimous about it, and what a long time it went on for! This was a character, not a worrier like Tetsukichi, nagging at the nurses as he did his rounds, wearing that sullen expression on his lowered face. Tetsukichi might be the Director now but he was, after all, only an adopted son. The Deputy's ideas began to gain ground among the other members of staff without needing any prompting from him, and they finally even spread to some of the patients as well. The latter had no close contact with Oshu since he took no part in the running of the hospital, but they would get the occasional glimpse of him from afar, and they felt for some reason that he looked dependable.

The Deputy would sometimes show him some plan for the improvement of the hospital and ask him for his opinion, although there was no need to do so since any such plan would have been fully worked out already and the matter quite settled. Since Oshu was in no position there to give any opinion, he would look bewildered and reply brusquely that it seemed to be all right. The Deputy would indicate his acceptance of this important contribution and then leave. But to anyone he chanced to meet on the way, he would say in surprisingly emotional terms:

"Just as I'd hoped, Master Oshu believes in straight talk and getting on with the job. No hemming and hawing from him. That's the mark of a great personality, believe me. There you can see the working of his father's blood."

Whenever Tetsukichi visited the hospital now, the Deputy, although maintaining some outward show of respectful politeness, adopted a definitely offhand manner, apparent to any bystander who was in the know. As he paced around with the Director, whose hair had recently turned almost completely gray and whose figure had also become slightly stooped, the Deputy would join his hands behind his back and assume his dignified, crane-like gait, his rimless spectacles flashing. Each motion of his small frame indicated that the person he was now accompanying was no more than a temporary director, whereas he, Hidekichi Katsumata, was the controlling power here and would remain so, glorying in the traditional title of Deputy Director of the Nire Hospital. Perhaps he believed that all this further sanctified the late Kiichiro, and that the noble ghost himself was gazing on this spectacle, his face wreathed in ghostly smiles, telling him that this too was well done, well done.

Tetsukichi's home life was also unhappy. His main impulse was to love his children in the innocent, doting manner of the normal parent, but something had changed inside him since he had returned from his stay abroad to find that the image he had cherished of his eldest son during those three and a half years did not coincide at all with reality, and Shun'ichi appeared to regard him as a complete stranger. This was certainly not the only reason for what had happened to him as a person, but one had the feeling that whatever it was inside that made him tick had gone wrong somewhere, as if the complex wheels of that spiritual machine were failing to mesh in the way they used to. The result was that his days had an emptiness he could never have imagined before.

He still lived in the same house in Aoyama, the house that had survived the flames and had been rebuilt and extended, but the only people who lived in it now were himself, his wife and children, and the maidservants. His adoptive mother, Hisa, had moved with her sons, Oshu and Yonekuni, to the new hospital in Matsubara. The only exception in this exodus to the west was Kiichiro's youngest daughter, Momoko, who was living just south of the Aoyama hospital, in a rented house in Kasumi-cho. Since his return from Hankow, her husband Shiro had been employed at the old hospital.

This was therefore the first time in his life that Tetsukichi had been able to live in a household of which he was the head, and where he was untroubled by the presence of people about whom he was obliged to be careful. But ever since the tribulations connected with the rebuilding of the hospital had begun, he had had no time for his family, nor even for himself, and this had destroyed something in the depth of his being, altering his character or perhaps simply revealing something that had always been dormant there. Whatever the case, he was now chronically withdrawn, unfriendly and unlikable in manner. Once he had finished his day's work he would return home exhausted, without even the energy to open his mouth in simple greeting, let alone indulge in that friendly exchange with wife and children which is part of the normal idea of home. Not only was he excluded from the world of his wife, whose character was alien to him, but also from that of his children. In Shun'ichi's case this perhaps had been inevitable, since he had been absent while the child was growing up. But with Aiko, born a year after his return, and Shuji two years after that, things were surely different, yet they showed no affection for their father whatsoever. What annoyed him more, to the point of fury, was their closeness to their mother, although she hardly took any trouble over them at all. Certainly Ryuko bought them presents, and as the financial situation of the hospital improved these became quite lavish. But a child's affection is not bought by presents, no matter how expensive, and just as he had lost confidence in himself as a practicing physician, Tetsukichi began to have doubts about himself as a family man. He came to the conclusion he was not cut out for this role either, that he was of no use as a man or as a father; a view of himself which was no doubt one-sided but seemed, all the same, real.

In this empty and disconsolate state of mind he would go upstairs to his room, which at first had only the few books that had survived the holocaust, sit in front of his desk, and enjoy a sense of being able to unwind, of having for the first time that day some hours that were his alone. It gave him the opportunity to consider himself as he was, a man now growing old who was obliged to live in an atmosphere that totally lacked any healing warmth. But he was free from it here for a while, for this was his own place and his own time, a time all too brief but real, where he could weep those tears that age and manhood should forbid.

The first time he reached out his hand to take a book from the shelves at his side he experienced a definitely unpleasant sensation, even one of repulsion. After the fire, when he had seen what had happened to all those volumes he had got together with such patient labor, he had felt something close to hatred for the written word. He detested the books that flames had transformed into charred fragments and ashes, and he detested the feelings he had to endure—that it had been pointless to collect them and that the years he had spent doing so were meaningless. He told himself that he need never acquire another book in his life, for he was now condemned to an existence in which scholarship and research would never have a part.

But the ache of emptiness inside him made him take up one of those books, and as he turned the pages and read a few lines here and there he became aware that he was once again being seduced by his former obsession. He experienced a slight shudder at the thought, but returned to his reading, to that consolation too deep to be explained. He turned over the page with mingled dismay and fascination, knowing the fascination might prove irresistible. And so he read on, confused and suspicious of himself; but then with other feelings, with a sense of awakening and, mixed with that, one of regret, an awareness of something that had been lost or not performed. Ought he to be doing this? Should he yield to sensations of this kind? His position was delicate now that Kiichiro was dead. The hospital was in a tricky situation, too. There were debts to be paid off, new wards to be built, queries from the police to be answered. Was it right for the new Director of such a hospital to be behaving like this? Wasn't it dangerously escapist and unproductive, this obsession with bundles of paper with ink marks on them? But he still turned over the next page.

When at last a certain stability had been achieved in the affairs of the hospital, and a sense of assurance about the future had been gained, Tetsukichi had already made up his mind. He had worked his fingers to the bone for the hospital. No one could deny that. Surely he was now entitled to do something that would give him a sense of relief, some relaxation from his daily task? Research would afford him a kind of comfort, even if only a cold one, and he saw no harm in continuing his studies a little. Obviously he couldn't hope to do any research on a scale that would interfere with his work, but there could be nothing wrong with writing a few minor things as a form of amusement. Recently he had noticed the first symptoms of potential nervous breakdown in himself, and research would be a simple, inexpensive and meaningful way of checking these symptoms. So the time he spent shut up alone in his room became gradually longer.

He had first thought in terms of writing a short history, or account rather, of the beginnings of modern psychiatry in Japan, something of article length that could be published in a general medical journal such as the *Monthly Bulletin of Medicine*. During the Meiji era these beginnings had meant the mere transference of European knowledge to Japanese soil. First, Bunsai Kanbe translated Henry Maudsley's simple textbook, *An Outline of Psychiatry,* rendering the writer's name in an exotic and almost unreadable sequence of Chinese ideograms. Then Jo Eguchi brought out a book called *Psychiatry* which consisted mainly of translations from German authors; Hajime Sakaki set up the first course of studies on the subject at a Japanese university; and Shu Miyake produced a book called *Essential Psychiatry,* which was a restatement of the ideas of Krafft-Ebing. The most striking thing about these works was the terrible struggle the authors had in translating the basically German terminology into Japanese. A concept like "*Blödsinn,*" for example, was first rendered into the Japanese equivalent of "trance" or "fainting fit" before finally achieving something like its meaning of "dementia." "*Sinnestäuschung*" came out as the pleasantly poetic "illusions and misunderstandings of the five senses" before a word was arrived at that indicated something like "hallucination." "*Katalepsie*" was rendered in a variety of newly coined terms which used so impressive an array of rare ideograms they tended to conceal the meaning of the word rather than clarify it. Of these early scholars, perhaps the most important had been Shuzo Kure who had studied in Germany a few years before Kiichiro, although, instead of returning encumbered with German beds, pianos, VIP chamber pots and steelware ranging from knives to nail scissors, he had brought back knowledge relating to cerebral anatomy and cerebral pathology, an amalgamation of the ideas of the Viennese school (whose leader at the time had been Obersteiner, the same aged professor emeritus who had appeared behind Tetsukichi one afternoon and advised him that any work worth doing could never be completed in a month) and those of the Heidelberg school, at that time dominated by the figure of Nissl. In addition to this, Kure helped spread the theories of Krafft-Ebing, and also of Emil Kraepelin (a person whom Tetsukichi recalled vividly and was not likely to forget in a hurry) on clinical psychiatry. These were the ideas put forward in the sixth edition of Kraepelin's *Textbook of Psychiatry,* including the concepts of manic-depression and *dementia praecox,* which were still, even in the Europe of the time, original and as yet unexplored. The Kure school of psychiatry, which followed reasonably faithfully the mainstream of Kraepelin's ideas, thus came to dominate and unify the whole of psychiatric studies in Japan. Kure was aware that a genuinely Japanese school must be created if the subject were to develop in, or even be relevant to, Japan, so he insisted that his disciples and students should record everything, their clinical records and journals, their patients' charts, in the Japanese language, at a time when the translated German terminology was much harder to handle and make sense of than the original German.

Tetsukichi soon realized that some account, even if only a superficial one, of early nineteenth-century German psychiatry was called for if he was to write of these Japanese developments, since the real creators of the Japanese school, Kraepelin, Bleuler and Kretschmer, had their roots in that period. This meant a study of the writing of Nasse, Friedreich, Groos, Blumroeder, and the great Wilhelm Griesinger who had declared that all forms of insanity arose from malfunctioning of the brain. But if one went back that far, it became necessary to go one stage further to the previous generation of French scholars, who included the legendary figure of Philippe Pinel, the physician who finally released so-called lunatics from their chains and manacles and insisted that they have humane and caring treatment. Although he was almost entirely ignorant of this period, Tetsukichi felt it could hardly be ignored, and on studying it he found a number of physicians whom no historical treatment could afford to overlook, including Pinel's disciples, Ferrus and Esquirol, and others who had made definite contributions to the subject.

But having gone this far back, where was one to stop? He felt a strangely irritating exhilaration mingled with a sense of physical fatigue at the thought. Perhaps he ought to be thinking in terms of a really inclusive history, going even further back, as far as the early Greeks, to the father of medicine, Hippocrates himself. There had been a number of medical histories written, but surely there was no history of psychological medicine, in particular not one that was specifically concerned with the subject insofar as it related to modern psychiatry? But the whole idea was absurd. How could he possibly do anything like that? He should be ashamed of himself for even thinking that he could. It was nothing but some monstrous self-delusion. Then he was the Director of a hospital which he was trying to rebuild. What did he think he was doing, indulging in nonsensical flights of fancy of this kind?

These doubts and misgivings had no effect. He started ordering books, either through Maruzen in Tokyo or directly through a large dealer in Germany, and they began to arrive from secondhand bookstores in Munich and Berlin that he remembered well; and then more and more books, which crossed the oceans to fill his bookshelves and spill over onto the floor; and all this happened without his seeming to will it, as if it were some kind of natural process.

It was clear from Tetsukichi's researches, if they could be given that name as yet, that the ancient conception of mental illness was of possession by devils or evil spirits which were beyond people's control; it was regarded as an occult phenomenon. This was seen conclusively in ancient Indian writings—the *Vedas,* the *Laws of Manu,* the *Mahabharata,* the *Ramayana*—and elsewhere. According to these works, the soul dwelt in the hollow of the heart and used the body as its tool, its attributes being *buddhi* (intelligence) and *ahamkara* (ego-consciousness). At some time in its progress this soul would be absorbed into the breath, leaving the body and seeking a home for itself elsewhere: this was transmigration.

In ancient Greece there were the rituals performed before the temples of Asclepius, the god of medicine. In order to cure mad people the priestesses would perform solemn ceremonies culminating in wild ritual dancing, in which their own sanity became as suspect as that of the people they were attempting to cure. But the rational, positivist spirit of the ancient Greeks ensured they would move away from the concept of illness as something that affected only the body, to a new one that saw it causing distortions in the functioning of the mind. Thus a new kind of intellectual came into being, such as Alcmaeon, probably the first man to carry out anatomical surgery on the human body, who exenterated an eyeball and became aware that our senses are connected to the brain and that the mystery of the human intelligence lies somewhere in that region. On the other hand, there was the philosopher Heracleitus, who criticized the physicians of his day for their fanciful ideas—and they certainly appear to be so from our vantage point—and insisted that human reason existed in the universal fire from which each individual soul was formed. When that fire burned with a dry flame, the intellect and individual soul remained healthy, but when it was damp it smoldered and the mind became ill; and should this dampness be extreme it resulted in a diminution of intellectual powers and perhaps in madness.

Hippocrates still appears centuries later as one of the summits of the human mind, and concerning the "holy illness" of epilepsy he made some prophetic remarks:

> The illness is considered of a more holy nature than others, but this is most certainly not the case for, like them, it arises from natural causes. . . Those who first connected this illness with demons and thus attempted to sanctify it were a rabble of magicians, necromancers, confidence tricksters and other idle, loud-mouthed braggarts who pretended to a non-existent depth of piety and breadth of learning. Since they were totally incapable of curing the disease they announced that it was incurable, and covered it with a veil of holiness.

A scientist devoted to clinical observation, Hippocrates noted examples of puerperal dementia, forms of phobia, delirium, defective memory and other kinds of sudden mental disturbances that occurred after copious bleeding. He also worked out a classification of some mental illnesses, such as epilepsy, mania, melancholia and paranoia. According to him, hysteria was a physical complaint restricted to women, and arose from the shifting of the womb within the body. But he also thought that mania was dependent upon a kind of bodily fluid consisting largely of yellow and black bile. He stressed the important role of seasonal changes in mental disease, and saw mania, melancholia and epilepsy as illnesses connected with spring.

There were numerous other Greek savants with encyclopedic knowledge and brilliant minds. Socrates himself seems to have been one of the great schizoids of history, showing all the symptoms of auditory hallucination and of stupor. Plato made his own acute analysis of the human essence. But, from a purely medical point of view, neither can be considered to have matched the achievements of Hippocrates. The Platonic system saw illness as something the irrational soul could undergo, classifying madness under the three categories of melancholia, mania and dementia, with two kinds of idiocy, namely madness and ignorance. Madness was sometimes a form of illness, sometimes something bestowed by the gods. Aristotle believed in the dominance of the heart over all the other bodily organs, and was convinced that neither the intellect nor the senses were connected in any way with the backbone or the brain. He modified Hippocrates' theory of the workings of bile, and asserted that black bile itself was not the cause of madness, the true cause being variations in heat and cold, and bile merely served to transmit the illness. Even so, a disciple of his laid greater emphasis on the workings of the brain.

Having been thoroughly confused by the works of the philosophers, Tetsukichi turned his attention to a proper physician, Soranus of Ephesus, who is believed to have practiced in Alexandria and Rome during the first and second centuries A.D. His two major works on acute and chronic disorders are preserved in their Latin translation, but Tetsukichi could only read them in a much abbreviated English version. Fortunately he had an acquaintance, a philosopher and linguist who had a personal library of more than ten thousand volumes and knew a dozen languages, including Latin and Greek. Since he had all this knowledge crammed inside a not very large skull this remarkable scholar suffered from constant headaches and would come to the Nire Hospital to obtain medicine. At Tetsukichi's request, he dug out the musty, mildewed volumes, and translated them orally for him with an expression of acute distaste on his face, like that of a child being forced to swallow something extremely unpleasant. But Soranus turned out to be an interesting and worthwhile writer, at least for Tetsukichi who was, after all, a mere medical man and therefore able to grasp and absorb the writings of other medical men more easily than far superior works in other fields. He appreciated the writings of Soranus, although they consisted in little more than perpetual bickering involving the writer and people like Diocles and Erasistratus and Heraclides over the question of what proper medical treatment should be.

Then there were the Alexandrian scholars who later moved to Rome and who created, if only for a short time, a sanctuary of scientific learning. Of particular note was Asclepiades who had called mental illness a "disease of the senses" and who had been able to draw a clear distinction between delusion and hallucination. However, Cicero, a devotee of the Stoic school and fanatically opposed to all that the rival Epicurean school stood for, asked the very pointed and natural question why, if we believed that human beings were created with both a body and a soul, we believed that only the former was an object for the healer's art, and that the latter lay beyond it. His own answer was that we did have an art that could cure the soul, namely philosophy; even so, he clearly took a much more creative and individual approach to mental illness than had the medical men of his time. One only had to look at the encyclopedia compiled by Aulus Cornelius Celsus, *De re medicina*, to come across a number of suggested treatments for lunatics, a typical one being that the head should be shaved and anointed with oil of roses. Perhaps the best summary of what these doctors thought is the sentence written by one of them: "It is impossible to cure all those who are sick, for to do so would mean that doctors were superior to the gods."

There were more scholars of medicine to be found, many more; so many that Tetsukichi, who was coming across them for the first time in his life, was dumbfounded. The ideas of these scholars, their lives and their achievements became a tangle in his inadequate mind, so that he lacked any sense of historical continuity, and he had to try to straighten it out right from the beginning. This, laboriously, he did, and his account of the Graeco-Roman tradition of medicine came to an end with the work of a man who was the very last in that tradition: Galen, who died some six centuries after Hippocrates in the year A.D. 200. After that, medical history entered a long, apparently endless, dark age.

Tetsukichi had meant to treat the whole period up to the birth of modern psychiatry as a form of prehistory, a brief account of a background that was either only faintly lit or in pitch darkness, covering the Graeco-Roman period, the Middle Ages when that earlier knowledge had been lost or destroyed, then the reemergence of the science of the mind during the Renaissance, and through the seventeenth and eighteenth centuries into that final period when the signs of the dawning of a new age had appeared. He had assumed he need write no more than the briefest of outlines, something that would take up only a few spare hours and amount to about thirty or forty pages of manuscript. But things did not turn out like that at all. He was astounded to find that what he had started as a kind of throat-clearing operation before getting down to the main work, or as a way of retiring from the harsh world about him, had somehow been able to occupy him for more than two years. In fact, he had first started work on this two and a half years ago, and though the whole should have been completed last year, all that he had managed to cover had been the Graeco-Roman period. What had been intended as a mere preface had turned into well over three hundred pages of manuscript.

Tetsukichi felt gloomy at the prospects that now faced him. Was he obliged to go on with this? Certainly not. The whole thing was ridiculous, a childish piece of make-believe. This was not the kind of work he should be doing at all. It had virtually no connection with modern psychiatry, and was really no more than a string of complicated irrelevancies. But, like some pathetic person enslaved by a bad habit he knows he should be able to break, Tetsukichi kept up his slow plodding through the minds of the people of those distant times. Occasionally he would throw aside his books and laugh at the folly of what he was doing. What could the childish interpretations and nonsensical therapeutic methods of these people matter to him? Bloodletting and administering emetics and laxatives were perhaps the least offensive of their methods. Most of the time, they seemed to be making their patients suffer as much as possible, by means of the rack, flogging, incarceration in pitch-dark cellars, or by hurling them into cold water.

Nevertheless, he wondered how much he was entitled to laugh at all this. Take the modern age, in which Tetsukichi's "genuine psychiatry" had at last come into being. Had there been any real progress in the treatment of mental illness compared with those unenlightened times? Various forms of "shock therapy" had been in use even in the eighteenth century—"Darwin's Chair," for example, invented by Erasmus Darwin, grandfather of the more famous Charles. The patient was strapped into this special chair and spun about with such vigor that eventually he would bleed from the mouth, nose and ears. In Germany during the nineteenth century, doctors who were, by any standards, quite genuine and distinguished men of science recommended that patients should be put inside special sacks or forced to remain standing for long periods, and prescribed emetics to induce vomiting, or deliberately caused pain. It would be difficult to distinguish any of these forms of therapy from torture. One particularly talented doctor named Horn would pour ice-cold water over his patients, never less than two hundred bucketfuls at a session.

Was the present age any better? Progress had been made, for example, in the treatment of *dementia paralytica,* which was now known to be caused by changes in a particular brain cell, and the powerful device of fever treatment, which consisted in inducing malaria, was available. There was now a drug that could prevent epileptic fits. In the case of manic patients, although caring for them still presented huge difficulties, it was now known that the passage of time brought a gradual return to a state of quiescence, and they were treated accordingly.

All this could be put on the credit side, but what about the treatment of patients suffering from schizophrenia (or *dementia praecox* as it had previously been called), still surely the most vital of therapeutic issues? Sedative drugs were now given, not the cold-water treatment of old, of course, nor were these patients still chained together in gangs; but the isolation, the watching over, giving a little work to one, a strait-jacket to another . . . and what else was there? Well, there were the revolutionary discoveries of the 1930s, the insulin and electric-shock treatments; and these would shortly be available to Tetsukichi, though the many remarkable drugs that were to appear after the Second World War obviously would not. So it seemed to him that, despite great advances in our knowledge and understanding of mental illness and in our ability to classify and recognize symptoms accurately, we had progressed little, if at all, beyond the methods of the bad old days where treatment was concerned.

The fact was that the majority of those patients at the Nire Hospital who were lunatics in the narrow sense of the term simply seemed to show no signs of improvement whatsoever. Even small-town doctors buried deep in the country had the satisfaction of seeing their patients get better. Their lives had a sense of joy and fulfillment, and the patients were grateful, as were their relations. But how seldom was this the case with a doctor who looked after the insane. More often than not he was blamed because no cure took place. Tetsukichi would sit, sour-faced, interviewing the parents, the brothers and sisters, and hear them complain about what he was not doing; yet, in terms of the psychiatric doctrines he had learned, these people were often sicker than the patient they were supposedly concerned about. Of course you could always maintain that the proprietors of mental institutions did well financially precisely because cures did not take place, which ensured that patients remained with them for an indefinite period of time. And doubtless there were people—the Deputy, perhaps—who were willing to exploit this aspect of their work. But for Tetsukichi it was only a source of pain, responsible for a number of scars he bore within him.

He remembered the occasion when a patient had almost knocked him cold. It was while he was doing his rounds and was looking into the face of a schizophrenic who had entered an acute state of catatonic withdrawal, remaining rigidly motionless and silent. Quite suddenly, he had thrust out his fist and punched the Director between the eyes. This was surprising, to say the least, for the patient was supposed to be in a state of total withdrawal; and since the blow was delivered with considerable force, Tetsukichi, who had been stooping forward to peer at the patient, was knocked flat on his back, a very unbecoming posture for someone of his standing in the hospital. The doctors and nurses who were doing the rounds with him quickly surrounded the patient and got him under control, but one young trainee nurse who had been trailing along at the end of the party found the whole thing beyond her control, and she spent some time afterward staring down at her feet and struggling unsuccessfully to stifle her giggles.

The pain in Tetsukichi's forehead persisted after he had completed the rounds and returned to the outpatients surgery, where a number of people were waiting to be seen. There was one in particular who had paid regular visits to the hospital in Kiichiro's day, a loud and overdressed woman who talked interminably and showed little inclination to leave.

"Now, Doctor, what is this illness of mine called? I mean the whole syndrome? I know it's not one of those ordinary, common or garden names, I'm sure of that. What do you think, Doctor?"

Tetsukichi replied that it was a form of mental indisposition and nothing like as serious as she seemed to think.

"I'm sure that can't be right. The old doctor never used to say that. I was half *luxuria extravaganza,* yes, that's right, *luxuria extravaganza* is what he called it, and the other half. . . Now it's that other half that I just can't remember, although I do know that it was certainly not one of your ordinary, common or garden names, that I do know. It was some kind of foreign name. Why, the old doctor, Dr. Kiichiro, said that name to me on I don't know how many occasions, every time I came I shouldn't wonder; and now I can't for the life of me remember it. Doctor, do you think it's my illness that's affecting my memory in this way?"

Tetsukichi produced a number of German names to see if one would do the trick.

"Well, no, I don't think so. I'm sure that's not it. Quite positive it was none of those. It wasn't so ordinary sounding as those. It was one of those extremely rare sounding, extremely difficult to remember kind of names. You know, I only had to hear the name and I would go all of a tremble, and my heart would go pitter-pat. I often wonder if there's anyone else in the world whose heart goes pitter-pat the way mine does. I'm sure it must be most unusual. You know, Doctor, the old doctor named it right away without any trouble at all. I mean, I wonder if you really understand what's wrong with me. It was certainly not one of those commonplace names. The old doctor always used to give me very special treatment, and he would only give me very special medicine from abroad. Now, can I get some of that medicine today? Is the same person still working in the pharmacy? You know I feel so worried these days, so nervous. . . It's my heart. I sometimes wonder how I manage to endure it. Are you quite sure you don't need to take my blood pressure again? The pills the old doctor used to give me were white; not an ordinary white but with a yellow tinge to them. And they were a little bit shiny here and there, because there were lots of different medicines all mixed up in the same pill. Of course they had come from abroad. . .''

Tetsukichi's forehead still ached, and he replied that he would have some foreign medicines prepared for her immediately.

"Well, I just hope they'll make me better, that's all. The old doctor always used to give me five or six different kinds. . . Oh well, I suppose it doesn't matter. I'll know when I take it. I imagine, Doctor, you realized when examining me how sensitive I am? I mean, I wouldn't like to think I might take some pills you gave me and just drop down dead, would I? Well, thank you anyway. Incidentally, what sort of effect would they have on a person who wasn't actually ill? I thought I'd just try them on my niece first. Not that I don't trust you, Doctor, but I am so very sensitive, not in an ordinary way at all, I can assure you, and Dr. Kiichiro understood that very well and me and my little ways. Oh, Doctor, I do wish I could get you to understand how ill I am. It's my heart going pitter-pat like this in such a peculiar way, and then there's this feeling as if I had a bowl placed over my head, it does so press around here. . . Oh, but it's no use. I just can't explain, and I can't expect you to understand how I feel, I know I can't. It's quite hopeless, quite impossible. . .''

Tetsukichi had listened to all this with great perseverance, and he finally gave it as his considered opinion that she was suffering from some maladjustment of her vegetative or autonomous nervous system. That, however, was a great mistake on his part, a grave error of judgment. She appeared to take the word ''vegetative'' as a deliberate personal insult, and insisted that he kindly explain the connection this vegetable thing had with the peculiarly rare complaint from which she knew she suffered.

So he explained. Or tried to, because she insisted on making constant interruptions with the result that he could hardly get a word in edgeways. Whenever he managed to do so, she seemed to steer these words so far away from their original goal that they ended drifting somewhere way off in the distance. He had to start all over again, twice, three times, it seemed dozens of times, while the same pointless and infuriating questions poured in from her direction. He began to toy with the idea of strapping this woman in a Darwin's Chair and spinning her round and round until she fainted. Or pouring two hundred bucketfuls of ice-cold water over her, a form of therapy that would still stand us in very good stead in the modern world. But these methods were not permitted, and he would have liked simply to say to her that he was not the right kind of doctor for her, that he advised her to leave this place forthwith and find some other doctor more to her taste. But this was precisely the sort of thing he could not say. It was an unfortunate fact that the Nire Hospital needed to make every penny it could, and the words that came to the tip of his tongue had to be swallowed down again. From a financial point of view, this woman was a rare and superior type of client, for she would buy their medicine no matter how expensive it was. Indeed, the more expensive it was, the better she was pleased with it.

About a week later (it had taken that long for the pain in his forehead to subside), Tetsukichi began to think about his handling of this particular patient, and he decided he had failed with her as he had failed with others and was not suited to be a consultant doctor. That kind of patient was a daily occurrence in a mental institution, and if a doctor could not handle such patients with smiling ease then he must simply consider himself not qualified for the job. But Tetsukichi was not in a position to throw in the sponge now. The main result of his ruminations was that he tended to live his real life more and more in his book-lined room. He was aware of the escapist nature of this other life; his relief on finishing his work and getting back to his study, the joyous sense of being alone, was very much like the feeling of restful assurance a drug addict feels as the soothing substance begins to circulate throughout his body.

So Tetsukichi pursued his untiring investigations of the history of psychopathology in ancient times, exploring those brilliant minds whose names had grown dim and finally vanished in the darkness of the past. Among them were scientists who had resisted the superstitions and denial of the intellect their times attempted to impose upon them. But even they had been unable to resist the historical trend gradually transforming the science of mental illness into the study of the Devil and all his works. Therapy was replaced by exorcism and incantations as the priests had psychiatry excluded from the medical sciences and gave it the name of demonology. An account of the treatment of hysteria in a tenth-century manuscript showed plainly that the Hippocratic diagnosis, which attributed it to a shifting of the womb, had been transmitted as far as that point in time. But a major difference in attitude between Hippocrates and the tenth century was apparent in a long incantation, appended as the accepted therapy for this complaint:

> In the name of the Father, and of the Son, and of the Holy Ghost. O Lord of the Heavenly Hosts, look down, we pray Thee, upon our weakness and upon our sickness, look in upon our true hearts and do not despise us who are the creations of Thy Holy Hand. Since Thou hast made us and we have not made ourselves, look we beseech Thee on this woman, and restrain Thou her womb, and cure her suffering therein for it doth move so cruelly. . . We beseech thee also, O womb, in the Name of the Holy Trinity, that thou return forthwith to thy former station and no longer trouble this person. And from thence to move no more. Hasten then, and be no more in anger but return to that place the Lord hath appointed for thee.

The incantation went on for much longer than this, but it was still of an essentially benevolent nature. This was not the case later, for there was a gradual increase in the demonic names given to mental disturbances until finally all were seen as instances of possession by devils, and the sufferers even ceased to be the victims of Satan but became his accomplices. They were either witches or demons in person. The climax of this process could be seen in a book by two Dominican friars on the subject of witchcraft in which they maintained the horrifying belief that there should be no attempt to cure or correct witches (most of whom must have been mentally unbalanced) but instead they should be destroyed by being burned to ashes.

As Tetsukichi continued with his reading of the apparently endless literature on his subject, scribbling on into the early hours of the morning, he would need to rest from sheer fatigue occasionally, and then he would clumsily make himself some strong green tea, gasping as he sipped down the hot stimulant. He would also sometimes pick up the newspaper, for he never had time to look it over properly in the morning, and read it through.

It was toward the end of January, 1933, when Tetsukichi read of Hitler's assumption of power in Germany. "*Meteoric Rise to Power: Hitler Takes Over Government*" was the headline in the paper, which also had a photograph of a man with his arm raised as he made a speech; the face gave the impression of someone calmly watching events as they happened. The name Hitler seemed familiar, and then Tetsukichi remembered the unsuccessful putsch that had occurred during his stay in Munich and wondered if this could be the same Adolf Hitler. If it was, and it seemed to be, the man had certainly risen in the world. Tetsukichi had been sitting with two or three other Japanese students, some time after the affair, when they were joined by a certain Major Takahashi, who was attached to the Army General Staff. The major made a comment which Tetsukichi recalled now, although he had been able to make little sense of it at the time:

"When I heard that Hitler had joined forces with von Kahr and Ludendorff I knew something very important had happened, but the revolution itself was mismanaged. He should first have got the army commander, von Lossow, on his side, and occupied the barracks. But that wasn't done, so the whole thing ended in fiasco."

Tetsukichi felt this created some kind of a bond between himself and Hitler. He had a friendly feeling of admiration for him and for what he had achieved, which was to have crushed the Communist Party in Germany just as it had been crushed in Japan. It was good to see a man who had definite beliefs and the ability to put them into practice. When he remembered the state of the German people after their defeat in the First World War, the confusions and corruptions of that time, it seemed to him that a man of this caliber was required if Germany was to be put on its feet again.

This euphoria did not last long. The obvious dictatorship which Nazi rule soon assumed took the form of burning anti-German books, and the announcement of this fact brought a definite frown to Tetsukichi's face. He could see the flames licking around the fragile bundles of paper, and this stimulated memories he would have preferred to forget. The newspaper report said:

> Wearing the uniform of the National Socialist Party, young party members, in an impassioned campaign to purify the national culture, made an enormous pile of books that had been designated as having anti-Germanic tendencies. Amid thunderous applause the names of each of the authors were read out, and numerous works of international reputation were given unhesitatingly to the flames. . . Among the more important works were the socialist writings of Marx and Engels, the French writer Henri Barbusse and the American Upton Sinclair. . . While this was happening

in Berlin a similar ceremony was taking place in Frankfurt am Main, where books were burned before a crowd of some fifteen thousand people.

Tetsukichi read almost nothing outside his own subject, and apart from the name of a German writer who had written on the science of sex, none of the writings of any of the long list of authors given there were known to him. It was also happening a long way away from home, so it was rather the articles specifically referring to Japan that made him appreciate the abnormality of the times. Banner headlines like the following appeared: *"Manchuria Not Recognized. Committee of Nine Countries Decided Yesterday. . ."*; *"Impassioned Speech from League Representative Matsuoka. Emphatic Rejection of Report. Urges League to Reconsider for Last Time"*; *"Japanese Army in Manchuria Opens Campaign in Jehol"*; and finally, *"Japan Quits League of Nations. Official Imperial Proclamation," "Farewell to the League."*

It seemed to Tetsukichi that his country had become as isolated and outcast as he was himself, and for some time he thought seriously about what might be going to happen. But he knew nothing about these things and had no way of even starting to think intelligently about the future. There was nothing he could do. Professional politicians and soldiers were there to look after that, in the same way that professional psychiatrists were there to look after the insane. It was not his business.

So he put aside these matters and returned to his own business, to an account of a doctor called Arnauld of Villanova, a passionate researcher into the writings of Galen, who maintained that a connection existed between epilepsy and the moon and between melancholia and Mars, for the rays emitted from the eyes go so far astray when searching for. . . But Tetsukichi's shoulders had become cramped and tired, and his head felt vague and confused. He curled up in the bed prepared for him in a corner of the room, totally exhausted in mind and body; but such was his fatigue it seemed to prevent sleep instead of inviting it. He got up again and took some sleeping tablets, double the amount he would have prescribed for any visitor to his hospital who complained of insomnia. Recently he had got into the habit of doing this almost every night.

Chapter

3

Ryuko's anger at her husband, at the fact that as Director of the hospital his handling of affairs was far inferior to her father's, was extreme. She had never really believed that phrase which had been so often on her respected father's lips about Tetsukichi's having "the finest mind in Japan," but, as she had once said to Seiko, she still thought he would come in the first thousand or, failing that, in the most talented ten thousand. Her latest ranking of her husband would no doubt have put him much lower down, around the million or ten million mark perhaps. For look what had happened to the hospital during his directorship: the Matsubara hospital had become the main Nire Hospital, and Aoyama, that proud domain in which the great idea had grown from just a seed to full fruition, was reduced to mere branch status.

Of course, Tetsukichi (or Tetsuyoshi to her) was still the Director of both hospitals, but that was merely on paper, for the actual property was in the name of Kiichiro's eldest son, Oshu. It is true that Kiichiro's will had stipulated that his property was to be divided equally between his adopted and his eldest son, but the way things were going now it seemed almost certain that the Matsubara hospital would go to Oshu and the one in Aoyama to Tetsukichi.

At first Ryuko had assumed the Matsubara experiment would be a temporary affair, a nine days' wonder soon to be abandoned, for what could that wretched area of cornfields, stinking of manure, have to offer compared with Aoyama, on whose land the drama of the House of Nire had been played out, and where the ghost of Kiichiro could not but choose to dwell? To cast aside the claims of Aoyama, to concentrate everything on Matsubara, even if the two remained the same Nire Hospital, to move all the experienced nursing staff, pharmacists and doctors there—this was flying in the face of nature and getting all one's priorities wrong. Someone like the Deputy, it was true, could well be spared. The smug, condescending, crane-like way he crept about the place had long got on Ryuko's nerves. But as she observed the transformation the Matsubara hospital gradually underwent as its buildings were completed and improved and the large area of unused land surrounding it was made into a sports ground and a hospital farm, she found that she was definitely not amused. In fact, she felt distinctly displeased at this obvious success. It was not because she sympathized with her husband in any way, but rather because she worshiped the land at Aoyama and the priceless memories it held for her. She also had not one trace of affection for her brother Oshu.

She could only think how different it would have been if her father had still been alive. Even if the Aoyama hospital had been reduced to this one tiny surgery, it would still have borne the proud title of "Main Hospital" written on a signboard so large and impressive that the entire structure might soon have collapsed under the weight and dignity of it. However skeptical one might claim to be about the value of appearances and titles, the decision to allow the "main" title to be transferred to the hospital at Matsubara was the act of a fool, a useless bumpkin.

Another thing that aroused her wrath was the state of the Aoyama hospital itself. Admittedly there had been a tragic fire, but that had been years ago and still the hospital was in the red and, most irritating of all when she heard about it, dependent upon the hospital at Matsubara for financial support. So one day she called to mind one of her mother's former customs and decided to summon Oishi into her presence, into the room that she alone referred to as the Western Wardrobe Parlor, in order to hear a detailed account of their finances.

She had no understanding of the account ledgers, but this did not prevent her from stabbing a haughty finger at one item and coldly demanding what it might be.

"Books, madam. The books that the Director himself has ordered. . ."

Oishi's head was as grizzled as ever. The only extra sign of age he showed was the recently acquired habit of putting on spectacles when he looked at the accounts. His various nervous mannerisms still persisted, but there could be no doubt that he had recovered a certain composure since the Deputy had gone to Matsubara.

"Oh, really. Foreign books, no doubt," said Ryuko, nodding her head. "Only foreign books would cost that much. Not that there's anything wrong with buying such books. Father bought a great many foreign books. Still, times have changed, you know. The Nire Hospital has changed, as has the world outside. This item really is rather excessive, wouldn't you say? Naturally I can't bring it up directly with Tetsuyoshi. I have my own position to consider. However, it is your role, is it not, Mr. Oishi, to maintain a strict control over hospital outlay?''

Ryuko clearly regarded her own extravagant purchases in a different light, and she soon dismissed the nervous accountant from her presence. She realized that it was no longer possible for Aoyama, with its few patients, to compete with Matsubara in terms of earnings. But, even so, to be still in the red like that! What sort of man was her husband to go shamelessly cap in hand to the likes of Oshu and the Deputy? If he was a proper man, a man with just a little backbone in him, he could never do a thing like that. Why, the thought would not even cross his mind.

Her husband's stock was fast diminishing in her eyes. He was a useless good-for-nothing, a mere hole in the air, a pathetic, incompetent nincompoop, and the fact so infuriated her that she unconsciously changed her posture. She straightened her neck and raised her head proudly, and her face took on the stern and frigid expression of some inspired priestess. Her annoyance was so great that some of it persisted until the following morning, confirming her in a resolve to buy a squirrel fur coat she had had her eye on for some time. Such extravagances were all committed from the splendid motive of enhancing the dignity of the Nire Hospital which had fallen into so sorry a state.

Ryuko no longer felt the need to maintain even a pretense of goodwill toward her husband. She had simply done with him, and no doubt Tetsukichi would have expressed similar sentiments if he had been asked about his attitude toward her. One result of this falling-out was the sudden interest she started to take in another man, a man whose face alone had formerly filled her with loathing: Tatsuji, or Zaosan, the Sumo wrestler. *He* had certainly not betrayed Kiichiro since he did still seem to be the largest man in Japan, although his abilities as a wrestler could not be judged so favorably.

If one considered his case coolly and objectively, it was probably cruel to dismiss him as a failure, as an incompetent wrestler. After all, it is a definite achievement to make it as far as the first division (*maku-uchi*) in the Sumo world, and to that extent he had to be considered a genuine success. The trouble was he was so monstrously huge that people, both the Nire people and people in general, had expected far too much of him.

Zaosan had reached his peak right at the beginning of the Showa era, in 1926 and 1927, just when the Nire Hospital was going through its worst period, and he made it right to the top of the *maegashira*. These are the wrestlers in the first division who are below the more or less permanent ranking of *yokozuna* (Grand Champion), *ozeki* (Champion) and *sekiwake* (Junior Champion). During the two-week tournament that had resulted in this achievement he had even managed to defeat a real Grand Champion, thrusting out his long forearms in a flurry of blows and sending the proud *yokozuna* sprawling out of the ring. It was an impressive display of strength, one that had onlookers wondering which of the two should hold the title of honor. Flailing his arms in this way made good use of his long reach and was the main weapon in his limited repertoire; unfortunately, he injured one of his opponents doing this, and further use of the technique was forbidden him. Even so, he was expected to do well enough at the next meet to achieve the position of *sekiwake* (in fact most people thought it was an absolute certainty), but he performed surprisingly badly and went down a number of places.

The trouble was that his wrestling lacked consistency. He had no fighting spirit and would lose to some quite indifferent performers. Then he injured his knee on a provincial tour, and that proved to be fatal. He had always been too tall up top; his legs and thighs had never been adequate to support his mountainous torso, and the injured knee simply accentuated this weakness. So he began to slide down the first division, ending up near the bottom. Here he managed to remain for quite a long time, however, always just about avoiding relegation to the division below. Nevertheless, he retained a remarkable popularity, for his amazing height obliged people to look up to him in a sense, and his sluggish wrestling techniques provided something to amuse everyone, particularly small children, who gave him the kind of vocal support a Grand Champion need not have been ashamed of. But despite this encouragement, which was of an ambiguous and half-joking nature anyway, he failed to win enough of his contests. The inevitable result was that he dropped down into the second division (*juryo*), and was now at the bottom of that and in danger of falling even further.

During one of the two-week Sumo tournaments, Ryuko summoned to the Western Wardrobe Parlor the head of the hospital pharmacy, though since there was only one person working in the pharmacy his title was perhaps something of a misnomer. This was none other than Yasusaburo Sugano.

"Now I want to know," she said in the perfunctory manner she always adopted when she was displeased, "—why is Zaosan so awful? It's an absolute disgrace, losing in that sloppy way and making himself a laughingstock."

"Well, madam, he isn't in fact doing so badly this time. He's won more bouts than he's lost. If he keeps on like this he should start moving up again," replied the faithful Sugano.

It is true that Zaosan did tend to be treated in a special way by Sumo enthusiasts. He was so enormous that everybody assumed he need only put his monstrous strength to proper effect and he was bound to win, and when he didn't he invited ridicule and provided material for ribald comment of the following kind, which often appeared in the newspapers:

> "Tatsu" Zaosan was again bowled over on the fourth day of the Grand Sumo Tournament, suffering one more ludicrous defeat. The poor lump is laughed at when he wins and when he loses, as if he had been born into this world simply to provoke mirth. Since he can only arouse laughter and little respect in others, our Tatsu, whose heart is as timid as his frame is large, likes to be on his own and spends whatever spare time he has fishing. On trains, he prefers to stand, not wanting to hear comments about taking up enough space for three, but then he leans against the brass pillar in the carriage, which makes it shake mightily, producing appreciative chuckles all round. Tatsu certainly has no idea what to do with that great bulk of his. . .

Ryuko did not smile in response to Sugano's encouraging appraisal.

"He's winning at the moment, you say. I should think so. It ought to be a matter of course, I would have thought. He was supposed to become a Grand Champion, wasn't he? Everybody used to say so. And now look at the state he's in. Ridiculous. He's six foot eight—or is it nine?—and he still manages to lose. It's incredible. I can't imagine what he thinks he's up to."

"He's weak in the hips, madam, that's the trouble. He injured his knee, you see," replied Sugano, continuing his apologia.

"His knee? A sumo wrestler must expect to suffer the occasional injury. A strong person would get over it, show what he's made of, wouldn't he?" retorted Ryuko, narrowing her eyes, her voice rising recklessly. "Why does he keep on losing? There must be a better reason than that."

"His opponents are too small," suggested Sugano, who was struggling to find something to say but perhaps half believed the reason he had just given. "He's very sluggish in his movements too. I think it's something to do with his nervous motor system. Perhaps it doesn't extend properly throughout his body, because it's so large. Then he's so slow getting started the other wrestler jumps in at him low down, gets hold of him around the waist" (and Sugano started unconsciously going through the motions) "—like this, like a bug clinging to a tree. So he just starts pushing him out gradually, and Zaosan is weak down there and out he goes. Once someone gets under his guard and gets hold of him like that he's finished."

"Finished? I've never heard such an irresponsible remark. Finished indeed! In that case he ought to make sure that people can't simply jump in at him and get under his guard. I should have thought that was rather obvious. He should thrust them away with his hands stuck out in front of him. Just brush them away. With long arms like that he shouldn't have any trouble."

"Well, madam, he took a great deal of criticism about the way he used his hands in the past. Then, as I said just now, he's so slow. He's always late getting his hands up, and by the time he does the other man has got in under there. . ."

"Then he must learn to keep his head down. What if he has his head so low it's almost on the sand and he simply rushes forward? Then he could thrust his hands out at the same time. There's no other wrestler with arms as long as his, after all."

"By all means, madam," said Yasusaburo, who was embarrassed by the whole conversation. "But if your hands touch the ground in Sumo you lose."

"I am perfectly aware of that. It's called a knockdown, or rather a slap-down. You seem to think I know nothing about Sumo at all. Let me assure you I often used to go to watch the wrestlers practicing when I was a young girl. The old Dewanoumi was extremely kind to me . . . used to make the most tremendous fuss of me. Why, when they went on a tour of Manchuria he said he'd bring me back anything I wanted. I asked for a horse. And, do you know, he actually got one for me. It was only one of those wretched little Korean ponies, though. I can also clearly remember when Zaosan first joined the world of Sumo, although I can't say I actually went to watch him practice then because naturally I had other things to do. Father was terribly worried about him because right from the start he used to lose to these ridiculously small people. I assumed it must be because he wasn't accustomed to the sport yet, but Father was so very upset about it that I went to talk to Dewanoumi about it—not this one but the one before him—on a number of occasions. I asked him quite frankly what kind of prospects there were for Zaosan. He told me not to worry and that everything would be all right because Zaosan was exactly the same type as a wrestler called Taiho who had been a Grand Champion. That's what he told me. He expected Zaosan to become a Grand Champion just as Taiho had done, and Dewanoumi was a man with a very good eye for a wrestler. He understood these matters. Even Father was convinced about that. He certainly knew how to train his wrestlers, really tough training, giving them good hard thwacks on their buttocks with the shaft of the ceremonial bow. Now, here we have a man of that caliber who devoutly believed in Zaosan's future and who plainly said so to me. Zaosan should have become a Grand Champion. Father left this world still believing that he would. . . And now you talk about people slapping him down. It's quite absurd. . . Surely he could still rush forward in the manner I suggested and find some way of avoiding being slapped down. I'm quite sure if Dewanoumi were here he would know what to do. Yasusaburo, have you no ideas on the matter?''

"Well, madam, his present coach is giving him plenty of good advice, I'm sure; and Zaosan himself keeps on thinking and worrying about it, I can assure you.''

"Yes. But what I am really concerned about is not that Zaosan keeps on losing because his opponents leap in at him or get under his guard or slap him down or anything of that kind. I don't see that as the real question at issue. I know Tatsuji well. It's true I find his face repulsive to look at, but I still know him well from a distance. He's cowardly. He's got no spirit in him, no go. He's been like that ever since we sent him to primary school; a huge body but all weak and timid inside. . .''

Sugano nodded his head again, but this time in a clear and affirmative way. At last she had produced an opinion that was just and acceptable. He nodded once more.

"You are absolutely right there, madam. He has no spirit, no confidence in himself. He lacks the killer instinct. He's not pushing himself to win at all costs. In fact, to be quite honest, he's an absolute bundle of nerves. . .''

Ryuko's expression changed on hearing this and she suddenly looked supremely confident; some amazing plan had obviously formed in her mind.

"What did you say just then, Yasusaburo? You said he's a bundle of nerves?''

"Twitches a great deal. Highly strung."

"But those are surely the signs of nervous prostration?"

"Well, yes, I suppose you might say. . ."

"No doubt about it. Nervous prostration. He's obviously been that way since he went to school. Look how he used to cry, that disgraceful roaring like a lion. . . Incidentally, do we still have any K.N. pills in the hospital, the ones my father used to have made?"

"K.N. pills, madam? I'm afraid we don't make them any more. They've been superseded."

"Superseded? Ridiculous. Father must have cured countless patients with them. I can't imagine why they're not being made any more. Do you know how to prepare them, Yasusaburo?"

"Yes, madam, I do."

"Good. Then I must ask you to prepare some immediately. It's a matter of prime urgency. We will give Zaosan a dose. How long does it take for them to have an effect?"

"Well, er, well. . . ," replied the reluctant Yasusaburo, completely put out by that awkward question. "Since they're made for everyday consumption they pass direct from the stomach into the bloodstream, so they should take effect some fifteen to thirty minutes after being swallowed."

"I see. Direct from the stomach into the bloodstream. Fifteen to thirty minutes. Very well then, before the fight I want you to go to the dressing room and have him swallow some. You'll need to give him a larger dose than normal. He's so very big, you see. Now, Yasusaburo, have you got all this quite clear? You go to the dressing room and make him take the K.N. pills. As far as tactics are concerned the main thing is that he should come forward with his head down so that his opponent can't jump inside, but also not too low, to avoid being slapped down in the ring. Of course he really must get his hands out in front of him and get them working. Yes, that's the best thing. Although perhaps he might be able to stand up straight with one arm lowered to prevent any possibility of the other man jumping in at him and the other thrust out before him in attack? Maybe that's not feasible. Yes, not really feasible. He'll just have to crouch down and jab away with his outstretched hands. If his opponent is to get through a guard like that he'll have to get down very low, very low indeed, and it wouldn't take much gumption to knock down someone who assumed that creeping kind of posture. I mean he could simply fall on him and crush him flat. He's big enough, after all. All he has to do is really

306

go at him, crash down on him, with enough force to smash him into smithereens, absolutely flatten him. No matter how sluggish he is he can surely manage that? The trouble is, as you say, he lacks the killer instinct. He's lost before he's even started. No fighting spirit. No will to win. Well, the K.N. pills will cure all that. Then tactics. You'll have to teach him those. He simply has to crouch and thrust out with his hands. And there's no need to say whose plan this is. Just say you heard it from some Sumo expert. If he follows instructions he's bound to win. Can't help winning. Now, Yasusaburo, I rely on you to do all this as a matter of the greatest urgency and importance. I myself shall go to see him win."

"See him fight, madam? You really mean to go and watch him?" Sugano said in amazement, and in a voice full of anxiety, interpreting this promise as a threat.

Strangely, Ryuko had never once been to see an actual Sumo tournament. She had been to watch the wrestlers practicing at Dewanoumi's training headquarters, for the great man himself had been so very obliging to her, but she shared none of her father's enthusiasm for the sport itself. On the contrary, she had never had the slightest desire to watch a lot of dunderheaded Sumo wrestlers battling it out in the sandy circle. But she was extremely pleased with her brainwave of giving Zaosan K.N. pills and with the fight tactics she had worked out. And it was in a very elevated mood that she set off for the National Sumo Hall.

The well-situated box which the Nire family used to have had been disposed of long ago. There was, however, a box reserved for the "Zaosan Supporters Club," and Ryuko telephoned beforehand and found no difficulty in getting seats in it. It was now the penultimate day of the tournament and Zaosan, although not doing quite as well as Sugano had said, had still put up a plucky display and was in the very sensitive position of having lost one more contest than he had won so far. This meant that if he won his next two bouts he would complete the tournament with more contests won than lost, and so would be able to move up a place or two. If he lost today, though, he would have to go down, perhaps even into the division below.

When Ryuko arrived, wearing a white and purple kimono patterned with arrow feathers, the opening ceremony for the second-division matches had just ended, so it was still early in the day and most of the boxes were empty. The same was true of the public seating areas, where the striped cloth which covered the floor and the lines of multicolored cushions only intensified the feeling of listless vacancy. Some of the boxes already had their little piles of wrapped delicacies and presents in preparation for the guests who were due to come, but they would appear only after the first-division contests had got under way. Up in the gallery, however, way above the special boxes, were the seats for the hoi polloi, and these were already jam-packed with people who had been queuing outside the hall since last night.

But the people who had once filled the Zaosan Supporters Club box, intimates of Kiichiro who were blessed with riches and a high social status, were conspicuous by their absence. Ryuko needed one brief glance to grasp this sad and inexplicable fact, for there were only three people in the box and none of them fitted into the above category. There were two men in cheap suits who were clearly petty officials from some obscure department of the Yamagata Prefectural Office, up in Tokyo on some petty official business. There was also an old man in Japanese dress who was not so easy to place but who might well have been—not that Ryuko cared—some powerful man from the same backwoods area. Here he was no more than a bumpkin Sumo fan come all this way to indulge his crude rustic enthusiasm, an impression that was fortified by the rebarbative burr with which he greeted her. Most of what he said was unintelligible, but she did manage to catch the tail end of it, which was an unpleasantly slurred and drooling version of the phrase "well done." Presumably the fellow intended to thank her for having taken the trouble of coming here, as if she were some sort of stranger.

Ryuko found this particularly offensive. By what right did this slob-bering half-wit, who looked as if he might drop dead at any minute (as one fervently hoped he would), make this insolent greeting to her? Was he quite unaware of what the House of Nire and the Nire Hospital were? If it had not been for her father, this very Zaosan would still be burning charcoal at the foot of the mountain whose name he now proudly bore. By whose efforts had he been brought to Tokyo and, finally, after tremendous labors, been turned into a Sumo wrestler? And then to say to her "well done" in that impudent and boorish way. The phrase was her father's. He was the only one who was permitted to use it. Only an unprincipled lout, someone unacquainted with the demands of polite behavior, could have dreamed of using it, particularly to her.

So she turned her back on this clownish person. Of course, in the limited space of a box it is very difficult actually to turn one's back on anybody. But she turned a cold shoulder at least, a shoulder like ice, frozen with rejection and loathing. From then on she spoke only to Yasusaburo, who was sitting in front of her to one side of the box. The occasional drooling appeal or question was apparently addressed to her, but she made no response, not even twitching an eyebrow and certainly not turning in that direction. For she refused to engage in any small talk nor even to indicate she was conscious that some object in the guise of a human being happened to be there.

This does not mean that Ryuko was in a bad mood; perhaps the opposite in fact, for having commandeered the tiny *hibachi*, the size of an ashtray in a wooden box, as a footwarmer, she seemed happy enough in her own way, whispering to Sugano:

"Yasusaburo, I suppose you've done exactly as I told you?"

"Don't you worry, madam. He's taken his K.N. pills. He was suspicious of them at first, but when I told him they were recommended by Dr. Tetsuyoshi he nodded cheerfully."

"Very well. You remembered to give him his fight instructions?"

"Yes. The crouching position. That should be all right, too. Zaosan himself had been thinking along those lines. He's in pretty good shape today. Looking fit and healthy. Good gloss on his skin. He should be able to show what he's made of."

"Good. Then I won't have wasted my time coming all this way."

That remark brought back the worries Yasusaburo had momentarily forgotten about. Today's opponent, a wrestler called Futagoiwa ("Twin Rocks"), was having a very successful run at the moment, having lost only two of his last thirteen bouts (unlike Zaosan who had lost seven of his), and he would certainly be no pushover. Yasusaburo tried to drop a few hints about the quality of this tricky customer to Ryuko, but she was not prepared to pay any attention. She clearly had thoughts only for the efficacy of the K.N. pills and the crouching mode of attack.

She began telling Yasusaburo her impressions of the arena and what was happening inside it, for this was the first time she had been here. Most of her remarks were contemptuous. She commented severely on the faces of the wrestlers and the referee each time they appeared in the ring, and on the way they behaved. Goodness me, that extraordinary voice he uses to call out their names. Like a cat with laryngitis. What a remarkable mishap of a face that wrestler has. I have never seen a face so like a gargoyle as that one. . .

No doubt this steady stream of vituperation was an attempt to calm the excitement growing inside her, although it only showed that her excitement was not diminishing but merely fostering more complex sensations of expectation and misgiving.

Now at last there was considerable toing and froing in the aisles between the boxes; and up near the roof, in addition to the roars that greeted the contests from time to time, there was a constant hum and buzz, an indication of the stuffy turmoil that must prevail up there.

Then, as two wrestlers were in the ring doing the raising and stamping of the feet which serves both as a ritual and as a warming-up exercise prior to a bout, some apparently irrelevant and scattered applause rang out. This was a sign that two other wrestlers of note were coming down the two passageways from their respective dressing rooms to take their seats at the ringside and await their turn to compete. Down the passage from the West came a very tall figure, leaning slightly forward and proceeding at a surprisingly brisk pace. This was Zaosan. His face, with its distended jaw which delighted cartoonists, was directed at the floor in hangdog fashion, so it was impossible to see his expression and judge whether the K.N. pills had done their job or not. At the same time another wrestler came quietly down the passage from the East toward the ring. The route he took was not far from the box where Ryuko was sitting, so she was able to get a good look at him. He was very dark-skinned and so small by Sumo standards that he could almost have been described as slight.

"What on earth is that? Surely that's not Futagoiwa, that teeny little shrimp? Yasusaburo, do you really think *that* is capable of defeating Zaosan?"

"Futagoiwa is very small, madam, I know. But he's a real technician. You have to be careful with him," whispered Sugano who was himself beginning to be caught up in the same odd state of excitement.

Ryuko said no more. It was clear that she was absorbed in what she saw, although she was obviously not following what the two wrestlers now in the ring were doing, nor was she inclined to make tart remarks about the crudity of their features. What concerned her was Zaosan, sitting there on the West side of the ring, and revealing his long horse-like face and jutting jaw in all their stupendous reality.

At last the long awaited and long feared moment arrived. Zaosan raised his monstrous bulk, that body which seemed an embarrassment even to its owner, and lumbered into the ring. He was facing the moment of truth, and his body gave off a powerful sense of fatality. Immediately the whole hall was alive with excitement. Even the as yet sparsely populated boxes on the ground floor were astir as if a *yokozuna*, or at least an *ozeki*, had come into the ring, and up in the gallery a group of primary-school children started shouting out Zaosan's name and giving encouraging cheers.

This vocal support seemed to move Ryuko. She leaned stiffly forward, placing her tightly clenched hands on her knees, and shook her head in an irritated way at a young lad who was passing by at that moment and attempting to sell people pots of tea.

Now more voices rang out from behind her, voices that seemed to carry smartly—if voices can be considered smart—all the way to the ring; voices calling out the name of Zaosan. They were dignified voices, proper voices, voices it was a genuine pleasure to hear, and there were more than one or two of them.

One more would be welcome, though, so she whispered sharply to Sugano:

"Shout out something. Come on. Quickly."

So Sugano shouted "Zaosan," but in a squeaky, clownish voice that totally lacked authority.

"Stop! Stop, for heaven's sake. Everyone's looking in this direction," whispered Ryuko, savagely this time, emphasizing her imperious change of mind with a swift jerk of her body which made it clear that we wanted no more of that, thank you.

In the ring the leisurely preliminaries were going on. The wrestlers squared up to each other, eyed each other, then parted, swaggered to the ringside, loosened up, picked up a handful of salt, cast it with a casual sweep of the hand into the ring, then took up position opposite each other—only to begin all over again. Ryuko was now almost straining out of the box, muttering instructions in so muted a voice they seemed to be aimed at herself, although their real object was out there in the ring. For example, Zaosan's method of taking the salt from the bamboo basket hanging from one of the four pillars which in those days supported the roof above the ring, and casting it on the sandy floor, was not to her liking, and her useless criticisms of this act were as unending as they also seemed beyond her power to control.

"Oh no, not like that. It's no use throwing a silly little bit of salt like that. Look at the way Futagoiwa's throwing it, great arrogant handfuls. . ."

Then came the moment of decision. The two wrestlers crouched down, glaring at each other, touched their hands on the marked lines before them, and leaped at each other in the same instant, the huge wrestler with the face of a cartoon Punch, and his tiny opposite number.

Zaosan put everything he had into it. Nobody could have denied that. Whether he was keeping Ryuko's tactical plan in mind or not it would be hard to say, but he thrust out his long arms and battered powerfully away with the palms of his hands at the head and shoulders of his opponent. This was effective. One of the ramrod blows sent the dark, intrepid figure of Futagoiwa staggering right to the edge of the ring. But Zaosan was unfortunately unable to follow this up, at least not with the lightning speed and power that would have settled the contest there and then. He moved slowly and clumsily, and so left himself open. The wily Futagoiwa quickly recovered his balance and composure and was in there like a flash beneath those flailing arms. Immediately he had his arms around the huge trunk of the man mountain, and a firm grip with both hands on the thick sash the almost naked wrestlers wear around their waists. This position ensured that Zaosan was unable to get anything like the same hold on his opponent's sash, and Futagoiwa gradually started to work him toward the edge of the ring. Zaosan made a desperate attempt to throw his opponent down, but he was panicking now and the attempted throw was half-hearted and incompetent and only made his predicament worse, for he lost his balance and was simply trundled out of the ring without being able to make any further show of resistance.

A stir ran round the hall, with a clear undercurrent of suppressed laughter at seeing a great hulk like that losing in so helpless a way to an opponent only half his size. Gradually this laughter ceased to be suppressed, an indication of the indifferent curiosity with which most of the spectators regarded a sport that they wanted only to provide amusement; and also of their relief that a man so monstrous could lose to someone much like themselves. Their own sense of everyday failure was mitigated, for here was someone failing even more abjectly then they had; here was someone they could despise and jeer at with great self-satisfied guffaws.

In the box next to the Zaosan Supporters Club was an oldish man who had hitherto been sitting by himself gloomily drinking *sake*. But now he was delighted, rocking on waves of hilarity. It seemed the world could offer nothing more delicious than this moment, so total was his joy. He rolled about, with almost painful roars of "hoah, hoah, hoah" coming from his lips, which pouted with mirth so that they looked much like the mouth of the little porcelain bottle of *sake* from which he was making vain attempts to drink.

Ryuko had suddenly stiffened at the moment the contest was decided. She now raised her head sharply and then, in one swift movement, leaned forward and reached for her *zori* sandals.

"Are you leaving, madam?" asked the bewildered Sugano, who had been immersed in his own feelings of excitement and disappointment, and now looked up in consternation at the expressionless face of the mistress of the house. Ryuko deigned not one word of reply, but set off swiftly along the passageway toward the exit, humiliation and rage showing in the set of her shoulders.

Sugano swallowed hard and set off swiftly after her.

Much of Aoyama remained as it always had been, from the Seinan Primary School with its ancient, decaying, wooden walls, the kindergarten on the slope opposite, the police box on the corner, and then down the narrow lane away from the main road to the Seiundo shop where all was just as it had been years ago. It is true that the parking area for rickshas next to the Seiundo had disappeared and the stationery shop itself could hardly be described as prosperous. A much larger stationers, the Takashima, had been built on the main road only a short distance away, modern, neat, brightly decorated, and there was no competing with that. The shop front of the Seiundo had always been a jumble of objects piled up on two low tables, heaps of exercise books and cheap toys, and nowadays the dust seemed to have accumulated more thickly on them than in the past. But the two people who ran the shop, the tiny couple whose resemblance to each other had lately grown so great that they were virtually identical, remained the same, perpetually smiling with a benevolence that came genuinely from the heart.

Momoko still visited the place often, although she was no longer a carefree little girl but a wife and mother. She would come all the way from her rented home in Kasumi-cho simply to indulge in innocent, endless chat about the good old days with this now aging couple. She would pass through the shop, ascend the creaking staircase, which was dark even at midday, and enter the single upstairs room, one of eight mats in size. In the *tokonoma* alcove hung a scroll with the famous words, "This Single Action Will Determine the Destiny of the Empire," signed by Admiral of the Fleet, Count Togo, and written in his own hand. His message was the Japanese equivalent of Nelson's "England Expects. . ." and was also associated with a great naval victory, for Admiral Togo was the man responsible for sinking the Russian fleet back

313

in 1905. The scroll in the modest room was, naturally enough, only a reproduction, one of dozens produced after that great occasion.

This was a room in which Momoko could feel at home. The couple were extremely courteous, unlike her own family who had always totally ignored her. Here she was treated properly, for they made tea for her and, leaving the half-witted boy they had recently employed in charge of the shop, would both listen happily to Momoko's idle chatter for as long as she wanted them to.

Sometimes her son Satoru, who was now at primary school, would turn up at the shop and then, by prior arrangement, Nanny Shimoda would bring Aiko there as well. The two children were of the same age and would spend their time shouting and climbing up and down the steep, creaking staircase, or handling the merchandise just as they pleased, finally selecting some tops or glass beads or a colored picture (a heliochrome) to stuff into their pockets. Naturally they showed these things to the shop lady before they did so, and an entry would be made in the book which was taken to Mr. Oishi at the hospital at the end of each month.

Satoru had grown up into rather a different child from the baby Momoko had so despaired over. He was still dark, it is true, but his features were well defined. At first Momoko had doted on him, but as he grew up and people started to admire him and say so, her love for him began strangely to grow less. The main reason for this was probably that the whole cast of his features, in particular those protruding ears, not only took after her husband but was the spitting image of him. So, presumably in compensation for the loss of this obsession, she gained a new one.

She kept cats. First there were three stray cats she had found somewhere, and then these cats inevitably had kittens, seven of them. Nothing could have been more lovable than these little balls of fluff as they frisked about, playing with anything they came across; one could have died for them, they were so sweet and pretty. But the advent of these animals gave a great impetus to Momoko's natural leanings toward slovenliness or, if one prefers, to her noble indifference to the dictates of common sense and propriety. She knocked large holes in all the thin paper sliding doors to allow these creatures the run of the house. Thus cats and kittens, ten in all, now roamed at will; pillars and doors were scored with claw marks; in the corners of the rooms lay the scattered remains of saucers of food which Momoko put down with solicitous affection; and at a strategic point at the end of the cor-

314

ridor there was a sandbox for the convenience of the kittens. All this was accompanied by an appropriate stench.

There was another event which must be mentioned here, since it is related to all this, and had considerable repercussions. About a year before the point we have reached in our story there had been a violent clash between Tetsukichi and Shiro, Momoko's husband. "Clash" is perhaps not the right word since it consisted in a one-sided abusing of Shiro by Tetsukichi. It would have been difficult not to sympathize with Shiro over this incident and, indeed, over his situation as a whole. He was commuting every day to the hospital in Aoyama, and he worked hard and conscientiously. Inside, however, he was full of dissatisfactions. He was unable to repress the belief that he had been the victim of a major deception. Had not the suave, affable, reliable (as he had seemed and would have seemed to anybody) Kiichiro asked him to become his adopted son, promising him his daughter, with the bonus of study abroad thrown in? But what kind of daughter had Kiichiro bestowed on him? The author of a succession of disasters so embarrassing that one could not even mention them to anybody else. Then the hospital, that reliable-looking structure with its columns and seven towers, had gone up in smoke overnight. And the maker of these various pledges had himself chosen to depart with similar rapidity into the great beyond. Even if he wanted to complain now to the smooth-tongued Kiichiro, the latter was safely in a place where he could not be reached, whether realms of light or of darkness; though the man himself would doubtless be smiling happily wherever he was and performing further wonders of the rhetorician's art.

But the real problem brought about by Kiichiro's death was that once he had gone the people in the Nire Hospital paid little attention to Shiro. They seemed to feel he was not worth bothering about. This neglect led to something more serious, an awareness on Shiro's part that he was not interested in mental illness nor ever had been, and that years of attempting to accustom himself to the psychiatric profession had had no effect at all. What he most wanted to do was to get back to surgery. This was his main complaint against life, although one he tried to keep to himself. On top of all this, the home he had to return to each night was not only occupied by a wife who had no affection for him and neglected normal household duties, but was full of claw marks and the excreta of numerous cats. Shiro was working on his M.D. thesis at the time, so he might have been well advised to use the cats as subjects for his anatomical researches. In fact, he chose lampreys. At first Momoko could not for the life of her imagine why he should have been seized with this sudden passion to eat lampreys for supper. It was her house just as much as his, and she had a particular dislike of long, thin, squirmy things like lampreys. She had only to look at a snake and she would go weak at the knees. She even found a delicious and non-squirmy-looking dish like sliced, broiled eels on rice was inedible owing to the associations the word brought up.

Now here was her husband bringing back a dozen or more of these slimy, loathsomely writhing creatures. She could hardly believe her eyes, and she screamed out in protest, while her husband had more than a few overbearing remarks to make in reply. A full-scale debate then ensued concerning the respective merits and demerits of cats and lampreys, and whether they should be allowed into the house or not. Since the tone of this was mostly hysterical it was a flaming row rather than a debate and resulted in an explosion of all that pent-up frustration which Shiro was obliged to keep under control at the hospital. The climax came when Shiro suddenly found himself grabbing hold of his wife's hair and dragging her about the room by it. This occasioned tremendous screams that reverberated throughout the neighborhood.

So Shiro's subsequent verbal lapse at the hospital must be regarded as an inevitable sequel. One day at the Aoyama branch he could no longer restrain his grievances, and he said what he shouldn't have said. This expression of naked feeling was spat out from between tight lips, but unluckily it was loud enough to be overheard. He said he was sick up to here of dealing with idiots, and was just about ready to throw it in.

The "idiots" he was referring to were the mental patients at the Nire Hospital, and when news of this outburst reached the ears of the Director, it put Tetsukichi into a rare rage. Since Tetsukichi himself had experienced to the full the burden of dealing with mental patients, his wrath may seem mysterious; he had surely had similar feelings many times himself. But it had always been an iron rule at the Nire Hospital that under no circumstances was language to be employed by the staff that expressed contempt for the patients. Kiichiro had constantly insisted to his nursing staff that only polite forms of address should be used to the patients in their presence, and that they should be spoken about politely in their absence. The late Director had presumably been concerned not so much with the ethical or humanitarian question as with what was good for business; nevertheless, it was still absolutely forbidden in the hospital to use any of those contemptuous words that ordinary people use when referring to lunatics.

Obviously the word "idiot" came within that category. It was a plain, unambiguous word that should have been taboo to a doctor at the Nire Hospital, yet it had been quite brazenly used by one of them. It must also be added that Tetsukichi lacked that largeness of mind which would have allowed the whole matter to pass as a slip of the tongue. Instead he called Shiro to his office and, his voice trembling in a manner never heard before, gave him a severe dressing down, the finale of which was a demand that he remove himself from his sight forthwith. The whole speech was delivered in words as plain and unambiguous as the one Shiro had used.

Naturally the affair left an unpleasant aftertaste all round, and bad feeling between the two of them. It wasn't long, therefore, before Shiro was transferred to the hospital at Matsubara, and Seisaku Kanazawa came back to work at Aoyama. Momoko and her husband moved to another rented house near Shimo Kitazawa Station, a ten-minute walk from the hospital. She took with her only half the cats which had been the main cause of their quarrel.

The move to Matsubara did not prevent Momoko from visiting the Seiundo. In fact she visited just as frequently as before, leaving Satoru in the hands of a servant girl who was little more than a child herself, and taking the train to Shibuya and then the streetcar from there. She used her next-door neighbor's telephone to ring up Nanny Shimoda before she went, so usually her old nanny would come bringing Aiko, and sometimes Shuji.

"Satoru hardly ever goes to school nowadays. I really am getting sick to death of him. I suppose it's because he's had to change schools, but to be quite honest with you that kid has got on my nerves lately. I sometimes think I positively hate him."

"Well I never! And about your own child, the child you labored to bring forth into the world," replied Nanny Shimoda with great severity of tone, while she neatly sliced up the sweet, sticky, jelly-like cake which Mrs. Seiundo (whose real name was O-ume) had provided for them.

"That's it. You've hit it there. I made a mess of the child's birth and now I'm making the same mess of his upbringing. One long series of messes. That's a nice dress you're wearing, Mistress Ai. Very pretty. You were a lovely little thing when you were a baby, you know. So lovely I could have killed you. Just the opposite of Satoru. Was he ugly! But you were sweet. I could have eaten you. Much too sweet, of course. I couldn't stand you. You're pretty cute even now."

Momoko had not lost the habit of saying exactly what she felt, even in front of the children, although it was interesting that she naturally referred to her little niece in the traditional Nire Gakushuin manner she had so despised before. She seemed extremely cheerful, her plump cheeks plumper than ever, and as she smiled her narrow eyes became even narrower.

"Oh, Auntie, do you really think so?" replied Aiko in a cheeky, grown-up manner, sticking her tongue out saucily. Secretly she felt that although her Auntie Momoko talked a little too much and in a rather vulgar way, she was marvelous fun to be with, and she really liked her a lot.

There was one more child in the room, a little boy in short pants who was lying on his stomach in a corner of the room, writing away for all he was worth. This was Shuji, who was due to enter primary school next year, but was not attending kindergarten. His elder brother and sister had both been to Seinan Kindergarten, and when the head teacher came to his house, presumably to solicit his custom, he had readily accepted the sweet that was offered him. But this had not swayed his resolve not to favor the place with his presence, and the main reason for his success in this respect was Nanny Shimoda's plea that one should not force the child to go if he really hated the idea that much.

Since there was no one to take his education seriously in hand he was still ignorant of the relatively simple phonetic script in which Japanese can be written. A child learns this when young, and then gradually acquires the basic Chinese ideograms during the rest of his compulsory education. Shuji could now just about write his own name if he struggled hard enough, but he did know one ideogram, and one only, which was the comparatively difficult character for *kotobuki,* meaning both "long life" and "congratulations." Shuji had learned the complex traditional form of this character rather than the simplified one now in common use, his instructor being the impetuous intern who had replaced Sadaichi Sawara as the children's occasional guardian-cum-nurse. This individual had advised Shuji to master the most difficult Chinese character first, and though *kotobuki* would hardly qualify as this even by half-educated standards, it was probably the hardest one he knew or could write with assurance; so Shuji was immediately shown how to do it. The child was fascinated and determined to master this skill, so he set to work, producing a peculiarly distorted version of his own, since the brushstrokes were all made out of order. Nevertheless, it was a recognizable pastiche of this complicated character if

318

one was told what it was meant to be. Grown-ups praised the mess in their usual irresponsibly casual way, and Shuji became so proud of his accomplishment that whenever he had a few spare moments he would spend them perfecting the art of writing "*kotobuki*."

Lately Shuji had acquired another skill, that of obtaining things free from the Seiundo, although he could not yet manage this in the grand manner of his sister. Just now, for example, down in the shop he had taken one red pencil in his hand, asked in a tiny voice if he could have it, and looked greatly relieved when the lady had nodded her assent. While she was sharpening it for him, he had time to ponder the nature of this success, and so he tried his luck with a large sketchbook, but this time the kind lady shook her head and said he was still too small for something like that. Obviously, the more Shuji appropriated the more money the shop would make, but the Seiundo couple never seemed to think in such terms. So, instead of the sketchbook, she gave him a few sheets of advertising handouts which were plain on the back and could be used for writing or drawing on.

Momoko had observed this transaction and immediately felt the need to poke her nose into things:

"O-ume. Give him the sketchbook, go on. I can remember what it was like when I was his age. I used to love buying all sorts of things here. It didn't cost anything, you see."

"I should think you did, too. All those pencil sharpeners. . . And there was that time you took more than a dozen erasers in one go. Of course, I tried to stop you. . ."

This made Momoko curl up with laughter, and while she was chuckling away Shuji went on writing "*kotobuki*" on the white backs of the handbills: "*kotobuki*," "*kotobuki*," and again "*kotobuki*." This attracted comment from Momoko who always believed in saying what she felt like saying.

"Goodness me, Shuji, whatever's that? Is it some kind of pattern? Or a symbol, maybe?"

"It's '*ko-to-bu-ki*,' " replied Shuji, forcefully spelling out the word in Japanese syllabic fashion and in obvious annoyance at this aunt who didn't even know what "*kotobuki*" was. He kept his head turned away from her.

"My, he certainly can write some difficult things," said Nanny Shimoda, her voice manifesting a complacent delight in this child who, in her eyes, could do no wrong.

"Nanny's still sold on Shuji, I see," said Momoko, who was always prepared to mock this predilection. "Still, the boys in our family have never been any good, and that's a fact. Look at them. Oshu and Yonekuni have super names, I admit, but that's about all. Hopeless at school, both of them. Shun'ichi's not all that clever, is he? He doesn't look it anyway. In the Nire household it's the women who have class. They're the ones with quality. It's been the same since long ago. Only the quality seems to fall off as one goes down the list, I suppose. Still, Mistress Ai, you'll be all right, I'm sure. I'm sure you've got quality."

"Even so," Nanny butted in, seemingly put out by these remarks, "Master Shuji is certainly intelligent. Only the other day he went into the maid's room next to the kitchen and came out with fifty sen."

"What do you mean, 'He came out with fifty sen'?"

Shuji had grown tired of writing "*kotobuki*" and had gone downstairs with Aiko, so Nanny Shimoda began the story. It seemed that Shuji had lately taken to playing outside on his own much more than before, his great passion being the picture-card storyteller who turned up most days of the week, usually just before it started to grow dark. Compared with the other children, Shuji was in an unhappy position with regard to this form of entertainment, for he had no money at all. As soon as the children heard the sound of the wooden clappers with which the traveling showman announced a performance, they would swarm about him, jostling for the best positions in front, and fighting with one another to pass over the one-sen copper coins clenched in their fists. The picture-card man would take their money and give each child a stick of twisty red-and-white candy in return. Then, while they sucked their stick of candy, they would watch a succession of crudely drawn pictures the man showed them and listen to the narration that accompanied the pictures, usually some popular drama of the day, delivered in a weirdly raucous croak.

These children would get a good view of the proceedings and be able to follow the narrative without difficulty. Shuji, however, since he lacked the wherewithal to buy a stick of candy, was not allowed to taste these other privileges. Not matter how good a position he got he was always hauled unceremoniously out of it by the picture-card man, who would shout:

"Right, kids who haven't bought a sweet get right to the back, now, right to the back."

This meant that Shuji could only stand on tiptoe at the back, casting envious glances at the kids who had bought sweets and, by straining his neck, catching an occasional glimpse of the mystery man with the death's-head mask, the creepy long fingernails and the outstretched red cape:

"And now, who should appear but the man of mystery, friend of the good, justice in a monster's form, Golden Bat! Wah, hah, hah, hah, haaah. . ."

At such moments the drama was given added tension by the picture-card man rattling away on the drum he had with him.

Having submitted to this kind of brush-off with its concomitant inconveniences on a number of occasions, Shuji began to feel that without money one was bound to miss things in life, and his small head became dominated by the idea that it was necessary to have cash on one's person. It was in this state of mind that he chanced to spy a purse on a shelf in the maid's room. Naturally enough he opened it, selected the largest silver coin he could find, and went outside again to play. Since the picture-card man didn't come that day he walked a considerable distance looking for him, ending up in an area full of little cramped houses down an incline just in front of the Aoyama Cemetery, where he came across an old man selling the simple device and liquid required for blowing soap bubbles. It was obviously a very special liquid, for Shuji had never seen such beautiful rainbow-colored bubbles before. So he joined a small swarm of children who were all unknown to him and for the very first time in his life produced from his pocket some money of his own. The old man fished about inside the jingling leather bag that held his money, and gave Shuji his change, which consisted, although Shuji did not know it, of several five- or ten-sen silver coins and the rest all one-sen coppers. There were a great many of these coins, and as Shuji stood there with them almost overflowing from his cupped hands, he was struck by the enormity of the crime he had committed. While still standing there like this he was eventually apprehended by the maid who had come in pursuit of him, in a state of bewilderment close to physical prostration, the bamboo tube with the soap-bubble solution in it discarded on the ground, and the great heap of coins still held dangerously in his two hands.

"Why, the child's a thief!" shrieked Momoko, apparently aghast at what she had just heard.

"How can you say such a thing, Mistress Momo. He most certainly is not. Master Shuji has no idea of the value of money. He's just a very unhappy, very unfortunate child, that's all. I feel sorry for him. This used to be such a large hospital with plenty of space to play in and plenty of other hospital children to play with. None of the children

I brought up ever needed to go outside the hospital to play. They never needed to touch money, either. You, of course, Mistress Momo, always seemed to crave money even though you never needed it either, although I can't think why. And I gave you enough of it as well; a great deal, indeed.''

"I know, Nanny, I know. I owe you a lot, I know that. And, believe me, when you're dead I'll have a bronze statue put up in your memory.''

"There you go again. All I'm saying is that things are different now from the way they used to be. Poor little Shuji, getting told off like that even by those servant boys. . . Still, it's wonderful the way he understands about everything now. I give him one sen every day and he never takes any money from the maid's room any more.''

"What's so wonderful about that? He's big enough to know better than to take money, surely? He's going to school next year, isn't he?''

"Still, what I really did admire was that he knew absolutely nothing at all about money, and yet he picked out the fifty-sen piece. Any ordinary child would only have taken something like five sen.''

"Nanny, you are the absolute limit,'' said Momoko, doubling up with laughter.

But Nanny Shimoda's remarks about things not being what they used to be stimulated other memories, and since Momoko's nephew and niece chose that moment to come back upstairs again she regaled them with a highly colored account of life in the days of the old hospital. It had been just like a palace in a fairy tale, with its seven towers and dozens of huge columns which a child couldn't reach around with both arms, and the proprietor of this very Seiundo had played an important role in the solemn prize-giving ceremony which had been such wonderful fun to watch. . .

"There were masses of people around then, including lots who had nothing to do at all and nobody could think why they were there. Plenty of patients, too. There was one who made banknotes; not cheap ones but worth a hundred yen or more. I wish I had some to give you, Shuji. Then there was Billiken. . . Poor man, he went in. . . He used to read the newspaper, out loud. He had a wonderful way of doing it, like this. . .''

Momoko picked up the newspaper at her side and turned to the human interest columns:

"*Sailors Fall into Evil Clutches of Resuscitated Communist Party. Three Cat's-Paws Discovered in the* Nagato, *the* Haruma *and the* Yamashiro.*''

She read this with a peculiar modulation, then suddenly screwed up her face and resumed her normal voice.

"Gosh, the Communist Party is terrifying. They've even infiltrated the armed forces now. I once heard a story, can't remember when it was exactly, of some sailor in this ship crossing the Pacific, and there was some kind of organization and all sorts of secret communications. They go on arresting them, but they hide away somewhere. They go underground and still keep plotting away. . ."

This also seemed to spark off a memory, for she calmed down enough to forget these present-day dangers and return to her own past:

"I used to be well up on socialism when I was young. Words like 'anarchist.' And the blind poet Eroshenko. Nobody remembers things like that now; never heard of them," she said, looking dreamily upward with her tiny eyes, apparently entranced. "Of course, the Communist Party is a real menace. You never know what they're going to do next. I remember when I was once arrested as a Communist suspect. Oh you remember, Nanny, that red cloth which people nicknamed 'marxisme,' and I had a kimono made out of it and was stopped at the police box on the main road. I was given a real going over, I can tell you. A proper interrogation. And when I told them I was one of the daughters at the hospital they had the cheek not to believe me and rang up home to check up. Treated me just like a criminal; it was the worst experience in my whole life, up to then. It all goes to show what a terrifying thing the Communist Party is and no mistake. You simply never know what they're plotting to do next."

Momoko had a sip of tea, then opened another newspaper in order to continue her rendition in the Billiken style:

"*Ruble Swindler Strikes in Broad Daylight at Tobacconist*. . . Good heavens, the ruble rascal robs again! They still haven't managed to catch him."

This was a story that had been providing the newspapers with excellent copy for a little while now, a deception in which a Russian ruble note was folded so as to look like good, honest Japanese currency, and the clever or dastardly villain ran off with the change. This prompted some more Momoko memories:

"There was a time when I was thinking of buying rubles. Do you remember, Nanny, that man Senaga, the one with the special nervous problems? He had lots of ruble notes. I wonder what's happened to him? I suppose he couldn't possibly be this ruble swindler? No, not very likely. Too timid to commit a crime like that. He was always buying patent medicines. Did it all the time. Now, what were they? Ah, now I remember: 'Bulgarin, created under the supervision of Dr. Mechnikov,' 'New Cure for Beriberi: Essence of Silverhide'. . . I'm beginning to think I must have a pretty good memory. And his symptoms were quite fantastic. He used to say that at night he would suddenly wake up and find he couldn't breathe. Of course it was all nerves. Then he used to pound away at his own backbone, and eventually he'd start breathing again. . . Like goldfish, I suppose, the way they breathe in water. . . You know, Nanny, don't you think it was perhaps Senaga who had a bad influence on Yonekuni? He's been behaving very peculiar recently. Seems to be his nerves as well.''

In fact Yonekuni had taken a whole year off school with pulmonary catarrh, but after recovering from that he had gone to an agricultural college in Aoyama. Even after he had moved with Hisa and the others to Matsubara he still continued his studies at the same place, traveling backward and forward every day. It was obviously unusual for a son of the Nire family to go in for agriculture, and one of the reasons given for this was ill health, for he was always catching colds. Momoko's more blunt opinion was that his grades at school were so unbelievably bad that it was decided he would have no chance of entering any medical faculty anywhere.

Yonekuni suffered a hemorrhage of the lungs; at least he decided that's what it was. Since there was already the tragic example of Seiko in the family, everyone viewed the incident with grave concern until an investigation of his handkerchief revealed only a tiny spot of blood which had most likely been coughed up from somewhere in his throat. However, a lung specialist did say there were traces or suspicions of infiltration of the lungs, and Yonekuni himself decided he was in an advanced stage of consumption, so he had another long layoff from school. The result was that he had finally managed to graduate from his agricultural college only this year.

Momoko was never content to remain on any one subject for long, and she soon switched to another. Faced with this audience of a niece who understood little of what she said but still found it fascinating, and a nephew who merely gazed blankly on, she remained absorbed in her recollections:

''The place was full of interesting people, and they were all really nice to me, to your old Auntie Momoko. But nearly all of them have gone now. Kumagoro, the Pockmarked Bear, is still around, of course, over at the main hospital. He was always saying he was going to be a lawyer or a politician, and never once did a stroke of work. There were lots of people like him, and Father—your grandfather—fed and clothed them all. Then the hospital burned down and some people died and others went back to their home towns, and there were lots who just disappeared somewhere. After all, we couldn't go on feeding and clothing and giving wages to all those people, could we? Still, the old hospital was a fantastic place. There was never anything like it. Like a palace, a real palace."

Then she seemed to waken from this reverie as other thoughts and feelings came back, and she turned sharply in the direction of Nanny Shimoda.

"But I was always unlucky, Nanny, always. I wonder if there has ever been any woman in the world as ill-fated as me."

There were definite traces of the style of the old *benshi* at the silent movies in these words of hers. She did not look in the least ill-fated, but seemed to be cheerfully carried away on the mounting waves of her own rhetoric. Nanny Shimoda, however, felt that Momoko should restrain herself in front of the children, and she muttered something that could have been interpreted as denying the unhappy nature of Momoko's fate.

"Nanny, do you really believe that? Do you honestly think so? After all, you ought to know. You ought to know everything. Or perhaps you just don't want to know any more? You just don't want to listen, I suppose. I didn't think you were like that, Nanny. Anyway, the truth's the truth. Nothing good's ever happened to me, not since the moment I was born."

Nanny's efforts to hush her up had been of no effect at all, and Momoko now seemed to be urged on by a seriousness that had come into her voice from somewhere. Indifferent to the presence of her young niece and nephew, she suddenly let herself go in a breathless outpouring:

"Nanny, I'll tell you this; and you're the only one I would tell this to. The House of Nire is a cold, heartless place, and always was. I can't describe the extent of that coldness. Oh yes, the people on top, the ones with class and quality, they get treated very well, very nicely thank you. But that's not from love; that's just being practical. The only thing that matters for the Nire family is the hospital. It's not people, nothing with warm blood running through it. There's no warmth, no blood in any of them, no tears, nothing. Look at Father and Mother if you don't believe me. What blood or tears did you ever see in them? Mind you, I don't enjoy saying things like this. I don't want to say this. You see, if you're all proud and stuck up and behave as if you're really somebody, then you get on all right. But if you're not like that, if you know you're not really anybody and can't behave as if you thought you were, then you've had it. You're not even treated like a human being. All right, I'll admit it: I was never much good. I was never anything to be proud of. That's true. But that was no reason why I shouldn't have been treated a little as if I were human, as if I were alive with thoughts and feelings of my own, not just some object, some piece of merchandise they could do anything they wanted with. . ."

This was an amazing change from the cheerful, pleased-with-life and delighted-with-herself Momoko of only a few moments ago. There was a shining in the corners of her eyes that presaged tears, and immediately large tears were dropping one after the other onto her cheeks.

Nanny Shimoda seemed to lose all her normal composure. All she could do was stretch out her wrinkled hands in front of her and repeat the same mumbled phrases:

"Please, Mistress Momo, please stop. Whatever are you saying? I can't think what. . . And here of all places. . ."

Aiko and Shuji were both dumbfounded and uncomprehending, particularly Shuji, who could only gape with his mouth wide open as, half astonished and half fascinated, he watched the tears pour down his aunt's cheeks. But Momoko was further carried away by the emotions this flood of tears she had not wept for so long now brought into being. She spoke in short, broken clusters of words:

"If you're down you're no use to them. They don't want anything to do with you. . . You're inferior, no good. . . No one paid a blind bit of notice. . . Just kicked and trampled on all the time. . . Why me?. . . Why did I have to have this kind of life?. . ."

Fortunately this state, which had completely demoralized Nanny Shimoda, did not last long. As always, the great flood of tears soon mysteriously dried up, and although her face was still fraught with emotion, enough of the old cheerful Momoko was apparent when she said impressively:

"I always cry a lot. I can't help it. It doesn't mean anything. But you remember this, Mistress Ai, and you too, Master Shuji, remember it well. Your Aunt Momoko was star-crossed at her birth, a hapless woman born under an ill-fated star."

This splendid remark cheered her up enormously, and all her former good temper came back at once. The recovery was so total as to seem magical. So she began reminiscing about Hankow, about Chinese food which is so good for you and had made her so fat, about the peculiar hodgepodge the servants would cook up out of the leftovers which was very tasty too, about the old man who had taught her magic spells so that she should give birth to a son, and about the great adventure which had ended in failure when she had tried to run away and come home to Japan. She went on happily talking away, careless of details and apparently indifferent to whether she was talking to Nanny Shimoda or to her little nephew and niece. She also didn't seem to care if the language she used was slightly vulgar or not, and then she leaned forward and said:

"When our hospital got burned down it was in the *Hankow Daily,* which is a Japanese newspaper they have in Hankow, and it was all about me being the wife of our Dr. Shiro Nire, Chief Surgeon at the Hankow Benevolent Hospital, and the third daughter of Dr. Kiichiro Nire, Director of the Nire Hospital of Mental Pathology."

Momoko spoke with pride, as if she too had once enjoyed her moment of triumph and fame, wrinkling her nose and helping herself to another slice of the jelly-like cake that O-ume had provided.

At this point, the master of the Seiundo ascended the stairs, perhaps to entertain the children with a recitation of Chinese poetry as was his occasional custom. Even though his vocal powers were undeniably still those of the man whose sonorous voice had once dominated the Prize-Giving Ceremony, the children considered the special tones required for Chinese poetry eccentric in the extreme. Today, however, he was not going to recite poetry, but was going to play instead the *shakuhachi,* the fat bamboo pipe which looks like a large, primitive clarinet. He placed the wooden tube to his mouth, coaxing a strangely sweet, melodious sound from it; and yet when Aiko and Shuji, after a series of snatchings and squabblings with each other, tried to blow through it, all they could produce was the harsh sound of their own breath.

Observing this, Momoko remarked on how difficult it must be to play the instrument, and expressed her admiration for the splendid skill the master of the Seiundo had shown in being able to play it with such ease. Then, for no very good reason, she was overtaken by a sense of delight, amused by something that seemed to appeal to her alone and to no one else, and with her customary indifference to propriety she doubled up and rolled over on the floor, shaking with laughter.

Chapter

4

One comes back to the question of time, of what it is, of what we ourselves are, living in the midst of it, laughing like fools, suffering and in pain, or just idly getting through the days. Is it too unimportant to be worth mentioning, or is it the most vital of things, something we daren't overlook? And which of those two attitudes is true of us, assuming either of them is? Whatever time may be, one assumes it is recorded on the clocks we make; and the hands of those clocks undeniably move constantly forward. True, there are all kinds of clocks. Some stop every five minutes, some gain in a busy, haphazard way, and some only deviate from the true by thirty seconds in a year. There are even clocks like the one in the tower at the old Nire Hospital which are deliberately put five minutes forward. . .

If one leaves the mechanical world of clocks, however, in what manner does "time" exist? Is it some huge, immeasurable circularity, finally returning to where it was? Or does it really proceed forever forward, second after second after second, a dead-straight line moving into a future that recedes beyond some infinitely distant horizon?

But who could work out the answers to such questions? And who really thinks about them, and why should they? After all, what possible reason could there be for the people of, say, the Nire family and those connected with the Nire Hospital of Mental Pathology to bother their heads with such things? Time just passes, that's all. Certainly people make distinctions between present and past, but these tend to concentrate in a myopic way on objects that are supposed to represent some specific alteration; on a limited thing that tells us nothing about the overall movement of time itself. For example, the towers of the old Nire Hospital no longer pointed skyward, and in their place was a shabby new hospital occupying less than half the former land. And the bandy-legged figure of Toyobei, the porter at the gate, could be seen no more. A number of people—this, that and the other person—

had vanished, as had their faces, the way they behaved, and the sound of their voices. There were also some whom one might suppose to have disappeared but who were still around. Isuke, for instance, the man of influence in cookhouse circles, was still there at the Aoyama hospital. He stooped a good deal more, but remained as grimy as ever, as if ten years to him were but a single day.

Many would have claimed, or at least assumed, that Isuke had always stooped to that extent, and there had been no actual change. The people who saw him every day probably thought so. And if we moved across to the hospital at Matsubara, we would note that the Deputy's rimless spectacles still glittered as they always did, and that he still pressed his large (perhaps slightly larger) square seal with practiced and deliberate hand on various documents and papers. No doubt the very small number of people who had known him as an intern suffering from examination phobia would have said that Hidekichi Katsumata had altered, but for the great majority the Deputy had not changed in the least. One might assume that this majority would say that he had aged somewhat, but even that is unlikely, for they would see him as someone who had always been round about that age. At least, that's how they would regard him in their everyday dealings with him, and the same would be true of the Director, Tetsukichi. He had always looked tired like that, always been nervous and fidgety, always had that amount of gray hair. Only those who saw him again after a long interval of time would notice any striking change in him, and thus directly experience the fact that time had passed, if not time actually passing; but this perception was denied his colleagues, the people who saw him every day or at least once a week. For those enclosed in the world of the Nire Hospital, time was not a passing but a standing still, a stagnation, something that had halted or seemed to have halted. There was no change in the tenor of their lives. They were buried deep in a kind of time that seemed incapable of real movement.

Still, anyone can see the changes that occur in very small children, for they spring up almost overnight, like the shoots in the cluster of giant bamboos on the cliff behind the hospital. Shuji, for example, that true Showa child, whose birth and early years had passed while Kiichiro's adult heirs were still struggling with certificates and loans and interest rates, was now all of a sudden going to primary school.

As he had not been to kindergarten he was obliged to have a formal health examination, which he submitted to with a cold lack of enthusiasm. Since there was a general fear that Nanny Shimoda was methodically killing the child with kindness, an elderly maid who had only recently arrived at the hospital took Shuji for this test. It was done in the school gymnasium, and after his weight and chest measurements had been taken he had to stand in front of a table and answer questions about what illnesses and infectious diseases he had had so far.

The maid accompanying him had no idea about these things, so the doctor aimed the questions gently at Shuji himself. One by one he recited a list of illnesses, diphtheria, for example, and Shuji nodded and answered ''yes'' in a strong, clear voice. In fact he had never suffered from this affliction, the name of which was completely unknown to him, and it was the same with all the other diseases he was asked about. But the previous night, his mother, who normally paid him no attention whatsoever, had drummed into his head some simple instructions about proper behavior at school:

''Now the important thing at school is always to answer 'yes' in a big, loud voice. The worst thing you can do is stay silent. Even if you don't understand the question you must still answer. When teacher asks a question put your hand up. You mustn't let the other children beat you to it. You've got to win. When there's a question, you have to stand up right away with no shilly-shallying before any of the others do.''

Shuji had learned this lesson so well that he got a nice big tick on his health card next to the word ''diphtheria,'' and during his very first class at school his mother's instructions still maintained a powerful influence over his behavior. This was a get-to-know-teacher lesson, in the course of which a question was directed at the whole class:

''Does anyone know which side of the road you are supposed to walk on?''

Shuji was reluctant to stand up and raise his hand, but he was in the grip of a comprehensive theory of human behavior, so he did so. More than half of the other children also raised their hands, but they did this with much more confidence than he, and their arms were straighter and their hands higher. Shuji's wavering, bent arm and his half-standing, half-sitting posture caught the teacher's eye and he pointed at him, but all Shuji could do was stand there, saying nothing and staring down at his feet as if he might burst into tears at any moment. Nobody, Father, Mother or anyone in the hospital, had ever told him what side of the road you were supposed to walk on. To save the situation the teacher quickly pointed his finger at another boy who answered smartly and brightly, ''The left!'' Shuji remained standing in his place, just about managing not to cry.

This incident was not related at the hospital, so the normal cheerful questions about what Shuji had done at school were asked, with the natural reflection on the questioner's part that it was all different in his day, and the truth about Shuji's experiences and behavior in class were known to nobody until the first parent–teacher meeting. Naturally, neither Tetsukichi nor Ryuko bothered to go, so the teacher's words were addressed to the elderly and still ignorant maidservant:

"There's something a bit odd about young Nire. He keeps raising his hand when he doesn't know the answer. I don't know if it's pure vanity on the lad's part, or the result of some deficiency in the kind of education he's been getting at home. His writing isn't very good either. Well, 'not very good' is hardly the right expression. The fact is that although he seems quite incapable of writing the simple stuff he gets taught here, he still insists on writing this peculiar string of Chinese characters. Always the same characters, too: '*kotobuki*,' '*kotobuki*,' '*kotobuki*.' I'm afraid it does look as if the kind of education he's received at home has had. . .''

But this has little to do with our meditations on "time." We need larger means to seize hold of it. The people of the Nire Hospital may have been unable to distinguish the effects of time in their daily lives, but it was working there all right, an accumulation of minor happenings which turned into something, or occurring as a sudden, unforeseen and drastic event; working ceaselessly, creating things, creating change, a process of real alteration and adjustment although totally unseen by most people. . .

Of course, one aspect of time's whirligig was as clear to the staff of the Nire Hospital as it was to anyone else, namely those extreme events, those violent upheavals, and those pieces of irresponsible gossip and fantasy that appear in the daily newspapers; although it should be added that we are not concerned here with the extent to which the actual truth or underlying significance of these things were discerned by people.

A great many events took place during the first two or three years of the 1930s, causing much ringing of the handbells that announced special editions of the newspapers. The Manchurian Incident soon became a thing of the past, with the Shanghai Incident following hot on its heels, and the phrase "mufti corps," referring to those irregular volunteers who involved themselves in these incidents, even reached as far as the Nire Hospital: the nursing staff would say disparagingly of some sloppily dressed person that he or she "looks like a member of the mufti corps." Then, just when Manchuria seemed to have settled down nicely to independence under absolute Japanese rule, Prime Minister Inukai was boldly shot down in the May 15th Incident—quick as a violent patient might knock down a nurse. There was also the harshly critical Lytton Report on Manchuria which was submitted to the League of Nations and advised economic sanctions against Japan; but of much greater significance to the Nire Hospital people was the Tamanoi mutilation-murder case which occurred at about the same time in a shady district of Tokyo, and was immediately followed by a remarkable fire at a large store called the Shirokiya, where the customers who took refuge on the roof spent a number of spine-chilling moments listening to the mad roars of a lion that was kept somewhere on the premises, before clambering to safety by using ropes dropped down to them from a military aircraft which had turned up in the nick of time.

As report followed report of Communist arrests, with the imperial representative storming out of the League of Nations and a large tidal wave swamping the eastern seaboard, a special edition of the *Yomiuri Shinbun,* a leading newspaper, was published with the headline, "*Successful Exploration of Worldwide Significance*": a member of the staff had been down the crater of a live volcano. There were a number of scandals, about the military, about judges, and the assault on one venerable politician had just been announced, it seemed, when the wail of sirens heralded another announcement at which nearly the whole nation was able to rejoice: an heir to the throne, Crown Prince Akihito, had been born. But early in 1934, the year that Shuji entered primary school, something caused a huge stir in cookhouse circles both in Aoyama and Matsubara, although it is rarely mentioned in the history books now: this was the business of finding a bride for an Ethiopian prince.

This prince, who was undoubtedly black but also agreeably young, was intended for some Japanese young lady. More than a hundred young ladies either applied or had their names submitted as possible candidates—Momoko herself thought she might well have done so had she been young and celibate—and Viscount Kuroda's second daughter, the Lady Masako, was decided on. Up to then not one person in the Nire Hospital (with the possible exception of Tetsukichi) had even heard of Ethiopia. But to their consternation this "engagement of the century," which had become a talking point over the whole length and breadth of the land, came to nothing owing to the machinations of the Italians. In 1935, Italy, later to become Japan's ally, invaded Ethiopia, an event that attracted much more attention in Japan than Germany's disavowal of the Versailles Treaty and its announcement of rearmament plans in the same year. Not only everyone in the Nire Hospital but the entire Japanese public, or so it seemed, sympathized with this obscure country where lots of poor black people lived. It was the wicked, hateful Italians against the poor, helpless Ethiopians; loathsome might against pathetic weakness. And much useful advice was offered:

"When those lousy Italians attack they want to ambush them with specially trained lions. Lions would do the job all right. Or better than that, poisonous snakes! Drive them back with armies of poisonous snakes!"

So, many things happened, at home and abroad in the great wide world. That in itself is hardly surprising since a world, any world, is a place where things happen. What is surprising is our inability to find a line or plot that would bestow some kind of meaning on what looks like a mere accumulation of pointless irrelevancies. After all, if we cannot make such sense of what went on at the Nire Hospital, how can we hope to grasp the meaning of human history or life as a whole; and what chance do we have of that if the process of time, which is the real controller of these events, constantly eludes not just our understanding but our actual experience itself?

Still, there were developments in the world at large, and developments at the Nire Hospital as well. Some things happened only within the Nire family itself, passing unnoticed by cookhouse Isuke or the lower nurses, but happen they most certainly did. Compared with what went on in the great world, these were doubtless trivial affairs, but in the eyes of the Nire family they could not be disregarded nor made light of.

The corridor was gloomy, dark and bare, with nothing warm or welcoming about it. The coldness of the hard concrete floor could be felt through one's footwear.

Momoko stood there waiting, scared, hopeless and bewildered. Sometimes she would smooth the blanket covering the man who lay on the trolley beside her groaning in pain, but it served no purpose.

The nurse who had pushed the trolley this far had disappeared through the swing doors, and left Momoko with no one she could ask questions of. There was only the man lying beside her in agony. When she tried to comfort him he made no response, although he was still half-conscious.

She knew the man was her husband, Shiro, but it was hard to believe that anyone's face could become so unrecognizable, so haggard and emaciated, in such a short space of time. And his face was also cruelly contorted with what could only be fear, a fear at the very heart of consciousness, so terrifying that all restraint had been set aside. And now this fear flickered plainly in the dull whites of his eyes, arousing the same emotion in the one onlooker, and sending such chills along Momoko's spine that she knew she could no longer stand it and must soon try to escape. There were cold, minute beads of sweat covering her husband's broad forehead. She wiped them away with her handkerchief, but they kept returning, little specks that grew into small, clear beads.

Momoko's normally cheerful face was as hideously contorted as her husband's, and she went on patting and stroking the blanket, overwhelmed by fear and mouthing a string of meaningless apologies.

Her husband did not reply, but let out so dreadful a groan, like a wild animal's, that she wanted to put her hands over her ears and run. Instead she continued with her hysterical apologies for something done or not done, and at the same time, in one part of her small brain, she was thinking of what others had not done, and irritation and then rage at that arose.

Why were they so late? What were they taking all this time about? Weren't they ready for the operation yet? It was just her luck again; just the time for something like this to happen. Why did everything always have to go wrong like this? On Sunday night they only had one doctor on duty. Someone had raced away to find more of them. Obviously it had to be a major operation. Even so, why were they taking all this time? It was taking them absolutely ages.

Nobody had arrived from home yet, either. They must have been told about it. She couldn't really expect her mother to come, but surely some of the family should have been here by now. But she was always alone. Even on a terrible day like this she would be left all alone. It just wasn't possible to be so frightened and helpless and lonely, with her mind going round and round as if she were going mad with not knowing what to do, and then she could see the cold sweat had started up on his brow again, and his face had changed completely, it just wasn't possible, and that awful agony written all over it, she couldn't bear to look at it it was so horrible. . .

She then had a flash of appalling insight. Nobody was going to come. They had always despised the two of them, or simply ignored them. Why should anyone bother to come now? In normal times people might have put in some kind of token appearance, but the Nire household was otherwise engaged, and nobody was going to bother about the dregs of the family, the adopted son Shiro and his wife, who was lower than a menial, even if it were a matter of life and death. At a time like this they just didn't count one tiny little bit. No one would take any notice, because the eldest son of the family, Oshu, was getting married tomorrow.

For some time the whole of the main hospital had been totally preoccupied with this matter, everyone active and excited about the myriad tasks that had to be performed. Debates continued endlessly over a table covered with pieces of paper in the inner room of the new house concerning seating arrangements at the wedding reception and which guests were to be asked to say a few congratulatory words. These discussions were of tremendous length, and were solemn or ludicrous depending on one's point of view. Whichever the case, they were unquestionably exhausting; quite minor problems would occupy leading members of the household for hours, causing frowns as the mystery deepened or smiles as it seemed to clear up. For example, there was the problem of whether the Director's brother, the uncouth Shirokichi Mihira, should be allowed to make the recitation which he himself had asked to do. This was debated with some seriousness. Opinion was at first divided, but after a while agreement was reached by all. Since he was the brother of the Director, there could be no question of not allowing him to give this performance, but only on the condition that he did not drink while the formal part of the reception was in progress, though he could of course have his customary five or six pints once that was over.

Oshu had been engaged for about six months. The engagement had been mostly arranged by his mother Hisa, but it had the backing of the hospital as a whole, and Oshu himself had generously agreed to the match almost as soon as it was put to him. He had just gained his license to practice as a doctor, but his academic career, as the critics among his relatives so constantly observed, had been such a succession of failures and repeated attempts that he was already in his mid-thirties. So he expressed enthusiasm for the idea of taking a young wife, and his features, which were as well fleshed as his corpulent body, were wreathed in smiles at the thought. He also felt it would be as well to use his marriage as an opportunity to set himself up in a new house, which would be next to the hospital but separate from it. This was a very reasonable request. At the present time the members of the Nire family at Matsubara, consisting of Hisa, Oshu and Yonekuni, were living within the hospital, on the floor above the comparatively smart entrance hall. This was very cramped accommodation, with few rooms, and people were constantly bumping into each other; on top of which the noise of the hospital could be heard day and night. Oshu had been dissatisfied with his living quarters ever since he had returned from Sendai, and his great hope was to have his own place, a home where he could get away from the hospital once the day's tasks were done, and relax in peace.

Hisa was not opposed to this; in fact she said she was completely in agreement with the idea of a new house for her eldest son in which he could welcome his new bride. However, she also made it quite clear (if the vague mumble in which she talked permits the description) that should such a house be built she intended to remain where she was now, inside the hospital. After all, both Kiichiro and herself, ever since the opening of their first surgery in Hongo, had never once lived away from the hospital. The hospital was a part of herself, and she was a part of the hospital. It was all right for Oshu to sleep in his own house if he wanted to. But she would never leave the hospital. If she just stayed where she was, she wouldn't cause any trouble for his young bride when she (Hisa) came home late at night or whatever. That would take a load off her mind; that would be much nicer. After all, the quarters "within" had been something special. One couldn't expect anything like that again. Compared with the cramped life she had led in Hongo, her present room was paradise.

Words of this kind might, of course, have meant exactly the opposite of what they seemed to say, and so required serious attention. But Oshu had his own ideas about life, as well as a life-style acquired during the long and leisured years of his student career, and he did not intend to spend time pondering whatever Hisa might have had in mind. So the building of his new house next to the hospital was got under way with great dispatch although, unlike his late father, he lacked the ability to draw up architectural plans and left all that to someone else. Inevitably, what at first had been expected to be a snug little love nest became something of much grander proportions. Oshu felt he had to think of suitable accommodation for his mother when she became too old to remain alone in the hospital. And then there was the kitchen. Oshu was an enthusiastic connoisseur of food and a cook into the bargain, and he wanted a kitchen of considerable size, which in turn demanded an appropriate dining room, quite apart from the living room and their bedrooms. In his own estimation a house of definite size was required, and once the very strong opinions of the Deputy on the subject had been allowed to influence the outcome, a stateliness began to infiltrate everything. The result was that a major product of the builder's art gradually came into being.

The Deputy's view was that the new residence of the true heir of the Nire family could not be constructed in any halfhearted manner, since that would be to desecrate the memory of the deceased Kiichiro. Even if this meant a temporary increase in hospital debts, the foundations of the hospital, now under the protection of his own unworthy self, would not be shaken. So they finally decided to build a very luxurious kind of house, sparing so little expense that Hisa knotted her brows a good deal even while accepting the principle of the thing. The spacious house was to have an inner garden too, trite and unoriginal in conception no doubt, with its carp pond and rocks and stone lantern for snow viewing, but a genuine garden all the same.

Once this decision had been made, Oshu ceased to have any say in the matter. The man who, from start to finish, personally supervised the construction of the new house was Hidekichi Katsumata, with a passion that amazed those about him. Despite the fact that no one had entrusted him with the business, he gave his word to Oshu and Hisa that it would be all right on the day, that the house would certainly be ready in time for Master Oshu's wedding day. And when the work was begun, he was continually at the scene of operations, walking with slow-motion wading-bird strides, hands clasped behind his back, his jaw resolutely protruding from his bespectacled, pallid face.

The master builder, who had been working on occasional jobs for the Nire Hospital for years, was well acquainted with the Deputy, and had paid scrupulous attention to the various mutations that had taken place in his character as he grew older, so no particular problems arose between them. But the Deputy was much resented by the other carpenters, plasterers and gardeners, for he ran here and there with a nagging zeal which had his jaw perpetually in motion, questioning, giving his opinion, suggesting that this might be done in a different way and wondering what that wall would turn out to be like, and generally arousing disputation and confusion. He would stand before one of the wooden pillars, portentously scrutinize it, and then say with the authority of an expert:

"Yes. That's a fine piece of wood. An excellent piece of wood. I'm sure that Dr. Kiichiro would be delighted with this."

He would then go off to where the plaster was being mixed, asking if it was good quality plaster or not, and how long a wall would take to dry out at this time of year. He wrinkled the tip of his nose as he wondered what might happen if it rained, and looked anxiously across to the other side where there were still only wooden supports and no sign of any wall, feeling very suspicious about the whole thing, for surely the roof would come crashing down if they didn't have it held up more solidly than that. One could have filled a book with a transcription of the disputes he had with the landscape gardener, which the latter would always win. After the Deputy had been scornfully ruled out of court a few times by this determined man and sent roundly about his business, he became so bitter and depressed that he made his bedside reading a book called *The Secrets of Rock Garden Creation*. He read it faithfully from the first page to the last in the hope that it would allow him a resounding success in future conflicts. But so far he had never been able to find an answer to the last dismissive statement with which the gardener always clinched his arguments: that it was simply in better taste if it was done his way. The Deputy had great respect for the demands of good taste.

Perhaps as a result of the Deputy's painful labors, though certainly in spite of the countless irrelevant suggestions, hints and proposals he had made and the debates and confrontations he had initiated, a splendid new house was completed well in advance of the day of the wedding. The pond in the garden mirrored the foliage of the newly planted trees and shrubs, and inside the house the fragrant odor of wood and the cool scent of fresh, green *tatami* more than made up for the smell of plaster that lingered there.

Here was a suitable house (much more than suitable in fact) for the Nire heir's new bride, who had, in fact, visited the hospital once or twice already; the general opinion was that she was "just like a doll," the kind of boring, uninformative cliché to be expected of general opinion at the Nire Hospital. The Deputy certainly thought that the house was very suitable, and muttered to himself that now he could look the old doctor in the face again.

It was in this new house that, night after night, the plans for the wedding reception were worked out, mulled over and reconsidered; and the seriousness and frequency of these family cabals only increased Momoko's awareness of how little she counted. It was her brother Oshu who had told her that the coral in the Coral Room was fake and who had misinformed her about the titles of books, and yet they had built a house like that for him just because he was getting married, and the whole family was in a commotion day and night. All she had was a tiny rented house for herself and her precious cats to live in, and her husband Shiro, a mere adopted son, had to walk to work and back and just about managed to scrape by on the measly salary they gave him. The difference was outrageous. She and her brother were treated as if they belonged to completely different orders of being. And it wasn't just her brother: all that little clan liked to think they were members of some superior elite. . . Momoko's feelings of righteous indignation toward the rulers of the house had reached this pitch of intensity when the tragedy took place.

At first it had seemed to be nothing, just one of those inconsequential things that can occur any day. One morning Shiro complained of a stomachache and said he would take the day off. He lay there with the bedclothes over his head in an even worse mood than normal, so Momoko naturally decided to leave him alone. She did not feel he was particularly ill, and neither did he. But next morning the pain suddenly got much worse, so he asked her to call Shimada. His voice sounded as if he was in considerable pain.

"Shouldn't we call Dr. Nirasawa?" she asked.

"No. Shimada will do," he replied, wincing.

Shimada was a very old, rather decrepit person who had graduated from one of the first medical colleges way back at the beginning of the Meiji era, and he had recently been taken on at the Matsubara hospital as a night-duty doctor. Since Katsujiro Nirasawa, who was bound to be Assistant Director someday, was at the main hospital, as also were a number of doctors Shiro had known for a long time, plus some bright young doctors from Keio Hospital who worked at Matsubara part time, Momoko could not understand why he should choose to rely on this antiquated specimen. Because of the outsider treatment Shiro received at the hospital, he perhaps had mixed feelings about asking such people and found it easier to deal with someone he could have a simpler relationship with, one based on casual friendliness and also, no doubt, on a sense of personal superiority.

So she telephoned from next door and Dr. Shimada came at around lunchtime. Shiro, in his usual morose, unfriendly way, made Momoko leave the sickroom when the doctor came, but she managed to hear what was said:

"Well, it's not what you think it is. You've almost no temperature. It's nothing but wind. There's a pocket of gas in there. As soon as that's gone you'll be all right."

Shimada had a peculiar voice that seemed to ooze slowly from between his snaggle teeth, so his words were rather difficult to make out, but those she did catch made Momoko feel there was nothing to worry about. In fact, after the doctor had gone her husband's symptoms did seem to get better, and even his bad temper improved. But this illusory state of affairs did not last long. The mysterious thing was that a doctor of Shiro's quality, once so highly thought of that the perceptive Kiichiro had marked him out, even made him his son, should have been so wrong about this. It was a failing that occasionally afflicts all doctors, an inability to diagnose oneself.

When the pains came back again it was obvious even to someone like Momoko that his condition was serious, and a specialist should be called in right away. Shiro, however, adamantly opposed the idea, even losing his temper:

"Don't poke your nose into things you don't understand. I know perfectly well what's wrong with me."

Late that afternoon, when Shiro had vomited for the second time, Momoko stole out of the house and talked to Dr. Nirasawa on the next-door telephone. She felt she couldn't altogether ignore her husband's comment, so she spoke without urgency, not asking him to come immediately but whenever he was free. So he came later that evening, and it was from this point that Momoko's real trials, a whirl of nightmarish activity that stretched her nerves to breaking point, began.

Nirasawa's face became frighteningly grave:

"Get a taxi or something right away. Hurry. This is urgent. We'll have to operate right away. . . Don't be stupid. It's abdominal dropsy. There's an enormous amount of liquid in there."

Nirasawa said he would phone and make all the necessary arrangements, so Momoko struggled with her agonized husband out into the cold night air, bundled him into a taxi, and then set off for Keio Hospital along roads that looked frozen. He was now writhing in pain. It was not a short journey, and as they were going up a rise just before Dogenzaka a sudden change occurred in his condition. He gave a short

340

scream, enough to make the driver start and glance back apprehensively. This cry, although Momoko did not know it, was a purely physical reflex announcing the fatal perforation of the peritoneum. His body slumped down and his mind seemed to grow muddy and confused, only his hands and legs started to thresh about automatically like the dying convulsions of a stranded fish, jerking horribly under her own hands as she struggled to restrain them.

And now she was still alone in the dark, empty corridor, standing despairingly by the side of her dying husband, stroking his body and pleading with him in vain, pleading for nothing as if she felt that the pointless act of saying she was sorry would soothe his pain and perhaps even make it go away.

Her apologies were abruptly interrupted by someone moving quite near her, and she felt a momentary shock as at the appearance of a ghost. But the person peering at her in a nervous way was her younger brother, Yonekuni, now twenty-six and a grown man. He was clearly appalled by the pain his brother-in-law was suffering. It went far beyond his worst imaginings, and he was soon reduced to a greater degree of terrified helplessness than his sister. He looked as if he sincerely hoped he might shortly be allowed to leave.

The spectacle of this helpless creature gave a lift to Momoko's flagging spirits, and she herself was surprised at the severity with which she interrogated him:

"Yonekuni, who else has come? There must be others, surely? You can't be the only one?"

Yonekuni cast another horrified glance at the sick man on the trolley, and mumbled and stuttered in reply:

"Katsujiro came with me. He said he was going to telephone the chief surgeon and he's doing that somewhere. . ."

"Well, what about the others? I don't expect Mother to come, I suppose, but where's Oshu? And the people at Aoyama? I imagine they've been told about this?"

"I . . . I don't know anything about that. I just came with Katsujiro. . ."

It was all perfectly clear. No one was going to take any notice. With the wedding tomorrow nobody in the Nire family was going to bother about Shiro and herself. They couldn't care less whether he lived or died, and she was now filled with a deep pity for him and for the waste that had been his life. He had only been married to her a short while when her father died and he had become a nobody. He had been bawled out by Tetsukichi, who was, after all, only an adopted son like Shiro, and given some rotten little job in the hospital. It wasn't surprising that he should have gone on grumbling like that all the time, and even pulled her hair. . . It was natural, really. The awful pity of it. . .

This awareness, mixed with a sense of her own guilt, flooded through her, moving to the extremities of her plump body. And so she wept. She let herself go and wept, and those enormous tears of hers trickled down her face. She crouched desperately over the body of her husband, that husband for whom she had never once felt any love or affection since their wedding night, whom she had sometimes genuinely wished were dead, and she poured out desperate pleas and regrets, breaking into a hysterical sobbing that was hideous to watch. But in another part of her mind she was hating her family, hating those people who headed the Nire clan, all of them, hating them from the bottom of her heart.

The doors in front of her opened and two nurses appeared who swiftly pushed Shiro away into the operating theater. As she stood there stiffly and watched him go she was aware that he was going to die. He was certain to die because he was that kind of person, unlucky and doomed, just like herself.

Momoko's bitter prediction was correct. Two days later, just as Oshu and his bride had at last managed to get away from it all at their honeymoon hotel, Momoko's husband, Shiro Nire, who had once been Shiro Takayanagi, stopped breathing in the new surgical ward at Keio Hospital. Momoko was now a widow at the age of twenty-eight.

Another incident occurred three months later, this time at the house in Aoyama. It took place in Tetsukichi's study, that book-dominated room where nobody except the cleaning woman ever set foot, so the truth of what happened was known only to the two people involved, Tetsukichi and Ryuko.

Recently Tetsukichi had reduced the number of his working days at the Aoyama hospital to three a week, and his visits to Matsubara to one weekly trip. By anybody's standards this showed a lack of application unexpected in the Director of a hospital that was still trying to regain its place in the world. Tetsukichi would probably have agreed with that judgment himself. However, he had decided he must begin his history of psychological medicine "at the beginning" as Alice would have said, and, having advanced halfway, he was determined to battle on till the end. So he needed time, he was desperate for time.

He had now reached the Middle Ages at last, the age of devils and witches, manifestations of group hysteria, mortification of the flesh with whips, St. Vitus's Dance, Children's Crusades, Jewish pogroms, and entire monasteries possessed by devils; and he wrote it all carefully down. He then moved on to the Renaissance, whose splendid achievements in other fields seemed to coincide with a rise in the persecution of witches. The number of people burned at the stake during the whole of the Middle or Dark Ages was in fact less than those cast into the flames during the fifteenth century alone, and also less than the number massacred for not altogether different reasons in our own twentieth century. However, the Renaissance also produced what Zilboorg was to refer to as "the primary revolution in psychiatric medicine" with the work of scholars like Cornelius Agrippa, Paracelsus, della Porta and Johannes Weyer. Despite the fact that they never freed themselves from the intellectual atmosphere of their age, they showed an understanding of things very different from the common enslavement to illusion. Weyer, in his *De Praestaiis Daemonum* for example, although accepting that the Devil and devils existed, maintained that they were not omnipresent. He denied their influence in the sexual act and insisted that the claims made by witches were not actual deeds but fantasies and illusions breathed into the mind by the Devil, that a witch's illusions would disappear if some belladonna ointment was applied, and that lycanthropy (the werewolf phenomenon) was not a form of sorcery but simple hallucination. Paracelsus certainly seemed to later generations to have held a number of peculiar theories, producing mysterious ointments like that made out of unicorn's horn, but his written works contained genuine observations and intelligent deductions, and he remarked of St. Vitus's Dance that it could not be something induced by angels since it was not conceivable that angels would cause illnesses. . .

One shelf of the bookcase next to Tetsukichi's desk was now completely taken up with bulky piles of written manuscript. The task so far had been too much for him, and yet it was all a mere preface to what lay ahead. Time and time again he had gloomily asked himself what he thought he was doing, for at this rate the project would go on forever. In the seventeenth century the Swiss Felix Plater awaited him, as also did Harder of Basel and the great English physician, Thomas Sydenham. Then finally in the eighteenth century psychiatry became an independent branch of learning for the very first time, and he would encounter a medical tradition that had genuine links with the modern age he was mainly concerned with. Here there was an intellectual development that could be properly traced. But it meant that an enormous number of books had to be investigated.

Just thinking of the task ahead was enough to make his head swim. He was no professor living secluded from the world and able to work calmly as his own will dictated, but a practicing doctor responsible for the running of two hospitals. Again he asked himself if he still meant to struggle along under this additional burden; and again he found that he did, or at least he felt he probably would. He had no idea when he would be able to complete the work, nor even if it would be worth anything when done. He simply felt it was something that had to be done, so he would do it.

One strange thing was that he seemed recently to have grown accustomed to his burden. At first he had been in a constant state of anxiety about the suitability of this work for someone like himself. Now the weight had become his own, and the doubts were numbed as carrying the burden became an everyday thing. The burden was heavy and it hurt, but there was an intoxication and joy at the center of it, an almost painful exultation of the spirit that he knew from the past.

Once he had reduced the amount of work he did at the hospital, he found he had time to go elsewhere, not back to his old laboratory at Tokyo University but to the Department of Psychiatry at Keio Hospital. Keio was not far, and he got into the habit of dropping in occasionally. He even attended study groups. He had no particular connection with Keio, but for years young doctors from Keio had been supplementing their small salaries by working two days a week at the Nire Hospital. This had been going on for so long, in fact, that some of the Keio professors had done the same when they were young, and Tetsukichi was given deferential treatment when he went there. He wanted access to a university because medical knowledge increases almost from one hour to the next, and he feared that he might not be keeping up. Also, the library there was fairly well stocked with works relating to contemporary German psychiatry, and since a former assistant professor had specialized in the French contribution to the field there were quite a few French books too.

The young doctors who had just been taken onto the staff there were not sure what to make of him. The gray-haired man was obviously their senior, both in years and knowledge, or so it seemed. But whenever he appeared in the classroom he would discuss matters of a wholly uninteresting kind with the professor, and though he supposedly went into the library to investigate something or other, if you had a close look at him he had invariably dozed off in his chair. Every time he went into the library he would have a short nap, then get up and go home.

At home, too, there were various changes in Tetsukichi's habits and behavior that could hardly be considered improvements. The most noticeable of these was that he had become forgetful, despite the fact that he was not old enough to have begun his dotage. He would entirely forget things that he had to do at the hospital, and at home he would do things like leaving his glasses somewhere and forgetting where he had left them. He would come charging down the stairs, with an impetuosity reminiscent of Ryuko's, but by the time he had arrived at the bottom he would have forgotten what he had come downstairs for. At suppertime he would, like any normal father, ask his children what they had been doing at school that day, and Shun'ichi, who was now faced with high-school entrance exams, would reply vaguely, while Aiko would chatter cheerfully away, and Shuji would stare down at the table and mutter something incoherent. In fact the style of their replies was a matter of indifference since Tetsukichi never paid any attention to what they said. One could tell from the vacant expression on his face that he was far away, thinking about something else and not listening to a word.

There was worse to come. One evening Tetsukichi was having supper alone with Shuji, and they were eating some kind of fried pork. Like Yonekuni when he was young, Shuji had a parsimonious side to his character which took the form, among others, of saving the food he liked best until last; so he had left his slices of pork untouched and started with things he didn't much like, the nastiest bits first. This meant that by the time he had finished even his rice, which is normally the last thing to be eaten, he still had half the slivers of pork on his plate; nice, fat, juicy slices which he was eyeing with considerable satisfaction.

At that moment, however, fate took a hand in the shape of his father's chopsticks. Tetsukichi had already drunk his tea, and when he glanced across at Shuji's plate he must have assumed that the boy intended to leave the pork.

"I'll eat that up for you," he said quite unexpectedly, yet in such an eager tone of voice that Shuji didn't know how to say no. He didn't say yes, either, but merely sat there, looking down and saying nothing, as his father reached out with his chopsticks, picked up a sliver of meat, and gobbled it down. This happened three more times, and all the meat Shuji had so carefully saved was gone. Then, ignoring the child, who was in a state of shock and on the verge of tears, Tetsukichi swiftly downed another cup of tea and left the table. No doubt from Tetsukichi's point of view this action was justified, since the long hours of mental and physical toil that awaited him demanded the extra energy those slices of pork would give him. But from Shuji's point of view it could only be called an act of calculated cruelty.

Ryuko, although ignorant of the pork-pilfering episode, had her own dissatisfactions with her husband, and she became more and more displeased with the way he was reducing the number of hours he spent on hospital duties. But it was with no intention of starting a quarrel that she went up to his room, fairly late one night, wanting merely to discuss what to do about their eldest son, Shun'ichi, who had, as she had feared, failed to pass his first high-school entrance exam.

Tetsukichi was in the habit of going to the toilet a lot, particularly at night. Since constantly going up and down stairs merely to urinate seemed a pointless waste of time, he had recently adopted the custom of keeping a child's chamber pot in his room, not discreetly in a corner but quite blatantly by his desk. Ryuko, as soon as she entered the room, showed a marked distaste for the confusion on and around his desk, in particular for that child's chamber pot, but this caused no immediate ruction between them and they had one of those conversations about things in general that married couples tend to have.

Normally Ryuko would have left the room as soon as they had finished discussing the matter in hand, but today there were a number of things she had on her mind and she felt a sudden desire to talk a little longer. So she said very casually:

"Over at the Matsubara hospital they've started having entertainments again, like we used to have here. I went to look the other day. Well, they certainly do it in style, I must say. They've also got a tennis court now. . . The patients seem to be having a good time, anyway. I suppose that sort of thing has a good effect, from the therapeutic point of view?"

"Certainly it has," said Tetsukichi, whose thoughts were drifting toward work again.

"I gather they use the big room there not only for entertainments but for the patients to make boxes and things in. Occupational therapy, or something. Is that true?"

"Yes. They are doing that."

"We always used to introduce new therapeutic methods here as soon as they were available. That was Father's idea," she went on. "It does seem now that only the Matsubara hospital makes any progress while we stay just as poor and shabby as ever. I must say I find it all most irritating."

"Don't be stupid. It's all the same hospital, isn't it? The way things are now I should have thought it's pretty obvious that our main efforts have to go into the Matsubara hospital."

"Still, the fact is that this hospital at Aoyama was the main hospital and should have remained so. But of course we don't make a profit here. After the fire I suppose that was to be expected. Nevertheless, we have wards now with patients in them—and we're still in the red. I find that a little strange."

"We are not in the red," Tetsukichi replied bluntly, for his wife was beginning to get on his nerves.

"Yes we are," Ryuko contradicted him, suddenly becoming defiant and speaking very stiffly. "I am well aware of it, thank you. I have been anxious on this score for some time, so I paid Oishi a visit. He is only able to balance his books because of assistance from Matsubara. It's perfectly disgraceful."

"Disgraceful? What's disgraceful? What do you mean by that?" Tetsukichi was needled by the remark, and he had unintentionally raised his voice. But he was able to restrain himself. "Look. One of the problems with running a mental institution is the question of scale. You can get by all right with a small clinic. A really big hospital, of course, is even better. But if you're neither one nor the other then you have problems, real financial problems. Make a few mistakes and you're bankrupt. Now, this Aoyama branch is a prime example of an institution that's neither one thing nor the other. The money we get from City Council-supported patients is practically nothing. Given the numbers of these patients it makes little difference if the odd one has expensive medicines, for financially we still gain nothing from it to speak of. The only way you can really do it is to have a great many patients. You've got to have a lot of patients, and you need a hospital the size of the one at Matsubara to make that possible."

"Very well then. But I shall just say this. You seem to be a little too casual about the affairs of the hospital. I can say this to you because we're man and wife, and I'll say one more thing: if my father were still alive he would have made this into a splendid hospital."

Talk about her father annoyed Tetsukichi because it stirred feelings

347

of inferiority within him, and although he was aware of the foolishness of losing one's temper over a thing like this, he burst out at her:

"Women should keep their mouths shut about things that don't concern them. I've got my own plans and they'll be put into operation one day. I'll knock down all the makeshift stuff we've got now and put up a new hospital. Of course it won't be all that big but it will have all the latest in equipment, and we'll only accept high-class, very high-class patients. The rest will be sent to Matsubara. Even now most of the patients we get here are sent on to Matsubara. It's happening all the time. We're helping them as well, you know. It's not all one-way traffic from their end. Anyway, who was responsible for building the hospital at Matsubara if it wasn't me? You ought to know well enough how I damn near sweated blood doing it."

"Yes. But the scheme itself was my father's. It was the force of his spirit behind it."

So this constant harping on her father, with multiple honorifics thrown in for effect, raised its ugly head again, making things much worse. Their conversation ceased to be a succession of questions and replies and degenerated into what could only be considered a ludicrous squabble; but since both of them were mature in years it eventually came to a close. Then they started to talk about the future. At some time or other they would probably set up a branch family, separate from the main House of Nire, which raised the question of how much of the family fortune they would receive. It was Ryuko's opinion, no doubt fostered by her dislike and distrust of her brother Oshu, that the hospitals would be divided between them just as they were, and it was consequently essential to make the Aoyama hospital rich and prosperous in preparation for that day. Tetsukichi replied that Oshu was too easygoing for that, lacking in ambitions of that kind, and they could rely on him to make some arrangement like having the cottage in Hakone registered in their names, or to offer some other perfectly satisfactory concession. Ryuko insisted she was not trying to cast any aspersions on her mother or her brother, but was thinking more of the fact that the Deputy was over there now, though even she smirked a little when she said that.

"Anyway," she continued in what was now a very good mood: "I think your plan is excellent. I mean your plan to turn the Aoyama hospital into a splendid building with the most up-to-date facilities and equipment. There is one thing I particularly want you to do, though, and it concerns the radium bath. I think we really ought to set one up again. The hospital simply can't do without it.''

"The radium bath?" replied Tetsukichi, somewhat taken aback and raising his voice again. "What do we want *that* for? It had no effect at all.''

Presumably Tetsukichi was reacting to the frequency with which Ryuko introduced the subject of her father, and for that reason his tone was perhaps a little too scornful of what had been Kiichiro's pride and joy. But his comment was unacceptable to this paragon of filial piety.

"That is quite untrue," Ryuko replied, returning to a stiff formality. "I know because I have researched the matter in my father's book, *The Medical Cure and Prevention of Mental Asthenia*. It is referred to in that excellent work as hydrotherapy. . .''

The stupidity of his wife's statement aroused Tetsukichi in the worst possible way:

"What incredible nonsense! That book's hopelessly out of date, anyway. It's a joke, the whole thing. A radium bath is just a swindle. It's a complete and utter fraud.''

On the surface Ryuko seemed coldly in control, but this was merely an indication of things seething within.

"Now let me tell *you* something," she said, pausing at this point to let her words sink in, and then continuing. "No doubt that book is old, which is not surprising considering it was written well before you went to study in Germany. However, if you see that as an adequate reason for offering insults to my father's memory, then I must inform you that you are very much mistaken. Wasn't it Father who brought you to Tokyo when you were a boy? Wasn't it he who did everything for you and made you what you are today? I am my father's daughter, but let me assure you that if I were in your position I would let my tongue fester and rot in my mouth before I would say what you have just said. My father was a great physician. I know of any number of people who have been cured by that radium bath. Every time I have the honor and privilege to meet any of those excellent patients who attended our hospital long ago, they all, inevitably and without fail, say the same thing: 'If only the good doctor were still alive today'. . . Perhaps it is strange for me, his daughter, to say this, but Dr. Kiichiro Nire was a great man. He became a Diet member. . .''

Tetsukichi had been listening to this with mounting anger. In a sense what she said was true, for he *was* obliged to Kiichiro. But that was not the real point. What he could not stand was the smugness of the woman, her talking down to him in that overbearing way, and when he heard her talking about her father's being a member of the Diet all the pent-up feelings in him exploded into the next few words that he spat out at her:

"A Diet member . . . that's lower than the monkeys!"

At this even Ryuko lost her surface calm. She had no great respect for politicians herself, but since Kiichiro had been one it was imperative that Diet members should be ranked considerably higher than monkeys.

"You can, I suppose, say whatever you like. But I wonder if you are aware of what people are saying about you behind your back? They think you are a disaster, an absolute failure as Director. I have heard it said myself."

She adjusted her position and proceeded to run through a list of items that she was certain would hurt him. He, on his part, retaliated with another eruption of raw emotion, telling her that she was a vain bitch without a trace of humanity in her; and gradually the whole argument not only lost any semblance of rationality but degenerated into a squalid free-for-all in which both were concerned only with how much they could insult and wound the other. Even so, Ryuko was certainly the more fluent of the two, and if a disinterested referee had been present he would no doubt have raised her hand once the contest was over.

Tetsukichi found his obvious inferiority galling, and consequently resorted to the male prerogative. First he signaled his intentions with the standard formula that no fool of a woman understands anything, and then he thrust out his arm and pushed her firmly just below the shoulder. Ryuko, who was in a formal kneeling posture on the *tatami*, went flat over backward, cracking her head against the bookshelves. This disturbed a dozen or so books that had been jammed in there, and these crashed down on her as she lay in disarray.

She brushed the books off her, stood up quickly, straightened her kimono and then, after a few moments of tight-lipped silence, she said in a slightly trembling voice:

"Nobody has ever once lifted a finger against me since the day I was born. . . And now to be knocked down like this. . . I am not the kind of person who will endure in silence an outrage of this kind. . . I shall . . . I shall leave this house."

"Leave it then," replied Tetsukichi automatically, struggling to keep his voice under control.

Then he opened one of the books on his desk, Pinel's *Traité médico-philosophique sur l'aliénation mentale,* a book that can be considered the epitome of eighteenth-century psychiatry and was thus distanced by many decades from what he was actually working on. Tetsukichi huddled over it. He could sense his wife behind him as she left the room, although he did not look at her. He was only just managing to hold down his wrath, as he endeavored to reenter the world of his books with as little delay as possible.

Ryuko's words indicated more than some passing difference of opinion, for she put them into effect. She did actually leave the house, and her three totally ignorant children, Shun'ichi, Aiko and Shuji, were left behind her.

Chapter

5

Oshu's wife, Chiyoko, was the youngest daughter of a long-established wholesale confectioners in Kanda. Kanda is in downtown Tokyo, and the ancient house in which she had been born, facing the main road with its streetcar line and wooden paving, had been burned down during the Great Earthquake, she herself escaping by running the mile or so, wearing only a thin *yukata*, to Shinobazu Pond at Ueno, and passing the night there in the open.

The house they put up after the earthquake was a replica of the one destroyed by fire, a traditional confectioners with a stall out front, living quarters for the family and apprentices behind, and the factory where the sweets and cakes were made beyond that. Toward the end of the Meiji era, around the year 1910, the Yoshida family had started to sell a slightly different kind of product called *Asahi-ame,* which fulfilled a medical function in that it was supposed to be good for moist coughs, and also served as a kind of sweet. The trademark showed a boy with a fringe of hair over his forehead (much like the way Chiyoko wore hers) sitting at a table, and the legend "Rice for the empty stomach, Asahi Candy for coughs" written at one side.

The "factory" out at the back was more like a kitchen, since it had no machinery in it, everything being made by hand. The rice gluten for the candy arrived early each morning in a large dray, was transferred into great tubs, and then various herbal medicines were added whose recipes had been handed down in the family. The mixture was stirred with a long spoon resembling an oar, the person who did the stirring walking around the tub as he did so. In years to come, the canning was performed by machines, but in Chiyoko's time it was done by girls who scooped up the paste with wooden paddles and slapped it into one can after another. Other girls put lids on the cans, which were then sealed and labeled. The cans were not entrusted to a conveyor belt, but when a certain number had accumulated a rope would be looped about them and they would be pulled together further along the table.

Chiyoko loved the factory and never grew tired of watching what was going on. There were companions in plenty, all boys at various stages of apprenticeship, and at the back of the factory was a narrow lane with that cheerful, vital atmosphere of downtown Tokyo, where she grew up playing hide-and-seek and hopscotch. At night they would play the card games that conventional families play only at the New Year. Chiyoko thoroughly enjoyed this life, and even after she had graduated from the nearby Ochanomizu Girls' School, and her elder sister had married and left home, it never crossed her mind that one day she would have to leave the home she loved so much to go and live somewhere else.

But such a life could not go on forever. She was twenty-two years old, petite, with fine, slightly sad features. Her mother was always telling her that in her day all girls got married when they were sixteen or seventeen, and it was into this situation that the name of the eldest son of the Nire family intruded. The lady who acted as go-between was none other than the old woman who had played so important a role on Momoko's "wedding day," the late Kiichiro's "Mom," our granny from Kanda, who lived close by and was still distinguished by the fact that she spoke with the traditional Edo accent. Since she was on friendly terms with both families things could not have been more convenient, particularly since Hisa from the Nire side occasionally put in an appearance at meetings of the Kanda Patriotic Ladies Club.

Chiyoko's mother was quite smitten with Hisa on their first meeting. She was so refined, magnanimous and courteous, and yet so modest with it that one could be quite confident about letting a daughter marry the eldest son of this charming lady. Chiyoko's mother was aware from her own experience that the mother-in-law was the crux of the matter for any girl getting married, and she believed that this lady could make Chiyoko happy. Hisa found the match more than acceptable, for she had been frustrated so often in the past when Oshu had been at an eminently marriageable age and yet persisted in failing his exams that she was delighted to get it all over and done with now.

Since both the mothers were so willing there was little likelihood of an objection from any other quarter, so Oshu and Chiyoko were married. Everybody, with the single exception of Momoko, attended the reception held in the Peacock Room at the Imperial Hotel. The only thing that did not go quite according to plan was the photograph of the happy couple. The photographer had asked the two not to wear the usual formal expressions on their faces but to smile, and he gave them the signal to do so just before working the shutter. Chiyoko was not the kind of person who could readily smile when told to do so, but Oshu, who was always willing to please, was able to produce an expansive grin immediately. The resulting photograph showed a bride in a state of considerable dejection and clearly loathing all the prospects that marriage had in store for her, and a bridegroom beaming all over his face with seemingly indecorous expectations.

Two things at the reception caused Chiyoko some surprise. First there was the appearance of Zaosan. She had heard rumors of his size, but had never thought that he could possibly be of such eerie proportions. The second was a man who gave a recitation in a voice that boomed throughout the spacious room even without the assistance of a microphone, but unhappily in so thick a northern accent that the whole thing seemed unreal. Afterward she learned this was Shirokichi Mihira, the brother of her own brother-in-law, Tetsukichi, and that he ran an inn in the town of Kaminoyama up north.

During her honeymoon Chiyoko enjoyed speculating happily about the life awaiting her in the new house with its fragrant odor of fresh wood, but once they were home the first dream to go was that the two of them would be allowed to live alone and undisturbed. During their absence Hisa had decided, for reasons best known to herself, to spend one night in the inner room of the new house just to see what it was like. This was a room that Oshu had built in the likely event that his mother would one day be obliged to come and live with him, and it was almost independent from the rest of the house. She was enormously pleased with it and, in complete contradiction to her previous fine words, decided she would not return to those cramped quarters in the hospital but would move in here, putting roots down as solidly as an ancient pine tree that intends to remain in place for centuries. Oshu pulled a wry face at this news, but Chiyoko herself was not all that displeased; in fact she felt more a sense of relief, for living with her mother-in-law would give her a chance to learn those arts of gracious etiquette needed by a wife in her position. These apparently normal expectations, however, would prove almost eccentrically unreal.

Chiyoko found that her respected mother-in-law, who behaved so impeccably when she was out of doors, was a very different kind of person when at home, particularly if one was obliged to live with her every day and all day. In fact she was gradually forced to realize that though the members of the Nire family might look all right on the outside, they tended to be pretty queer within.

The first time they ate together Hisa said:

"In the old days I never once tasted warm rice. By the time I was able to eat it was always cold, because I was obliged to think about other people all the time. That's always the case in a hospital."

Chiyoko admired this statement. Obviously Hisa must have been worked off her feet, although the experience had not, it seemed, given her any permanent taste for cold rice. Indeed, she would have been most put out if she had been offered any. Despite her spartan past, Hisa was strikingly fussy about her food, for she could eat nothing in the least bit hard or tough, and Chiyoko used to spend hours worrying about what kind of food she could serve her. It would have been all right if Hisa had been content with warm rice, but this was not the case because she liked to have lots of other things too. And owing, no doubt, to the remarkable modesty and restraint of her character, she had a great dislike of wasting any food that had been prepared for her. Consequently, if there was any dish that her teeth could not cope with, she would quietly push it to one side and mumble, "Yonekuni!" This youth (whom Chiyoko had never met until she came to live here, since the only people she had been introduced to had been Hisa, Tetsukichi, Ryuko and Oshu himself) would make a formal statement of thanks and receive the dish as his own. At first he would make no attempt to eat it, and on occasion he had even got away with this, but Hisa usually noticed and, by means of a very slight movement of her body, urged him to do his duty. Yonekuni would then gobble it down in great haste. On one occasion Hisa noticed there was quite a lot of soy sauce left on Yonekuni's plate, and she made another of her almost imperceptible movements, this time with her head, and mumbled his name again. He acknowledged this with alacrity and proceeded quite literally to lick the plate clean with his tongue.

Although he displayed a ceremonious obedience before his mother, Yonekuni's behavior was very different when she was not there. Once he told Chiyoko that he had been thinking about things and had decided to give up meat. The "thinking about things" which he claimed to have been doing gave Chiyoko the impression of profound intellectual torments beyond ordinary human comprehension, and it made her uneasy. Yonekuni then went on to state, as if he were communing solely with himself, that he suffered from tuberculosis and had to eat a great deal of butter. When presented with a fresh 200-gram lump, he proceeded to down half of it as if he were eating some kind of cake. Naturally this talk about being consumptive made Chiyoko even more worried, but when she mentioned it to Oshu he simply replied that Yonekuni always said things like that.

Then there was the younger sister, Momoko. The funeral for Momoko's unfortunate husband had taken place just after they returned from their honeymoon, but when Chiyoko had expressed her sympathy, Momoko had simply glared at her with eyes brimming with enmity. After that Momoko rarely came to the Matsubara hospital, and when she did she always seemed to be in a nervous fidget in front of Chiyoko and could hardly manage even a simple greeting. Chiyoko began to have the vague feeling that this was a strange sort of family she had married into. They had no unity at all, but lived simply as individuals with no real relation to each other. As individuals they were all a bit peculiar as well. She once asked her husband about Momoko, but he only curtly and wearily replied that she was just a mess; and when she asked what kind of work Yonekuni did in the hospital he said that he looked after the farm round the back.

Chiyoko had never really known what sort of place a mental hospital was, and at first always made a point of keeping well away from it. But now she wanted to see the farm and found herself obliged to go down the side of the main building, past a number of wards and the tennis court, which she did at great speed, until she saw a wide area of arable land planted with green vegetables and onions. One part had a bamboo fence about it, with chickens inside. Beyond was what looked like a stand of oak trees. If one walked a little further there was a pond, fed by a nearby stream, and then a fairly large sports ground. Much farther off she could see a low fence made of cheap corrugated iron that marked the boundary of the Nire territory. The land beyond still consisted of cornfields.

As Chiyoko was walking, feeling curious and still a little nervous, she saw Yonekuni. But far from looking after the farm in any practical way, he merely seemed to stroll about it, quite aimlessly, as if moving his legs for lack of anything else to do with them; or he sat on a log and watched the chickens, endlessly absorbed in their goings-on. There was another man who followed him about like a shadow, a very shady-looking character, dark, with a square face covered in spots and pustules, glaring eyes and a short, stubby, bull-necked body. This man didn't do any work either. His only gesture in that direction was a finger pointed at a vegetable patch, or a word or two with Yonekuni, and a loud clucking he made when he was standing beside him at the chicken shed.

The one person who did do any work was a very small man dressed like a farm laborer. The system seemed to be that Yonekuni would make some kind of suggestion to his square-faced, pustuled companion, who would pass on some kind of order which the small man carried out, whether it was hoeing the field or feeding the chickens. Unfortunately, Chiyoko did not have time to observe the ecology of this group all that closely, so her grasp of the matter may have been inadequate; for as she was walking toward the sports ground, she noticed a group of people in various styles of dress streaming out from the wards, with white-coated male and female nurses in attendance. And despite the fact that they were a long way off, she lost her nerve and quickly ran home.

"Who's that square-faced man who's always with Yonekuni?" she asked her husband.

"That's Kumagoro. . . He's been an intern here for years, since way back, well before the fire at Aoyama. He seems to have attached himself to Yonekuni as a sort of lackey," Oshu replied in his usual indifferent tone of voice.

Two or three years after Chiyoko's marriage the land at the back of the hospital had changed out of all recognition. The wards were surrounded with lawns and flower beds, there were two tennis courts instead of the previous one, the arable land was all fully cultivated, the number of chickens had increased to several dozen, their ranks being swollen by the addition of ducks and turkeys, and most of the oaks had been felled to make way for a pear orchard. Even the men working for Yonekuni and Kumagoro had increased over this period of time, to two and then three. But, though it seemed reasonable that Yonekuni should act as their supervisor, Chiyoko remained puzzled by the fact that Kumagoro persisted in doing nothing, not even deigning to wield a watering can. This began to prey on her mind, so, one day, being now quite used to saying what she liked to servants, she asked him outright why he never did anything.

"It's my piles, you see. . . ," he replied. "They're bad. They are in a very, very bad way."

Later, she asked her husband:

"I know we use the farm produce in the cookhouse, but surely there must be quite a lot left over?"

"There is. The vegetables and eggs are used in the hospital. But we pay for them. Pay Yonekuni, that is. Lower than the market price, you see. He seems to sell what's left over locally."

"I see. So Yonekuni uses that money to hire his laborers."

"No. They're on the hospital payroll. The hospital also provided the money to buy those turkeys and put up the chicken shed."

"In that case Yonekuni must be making a fortune."

"Not only that, but he gets a monthly allowance from Mother."

"Well," said Chiyoko, genuinely surprised. "He must be embarrassed by all that money."

"More than I am, anyway," said Oshu in his most nonchalant manner, fondling his small, round chin as if none of this could be helped.

Still, Yonekuni and Kumagoro caused Chiyoko no real trouble; that was the prerogative of her mother-in-law, the lady of whose ideal behavior in that role Chiyoko's mother had been so confident.

When Hisa was at home she spoke to the servants and anyone else she considered beneath her in a curt, even coarse-sounding way, but if an important guest arrived she would become polite, humble, even cringing, and her language heavy with refinement. Having been brought up in a tradesman's family, Chiyoko had at first found this so impressive that she had been almost too terrified to breathe, let alone say a word, although the occasional use of three honorifics when one would have done nicely (for the old lady was gradually becoming senile) had an upsetting effect upon her. She would hurriedly leave the room on the pretext of clearing away the tea things, and enter another room, any room so long as it was deserted. There she would sit, trying to control the laughter that was ready to burst from her. It was so hard, and so funny, and strangely sad all the same. She just had to wait there quite still until the fit passed away.

Hisa went out a good deal. She went to various charitable organizations, and there she would be obliged to buy tickets for functions connected in some way with those organizations, and she would attend those as well, making frequent use of the hospital's black Opel car. If the hospital car was not available she would sulk and give up the idea of going out altogether rather than call a taxi or hire a limousine. Taxis cost money, an expense that Hisa shuddered at the thought of. It seemed that she genuinely believed the hospital's own car cost nothing and that using it was a great economy. Consequently the car became virtually her personal property, and Oshu and his wife rarely had the use of it.

When Hisa left the house on one of her excursions, Chiyoko had to kneel with the maids in the hallway to see her off. The same thing happened when she came back, and when she had been to the theater this would be late at night. They would all troop out into the hallway, rubbing the sleep from their eyes, and Chiyoko and one of the maids would have to help her off with her kimono, remaining loyally with her until she had actually got between the bedclothes. Never once did her mother-in-law suggest in the normal way that Chiyoko need not bother to wait up for her.

Nor was Hisa particularly clever at handling the servants. The habit learned during the hard early years of the Hongo Clinic, the habit of doing everything herself, persisted in her old age. She would never entrust any present she received to the keeping of a servant, but would store it away in the cupboard of the room next to her own, and then hand something from this store to her occasional visitors. Ever since Chiyoko had become a member of the family there had been a flood of Asahi Candy, much as there had been one of plum jelly from Yamagata in the past. Hisa would put all the Asahi Candy carefully into her cupboard, and give the sweet medicinal stuff to the odd visitor of no consequence, or to the children from Aoyama on the rare occasions when they visited.

Chiyoko had been particularly surprised by Hisa's behavior as her first New Year in the Nire home approached. One evening just before New Year's Eve, Hisa stayed up until after midnight, seated before a pile of fifty-sen silver pieces which she proceeded to put one by one into small envelopes, one small envelope for each small coin. This was the conventional token sum given to dependents and children on New Year's Day, for although Prize-Giving Day had been abandoned ever since the great fire, the New Year present giving still went on, and Hisa would not entrust the preparations for it to anyone else. She did the task with excruciating slowness, but also with such painstaking care, such senile tenacity, that Chiyoko did not have the heart to suggest that someone else should be allowed to do it, and the result was that she was obliged to sit there helping with this dreary chore.

The Deputy was also difficult to fathom. Each morning he would come to dance attendance on Hisa in her room, and also to pay his respects to Oshu, tasks he performed with cringing courtesy, and yet he was all arrogance toward the hospital employees.

''Kanedon,'' he would say sternly to a maid who had been working there long enough to expect a more courteous mode of address than the dismissive use of a nickname. ''Tell the others to get this corridor a bit better polished than this. I want to see it really shining, enough to make people slip on it.'' Then he would fold his hands behind him and strut slowly back to the hospital.

One day he said to Chiyoko:

''It is the done thing on New Year's Day for all members of the family to attend the celebrations in the hospital. It's one of the old Nire customs.''

So when the day came she was in a nervous flutter as she was taken into the large hall with a wooden floor which served as a gymnasium or exercise area when it rained. This was, in fact, the first time she had ever set foot in the hospital building, and she was made to sit on one of a row of chairs that had been set at the back of the rostrum. From here, Hisa, she and all the others were to observe the ceremonials. All the staff of the hospital were assembled, including part-time carpenters and gardeners, in order to receive from the hand of the Director, Tetsukichi, who had come straight from a similar ceremony in Aoyama, those little envelopes with their fifty-sen silver coins inside that Hisa had prepared with her own hands.

Unlike the Prize-Giving Ceremony, there was no question of the Deputy handing these things to the Director for the Director to hand to the recipients. The envelopes were all placed in a box in front of the Director, who had none of the love of ceremony that his predecessor did, and after a perfunctory and only half-intelligible opening address, he simply passed them out in quick succession. The recipients contributed to the undistinguished tone of the proceedings by lining up before the rostrum, so that they resembled the trail of excreta a goldfish dangles behind it, and they received their envelopes briskly without any proper display of polite acknowledgment, then quickly pushed off.

The Deputy observed all this with obvious unease. The air of dejection on his face suggested that he was only just able to suppress a protest, that this was all wrong, and that it also grieved him to acknowledge there was nothing to be done about it at present. So he stood there, casting the occasional scathing glance at the profile of the undistinguished individual now so incompetently performing the role of Director as to trample underfoot all the glorious history and traditions of the Nire Hospital of Mental Pathology. His eyes, deep behind his rimless spectacles, were full of distrust and contempt, until he glanced in the opposite direction, where the main repository of his hopes and expectations, Oshu, was sitting stroking his chin in a bored manner, his back more or less turned on the proceedings.

Nobody could have hoped more passionately for a rebirth of a Nire

Hospital over which the ghost of Kiichiro could properly preside than the Deputy did, nor have dreamed of it day and night with such wholehearted sincerity. He was desperate to bring back all the glories of the Prize-Giving Ceremony at some time or other. Nineteen thirty-three had been the thirtieth anniversary of the founding of the hospital in Aoyama and he had almost swooned in rapture at the thought of the splendid ceremony they would be able to hold. Ever since the day in 1932 that marked the seventh anniversary of Kiichiro's death, the Deputy had been mulling over his plans, fostering them, and generally enjoying himself at the prospect. Yet this contemptible, unenlightened, benighted half-wit, this lump who had neither the ability nor the wisdom required to run an institution like the Nire Hospital, had rejected these carefully worked out plans on the pretense that the hospital was not yet on a stable enough footing to allow celebrations on such a grand scale.

But the Deputy now harbored an even greater dream. He had undertaken a scrupulous investigation of the origins of the hospital, and had become aware that the palatial hospital in Aoyama had what might be called a relevant prehistory extending back another fifteen years. He added on these years, adjusting his calculations accordingly, and came to the perfectly valid conclusion that the year 1938 should not be seen as the thirty-fifth anniversary of the hospital but as its fiftieth. Fifty years was a round half century, a good period to celebrate. It sounded significant. He felt a surge of excitement, a sense of being literally carried away at the thought. Also, 1938 would be the thirteenth anniversary of Kiichiro's death, although naturally that event was not one to be celebrated in the same way as the other. Yet it gave a peculiar significance to the year, as if it had been singled out for grand celebrations and observations, a year particularly favored by gods and buddhas alike. Luckily—or rather, naturally—the hospital was now firmly on the road to prosperity. Though the Deputy gratefully acknowledged that it was a misfortune for Japan's mental patients, there was a considerable shortage of beds in mental institutions, and now that the semi-incarceration of lunatics in country houses was ceasing to be normal practice, numbers of patients in the Nire Hospital were coming from very far afield. Setting aside the question of what went on at Aoyama, it was an undoubted fact that the Matsubara hospital was more than full, and each year saw some form of rebuilding or extension of existing accommodation to make room for additional patients. Owing to Dr. Kiichiro's foresight the hospital had ample land, and the land itself, although originally rented, had been bought outright and was now the property of the hospital; they had learned that much from the misfortunes following the fire at Aoyama. The day was not far off when the number of inmates would exceed those housed during its great days in the past and, with the approach of the fiftieth anniversary, it would not be long before the true heir to the hospital, Oshu, took over the directorship from Tetsukichi.

Since Hidekichi Katsumata was in thrall to so intoxicating a dream of the future, it is not surprising that he should have felt in no mood to excuse the pusillanimous display just given by Tetsukichi. When the New Year's ceremony was over he said to Chiyoko:

"Madam, I deeply regret that you have been obliged to witness such a slovenly performance today, but let me assure you that it is merely a question of time before your revered husband takes over the reins of the directorship, and then, together with my unworthy self. . ."

Chiyoko was not all that clear what he was talking about. Since she found this thin, unhealthy face faintly repulsive, she was the more inclined to find something sinister in the obsessive glitter of the small eyes behind his rimless spectacles.

As the long-awaited fiftieth anniversary drew nearer, and the prosperity of the hospital began to exceed that of the good old days in Aoyama, the Deputy opened a careful and determined campaign. This involved a mass of trivial detail, and even included additions and alterations to the list of hospital doctors on the metal signboard at the main entrance. He proposed, for example, that both Katsujiro Nirasawa and Seisaku Kanazawa should be written down there as Assistant Directors.

"They are both equally qualified for the post, and in a hospital of this size it would hardly seem inappropriate to have two Assistant Directors. . ."

"But Dr. Kanazawa belongs to the Aoyama hospital. . ."

"Yes, but that is beside the point. The Aoyama doctors are also registered at Matsubara, since they often come here to perform diagnostic work. No, we shall have those two recorded on this signboard here as Assistant Directors, and then the names of all the doctors employed at both the main and the branch hospitals."

The Deputy now read out all these names to Oshu, whose reluctance to hear any of this was plain from his expression. But he did interrupt at one point:

"Look here, Sato and Shimazaki are just on loan from Keio, and they're due to be replaced soon anyway. It all depends on what they decide over there. Surely we only need the names of doctors who have been, or will be, here for some time?"

"I don't see that at all. Should such changes occur, the appropriate alteration can then be made. The more names we have, the more impressive the scale of the hospital will appear. There's little expense involved in painting out one name and painting in another."

The popularity of tennis at the hospital had grown remarkably of late. Oshu was very good at it, no doubt because of his former skill at more martial sports, and he moved his corpulent frame about with incongruous agility. There was also a man working in the office who had played for his university. Even Kumagoro, who had never touched a racket before in his life, was now spending the greater part of each day playing tennis, and his game was rapidly improving. Many of the other doctors and employees would make for the tennis courts whenever they had time to spare, and would be joined by a few of the milder cases among the patients. So the Nire Hospital was more than moderately successful in tournaments with related organizations, and almost achieved an unbeaten record. The psychiatric departments of Tokyo University and of Keio were no problem since they consisted of relatively few doctors and were easily defeated. In contests with other private mental institutions the Nire team had no trouble in winning either. But there was one opponent the team could not defeat, and that was Matsuzawa, a large public hospital which was called a mental institution though in fact its services were more of a general nature, much as those of the Nire family had been. Thus it had a much larger staff than the Nire Hospital, and since a number of the male members of its staff were competent tennis players, even the powerful Nire team was no match for them. Oshu was officially on the staff at Matsuzawa since his medical education was still not complete, and on a more casual occasion could have been expected to play for them. Yet on the vital day itself he played for the Nire side, although even he was unable to put up much more than token resistance.

The Deputy was completely ignorant when it came to tennis and did not even understand the system of scoring, but as the number of home-team victories over other mental institutions mounted, so did his own interest, and he was often to be seen in the vicinity of the tennis courts. Anything that might raise the reputation of the hospital was a matter of concern for him, for he saw everything as a matter of prestige and publicity, and though he had no aptitude for the game himself he urged others to take part. He was determined that, by hook or by crook, the hospital should at least manage to beat Matsuzawa once.

One day, the Deputy went to the courts, paid undivided attention to the passage to and fro of the white ball for an hour or so, and then turned to the pharmacist at his side and said:

"He looks pretty good, doesn't he? Plenty of skill there, plenty of talent. I don't seem to have seen his face before, though. Is he a new member of the nursing staff?"

"No. He's one of the patients."

"One of the patients," the Deputy muttered to himself with obvious regret. "Doesn't seem to be anything all that wrong with him. Be leaving soon, no doubt? I wonder if there's any way of getting him on the staff."

Then a new young doctor started to come twice a week from Keio, replacing one of the others. He looked as if he were really cut out for sports, and the very day he arrived the Deputy asked him, in a casual manner that concealed his eagerness and expectations, if he played tennis.

"Tennis? No, hopeless."

"Really? I mean, Doctor, just looking at you, you look nimble enough. Just made for the game, I should have thought. Why don't you try your hand at it sometime, Doctor?"

"I'm afraid I'm just not good at games. Not my thing. I'm unbelievably clumsy. I often amaze myself at my own clumsiness. . ."

Whereupon the Deputy nodded stiffly twice or thrice, turned his back and clasped hands abruptly on the new doctor, and walked away as if he were about some business of pressing urgency. He had already lost interest in this fellow. He could be of no possible use.

Being made use of by one's mother-in-law was no doubt unavoidable; it happened in any household and was something one was obliged to accept. But Chiyoko's calculations were completely put out by the reappearance of Ryuko.

Ever since her first meeting with her sister-in-law, Chiyoko had felt she was not fated to get on well with her. She received the impression that Ryuko was one of those self-obsessed women who are completely indifferent to what anyone else might think or feel. That was before her marriage. Oshu had just received a bonus from the Matsuzawa Hospital where he worked, and had invited the principal members of Chiyoko's own family, the Yoshidas, and of the Nire family to a dinner of what is called "Genghis Khan" in Japan, a mutton barbecue in the Mongolian style. It was still a fairly uncommon way of eating at the time, available only in Chinese restaurants where it served as an entrée to the main Chinese meal. It was the first time Chiyoko had ever encountered mutton, and she found the smell of the meat repulsive, so she left it untouched and looked forward to the Chinese food that was to follow. But Ryuko, sitting beside her taciturn husband, announced in a tone of voice that proclaimed she was in charge of the day's proceedings, that we had all had plenty to eat with the mutton barbecue (for she judged everything by using herself as the only norm), so there was no need to order any Chinese food and we could go straight on to the final rice course. She then made a token inquiry as to the opinions of the others, although she had already decided their response. The result was that Chiyoko had to content herself with rice alone and a few bits of hard pickled vegetable. Hell hath no fury like a woman deprived of her dinner, and Chiyoko began to feel suspicious and negative about her sister-in-law from that moment on.

Ryuko, who gave most people the initial impression of being withdrawn and retiring, had immediately shown herself to Chiyoko in her true arrogant and high-handed colors, and it was this woman who turned up at the house in Matsubara and started living there.

For the first six months or so after Ryuko had left home following her tiff with Tetsukichi her whereabouts had not been clear, although it seems that she spent the time living with her uncle from Chichibu, who was now head of her mother's parental home. No doubt she was not all that welcome there, and eventually the point was reached where she felt obliged to pack up and leave, and thus she came to Matsubara. Hisa and others had done all they could to try to patch up the quarrel between her and Tetsukichi, but both of them were abnormally obdurate and nothing came of these attempts. Since Ryuko was her own daughter, and since she had never been really all that pleased with Tetsukichi for many years now, Hisa naturally sided with Ryuko. Oshu was well aware that he did not get on with his sister at all, but he could find no adequate reason for putting up any forceful opposition to her coming to live with them. So he agreed to her becoming one of his dependents, feeling bitter enough about it inside but on the surface making it look as if he were trying to accept it in good part; and he immediately set about having an extension added to the house. This was a suite of two rooms at the end of a long connecting passageway, and he had it built in great haste. Even though he had to have his sister formally living under the same roof as himself, he wanted her as far away as possible, living under as different a roof as he could contrive.

At first even Ryuko managed to be inconspicuous and behave herself, but she was unable to remain that way for long. Her natural character soon began to push to the fore. Her obsession with herself, her horrible confidence and pride ensured that she would look upon everything as her own property, and she was soon to turn the whole household upside down. Even before Ryuko arrived, the real authority in the house had been wielded by Hisa, and Chiyoko had been little more than the head maid; but with the advent of Ryuko and her totally self-centered declarations, further confusions developed in the power structure of the household, with the occasional breakdown in lines of communication. For example, there was the question of titles. Previously, the fact that the house had two mistresses had been handled by referring to Hisa as the old mistress and to Chiyoko as the mistress, but now it seemed there were to be two mistresses again. Ryuko solved the problem to her own satisfaction by instructing the maids to address Chiyoko as the young mistress and herself by the eccentric title (a nonce term if ever there was one) of "middle mistress," with the result that, behind her back, she came to be called "the honorable middle."

Thus it came about that the honorable middle found herself enjoying life in a household toward which she should have felt a powerful prejudice, since it belonged to her brother. Yet she showed no trace of restraint nor any sense of gratitude, and seemed to have no care in the world other than that of pushing the already unimportant Chiyoko even further out of the limelight. Chiyoko had never met anyone so arrogant, so lacking in manners, and so willing to say exactly what she liked regardless of everybody else. Before guests whom she considered important Ryuko would, of course, speak in a very genteel way, and her behavior was faultless. But once she found herself dealing with her inferiors (and she clearly considered Chiyoko her inferior) she would say things that would startle her hearer, using honorific forms of language about herself and her doings and never about others, as if all her respect was directed at one person with nothing left over for others.

In all this she was much like her mother, but at the dinner table she was exactly the opposite, polishing off her food at a great lick as if anxious to get the business over and done with, regardless of what the rest of the company might be doing. This remarkable indifference could be seen in the disgusting habit she had of casually tipping the rice from her own bowl back into the common pot, saying that she had not touched it. She would then stand up briskly, careless of the discomfort this caused the others who were still eating, and thoughtfully order the maid to clear up the dinner things straight away.

A little while after she had moved in at Matsubara, she was visited by the children she had left behind at Aoyama. The first visit was kept a secret from their father. Chiyoko had no real knowledge of what had happened at Aoyama, but the children had certainly been separated from their mother for seven months and they reacted in the normal way. Shuji cried out "Mama, Mama" and hid his face in his mother's skirts and went on crying. Aiko was the same at first, but eventually wiped her tears away with a heroic gesture and started to berate her brother for his lack of manliness. Shun'ichi, the eldest, remained awkwardly to one side looking flushed and embarrassed. And Ryuko herself stood there with one of her most dauntless expressions on her face, the face of the wronged mother for whom no words or actions could express the profundity and power of her feelings etc. etc. . . . But, perhaps for the very first time in her life, she did actually fondle the backs of her two small children with something that seemed like tenderness.

Eventually these visits became semi-official. The Aoyama car now often plied between the branch hospital and the main hospital with the children in it, although not on Wednesdays when the Director himself paid his weekly visit. Naturally he did not meet his wife on such occasions. The children usually drove over on Sundays, arriving in the morning and leaving late in the afternoon, though occasionally they would come on the Saturday and stay overnight.

Unlike most grandparents, Hisa showed no affection for her grandchildren whatsoever. The most she would give them was a can of Asahi Candy, and if she noticed them after that it was only to reprove them at table, in her almost unintelligible mumble, for the way they held their chopsticks. (This was not mere grumpiness on her part because even Chiyoko thought they were peculiarly inept at this.) But though the children received no marks of affection from their grandmother, their mother made up for this with public demonstrations of affection for them. These were perhaps only the working out of some mild whim of hers, although they were certainly more than they could ever have hoped to receive from their father.

The long separation from her children had also probably awakened Ryuko's maternal instincts. On the day before they were due to arrive she would march in and take over the kitchen, diligently causing trouble for everyone present as she baked cakes and made jellies for their visit. She would tell the maids that this was for the children from Aoyama, the honorable children from Aoyama, using such honorific language for these superior beings who were soon to bestow the largesse of their presence on them that Chiyoko found it hard to accept that Ryuko was actually talking about her own children.

Ryuko would also investigate all the cupboards and the icebox, appropriating the finest cuts of meat and marching off with the booty to her own room, there presumably to enjoy an undisturbed feast of *sukiyaki* alone with her children when they came. That in itself would not have been too bad, but when the children were about to leave for Aoyama, out would pour Ryuko's maternal instincts again, and she would gather up all the fruit and cakes she could find, and not only fruit and cakes but eggs and packets of dried fish, put them all in a large box or boxes, and send the children off laden with gifts. It would perhaps be unfair to suggest it was her displeasure at the prosperity of the Matsubara hospital that was responsible for this urge to transfer some of the spoils to the depressed house at Aoyama, but the fact remained that once the children had gone the house at Matsubara was as bare as if it had been plundered by Genghis Khan and his hordes. One day even the great pile of pears from Yonekuni's orchard had gone—small and rather sour pears, it was true—and the box of chocolates on the dresser had disappeared with them. As a result, Chiyoko would feel obliged to take various things, baskets of fruit received as presents and now prime targets for this maternal love, and hide them in her room. While she was doing so, she would wonder why she should have to behave in this petty way in what was supposed to be her and her husband's home as if she were living here on sufferance, whereas the person who really was here on sufferance was loud, insolent and overbearing, and had usurped what should properly have been her position. She found the whole situation simply beyond her comprehension.

Ryuko gradually began to infiltrate from her own quarters, occupying the living room in which Chiyoko ought to have been able to relax in private, and then the room next to that as well. She had taken to studying No recitation. This did not indicate any real interest in the traditional arts, but was more a piece of long-term planning on her part. She had heard that well-bred children were sent to a certain teacher's house for instruction, and it seemed an excellent place to start searching for a suitable bride for Shun'ichi. Naturally this teacher would be received at the Matsubara house from time to time, where he would be treated regally, all the maids being fully employed in this exercise. Even so, Ryuko seemed to make slow progress in her studies. No recitation is accompanied by a form of dance at which she was particularly incompetent, and listening in secret to the instructor's comments through the sliding doors in the next room was the one thing in this charade that provided Chiyoko with any satisfaction.

"Now, at this point, I'm afraid it's no use coming forward like that. . . 'The wind-blown spray'. . . We seem to be a little cramped there . . . more expansiveness is required . . . a slow pulling forward. . . Yes, but then we stop on our left foot and there's simply no balance . . . the whole rhythm is lost. . . Then we move backward again in that slightly doubled-over posture. . . No, it's the feet. . . It does seem to be the feet. . . We do tend to look a bit like a straw doll that's had its feet lopped off. . . In that kind of state it really seems. . ."

When this teacher eventually asked to be allowed to use the "small room" it was Chiyoko's job to show him the way.

That in itself was not particularly upsetting. What Chiyoko found hard to take was Ryuko's attitude, the way she treated her as an underling and constantly found fault. This was not done to her face, but there was a maid in the house who sympathized with Chiyoko, so she was able to hear a variety of insults relayed from this source. For example, as Chiyoko had not yet given birth to a child, Ryuko would proclaim: "In the old days they soon sent brides back where they came from if they couldn't bear children"; or "I can't think why Mother had to be in such a hurry when there were all sorts of girls from the aristocracy whom Oshu might have married"; or "Ever since we've had that tradesman's daughter in the house there's been a deterioration in the language people use." Chiyoko would burn with rage and vexation when she heard these remarks, but Ryuko was much too tough and awkward a character for her to take on, so she had to content herself with sharing sly remarks with the maid about the various things Ryuko got up to. They would refer to the middle mistress as plain "the Middle," and repeated use of this ironic title, with some tittle-tattle about what was wrong with her and her children, would eventually cheer Chiyoko up a bit. One result of this was that Chiyoko, once so meek and quiet everyone had thought she was "just like a doll," began to acquire a reputation among her relations as a cynical kind of person, a woman with a sharp tongue who liked to speak badly of people. In fact she had learned to see through people's pretensions to the rottenness within, and also how to give witty expression to these insights. Obviously the presence of Ryuko was a great incentive in the development of this talent.

A more central question, however, is how Chiyoko reacted to her husband, or at least what she thought of him. At first, with thirteen or fourteen years difference in their ages, she had formed only a vague impression. There was this generously corpulent body, and a man inside it who spoke little and that little with little interest, so she found his essence, if it existed, hard to grasp. Because they were man and wife, she obviously acquired some understanding of his various ways, but she could still not escape the impression that she did not really know what he was like, and could not fathom what was going on inside him, always assuming that something was. She never found out about his scholastic career in any detail. She assumed from his age that he had spent a very long and leisurely school life, but the reality of how many times he had flunked and how many years he was forced to repeat remained a mystery to her. This ignorance should not be blamed entirely on Oshu, for sometimes he did start to talk about his student days, but whenever he did so she had the ominous feeling she was going to hear something much better left unsaid, and she would quickly change the subject.

One thing that did seem certain was that Oshu was almost entirely lacking in any real desires or ambitions. He showed no interest in expanding the hospital nor even raising a succeeding generation of doctors as Kiichiro had done. In fact he showed no interest at all in the running of the Nire Hospital, and this was not because he had only just become a doctor and was lacking experience and the habit of command, for one could see by the reaction of the Deputy, who considered him to be of royal lineage, that he would be only too eagerly welcomed. The Deputy was still living the Kiichiro legend, and so were a great many other people, too. No, Oshu simply was not interested. He went to work as a trainee at the Matsuzawa Hospital, then came home and played tennis and, to the Deputy's chagrin, never gave the slightest hint that at some time in the future he intended to take over the management of the hospital. Even Tetsukichi urged the job on him, saying he himself was too busy and hoped he could at least entrust the directorship at Matsubara to him when the right time came. But Oshu did not nod his large head in reply; not once.

He saw the post as a dreary encumbrance. He simply wanted to lead his own life. He had managed to evade all the toils and troubles of the bad period in the hospital's history by being a student at the time; and now his life was easy and pleasant enough and he had everything he needed. It is true that, with the advent of Hisa and Ryuko, things at home had not gone quite as he'd expected, but this also had the advantage of releasing him from any feeling of responsibility in that area. Whatever he did now would have no effect, and he could safely assume that this sense of being free of everything and being able to live solely for himself would continue forever. His wife would complain about his sister, whom he couldn't stand either, but he would only frown a little. He had not the slightest intention of getting off his backside and trying to straighten things out because he knew it would only make the situation worse. To prevent any real dispute from arising (for he really could not bear things like that), he treated his mother with courtesy, nodded to whatever the Deputy might say, and did not interfere in any of his sister's affairs, letting her do exactly as she pleased. He turned his back on all the troublesome, awkward and irritating tasks that can occupy a life, and busied himself with more cheerful things. He decided to live for his hobbies, for his leisure interests.

Oshu had once said that Yonekuni had more money saved than himself, but he too was well provided as far as cash was concerned. In the event of his actually needing any money he would simply go and ask the Deputy, who might frown very briefly at the thought of a fresh loan but would generally be all smiles and order the required amount from the accountant. But Oshu had no great desire for money; or at least he hadn't at the time Chiyoko married him. His great hobby was cooking, and he liked to invite people to eat what he had prepared himself. He had a wide circle of acquaintants and friends in the small restaurant trade, and he would also ask the managers of hotels to allow him to visit their kitchens, where he would study the mysteries of European cuisine, gazing at the huge saucepans (known as red pans in the trade) in which chicken bones were boiled down into a kind of sludge, and then being persuaded by the chef to taste the resulting consommé. In the one room in the house that had been made to his own specifications, the kitchen, he would slice up the fish he had himself gone to buy with swift, skillful movements of the knife. Then he would chop up the giant radish at an astonishing speed, creating decorative, tasteful strings of it to go with the slices of raw fish. Chiyoko would be left at table to entertain the guests. Even if she felt like helping in the kitchen she was aware that her husband was much better at it than she was, and this added to her sense of being left out of things.

After a while, Oshu's interest moved in the direction of the cocktail, to which he gradually became addicted. He assembled various bottles of foreign alcohol on the shelves of his room and, just before dinner each evening, he would nonchalantly mix some of them together and enjoy jiggling them about in his cocktail shaker. Although he would sober up at the thought of the meal to come, going off to join his mother and sister at table with a glum expression, he never thought of dining alone with his wife, for that might encourage some minor dispute in the household, the kind of thing he most wanted to avoid.

When a very much longer period of time had elapsed and it seemed clear that their marriage was not to be blessed with children, Oshu began to indulge in an expensive hobby, hunting. He bought a number of shotguns, including the most expensive British makes, which he polished carefully and hung on the wall. He would take them down to stroke and fondle, and it was clear to Chiyoko that he was happy to have found one more distraction in life. Naturally hunting dogs were required, one, two and then three: thoroughbred pointers of apparently inexhaustible energy that would scratch away at the wire netting of their kennels and drag their long tails and whine and bark. As the kennels were near Ryuko's quarters, the middle mistress kept up a stream of complaints aimed at Oshu and his dogs, while Hisa mumbled that the boy had ceased bothering about his old mother once he had taken a bride.

Although Oshu had these first-class guns and dogs he did nothing very fancy in the way of hunting, nothing more ambitious than the occasional foray into a pheasant reserve—known as the easiest hunting in the country—or to one of the rural areas along the Odawara Express Line that could be easily reached from home, or up a nearby river. The booty he brought back—and each bird must have cost a small fortune if one calculated the expense of killing it—would be left dangling in the main parlor for as long as possible, and Oshu would display it with an expression of casual pleasure to his guests, although he doubtless felt as proud as the conqueror of an empire. At times like these, moreover, he showed symptoms of genuine ambition, this being to shoot a wild boar. He had had this desire for some years, and each season he would draw up plans, not neglecting to make contact with other hunters over the matter. Considering the time and money Oshu spent on this project he ought to have shot any number of the beasts, but something always seemed to go wrong. There was always some extraordinary and quite unforeseeable happening which resulted in his never once being able to hang up a wild boar in his house. Even so, despite his indifferent performance as a hunter, the excellence of his dogs and guns ensured that he was eventually made President of the Setagaya Hunters Association.

So Oshu turned his back as far as possible on the awkward complexities that reality presents, enjoying his harmless leisure pursuits, providing guests with the pleasures of the table or chat about hunting, and quietly polishing and fondling his guns or pausing to stroke the heads of his excitable spotted dogs. What could have been more innocent? As he saw it, he had been blessed with an unproductive way of life but he had managed to make it a full one with all these excellent amusements, and he was happy to keep things like that. Still, there was a victim of this dedication to pleasure, and that was his wife. It was not that he actually ignored her, but that she could never become a part of his life, for his life was his leisure, in which she never shared. So she was left outside on her own.

But all this is well in the future, and we must return in time to an event of great importance which took place before the developments just described, one that added another major burden to Chiyoko's life. The affair was kept as dark and secret as possible since it was the kind of thing one certainly did not want the world in general to know of. It happened at a time when Chiyoko's newly married life was not going the way she had expected, and a short time after the arrival of Ryuko had created further gloom in her daily existence.

The widowed Momoko had gone on living in the rented house at Shimo Kitazawa, but she disappeared one day, leaving her son Satoru behind her and her whereabouts unknown. Despite the fact that Oshu had no liking for his youngest sister (it was not surprising that Chiyoko thought the Nire family was remarkable for the way that nobody got on well with anybody else), he had previously urged her to come and live with them, but Momoko had declined. She visited them once to discuss putting Satoru into an expensive private school since he disliked going to his present primary school, but other than that she stayed away from Matsubara, living in squalor with a number of cats that did exactly as they pleased.

Oshu decided he would say no more about it. Hisa had ordained that Momoko's living expenses should be provided out of the Matsubara hospital funds, and Oshu felt there was no point in interfering in her life any more since it could only lead to trouble for all concerned. Then Momoko vanished, although it was not until three days had passed, when the very young serving girl turned up nervously at the Matsubara house to tell them the news, that anyone knew anything about it.

Momoko's house was in an incredible state, so filthy it was difficult to believe a woman had been living there, but they came across a letter she had left behind. Oshu read this with an unusually angry look on his face, then tore it up, so Chiyoko never learned what the full contents were. She had never imagined she would see such a bitter look on her husband's face; it was as if he had been forced to swallow something unspeakably disgusting. The always cheerful, almost idiotically relaxed and genial Oshu did not go so far as to start shouting and cursing, but he looked so furious that Chiyoko feared he might do just that. What he finally said, spitting out the words as if he could not endure to have them in his mouth, was:

"She's got herself a man."

He maintained a frightening silence for a while, then added:

"We'll have to take Satoru. There's no one else."

The act of speaking seemed to make him even more furious than before, but when he had finally calmed down a little he muttered, not so much to his wife as to himself:

"She was never any good. The dregs of the family. A good-for-nothing slut. If she should dare to come back she won't be allowed inside my door. Never. I wouldn't even let her stand outside in the cold."

Momoko did not come back. If she did, she certainly did not come to see Oshu and Chiyoko. Satoru was taken into the house at Matsubara, given a room, and brought up half like a child of the family and half like a serving boy. Despite the fact that he was still only in fourth grade at primary school, the boy had something unpleasantly grown-up about him, and already showed signs that he was going to be trouble, if not actually delinquent. He didn't like his new school and was always playing truant from it. Chiyoko had no desire to adopt him as a substitute for the child she herself could not have, but she could hardly desert him either. All she could do was feel despair at what was happening to her.

She began to think it had all been a mistake, and that she should never have married into this family. This was something she knew she should not feel, but she couldn't help it. Before this, she had on occasion felt a sudden desire to go home, but she had always been conscious of a deep, irrational sense of guilt at the same time, even if she only wanted to go for a few hours; so it had been in fear and trembling that she had approached her mother-in-law for permission. Hisa had always given her consent, but only after what seemed a lengthy and calculated silence. Unsmiling, with her face as expressionless as a No mask, she would say in a voice that seemed to come from somewhere beyond that mask:

"Very well. Just as you please. You may go."

Chapter

6

While these dramas of discord and dissension, grief and grievance went on in the grown-up world, the children still lived in a world of their own, where a simple object like a nail or a splinter of wood could take on a special, magical meaning. The Aoyama branch of the Nire Hospital of Mental Pathology was now being rebuilt and the building site was full of interesting things. There were six-inch nails, twisted cramp irons, even little pulley-like objects with wheels that went round and round lying scattered on the ground. Shuji scrupulously picked these things up and stored them in his toy box, an orange-crate with paper pasted over it. He was now going to school, but he was still interested in things like these.

One day, at lunch-break, his elder sister Aiko was with her friends in the playground of the Seinan Primary School, which had recently been rebuilt in concrete, when she noticed that Shuji, who was still in one of the lower classes, was not playing with any friends but wandering about by himself and staring at the ground. In contrast to her undistinguished brother, Aiko was becoming more and more precocious, with looks and clothes that put her near the top in the popularity stakes. She was already a person of authority among her fellows, and one could see in her clear signs of headstrong egotism, no doubt inherited from her mother along with other characteristics. For example, during the year that the school was being rebuilt (this had begun just after Shuji entered the school), temporary buildings had been put up in Moto-no-hara, the field next to the Nire Hospital. Since space was limited, teaching had to be done in two shifts, and there was a consequent tightening-up of teaching and break schedules. The brief lunch-break this led to was not to Aiko's liking, or so it appeared, for she always found some excuse for not bringing a packed lunch with her, and went home instead since it was now so close. Her reason for doing this was not that she would get a hot, more varied lunch at home, but simply that she liked to be different from everybody else and do things no one else was allowed to.

Aiko knew perfectly well why her brother was snooping about the playground in that pathetic way. He was looking for buttons, any kind of dress or shirt button. Although Aiko herself had long ago reached an age when she no longer needed the affection of Nanny Shimoda, Shuji still lived snugly under her wing. But Nanny was old now, no longer always healthy and good at everything; her eyes were not what they used to be, and in particular she had a great deal of trouble sewing since she found it hard to thread a needle. Shuji would sometimes do this for her, occasioning further bursts of admiration for this youngest child who could do nothing wrong, and her face would be wreathed in sentimental smiles. Then Nanny once happened to say that she didn't have a button to sew on a particular shirt, and this was overheard by Shuji who quite by chance picked up a button on the street soon afterward. This remarkable feat excited Nanny to such a degree that she had difficulty expressing her amazement, though this did not prevent her from explaining to all her acquaintances, from interns to maids, how well this demonstrated the remarkable benevolence and concern of the young master. It was out of a desire to give Nanny even more pleasure, and to reap even more praise from her, that Shuji set about looking for buttons.

He found that a close inspection of the playground revealed a surprising number and variety of buttons. So every playtime Shuji would leave the boisterous company of his peers (they tended to take little notice of him anyway) and walk about by himself, head lowered and eyes fixed on the ground. As Aiko was watching, in fact, he bent down and picked up something, and put it in his pocket. She knew it was a button because she had seen a flicker of something close to joy pass across his normally cheerless face.

Aiko frowned. She felt his behavior was an insulting reflection on herself. The kid really made her sick, slouching around like a tramp. Unfortunately Shuji's action had been seen by another girl, an underling of Aiko's who habitually followed her around.

"Isn't that your brother over there? I wonder what he's doing?"

Her curiosity was increased by the fact that Shuji bent down again, picked up something, and put it in his pocket. But Aiko found it no problem to refute with smart alacrity the suspicions of her friend:

"Oh, him. He's not my real brother, just a relation. Right, then, here we go, bumps-a-daisy!"

Whereupon she leaped sideways at the unsuspecting girl and jerked her buttocks smack against the other's, catching her completely off balance and sending her sprawling forward onto her hands. This unsporting attack, however, did not provoke any critical remarks from the other children, who tended to approve of the way Aiko acted swiftly and decisively in all things. Indeed, they laughed and clapped their hands in admiration. Aiko laughed too. She became pleased with herself again and forgot all about her scavenging brother.

Aiko was even worse than Momoko had been in the frequency of her visits to the Seiundo. She would simply appropriate anything she laid her eyes on, whether she had any need for it or not. Shuji had also acquired the habit recently of going to the shop by himself and buying things for nothing, such as slap-cards and marbles, although he would still look inquiringly at the lady's face whenever he picked up something like a toy pistol with caps that made a real bang when fired. Aiko couldn't bear to see her brother take anything, whether drawing paper or exercise books, that might be superior to what she had. If, for example, Shuji got a new set of twelve colored crayons, she would acquire one of twenty-four, including gold and silver, and she had such a stock of beads, colored paper, coloring pictures, transfers and erasers that she could have opened a store of her own. The coloring picture was an outline drawing on white paper of something like Mickey Mouse or Betty Boop which you filled in with colors as you liked. Aiko's capricious nature showed in the way she would soon lose interest, just coloring Betty Boop's lips, for example, and then throwing the picture aside. Shuji, on the other hand, had a parsimonious streak which he might well have got from Yonekuni, for he would pick up whatever Aiko cast away and carefully color in the hair and clothes. The same kind of difference could be seen in the way they played with transfers. Shuji would soak his carefully in water, consider what he would transfer it to, select his piece of paper, and create a neat picture that had all the permanence of art. Aiko, however, would roughly command her brother to keep still and attempt to stick hers somewhere on him, on his hands or legs or forehead.

The traditional "mistress" usage that Ryuko, or Mistress Ryu, had imported from Gakushuin and which had been so much to Kiichiro's liking, persisted in the case of Aiko. She was called "Mistress Ai" by everyone in the hospital, and she took a special pride in the puzzled looks that appeared on the faces of people who were not in the know.

Aiko also had a talent for making up stories. She used the song she

378

had often heard from Nanny Shimoda about the ghosts in Aoyama Cemetery to invent an experience of her own with which to terrify her young brother:

"There really are red ghosts. You know that big laurel tree in the small cemetery, don't you? The one right in the middle? Well, that's where I saw them. Really horrible, creepy faces they had, all pale and spooky, and they had these dirty old torn kimonos on, red ones; that's why they're called red ghosts, because of what they're wearing. They're really scary, I can tell you. I guess the white ones must be in the main cemetery. You'd probably see them if you went there, because that's where they must be."

The result was that Shuji never dared go near the cemetery until he was quite big. Seiko's grave used to be there, but Kiichiro's monument had been set up in the grounds of the Nichirinji temple in Asakusa and so hers had been moved there as well. The wide expanses of the Aoyama Cemetery with its innumerable gravestones seemingly jostling one another for room, its evergreen hedges with their musty smell, its clusters of dark trees—the playground of innumerable spooks and goblins—thus ceased to have any direct connection with the Nire family.

Aiko had often been compared to her dead aunt when small, but now she was certainly more cheerful, precocious and spirited than Seiko had ever been. There was one cold winter day, when snow lay thick on the ground, that had given her particular pleasure. It was a day toward the end of February, 1936, when detachments of the army led by young, idealistic officers from the Military Academy staged their February mutiny, attacking the homes of a number of cabinet ministers and occupying the Metropolitan Police Headquarters, the Home Ministry, the General Staff offices and the War Office. The next morning Sadaichi Sawara, who had come back from the army and was now attending night school at Senshu University in the Kanda area, appeared at the hospital in a state of feverish excitement. He said it looked as if there could be street fighting in Akasaka, and it was even possible that stray bullets might come this far. Nanny Shimoda had no idea at all what was going on but the color drained from her face. She made the two small children go into the inner room and ordered them not to dare take one step outside.

The children, of course, understood what was happening even less than she did, but they were delighted there was no school that day. In particular the idea of "stray bullets" stirred Aiko's curiosity and aroused her excitement to an uncommon degree, so she carried all the mattresses and bedding and cushions she could find into the inner room. She had always preferred the *Boy's Own Weekly* to the equivalent magazine for girls, and she was well acquainted with the exploits of that resourceful stray dog, Norakuro, plebeian hero of the honest Dog Army (the Japanese) in their battles against the wily Monkey Army (the Chinese), and the various other militaristic adventure stories that filled its pages. She built a huge pile of bedding to make a "dugout," and then bravely raised the upper half of her body above it, taunting her foes:

"Come on, then, you 'mufti corps' cowards!"

Shuji, however, had been reduced to a fearful state by the thought of "stray bullets," and was curled up right at the bottom of the padded dugout. He had been with the local children to "rifle hill," the firing range for the Third Regiment, and on a patch of earth amid clumps of bamboo grass he had picked up two spent cartridges. They were small, but felt solid and heavy in his hand. He imagined what they would be like stuffed with powder and bullets, and he went almost faint with excitement at the thought of these wonderful and dangerous objects. A bullet might arrive at any moment, tearing through the wall or ripping through the door. He drew in his breath and lay quietly, not daring to budge from the cover of the dugout.

This February mutiny, or Two-Two-Six Incident, as it came to be known since it began on the twenty-sixth day of the second month, was finally brought to an end by a dramatic appeal over the radio to the lower ranks, and with leaflets dropped from airplanes: "It is not too late, even now. Return to your units. All those who continue to resist will be shot as rebels. Your families are in tears, since your actions have made them traitors to their country."

These words achieved a certain currency within the Nire Hospital and in the outside world, though nobody seemed to have any real idea what had actually happened. Aiko and her brother, for instance, had been in the habit for a long time now of helping themselves without permission to the various sweets and cookies kept in one of the drawers of the Western wardrobe. One day there was clear evidence that Shuji had filched a considerable amount, so Aiko assumed her most grown-up and severe expression and said to him in a voice that bristled with authority:

"Come on, Shuji. It is not too late, even now. Own up!"

The highly competitive Aiko took great interest in the Olympic Games that were held in Berlin the same year. Since they were away in Hakone during the summer she was unable to listen to the short-wave radio broadcasts, but was still ecstatic about the victories of Son in the marathon, Tajima in the hop, step and jump, and Terada and Hamuro among the swimmers. The slogan "Come on, Maehata," and the image of Murakoso fighting gamely against the tall foreigners made a profound impression on her. Later she went to see the German documentary, *Olympische Spiele*, and watched it intently, her hands placed firmly on her knees and her head straining forward.

This was the occasion for a rare excursion with her father, for it was he who took Aiko and her brother Shun'ichi to see this fine, indeed beautiful film, which was also undeniably an attempt to portray the new Nazi Germany in as dignified a light as was possible, or even more than was possible.

In the previous year Germany had broken the Versailles Treaty agreements and announced its intention of rearming, and photographs of valiantly high-stepping troops had been appearing in newspapers and magazines for some time. Their martial bearing expressed this passion for rearmament, and perhaps something else. The Japanese, however, saw it only as a reassuring indication of the strength of a reliable ally, for both Germany and Japan had quit the League of Nations to become defenseless orphans in the world, and recently they had joined hands in a Mutual Defense Pact, which was to have such fatal consequences. Japan had learned a great deal from Germany in the past concerning military and academic matters, and a worship of things German had now come clearly to the surface, seeming likely to swamp and conceal other considerations, and affecting even quite ordinary people. Tetsukichi was naturally no exception. Japan had sent a contingent of 294 athletes to the Berlin Olympic Games, apparently as determined as the Germans to make a national propaganda demonstration out of it (the new field-service caps they wore made a fine contrast to the straw hats worn at the previous Games in Los Angeles), and Tetsukichi found himself supporting both the Japanese and the German athletes, watching the flickering screen with rapt attention and forgetting for a while the labors that had occupied him over the past years. During the women's 400-meter relay the German team were well in front, but a baton exchange was bungled and the receiving runner dropped it. The camera then switched to a shot of Hitler leaning forward in his seat and watching the race with keen interest. At the moment when the chance of a great German victory was thrown away the dignified Führer himself, his distinctive short-peaked cap pulled down over his eyes and a swastika armband prominent on his upper arm, slumped forward slightly, smiling wryly with an expression of regretful resignation on his face. This reaction brought spontaneous smiles from the Japanese cinema audience, since it gave the impression of someone who was human and likable.

Tetsukichi also approved. Hitler was a man who got things done. It was marvelous the way he had regenerated Germany. For a moment he recalled the putsch in Munich all those years ago, feeling that this leader of a Western ally was related to him in some intimate way he would have been hard put to define. At his side he could hear Aiko exclaiming what a pity, what an awful pity it was, and her much older brother Shun'ichi, conscious of the presence of other people about them, telling her to shush.

Aiko often visited the hospital, sometimes alone and sometimes taking her younger brother with her. The rebuilding of the hospital had been completed. It was no palatial structure like that which had formerly amazed the eye, but the facade of the neat two-storied building, from the smart little car porch to the entrance hall, was painted cream and had none of the gloom one normally associates with mental institutions. It looked more like a high-class hotel. Even Oshu had praised the place in his usual laconic manner at the opening ceremony, remarking that the ostentatiously good taste extended even as far as the umbrella stand. But this transformation did not apply to the wards round the back, which remained much as they had been, although they had been modified slightly and were now connected to the new building.

Aiko would go in through the main entrance, dropping in at the office with its variety of teapot mats made out of empty cigarette cartons to hold a few minutes' pert conversation with the accountant Oishi, or the hospital chauffeur Katagiri, or anyone else who worked there. She went next to the pharmacy, which smelled of iodoform and where Yasusaburo Sugano would be busily folding up doses of medicine in slips of paper. She would complain that she must have a migraine for her head hurt although she didn't know why. This was the same trick Aunt Momoko had played when she was a child; in fact, Aiko had learned it directly from her. Yasusaburo accepted anything she said, and would mix some colorless medicinal syrup in a glass with a certain amount of red wine, dilute it with water, and give it to her. It tasted nice and sweet. When she held the glass up to the light she could see strands of syrup that had not yet dissolved in the blood-red liquid, and she enjoyed watching them, as though observing something of profound import. She particularly liked the drink because it was something only made in this pharmacy, and you couldn't buy it in just any old store. Shuji had also developed a passion for this pick-me-up, as Yasusaburo called it, probably because the company that made Bordeaux, the soft drink he had patronized for so long just like his grandfather before him, had recently gone bankrupt and no one made it any more.

After drinking her pick-me-up, Aiko would run down the long corridor toward the rearmost ward, stopping at a thick, blackened door. She knocked on this and a nurse opened it for her with a great, jangling bunch of keys. Then she ran along the corridor beyond that. She was used to the dull color of its walls and the peculiar stench, and she would either go to the nurses' room to receive an orange, or talk cheerfully to any patient who might be wandering about.

"How are you getting on, Auntie?"

"Well, very well; always been well and always will be."

This particular old lady answered as if the question offended her. She had a frizzled head of hair reminiscent of spider's webs, with the odd strand hanging over her brow. Her kimono was open indecorously at the front. The only thing taken great care over was her make-up: layers of thick white foundation and plenty of lipstick. She often walked about the corridor nibbling a cookie. Still wearing the same offended expression, she would break the cookie in half and give half to Aiko, sticking out her disturbingly long red tongue and licking the corners of her mouth. When that long red tongue appeared her scarlet lipstick seemed to fade by comparison.

Aiko was not in the least afraid of the patients. Of course, the patients here were only mild cases, people who were allowed to walk freely about the corridors and play ping-pong in the recreation room, all the serious ones being sent to Matsubara. Aiko did not think of these people as particularly different from those in the ordinary world, but more as friends with whom one didn't have to stand on ceremony, though there were certainly some patients who behaved in an obviously abnormal way, like the woman who would never answer no matter what one said but merely laughed out loud in an idiotic way. Aiko found these people interesting as well. Admittedly, there was no one as fascinating as the lady who made banknotes whom Aunt Momoko had talked about, but there was still Sun Wu-kung, and he was great fun. Sun Wu-kung is the main character in the famous Chinese novel *Monkey* or *The Way West*, whose name, interestingly, means "Awareness of

Vacuity." But this Sun Wu-kung was a middle-aged man with a shaven head who spent most of his time sitting in an armchair in the recreation room. His legs shook uncontrollably, and Aiko liked sitting on his lap, for it gave her the sensation of riding a rocking horse. Sometimes he would talk to her, and during these long conversations he would often drop his usual Chinese alias and return to his original identity, a man called Shimaoka, only to reappear as a Chinese emperor at some stage in the tale. None of it connected at all well with what had gone before, and the longer he spoke the more incoherent he became. Aiko assumed that he made up this ridiculous nonsense on purpose because she was a child, and she would bite her lip in vexation and answer him in kind:

"You know, at our school, the one I go to, the playground, why, all of it's a cemetery. . . ,"she said, creating a fiction which she was determined should not be inferior to the ones he told her. People were afraid of lunatics, but to her there was nothing particularly strange about them. She was sure that if she were a nurse they would all get better in no time.

Certainly there was no patient in that ward who could have really scared the wits out of Aiko, although if she had gone there any morning she would have seen things that might have done so. Insulin shock therapy was being introduced into Japan at the time, and it was now often employed at the Nire Hospital, for it was believed that a genuine therapy for *dementia praecox,* or schizophrenia as it was now called, had at last been discovered, and Tetsukichi ordered its use on even the old patients. Insulin therapy induces a trance, but before falling into that trance or when awakening from it, patients would occasionally let out mysterious howls and screams which seemed more in keeping with the popular idea of what a lunatic asylum ought to sound like. But this would all be over by lunchtime at the latest, and the treatment was never used on Sundays.

Although Aiko did not believe there was much difference between mental patients and ordinary people, she would not say this to her friends at school when questioned on the subject. Instead, she created wild fantasies.

"They're a bunch of real weirdies. There's an illness called hydrophobia. It means being scared of water, because 'hydro' means water and 'phobia' means scared. Well, they are just terrified of water, those who've got it. One drop of water and they drop down dead. Then there's woodiphobia, and those are scared of wood.''

"But what do they do when there're all those wooden columns and things in the hospital?"

"Exactly. And that's why we have these special rooms in our hospital made entirely of metal, from the ceiling down to the floor. The ones with woodiphobia get put in those rooms."

Aiko loved to be the object of other people's curiosity, and enjoyed the sense of being able to freely enter and lord it about in a place others were not even allowed a glimpse of. She thought it was marvelous that she had been born into a family that ran a mental institution. After all, you didn't find lunatic asylums on every street corner, did you?

Shuji's feelings were different. True, he was not frightened of the patients in the way that Oshu's wife, Chiyoko, was. In fact, he probably played about with less restraint in the wards than he did outside them, for in the outside world almost nobody took any notice of him. He sometimes even went too far in this, stealing one of the hairpins from the head of the old woman patient with the idiotic laugh. She chased after him, maintaining an endless, loud chuckling. Shuji thought this was great fun and decided to evade her pursuit by dodging around the ping-pong table. Then suddenly everything changed. The woman's features were transformed into those of a totally different being, and she picked up the ping-pong bats and hurled them with terrifying force at him. Luckily they missed, but for some time after that Shuji approached the ward with trepidation.

His attitude toward the hospital most differed from Aiko's in that he felt no pride in having been born into a family running a psychiatric institution. Rather, he had a deep inferiority complex about it. The reason was that whenever he lost one of his rare fights with some strange boy in the neighborhood and took to his heels, he would always hear the same taunt: that he was the idiot boy from the loonybin. He would feel all the bitterness of having been born in such a place, and be reduced to the verge of tears.

Undoubtedly this youngest scion of the house was a hopeless and spineless case, as could be seen from his absolute refusal to go to the barber's. The neighborhood barbershop was a place where no qualms were shown about cutting the hair of the Nire Hospital patients, and Shuji would have been treated well, even royally, if he went there. But he had a neurotic fear of the glittering clippers the barber wielded. He knew he would cry out and tell the man to stop, and since he was ashamed of behaving like that in front of strangers he could not pluck up the courage to go.

Consequently Katagiri, the hospital chauffeur, had to acquire a pair of clippers and shave Shuji's head with his unpracticed hand, for most small Japanese boys at that time had shaven heads. Once, however, something went wrong with the clippers and they refused to move, remaining stuck in Shuji's hair. They were eventually untangled, but when Katagiri tried once more they got stuck again immediately. So Shuji was finally taken to the real barbershop with his head half-shaven and half-unshaven. Predictably, he discovered that this man was skilled at his trade and the operation here hurt much less, and at last he was able to start going regularly to a barber's like anyone else.

He did not do very well at school either. He lacked the desire to learn in general, and was particularly bad at arithmetic. That faithful retainer, the intern Sadaichi Sawara, thought of a plan to rectify this: he would make up ten problems that involved subtracting from one hundred, hold a stopwatch in his hand, and tell Shuji to try and see how quickly he could do them. At first Shuji took a very long time, but with constant repetition he became faster and started to grow interested in the exercise itself. He would excitedly wait for the stopwatch button to be pressed so that he could start, even blowing on his fingers as the suspense built up and his intellectual preparedness reached a peak.

This was not as effective as one might think, however, since Shuji seemed to be content with his considerable skill in the sole accomplishment of subtracting from one hundred, and showed little progress in other aspects of his schoolwork.

His parsimoniousness showed no signs of improvement either. In front of the Seiundo shop he occasionally played an unimaginative lottery game with his school companions, one that he had devised himself. It consisted in sticking lots of little envelopes made of newspaper with cards inside them on a large sheet of cardboard, and if the card picked out had "WIN" written on it the lucky person received a large color photograph of a sumo wrestler, and if it was blank a small, cheap, black-and-white one. Each competitor contributed one sen to draw one card. Shuji would draw a card, too. Since he was running the game, though, he did not need to contribute any money and he could also draw as many cards in whatever manner he chose. He would silently debate which card he should draw, his hand wandering from one envelope to another until he finally chose; but the card inside would inevitably be a blank, and the gasp of disappointment he gave was the same he used to make when being deprived of a top in his younger days, his mouth slightly agape in the same bemused, moronic fashion.

The others would compare the cheap photos they had won, all of leading Sumo wrestlers of the day such as Tamanishiki, Musashiyama, Minanogawa, Shimizugawa, and the rising star of the moment, Futabayama. Unfortunately there was no chance of Zaosan's photograph being among them.

Since we last saw Zaosan he had sustained a spinal injury that resulted in any number of missed contests and tournaments, and he had now fallen right down to the second grade of the preliminary division. It was beyond anyone's comprehension how a wrestler who had been near the top of the first division had fallen so low and still not retired, battling on in vain and exposing his monstrous bulk to a chorus of jeers rather than sympathy; but battle on he did for he still had faith in his future. He would be all right once his knees and spine got better, for had he not once hurled a Grand Champion out of the ring?

Zaosan preferred to visit Matsubara and see Oshu, a man who took a superficial interest in almost everything, rather than Tetsukichi who showed no interest in Sumo whatsoever. There were many generous perquisites forthcoming from the Matsubara quarter, too. Even so, he still appeared at Aoyama, and his visits were not infrequent, for round the back were a large number of potted azaleas he had received from fans at various times over the years, and he liked to look after them himself.

Shuji no longer cried when he saw Zaosan. He would slowly edge up to him and gaze at this unhappily large person in whose existence he could still only partially believe. On one occasion the now completely bowed figure of Isuke, who still cooked the hospital food despite his decrepit state, had appeared and started talking to him in gruff tones, rather as if he were talking to a son. Zaosan also replied gruffly, or so it seemed, to the effect that Isuke shouldn't have used oil cake or something while he was away because it didn't do azaleas no good. Shuji watched his thick lips moving but was unable to make out quite what he said, for the voice sounded as if it were reverberating from some cavernous depth. After he had made these lip movements, Zaosan spent a long time transplanting his azaleas into different pots, so he must have been dissatisfied with the way they had been treated. He then had old Isuke bring him a long hose. Placing his inappropriately sized hand on the thin nozzle he watered the long row of potted plants. He sprinkled the water with surprising sensitivity over all the plants, missing not a single one of them, changing the direction of the hose from time to time, and saying nothing to Shuji at his side, spraying endlessly, apparently forever. . .

Zaosan was not, for Shuji, a practicing wrestler but a visiting giant, an unintelligible being who for some reason came to water the azaleas at the back of the hospital. After all, a wrestler who did not appear in photos or on cigarette cards could hardly be called a wrestler at all. But the Sumo rankings were still delivered at the Nire house before each new tournament, and Shuji eventually discovered the name Tatsuji Zaosan right at the bottom among the small, jumbled, almost illegible type, and he felt a shock in the very soul of his being. At the time his own favorite wrestler, Tamanishiki, seemed quite incapable of matching the new star Futabayama, whom Aiko supported because she always chose the strongest, most successful wrestler as her champion. These two misfortunes in the Sumo world made Shuji look even more like a peevish old man.

In baseball the main focus of interest was the Tokyo Six Universities League, and here Aiko supported Keio and Shuji rooted for Waseda. At home there was a record of a commentary done by the star sports announcer of the day concerning a completely imaginary match between the two teams. They would play it on the box-like gramophone, which lacked the large horn of the one in the old hospital but still required a great many turns of the handle to make it go. Against a background of the two school songs sung by the rival supporters' groups, an extraordinary see-saw battle was played out, coming to an end at the seventh inning with the score standing at seven all.

When there was a live broadcast of a Waseda game, Shuji would clamber up onto the dresser where the radio was and listen to the commentary through the great crackling of static the loudspeaker produced. Having dragged himself precariously into position, he would write the names of the team members on the wall with a thick 4B pencil. Then he would do the scoring. If Waseda were losing, he would feel so frustrated and depressed that he would scribble his own version of the lineup in vigorous pencil strokes on the same wall. The names of Takasu, Nagata and Go would be put at seven, eight and nine. These were the three principal batters in the Waseda team, and Shuji's idea was that if they appeared right at the bottom of the order they might catch the opposing team off their guard, and Waseda would hammer the daylights out of them. Thus the wall near the radio became quite black, covered with the names and numbers Shuji had written there. Even this did not give Nanny Shimoda cause to rebuke him, but just one more excuse for beaming with pleasure and satisfaction. What a studious boy Master Shuji was, even using the walls for writing practice!

Shuji's sister allowed him to play with her only when she felt like it, mostly treating him as a menial, but he would often go to visit Shun'ichi in his room. He had feelings close to veneration for this brother who was eleven years older than he and seemed more of a grown-up living in a different world than a mere brother. But despite the attractions of the adult world Shun'ichi apparently embodied, the first thing that had attracted Shuji to him was probably a deluxe yo-yo that Shun'ichi handled with great skill.

Shuji's impression of his brother's room, at least as he remembered it in later years, must have been created during the year after Shun'ichi had failed in his first attempt at the high-school entrance exams and was preparing for them again. So he was around fifteen or sixteen years old. But in his young brother's eyes, he had certainly looked like a grown-up. He had grown taller and taller, and thinner and thinner at the same time, and his long, narrow face with its good-natured, credulous expression make him look the perfect example of Ryuko's favorite belief that the eldest son of the family was usually a cretin. Shuji remembered him sitting in front of a splendid desk in a swivel chair that was surely too grand for someone who had just graduated from junior high school.

Shun'ichi was indeed a gullible person. At school when playing at Sumo wrestling in the schoolyard he would assume the name Zaosan. Although it had definite associations with his family, it was not a name that inspired visions other than of incongruous size and perpetual, degrading defeat, and one might think he would have hesitated to identify with something of which he should naturally have felt ashamed. But he had been egged on to it by his classmates, and they were then rewarded by the sight of this lanky object staggering under the blows of his opponent and being unceremoniously trundled out of the ring in true Zaosan fashion.

In addition to his monthly pocket money Shun'ichi received a considerable allowance for books to assist him in his studies, and he would drift down to the bookstore area in Kanda and buy up dozens of the reference works that were deemed desirable by the many students throughout the land who were preparing for similar exams. He was a very methodical sort of person, and he would carefully arrange these volumes on his bookshelves, even taking such aesthetic considerations as the color of their spines into account. Then he would begin work, opening a book and reading the preface with great attention, bracing himself for the task to come, the actual body of the text, where he would draw red lines under those sections and passages that seemed to be important and needed to be thoroughly learned. He took great care over this, even using a set square to rule these elegant lines, and he was at pains never to exceed a proper degree of aesthetic relevance. Naturally this was very tiring work, and the resulting exhaustion meant that he had little energy to turn over the many remaining pages. Thus all his books had the same characteristic of having the first few pages full of artistic underlinings in red, and the large remainder left pure, intact and, one is obliged to add, unread.

Once when Shuji went to see him he was absorbed in the study of geometry. With his compasses he had been able to draw a circle with such remarkable precision that he contemplated it in admiration. Then with his set square he drew a straight line of superb accuracy. He felt so satisfied with his brilliant execution of this figure that he lost any desire to solve the problem itself. The entry of his brother gave him an excuse, therefore, to close his exercise book with casual ease.

Then he took his cigarettes out of his desk drawer. These were not the brand Shuji had seen Oishi and the others smoking in the office, Golden Bat, but a smarter kind known as Cherry. Shun'ichi took one from the pack in a leisurely way and tapped it on the arm of his swivel chair. His gesture indicated that everything was going according to plan today, as always. If his father had caught him smoking he would certainly have got into trouble, but he was prepared to take the risk since there was a great attraction in smoking secretly in the privacy of his room before the admiring audience of his brother. After casually twiddling the cigarette for a while, he finally lit it. There was now the question of what he should do about his brother. He could talk to him, or he could show him the new pictures. Ideally he should wait for his brother to ask him to show him the new pictures, and the mental conflict this dilemma aroused, plus the efforts he was taking to retain a relaxed pose, brought an unnatural grimace to his face. The dilemma was only resolved by Shuji asking breathlessly if he had done any more pictures. Shun'ichi immediately cast aside any pretense of being grown-up and grinned all over his face, responding with an eagerness that would have done credit to a primary-school child.

"I should say I have. Three of them."

He stood up and removed from the cupboard a number of sheets of drawing paper which had pictures of airplanes on them, beautifully painted in watercolors. He had always been good at drawing, gaining the highest marks at primary school in that subject, and that subject only. Though drawing airplanes had nothing to do with any of the subjects required for his entrance exams, he would spend much of his considerable spare time doing so. More than a hobby, it was a craze. Every picture he drew was magnificently executed, and much more than a simple reproduction of the photograph or illustration he used as a model.

His younger brother gave a gasp of admiration, and Shun'ichi was just about able to contain the justified conceit that rose within him:

"Do you know what this is?"

"It's a Curtiss fighter. . . The F-11 Goshawk," replied Shuji, who had learned about aircraft from his brother and now knew a certain amount.

"Okay. Then what about this one?"

"Kawasaki Type C-5."

"Um," Shun'ichi said. Though his brother's knowledge was not all that amazing, it still reflected considerable credit on himself. "What about this one, then?"

"It's the Douglas . . . the Douglas passenger plane. . . ," Shuji mumbled, unable to recall the complete name.

"DC-2. It's the DC-2. The one Japan Air Lines have finally decided to buy. The days of Fokker Universal are over. You'll notice you can't see any wheels on this one, can you? We're at last getting planes with retractable undercarriages in this country."

Shun'ichi expounded at some length on the question of the undercarriage, of the various problems caused by wind resistance, giving a specialist account of the changes that had taken place up to now, and those that could be expected in the future. At first the wheels had simply stuck out on the ends of fixed legs, and then these had been covered with things that looked like spats, and finally the American Army's Curtiss A-8, the Shrike fighter plane, and then the Kawasaki Type C-5 had the whole undercarriage and most of the wheel covered with something that looked like a trouser leg. This led to a discourse on the wings and struts of a plane, with the progress from biplanes to monoplanes, first the high-wing and then the low-wing monoplane, at which point the problem of struts naturally disappeared. The flying machine of the future would no doubt be like the rocket of science fiction.

Shun'ichi's passion for airplanes was of long standing, and his vivid and numerous recollections could have served as an accurate account of the history of aviation in this country. At first this was nothing more than the normal boy's attraction toward machines that fly in the sky. When, back in 1923, the British test pilot for Mitsubishi successfully landed on the aircraft carrier *Hosho* and took off from it again, the eight-year-old Shun'ichi was much more interested in the prize money of 100,000 yen than in the achievement. But in the summer of 1930, the incredible Zeppelin appeared in the skies over Japan. Shun'ichi observed it with his first feelings of seriousness, though he looked like an idiot as he goggled up at the monstrous yellow shape drifting slowly across the Tokyo sky.

There then began an age of tremendous progress in the design and manufacture of airplanes, and in their capabilities. Various advanced models visited Japan from a number of countries. But what really caught the imagination of this schoolboy was an event calculated to appeal to the purist among aero-fans, a competition extending from 1930 into 1931 and sponsored by a Japanese newspaper company, the Transpacific Flight with its various glories and mishaps.

The first attempt was made by two American pilots, Bromley and Gatty, in a high-wing monoplane, the *Tacoma City,* and it was fraught with danger. They set off from Kasumigaura, but found the runway was too short since they had loaded their plane with every drop of gasoline they could get on board. At the last moment they were obliged to jettison some of the load to avoid disaster, opening their tanks and leaving a long cloud of gasoline trailing behind them as they took off. Their second departure was from Sabishiro in Aomori Prefecture. They got away all right this time, but bad weather encountered in the vicinity of the Aleutian Islands forced them to abandon their attempt. In 1931 two more Americans, Thomas and Ashe, rebuilt the *Tacoma City* and named it the *Pacific.* They set out from the same Sabishiro, or rather attempted to since they failed even to get off the ground. In September of the same year two more Americans, Allen and Moir, flew from Sabishiro in another rebuilt and renamed version of the same plane. Shun'ichi felt his heart flutter when he read the headline, "*Madge Sets Off in Attempt to Conquer the Mysterious Pacific,*" but in the evening edition of the same paper an article appeared raising serious doubts about their fate: the plane seemed to have taken the southern route and yet radio communication with it had been lost. The next day's edition had: "*No message as of noon today. Weather conditions remain poor.*" Later editions said: "*The silent Pacific. Still no word from Moir's machine after more than forty hours' flying time,*" followed the day after by: "*The mysterious Pacific keeps its secret. Two and a half days with still no news. Are*

these the first heroic victims? Hopes of a safe landing in Seattle now seem remote.''
This caused even more terrible perturbations in fifteen-year-old
Shun'ichi; but it turned out that the two airmen were both alive, as
the newspapers announced in banner headlines: *"THE PACIFIC
SPARES THEM. A MIRACLE. ALLEN AND MOIR DISCOVERED
ON DESERT ISLAND.''* The two had made a forced landing and been
picked up by a Russian steamer.

Eventually the first non-stop flight across the Pacific was performed
by Clyde Pangbourn and Hugh Herndon in a Bellanca aircraft, the
Miss Wild, which lost its undercarriage on takeoff and so had to make
a pancake landing at Wanatchee, Washington, bringing the long saga
to an end. In Shun'ichi the whole dangerous episode had aroused pas-
sions that words could not express, ideas that made his mind grow
numb, and he was transformed into a youth whose eyes would almost
start out of his head at the mere mention of the word "airplane."

Aircraft, airplanes, aeroplanes, it didn't matter what word was
used or what form they took, whether passenger planes or fighters,
bombers or flying boats, of Japanese or foreign make—Shun'ichi
loved them all. Anything connected with flying machines, their wings,
fuselages, struts, wheels, even a rivet or a piece of wire, aroused in
him the fond desire to stroke and handle. So he scanned the sky with
great interest and watched any airplanes flying there, Japanese planes
in a Japanese sky, although most of them were in fact foreign imports.
And he wondered why they all had to be old-fashioned biplanes with
great networks of struts between their wings and fixed undercarriages,
capable of only the most feeble performance, whereas in foreign countries they kept on producing more and more marvelous new prototypes
whose photographs alone were enough to fill one with joy and longing.

At New Year in 1932 a military review was held for the first time
by the army at the drill ground in Yoyogi, and it included the first
public appearance of the new fighter plane, the Nakajima Army Type
91. The flypast consisted of a mixed squadron of ancient Nieuport
fighters, Salmson B-1 scouts and Type 87 bombers, but right at the
tail were three of the new high-wing monoplane fighters, the 91s, which
suddenly opened their throttles and with a screaming metallic roar
zoomed past all the planes ahead of them. How smart they were, how
reliable they looked, and how fast they flew above the marching troops,
above His Majesty the Emperor and all the crowds of watching people! Shun'ichi looked up and felt the whole length of his thin body thrill
with excitement and nameless emotions. And so it was that the

schoolboy who had always produced the ten sen required for baked potatoes before anyone else did, who had assumed the unlucky name of Zaosan and been pushed and pummeled about the schoolyard, was transformed into a patriot. His was a puerile kind of patriotism, no doubt, which as yet only existed through the medium of the airplane, but a genuine patriotism all the same.

In the summer of the next year the first air-defense maneuvers were held in Tokyo. Shun'ichi had gone to the cottage in Hakone, but came all the way back to Tokyo just to watch them, and stayed up all night, obsessed, his whole body alive with pleasure and expectation. He thought how wonderful it would be if real enemy airplanes, like the Curtiss and the Grumman which were still biplanes at the time, should actually appear in the sky. He was always looking at pictures of airplanes, both of foreign and Japanese make, and thought only about copying them in detail on paper.

Now that he possessed the spare time that a year of preparation for an exam provides if one has already failed it, he found that he wasn't satisfied with simply copying photographs of aircraft. He wanted to see the real thing in action. In particular his longing to see the brand-new prototype which had been announced in newspapers and magazines proved irresistible, so he began paying visits to the airfield out at Tachikawa, some twenty miles away to the west. Sometimes he took his younger brother with him, and Shuji was surprised to see how excited Shun'ichi became as the train approached Tachikawa and they could see, far off, the tiny shapes of Type 93 bombers and other planes taking off and landing. He would even start to stamp his feet with impatience at the slow progress of the train.

Mostly, however, Shun'ichi went by himself. This was not only because it was a secret pleasure that he found hard to communicate to others, but also because what he was doing could be considered an infringement on military secrecy, and if he was not careful there was always the risk of being suspected of spying. This gave an additional allure to these visits to Tachikawa, a sense of adventure that was irresistibly attractive. He would wander as nonchalantly as possible along the dusty road past the base. The air was filled with the roar of engines, but all he could see was a perfectly ordinary Type 92 fighter plane, its propeller slowly beginning to tick over. He also saw an old-style Type 88 scout plane idly standing there. But his professional eye was quick to notice a difference: it now had a metal propeller instead of a wooden one, and he realized with excitement and satisfaction that the military must be carrying out various aeronautical experiments. Since he knew it was a bit dangerous to spend too much time near the base he walked beyond and away from it, doubling back by a different road and finally concealing himself in a mulberry field that stretched right down one side of the airfield. He drew out a small camera as, immediately overhead, a Type 93 bomber flew in to land, its engines rattling and groaning like an ironclad warrior in full cry (if one took a positive view of the matter) or like a clumsy lump of dead weight trying to stay airborne (if one did not).

As yet, the new prototype he wanted to see and photograph if that were possible had not shown itself. Right on the other side of the dusty airfield and farthest away from the mulberry field in which he was lying were some great black hangars, and he had no doubt that the top-secret prototype, the result of so much research, must be concealed behind those closed doors. If only those doors were to open so that he could be allowed to gaze on the secrets within—he felt he would be prepared to give up anything, make any sacrifice that was asked of him. . .

This way of life was hardly the right one for a student preparing for an entrance exam, yet his success in the following year exceeded everyone's expectations. It was probably the result of some incredible fluke, but he gained entrance into the preliminary course of the Medical Faculty of Keio University. When people praised him for this, his long, narrow face would break into smiles and for some reason he would put on the new cap he had been twiddling in his hands. The odd thing was that it suited him perfectly, and he looked exactly the way a "Keio boy" was traditionally supposed to look. During his year of cramming, even Shun'ichi suffered certain qualms of conscience concerning his behavior, but now that it had all ended with his entry into what was unquestionably a good school he was able to cast all doubts aside. His visits to Tachikawa became more and more frequent, and he even went off to the seacoast at Oppawa to watch the naval planes in action. So he spent his days boldly cutting classes, buying a return ticket each morning, and traveling to both the army and navy bases, his heart trembling with secret pleasure. He looked up constantly at the sky in exultation and also with a kind of fear.

Now more and more new prototypes were appearing. He watched the trial flights of the Nakajima Ki-11 single-seat fighter and the Ki-8 two-seater, although he did not yet know that those were their names. From his concealed vantage point amid the mulberry bushes he saw the Ki-11 suddenly lose speed as it came in to land and become entangled in telegraph wires like a child's kite. The plane did not catch fire, nor was it particularly damaged, but Shun'ichi forgot his fear of being taken for a spy and ran over to look, arriving as the apparently uninjured test pilot was shinning down a broken telegraph pole.

These particular prototypes did not, in fact, go into production, but there were many others that did, and they were produced in considerable numbers, making air power the principal weapon in the Japanese armory. Each revolutionary development of military aircraft in Japan was thus imprinted in vivid and passionate detail on Shun'ichi's mind . . . and also on the film in his camera. And more breathtakingly new planes appeared, the army's Type 94 scout, Type 95 fighter, the navy's Type 95 carrier-borne fighter, Type 96 sea-attack and land-attack fighters, and others, too, as year succeeded year.

Even so, it was still not possible to feel safe; it was dangerous to be too confident about all this. Just as had happened in the mid-twenties with the uproar over the Immigration Act, the idea of a war between Japan and the United States once more became a subject for the fiction writer, leading to an inundation of popular novels and short stories with that as its theme. But if one were to imagine an air battle between the Japanese and American forces now, it was clear that the Japanese flying machines were inferior. The carrier-borne Grumman had been equipped with a retractable undercarriage for some time, the wheels folding not inside the wings but up into its plump fuselage. The carrier-borne bomber, the Curtiss Helldiver, was the same. The American Army single-seat fighter, the Boeing P-26, still had a fixed undercarriage, but the wheels were held by sturdy, strongly armored legs, giving an impression of ferocity, of tremendous toughness in a scrap, and Shun'ichi could only sigh in envy.

So it was that this good-natured, slightly foolish airplane enthusiast was transformed first into a patriot, and then into a fully-fledged militarist, a prey to any nationalistic wind that might blow. All the ideas that Kumagoro had drummed into him when he was a child about the "eight-eight fleet" now came back to him, and he became an avid reader of the "if Japan should go to war" variety of books.

One evening he came back from Tachikawa tired but in high spirits, and called his young brother to his side:

"Shuji, at last," he said, so elated that the words would not come out at first, and grinning even more childishly than before, when he was an educational outcast cramming for his exams. "At last Japan has a low-wing monoplane fighter."

This had still not been made public, but Shun'ichi had braved possible arrest to discover the secret by himself.

In January, 1936, when Japan walked out of the London Disarmament Conference and decided to build warships from the following year without any regard for the Naval Treaty agreements, Shun'ichi talked to his brother about the matter as if he were the Navy Minister himself:

"Look, it's like this. We, Japan, have had this five-five-three ratio for capital ships imposed on us. Now, if we start building warships again we'll be unbeatable. Before, when we were building what was then called the eight-eight fleet, the Americans got upset about it and told us to stop. Get this clear, Shuji, none of us can afford any luxuries any more. Everyone, civil servants, people in offices, will have to contribute a part of their salaries, because we've got to build the eight-eight fleet again. Then we've got to have airplanes, lots of them, too."

He proceeded to give Shuji a lengthy account of the very awkward customer called the Curtiss Helldiver that the enemy, the U.S. Navy, possessed. This led to a disquisition on the special ring formation the fleet had worked out to counter it. Shuji listened with rapt attention to the brother he idolized, and finally asked:

"Will there really be a war with America?"

"Must come sometime or other." Shun'ichi felt a peculiar elation at the thought, which it never crossed his mind to question.

"When will it start, then? When exactly?"

"Bit difficult to say," replied Shun'ichi. But then he added in a sudden irresponsible flash of inspiration, "Round about 1939, I should think. Yes, 1939 looks the most likely year."

He looked calmly up at the ceiling with a peaceful expression on his long, narrow face, lost in complex considerations and mingled misgivings and expectations concerning the performance of the enemy's aircraft and the degree of progress Japan's own military aircraft had made in response to the swiftly growing American threat. His reflections were of a specialist nature for he was, at least in his own judgment, as well informed on modern aviation as anybody in the military's inner circles. It would have been difficult to imagine a person who believed more sincerely in the reality of this coming conflict, nor one who awaited it with such eagerness. And Shun'ichi was to be proved right, for Japanese and U.S. fighters were to fill the air with skirmishes and dogfights, not in dreams and fantasies but in harsh reality.

As for the other two children, Aiko and Shuji, their experience of true joy was restricted to the forty days of the summer vacation which they spent in the mountains of Hakone, freed from the various fetters of school.

Normally they took the steam train from Shinbashi, accompanied by Nanny Shimoda and one of the student houseboys, or sometimes a maid. The train always made Nanny Shimoda feel sick, and she was soon prostrate in her seat, placing the small bucket that she had brought in readiness a littler nearer to hand, though this did not prevent her buying the children their ice cream at the various stations where it was available. The children were totally unaffected by travel sickness, although Aiko would express her sympathy for poor Nanny when the mood took her by rubbing her old, round back with a gentle hand. Since they never felt sick, the children would have been content if Hakone had been miles further away, even right on the other side of the world, for that would have meant stopping at hundreds, even thousands, of stations, and before they arrived they would have eaten lots and lots of ice cream, perhaps all the ice cream in the world. At Odawara they got on an electric tram that went even slower than the most dilapidated Tokyo streetcar, but finally at Yumoto, just three or four miles west of Odawara, there was the Hakone Mountain Railway.

The Hakone Mountain Railway! The very name made one thrill all over. So they changed into carriages that had been imported from Switzerland and made especially to climb up steep gradients. Off they went, the electric train giving off its special rumble and roar, which was particularly powerful and wonderful when going up a really steep incline. As the green, jaggedy, up-and-down landscape opened around them a coolness came in through the windows. Now the iron bridge they had crossed a little earlier was way below them, small and toy-like, and the water was white and foaming in the deep ravine. The train passed through a number of tunnels. They always tried to count the number on their fingers, and each time at some point they would lose count. At one of the stations the train stopped and the driver and guard changed places, the train mysteriously setting off in the opposite direction, although this did not mean it went back down again but only further up on a different line. At another station, where banks of

398

yellow-fringed mountain lilies attracted swarms of black swallowtails, the descending train waited for them to pass, for this was a single-track railway. Here the two guards exchanged leather satchels with huge rings on them, after which the two trains proceeded on their way, one down and one up, each making its own clatter and hum.

Once they had passed Miyanoshita they were really in the mountains, and on a far slope amid deep greenery was a cluster of white buildings among which a hotel with a red roof was particularly prominent. This was Gora, where they were going, and the end of the line.

After passing the souvenir shops near the station and the row of houses that extended a little on from there, they walked up a fairly steep rise to the cottage Kiichiro had built all those years ago, puffing and blowing because of the heavy luggage in their hands. The ditch by the side of the road was full of overflow water from the hot spring, and the stones had turned a yellowish brown and gave off a smell of sulfur. Clear-toned cicadas were singing in chorus from the dark cedar woods that lined the roadside. This was where they were to spend their summer days, untroubled except by one holiday task set by their school, a place where some small and unimportant dreams could be fulfilled, a secret place, a paradise.

The cottage had been very modern when it was first built, but the damp of the mountains had taken a swift toll on it and now it looked decayed and old. From the side of the veranda, with its glass sliding doors where the putty had come off in a number of places, a partially enclosed walkway led across to the bathhouse where a constant spring of sulfurous hot water bubbled noisily. The children bathed a number of times each day, prancing about in the murky water and splashing it over each other. The hand towels which had been white when they arrived gradually changed color, becoming a dull yellow by the time their stay came to an end.

The cicadas sang most vigorously at dawn and twilight. They would also sensitively reflect the changes in the weather, taking on a more doleful tone when the sky clouded over, or when black clouds started to build up for a storm. This green cicada, *Tanna Japonensis,* with its uniquely clear voice, was somehow symbolic of Hakone, although it aroused the comment from Aiko that its voice was very sad, even sadder than the sound of the bugler of the Third Regiment playing "lights out." She said this in her usual pert and grown-up manner, and although all the real grown-ups responded that it wasn't sad in the least, the comment had its effect on Shuji, and for a while he could not hear the song of the cicadas without feeling there was something unbearably strange and unsettling about it. He would wake up around dawn when it was still not light. He wanted to go to the toilet, but all about him was dark and lonely and creepy, and he didn't quite have the courage to get up. He tried to stay absolutely still in bed with his eyes wide open, for in the half-light he knew there was a big daddy longlegs high up on the damp-stained wall, all thin body and long legs, and it was stretching out those long legs and crawling about. At the moment of dawn, the first cicada would suddenly start up in a low voice far off in the cedar woods. At first the voice would be wavering and uncertain, but it was soon followed by another, and another, until the whole chorus had sprung into life. The thin, cool sound made him feel more and more forlorn, although strangely it never had any effect of that kind during the day. It also made him feel unable to do anything, so he curled up in the warmth of his bed for a little longer, until making up his mind at last and forcing himself to get up.

The toilet was at the far end of the corridor, and on the way there he passed the room that served as his father's study and bedroom. Every time he did so, he noticed that the desk light was on. Tetsukichi handed over the whole business of the hospital to the Assistant Director, Seisaku Kanazawa, for two months every summer, and shut himself away in this house in Hakone. Shuji found his father very distant and hardly knew him at all, although he did know that he came to Hakone a little before they did and that every day he was doing some kind of work that Shuji understood nothing of. His father had already begun at this early hour of the morning.

Momoko's child, Satoru, whose father had died and whose mother had abandoned him and who now lived in the house in Matsubara, also came up to the cottage that summer. Although Satoru was a constant trial to Chiyoko with his powerful aversion to school, he was a marvelous playmate for Aiko and Shuji since he possessed a talent that they did not have, the ability to remember and repeat perfectly all the popular songs of the day, cleverly putting in the guitar accompaniment with a neat rolling of his tongue whenever that was possible. His features were now clear and well defined, a great improvement on those of that ill-favored infant over whom his mother had lamented. But his ears were too large and prominent, and there was a look in his eyes that was far from the imagined innocence of childhood. It was a sly, cunning glint of an unpleasantly grown-up kind.

The three of them played in the neighborhood as if the whole area belonged to them. In the local park at Gora, after messing about among the rocks and the moss-covered trees for a while, they would go to the pond with the fountain and make wild attacks with sticks on the pond skaters that slid around on its surface. The idea was to splash these insects out of the water onto the bank and catch them, which they sometimes managed to do, and then feed them to the monkeys in the cage nearby. They had already named each monkey after someone working in the Nire Hospital, and this added to the fun. The carp and goldfish in the pond could be fed with large globs of wheat gluten, which were available in a box. On the box was written "Goldfish food: two for one sen," but there was no one about to watch over any transaction so Satoru soon hit on the plan of pretending to put a coin in the money box and taking the food for nothing. The other two decided to ignore the pricks of conscience, and when no one was around they helped themselves as they pleased, only they didn't feed the goldfish but stuffed it into their own mouths.

The next thing was to occupy and establish complete control over the park swings. There were only three of them, and when they had each taken a swing and were competing with one another there was no swing for anyone else. Once, two or three other children came over, and the oldest boy among them suggested that Satoru and company should all ride on the same swing so as to give someone else a chance. The suggestion sounded much like a command, and this offended Aiko; her expression suddenly hardened, and she delivered one of her famous spontaneous lies:

"What are you talking about? My grandfather donated these swings to the park, if you must know. Go and ask at the office of the Hakone Land Company if you don't believe me."

The enemy withdrew crestfallen, much to Aiko's delight, and she urged her swing higher and higher, right up into the sky, so high that her skirt was blown up by the wind, revealing the whole expanse of her thighs as far as her knickers.

On hot days they swam in the park swimming pool. At first all three used water wings, although Satoru soon claimed that he could swim without them. He proceeded to give a demonstration before an attentive Aiko and Shuji, choosing a shallow place where the water only just came above his knees. He closed his eyes, plunged his face into the water, and made a tremendous and uncoordinated thrashing with his arms and legs. This raised so much spray that he disappeared in the midst of it for a moment, but it was only for a moment, and he soon raised his dripping face with an expression that plainly invited the applause this wonderful exhibition richly deserved. In fact he was standing exactly where he had started, not having moved six inches. Nevertheless, all three of them did learn to swim that summer.

If they went on any long excursion, like the one to Owakudani, it was always with a grown-up. They took the cable car from Gora to the summit of their local mountain, Sounzan. Halfway up, the single track divided to allow ascending and descending cars to pass, and Aiko noticed, as she had in previous years, that the driver of the descending car was the same man, a very broad man who looked remarkably like a hippopotamus. Several years later she noticed him in a different role, this time wearing a stationmaster's hat on the platform of one of the minor stations on the Mountain Railway. This discovery gave her a profound shock, she said, for he had never looked the type who was fated to succeed in life.

At Sounzan Station they each bought a walking stick or a staff and began a long trudge along the mountain path. Their surroundings gradually became more desolate and blasted. Trees, bushes, and finally grass disappeared, and a valley opened before them, plainly revealing the cruel, red-brown entrails of the earth. Bursts of white, sulfurous steam shot up here and there. There was a teahouse right at the summit, and here you could order eggs and have them placed in a basket which was lowered into one of the rumbling, bubbling, natural cauldrons nearby; they were hard-boiled by the time the basket was pulled out again. On the way, they had walked past a number of teahouses, but only this one on the summit and the one by the station still remained open; those in between had fallen into decay and finally closed. There was one in particular which had been open last year, but was now boarded up. These boards and the long bench in front were weathered and rotten, and tiny mushrooms were growing out of them. And Aiko, whose conceitedness was matched by a sentimental streak common in young girls of her age, was moved to comment:

"Oh look, that shop's closed now. I wonder how the people who ran it are managing? If only we'd drunk more lemonade when we came last time."

The world these three inhabited was quite different from the one the grown-ups in the same cottage lived in. It wasn't even contiguous but far off, removed. Even their elder brother, Shun'ichi, now enjoying a few weeks of leisurely mountain climbing, was excluded from the children's world. The only adult member of the Matsubara household who ever appeared at Gora was Uncle Yonekuni, who always had a lengthy stay here, having spat up a minute quantity of blood again, which had made him very worried and depressed. Naturally he had had a number of thorough medical examinations since then, but he was always told there was nothing much wrong with him, which only increased his dissatisfaction. Nobody, it seemed, was prepared to worry about him, nor, on reflection, had they ever been. So he was obliged to worry about himself, to give this serious illness of his the consideration it deserved, and he resolved to treat himself with the utmost care. Unhappily, since he spent his days wandering about the hospital farm, his face had acquired a very healthy suntan; and this was another reason for secret regret.

All Uncle Yonekuni did at Gora was lend the occasional hand with the garden, which meant looking after the very smallest of the potted plants. A certain amount of exercise, plus a far greater amount of healthy nourishment, were obviously essential. In addition he had quiet, recuperative periods, postprandial rests that lasted precisely three hours. There were, admittedly, country walks, on which he would be accompanied by one of the pointers that his brother Oshu had entrusted to him; but a time was always chosen when the rays of the sun were not too strong. On the one occasion Shuji went with him, he was impressed by the very leisurely and composed way in which his uncle walked, sometimes sitting down on a rock in the shade of a tree and quietly closing his eyes, while the dog pushed on ahead, racing ecstatically about and disappearing far off into the darkness of the woods. Then the animal had started barking and the shadow of a large bird passed across the clearing. Yonekuni immediately picked up his walking stick, held it to his shoulder, and went through the motions of firing. He had once been taken by his brother on a hunting expedition, but it had been an extraordinarily strenuous affair and full of remarkable misfortunes, all too much for him, and he never went again. He now restricted his enjoyment of the sport to the occasional raising of his stick and mock firing at shadows.

Uncle Yonekuni used to spread lots of butter on his rice at mealtimes. One reason for this was that butter was good for the consumptive condition he had convinced himself he had, and he would have felt very uneasy if he could not have as much as he thought he needed. Another reason was that the Aoyama cuisine was much inferior to what he enjoyed at Matsubara. One summer, however, Yonekuni started on a completely different diet. He brought his own supply of barley, which he boiled up with rice in a little saucepan. Since barley has no particular effect on the illness he claimed to suffer from, or on any illness at all for that matter, one can only assume he had been encouraged in this nutritional adventure by readings in obscure, specialist volumes, or had received spiritual insight from some profound and hidden source of wisdom. In any event he was now all for restraint and simplicity in these matters, and when Aiko once complained about the inadequacy of her own dinner he assumed a serious, almost angry expression, though his deep, staring eyes remained unaltered:

"Now, see here. Extravagant eating habits never did anyone any good. Look at your uncle, now. All I eat is barley and rice. I don't have anything else; no extras of any kind. I don't care how poor my diet is, so it doesn't matter to me how badly off I become. Whatever happens I know I can manage; I can get by."

Perhaps as he said these fine words he may have remembered that evening long ago when, out of sympathy for those unhappy, hungry German children, he had determined to eat only rice and hard pickles. The odd thing was that he resolutely persisted in his new diet for that summer at least, refusing to show any inclination for anything that might have pleased his palate. Even on the rare occasions when people came all the way from Odawara selling fresh fish in shallow trays, he showed no interest. He simply shook his head, indicating by his expression that it was of no concern to him. So he went on eating his own plain meals of barley and rice, perhaps allowing himself the odd sprinkling of something like grated eggplant (previously boiled stone-hard in soy sauce); and consuming this unappetizing meal with the distaste it deserved, masticating slowly, carefully, and with determination.

Nanny Shimoda soon recovered from her travel sickness once she had got into the cool air of the mountains. Her fat, wrinkled face looked healthy again, and she said she was sure to live to a hundred if she were lucky enough to continue to be allowed to spend the hot summer days up here in the coolness of Hakone, and how grateful she was for the kindness shown her in allowing her to do so. She went on tirelessly working away in the kitchen and doing the washing, despite the fact that there were enough hands to do everything without her, spending the whole day shut up indoors, except when it got dark and the children were late coming home, when she would go out to the gate, then a little beyond it, and finally totter down to the bottom of the slope and wait there until the figures of Aiko and the other two appeared in the distance. The children of the house now provided the principal meaning of her life, and when she finally saw them her old, wrinkled face would dissolve in an innocent and doubtless ridiculous way. Her features had never been beautiful, in fact it would be truer to call them ugly, but the gentleness of her face was unrivaled. No portrait of the compassionate mother by any of the old masters ever had such gentleness, for these children had no mother, or only one they hardly ever met. So as they ran along the evening road toward home, her face began to tremble, for of late she had become very prone to tears and she felt things from the bottom of her honest heart, and when she looked at the dragonfly that Shuji, who had come dashing up to her, held in one of his hands, his pleasure became her own.

"Why, Master Shuji, what a lovely, great big dragonfly. You *have* been clever to catch a big one like that. . ."

"He didn't catch it," interrupted the flint-hearted Satoru at Shuji's side. "I caught it for him."

Once a toad appeared in the garden, causing a great commotion among the children, who ran about shouting with bamboo sticks, determined to wreak havoc on it. But the barley-and-rice enthusiast, the believer in the simple life, Uncle Yonekuni, made them desist, telling them the toad was a friend of man, a guardian deity of the garden who consumed very harmful insects. This sermon had some effect, but Satoru had conceived so strong a loathing for the beast he sought it out later and finished it off himself by dousing it with some alcohol he had found in the medicine chest and setting it alight—an action that brought down hysterical reproaches from Aiko when she found out:

"Satoru, I loathe and despise you. I won't stand cruelty like that."

Satoru never took Shuji seriously, but Aiko was the same age as himself and tended to be the boss of their small gang, so he had to be careful with her. He spent half a day making a grave for the toad with conspicuous care, even building a headstone and setting offerings of white trumpet lilies and faded evening primroses before it. And, sure enough, the capricious Aiko soon revoked her judgment.

"That is nice of you, Satoru. You've a kind heart after all. I really like you, you know; you're really sweet."

The great attraction of the holidays, the event for which the children waited with beating heart and bated breath, was the Gora Festival. It was held each year on the 16th of August, and consisted during the day of a naive dramatic performance, as well as some amateur Sumo wrestling. During the wrestling, a man of remarkably ugly and evil countenance defeated five opponents in a row, much to the delight of some local youths who were supporting him. Satoru felt particularly frustrated when he heard them claim that this triumph was only to be expected since the man was no amateur but a real pro who had once made it as far as the second division, for he was convinced that if they had only brought Zaosan with them he would have been able to dispose of at least ten opponents.

At night, however, it was really magical. Pitch darkness descended over the tall branches of the cedars; not the usual darkness that filled Shuji with fear, but the precursor of excitement, and in the normally frightening peace of the countryside he could hear the murmur of a crowd down there in the direction of the station. Fireworks began to sparkle in the starry sky. There was a succession of cheerful explosions and then a chrysanthemum opened and faded in the dark immensity or spread astonishingly through the great expanse, lighting up the night entirely; or a number of bright arcs like fishing rods streaked across the darkness, all different colors, leaving momentary trails behind them as they fell. Then, when the night had grown late, near the summit of Myojogatake, which was a black shape in the darkness visible from the front veranda, a small light suddenly shone out, then others, spreading and forming the three thin lines of the character for "great." This was in imitation of the famous Daimonji Festival in Kyoto, and was done every year by the members of the local Young Farmers Association, who set fire to huge quantities of brushwood which had been sprinkled with kerosene. During the day, if one allowed the eye to travel around the whole panorama of the surrounding mountains, one could see that the grass and undergrowth had been cleared away in the area close to the summit of Myojogatake, forming the vague outline of the character "*dai*."

This year, however, there was a minor incident. The great, fiery letter was just beginning to die down as it did every year, fading back into the blackness of the night, its shape now broken in places, when the top half of the letter began to flare up again, advancing up the hillside like a fiery snake and gradually expanding as it did so.

"What's happened? Has it spread?" asked Aiko, her nose glued to the window of the veranda.

"Looks like a forest fire," said her elder brother in a solemn sort of voice. "Still, it'll soon die out," he added, in what seemed to be tones of regret.

Shun'ichi was only taking the preparatory course at Keio University, which made him, in effect, still a high-school student. He had invited one of his friends from junior high school to spend a few days at the cottage, a youth with a dark complexion and slightly prominent cheekbones who wore a very grubby version of the cap with one white stripe that marked a student of the prestigious Tokyo First High School. His name was Tatsunori Shiroki, and it was he who, as deputy class leader, had thrown the baked-potato basket heroically out of the window on that famous occasion when Shun'ichi had produced his sensational nosebleed.

The two young men talked with considerable pleasure about the fire, Shiroki commenting that he was a little surprised to see Shun'ichi deriving so much enjoyment from watching what was, after all, a small disaster.

"You used to be such an innocent, friendly person; almost stupidly so. Look at the way you'd always produce the money for the potatoes way before anyone else did."

Aiko listened with attention to this remark, hoping to hear more, but Shiroki looked back toward the fire, and merely added:

"Still, there's not much to burn up there. There's only grass on the summit."

A couple of days before, Shun'ichi and Shiroki had climbed to the summit of Myojogatake, and what the latter said was true. The wildfire was probably little more than some nearby bushes catching alight, and it gradually burned down until only a few points of flame remained. Then those too were gone. Darkness reoccupied the mountainside, and no more fireworks went up into the sky. The veranda was suddenly dark as well, for they had turned off the lights to see better and so as not to attract the moths. One could hardly distinguish people's faces, and the night air had grown cold.

"Let's have a bath and go to bed," said Satoru, yawning.

But Aiko was aware of the courtesy due to a guest and, looking toward the other window where Shiroki and Shun'ichi were two dark shadows, she suggested, in a pert, affected tone of voice, that her brother and his friend should go first.

So the last day drew nearer, and the long festival of the summer vacation was fading like the great fiery symbol on the mountainside. Suddenly their days in Gora were numbered, easily countable.

There were noticeably fewer cicadas singing now. Their clear voices which, at the height of summer, could be heard even at the hottest hours of noon, now no longer formed a chorus. Instead, there was a small, easily distinguishable number of voices, away in the woods or over in the shadow of the mountain, as the afternoon drew on. The number of evening primroses that attracted notice as night began to fall had also swiftly decreased. The wild plants had taken on the tones of autumn, and young, black crickets leaped upward and away as one walked. Even the interior of the house seemed old and shabby now, as if it shared in the general desolation of the approaching season. The husks of cicadas and dragonflies that Satoru and Shuji had collected and put in a box in a corner of the corridor were crumbly and decayed, with scattered wings and legs. The yellowish brown hot-spring water poured out as endlessly as ever from the bamboo pipe, but the bathhouse seemed damp and uninviting, strangely wide and empty. Only a few now yellowing towels hung from nails on the wall, unused.

In those last days the children were obliged to set about their homework. They looked as if some curse had suddenly descended on them. The tasks they had been set were nothing in themselves, but having been left so long undone they towered above them like overhanging cliffs. Shuji's had been to record the weather of the holidays, noting merely which days had been cloudy and when the sun had shone, but he had kept putting it off. Now he was worried sick about it. Aiko tried to cheer him up:

"Don't worry about it. You can make it all up because the weather in Hakone is quite different from Tokyo, and teacher's not likely to have come to Hakone, now, is he?"

Still, Shuji was not happy about making it up. He considered his teacher the fount of all knowledge and felt sure he would see through this fraud. On the rare occasions when he had been obliged to submit homework in the past his hand had always trembled.

Finally the last day came, and it was time to say farewell to this land that had taken such gentle care of them during the summer days. They measured one another's heights on a pillar in the corridor as a reminder in years to come. They took a last look around the house until they were told to hurry up, and then they stepped down into the entrance, out through the door, and onward down more steps. The bush clover was so thick now it had almost overgrown the path. Red dragonflies stopped and rested on the full ears of pampas grass, spreading poised wings, but there was no time left to catch them any more.

The rumble and roar of the Mountain Railway that had so thrilled them when they had arrived was now a gloomy, empty rattle and clank. As the train descended through the tunnels whose number they never managed to count they looked once more at the green mountains, the abrupt cliffs and crevices, the foaming torrents and the streams. But the main thing was to avoid useless regrets and concentrate on the stations at which the steam train would stop and the ice cream they would eat at each one.

It was already stinking hot at Odawara, and even worse at Shinbashi Station. Tokyo was still steaming slowly in the summer heat. The hospital chauffeur, Katagiri, had accompanied them on the journey back, so the car was in Aoyama. But he would not let them get straight into a taxi. There were plenty of taxis lined up in front of the station, but Katagiri insisted on asking each driver how much he would charge to take them to Aoyama. The first raised his outspread hand, indicating fifty sen. Being a driver himself, Katagiri found this exorbitant. He offered thirty, and the driver turned his face abruptly away with an expression of scorn at the absurdity of the offer. Katagiri was managing the heavy suitcases, but the children also had as much luggage as they could handle. There was a limit to how long they could stand it as a succession of cabs pulled up and were sent on their way by the obdurate Katagiri. Aiko pouted and said that she would put up ten sen of her own, so he finally made a deal for forty sen. He still looked unhappy about it as he loaded the children and the luggage into the taxi.

The house at Aoyama looked deserted and worn out by the heat. The sound of the large brown cicadas filled the late summer sky, which seemed to sag down over the earth. But that was not the only sound. Shuji also heard the restless, thin screech of the autumn cicada, and through the confusion that had reigned in his mind since early morning, he finally realized that the holiday was over, and summer was gone for another year. This realization was intense, and lent an added dullness to a face that was lacking in cheerful energy at the best of times. A peevish gloom emanated from his bowed head.

These had been good days for the children, a reflection in some ways of the age itself, for those few years of the early Showa era had been relatively happy ones. Bad things seemed far off, unintelligible or unreal. The harvest failures in the North, the oppression in the world of ideas, and all the other rumors that grew as the dark clouds gathered were things that never reached the children's ears, and would have meant nothing to them if they had.

But one rifle shot fired late one summer night, and the many shots that followed it, certainly did reach their ears, for this was the summer of 1937 and the shot that was fired at the Marco Polo Bridge on the outskirts of Peking signaled all-out war with China. Even so, the news seemed at first to be about something remote, and the children set off as usual for the carefree pleasures of Hakone. But while they were there the flames of war leaped southward to Shanghai and continued to spread, and what had first been called the "North China Incident" was renamed the "China Incident." It was always referred to as an "incident" after that, but this was unquestionably full-scale warfare, an endless, muddy swamp of war, the unmistakable beginning of what would drag the whole nation into an abyss of destruction, though nobody seemed to realize this at the time.

At first the war was greeted with a noisy atmosphere almost of celebration. Patriotic cheers resounded at the stations as troops entrained for the front. Among those troops was an intern of the Nire Hospital, Sadaichi Sawara, who was one of the first to be drafted. A soldier going to the front was given a *senninbari,* a lucky belt that had stitches sewn into it by a thousand different hands. All the staff of the hospital and even some of the patients had contributed to Sadaichi's, and they also wrote their names on a huge Japanese flag inscribed with the motto "Fortune in Arms." But Sadaichi Sawara was not only one of the first troops to leave, he was one of the first to die: he died very promptly during the storming of Nanking. He had always been extremely serious, and was remembered chiefly for such things as teaching Shuji how to subtract from a hundred. He was a good young man with a future, the first victim of the war from the Nire Hospital, and a very early one.

The war affected Shun'ichi, now a twenty-two-year-old medical student, in a different way. It filled him with a huge, solemn elation. In the spring of that year an airplane sponsored by the *Asahi Shinbun,* the *Kamikaze,* had established a new world record for the flight from Tokyo to London, covering the distance in a time of 94 hours 17 minutes and 56 seconds. The newspaper had run a competition among its readers for the most accurate prediction of the time and Shun'ichi had sent in dozens of entries, but since he had been overoptimistic in his calculation that the plane would fly at around 300 mph, each forecast he had submitted had been in the region of seventy hours, and all of his postcards were wasted. But none of that mattered to him now, for immediately after the "Incident" had begun the navy carried out transoceanic raids using the Type 96 coastal bombers that he knew all about. All his long years of waiting seemed justified, for he had been following the development of the airplane since a time when there were only a few of them in the country. He felt like one of the founding fathers of this military device. With the outbreak of hostilities, air defense also became the subject of statement and counterstatement, and the importance it acquired seemed an indication that at last his own views on the subject were gaining general acceptance. He saw himself as a prophet, aware that his own farsighted vision put him in a quite different class from those contemporaries of his who were only now beginning to notice, with excited consternation, the military potential of the flying machine. Consequently, when he went to see a film about air defense at the local Youth League Hall, he not only felt obliged to click his tongue in contempt at the childishness of the film itself, but received even stronger confirmation of the belief he had held over the years, the blind conviction that Tokyo would be bombed at some time in the future. He knew that the planes would come one day, and although it did not really matter which country they came from, they would probably be American planes.

He went to a special shop in Kanda and acquired a gas mask. Despite the fact that it was labeled for civilian use, it was a perfectly normal gas mask, and Shun'ichi enjoyed fondling the concertina-like rubber hosepipe part of it, putting it on a number of times and even wishing that he could have the opportunity to try it out. So he lit a whole box of mosquito-repellant coils, put on his brand-new and by no means inexpensive gas mask, and looked through the smart visor at the smoke-filled room, gratified to find that it gave him one hundred percent protection from anti-mosquito fumes. Even if there were a gas attack on Tokyo at least one person, the farsighted Shun'ichi, would survive. But there was also the problem of food for the survivor, and he gave the matter of emergency rations a good deal of thought. The result of this brainwork was a decision to buy large quantities of hard tack or crackers, which he wrapped in cellophane and packed away neatly in a small case. He then forgot about them completely, only remembering them more than two years later. But when he opened the case he was horrified to find only a few crumbly remains and weevils swarming over the cellophane.

Well before this, however, when the crackers were still quite fresh, an amazing thing happened. Shun'ichi was unceremoniously arrested by the Military Police.

A year before his arrest, Shun'ichi had joined a club of aviation enthusiasts. There are all sorts and sizes of enthusiasts, but these people were just like Shun'ichi, though their ages varied considerably, ranging from people even younger than himself to men of venerable antiquity. It was not a particularly large club, just fifteen or sixteen people living mostly in the Tokyo-Yokohama area, aeronautical buffs who produced their own monthly journal, a flimsy, mimeographed affair. Most of the material in this journal consisted of the latest information found in foreign magazines, but there were also accounts of what they themselves had seen or heard, and naturally this meant that they often dealt with military aircraft. It was exciting to come across a plane being tested that they had never seen before, and they would construct a plan and drawing of it, and publish this boldly in their journal, giving the plane a nickname (for there was no way they could know what it was really called) and adding estimates of the aircraft's capabilities. For example, someone might comment that he had seen a fighter on a test flight, a low-winged monoplane with fixed undercarriage and an air-cooled engine, and the sound of the engine suggested it was a Kotobuki; or someone else would write that he had seen a single-seat low-winged monoplane with water-cooled engine and fixed undercarriage with spat-covered wheels at Tachikawa, and it was remarkably like the French Dewoitine as in the picture on the left; and so on. But the behavior of one of their members attracted the attention of the ever-vigilant Military Police, so in swift succession they were all arrested.

The house at Aoyama was also searched. Shun'ichi's room was given a thorough going-over, and the three albums that contained all the photographs of aircraft he had taken with such pains over the years were, of course, confiscated. If that had been all, it would have been a simple case of Shun'ichi calling down misfortune on his own head, but the two policemen spent a considerable time in Tetsukichi's room as well. No doubt all the books jammed in there and the damp, mildewed smell of the place had aroused their suspicions. So they rifled through the dusty piles of manuscript paper which were Tetsukichi's history of psychiatric medicine, and opened and closed one after the other all the foreign books that lay scattered about the room, almost certainly without being able to understand a word of what was written within. They acted out of no respect for the written word, but out of the suspicions that these unknown, un-Japanese objects aroused in them.

Shun'ichi spent two days with the others in the custody of the Military Police. They were not interrogated in any severe fashion, since it was clear that whatever had been going on was of no real consequence. Their patriotic sentiments were accepted at their face value, but since such actions could prove to be beneficial to an enemy, they were released only on condition that they swore never to try to take photographs again of military aircraft still on the secret list. Shun'ichi's albums were returned to him with the photographs of the military aircraft removed and only those of civil aircraft left, although he was pleased to find that one photo of an army plane remained since it had been mistaken, ludicrously in his opinion, for a civil passenger plane. He had also been amazed and frustrated by the small understanding of aviation matters the officer who had interrogated him had shown. Even so, he returned home in high spirits, for had not the Military Police, whose reputation was so terrifying that their name could reduce the most fractious child to silence, recognized his patriotism to some degree, and even praised him for it?

His father, however, reprimanded him in surprisingly strong terms. Normally Tetsukichi was absorbed in his own work and totally indifferent to the education and upbringing of his children, but his wrath had been aroused by the way his study and the manuscript, the repository of his spirit, had been so roughly manhandled. He maintained a solid onslaught on his astonished eldest son until the early hours of the morning, furiously remonstrating with him in even higher pitched tones than he had used during the final quarrel with Ryuko. Whether it was because this scolding had some effect or because the implications of his stay at Military Police Headquarters finally got through to him, Shun'ichi did not visit airfields very often after that. But perhaps the main reason for this change was that the situation had altered in other ways. One difference was that instruction at the Faculty of Medicine was quite unlike the preparatory course and included a great deal of practical work, which meant it was nowhere nearly as easy to cut classes. Still, what probably mattered most was that Japan's antiquated air force, which had filled him with such deep depression and shame before, had now been transformed into something genuinely up-to-date and, as the recent overseas bombing raids had shown, it was only a matter of time before they caught up with the Europeans and the Americans. It was this realization that largely released our very tall and very childish airplane enthusiast—no doubt all such enthusiasms are a sign of immaturity—from an obsession that had been fostered by a sense of frustration. Now that his expectations were being satisfied, the obsessive concern started to disappear.

Shun'ichi's brother and sister knew nothing whatever of his being arrested. Their ages were so different they found nothing particularly

413

odd about his not being around for a couple of days. And despite everything, Shun'ichi himself obviously felt some sort of shame at this escapade, and didn't so much as mention it to Shuji, who could be considered his disciple in aviation matters. The grown-ups, of course, made every attempt to keep quiet about what they considered an unseemly, un-Japanese activity, though he did not regard the matter in so unprepossessing a light.

In Shuji's classroom at Seinan Primary School a large map of the Chinese continent had been pinned up on the wall. The teacher, encircled by his pupils, would stick little Japanese flags on the map to represent the towns the troops had occupied in their spectacular advance. He then made the following suggestion: in order to get a better idea of the privations of our boys out there at the front, once a week all the children should bring to school a plain lunch consisting of just rice with one dried plum in the middle of it. The gesture would be particularly patriotic, since the round red plum on a white rice background was the same design as the national flag, and the meal was known as a *"hi-no-maru bento,"* *hi-no-maru* meaning "round sun" and *bento* "lunchbox." As Shuji ate his unappetizing *hi-no-maru bento*, whose only real virtue was its splendid-sounding name, he recalled what his uncle Yonekuni had once said, realizing he must have been accustoming himself to that meager diet of barley and rice for just such a contingency as this.

In the Aoyama hospital office, too, one could notice war impinging on life, as Oishi the accountant, Yasusaburo Sugano from the pharmacy and the chauffeur Katagiri talked eagerly of the progress of the imperial forces. The Deputy, Hidekichi Katsumata, on one of his very rare visits here from Matsubara, with rimless glasses glinting, praised the cunning ruse employed during the landing at the Bay of Hangchow, when the enemy had been plunged into confusion by the sight of advertising balloons carrying the exaggerated information that a million Japanese troops had landed.

"Marvelous idea. Worthy of Dr. Kiichiro himself. Absolutely. You know, the old doctor, that was his way of doing things. That was his way."

Oishi then nervously raised a point with the Deputy. In the area where the Aoyama main road led into another main road, Miyuki-dori, there was a house commonly known as "The Soldiers' Nurse." Some time ago, a comfort station had been set up in front of it for the soldiers of the Third Regiment as they returned to their barracks from training. Since the "Incident" a number of large houses had followed suit, and he wondered if it might not also be appropriate for the Nire Hospital to do the same, providing hot tea in the manner of "The Soldiers' Nurse."

"Well, you see the point is this," replied the Deputy with an attempt at introducing an authoritative note into his nasal whine. "We were, in fact, the very first to provide tea for soldiers, many years ago of course. We used to be the resting point for soldiers and also for the portable shrines at festival times. Which is why we received that specially courteous treatment from the military at the time of the Great Earthquake."

Oishi himself was perfectly aware of this aspect of Nire history, and although he was some years older than the Deputy, as his bent back showed, he was happy to defer to the other in these things. So the Deputy went on:

"I see no real need to provide tea at the present time. If we were to do so now, it would seem very much that we were merely running with the pack, you might say. Dr. Kiichiro would never have done anything like that. He believed in the exact opposite, in being ahead of everyone in everything, always miles ahead, and attracting attention that way. After all, insofar as tea is concerned, we are the ones who thought of the idea in the first place. . ."

The Deputy then went on to talk of the recently signed Tripartite Pact between Germany, Italy and Japan, pointing out that Dr. Kiichiro had always had a very soft spot for Germany, and had also availed himself of the services of an Italian make of car, a Fiat. It seemed likely he had foreseen that some such connection would be forged between the three countries. Thus, even in this innocuous conversation, the Deputy had managed yet again to add a flourish to the Kiichiro legend.

The news of this pact was received in the streets with avid enthusiasm. The flags of the three nations were everywhere, and there was an inundation of objects with that design on them. In Shuji's class at school, they made cardboard pencil boxes during the handicrafts lesson, and nearly everyone decorated theirs with some kind of design based on the three flags. It was almost as if they had conspired together to do so. The teacher in charge of drawing and handicrafts was a small man with a moustache, and by the time he had got around to Shuji he seemed to have had his fill of the three-flag motif. Shuji had done his with scrupulous care, but the teacher only glanced at it, muttering something about it being those flags again, and did not draw the four circles that

Shuji had hoped for—the equivalent of "excellent"—but only gave him three.

This was soon followed by the national holiday to celebrate the occupation of the enemy's seat of government, Nanking. The streets were almost drowned in a sea of flags, wave after wave of them. There were shouts, people singing the popular military song of the hour in hoarse voices, and sudden, spontaneous, almost manic bursts of cheering which swept through the marching crowds, encouraging the bystanders at these mass processions to wave their flags in response. Among these were rows of primary-school children, including Aiko and Shuji who were as yet unaware that the kind, generous Sadaichi Sawara had been killed in the battle they were celebrating. Aiko waved her flag so vigorously that she went red in the face with the effort, and the flag looked as if it might get torn off with the wild motion. Her brother Shuji had only been able to get hold of the cheapest paper one, and his had come off already. All he had left was the stick, which he was holding in a confused, embarrassed way. But the top of the stick was moving back and forth from left to right and right to left, so he was still waving it to some extent.

That night there was an exotic, cheerful lantern procession on the same kind of scale. So the two of them got home quite late, and when they finally got to bed in their seven-and-a-half-mat room (where even Shuji was too old to sleep with Nanny Shimoda any more) they could still hear the dull reverberation of cheers and shouts coming from the main road, distant murmurs of triumph that sounded as if they would never end.

Chapter

7

One early spring day in 1938 Momoko got off a train at Shinjuku Station. She was dressed in a rather dirty kimono, on top of which she had the short coat traditionally worn in Japan for carrying babies on the back, and she had a baby in hers, a one-year-old girl. She was going to do some shopping at one of the department stores. The square in front of the station was crowded, and here and there people were standing asking passersby to contribute to the *senninbari* they were holding, the cloth belts given to soldiers bound for the front. This had now become a familiar sight, and Momoko went up to one of them and quickly made her own contribution, sewing a small circle with red thread. The belt was already half-completed, and Momoko noticed that some people had sewn five-sen coins onto it. She was not tempted to do the same. She was not in a position to give five-sen coins away.

The baby on her back was sleeping quietly. Unlike Satoru, this little girl gave her no trouble at all, perhaps because Momoko was used to bringing up children now. The father of the baby was a man three years younger than she who worked for a small company that handled cotton goods, her second husband, Inosuke Miyazaki. He was much taller than Shiro had been, and he had a perpetual frown which at first made him seem unfriendly, but his long, slant eyes were gentle. At least his ears did not stick out sideways. He had appeared at a time when Momoko had lost one husband and was worn out with trying to bring up the fractious, school-hating Satoru, and her life had become a sordid matter of complete indifference to her. So she had left her child and run away with this man, becoming what society would term an abandoned woman. But Momoko loved him for having saved her from the empty life she had fallen into. The only thing she was unhappy about was his name, Inosuke, since it called to mind the filthy, hunchbacked figure of old Isuke of the cookhouse, who was apparently even more horribly bowed these days than ever. She had spoken to her husband about old Isuke on a number of occasions, rolling about with laughter in their small, cheap room. He would respond cheerfully to her amusement, a smile appearing on his tired face.

Her husband's salary was not all that bad, but his old parents were still alive in the Shinshu countryside to the west of Tokyo and he was obliged to send money home, so they were always hard up. They lived, the three of them now, in a cheap, broken-down apartment house in Mejiro, two miles northeast of Shinjuku, a place of crumbling walls where each window was perpetually cloaked in rows of babies' nappies and other articles of drying laundry. They had to share the kitchen with the other people living there, and Momoko put up with a variety of vexations she had never even imagined before. Even the life of her hapless sister Seiko, for whom she had once felt such sympathy and indignation at the injustice of a world that could allow such things, had been far better than hers was now, at least in terms of material comfort. Besides, she was even more outcast than Seiko had been, since she would certainly never be allowed to see any of her family again. She had, of course, been well aware of this when she took the decision to run away, since her crime could only be met by such a punishment, but as time passed she sometimes felt a desire like a physical longing to meet her relations again, even though she had no great affection for them. In particular, she longed to pass once more through the gates of the Nire Hospital of Mental Pathology.

For more than a year and a half she had kept her whereabouts hidden from everyone connected with the hospital, and had made no attempt to get in touch with anybody; but she found she could no longer endure the isolation, and she arranged a secret meeting with Nanny Shimoda upstairs at the Seiundo. Nanny was so pleased to see her that, for a while, Momoko could only sit with her head lowered and cry. The couple who ran the store also welcomed her just as they had always done, so, very occasionally, she would meet Nanny Shimoda there. Once, Aiko happened to drop in at the shop on her way home from school when Momoko was upstairs. Since Momoko's behavior had condemned her to being someone whom Aiko should not meet, Nanny Shimoda had to warn Aiko that this must all be kept absolutely secret, and as Momoko listened to her repeated injunctions, she recalled the times she had gone to visit Seiko with Nanny herself, carrying parcels of rice and vegetables.

So history started repeating itself. Nanny Shimoda enlisted the support of Katagiri, the chauffeur, and deliveries of rice and vegetables were made to the cheap apartment in Mejiro. The cottage at Hakone would be closed each year on the 10th of September when Tetsukichi returned to Tokyo, and since the remaining charcoal and rice would only be ruined by the damp if left in Hakone, it was Katagiri's task to load all of it into the car and bring it back to Aoyama. This he did, but he took it to Mejiro and gave the lot to Momoko.

Nanny Shimoda came a few times to the Mejiro apartment, and on one occasion she brought Aiko with her. It was when Aiko had just left primary school, and her sentimental streak seemed to have been given a powerful stimulus by her aunt's sad case. Even before this, a present from Aiko had usually been among the various gifts that Nanny Shimoda brought, a box tied with a beautiful ribbon with a pretty card attached saying "To Auntie Momoko" on it, and full of chocolates and cookies. She appeared shyly from behind Nanny Shimoda and entered the cramped room a little hesitantly, then gave her exactly the same kind of present wrapped in an identical way, for Aiko seemed to believe that shiny green ribbon bestowed a romantic air on any package.

When she saw her niece's tiny hand, and heard her artless, prattling voice (specially assumed for the occasion), twice married Momoko, mother of two children, was quite overcome, and her friendly, fat face twitched with emotion as the usual large, bogus-looking tears coursed down her cheeks.

"Mistress Ai," she sobbed, uncertain how to address this niece who was a couple of decades younger than herself. "How kind you are to me, how kind! The Nire people are so cold, so horribly cold, heartless, unfeeling. . . They know nothing of warm blood or tears. . . And yet you were born into that family. . . How, I don't know . . . a kind, sweet, gentle child like you. . ."

Momoko soon calmed down after this outburst, wiping away her tears with the back of her hand, and pressing on with a confession she had already made numerous times in the past:

"To tell you the truth I used to hate you when you were a baby. You were such a lovely baby and all anyone thought about was you. My Satoru was so ugly that nobody paid any attention to him. . . Still, Mistress Ai, you'll forgive me if I say straight out what I think because that's my way, but although you were a lovely baby you weren't anything all that special by the time you went to school. You'd become a right gawky little thing, I can tell you, not in the least like your aunt, Mistress Sei, who died, because she was a real beauty. But you're much better now. I'm not just trying to flatter you, you know, but you're not bad at all now. A girl's face keeps on changing during her life. With a bit of luck, dear, it wouldn't surprise me if you turned out to be just as beautiful as Mistress Sei."

Aiko wasn't sure whether these bold words of her aunt's were meant to be insult or flattery, so she murmured a shy disavowal as a safe way of handling the situation. Momoko bustled about preparing some nominal refreshments, suddenly saying with studied casualness:

"Do you ever see Satoru, Mistress Ai?"

"Oh yes. I was playing with him at the main hospital just a little while ago. He's fine; he's just fine."

Momoko said nothing after this, but became even busier with the teapot for a while, pouring in the hot water, and then peering to see if the baby was still asleep, which luckily she was. Momoko was thinking that, even though she was always condemning the Nire family as a bunch of cold fish, she was really no better herself. Biting her lip in vexation, she acknowledged that fate seemed to have forced her to become the sort of person she most disliked. She was self-condemned, on account of an abandoned son.

But Momoko was not the kind of person to be downhearted about anything for very long. Just as her great floods of tears would suddenly dry up, so her quiet reflections soon gave way to innocent chuckles and loud belly laughs, so that any third party might well have wondered what she had to be so happy about. She was talking to her niece about Hakone. It only needed a minor detail, such as the way the guard on the cable car always signaled to the driver by touching the electric line with a stick, to bring back all Momoko's memories in one vivid rush. All the shadows passed from her face as she rattled on with the cheerful fluency of a schoolgirl:

"I remember that pond in the park, it had goldfish in it. . . . Used to eat the goldfish food, did you? Well, that's not much. I used to go fishing for goldfish, at night, trying to catch them in my kimono sleeve. All it meant was my sleeves got soaking wet. Still, I envy your generation, I really do. The very first year that cottage was built they didn't even let me go there. That's what the Nire family used to be like. All sorts of formalities and ranking in it, and if you were at the bottom like me you got nothing. I was treated like dirt, as if I was the child of a servant or something. No one took any notice of me—oh, I'm sorry, except Nanny, of course—but at least I managed to see plenty of movies. I got my fair share of those. This old guy used to come in all dressed up in those old-fashioned clothes and start off in that super, weird voice about the *Curse of the Iron Claw*. It was marvelous. The talkies ruined all that. You would have loved it."

Momoko slapped her thigh and rocked forward in a vulgar display of joy.

"Come to think of it, I was there in Hakone at the time of the Great Earthquake. You wouldn't remember that, Mistress Ai, would you, because you weren't yet born. Amazing to think that someone not born at the time of the earthquake should have grown as big as this. Still, I was in Hakone when we had the Great Earthquake. That morning, Father and Uncle Shirokichi had gone back to Tokyo, and Mistress Ryu and Yonekuni and some of the others had gone back the day before—or was it the day before that? School was just about to start, you see. So there were only about four or five of us left in Gora, I think, and—yes, that's right—we'd ordered pork cutlets and rice from the shop and the delivery boy had just turned up at the back door, saying he was sorry he'd kept us waiting like they always do, when suddenly everything started shaking and rocking. We all ran out of the house, and you know that big pine tree in the middle of the garden, well we all clung onto that. I had this idea that fissures always opened up in the earth, so I'd got hold of one of the branches and was hanging on to that like grim death with my feet off the ground. Then we realized that Mother was missing. Someone said she'd been in the bath, so Seisaku—no it wasn't him, it was Yasusaburo—went off to look for her during one of the intervals when it had all died down a bit, and when he found her she was just very casually tying her bathrobe sash. Quite calm and collected she was, an old lady like that. Plenty of coldness to go with her coolness, too. I mean she hardly ever had a word to say to me, since I was the youngest daughter and all that and didn't count for anything; although she nagged me enough once she got going. Anyway, the house started tilting over. The cottage you've been to is how it became after it was repaired. So a man came from the Land Company and put up tents and people came from the cottages round about and all lived together in the tents. There was this tremendous fuss about somebody's house having collapsed completely. Then that evening there was a rumor—a pack of lies, of course—about Korean laborers rioting in Miyashirono, and people made bamboo spears and stayed up on guard. All we had to eat was balls of rice, sort of emergency rations. And the aftershocks going on all the time—it was incredible, I can tell you. So finally, because there were no provisions in Gora, we had to get away across the mountains to where there were some. We split up into three parties and went over the Otome Pass and down to Mishima. Everyone tucked up their skirts and just wore *tabi* socks on their feet because *geta* are hopeless for walking. My trouble was I just couldn't wear my kimono up high like that, showing everything, you know. I mean my face was okay when I was young, but my legs . . . well, the girls at school used to call me 'Horselegs' because I was a wee bit fat around the thighs. With schoolgirls that age, it's a very peculiar, special period in life, particularly at that time, you know, you just can't put it into words really, but anyway you just hate to expose yourself before people, and at an awful time like that to go around with your skirts all tucked up and showing . . . well I just couldn't, so you can imagine how absolutely awful it all was, going over the mountains like that. . . But, believe me, Mistress Ai, worse things than that have happened to me, far worse—things I could never reveal to anybody. I simply can't talk about them. When I think about myself and the life I've had, it seems there's been nothing but suffering. It makes me sad just thinking about it.''

While Momoko was cheerfully relating all these things, including some that were not really proper conversational topics with which to entertain a small niece, her face had a wonderfully outgoing, relaxed expression, and she spoke of all her sufferings in a tone of voice that made it sound as if she were proud of them. Finally, as her two guests were preparing to leave, she said:

''And Shun'ichi's going to medical college? Time does fly, doesn't it? It's amazing he managed to get through his exams. It's a tradition in the Nire family for the boys to flunk their exams. Look how many times Oshu failed. Heaven knows how many times. He'd a genius for it. The women have always done much better. They've got more class. Now *you've* certainly got class, Mistress Ai, so you're bound to be clever and do well. You mark my words, you'll grow up into a real beauty as well, I'm sure. You'll be a lovely girl, you take my word for it.''

''Oh, Auntie, you do say such awful things,'' replied Aiko in a slightly perplexed whisper, not quite sure how she should reply since, as her face showed only too clearly, she largely agreed with what Momoko had said. . .

Momoko made her way through the crowds in front of Shinjuku Station, feeling the weight of her still sleeping baby on her back, walking along the main road past all the various shops until she arrived in front of the Mitsukoshi Department Store. She was poorly dressed, her hair unkempt, her hands chapped and sore, and on her face, which had always been so frank and open, she wore an expression of gloom. She looked a quite different person. Her mouth, which used to be in perpetual motion, was tight-lipped now, as if she were angry about something. Recently this had become her habitual expression when she was not in conversation with someone, for she had a serious problem on her mind. Her husband had suddenly started talking about going to China. He didn't want to spend his whole life being told what to do by other people, but wanted to branch out on his own. There was good work in Shanghai. A friend of his, a little older than himself, had asked him to come and join him out there as a partner. It seemed a good idea, now, to move over to the continent and make a success of life, instead of just sticking it out here. . .

Momoko's first reaction had been to comment that she still remembered something of the Peking dialect, but she had not been able to make up her mind to go. She could recall in vivid detail how desperate she had been to get home when she had been in Hankow. Although she now had no home to return to in Japan and genuinely loved her husband and knew she was bound to live with him wherever he went, she felt reluctant about going abroad now that the opportunity had presented itself. In fact, deep inside she was terrified at the prospect, not out of concern for herself, but because she didn't want to be too far from the Nire Hospital, even though she had run away from it and had nothing but constant abuse for the place. She had the same illogical feeling about many of the people connected with the hospital.

Her husband had no intention of forcing her to go, but he did point out that this was a chance to make good, and also that they would probably be going only for a few years. There was no great hurry, for they would certainly not be leaving in the next week or so. She should think it over nice and slowly and then decide. But the more Momoko thought it over the more confused she became, until she had no idea what she should do, and things had dragged on until today with no decision made, except for the thought that she could make it her excuse that Sachie, the baby, was still too young to travel.

In fact, Momoko had meant to go to the Seiundo again today and talk the matter over with Nanny Shimoda, but when she had telephoned Aoyama (in a disguised voice and under an assumed name) she had been told that Nanny was out at the moment but would be back fairly soon. Momoko decided she would go to the department store and do some shopping for the baby first.

Once away from the immediate area of the station there was nothing much to indicate that a war was going on, and one came across the occasional person with permanently waved hair, despite the fact that it was now forbidden, or even someone wearing a long-sleeved kimono although this too was frowned upon. There were still no charcoal-powered automobiles (those symbols of wartime austerity) on the roads, and the cars gave off a good stench of gasoline, while streetcars rattled cheerfully and peacefully along. The shops were still crammed with goods that almost overflowed into the street outside. And they were crowded with customers too. As Momoko walked by she felt envious of this bustling prosperity in which she had no part.

When she reached Mitsukoshi she saw something that brought back the past, for parked in front of it was a car exactly like the gray Opel of the Matsubara hospital. Then she realized it not only looked like that car but was undoubtedly the car itself, for the man who stood beside it working on the windows with a feather duster was none other than the Matsubara chauffeur, Shigematsu Shimoda. Momoko was stopped in her tracks by this discovery, and looked swiftly about her to see if there was anyone else she knew. She glanced back at the car and saw that Shigematsu had already recognized her and was running toward her.

"Miss Momoko? It is Miss Momoko, surely?" he said, stopping two or three paces from her, and scrutinizing her closely.

Momoko was so shaken she could say nothing. She had never been on particularly friendly terms with this chauffeur, but he had known her straight away despite her shabby clothes, and had come running over to her, his duster still in his hand, calling out her name in that breathless, excited way. Momoko was suddenly overwhelmed with the feeling that the whole Nire Hospital was welcoming her with open arms. An image of the hospital as strong, dependable and loving took immediate possession of her mind.

Shigematsu Shimoda was a middle-aged man who had been the chauffeur at Matsubara for a long time, and he had some idea of the way Momoko had left home and why. He may not have been able to work out exactly what the baby on her back implied, nor the conditions in which she lived, but he seemed to grasp the general situation quickly enough. He came another pace nearer and said hurriedly:

"The old lady is shopping at the moment. She's all by herself. Miss Momoko, you must see her. Come and wait with me and just apologize for everything, and I'm sure your mother will forgive you."

His words were so kind and considerate that Momoko was suddenly convinced that they must also be true. She was bound to be forgiven;
it stood to reason. Of course she would be roundly abused; she would
be dealt with as a useless good-for-nothing. But she would humble
herself and say she was sorry, and eventually she would be forgiven.
How far she would be forgiven she did not know, but at least she would
be allowed to return to Aoyama and Matsubara. She was sure she
would.

In this state of wishful anticipation she went and stood by the car,
and almost immediately, much sooner than she had expected, she saw
her mother approaching. Hisa had certainly grown older and looked
it. She was now seventy years old, but she was still presumably energetic
if she could go out shopping like this. She was dressed in black, holding
nothing in her hands, and she walked in a straight line toward the car
with short, mincing steps. Her old-fashioned face remained as blank
and expressionless as ever, a mass of small wrinkles now with the same
off-putting hooknose. Momoko stepped forward two or three paces,
but then her body went stiff with a sudden shudder of realization. Her
mother had known for some time that someone was there, and she was
also well aware who it was. But she was not even going to glance in
her direction. As that expressionless, emotionless profile passed directly
in front of her Momoko knew exactly what its message was, just as
if it had all been put into words. It was telling her that her mother
did not wish to look upon her face. It was telling her that she would
be wise to go away at once.

Shigematsu opened the rear door of the car and Hisa bent down
and crawled slowly inside. The chauffeur closed the door after her,
looked around at Momoko, hesitated as if he had something to say
to her, but changed his mind and opened the driver's door instead.
Momoko looked away. She looked up into the sky, into the blank space
beyond the roof of the department store. The car started and for a while
she could hear the sound of the engine. When she finally lowered her
eyes to the world about her there was no sign of the gray Opel.

It was strange there were no traces of tears on her slightly haggard
but still plump cheeks; but not really strange, for she had opened her
small eyes as wide as she could to keep the tears back. What was also
strange was that although she felt desolated, she also experienced a
sense of finality, of having finally been released. So she made up her
mind at last. She would go to China. She would go to Shanghai, or
anywhere else for that matter. She would live there with her husband

425

and with Sachie and, somewhere, at some time or other, she would die, and it would probably be a wretched death. But at least she would never die in a place that was connected in any way at all with the name of Nire. She vowed she would never do that. On her back she could feel her child, who had woken and was stirring restlessly.

The affairs of Tatsuji Zaosan remained as doom-laden as ever. Ever since the "Incident" the world of Sumo had become even more popular and prosperous, for it was regarded as a sport that was part and parcel of the country's traditional way of life. But the monster of incomparable size hardly shared in any of this because his injured knees and back refused to get better; he kept missing contests, and when he did manage to appear in the ring the results were less than indifferent. Consequently, he dropped down into the preliminary third division, while people who had once waited on him in his great days were now right at the top, true giants of the Sumo world. His popularity remained in the sense that he still attracted plenty of attention, but only as a freak whom people observed with contemptuous amusement.

When it had looked as if he might make it to the top of the Sumo ladder, he had been royally treated by his manager, and when he arrived back late at night, perhaps after drinking with some fans of his, the manager's wife herself would come rushing to let him in even if it was long after the doors were locked. How different it was now. Everyone looked at him as if he was mad not to retire after falling so low, and all he seemed to hear nowadays was people telling him he really ought to call it a day and asking him what it was like to have a heart and head both made of concrete.

That summer, however, he made one of his rare appearances in the ring. Although most people at the Nire Hospital found him preposterously comic, Oshu was comparatively sympathetic, and it was before Oshu that Tatsuji had awkwardly bowed low and asked to be given one last chance to fight. Consequently, a number of people from the hospital went along to watch him, and even Tetsukichi made one of his rare appearances in support of the man mountain.

Since Zaosan was so low in the ranking he appeared very early on in the morning, around half past ten or eleven o'clock. At that time of day, the Sumo contests were very simple affairs, each having to be completed within five minutes. There was no ritual salt throwing or drinking of water. The boxes on the ground floor were almost all empty, though the popular seats near the roof were already packed. At last Zaosan appeared before the nervous gaze of Oshu and Yasusaburo and to the roars of the distant mob. His opponent was some emaciated apology for a wrestler, yet even this shrimp had no trouble at all in gradually easing Zaosan out of the ring. One could hardly bear to look. It was so pathetic one couldn't feel angry with him.

Since the suggestion had already been made by his manager, Oshu and Tetsukichi, and other zealous members of the Zaosan Supporters Club, arranged that he should retire and be made a senior wrestler, which would put him on the "managerial side" of things. This "managerial side" in fact meant he collected tickets at the door, and was thus obliged to endure the insolent stares, the pointing fingers and snide comments of anyone and everyone, adults and children. One can well imagine how humiliating this must have been for him, for ever since he had been taken up by Kiichiro his main aim in life had been to avoid appearing before people and revealing the monstrous body with which he had been cursed by who knows what strange karma.

He still paid occasional visits to Matsubara. Sometimes he even came to the house at Aoyama, where he would spend most of the day sitting in the garden, attending to his two hundred potted azaleas. After Kiichiro's death, he had ceased to receive the sort of warm attention he had once been given by the Nire household, but there were houses where he was always given kind and courteous treatment: a doctor's in Hamacho, and a noodle shop in Senju. The son of the noodle shop proprietor suffered from polio and was unable to stand up. One day when Tatsuji was playing with this child, he picked him up in one huge hand rather as if he were holding a large fan, and muttered to himself through unpleasantly fat lips: "If only I'd been a doctor."

In the same year, 1938, another man's dreams and enduring hopes were finally realized, for the fiftieth anniversary of the hospital was celebrated in style grandiose enough to suit the Deputy. It is true that some complained that there might be a suspicion of trickery involved in tacking on those fifteen years of the clinic in Hongo before the hospital was actually built, but the Deputy remained adamant on this question of principle. In previous years the opening of the hospital had been celebrated on the 14th of December with the great Prize-Giving Ceremony, but the Deputy proposed that this date should be changed to the 18th of June, the day of the official opening of the main hospital at Matsubara, and this was accepted. One reason for this change of date was that Hidekichi Katsumata simply could not bear to wait until winter, and another was that you couldn't hold a large open-air sports meeting, which is what the Deputy wanted to do, in December, owing to the inclement weather.

Once the thirteenth anniversary of Kiichiro's death had been safely observed at the Tokyo Hall in April before a number of invited guests, the Deputy launched himself into the preparations for the fiftieth anniversary celebrations with unparalleled zest. The principal members of the House of Nire showed no particular interest, but seemed to find the enthusiasm of the Deputy irresistible to the extent that they agreed to everything he said, giving the impression that the Nire Hospital of Mental Pathology belonged less to the Nire family than to the Deputy.

Nevertheless, the Deputy's ideas on most matters were those that had been handed down to him by the example of Kiichiro, even if they sometimes surpassed his in absurdity, and it was this conformity to a grand tradition that gave him such confidence in the soundness of his own judgment. He was aware that they were now facing a new chapter in the history of the hospital, a second golden age in which the Nire Hospital would be, as indeed it now was, the kingpin of private mental institutions. As he sat facing his desk with its many stamps, among which was, of course, his own "Deputy Director of the Main Nire Hospital of Mental Pathology," Hidekichi Katsumata contemplated what could be done to make this signal fact clear. The glory of the past was beyond recall. The former hospital had possessed grandeur and dignity; it had had style. It had had seven towers and dozens of Corinthian-type columns. Clearly that could not be emulated. But in terms of the number of patients, the old hospital had been surpassed by the hospital at Matsubara alone. The Aoyama branch was, of course, a complete mess, but the hospital at Matsubara, which happened to have been entrusted to the care of his unworthy self, though no imposing edifice, was superior to the old hospital in terms of its size and amenities. There were tennis courts, a large sports ground, a lake full of carp, a farm, a chicken house (which also contained turkeys) and even a pigsty. This was all owing to Dr. Kiichiro's foresight in acquiring so much land. The Deputy glanced up at the photograph of the former Director on the wall, a photo dominated by that Kaiser moustache whose waxed and upturned ends would always maintain their proper station in life and never droop.

"Carp, chicken, turkey, pig," the Deputy muttered meaninglessly

428

to himself, adding cryptically: "A turkey would be no good."

Turkeys were obstinate, ill-tempered birds. If children or people they weren't used to came near, they would ruffle up their tail feathers and go for them. Why, only the other day, he himself had been strolling casually about when he had suffered such an attack. The Deputy had, of course, a crane-like style of walking, but he had been obliged before the eyes of Yonekuni's hired hands to flee for his life in the manner of an ostrich, resulting in a considerable loss of face.

"Now a pig could be used," he muttered again.

Having reached this decision, whatever it might be, the Deputy rested his head in the palms of his hands and thought long and seriously about the question of the resuscitated Prize-Giving Ceremony. The selection of prizes would be left, naturally, to the grande dame, Hisa, but some plan was still required if the dignity and style of the old ceremony were to be restored. Tetsukichi wouldn't do—one couldn't even entrust him with the simple task of handing over New Year envelopes to the staff and expect him to do it in anything like a satisfactory way. Obviously one would have to persuade Oshu to take over the role of giving out prizes. . .

Now, there was nothing particularly rare or novel about any of the things the Deputy was planning, since he was not blessed with even a hint of the creative imagination. He intended to revive the Prize-Giving Ceremony, and he wanted to have entertainments extending over three days, although these would only be an extension or inflation of the lesser concert parties they already held from time to time. He would make use of professional artists, and give all the volunteers from among the staff and patients the opportunity to perform. He also wanted the annual sports day to be on a much larger scale than before, so . . . he would ask people from the neighborhood to take part, or at least come and watch. This last idea came in a sudden flash of inspiration, and he burst out of his office at unparalleled speed and seized hold of one of the young clerks:

"Look, I'm thinking of having leaflets announcing the sports meeting distributed in the neighborhood, so I want you to find a suitable printer."

"Distributed in the neighborhood? Isn't that a bit strange, inviting people to a sports meeting at a mental hospital?"

"Let me assure you I am perfectly serious," retorted the Deputy, rimless specs aglitter and chest puffed out. "Where the Nire Hospital is concerned we consider ourselves an integral part of the community.

You, of course, will not know about this, but in the old days at Aoyama—this was when Dr. Kiichiro had just returned from America—we threw a huge garden party in the next-door field. Scores of carriages lined up; Sumo wrestlers in their dozens; so many casual onlookers from the neighborhood that we put on a procession of floats for them. A procession of floats! That was the sort of thing that happened when the Director of the Nire Hospital came back from America. It was a grand local event. Now, I realize times have changed. We can't expect horse-drawn carriages and we can't send horse-drawn floats around the town to advertise ourselves as we most certainly did then. No. But we can distribute leaflets, and this is what I mean when I say I am serious, I am in deadly earnest. After all, it's excellent publicity for the hospital. We shall also need considerable numbers of balloons. I wonder how much they cost? Then there's the question of bunting; the flags of all nations, of course; bunting. Shouldn't cost much, that sort of thing.''

But as he folded his arms and pondered the matter, there still seemed to be something lacking. Some centerpiece was missing, something that would hold the whole thing together, something that would add further glory to the hospital's tradition. After days of racking his brain, some semblance of creative genius began to work in him. He hit upon the following ideas: the hospital would have a special hospital flag, and it would also have a special hospital song. But this turned out to be easier said than done, for despite the mobilization of all the intellectual resources of the hospital, an appropriate design for the hospital flag was not forthcoming. The Deputy had been hoping for something on the grand scale, resembling the exciting national flags of those two allies of theirs, Germany and Italy, perhaps, but all that was achieved—it seemed inevitably—was a plain blue flag with ''Nire Hospital'' dyed on it in white. The words ''of Mental Pathology'' had been left out because it was claimed they would create an illegible huddle of script. The Deputy was certainly none too happy about that, though he tried to keep his dissatisfactions to himself.

Since something as simple as a flag had produced problems of this order, it seemed most unlikely that the creation of a hospital song would meet with any success. Somebody had to write some appropriate words; these would then have to be entrusted to a composer; and the resulting composition would have to be learned by all the staff and patients before the actual day of the celebrations. It seemed a hopelessly tall order.

While the Deputy was clasping his head in despair over this, his problem came to the ears of one of the patients. This was a fifty-year-old man called Yashiro, who happened to be a composer. Nobody had any idea what kind of music he composed, but there was no doubt at all that he was a musician. He was a manic patient, which is a very noisy way of being ill, marked by an inexhaustible and overweening self-confidence, and an extraordinary exaltation of the spirit. This was Yashiro's third spell in the hospital. On the previous two occasions he had recovered within two months and been discharged (or had discharged himself), but within a year it had all started again. He would begin spending money in a wild way and cause distress of various kinds to his friends, so that his relations were obliged to drag him forcibly back to the Nire Hospital again.

On this third occasion he had strutted and swaggered into the hospital, treating the nurses as idiots and the doctors as his minions, and when he was eventually locked away he had made speeches and sung at the top of his remarkably deep and sonorous voice, upsetting everybody in his immediate vicinity. But within a month he had improved considerably and was allowed into one of the general wards, although he was still by no means normal, retaining a bumptious, unstable attitude toward life which, so long as it persisted, meant that he was not prepared to organize his day in accordance with the directives of others. Since this was his third visit here, he had a pretty good grasp of what was going on. He made his own observations of the illnesses of other patients and prided himself on his ability to name the complaints from which others were suffering. On top of this, he was in the habit of leaving his ward without permission, wandering outside, entering the hospital building again through the main entrance, relaxing in one of the waiting-room armchairs or going into the office without a by-your-leave and chatting there for a while, or peering in through the pharmacy window. Obviously, he could not be allowed to get away with this kind of behavior, but when he was threatened with being locked up if he did anything unauthorized again, he calmly replied:

"If you do that I'll only start going off my head again. In that case you'd be deliberately making me worse, wouldn't you? Funny sort of way to treat a patient, I must say. Do you really think that's the right way to run a hospital?"

What caused the most trouble was the habit he had of cornering outpatients, and sometimes the people who had merely brought them, and telling them what was wrong with them.

"Would you like me to inform you what's wrong with you? Well, you're schizophrenic, that's what you are. *Dementia praecox* and no doubt about it."

Or he would say, "I imagine you suffer from epileptic fits? No use trying to hide it from me, because I'm manic myself, you see."

Thus this man who was only half-cured, if cured at all, heard about the problem of the hospital song and promptly said he would compose one. He then pushed his way self-invited into the Deputy's office. At first the Deputy viewed the idea with skeptical distaste, but after thirty minutes he began to show a genuine enthusiasm for the project, and somewhat revised his view of manic patients in general and this one in particular. Finally he agreed to what Yashiro suggested. Perhaps he had recognized some kind of kindred spirit in this excitable person. Yashiro also knew how to play his cards right. He praised the hospital, insisting that although he was now perfectly cured, he liked it here so much—except for that organ in the recreation room, which was a load of cheap rubbish—that he intended to stay for another six months or so. He went on to say that if a hospital song was required he would be only too happy to compose one, and nodded curtly in agreement with his own suggestion.

"Well, you know, I must say, look here," replied the Deputy, still feeling a bit doubtful about the business. "I mean, can you, I mean you, Mr. Yashiro, really compose this for us?"

"Leave it to me. Just leave it to me, Mr. Deputy. If you don't like it when you see it, then you don't have to use it, do you? Always assuming that you possess the critical ability for judgments of that sort."

The result was that the Deputy dashed off to see the doctor in charge of Yashiro's case, to ask him if Yashiro really was a composer. He was told that the man was indeed a composer.

So Yashiro went back to his room and set to work, giving his fertile fancy free play, and after a quarter of an hour he had produced three four-line stanzas. He composed an appropriate melody for them in the next ten minutes, and set off to see the Deputy again, whistling his new composition as he went. The Deputy was astounded by the speed at which this had been done, and felt extremely suspicious. But as soon as he actually read the words he was pleased to find that, in terms of his own unreliable taste at least, they were not at all bad.

> Far from the city's madding roar,
> Far away from its strife,

> Treading these lawns of brilliant green,
> We lead our simple life.

That was how it started, and although the Deputy was happy about that "brilliant green" because it was so gross an exaggeration of reality it had to be poetical and romantic, he hesitated over the opening statement that the hospital was far from the city. Setagaya might be a suburb, but it was still a genuine part of the city of Tokyo. He expressed these doubts to the composer, who shot out an immediate reply, having apparently recomposed the first two lines on the spot without giving any thought to the matter at all:

"In that case, then, what about: 'In Matsubara where the wind / Blows softly through the pines'? That should do, shouldn't it?"

The Deputy was struck by the lightning of this reply. The man must be a genius. His mind worked at phenomenal speed. After this Yashiro sang the song two or three times. So far as the Deputy could judge, the melody was perfect for mental patients, for it was very light and cheerful, and should help them relax and recover from stress. And he was pleased to join in, clapping his hands and jogging his jaw up and down in time with the rhythm.

Just to be on the safe side he went around showing the song to a few other people, but nobody had any particular objection. After all, Katsumata looked so pleased with it, his whole face wreathed in smiles. Who could possibly object?

At last the great day came, the opening of the fiftieth-anniversary celebrations. The Deputy's original plan that the entertainments should extend over three days had been modified a bit, for the Medical Department had complained it would do psychiatric patients no good to watch stunts and make-believe on three consecutive days. So the festivities were reduced to a mere two days, with the traditional, if slightly unexciting program of the Prize-Giving Ceremony and the entertainments on the first day, and the sports meet and staff party on the second.

The Deputy believed in no slow buildup, no gradual crescendo, but liked to start as he intended to carry on—with a bang. Early that day he proposed to get together, if not the whole staff at least all those who had nothing in particular to do, with both Oshu and Hisa also in attendance, and then, before the assembled throng, raise the new hospital flag slowly and solemnly on the iron pole on the roof, and all would see it fluttering proudly in the breeze. That, at least, was the idea, but the first thing he noticed on going outside that morning was that some overenthusiastic, officious person had already raised it some time ago. Moreover, it wasn't fluttering in the breeze at all, but just limply hanging there.

Even the resuscitated Prize-Giving Ceremony was not entirely to his satisfaction. Not that there was anything wrong with the way it had been organized, nor with its scale. The recreation room here was larger than the one in the old Aoyama hospital, and the number of full-time and part-time employees present compared very favorably with the past. In order to preserve some of the former old-world atmosphere, the master of the Seiundo had been called out of his long retirement, and he came wearing the frock coat that was still too large for his small frame, and read out the names in mellifluous tones that had not altered one iota.

"Isuke Matsubara, Esquire," sang out the voice, and old Isuke, one of the prizewinners from the branch hospital, stepped forward from the ranks. He proudly wore the *haori* and *hakama* he had received at the fifteenth anniversary twenty years ago, but the doubled-up posture old age had imposed on him, not to mention his hunch, made him a somewhat eccentric spectacle, particularly to the many members of the main hospital who had never seen anything like it before.

"Tatsusaburo Oishi, Esquire," the proprietor of the Seiundo called out with particular strength, still retaining his clarity of tone, and Oshu's wife, Chiyoko, who had been made to sit on a chair at the rear of the dais, felt she was going to die of embarrassment. What fate had ordained that she should sit here, listening to this tedious voice and having to watch this absurd spectacle?

But Seiundo pressed tirelessly on:

"Miss Tazuru Takarada."

This was the pug-faced nurse who had always kept up such a mad cackling for little reason in the Aoyama cookhouse, now much older and holding the post of chief nurse in the main hospital.

Each person left the ranks when called and sheepishly ascended the steps of the dais, where the Deputy waited, nodding gravely and taking the prize from the stand before him in the approved leisurely style. But the principal player in this drama was no longer present. Only the former Director was really made for this role, only Kiichiro could have puffed out his chest proudly and twiddled his curled moustache and handed over the prizes in that overweening manner as if his principal aim in life was to prolong the ceremony for as long as human ingenuity could manage. . . Instead, what had we in his place? Tetsukichi. With his hair gone totally gray now and his weary, stooping back. Tetsukichi, who took the prizes from the Deputy in a purely mechanical way and handed them over to the recipients with no dignity, no grace. The Deputy was forced to frown on a number of occasions as Kiichiro's sad loss was made more poignantly clear than ever, and his judgment of the hopelessness of Tetsukichi's case was reaffirmed.

That evening's concert party, however, was a great success. More than two hundred and fifty patients had been allowed to attend, and they packed the recreation room. They sat jammed together on the *tatami* floor and watched the proceedings with passionate interest, laughing and clapping without restraint. Before the professional entertainers came on, a few short sketches were performed by volunteers from among the staff and patients. The Deputy, also watching with great interest, was amazed at the skill and ability of these people. It was difficult to believe they were mental cases. But then the patients of the Nire Hospital were bound to be of a superior kind; and he nodded happily to himself at this astute perception.

Eventually, however, there was an unfortunate incident. One individual, a male patient, took the stage billed as a narrator of comic stories. Curiously, there was not one single remark he made that could possibly have raised a laugh. The packed rows of the audience responded to this by producing not even the suggestion of a titter or snicker, simply sitting there in glum, serious silence. This encouraged the self-styled humorist to new extremes of dullness: his tone became downright earnest, and, going well beyond the time allotted to him, he showed no signs of putting an end to his monotonous drone. Finally one of the male nurses was obliged to go up onto the stage and drag him off it, making attempts to placate the man as he did so.

But the high spot of the festivities, the performance that attracted the greatest and most deserved attention during these fiftieth-anniversary celebrations, which had, let it be admitted, no real focal point, was given by the Deputy, Hidekichi Katsumata himself. This took place on the following day, a Sunday. The leaflets distributed around the neighborhood seemed to have had some effect, for a number of the local children had been drifting in through the hospital gates since morning. At the gate they received a small container of Asahi Candy (as efficacious for the cough as rice for the empty stomach), which had started appearing recently in the shape of "drops" rather than the large lumps of old. The children, with some of these stuffed in their mouths and holding a free balloon, made their way to the sports ground and were soon running their own races outside the roped-off enclosure. There were also a number of adults, either accompanying the children or just there out of curiosity. These people added to the festive atmosphere already created by the excessive amount of paper bunting all over the place, and by letting off the odd firework.

Then, at a nicely timed moment, the figure of the Deputy appeared, walking toward the band, a motley collection of ten instrumentalists who were waiting alongside the VIP seating. A rostrum had been set up here and the Deputy, dressed smartly in frock coat and a dazzling high collar, made a beeline for it, mounted it, and stood erect, his minute body stretched to its highest extent. Then he assumed a very strained posture and raised his right hand above his head, a hand that trembled with the pent-up emotion of years. And in this hand he held a thin black stick.

The stick was a conductor's baton. As might easily be guessed, he was about to conduct the piece of music that would serve as a prelude to the games. If pressed, he would have had to admit that this activity, for which he was totally unsuited, had not been a part of his calculations, nor even of his wildest dreams, but the excitement of the anniversary celebrations had produced an abnormal zeal in him, and a half-joking suggestion from one of his office staff had done the trick; for a gap existed that someone had to fill.

The sole perpetrator of this ensuing composition, the manic Yashiro, was no longer a patient in the hospital. Despite the fact that he had announced, in the Deputy's presence, that he intended to stay for another six months, the composer of the hospital song, author of both words and music in twenty-five minutes of free associational activity, had taken it into his head to pick up the telephone one day and call his relatives, then call a chauffeur-driven limousine and drive away in it, ignoring his doctor's remonstrations that he should remain under treatment for another month. He had, however, left his scribbled piece of music behind. There was no one in the hospital who could read music, so they had to call in a music teacher from the nearby primary school to play the organ, while such members of staff as could be spared from their duties and the less serious cases among the patients practiced singing the song in chorus. It was all very much like a singing class at school, although the music presented unique problems of its own. It was in the key of F and in quadruple time. But its brisk, cheerful banality was, unhappily, not maintained throughout, for the final refrain showed a sudden change of key to D Flat Major. Presumably the composer had experienced some kind of sportive impulse just at the point where he would have been better advised to let the work run on to its banal, foregone conclusion. This abrupt switch of key made the passage extremely difficult, not to say impossible, to sing. With the anniversary so near, people could not spend all their time in singing practice, and there were doubts as to how well the vigorous unison at the beginning of the work could be handled, that point where the voices blended in powerfully with the instruments. Given the problems of the final refrain, it was natural that there should have been a sense of misgiving about the whole project.

So the Deputy, since it had been his idea to have the song, was now obliged, despite his total ignorance of music, to stand on a rostrum before a ten-piece orchestra with a baton in his hand. Behind his rimless spectacles the eyelids of his tiny eyes were trembling, and his normally pale face was now a livid hue. Perhaps the neurotic faintheartedness that had plagued him as a young man in the grip of examination phobia had chosen this moment to return. But he stretched himself up on tiptoe, straightened his back in a show of determination, and brought down the baton with a desperate flourish. Obligingly the band, little more than a group of glorified buskers, struck up, producing a splendid cacophony that clearly gave the Deputy fresh heart, for he waved vigorously away, mechanically reproducing the gestures that had been drilled into him the day before. His half-closed eyes and jerky movements gave the impression of a person who was struggling for breath.

Once the brief introductory passage had been completed, the chorus was supposed to join in. This to some extent they did, but in a faltering, uncoordinated way that suggested a considerable lack of confidence:

> "In Matsubara where the wind
> Blows softly through the pines,
> Treading these lawns of brilliant green. . ."

These opening lines were about as much as anyone could make out. Some of the singers couldn't remember the rest of the words, some couldn't follow the melody, some had become bored with what they were doing; most were merely going through the motions of singing, opening and shutting their mouths in an embarrassed way. The grand chorus of voices the Deputy had expected to echo through the sports ground thus failed to materialize, and the singing began to tail off, becoming fainter and fainter. By the time they reached the second stanza nobody was singing at all.

The Deputy was so passionately involved in his task that he was unaware of what was happening. His doubts and hesitations had been limited to the moments before he began to flourish his baton. But now the veil of his soul's temple had been rent asunder and he was in thrall to the melodious boom of the trombone, the high-pitched clarinet's rise and fall, and the brave rattle and clang of drums and cymbals. Thrusting out his chest, he continued to conduct, waving his baton with might and main.

"What a mess!" one astonished spectator was heard to say. And his neighbor complained about the opening lines, maintaining that there weren't any pine trees in Matsubara despite its name (for Matsubara means "pine field"). The only trees in the area were oaks. The remarks were no doubt reasonable, but vulgarly outspoken on an occasion like this.

Despite the amazement he was arousing in his audience, the Deputy remained exalted, above the throng in spirit, solitary, completely involved in his unequal struggle. The way he handled the baton was more reminiscent of gymnastic than musical accomplishment, and as the piece proceeded this became more marked, for his arms worked faster and faster, until he had left the orchestra way behind. Finally the hectic motions of his arms ceased to have even a marginal connection with the music, but by then, of course, no one in the band was paying the least attention anyway.

Then suddenly the music stopped. It stopped because the piece had come to an end. The Deputy, still conducting, eventually became aware of this, lowered his arms, and wiped the sweat from his brow. Immediately a number of fireworks were set off, bringing a more cheerful air to the proceedings, and the band broke unaided into the *Patriotic March*. Sports day had officially begun. It was like most sports days, before or since: a number of contests whose banality didn't prevent grown men from getting excited about them. There were obstacle races in which one was burdened with a crude costume made of plaster of Paris and staggered awkwardly around the track, attempting to eat buns dangling from strings or trying to pick mudloaches out of tubs of slime as they squirmed away through one's fingers. . .

One sign of the times was that many of these contests were so labeled as to suggest the irresistible Imperial Army wreaking death and destruction upon the immoral, plundering Chinese forces; but the contests themselves were quite innocent in character, unrelated to the bloodthirsty events they were supposed to mimic.

Among the crowds of people absorbed in these childish pastimes were Aiko and Shuji from Aoyama, and Satoru from Matsubara. Since they were hospital children, they took advantage of their privileged position and participated in nearly every race and contest, yet none of them won a first prize, not even the fleet-footed Satoru. The reason for this was that the majority of people taking part in the obstacle races were, in some way or other, queer in the head, and although some of them showed a consideration for the children and slowed down accordingly, most seemed to be incited by their presence into pushing them out of the way and zooming off toward the tape, teeth clenched in a fierce determination to win.

There was a tug-of-war that went on inconclusively for ages; an inter-ward competition that involved throwing a lot of little balls into a large basket; an egg-and-spoon race open to all comers; and then the *pièce de résistance,* the "Pig-Catching Contest." This was the Deputy's brainchild. It consisted in letting one of Yonekuni's piglets loose in an arena, and offering a prize of Fourth-Issue China Incident Bonds to the person who caught it. An announcement was made and the piglet was released. A pack of bloodthirsty, howling patients then set off in pursuit. They ran fast, but the piglet ran faster. Who could have imagined that a piglet could run so fast? But even this Mercury of a piglet was bound to be caught in the end, disappearing in a scrum of patients that made it impossible to decide who had captured it.

Finally the setting sun bathed the sports ground in its long rays, and the noise and the people seemed to vanish away. All that remained were the dangling lines of bunting, and here and there an empty container of Asahi Candy or some paper wrapping thrown away by a child. The fiftieth-anniversary celebrations were coming to an end.

The staff party in the recreation room had gone on noisily until late at night. Oshu had put in a brief appearance, and the Deputy had put in a much longer one even though he never touched a drop of alcohol. Some of the doctors had also turned up, but now only six or seven male nursing staff and pharmacists remained. The one drinking with the most confidence was the Pockmarked Bear, Kumagoro Sakuma, most of whose pimples and eruptions had now disappeared from his face, although when he drank the scars they had left showed indistinctly through the general redness.

"Next after Hsuchow will be Hankow. Hankow will be next. . ." he said importantly, glaring about him with drowsy eyes in an obvious attempt to cow his companions into agreement. "Then Chiang Kai-shek will surrender. But that won't be the end of it. There's still the Soviet Union; there's still Britain and America. We've got to beat them all. . ."

"Because Chiang Kai-shek's no longer the real problem any more," added a young pharmacist in properly sycophantic tones.

"That's it. The real enemy is America. Just recently they got together ten million dollars in subscriptions for China. Had a few dance parties, raised a cool ten million. Ten million dollars, that's quite a sum. Let me tell you, gentlemen, it's nothing to be sneezed at. Ten million dollars, well. . ."

Kumagoro still had no real employment in the hospital, but that didn't prevent him behaving with an air of assurance, even arrogance. He was as sly as they come, and those who had recently been taken on the staff were well advised to pay him a certain amount of attention. He was forty-two years old, an age at which one can finally be considered grown-up, and was genuinely proud of this fact. Three years ago he had married one of the nurses, a late marriage for both of them, and they lived in one of the hospital houses.

He had ordered one of the youngest male nurses to go around all the tables a little earlier and bring back whatever remained of any value, which principally meant all the remnants of alcohol; and now, after a few more drinks, his eyes had glazed over and his drunken mutterings were only just intelligible.

"The trouble with you lot is, all you do is complain. Moan about everything. So you don't find the work here interesting? All right. But it takes more than a year or two to work out what's going on . . . what's going on in a mental hospital, I'll tell you that. Takes more than that. Look at me. Just look at me. I've been in the Nire Hospital twenty-three years. Came in the spring of 1917. When they had the fifteenth anniversary . . . but you wouldn't know anything about that. No idea what the old hospital was like. There's no one left in this place who knew the hospital then. They've all gone; all of them; all the old crowd. . . Anyway, the old Director, he had his eye on me, I can tell you. He noticed me. He saw me standing there in the corridor, and

'Well done,' he said, 'well done.' I was a bit of a reformist at the time, though. Took it on myself to bring about reforms. Only had to say one word and you soon saw an improvement in the cookhouse food. Still, staying twenty-five years in a place, you get used to it. You feel at home. At home, you know. I sometimes feel like I was born in this hospital, like one of the family. When the Deputy dies they'll make me the next Deputy. The creep talks in a funny way too, all through the tip of his stinking nose. . .''

"How about another drink, Mr. Sakuma?"

"Sakuma? My name's not Sakuma. I'm Kumagoro Nire. Still, mustn't drink too much. Get the piles if I do. Anyway, gentlemen, from today I assume the surname of Nire. That will make Yonekuni my brother for a start. When you've been somewhere twenty-five years it's the least you can expect. Sort of thing that's bound to happen. Like me becoming Deputy. I like it here. I like this hospital and I'm going to become Deputy someday. This present creep is trying to sneak his own son into the office here. Means to train him up for the job. Won't work, though. Won't be allowed. Shouldn't be, anyway. It's not a bad place, this. It's all right here. Feel at home. Been here twenty-three years. You lot wouldn't know about that. . .''

No doubt Kumagoro did feel at home in the hospital. It would have been strange if he hadn't. All he did was wander after Yonekuni around the chicken coop and the farm, never once doing a stroke of work on his own accord, and after this one supervisory doing of the rounds was over he occupied the rest of his day as he pleased. He would spend the whole time playing tennis if he felt like it.

His intoxication seemed to have got worse.

"The enemy's destroyed the banks of the Yellow River. Well, they're giving it a go, I'll say that. Can't think what you lot are doing sitting about here. Ought to have enlisted. Ought to be out there, not just idling about. The kids are fighting out there, you know. 'Father and I, both warriors bold. . .' How does it go?. . . At least get out to Manchuria. Go to Mongolia. In the old days, when I was young, I had my ambitions. I thirsted for glory. Bit different from you lot. Totally different attitude toward life. Toward society as well. I don't want to make a big deal of this, but I tried to reform society. I felt I had something to contribute. All right, perhaps I was wrong. But before that I had been right. I understood the path the good old country must take. . . 'Having completed beforehand their BLANK BLANK at BLANK, now regrouped in BLANK BLANK BLANK of BLANK, rendezvousing at BLANK, and the imperial warships BLANK, BLANK, BLANK and BLANK. . .' You don't have a clue what that means, do you? Not a clue. That's why I say the young people nowadays are hopeless, just plain useless. . . 'Father and I, both warriors bold' . . . 'raised anchor at BLANK and set off majestically in line-ahead formation for BLANK. . .' That's how it went. Ten million dollars. It's a disgrace. Won't get away with it, ten million dollars. . .''

The squat, podgy frame of Kumagoro Sakuma slumped forward and collapsed. His eyes had closed and his square red face with its even redder pockmarks and pimple scars was ready for sleep. He was apparently quite happy to drop off where he was.

''Mr. Sakuma. Mr. Sakuma,'' one of his companions called, shaking him by the shoulder.

Kumagoro opened his eyes a fraction and answered in a sleepy, irritated and pompous voice:

''Nire. Kumagoro Nire, that's my name.''

Chapter

8

Tetsukichi's work was approaching its final stages. Already the first volume of this long, daunting *History of Psychiatric Medicine,* from the Graeco-Roman period to the eighteenth century, had been published, and the galley proofs for the second volume, covering the period from the French school of Pinel and Esquirol to the German school of the first half of the nineteenth century, had started to appear. It was being brought out by a small publishing house that specialized in medical books, and since one of the clauses of his contract was that no royalties should be paid on the first edition, and the book had required a great number of illustrations, charts and diagrams, he had been obliged to pay a certain amount of money out of his own pocket toward the cost of publication. As an appendix to this massive work, he had published, toward the end of last year and from the same publishing house, a much slighter work in paper covers, 230 pages in length. This was his *Introduction to the History of Psychiatric Medicine in Japan,* the projected work that had started him off on his laborious researches, and had been written during one summer vacation in Hakone.

At last he was entering a period toward which he felt a genuine commitment, the era of modern German psychiatry to which all Japanese psychiatrists inevitably looked for instruction. Here were any number of magnificent scholars with whose work Tetsukichi had been acquainted since his student days, and of whose relevance he was convinced. Among them were a number he knew by sight, and some he had even met in person.

In January of 1939 the Sumo Grand Champion, Futabayama, who had previously driven all opposition before him, was finally stopped on the day he was expected to record his seventieth consecutive victory. A new star, Akinoumi, managed to throw him by using a swift leg movement, and as the Grand Champion crashed onto his back the whole stadium, indeed the whole country, exploded into a babble of excitement. While this encounter and its repercussions were going on, Tetsukichi was reencountering one of the giants of modern psychiatry, Emil Kraepelin, whose achievement seemed so unshakable, his reputation so firmly established. This was the savant with the looks of a wandering samurai who had declined Tetsukichi's proffered hand, turned his back on him, and walked away.

He looked at a photograph of Kraepelin he had. The hair was thin and white, the eyebrows still black and the eyes piercing. The beard was sparse and straggling like an old-fashioned broom. As Tetsukichi looked at it, he felt all the humiliation of that terrible moment fifteen or sixteen years ago as vividly as if it had happened yesterday. He was surprised to find that he possessed such persistent feelings of hatred for this foreign scholar who had died some years ago. He had to laugh at himself, although he did this against his own bitter inclinations. He leaned his elbows on the desk among the scattered papers and books, closed his eyes, and tried to recall that period in his life when he had spent hours gazing through the lenses of a microscope. There were the jackdaws returning to the old gray cathedral in Vienna, the ice on the Danube and the harsh sound it made, like the rubbing of coarse cloth, and the old man in Munich who had ignored him, standing up immediately he had tried to sit down at the same table in that small cafe; or there was the simple, perpetually smiling face of the "Japanese granny" whom he would also never see again.

Then a clear image, undesired yet precise, of Kraepelin arose, black-suited, back toward him, disappearing through the exit of the lecture hall. Much clearer than that image was one of another person who was watching him go. That person was himself, standing transfixed, except for his clenched hands which were trembling. . . As he remembered, he felt his body going tense again, now, in this distant present, and he forced himself to produce a wry smile once again.

Besides being the most distinguished scholar of his day, Kraepelin was also well known as a devout prohibitionist. The anti-liquor campaign he had conducted energetically over so many years was obviously connected somewhere with his psychiatric studies, and also no doubt an expression of patriotic concern for the state of the nation. Unfortunately Munich was the center of the brewing industry. No article Kraepelin wrote championing the prohibitionist cause was ever printed by any local paper; indeed the press had various nicknames for him, such as "the teetotal professor" or "leader of the lemonade faction." And these must have had some effect, for Tetsukichi had heard students in one of the beer halls singing as they waved huge three-liter mugs in their fists, "*O Kraepelin! O Kraepelin! Wo gehst du mit dem Wasser hin?*" ("Oh Kraepelin! Oh Kraepelin! Where are you going with that water, eh?")

He also remembered a satirical cartoon he had seen in one of the magazines. There was a modern German poet who had written a number of imperishable masterpieces. However, Germany had been defeated, a revolution had taken place, and the exchange rate kept on falling. This poet, despite his being the greatest genius since Goethe, had finally starved to death. His corpse was dissected and the brain sent off to the psychiatric department, where the director was so delighted to receive this famous brain he danced with joy and inadvertently drank down a whole glass of red wine, the first time he had ever done so in his life.

It was now past midnight and Tetsukichi could feel a cold draft of air from somewhere; so he leaned over the *hibachi* in which most of the charcoal had burned down into ash, cupped his hands over the remaining warmth, and half hummed to himself the words he had heard those foreign students sing more than fifteen years ago.

"*O Kraepelin! O Kraepelin!*
Wo gehst du mit dem Wasser hin?"

But the expected sensation of release, of amused, smiling relaxation did not come. He felt, rather, a strong and irritating sense of pathos. Where had the great man gone? He had left his achievement behind him, and then where? And what of himself, on this small, unimportant island in the eastern seas? What was the small, insignificant Tetsukichi doing, exhausted, struggling on, nervous and apprehensive, creating something of his own that he hoped would remain after he had gone?

There had been a period when modern psychiatry had seemed in danger of losing itself in an enormous, inflated and verbose system of classification, reaching a nadir in the mid-nineteenth century when Heinroth had proposed that Plater's classification of twenty-three illnesses should be increased to forty-eight. Kraepelin's real achievement had been to refuse to be seduced into classifying an illness merely in accordance with the symptoms it showed, but to concentrate instead on the whole syndrome of the illness as it developed and changed. Kraepelin hated the word "philosophy," and asserted that Daquin and Pinel had been philosophical in their attitudes (although it should be borne in mind that the term "natural philosophy" at the time meant something more like "biology"). He contrasted their approach with what he called his own "natural science mentality." In the second edition of the standard work in which he first gave expression to his ideas, the *Kompendium der Psychiatrie,* Kraepelin divided mental illnesses into two basic types, those brought about by external causes and so capable of cure, and those that resulted from inner causes and were incurable. He showed that in any group of patients some would recover quite naturally, while others would merely deteriorate, with no suggestion of improvement. Diagnosis should depend on prognosis, the validity of a diagnosis being determined by the course the illness took. This clear-cut view of the matter was, no doubt, a simplification that ignored any number of individual differences, but it had the virtue of conferring uniformity and clarity where before there had only been confusion, and possessed all the persuasive power of a system that held together from beginning to end.

The fifth edition, published in 1896 and attaining a length of 825 pages, presented his system in virtually complete form; but in the sixth edition of 1899 an illness called "manic-depressive psychosis" made its first appearance. His classification of mental illness into two large groups was now under the major headings of *dementia praecox* and manic-depressive psychoses. From then on he made a series of gradual emendations of his system, aiming at greater soundness and clarity, until by the time of the ninth edition in 1927 the work was in two volumes and ran to 2500 pages. This edition appeared in the year after his death, jointly edited by J. Lange.

There were more than a few voices raised in opposition to Kraepelin's theory of diagnosis. With regard to the question of *dementia praecox,* Pappenheim, Ernst Meyer, Korsakov and others were in strong disagreement, and it was pointed out that about thirteen percent of such patients do in fact completely recover. As for Kraepelin's treatment of manic-depressive psychosis, Mendel and Kahlbaum indicated that there were contradictions in the concept itself. Even so, the basic distinction between the two kinds of psychic illness was incorporated in most of the textbooks and eventually took on a classic status.

During his reading, Tetsukichi came to realize that Kraepelin's theories were not the completely independent creation he had once assumed them to be. The term "*dementia praecox*" had already been used as early as 1860 by the Frenchman Morel. Gauthier, Saury and Legrain had also made use of it. The concept of manic-depression had been put forward by Falret, Baillager and Kahlbaum before Kraepelin had taken it up. It became apparent that Kraepelin's work was an amalgam of a century of research done in both France and Germany, a natural outcome of the knowledge that had been gained over that period. It was as if an intellectual giant had been required to impose form on all this knowledge, a man who possessed tremendous will and aimed at the creation of a total system out of the mass of data and individual case histories.

But, once completed, the system became a formal ruin, a blind alley from which the brilliant minds that succeeded him were fated to try to escape. In particular Eugen Bleuler revised the whole concept of *dementia praecox* and renamed it "schizophrenia." Another critic of Kraepelin's, Ernst Kretschmer in his *Konstitution und Charakter,* developed and extended his conclusions in a manner that Kraepelin could not have foreseen.

Even a limited field of human activity such as psychiatric history can tell us about humanity, and give an account of the history of the human race. Here as elsewhere one finds a precise record of human intolerance and illusions, and also of human perseverance and struggle that verges, at times, on the heroic. From ancient times, society has constantly shown examples of people considered mentally abnormal, and whether we see abnormality as a complete aberration from normality or merely an exaggeration of it, these people still present us with a clear image of the human. The way a society responds to them is also a real reflection of that society; an extreme reflection, no doubt, but still a totally human one. Indeed, one thing that Tetsukichi particularly noticed was that when something that he could only call the "democratic spirit" (although he was not at all sure that "democratic" was the word he wanted) disappeared from a society, psychiatry inevitably entered another period of stagnation.

The contemplation and recording of such a history should naturally be linked to some critical awareness on the part of the researcher, and should stimulate and strengthen that awareness. But in Tetsukichi this process did not seem to take place; or if it did, only to a minimal extent. Certainly, he had read a great many books with scrupulous care, and was acquainted with various individual histories and cases. But the accumulation of knowledge seemed to add neither width nor depth to his understanding. In this, he was much like those scholars who had been so obsessed with their intricate classifications they had gradually estranged themselves from the problems that really mattered, their patients, and so finally from humanity itself. In Tetsukichi's case, this did not result in any objective distancing of himself from the object, allowing a cold, impartial scrutiny of it, but was more like an excessive adhesion, a clinging embrace that eventually suffocated the object and buried it under an accumulation of detail. The world he had so labored to produce, the world created from all the studious effort he had put into assembling these fragments of knowledge into a whole, was a world apart from any other, a world cut off, closed in. So it lacked any light or warmth, and seeds received no chance to bud and flower. For all its brilliance, it was a world that was ultimately barren.

Not that Tetsukichi would ever have seen it in such terms, not even in his worst dreams, for he was now proceeding at an ever quickening pace, occasionally abandoning his everyday duties to press on with his research. The book grew like a snowball rolling down an incline. He had a look at the work of Adolf Meyer, Karl Jaspers, Binswanger and Straus, but their ideas seemed too new, too raw for his psychiatric history; it would take some years before they could be fully assimilated, described and evaluated. And there was one body of research that would prove much more difficult to handle but could not be ignored: the work of Freud and his colleagues and disciples. Despite the fact that Sigmund Freud was clearly the most famous medical man of his age, in Germany his ideas had been subjected to vilification and ostracism for years. Since the medical world in Japan was little more than an offshoot of the one in Germany, the same applied here as well, and Tetsukichi too had never had the least inclination to take his psychoanalytic theories seriously. In 1930, however, Freud was awarded the Goethe Prize, which seemed to indicate some weakening of the hatred his theories had aroused, but Hitler's accession to power cast a shadow over the last years of his life. During the burning of the books in Berlin, Freud's writings were among the victims, and with the German takeover of Austria in 1938 he was driven out of Vienna, the city in which he had passed most of his life. Tetsukichi knew that Freud was now living in London, but he had no sympathy with his theories and gave them only a very rough, general treatment in his history, unaware that this undoubtedly great man would be dead within a few months.

Sometimes Tetsukichi would take a rest from his work and go for a walk, usually as far as the Meiji Shrine. He had seen how eager his German teachers had been to make use of their legs and to take proper exercise, and he appeared to have picked up their habits without really knowing he was doing so. One day, the tree-lined avenue leading to the shrine seemed suddenly alive with fresh, green leaves. He bowed his head before the outer shrine and prayed for the successful completion of his work and good fortune for the Imperial Army. He then passed through the shrine and out onto the road at the back, where he sat down on a bench for a long while. The color of the new leaves seemed to sink into his eyes, so he half closed them and thought about his work, which was finally approaching its conclusion. At times, almost unbearable surges of excitement came over him, and at times waves of vague sleepiness. He had been working for ten years now and he was satisfied with himself and what he had done. He had done it as well as he was able. When he had been much younger, he had dreamed of such work as being special and unique, the product of strange workings of the mind, created under conditions of passionate solitude in a realm far removed from the everyday world and its spiritually debilitating problems. But now he could see that his work was simply an aspect of the trivial everyday, or at least no more than the accumulation each ordinary day had left behind. The energy he used when doing it was no different from the kind he used in other aspects of his daily life: when eating his three meals, or when he had quarreled with his wife, or when disillusion sometimes overcame him at the thought of how distant his children had become. It was no more than his response to any other occurrence of the day that caused him anxiety and concern. So it aroused no sense of something taking shape, of something cold and pure and hard within him. But neither did it give a feeling of emptiness and nothingness. His work was no more than an expression of the obstinate determination of a man who was, in the end, ordinary and commonplace, as ordinary and commonplace as his life had been.

A fly settled on his knee, moved around a little, flew away, and then returned and settled there again. He did not try to brush it away but watched it until it flew off of its own accord. Then he stood up and took the road back home, hearing the gravel crunching beneath his shoes. When he reached the main road, he saw that a group of girl students were sweeping the gravel approach to the shrine. They were volunteers, and their young, almost childish figures made him feel his age, yet also a simple, unalloyed sense of gratitude that such young people should still exist and be willing to expend such energy on keeping the place clean.

He walked the mile or so to Shibuya and went into a small cinema that showed foreign and home newsreels. He did this quite often now.

The conflict in China had reached a stage where it seemed it would go on forever, and new fighting had broken out in Nomonhan. The foreign news consisted of a Paramount newsreel showing the grim concrete fortresses of the endless miles of the Maginot Line. A hole opened and a heavy piece of artillery poked its barrel through. Even so, the forests of short iron stakes in the tank traps below these gun emplacements were overgrown with grass, and the sentries walking about behind barbed wire seemed relaxed and at ease. Sheep could be seen grazing just a short distance away. Then the news showed the German Siegfried Line confronting this. Hitler had built this system of underground defenses, in no way inferior to the Maginot Line, in one year, using one-third of the country's civil engineering capability to do so. Both lines gave the impression of being unbreachable walls of steel, capable of absorbing any attack launched on them. Tetsukichi, however, who had once traveled by train across that border, could sense only crisis in the landscape now. It aroused no warm sense of the past in him, but only a peculiar and causeless elation, and he realized that he was betting on the Siegfried Line to win.

When he left the cinema, the blue-gray clouds were dazzling with the light of early summer, but the feeling of wartime austerity had grown stronger of late, as more and more men seemed to have shaved their heads, and charcoal-driven automobiles with that clumsy-looking contraption at the rear had appeared in the streets. He went down the slope to the river, standing awhile at one end of the bridge. He looked down at the black, polluted surface of the water and watched as a broken eggshell was carried toward him and away. Then he walked briskly toward the streetcar stop.

The great day came in the last week of June. His ten-year labor was at last ended. He had always known that this day would come sometime, that it would eventually approach and not seem to go on receding forever. But the work had lasted for so long that he had always found the thought of its ending uncanny; deep down inside he seemed unable to believe in it. Whenever he thought back over the road he had come, he would feel moving inside him the emotions and attitudes that had sustained him for so long, the sense of burden and strain, the exaltation and joy, an unpleasant yet proud complex of joy and sorrow that stirred and flowed within him. And yet what an awkward, uneasy sense of joy it was; and what a feeble sense of sorrow.

When he had first set out on this task, it was as if he had condemned himself to attempting to drink the ocean dry, so desperately impossible did it seem, with only defeat and failure awaiting him. But he had given himself over to it completely; moved forward, even if slowly, and while moving at his snail's pace he had arrived where he was now. There had been numerous times when he could no longer move forward, when he had lost heart, but those had alternated with days of exultation, with days when something real seemed to have been achieved. There had been endless obstacles as well, in particular that long-standing doubt as to whether the Director of the Nire Hospital should properly be engaged on an undertaking of this kind.

Then the end had drawn near, and he knew for certain that he was soon to be released from this long labor. But would it really end? And when it did, what kind of joy, what delirium would he taste? He had, of course, occasionally pondered this question during those long years, but the day had seemed so far off that the question had no immediacy, and he had dismissed his thoughts as profitless. But it was real enough now, for it was about to happen. The end was approaching and would come as inevitably as day turns into night, as one season fades into the next or as a new year starts again. It was just a step away, kept from him only by the thickness of a piece of paper.

He had felt heavy and dull since morning. For some days he had been afflicted with a head cold, a stuffiness in the nose rare at this time of year, and perhaps that was the reason. Perhaps it was tiredness from the day before, which had been a full schedule at the hospital, followed by a directors' meeting, and then by his own work, which he had pushed himself into continuing well past midnight. Today, as usual, he took up his accustomed position before his desk, with the pages he had written yesterday spread out before him. He looked hesitantly at his own round handwriting. It was precisely at this moment that what he had written always seemed particularly unreal and dead, the matter dry, pedantic, empty. He remained there like that for some time, feeling no particular desire to get down to work. His brain felt dull and leaden, his stuffy nose filled him with a depressed fatigue. He picked up at random one after another the books piled at his side, and flicked hurriedly through their pages. Finally he blew his nose a number of times, and although it had been completely bunged up until a few moments ago, it now deigned to discharge a certain amount of thin, watery mucus.

By lunchtime he had got into his stride at last, and had written a page and a half when he was told that the plain noodles he had ordered had arrived. He dashed downstairs so as to get this down quickly and then return to his work, but as he sat at the table his nose started running again, and he was only just able to stop it dripping into his food. This put him in a bad mood, and the impetus he had built up before lunch had completely gone by the time he went back upstairs again. He spent the afternoon sniffing and feeling generally depressed with the world and his own inability to handle it better. Just after four o'clock he lay down and slept until dinnertime.

When he got up, he was still not in particularly good shape, and began to feel he had better get used to the idea that this was going to be a wasted day. He went slowly downstairs and noticed that preparations for dinner had already been made in the living room, and they were having a rare treat of *sukiyaki* tonight. There was a plate piled high with beautifully fresh, paper-thin slices of beef, and as yet no sign of the children. He felt he would much prefer to eat his food quietly by himself than together with the children, so he lit the portable gas ring, put a lump of fat in the iron pan on top of it, adding vegetables and meat in just the way he liked. He broke a raw egg into his bowl and started helping himself to meat even though it was not quite cooked yet. Despite his head cold and general feeling of stuffiness, the meat tasted marvelous, and by the time Nanny Shimoda and the children turned up he had already disposed of half of it. He reminded himself that it would do him no good to overeat, so he did without his rice and went back upstairs again, leaving the table just as the children sat down.

Perhaps it was because he could still taste the sweetness of the meat on his tongue, but that evening his pen glided over the paper, gradually increasing speed until it was racing passionately ahead, filling up page after manuscript page. Just before midnight, he found that the number he had affixed to a fresh page was 3000. He felt a brief surge of emotion at the realization that his work would exceed 3000 pages, but he decided he would leave the rejoicing to later and get on with the task in hand.

At one in the morning he had reached page 3004, and then he called a halt. Tomorrow he would add a short account of what could be hoped for from more recently established methods of psychiatric therapy, intending to bring the work to a close without any general concluding remarks. Compared with other branches of medicine, psychiatry had been particularly late in starting and, in contrast with general medicine, even a basic standard as to what could be considered an illness was lacking. It was only now becoming a genuine branch of medicine and still clearly in a lengthy transitional stage, so that it would be unreasonable to forecast how it might develop in the future.

Anyway, he would certainly stop here for today. He was aware of his own physical exhaustion. There was a dull ache from his backbone right through his shoulders, and his eyes were tired and bleared. But there was still a portion of his brain that was alive, active, burning away, and this tempted him, despite his tiredness, to go on for a little longer, to do a few more pages. Out of sheer inertia, although half-dubious of what he was doing, he responded to that inviting voice.

At the beginning, his hand moved slowly, if at all; and then suddenly it began to race away at an almost suspicious speed, writing with such unaccustomed fluency that he felt almost positive it would turn out to be unusable when he read it through again. By two thirty in the morning he had forgotten all about his tiredness. The tingling sensation in his brain seemed to have numbed his senses, but his eyes had lost all their heaviness and were now bright and clear. He found he could write with a swift efficiency he had never imagined before, and as he finished each page he began to feel it would be as well, if not actually unavoidable now, to keep on right to the end. In the past he had always tried to avoid writing on through the night, since it usually turned out to be unproductive in the long run, but since he was rapidly approaching the end these objections ceased to have any relevance; so on he went.

At three forty he heard a cock crow. It was still dark outside, and the repetition of the sound he found annoying, even ominous. He kept on blowing his nose in what was now a wholly mechanical fashion, just as he kept on adding more pages to the pile. At last, when a whiteness was coming into the night sky, with a final sudden spurt the work was brought to an end. He placed the last period on the three thousand and fifteenth page, and because that page was still half-empty he wrote "The End" at the bottom, but then found that it seemed to make the page look unbalanced, so he crossed it out. His head seemed numb, his body sluggish; only his eyes remained eager and alive. Anyway, it was finished; it was over. He nodded to himself in acknowledgment of the fact.

Then the tiredness started to overtake him. His long travail was over. The book he had dreamed about, his *History of Psychiatric Medicine,* was complete. Now he awaited the elation that should have come with this, but he felt nothing, no joy, no satisfaction or fulfillment even. How was it that, after laboring so long to produce this 3015-page work, all he should have achieved was an exhausted and ambiguous emptiness?

For a while he sat vacantly in front of his desk. Then he stood up and looked around his study. An irritated distaste for this drab room occupied by nothing but books arose in him, so he opened the door. He suddenly wanted to get outside, out into the open air.

There was only a faint light in the corridor, and it lit up the rows of books that lined these walls too. But the light only extended halfway down the stairs at the end of the corridor, dimly revealing their worn carpeting, so he had to grope his way very slowly down. Everyone in the house still seemed to be asleep; there was no sign of even the maid getting up yet. He walked as quietly as he could to the hallway, where the white light of dawn was entering vaguely through the frosted glass of the sliding front door. He put on his *geta,* unscrewed the lock, and carefully slid the creaking door open.

The sky was milky white, the air full of a pale, pellucid, pre-dawn light. The ancient, faded brick wall concealed the outside world, and the leaves of the ivy covering it were soaked with dew, as was the earth beneath his feet. He had not seen the dawn in Tokyo for years now, for he only got up early to work when he was in Hakone. The cool, damp air was pleasant to the touch, reviving his heavy limbs, curing the numbness at the center of his brain. He felt a strange dissatisfaction at not hearing the chorus of clear-toned cicadas here, just as he had felt a similar dissatisfaction once when awakening in Munich and not hearing the blackbirds; but this was Tokyo, not Hakone, and sparrows were gathering on the roof, busily chirping before flying off toward Moto-no-hara.

He walked along the side of the house toward the rear of the hospital. In the pleasant chill of the dawn and the sense of reawakening it gave him, he wanted to experience again the fact that his work of many years had come to an end. There could be no doubt that it was a genuine achievement. It was the first time anything of this kind had been done in Japan, and even abroad he did not know of a work that was so complete in its scope as his. However, he could not be sure. He thought of the library of the Neurological Institute in Vienna, just one library among so many over there, and how jammed tight its shelves were with publications. He envied the people there. They were lucky to be able to study in an environment like that, and above all they had no language problems like himself. He thought of the amount of time he

454

had been obliged to spend reading just one research paper or essay if it was written in French.

He suddenly felt depressed again, and a sense of desolation overtook him. He had wandered past the hospital kitchen, and just ahead of him was a brick building that looked like a ruin. It was what remained of a ward that had been burned down in the fire and was now used as a storehouse. Right next to it, with no space in between, was one of today's wards, one of the temporary buildings put up after the fire, a cheap and shabby construction that seemed even worse because he was looking at the rear of it.

There was a long row of barred windows, and from behind one of them he could see the vague outline of someone looking out. It was the face of a patient, a woman patient, who was staring vacantly into space. He went up to have a closer look, and realized it was a middle-aged woman whom he knew quite well. She was a patient who had failed to respond to the new insulin therapy, and all that could be expected of her was a gradual decline into total imbecility. No doubt she would spend the rest of her life shut away in a ward like this, and she was certainly much younger than he was.

As he approached, she showed not the slightest change of expression. Her blurred features were immobile, and it seemed unlikely that she recognized this man in Japanese dress as the Director of the hospital. As he stood looking at her, the doctor in him took over from the scholar, and he thought he would try to say something to her.

Just as he was about to do so she suddenly burst out laughing. The laughter was not only totally unexpected, but possessed all those peculiarities one finds in the laughter of such patients: vacant, moronic, with no rise or fall, no heights or depths; a laughter that made nonsense of any human attempt to understand it.

Tetsukichi was completely taken aback. He knew this was something about which he could do nothing. Before she had finished laughing, he had turned away from her and was walking in the direction of home. As he walked away, shoulders hunched, there was something awkward and ungainly about him, the impression of a man trying perhaps to escape from something.

Tetsukichi had planned to relax in Hakone that summer, gradually allowing all his tensions to unwind, but the habits of many years were not easily cast aside. He still found himself getting up early, before the chorus of cicadas had begun, and reading some book or other. In fact, he felt a sense of relief at the thought that he still had the index and bibliography of the third volume to write.

Although the summer vacation had begun some time ago, there was no sign of the children. Since last year they had started spending the first half of the summer holidays in the hotel at Hayama where Oshu and his family stayed. This was done at the instigation of Ryuko, and Tetsukichi had given the plan his implicit consent, for he was well aware that his children were much closer to their mother than they were to him and it was natural they should want to spend some time at the seaside with her, particularly as he had not the least intention of putting an end to the long separation from his wife. The children needed their mother, and he knew he had discharged few of his real duties as a father and his children had no affection for him at all. Still, he felt lonely here without them, even though they had always got on his nerves as they rushed about the house and he had done little but shout at them to keep quiet.

But he did make efforts to go outdoors this summer, in contrast to the years before, when he had always remained cooped up in the house. He went to the local Gora Park and sat on a bench with peeling paintwork and watched the sun shining through the branches of the trees. After that he went and looked at the monkeys in their cage. Then he wandered along by the pool and watched other people's children splashing about in the water. This was the routine he worked out for himself, and he stuck to it, just as in previous summers he had never deviated from his fixed course of study.

Sometimes he did break free by walking as far as the mountain that towered up in front of the house, wandering through the gloomy cedar woods, or into clearings where the trees had been chopped down and white umbellate flowers bloomed and the tree stumps were powdered with sawdust. Or he would go wandering along the paths that led up the mountain. Small mountain streams splashed across the road and he would follow one of them into the woods. The rotting foliage sank beneath his feet and the dead leaves of the cedars gave off a damp, musty smell. Today he sat on a rock and watched the surface of the water as it flowed past him. The dark woods, the constant sound of water reminded him of that remote mountain village in the North where he came from. He put the two peaches he had brought with him into the running water and waited patiently for them to get cold. Finally he peeled one of them and, since no one was around to watch him, he opened his mouth indecently wide and bit deep into the fruit. It was full of sweet, juicy goodness, and he regretted the amount inevitably spilled and wasted.

Having wolfed down both peaches, he wiped his mouth with the back of his hand and wondered if there wasn't something of the sensualist in his character, for what happiness it was just to eat two lovely, ripe peaches, alone like this with no one to bother him. In the village where he had spent his childhood, there had been no experience of this kind, the only sweet thing available being a kind of starch syrup called *mizuame*. The salted fish which was brought all the way over the mountains was the nearest thing to a feast they had, and sometimes there would be a sweet-tasting fish among all the salt, which was the height of luxury. When his father had taken him to Tokyo at the age of fifteen, they had walked the forty-odd miles to the hot spring of Sakunami on the first day, and then on to Sendai, and in the inn there he had tasted a cake called *monaka* for the first time in his life. *Monaka* is a wafer-like cake filled with sweet, sticky bean jam, and Tetsukichi had been astounded that anything so delicious should exist. Then in Tokyo, when he arrived at the Nire Clinic in Hongo and saw the guest parlor with its red carpet and huge lamp brilliantly shining, he felt he had arrived on a different planet. *Monaka* ceased to be anything special, for when he first ate flavored *soba* (which are noodles with various delicacies added) he thought it tasted even nicer. Just before he had left home, his mother had quietly given him a meager amount of hard-earned money for himself, telling him there was a thing in Tokyo called "baked sweet potato," and that he should eat that if ever he felt hungry.

Having eaten his two peaches, Tetsukichi felt satisfied, even fulfilled. He had all that he wanted. When the woman with the basket of peaches on her back had arrived yesterday, he had gone to the door himself and bought a whole box off her. Perhaps it was just as well Shuji and Aiko weren't here. They would have polished off the lot in no time. It was amazing how quickly they got through things like that. . .

But the younger children did come eventually, and they were no longer all that young. Even if one discounted his eldest son, Shun'ichi the medical student, as being well outside that category, Aiko had left primary school the year before and had been going to girls' school for more than a year now. She had become a pupil at the Toyo Eiwa Girls' School, and had apparently grown overnight into a young lady of the kind her aunt Momoko (who had already left Japan, unknown to anybody) had predicted, sweet and charming in the eyes of all, both her classmates and her teachers. The school uniform, particularly the maroon scarf, suited her wonderfully, and she herself was very pleased with it, as she was with everything in her new surroundings.

She liked, for example, the way the children called each other by abbreviated forms of their surnames (such as Sai instead of Saito, Muko instead of Mukoyama), though nothing could be done with Nire and she had to make do with the nickname Ako. She liked the headmistress, in fact worshiped her to excess; she was a large, red-faced Canadian lady called Miss Hamilton who spoke the most primitive Japanese and wore a dress with a belt that mysteriously buckled at the back. But Aiko did not think much of the Japanese members of staff, such as the English teacher who refused to pronounce Chopin in the proper manner of "show" and "pan" but in what she imagined was the orthodox English style of "chop" and "inn"; or the physics teacher with a scar on her forehead which it was widely rumored she had received when struck by a plate hurled by her husband during an argument over religious matters. For these two, and for many others, Aiko concocted some malicious nicknames which were so imaginative and ingenious they were rated superior to those already bestowed by the senior girls and thus achieved a currency beyond Aiko's own year.

This summer she had spent some time with her mother at Hayama, a seaside resort south of Tokyo, and then gone to a school camp at Lake Nojiri in the Japan Alps. There had been a group from the YMCA in the neighboring campsite, and she had learned a song from them that she insisted on singing constantly as soon as she was in Hakone. The song was of a cheerful, barking kind, about camp, camp Nojiri, our strength and joy, and doing our best and never say die. . . It fairly bubbled over with youthful high spirits, and when sung in a high, piercing screech by Aiko, with Shuji and Satoru eventually joining in, filled the cottage with so much life that it was not surprising the old frown soon returned to Tetsukichi's face.

Aiko did other things, of course. She would assume an unnaturally soulful expression, no doubt meant to be very grown-up, and recite scraps from the holy scriptures. She sung hymns in her squeaking voice, but her real favorite was the Lord's Prayer, which she would chant with a look of the utmost piety on her face, although it was obvious, given the old-fashioned style of the Japanese version, that she did not have a clue what it meant. Naturally she said grace before meals as well, and considering how slim she was, it was remarkable how robust an appetite she displayed afterward. This was also something she seemed to have picked up at school. School lunches were served in the cafeteria, but since most of the food on offer was very unappetizing, the greater portion of it tended to be left. This led to a ''Meals List'' being put up in the classroom which recorded achievements in eating. One round mark was received if you ate all your lunch, and a second round mark if you asked for a second helping and successfully disposed of it. Aiko, with her constant urge to be top, received more and more double round marks, and this may have led to some kind of expansion in stomach capacity.

Tetsukichi would watch his children playing, aware that he had nothing to do with them now and occasionally experiencing a slight pang of sadness at the thought. They had all grown and he had hardly noticed it. Aiko's behavior occasionally brought home to him the fact that she was turning into a woman, and this provided another source of anxiety. He recalled how last year (or was it the year before?) she had played around in the bath with the two boys, but now she made a point of bathing alone. Well, it was a mysterious thing, he thought, platitudinously, and slightly irresponsibly considering she was his own daughter; and then he was suddenly aware that she really would soon be of an age when she could marry. No doubt his charming wife, whose detestable visage he had no wish to look upon, would tidy up that problem for them all in good time. Just as well, perhaps, since he doubted whether he had any talent for dealing with that kind of thing.

He did not spend much time worrying over his daughter's future, since there was a much more pressing problem at hand. This was something that occupied him most of the time, whether he was idly sitting in a cane chair on the veranda and listening to the voices of the children playing in the garden, or just gazing at the ripples spreading out from the fountain in the pond in the park, or when the moonlight filtered through the black shadow of the cedar woods and came in through his window. He was thinking about the necessity for a Japanese psychiatry textbook. A variety of textbooks were already in use in the country, but these were all Japanese translations of foreign, principally German, originals. Yet in Japan they were dealing with Japanese psychiatric patients, and these people's symptoms showed genuine differences when compared with their foreign counterparts. The proportion of manic and depressive illnesses was different, for example, as also was the form in which hysteria appeared in Japanese patients. And

459

even within Japan itself there were regional variations, variations that recurred and could also be seen in different historical periods.

He knew he was a fool even to dream about doing something he should leave to others who were more competent. But he kept finding himself brooding on the subject, indulging in fantasies in which he was firmly embarked on his course even though he feared he would make a dreadful mess of it. Finally he became enslaved by the idea and asked himself what reasons he had for not doing it, since he possessed the medical records of thousands of patients at the Nire Hospital and had easy access to thousands more in Keio and Tokyo universities. And why shouldn't he go all round the country, to mental institutions in every district, searching out case histories of particular importance? Japan was the leading country in Asia now, no longer a small, insignificant island in the eastern seas, and would soon be one of the major powers in the world. Obviously it must have a textbook of psychiatry that was a product of the land itself. He remembered the example of Professor Kure long ago, insisting that his students write down their patients' records in the Japanese language. He thought of him not only with the affection due to an old teacher, but also with a feeling close to awe and reverence. On the occasion of a *Festschrift* for Professor Kure, had not Professor Obersteiner (the retired professor who had once stood behind Tetsukichi in the laboratory in Vienna telling him to keep at it, for no good work was ever done in a month) taken up his pen and written to him expressing admiration for his achievements and offering his felicitations?

Tetsukichi remembered that in his message the old German scholar had referred to Japan as the Land of the Rising Sun. Obviously, this was only a special European form of compliment, but Tetsukichi felt it was a true description of the country. In many ways Japan might still be inferior to Europe and America, but it clearly possessed the potential for great achievements in the future. He felt a brief surge of pride and elation, soon to subside again, although at the time it seemed to him undeniable that this was true.

But a nerve-racking experience was awaiting him at the end of the summer vacation, and this was not related to his self-centered and as yet mostly imaginary fears and hopes and ambitions. Nanny Shimoda, the loyal servant who had worked in the Nire Hospital for so many decades without one day of serious illness, finally became ill, quite seriously ill.

She was seventy-one now, an age at which she really ought not to have worked, but she still seemed to be in excellent health and nobody could persuade her to relax her detailed direction of the other servants' activities and her insistence that she be allowed to go on with her busy sewing. But just before summer (or, at least, so it appeared in retrospect) the wrinkles on her face suddenly grew deeper and for longish periods she did not feel very well. The pain she later complained about in her stomach was probably something she had started feeling then, although she herself had only said:

"Well, I'm getting on a bit now, and I never could stand the heat; but once I'm back in Hakone, and grateful I am, I'm sure, to be given the opportunity to go there, I'll soon be better again and very sorry I am to cause all this trouble."

Although she had always suffered from travel sickness, this year she was much worse on the train, vomiting a number of times before she reached the cottage in Gora. Still, as she had predicted, she soon seemed to recover her spirits, preparing Tetsukichi's meals along with the young maid, and tirelessly performing a number of other tasks as she had always done every year. No matter how often she was told to rest or take it easy, the stubborn old woman would never listen.

Then, when her beloved children arrived in Hakone, the familiar smile came back to her wrinkled face. After a few days, however, around the middle of August, she came to see Tetsukichi with a very hesitant, apologetic look on her face, but obviously exhausted and in considerable pain, to tell him that she had been having these pains in her stomach for some while now and she could not sleep at night. As he listened to what she said and looked at her thin, drawn, unhealthy features, Tetsukichi was appalled at how unobservant he had been.

That same day he had Yasusaburo Sugano, who had very conveniently just arrived in Gora, take her back to Tokyo and place her in the Keio Hospital. The Assistant Director, Seisaku Kanazawa, would be able to take care of things after that. But a communication came a few days later, one he had feared and expected. It was cancer and too far gone to permit an operation.

Since Tetsukichi had no work to keep him in Hakone that year, he was free to take the children back to Tokyo at the end of August. During that fortnight Nanny Shimoda had grown much thinner. She was in obvious decline and so emaciated it was clear at a glance to any of her visitors that it could only be a question of time. But Nanny herself, on those occasions when an injection had given her temporary relief from pain, would say with a smile on her now completely wasted face:

"I'll be better again soon. I'm strong enough right inside, you'll see. I feel fine today; much better. I'm only sorry you've had to waste all this money on me, putting me in this hospital and everything. . ."

When she was visited, she would often insist on raising herself painfully in bed and urging her guests to eat some of the fruit on the bedside table. It was so terrible to look at her that people would turn their eyes away and hurriedly peel a pear in the hope that conforming with her wishes would put her at ease. For this reason, Shuji managed on one occasion to eat half a melon all by himself. Nobody scolded him for doing so, and he felt a strange sense of happiness.

Eventually, however, she came to understand she was going to die, and that her death was not far off. Once she had made up her mind about this, she was obstinately convinced it must be so, and anything anybody said to try to console her was utterly rejected. She insisted she wanted to go home and die there, and she went on insisting. The Nire house might be anathema to Momoko, but for Nanny Shimoda it was the best place in the world; a home, a heaven. Her desire to return there had something unreal about it: the unpleasant, slightly hysterical air that accompanies any form of delusion.

At the end of September, Tetsukichi sentimentally decided to do what she asked and allowed her to leave the hospital and come home. The inner room was turned into a temporary sickroom for her, but as soon as she was back in Aoyama she visibly deteriorated, and at times her mind became confused and she would stare blankly and suspiciously about her:

"Where am I?. . . Is this Hakone?. . . Yamagata?"

Her face had already become jaundiced, and this combined with the hideous pathology of cancer to produce a total change in her appearance, so one tried one's best to avoid looking at her. It was horrifying to see how emaciated she was when one thought of the plump, round person she had once been. Her ribs stuck painfully through her chest, her arms and legs were unspeakably skinny, and the skin that seemed to drape these bones was of a loathsome color, the muddy, dried-out color of skin that has started to die.

Now she began to complain about the pain, and complain frequently, for the capacity for endurance she had always had was gone. She lost all control of herself, writhing and groaning in her agony. This was the Nanny Shimoda who had been so strong, so stoical, and had never once been heard to utter a complaint.

After a week of this, she was in the critical stage and expected to die at any time. A great many people came to see her, not only from the Aoyama hospital but from elsewhere, including the old couple from the Seiundo, old members of staff from Matsubara, and Oshu, Yonekuni, the Deputy and even Kumagoro. No one else in the Nire Hospital could have aroused such concern at the approach of death. Different people responded in different ways as they observed the inevitability of what was happening to her, but what these responses all had in common was a kind of blank dullness, expressed only in sighs.

The one exception was Yonekuni. He looked into the sickroom from the passage outside, hesitated about going in, and finally decided not to, going to the bathroom instead and washing out his mouth. While he was doing this, Shige, the maid who long ago had been employed "within," happened to pass by and he asked her nervously:

"Do you think Nanny Shimoda knows us?"

"I don't suppose she does any more."

"But she must have some idea what's going on?. . . I don't see how they can all bear to be in there like that. . . Making all that fuss when someone's dying. . . She ought to be left in peace. . . Do you think she still feels the pain, I mean right inside herself?"

"Don't upset yourself about it. She's all right. She's going to a better place."

"What's all right? What's supposed to be all right about that?"

Yonekuni's staring eyes wandered wildly about, an expression of great seriousness on his face as if he had much more to say, but Shige had already gone. He turned the tap on again and gargled a second time. In the end he went home, without seeing the patient.

She still did not die. She was unconscious but continued to breathe for more than a week. Each day when the children came home from school they would whisper as soon as they were inside the door:

"Isn't Nanny dead yet?"

The question sounded particularly cruel and unfeeling to the adults since it so well reflected their own wishes, which were that the sooner she died the better. Nanny Shimoda would be released from her suffering and they would be released from what had become a tiresome ordeal. Even Aiko and Shuji could no longer recognize or feel affection for that haggard face. They were not allowed into the sickroom, but that didn't stop them peeping from the doorway and gazing at her as she lay there sleeping quietly after an injection. Tetsukichi regretted having allowed her back.

Then one night, the night before she died, he went to see her and found Katsujiro Nirasawa from Matsubara at her side, along with a nurse, and also Aiko and Shuji. He scolded the two children and made them go out into the passage, but they stayed looking into the room from the doorway.

Nanny Shimoda's parched, deathly lips trembled as she tried to say something:

"Where . . . where am I?"

Then suddenly her small, glazed eyes flickered wide open and stared:

"Mistress Sei. What are you doing, Mistress Sei?"

And then:

"Oh . . . oh . . . it hurts so much. . . Where am I now?. . . Where are you, little Shuji? Shuji, where are you?"

Then what seemed to be agony, although it may only have been a physical reflex causing more pain to those watching than it did to her, contorted her face, that face now discolored beyond recognition. She was certain to get worse during the night, so Tetsukichi told Katsujiro to increase the number of morphine injections. These were already having a bad effect on her physically, but it was the only thing they could do to help her now. He left Katsujiro to look after her and went out of the room. The children had vanished somewhere.

As he walked quickly along the passageway, he recalled Nanny Shimoda in her younger days, when he himself had been a young boy new to Tokyo, and she was telling him in slightly arrogant tones the correct words in Tokyo for various everyday things which he was apparently getting wrong. He then went into the toilet, but as he was urinating he became aware of someone behind the door of the inner lavatory. He was quite sure there had been no light on in there before he came in, so whoever it was must have been sitting in the dark. He paused a moment, and could hear the voice clearly now. Someone was sobbing and trying to restrain those sobs. The voice was that of the youngest child of the house who always used to run away and hide here whenever he had been frightened by the giant figure of Zaosan. Shuji was a big boy now, and next year he had to sit his junior high school entrance exams. . .

A few weeks before this, while death was still toying with Nanny Shimoda, the German Army had stormed across the Polish frontier at first light on the 1st of September, and another great European war had begun.

"Zao was in tears. Someone like him being able to get married. . ."

Oshu had just returned home on a bitterly cold night in the middle of February, 1940, and was reporting to Hisa on Zaosan's wedding which he had been to that day.

He was wearing a khaki "people's uniform" made out of shiny rayon, and his head was close-shaven. The shape of his skull was clearly exposed now it was disencumbered of its hair, and it gave the impression that it had been squashed down from the top to produce a marked sideways extension. Oshu, well known as a man of fashion and taste, certainly looked awkward sitting there in this garb at the living-room table, and it could hardly be said to have suited him. But this merely showed one more aspect of that passion for the new which he, with the blood of Kiichiro coursing through his veins, had always had. Probably he had felt certain misgivings at all his energies being expended on the sport of hunting at a time of national crisis like this, and was determined that at least his appearance should be up with the times. His decision to wear the uniform at Zaosan's wedding had thus been one with a purpose.

In accordance with the old principle of marrying the girl next door, Zaosan had married one of the women servants at his manager's place, where he had been living ever since he had become a wrestler. As already mentioned, in Zaosan's heyday the manager's wife herself used to come and open the door for him when he came back late at night, but since entering his period of decline, the woman had confined her efforts to merely mouthing complaints about the lateness of the hour from the shelter of her bed. The person who always got up and let him in had been this servant, and it was this that had brought about her role as the girl next door. In fact the idea of marrying this giant, popularly considered a monster, had been all her own.

"That's all right, then," mumbled Hisa, with back bent and hands cupped over the meager warmth of the *hibachi*. "It looks as if Tatsuji will, well. . ."

What it looked as if Tatsuji would well . . . remained unknown, for her sentence tailed off into unintelligibility. Her voice had always been lacking in clarity and had grown even harder to understand. Her wrinkles had also increased until her whole face was a mass of tiny lines, their presence accentuated by the unnatural blackness of her dyed hair.

"Such a nice, kind-looking bride," put in Chiyoko, who was now a totally accepted member of the family. "Yonekuni, don't you think it's about time you got yourself married as well?"

Yonekuni raised his ruddy, healthy face. His staring eyes, however, expressed anxiety and amazement at his sister-in-law's words. He looked like a person living in acute poverty who has suddenly been requested to donate a considerable amount to some worthy cause.

"Well, I don't know," he muttered awkwardly. "If I could only have something like normal health. . ."

"Normal health?" interrupted Oshu. "Your health's a bit better than normal. All this talk about consumption; it's nothing of the sort. All right, just assuming—assuming, mind—that you had some slight seepage in your lungs, marriage still wouldn't do you any harm. . ."

"You don't know what you're talking about," shouted Yonekuni, interrupting his elder brother in a tone that suggested he was genuinely annoyed. "I've got my own ideas about life, my own philosophy. I never became a doctor. I'm in a very special situation in this household; in very peculiar circumstances. Still, I've got my own way of life, which I manage by myself. I don't cause any trouble to anyone and I don't need anyone to look after me."

This proclamation of rugged independence caused Chiyoko a certain amount of inner amusement. She was accustomed to these weird, irrelevant statements about life that Yonekuni was in the habit of making these days. But this was not the case with Oshu. He had few opportunities to talk with his younger brother, and he was clearly taken aback by these remarks, saying with a dumbfounded look on his face:

"I don't see why you should talk like that. There's nothing particularly wrong about your not becoming a doctor, is there? After all, you're looking after the farm all right, aren't you? What are you talking in that peculiar way for, as if you had some kind of grudge against everyone?"

"It's not a grudge or anything. It's just that I want to be in charge of my own life, that's all. I mean, I've got a pretty good idea how much time I've got left."

"How much time you've got left? Sounds as if you're expecting to drop dead any minute."

"Well, nobody can be sure how long I'm going to live. I'm not talking about my consumption, of course. That's not the real problem. I've been dieting over the years, and at last it seems to have settled down, sort of capsulated."

The "sort of capsulated" caused Chiyoko a flutter of concealed annoyance and she put some more hot water into the teapot. Oshu, however, seemed rather put out by the strange seriousness of his brother's remarks.

"Then what is it? Are you saying you've got something else wrong with you?"

"I'm afraid I can't tell you," Yonekuni replied with a completely serious look on his face, a face glowing with health despite its somewhat tragic air. "I don't want lots of people worrying themselves about me. It's my life and that's the way I like it."

"But look here: I *am* a doctor, you know," said Oshu, who was beginning to lose his temper.

"Yes, but there are illnesses that contemporary medicine can do nothing about."

"Things like cancer, you mean?" said Oshu, showing the professional's scorn of the amateurish statement, but also sounding a little worried.

"No, nothing like that. It's still not quite clear. Of course, once I really know what it is, then. . . Still, I don't want to talk about it."

"Look here, Yonekuni," said Oshu, producing a rare bellow that suited his tubby form. "What has got into you? Why do you have to talk in that pretentious, devious way. . . ?"

"That's enough. That's quite enough," Hisa chose this moment to mutter. "Yonekuni will go to the hospital and have himself examined."

This brought an end to the dialogue before any conclusion had been reached, but Oshu's normal cheerfulness was soon restored. As he drank his tea and ate his cake, he changed the subject to the *magnum opus* his adopted brother Tetsukichi had completed last year. It seemed that the *History of Psychiatric Medicine* had been highly acclaimed by the experts. The director of the Matsuzawa Hospital had even been good enough to say that Tetsukichi's name had been put forward as a candidate for membership of the Japan Academy.

"What's this Japan Academy? Is it some kind of honor?" asked Hisa bluntly.

"It's an honor bestowed by the government; the highest honor a scholar can receive."

"Well, Tetsukichi always did work hard at his books," Hisa mumbled to herself, making an almost imperceptible movement with her eyes which indicated she was about to rise. Then rise she did, very, very slowly, and she returned to her room with Chiyoko in close and helpful attendance.

This talk about Tetsukichi's being a candidate for membership of the Japan Academy eventually reached Ryuko's ears in a slightly exaggerated form. She was delighted at the news and smiled broadly despite the fact that she had been separated from her husband for so long and was no more thinking in terms of reconciliation than he was. Her joy had nothing to do with their being husband and wife, but concerned the honor that would be done to her father's memory if the son he had adopted were invited to join this august body. It would also be an honor for the Nire Hospital, and while she thought long and deeply along these dignified lines she was obliged to admit it was only natural that even a person like Tetsukichi should have been able to do something for the hospital.

She also felt she would like to see the work in question. So far she had not so much as laid eyes on it. There was a copy in Oshu's room, it seemed, but it would be mortifying and much too far beneath her dignity to go and borrow it. Consequently, when she was out one day she called in at the Maruzen Bookstore and acquired those three fat volumes. She then carefully read the preface and acknowledgments, and even managed quite a lot of the almost unintelligible introductory pages before giving up the unequal battle. Nevertheless, she had received the impression that it was a unique and remarkable work of which she could be proud. Since she had nowhere to keep any books, she put the three volumes carefully on top of a small chest of drawers.

In the spring of that year the long-awaited announcement of new members of the Japan Academy was made, and Ryuko felt she must be the victim of some deception, for the name of Tetsukichi Nire, Director of the Nire Hospital and Her Husband, was nowhere on the list. Ryuko pulled her neck up straight and firm, nodded portentously in recognition of the fact, and was in an unpleasant mood for a while. The offending three volumes on top of the chest had now become an eyesore, so she put them in the long, low space for storage beneath the window which was rather like a window seat but much longer. Naturally various boxes and bags accumulated on top of the books, and even a chamber pot that Ryuko had used when she was ill in bed with a cold. Thus did Tetsukichi's bulky masterpiece sink into oblivion.

Aiko was in the basement cloakroom (or "crock-room" as the girls called it) of the Toyo Eiwa Girls' School, chattering to her friends and preparing to go home. She had entered the third year that spring.

When she opened her shoe box, she found placed beneath the slightly worn heels of her shoes a small, pink envelope. She didn't need to look at the contents to know that this was from someone with a crush on her, but since she received a great many such love letters she was able to view it with a certain indifference. When she turned it over, however, and saw that the name written on the back in a strange, wavering script was that of Agnes Nielsen, she slipped it into her bag with a stealthy care she rarely displayed on such occasions.

Agnes Nielsen was a girl who had originally been in a different department of the school and had only recently joined the same class as Aiko. This "different department" was a special class consisting of children who had spent some time abroad. Most of them were Japanese children whose fathers' work had kept them away from Japan; and once their Japanese had reached a suitable standard, they were put in an ordinary class with people of their own age group. But, either because they were fluent in English or knew some French, or because they wore smart clothes of their own instead of the school uniform, these students were considered a very special breed in the mission school, and were often the objects of considerable envy. On top of this, Agnes Nielsen was of Swedish-Japanese parentage. It is true her skin was all freckles and she was almost absurdly tall, so that she could hardly be called a pretty young thing; but her eyes were so blue they looked quite unreal and her hair was flaxen, so she was the focus of a great deal of speculation and rumor.

The fact that this exotic person should have sent her a letter did things for Aiko's ego. Aiko liked anything that looked different, and Agnes Nielsen's blue eyes and crude Japanese script were made to appeal to this taste. She was also having a love affair with anything foreign at the time, with a particular craze for French movies, and Sweden was a country almost next door to France, or so she assumed.

Despite the dark war clouds building up all over the world, the French cinema had reached a high point during these late years of the 1930s, and many of the films were shown in Japan, usually a year or so after their appearance in France. So Aiko had seen Jean Renoir's *Les Basfonds* in 1937 and Julien Duvivier's *La Belle Equipe* in the same year, with the same director's *Un Carnet de Bal* in 1938 and *Pépé le Moko* in 1939. In 1939 she had also seen Leonid Moguy's sensational *Prison without Bars* about a reformatory for girls. Most of these films she saw more than once, and she was thrilled to death by Louis Jouvet in *Un Carnet de Bal* and Jean Gabin in *Pépé le Moko,* for she was at a fickle age and was more star-struck by all this kind of thing than by watching the Takarazuka Girls Opera, where actresses in male costumes strutted and sang in romantic period dramas that could be relied on to send girls of her age into enthusiastic hysterics. Aiko thought all the women who appeared in these French movies were absolutely wonderful, and although Agnes Nielsen could hardly be considered a fine figure of a woman, she certainly had blue eyes and flaxen hair and undoubtedly had some sort of connection with those distant beings whom Aiko found so emotionally rewarding.

She was a bit scornful of the fact that Agnes Nielsen should have written her name on the back of an envelope containing a letter of this kind, showing her ignorance of proper etiquette in these matters. But Aiko did not seriously blame her for this blunder, and called to mind that long, freckled face. . .

Her thoughts were interrupted by a sudden loud burst of laughter near at hand:

"Come, you evil child, most wicked of all since creation dawned, and carry my bag a bit for me."

"No I shan't. You carry mine for me, most monstrous child since the beginning of time."

The heartless Aiko promptly forgot the letter she had just received, and in the rough tones appropriate to a tough gang leader she soon had this noisy rabble under control:

"Quiet, you, you delinquent dregs. Remember that this here is a prison without bars."

The elaborate style of this exchange could be traced to the following incident. The teacher with the plainest nickname among all the staff was a male music teacher with a bald head who was known as "the Mazda Bulb." The girls tended to have a lowish opinion of any male teacher, unless he was a very attractive man indeed. The Mazda Bulb,

470

who seemed to find it impossible to scold anyone in a loud voice, also had the disadvantage of having recently got married, and he was a constant butt for their practical jokes. One day Aiko and her friends raised a stout barricade of desks and chairs in front of the door in the music room so that it could not be opened from the corridor. This most tormentable of teachers struggled awhile with the door in a fruitless attempt to open it, and then went to ask for the support of other teachers. This is what Aiko and her friends had been waiting for. In no time at all, with perfectly coordinated teamwork, they arranged things so that when the posse of teachers turned up all the desks and chairs were back in their places, the children all sitting quietly as if nothing had happened. But a short, sturdy-looking spinster, a house mistress who went under the name of "the Bulge," worked out what they had been up to. She stormed to the dais, thrust out her pudgy arm at the girls, and shouted:

"You people . . . you people are the most wicked girls since the dawn of creation!"

Certainly the best part of this performance had been her striking resemblance to a crowing cock, but the phrase itself, delivered in a voice trembling with rage, had won popularity among the girls as well.

"Still, I was really amazed at the size of the Bulge's mouth."

"The grandmother transformed into the wolf," said Aiko very coolly, and then curled one corner of her lips slightly and, as was her habit, added one of her freshly created fictions. "Do you know, any of you, the real reason why the Bulge was left on the shelf? Well, I'll tell you. . . She was born in an unlucky year, the year of the fire horse. And with a mouth that size—bound to scare off any man."

The year of the fire horse occurs, according to the Japanese system of year naming, only once every sixty years, and this would mean the Bulge was born in 1906 or 1846, neither of which seemed a likely date given that it was now 1940. The common belief is that a woman born in such a year can "eat up forty men," and will thus find it difficult to get married (hence the joke about the big mouth).

"Was she really?"

"Of course. It's a well-known fact. Once upon a time the Bulge was in love with a man. Still, all the love was strictly in one direction only. The man married another woman. And this didn't happen only once but over and over again. Each time she shed tears, finally vowing revenge on the whole of womankind. That's where she gets the passion from when she's tormenting the life out of us."

The girls always listened to Aiko's tales with keen interest, almost as if they were really taken in. Perhaps they were, since although the details were obvious fabrications, there was something about her stories that made them sound as if they ought to be true. It was on this that her popularity was founded. For example, when they had all been in their first year there had been a fantastic rumor current about a leprous monster known as "the Red Cloak" who attacked young girls by digging its fangs into their throats and sucking their blood. For a time this had caused a stir at the Toyo Eiwa Girls' School and Ako, alias Aiko Nire, reported that she had seen it. One evening she had been passing by the Seinan Primary School near her home, and there she had seen a little old woman standing about by a mailbox, wearing something like an Inverness cape. She seemed to have a very refined face, but Aiko was blessed with almost supernatural powers of intuition and she was overcome by an ominous premonition. Then she noticed that when the old woman smiled at her in inviting fashion there was just a glimpse between her lips of sharp, pointed teeth like a dog's. Aiko immediately dashed off down a side street and went quickly home without once looking back, for she had also noticed the color of the lining of the old woman's cloak. It was a horrible red lining, red as if it had been dyed in blood!

"All that stuff about its face being all disfigured and hideous, well that's completely untrue," Aiko announced to the crowd of classmates gathered about her in the playground. "She had a really kind, really gentle face. That's what's so terrifying about the Red Cloak."

Among these innocent fabrications of hers there was one that no one knew about and that was not entirely beyond reproach. This was when she was still at primary school and used to send parcels of comforts to the troops at the front. The parcels themselves were made up by one of the maids and contained bits of free stationery from the Seiundo, but also caramels and chocolates from the Kimuraya, a local candy store which had also recently become a place where things could be acquired without having to hand over hard cash. So all Aiko actually did was provide these free contents. She also wrote a number of letters to soldiers whose names she did not even know and who were fighting somewhere on the Chinese mainland. Since the gifts she sent cost her nothing, Aiko assumed that the soldiers who received them would not appreciate them much either, so in order to heighten the emotional impact she enclosed a letter with one of the gift parcels written in a deliberately naive style:

I get up early each morning and clean the shoes of everyone in our house. Then I sweep the street in front of the house nice and clean as well. My daddy gives me some pocket money for doing this, and I use it to send gift parcels like this to the brave soldiers.

Some months passed and she received a very sincere, heartfelt reply to this pack of lies. She was pleased with this result, and was so carried away by her success she sent off another letter to the same soldier:

Our house is very poor. I am afraid we have nothing that could make our soldiers really happy. So I go about the streets selling fermented soybeans and with the little money I receive I. . .

The response to this, all the way from distant China, was almost passionate with gratitude, asking questions about herself of so serious a kind that even Aiko lost her nerve and stopped writing.

But at the moment she was standing with a perfectly innocent look on her face, her mouth curled slightly at one corner, and giving her friends insight into another problem:

"The Bulge is a really tragic case. It's up to us all to sympathize with her, to help her. Lo, as the maple trembles in the breeze, the beauteous maple leaves which are so fair, and all that stuff. So that's the way we'll be from now on."

Finally the girls started to leave the cloakroom in twos and threes, drifting across the playground and out through the school gates. Normally Aiko would turn right to the stop at Roppongi, where she boarded the streetcar, but today she turned left instead with a group of her friends. Just down Toriizaka there was a shop selling ice candy which they often went to; it was one of the most advanced fashions among them to walk back past the school sucking this ice candy in the most vulgar way possible. The ice-candy store also sold fried buns even out of season, and although eating one of these crude objects could hardly be considered as satisfying even to the most perverse standards of elegance, they found them irresistibly delicious.

Aiko walked along in the midst of her friends swinging both arms freely. She was able to do this because she was not carrying her school bag: one of her underlings was holding it with great care. So, accompanied by her bag carrier and other henchwomen, she arrived at the top of Toriizaka and saw three schoolboys coming up the slope toward them. She could tell at a glance they were from the Azabu Middle School, which had fairly close links with the Toyo Eiwa Girls' School since it was in the same vicinity. These three looked pretty wet to Aiko and her friends, for they had very white, brand-new satchels dangling from their shoulders, and were obviously in their first year. Despite that, they had the impudence to be holding a large greasy bag between them from which they were extracting fried buns as they walked along.

"The cheek of it!" said the girl who was carrying Aiko's bag, giving an exaggerated gasp.

Even so, they were certainly taken aback by what their leader now did. Aiko went straight up to the three boys and brusquely ordered the smallest of them, who was just putting his hand into the bag, to hand one over. "Come on," she said, sticking out her hand as she did so. The girls were quite certain they heard her say that. The boy looked up at her, his face filled with consternation, and gave the whole bag to Aiko as if he had no choice. Aiko swiftly took one of the buns and gave the bag back to him, walking away with a look of complete unconcern on her face. The other bun-eaters were obviously too startled by this transaction to be able to do anything about it and merely stared vacantly after her retreating figure.

This bold exploit of Aiko's was looked on with amazed admiration by her friends, although only she herself knew that they were the victims of a deception, and this added to her pleasure. For the boy she had seized the bun from was her younger brother Shuji, who was indeed in his first year at Azabu Middle School.

While his sister was enjoying this cheerful, exciting life, Shuji's schooldays consisted almost entirely of gloom and anxiety. The age demanded above all spiritual aspiration and physical strength, and this youngest child of the Nire household, with his sniveling temperament, was only able to respond to these demands in a very incompetent fashion.

In 1940 Japan was entering the fourth year of her Holy War, which happened to be the year 2,600 according to the imperial calendar, the first Emperor, Jimmu, having supposedly ascended the throne in 660 B.C. This was to be celebrated in style, for the solemn figure of 2,600 gave the media an excellent pretext to laud the immaculate nature of the nation's constitution, to proceed with the further sanctification of the uninterrupted imperial lineage, and to make the Western calendar with its inferior number seem more and more remote from the country's needs. For example, the *Asahi* newspaper, in accordance with its custom of announcing its plans for the coming year in its New Year's Day issue, gave them under the heading of "*New Projects in Our Paper for the Imperial Year 2,600*" and listed them as follows: "*Consecrating a Seminary Hall for Shintoist Practices, Prayers to be Offered at All National Shrines for the Prosperity of the Country, Sponsorship of the National Tournament of Martial Arts, the National Gymnastic Tournament and an Exhibition of Japanese Culture.*" Even the cartoon series "Fuku-chan," which had been popular for years now, was to be given a more positive character by being re-entitled "Forward Fuku-chan!" And the *waka* poet Mokichi Saito had contributed some verses to this New Year's Day number:

> Beneath the heavens how great
> The heart that beats as one all these
> Two thousand and six hundred years.

> In this East Asian dawn
> What is it that they cry, those
> Voices all in unison?

The entrance requirements for middle school were also changed this year. There was no longer any written exam, but entrance was permitted on the evidence of a report from primary school, an interview, and a physical examination. Since Shuji was hopeless at things as simple as pulling himself up on the horizontal bar, Tetsukichi had one put up in the garden. He was also anxious about Shuji's inability to open his mouth before strangers, and decided he must be given practice in interview techniques. Feeling that it would be better to have this done by someone Shuji did not know too well, he asked Kumagoro Sakuma from Matsubara to do it, since he always seemed to have plenty of time to spare.

"Where were you born?" Kumagoro asked this youngest child of the Director as he stood before him, assuming a special deep voice for the occasion, which was meant to be brusque and offhand at the same time, so there was a certain lack of conviction in the sound he produced.

"In Tokyo, in the Red Cross Hospital. . ." Shuji's voice soon tailed away, but Kumagoro simply told him not to be too precise, although he gave him no hint as to the proper mode of reply.

Kumagoro cleared his throat and began to get into the swing of things. He was finding the business interesting, and he assumed the haughty attitude of the genuine schoolmaster:

"Before replying to each question you'd better say 'Yes, sir.' In a good, sharp, clear voice. Sound as if you mean business. . . Right, then. Now, my boy, what people do you particularly admire?"

Shuji replied speedily and unwaveringly:

"Yes, sir. Masashige Kusunoki and Hideo Noguchi."

Kusunoki was a soldier who had restored the Emperor to the throne in the fourteenth century, and Noguchi was a doctor, a cytologist, who had died in Africa in 1928. Both had struggled manfully against adversity.

"Very well. Now, in what way . . . in what manner were these men great?"

This put an immediate stop to Shuji's eloquence and all he could do was blush and stare in silence at the floor.

So when Kumagoro got back to cookhouse circles at Matsubara, it was not surprising he should have expressed his frank judgment of the boy's performance:

"He's hopeless, the Director's youngest. He hasn't a hope of getting through."

But this forecast was proved wrong, and for some unknown reason Shuji was able to enter the school of his first choice, although, unlike most schoolboys of his age, he was unable to take any pleasure in the long trousers he wore for the first time in his life, being merely irritated by the itching they caused and unable to see this as one more joyous step along the road to adulthood.

This spineless attitude was reflected in his behavior each morning. He would get up early enough, even earlier than necessary, but then he occupied himself with so much pointless time-wasting he would only dash out of the house at the last possible moment. Because there was no streetcar from Aoyama to Azabu he was obliged to walk the mile or so there. His face already showed the anxiety he felt at having set out so late, as he walked down past the smaller cemetery, where the air always tasted so dank and musty at this time of day, and then on through the jumble of slum-like streets, looking straight ahead of him. When he arrived at Kasumi-cho there was usually a sudden increase in the number of boys hurrying to school, for they were not allowed to get off at the streetcar stop by the Red Cross Hospital that was nearest the school. It was a rule that they get off at the stop before that and cover the remainder of the distance on foot. If there were plenty of other boys about it was all right, but if Shuji noticed almost nobody around at this point his heart would begin to pound and he would break into a trot, looking nervously about him. If only he had got up five minutes earlier this need never have happened; and while thinking this dismal thought he would arrive at the Red Cross Hospital stop and perhaps see two or three boys from his school jumping off the street-car there. They were seniors who realized they were going to be late if they kept to the rules, and had taken the risk of being found out. So they leaped from the streetcar while it was still moving and dashed up the slope toward the school, holding their grubby satchels down with one hand as these bumped heavily up and down on their but-tocks. If they missed the morning assembly they would be called into the gym by one of the P.E. or drill instructors and given a terrible dressing down. These teachers all had nicknames like "Snapping Tur-tle" or "Louse" because once one of them had his eye on you he would have his teeth into you as well, never letting go until you graduated from school.

Now Shuji really began to run for all he was worth, but the senior boys gradually widened the distance between them. He found it dif-ficult to breathe. He wondered why he always had to be subjected to this kind of misery as he toiled up the slope gasping for air. When he did finally make it through the school gates just before the siren went, he was soaked in sweat, a mixture of the sweat that exercise brings out, and the cold sweat caused by chronic anxiety.

This manner of going to school was typical of his school life in general, and he was unable to avoid the guilty feeling that he wasn't really suited for anything. He had never realized, for example, that the position of "attention" in drill, which surely ought to mean just standing still, could involve so many difficulties. It transpired that it was a unique and solemn form of behavior, known as "the soldier's basic position and attitude," one that "must at all times express by external rigor and correctness the constant presence and latent vitality of the martial spirit."

The warrant officer walked about with a bamboo cane in his hand and returned one's salute in a very slack manner with his fingers all over the place, but he had an incredible memory for all that was in the drill manual. He could tell one what "attention" meant, and it meant the following:

"Both heels are to be placed together in one straight line whereupon the feet are to open from that position at an angle of approximately sixty degrees. In accordance with this, the knees shall assume a similar posture, without strain but properly extended, and the upper half of the body shall rest poised and settled upon the waist, the back straight and extended but leaning slightly forward while the shoulders press backward as a counterbalance to this. The arms shall be allowed to hang in a natural manner, the hands touching the thighs and the fingers lightly extended, the middle finger of each hand lying generally along the seam of the trousers. The neck and head should be held in a straight line, the mouth closed, and both eyes correctly open and looking straight ahead in a forward direction.''

The warrant officer, who was known as a ''New Special,'' an abbreviation of ''New Special Duty Sergeant'' (although the title was already out of date so ''Old Special'' might have been more suitable), would often spend a whole hour trying to get them to achieve this apotheosis of the position of perfect poise. His nickname was ''the Imperial Calendar,'' so it was to be expected that he would go on for a long time about such things:

''Look here, you numbskull, what does it say in the drill manual? 'Both eyes correctly open. . .' Do you call your eyes correctly open? Do you?''

Marching, which should have been just plain walking, turned out to have a truly problematic nature that Shuji had never foreseen, for this had to be a noble gait which expressed a ''bold and indomitable spirit.'' If the instructor questioned anyone about the proper length of stride it was no use answering ''thirty inches'' or even ''approximately thirty inches'' or ''about thirty inches,'' for only ''on a basic average of thirty inches'' would satisfy him. Luckily there were people who found the actual marching even more difficult than Shuji did. One of them, for some reason or other, naturally seemed to walk with his behind stuck out and his head thrust forward, a posture that became so accentuated in times of stress that he gave a remarkable imitation of a waddling duck. Another one had hands and feet of an inhuman length that only seemed to move with a strange, jerky motion as if they were run by clockwork. The drill instructor naturally picked on him to howl at, and the abuse seemed to affect the motor function of his nervous system, so that his right arm came forward with the right leg and the left arm with the left leg, producing an even more remarkable clockwork effect. The third object of the instructor's wrath was Shuji.

Another thing that caused Shuji great trouble resulted from the fact that he had not practiced winding on his puttees with sufficient zeal. When they were marching in file, his puttees would choose to unwind as if on purpose. They gradually sank down to his ankles, where they formed little circular heaps, and then the ends began to trail along the ground, flapping malevolently in the air each time he brought a foot down. In fact, one of the senior boys, in true old-soldier fashion, had advised him not to tie up his puttees too tight, because when they came undone you had a nice opportunity to take a rest. Shuji, however, had not been aiming at this result, when one day he did make up his mind to fall out and squat down in the schoolyard and tie them up again. Since he lacked the idler's motives of that senior boy, he was in a desperate panic to do them up as quickly as he could and resume his place again. But he had been in too much of a hurry, and as soon as he completed the task and stood up his puttees started to fall down again. So he had to start from scratch, which he did, suddenly becoming aware that the instructor was standing over him, and for a moment he felt the core of his brain go completely dark. The instructor, however, who had assumed that any pupil fumbling and blundering about in that fashion must be deliberately idling and had come to observe his progress, soon noticed the horrible pallor of Shuji's face and the frantic and useless efforts his trembling fingers were making. Satisfied that this display of terror and frenzy was proof of the very highest kind of sincerity, the instructor left him without saying a word, and finally Shuji managed to make it back to his squad in some sort of soldierly shape.

Somehow or other, Shuji badly wanted to stop always being in frustrating situations of this kind. He had a great desire to become a genuine middle-school student, one who was accepted by his peers, and to have it said of him, if only for the most delusory of reasons, "he's a pretty amusing sort of guy."

A clue as to how he might achieve this was put into his head by the drill instructor known as "the Snapping Turtle," who one day chose to lecture the senior boys on the habit some of them had "of going to this fruity something or other." He was referring to a local snack bar or "fruit parlor," but the habit of calling such places a "fruity something" spread through the school. So one day when lessons were over and Shuji was filing out through the school gate, he called to two of his friends and asked them if they would like to go to the fruity something, adding swiftly that he would treat them. Having made this bold proposal, he felt himself going tense all over, and his face took on a somewhat sour, frigid expression. The two of them looked at him suspiciously and Shuji, who was already imagining the worst, avoided their eyes. However, the two agreed to go, although it was decided they would do well to avoid the Kasumi-cho area where there was every chance of being seen by one of the teachers. So they set out in the opposite direction, toward the Toyo Eiwa Girls' School.

Each step they took, Shuji could feel his legs growing heavy and his mouth going dry. Suppose they were caught, what sort of punishment would they get? They might even be expelled. Even so, it would be a bit too cowardly to go back on his own proposal now, although finally that was exactly what he did.

Overpowered by feelings of self-loathing, he finally said in a wretched, hoarse voice:

"Perhaps we ought to drop the idea today. . ."

"What?"

"There's only just recently been a warning. . . There're bound to be people from the Guidance Committee about."

His two companions complained that they knew all about that before they had agreed to come with him, and now gazed at him with obvious contempt. It hadn't been their idea to go to a fruit parlor, after all, so they stared balefully at the person who had contrived this atmosphere of gloom and misery. Luckily they were just passing a shop that sold fried buns and Shuji suggested in a strangled voice that he would buy some.

For middle-school students at that time, in particular for one like Shuji, something like buying fried buns was a tremendous undertaking, and it gave a powerful sense of achievement when successfully performed. Now at last he could get his breath back again, and he swaggered along stuffing the spoils crudely into his mouth. All three of them were doing this when a schoolgirl suddenly appeared as they were going up Toriizaka and seized one of his buns.

The incident certainly made Aiko's stock rise at the Toyo Eiwa Girls' School, but it had an adverse effect on Shuji's chances of being referred to as "an amusing guy." He could not say that it had been his sister, nor would anyone have believed him if he had; so he was simply despised as a weed, a washout, the kind of useless creep who has a fried bun taken away from him by a girl.

That year Aiko and Shuji spent part of the summer with their mother at Hayama, the last summer they were destined to spend by the sea. Ryuko was forty-six years old now, but she wore a very striking white swimsuit and white swimcap, and spent more time in the water than out of it. Her habit of ignoring what anyone else thought had grown stronger with the years. When she had been approached on the Ginza just before coming here by a member of the Women's League with a leaflet calling for restraint in dress, Ryuko had given her so frigid a look that the woman had looked away as if she felt *she* was doing something wrong.

Ryuko had taken swimming lessons that year at the YWCA, joining a class with a number of women who were all young enough to be her daughters. She showed her usual energy in commandeering the attention of the instructor and endeavoring to master all the secrets of doing the crawl. The young man responded nervously:

"That's it, madam. When you raise the one hand from the water the other should be ahead of you in the water at an angle of forty-five degrees. I'm afraid madam's hand tends to be right underneath her. And before you push your head into the water it is advisable to take a deep breath and hold it in."

For this reason Ryuko felt qualified, now that they were all together at Hayama, to give the children dreary lessons in the crawl, demonstrating with arms no longer young the correct way of doing it. It was on her account, too, that Aiko and Shuji were obliged to go through a very humiliating experience, which happened as follows.

Some distance beyond the diving platform floated a wooden, painted buoy, and Aiko and Shuji swam out to it one day. The slap of the waves on the sides of the buoy, and the slight chill of the sea breeze on the skin when one climbed out of the water, gave the two children an exciting sense of being far out at sea, and the tiredness of their limbs was so pleasant that they would have been happy to lie there dreaming in the sun. But a babble of voices started up at their side. These belonged to three young men who had arrived at the buoy before them and were now shouting excitedly to each other:

"Hey, look at that! Just take a look at that!"

"Yeah. I see what you mean."

"She's not moving at all."

"Wow, look. She's a real old granny!"

When Aiko and her brother looked up, they saw a white swimcap among the waves headed in their direction. They knew straight away it was their mother. Ryuko was doing the crawl, the orthodox crawl as she was in the habit of calling it. Stylistically she seemed to have got it right, but her arm movements were remarkably sluggish and she was only making very limited headway. She plunged her head deep into the water, and each time the face surfaced horizontally she opened her mouth in orthodox fish-like manner and took a deep gulp of air, plodding on stroke by stroke at an almost imperceptible rate of progress. Her two children were so appalled by this sight that they dived into the sea and swam off toward the shore in frantic haste.

The beach was emptier than it used to be, and there were fewer kiosks with reed screens set up before them, but it was still full of life. There were multicolored beach parasols, and fair-haired foreign children ran about, small boys holding duck-shaped water wings. A heat shimmer rose from the dry sand, and if you trod on any of the dry, white shells scattered here and there they were so burning hot you could easily blister the soles of your feet.

Aiko stretched her elegant, perhaps overly slim body on the sand, feeling the sunlight slowly burning into her back, and lay quite still. She was thinking about the phosphorescence she had seen in the sea last night. A great swarm of those animalcules had turned up near the beach, and the crests of the waves had shone bluish white, sparkling as they fell, spreading a sheen over the whole expanse of water. She had paddled into the sea until she was wet to her thighs, trying to catch hold of this delicate, ghostly shining, but whatever it was simply dissolved in streaks across the palms of her hands and slipped back into the water. Then that brother of hers had to come running up and be idiotic enough to claim he had found out what it was. He said it was like a small grain of rice. How stupid can you get, she thought. Her next thought was about something else: iced sherbet.

She still had the same demanding appetite, although luckily it did not seem to affect the girlish slimness of her figure. Meals were no longer provided at school so she was unable to go on winning double marks on the meals chart. One reason for this was that there had been an outbreak of dysentery at the school once, but the main one was probably that the food situation in the country had gradually deteriorated until school meals had become an impossibility. Before coming to Hayama, Aiko had been taken by her elder brother, Shun'ichi, to a department store, along with his friend of schoolboy days, the hero of the baked-potato incident, Tatsunori Shiroki. The three of them had gone to the store's restaurant, but it had been a "No Rice Menu Day" and there had not been a single thing they had wanted to eat.

Eventually they had settled for sardines with flowers of egg. "Flowers of egg" was, in fact, only the lees of beancurd and hardly renowned for its flavor. Still, it had been tasty enough. She couldn't for the life of her think why her brother and his friend had eaten it with such marked disrelish. She moved slightly, and the dry sand ran down her arms and legs like hundreds and thousands of tiny, invisible crabs.

She started thinking about Shiroki. For some odd reason he got on with that elder brother of hers, and they sometimes went to baseball matches together. She started to recall his face in detail, unconsciously scrutinizing it for faults. The brow was certainly too high, so he was bound to go bald early. His eyebrows were very bushy as well. His jaw jutted out too much, a bit like that trademark for Kao soap. Still, on the whole, Aiko cheekily concluded, he wasn't too bad, as she lay there on the sand with her head resting on her arm. He was certainly an improvement on what he had been when he had come to Hakone. He was more grown-up now. What she most liked about him was his slight swarthiness and the width of his shoulders.

She then remembered something she had said to him, it must have been at New Year, when they went to see the big rugby match between Keio and Meiji; and there, on the beach in the brilliant sunlight and with the chatter of voices all about her, she poked out her tongue slightly at the thought of it. She had said, in response to some remark, that if he became a full university professor she would be prepared to become his wife. When he smilingly asked her why it had to be a professor, she replied that it was her duty to marry a medical man twice as good as the average. This was the Nire concept of marriage, which had been fed her as a child by that unreliable source, Aunt Momoko, and she repeated it with no apparent qualms or doubts as to its truth. Shiroki replied that if this meant having to become an adopted son (and she said that it did), then he wasn't too keen, which made the two young men roar with laughter.

She wondered what Shiroki would write if he were to send her the sort of letter she had received from Agnes Nielsen. This led her on to reflections about the letters from various girls she kept receiving at school, and how much she would like to show them all her preposterously suntanned face now. She could feel the dry heat of the day penetrating the whole of her body, front, back and both sides, and sand, sea, sky were full of dazzling light. When she closed her eyes she could see in the blackness fairy-tale globules of fire that rose up and moved about incessantly. Her arms, her legs and the nape of her neck were burning, tingling, yet deep within her body she felt a weariness, a heaviness. . .

Still, that had been a bit too awful, saying she'd become his wife.

Behaving like a primary-school kid, and she poked out her tongue again, acknowledging her blunder and demonstrating her indifference to it all now. Then she suddenly rolled over. The sun's great, incandescent disc was almost dead overhead. Fierce rays that put an end to thought poured down, and the beach about her seethed with heat and light. The sound of the waves approaching and receding was mingled with meaningless, shrill cries.

Then suddenly there was a roar in the sky way off to one side, finally turning into a metallic scream that seemed to pierce right down into one's veins, and three small planes in close formation, the sunlight glinting on their duralumin wings, flashed over the crowds of semi-naked people on the beach to recede into the distant sky.

Aiko scowled. Airplanes really got on her nerves. What a nuisance they were. She scowled again, contorting that tiny, oval, perfect face her school friends found so charming; and then she jumped up, brushing the sand off herself with one hand.

Much further along the beach, near the hotel, her elder brother was standing in the water. He had arrived in Hayama that very day and had gone for a swim. Shun'ichi the medical student, due to graduate next year, seemed to grow in no direction but upward, and his awkwardly tall, thin body stood there like a pole, quite motionless, watching the three planes until they became black specks in the far sky. Drops of salt water dripped from his face and arms. His normally stupid-looking face took on an expression of rare seriousness in that moment when the planes zoomed by, and as he gazed at the thrilling sight a kind of ecstasy rose within him.

He had paid no visits to military airfields these past two years, so it was the first time he had seen this particular aircraft. He had memorized all the details during that brief sighting; the deep cowling of this low-wing monoplane fighter was of a kind he was unfamiliar with, as was the beautiful line formed by the filleting of the wings and the fuselage like that of a fast-swimming fish. Then there had been its startling speed, although what had made the greatest impression was the smooth underside of its fuselage and wings . . . so smooth and bare . . . there was nothing there at all. The undercarriage had been retracted!

Shun'ichi looked behind him. Standing there was his much smaller brother, Shuji, who had come swimming with him and had also been standing in much the same posture until just now. The two looked at each other. Shun'ichi's foolish but friendly face was contorted in a weird

484

fashion. It was the kind of expression one might expect to find on the face of an old lecher on his deathbed, granted a last fleeting vision of a paragon of female beauty.

He spoke in a tone of almost religious reverence:

"Did you see that?"

Shuji grunted and nodded his dripping face forcefully in reply. Then the two brothers, despite the many years between them, automatically thrust out their hands at the same moment, and shook. They had just seen something they had never expected to see, a new fighter plane that realized all their dreams of what such an aircraft should be, and it had suddenly appeared out of the blue like that. This was, although the two of them did not know it then, a carrier-borne fighter which had formally been introduced into service that July, and which was to become known all over the world. They had just seen the Zero Mark II.

Chapter

10

In the office of the Aoyama branch of the Nire Hospital, the Registrar, Oishi, who had recently acquired this new title, was reading the day's newspaper with passionate concern. The same sight could have been seen in cookhouse circles, among the nurses, both male and female, and in Matsubara as well as in Aoyama. All of them were people who tended to take little notice of any wider world beyond their own small circle, so this ravenous consumption of newsprint had not occurred for well over a decade. Back in the past, particularly during the period when Kiichiro had been a Diet member, the interns had often debated political questions, but nowadays the political situation was not such that the fate of the nation could be entrusted to the care of any one individual, nor was there anybody to read newspaper articles aloud in the style of Billiken. Yet numerous people could be seen reading the newspaper with serious expressions on their faces.

A great many things had happened since the spring of 1941: the American restrictions on Japanese assets, the signing of the Japanese-Soviet Neutrality Pact, the inauguration of Japanese-American negotiations, the breaking-off of talks between Japan and the Dutch East Indies, and the German invasion across the Soviet border. All these had been sudden and unforeseen events, and left people with the feeling that they had no idea what was going to happen next. However, a general idea of what might befall them had been created by all this, even if only deep down inside people, perhaps only in the semiconscious parts of their beings, and they could sense the future as something heavy and oppressive hanging over their heads. This obscure knowledge was gradually given precise outlines in each day's broadcasts and newspaper articles. Everyone in the Nire Hospital gossiped and argued about these things, until even some of the patients were no longer immune to what was in the air, though what it was seemed to defy the normal processes of their imaginations. Usually these people treated information as a starting point for free, sometimes wild fantasies, but the only reality these great world events seemed to possess was their appearance in the newspaper headlines, and these seemed so alien to the everyday world that there was nothing for the imagination to hold onto. The events were too large, too far beyond the powers of the individual to influence, and the truth of them seemed to be settled elsewhere. As the various Nire people gazed at newspapers they were not accustomed to reading with any attention anyway, the only impression they received from these carefully supervised pages was that everything seemed oddly similar. But though the official interpretation of what was happening imposed an unchanging uniformity, the events themselves certainly showed a startling development from summer to autumn, when even people who were bored stiff by newspapers could be seen reading them. All this happened at an unprecedented pace as history rushed headlong toward some kind of goal. The headlines they read were these:

July

German Army Announces Further Triumphs. 4,100 Soviet Planes Shot Down. 40,000 Prisoners Taken. 2,200 Tanks Destroyed.

Imperial Conference Held Today. Decision on Supreme National Policy. Unshakable Resolution concerning Present Conditions.

Army Announces Achievements of Past Six Months. Twelve Major Battles. Retire to Chungching. Front Line More Than 2,000 Miles Long.

Medals Awarded to Survivors of First China Incident. Special Awards of Glorious Order of Golden Kite. 8,009 from Army, 46 from Navy.

Switch to Dining out, Sugar Supply Mishap. Should Be Enough but Cut in Ration to Make Up Deficit.

Imperial Mandate: To Strengthen Country's Internal Situation Konoye Cabinet Resigns. Prime Minister Konoye Submits Request to Imperial Majesty Last Night.

Prince Konoye Reappointed. Sets about Creating Third Konoye Cabinet.

Joint Defense of Indochina. Complete Accord Reached between Japan and France.

Britain and America Freeze All Japanese Assets.

Dauntless Response of the Empire. All Foreign Assets in Japan Frozen. Control of All Foreign Transactions Promulgated Tomorrow, in Effect Same Day.

Britain Suddenly Abrogates Anglo-Japanese Commerce and Navigation Treaty. Together with America Imposes Embargo on Japan.

America Creating Needless Alarms. We Believe in Peaceful Methods, Says Cabinet Chief Ito. Asks West to Think Again.

Dutch East Indies Follows Anglo-American Lead as Expected, Suspends Credit Pact and Freezes Assets.

Dutch East Indies Suddenly Announces Suspension Last Year's Dutch-Japanese Oil Treaty. Great Concern over What Other Steps May Be Taken.

August

Supreme Commander Armed Forces Boldly Proclaims Japan Will Defend Indochina. Sea Eagles Arrive Outskirts Saigon.

Thai-Japan Loan Deal. Countermeasure to Anglo-American Asset Freezing.

President Roosevelt Announces Stepping Up Anti-Japanese Oil Embargo. Soviets to Be Given Preferential Treatment.

Britain Mistakenly Assumes Improvement in Own Global Situation. Calls for More Forceful Measures in East Asia. Main Objective Is Appeal for American Strength and Support.

Constant Anglo-American Intimidation of Japan. British Official Circles Maintain Choice of Peace or War Up to Japan.

Effects of ABCD Encirclement. On the Spot Reports by Phone. Barbed Wire Seals Singapore Border: Japanese Business Community Prepares to Leave. All Night Air Exercises in Philippines: Tragic Plight of Resident Japanese.

Joint Communiqué from Britain, America. Obvious Plans for World Domination. Entire Japanese Nation Will Resist.

Anglo-American Enticement Attempt of Soviets into Anti-Japanese Strategy. Promise All-out Economic Military Aid in Return. Tripartite Conference Planned.

Only Vehicles Using Synthetic Fuels to Be Licensed. Restrictions Stepped Up on Buses and Taxis.

No One Shall Be Idle. Mobilization of Entire Nation.

British Prime Minister Boasts Britain, America to Take Concerted Action in Event Crisis East Asia. Churchill's Wild Accusations against Japan.

Infallible Guide Air-Raid Drill. Lt. Colonel Nanba Explains. Evacuation from Cities Must Not Be Allowed. Neighborhood Groups Must Put Out Incendiaries.

Ambassador Nomura Relays Japanese Viewpoint on Pacific Problems to America.

Collection of Iron and Copper Household Goods. Provide Armaments for Your Country. Hand Over All Those Things You Don't Need.

America Hastily Preparing for War, Says Envoy Wakasugi on His Return.

America Gives Serious Attention to Konoye Message. Next Few Weeks of Major Importance.

September

Now at Critical Turning Point in Empire's History. One Hundred Million People Must Rise Up This Autumn. Military News Chief Mabuchi Urges Readiness to Defend This Land of Our Ancestors.

Siege of Leningrad. Key to Military Situation in Russo-German War. German Army Launches Determined Attack on Red Army Defenses.

Japanese-American Negotiations to Continue, Secretary of State Hull Tells Journalists.

Japanese Nationals in England to Leave. Two Passenger Ships Sent to Europe.

489

Chungching Problem Vexes Japanese-American Talks. Chiang Kai-shek Plea to American Government.

October

Imperial Army Occupies Chengchou. Front Extends More Than 3,000 Miles.

Anglo-American Manila Conference Debates Joint Air Strategy. Maneuver to Strengthen Anti-Japanese Encirclement.

With Increasing Restrictions Living Standards Must Decline. Trade Minister Requests People's Understanding and Readiness.

Three Passenger Ships to Restore Interrupted Services to U.S. Talks Set Up between Japan and America.

The Japanese Ships Are Coming! Our Brethren in America Rejoice.

Fate of Imperial Army Now in Balance. Navy in Fine Fettle, Says Colonel Hiraide in Lecture. Stresses Crisis Nature of Japanese-American Relations.

Konoye Cabinet Resigns Three Months after Formation.

Dramatic Last Moments of Konoye Cabinet. Cabinet Chief Ito's Voice Trembles during Announcement.

Imperial Mandate: Army Minister Tojo Resigns. Will Form New Cabinet. Almost Complete as of Early Hours This Morning.

Expresses Indomitable Resolve. Demands Iron Hard Solidarity. Important Directive from Prime Minister Tojo.

Graduation Next Year in September. This Includes High Schools. Become Branch of National Defense.

"I Will Not Shirk Responsibility." American President's Grave Attitude to Japan-America Situation. Broadcasts Tomorrow.

Shooting War Already Begun. Roosevelt Asks Congress Rescind Neutrality Act in Challenging Broadcast.

Immediate Anti-Air-Raid Measures Handbook. Expect Some Slight Bombing in Your Neighborhood. All Who Can Work to Register at Local Center.

November

America Somewhat Appreciative Our Resolve but No Real Change in Awareness.

Air Treaty Due Soon. Complete Australian Dependence on America. Panic-stricken by Specter of Danger.

Envoy Kurusu Sent to Break Deadlock Japanese-American Relations. Support for Ambassador Nomura.

American Covert Maneuvers. Network of Hostile Bases Encircles Japan.

Soviets Appeal Britain, America Create Second Front in Western Europe.

Tatsuta Maru *and Sister Ship Set Sail from America. 1,680 Japanese on Board.*

American Newspaper Declares Little Hope of Success in Japanese-American Negotiations. Demands of Both Sides Diametrically Opposed.

America Considers Withdrawal All Navy, Army Units in China.

Unprecedented Outrage by Panama Government. Expulsion of Resident Japanese. American Puppet President Ignores Our Protests.

Imperial Government Urges Reconsideration in Matter of Gravest Possible Concern. Absolute Refusal Accept Such Measures.

Desperate Japanese Business Community. Panama Government Refuses Comply Request to Think Again.

Desperate Attempt to Stir Up Anti-Japanese Feelings. British, American Leaders' Constant Irresponsible Statements and Deceit.

Widescale Amendments Military Draft Law Procedures. Class C Category for Call-up. Secondary Militiamen to Be Enlisted.

Passengers on Tatsuta Maru *Weep on Reaching Homeland. America Totally Intent on Entering War. All-out Preparations for Anti-Japanese Conflict, Say Returning Passengers.*

We Must Endure Winter Cold. Heating below Following Levels.

Envoy Kurusu Arrives Washington for Talks with Secretary of State Hull.

Totally Prepared for Any Eventuality. Army and Navy Ministers Stress Resolution of Armed Forces.

Prime Minister States Three Principles for Foreign Diplomacy. Total Exclusion of All Hostile Activity. Positive Enforced Containment of Present Conflicts. No Interference in Our Task of Bringing China Incident to Successful Conclusion.

Foreign Minister's Address. Limit to Ability to Cooperate with America. Will Not Press for Extended Talks.

Ambassadors Nomura and Kurusu in Late Night Conference. Talks with Secretary of State Hull to Continue.

Britain Feels Little Chance of Avoiding Crisis.

Third Japanese-American Talks Today. Discussions Continue Record Length of Time.

Refugee Ships from Southeast Asia and Philippines, Hie Maru *and* Hakone Maru, *Arrive Kobe Port.*

Both America, Japan Concerned Maintaining Peace in Pacific. Informal Talks Last Two and Half Hours.

Refugee Ships to America Again. Tatsuta Maru *Leaves at End of Month.*

Crisis Point in Japanese-American Talks Approaches. Outcome Depends on American Attitudes. Decision Due Soon.

Climax of Negotiations. America Submits Written Document. Fourth Meeting. Summary of Attitude toward Japanese Demands.

Facing Serious Situation. Fifth Meeting. Presidential Conference Requested. American Draft Outline of Final Propositions?

Atmosphere in Washington Pessimistic. America Dogmatically Refuses Alter Principles. . .

Sometime around the middle of that November Tatsunori Shiroki, who had just been made a lieutenant junior grade in the navy, left Tokyo Station with his colleagues from Military Medical School in a great hurry. He had been posted to the aircraft carrier *Zuikaku*.

He had exchanged a few meaningless conversational phrases with his parents, who were of advanced middle age, and his one brother, who was younger than himself. His uncle, who arrived late, had then dashed up and occupied the remainder of the time with various witticisms and words of encouragement. The train soon left.

Everything was confused and hurried, like dreams on a restless night. All he had been able to do was submit unresistingly, almost unconsciously, to the movement of time that had carried him forward in this dizzy manner through the chaos of the past days: the purely formal examination at the Military Medical School, the graduation ceremony there, the tea party afterward, the packing, the quick return to his old medical department to pay his respects and say his good-byes, the formalities of having his name taken off the school register, and now this departure.

Still, it had really started, all this rush and panic, in the spring, when he had graduated from the Medical Faculty at Tokyo University and been taken on at a surgical hospital. Shiroki, although really a freshman there, had a first-class degree and had volunteered for two years' service in the navy, and since he was already of ensign rank his professor not only gave him appendectomies to do but also stomach operations that would normally have been entrusted to a more experienced hand. In September he joined his naval unit and spent a month doing arms training and marching. Then at the Military Medical School in Tsukiji in downtown Tokyo he took a crash course in naval hygienics, which was literally drummed into his head in the form of instant knowledge. While this was going on, the world situation was changing day by day, and this added to the already stifling sense of pressure. An oppressive atmosphere built up in the Military Medical School itself, the feeling that something was bound to happen, that it was no longer a question of whether there would be a war or not but only of when it would start and where. Japan had been forced into a situation where some solution had to be found and put into effect, for there was now no other way. At least, that was how Shiroki felt about the matter, though one part of himself found it impossible to believe it would actually happen, and that belief was more firmly rooted than the reasons that told him it had to. In particular the idea of getting mixed up in a war with a country like America was surely unthinkable, absurd. . .

The constant motion of the compartment and a funny sense of endlessly traveling but of having as yet covered only a short distance altered as the train slowed down and came to a gradual, screeching halt at a station. While the train was stopped, Shiroki had a sensation of returning to his true self, but soon they were moving again and he gazed idly out of the window at the hills and woods as they filed by, sometimes following them with his eyes as they moved away from him. The period just before, when the rattle of the carriage wheels had ceased, seemed to take on a dream-like existence. Only this present was real. The sky was bright with the artificial clarity of early winter, an almost cruel blue, and the leaves of the trees were faded and yellow, with pale sunlight spilling and playing among them. A number of towns went by. Finally a wintry paleness came into the sky with the approach of evening, and then twilight was over all.

This second-class compartment was full of people like himself from the Military Medical School. There were even instructors who were seeing them off. But the rich, endless laughter and the idle talk had come to an end some time ago, and it was now night. The train ran on, apparently gathering speed all the time. Most people were sleeping, since they had not had much time to sleep the night before. Shiroki was dozing, his chin resting on the breast of his number one uniform.

At Kure, the naval base south of Hiroshima, about half the passengers got off. They were due to board ships at Kure port or at nearby Marifu. A few words, a shake of the hand, and then they had descended onto the dark platform, their sea chests on their shoulders. Civilians got on and soon filled the vacant seats they had left.

The ferry crossed the Kanmon Strait between Honshu and Kyushu at dawn. It was the first time Shiroki had done this. Most of the others got off at Moji on the Kyushu side, since they were going across the island to the port of Sasebo on the west coast. The train began to feel empty at last, despite the fact that there were few empty seats. Only four of these young men were left on the train now, including

Shiroki, as it traveled down the east coast of Kyushu to the port of Saeki, where their ships were waiting.

At Saeki, three of them were able to proceed as planned. One was to board the battleship *Mutsu* and two the aircraft carrier *Akagi,* and all three took the regular motor launch, waving good-bye to Shiroki as he saw them off. The ship he was supposed to be boarding, the *Zuikaku,* was no longer there.

"A great way to start," he muttered to himself. "About turn and back again." And he picked up his baggage and started walking.

The *Zuikaku* would be in Kure through the eighteenth, setting sail on the nineteenth. His orders were to proceed "with all dispatch" to Kure, but he was exhausted in every fiber of his body so, having obtained the permission of the Saeki military command, he checked the train times and decided to spend the night in the nearby resort town of Beppu. After he had taken a bath, he felt relaxed again as if nothing really untoward had happened, but that night he had a bad, suffocating dream from which he awoke any number of times. He could see the *Zuikaku* heading for dark, wide-spreading waters, and he was in a small boat trying to reach it, but all the time the ship went further and further away.

The next day was the seventeenth, and he caught an early train that morning, back across the Kanmon Strait. The sky was quite clear again today, so high and blue it seemed to extend forever. On his right lay the peaceful sea, and on his left were the gentle undulations of the western Honshu mountains. How innocent it all seemed, how quiet, how deeply asleep. Last night, for the first time in some weeks, he had been quite alone, finally separated from his classmates. Now, swaying on the train, he was alone again. He looked at the placid grandeur of the natural world as it calmly awaited the coming of winter and a sense of irritation rose within him, stirrings of unrest and dismay. And yet the green of the pine trees seemed so soft, so gentle, so calm. He seemed never to have seen such delicate shadings of green in pine trees before, never felt such closeness, such intimacy with them.

Late that afternoon he reached Kure. When he arrived at the motor-launch office to find out what time he could board, it seemed the *Zuikaku* was no longer there either. It had left port before the scheduled time and he was again too late. He felt the same weariness that had overtaken him yesterday, only it seemed worse this time. It was as if his head had gone completely numb. But this was no time to hang about.

He hurried to the personnel office of the naval station and waited twenty minutes or more while they found out what had happened to his ship. Apparently it was to be in Oita, which was very near where he had come from, until midnight on the eighteenth. Things must be happening to make the ship behave in this frantic way. He had to get a move on, get his baggage together again and go back. While waiting for a connection at Hiroshima, he walked the midnight streets of this town he had never visited before, and the sense of strain and foreboding caused by this unique journey seemed to be reflected back at him from the dark streets, advancing like a slow, black tide.

As the train set off to take him toward the Kanmon Strait for the third time, he thought of how it must be at home. The house would be fast asleep now. He felt that same quietness, an unbroken absence of sound, in his thoughts about his parents and his brother. He thought about two or three of his friends as well. He remembered Shun'ichi Nire, with whom he had kept up a friendship ever since their junior high school days.

Shun'ichi had graduated at the same time as himself, though from another university, and started work as one of the medical staff in the Department of Psychiatry at Keio University; but he had been drafted at the beginning of September and joined the 7th Unit of the Eastern Army. Unlike Shiroki, who had volunteered, for Shun'ichi this had come as a bolt from the blue. He had been given B classification and had assumed that, even if he were to be drafted sometime, it was still way off in the future. When Shiroki had first heard about Shun'ichi's being drafted, his immediate reaction had been to find it very funny. When he thought about Shun'ichi, he remembered the long obsession with aircraft and the refusal to read any kind of book except those about the coming war with America. But it was his friend's elongated body and face that came to mind—it was hard to imagine anyone like that actually involved in fighting. He seemed totally unsuited for war, nor likely to be of any military use if he did take part. Once he had been called up, Shun'ichi had immediately applied to become a trainee officer, but it seemed he would have to remain an ordinary private for some time at least. Shiroki remembered what his friend had been like during military training at school, and could not help feeling sorry for him any more than he could help the feeling of mirth the prospect aroused.

Toward the end of October, when he had leave one Sunday, he tried telephoning Shun'ichi at his home, hoping he could arrange to meet him somewhere that day. This he wasn't able to do, but he did meet his sister Aiko instead. It was Aiko who had come to the phone and said, in a surprisingly serious tone of voice, that she would very much like to see him; surprising in someone whom he had thought of merely as a cute little girl. Aiko came to meet him at Shibuya and they had tea in a cafe there. This was the first time he had been with her without Shun'ichi's being present, and when he saw her waiting for him by the statue of the faithful dog Hachiko in front of Shibuya Station, he was struck by how much she had grown up in so short a time, and felt disconcerted for a few moments. But he soon realized she was only an innocent schoolgirl.

"Shun'ichi's lost weight, got really thin. Isn't it awful being in the army?" said Aiko, frowning a little in what was still a childish way.

"The navy's just as bad."

"Well, I personally dislike the army. It all seems so crude in the army, so vulgar."

When Shiroki said he would soon graduate from the Military Medical School and then join his ship, the face of the young girl before him grew suddenly and almost comically grave, and this unlikely seriousness made her look years older all at once.

"You mean you already know what ship you'll be on?"

"No, not yet."

"When you do, you will let me know, won't you?"

The tone in which she spoke was still serious, but this time it was an innocent, childish seriousness that affected him in such a way he could only grunt a brusque assent.

When they said good-bye, she again mysteriously spoke in the polite tones of an adult, wishing him well and advising him to take good care of himself. As he sat there in the darkness of the swaying train, he recalled the oddly faltering manner in which she had spoken, and then he tried to get some sleep.

He arrived in Oita around lunchtime on the eighteenth, and went straight to the naval wharf. This time the *Zuikaku* was there. The great, gray, flat vessel was lying quite close in, along with her identical sister ship the *Shokaku*. The huge flight deck and the comparatively small, tidy superstructure made a striking contrast, stressing how special this ship was, as if it possessed secret powers and belonged more in legend than in the real world; but now it was resting motionless on the waves, concealing its strength. Unlike his friend Shun'ichi, Shiroki had not the least interest in aircraft or warships, but the sight of the *Zuikaku* seemed to lay to rest the anxieties and fears of the last three days, for he had been genuinely starting to think that the dream he had in the inn at Beppu of not being able to join his ship might be coming true.

He found out what time the next launch was and then went into town to a small *sushi* restaurant. The wedges of rice, fresh fish and cucumber tasted marvelous. He felt he had not eaten *sushi* as good as this for months, and a sense of relaxed happiness swept through him. Then the man, also in uniform, sitting next to him at the counter suddenly asked him where he was bound, and showed great pleasure when he heard it was the *Zuikaku,* for he was going there too. His name was Lieutenant Tsukamoto, he said, laughing in a bluff, high-spirited way that revealed a mouthful of stained, irregular teeth. Shiroki felt another burst of relief when he heard that his neighbor had also dashed onto an express at Kure in pursuit of the ship.

Lieutenant Tsukamoto may have had filthy teeth but his eyes looked very friendly and Shiroki felt, for no good reason, that he could rely on this heroic-looking character. He called himself a "flier," and now that he had appeared all the loneliness Shiroki had experienced during the past three days was gone. Tsukamoto stuffed his two platefuls of *sushi* into his snaggle-toothed mouth with remarkable speed.

"Great stuff, this *sushi*. . . Marvelous. The rice is good in these parts. Nothing like Kyushu rice."

They took the late afternoon launch out to their ship, together with a number of higher-ranking officers. The *Zuikaku* could only be boarded from the starboard side, and as the launch approached the steel bulk of the carrier, Shiroki received no impression of a place that was to be his home from now on, but only of a gray, steel vessel, completely alien to all human needs and emotions. The launch went into reverse, sending out a short, white burst of foam, then bumped alongside the towering height of the great carrier, which sat there unmoved by this slight commotion below.

The executive officer introduced him to the first and second officers' messes, where Shiroki formally announced his presence. After dinner, together with the new cadets, he went to pay his respects to the captain, and after that to the principal medical officer. He was to share a cabin with a paymaster lieutenant, but since no bunk had been prepared he had to bed down for the first night in the officers' sick bay. He felt so exhausted and yet so excited that he wondered whether he would be able to sleep. There was a constant noise from the engine room, a ceaseless, dull rumble that seemed to fill the whole ship. But as soon as he had pulled the blanket over his head he fell immediately into a deep sleep. At almost the same time the *Zuikaku* raised anchor, and the 29,800-ton giant began to move quietly toward the open sea.

The ship looked quite different when viewed from inside. The steel dividing walls and partitions, the ceilings, the pillars and girders all seemed to have an independent life of their own, while the human inhabitants were like mice living inside the belly of a monster, scuttling here and there in constant confusion and bewilderment. There were ladders and ramps and hatches and long, narrow, cramped gangways and innumerable rooms, all made of steel and all with the same bleak appearance. It was a maze of extraordinary complexity where everything looked the same, yet where the door of one's own cabin looked different every time; and for the inexperienced newcomer shut up inside it, the awareness of right and left, of forward and backward, even of up and down, became confused and unreliable. Shiroki was eager to get a grasp of the geography of the place and did a tour of inspection at night, which it would be no exaggeration to say was a kind of voyage itself.

There were three decks. On the two lower decks the aircraft were all neatly stowed away in packed rows with their wings folded, and here the mechanics swarmed and the three airplane elevators rattled up and down. It was not like the interior of a steel building, as he had imagined it, but more like being in a great factory. In the corridor to the engine room the already stifling air became heavy with the stench of oil and filled with the great rumble of the machines as they turned over and groaned incessantly. When he tried to get back to his cabin on his own he lost his way in this deliberately planned maze, 886 feet long and 121 feet wide, although that was merely the size of the container holding this winding enigma.

Shiroki wrote an amateurish *haiku* in his diary:

> Walk as much as you
> Like, this ship's inside will
> Not be found out.

He had not kept a diary for a long time, not since he was a child. As soon as he had heard of his posting to this ship he decided he would, even if it was only a bare record of each day. It was a cloth-covered notebook of particularly poor quality paper.

Since he had so little grasp of the world about him, not even being able to distinguish east from west, his daily routine was a very restricted one. The mornings were spent in the sick bay examining patients. At first his role had been that of a looker-on, but with the regular health checkup for the crew he became more directly involved. This included an inspection of the private parts of a great many men, which caused the senior doctor little trouble since he was bothered by no sense of delicacy in such matters.

"Out with it!" he would briskly order the man in front of him, who just as briskly obeyed, although the doctor was often obliged to scold the object once it appeared:

"You're issued with rubbers. What do you mean by getting in a filthy state like that?"

Shiroki could not yet command that tone and form of language. When he was diagnosing someone he seemed to forget at times he was a military man, feeling much as he had done when working in a civilian surgery. Next door to the sick bay was an operating room with X-ray and other machines, and he was secretly hoping that someone would soon get appendicitis, for only by taking a scalpel in his hand could he hope to get some bearings, give some meaning to this alien new existence. It was the machine-like systematization of the life he found most difficult to get used to, a sense that nobody existed in his own right. So when he discovered one of the men had a concretion in his right seminal passage, and he was probing this hard lump in the man's testicle, he felt for a moment a trace of satisfaction in his work much like he had experienced in civilian life.

When his morning duty was over, he could either go to the mess or to his cabin. There was nowhere else. If he had gone up to the bridge he would have gained a little more understanding of what the ship was doing, but he was only a brand-new medic and did not feel he should.

The ship had very little movement; one could only feel a slight swaying. On the first morning, Shiroki had got up and looked out of the porthole, and immediately below him were the waves, so close it seemed he could have put out his hand and touched them. He could see the horizon, but nothing else besides the sky and sea. He heard they were passing south of Shikoku, and on the next morning he saw the island of Hachijojima away on the starboard side, which meant they must be about a hundred and fifty miles south of Tokyo. That was the only sign of land; otherwise there was the gently swaying sea on which occasionally one white-flecked wave traveled slowly and mysteriously backward to mingle with the following wave.

The one thing he did understand was that they had started to move north now. He knew this because it had clearly become colder. When they had first left port he had felt hot with only one blanket, but now he was cold even with two. He opened his sea chest and dragged out the heavy quilted kimono he had packed right at the bottom.

He did not feel much inclined to try guessing where the ship might be going. His cabin companion, the paymaster lieutenant, had his theories, however:

"I reckon we'll be heading south. That's after we've joined up somewhere with the rest of the fleet. We'll carry out the southern strike regardless of how the Americans respond. If we go on the way we have been, we'll just keep on slowly losing out."

The "southern strike" he was referring to was an assault on Southeast Asia. The old sailors in the mess, however, tended to talk more cynically. They explained that the *Zuikaku* had been built with the emphasis on speed and storage for as many planes as possible and that the armor plating of the ship was lousy. One good smack from a torpedo and she was a dead duck. It was also a new ship and so the working schedules had not been gone over thoroughly enough. As it was, some of the aircraft personnel had their hands more than full with just the basic business of taking off and landing.

"Well, Lieutenant, we seem to have embarked on an unlucky ship," said Lieutenant Tsukamoto, Shiroki's acquaintance from the *sushi* restaurant. "Another six hours late and we could have missed her, too. . ."

He grinned with his snaggle teeth as he said this, provoking a response from one of the old sailors, who was no older than either of them but had seen some slight service on the carrier:

"Still, she's fast, I'll say that. When she starts moving at combat speed the walls start to creak and rattle. They rattle like hell."

Shiroki was put in charge of the coded messages concerning medical matters and, together with a newly appointed paymaster petty officer, he learned how to decipher and construct the naval A codes from the chief cipher officer. It looked extremely difficult at first, but when he tried making an actual message he found it surprisingly simple. It was pleasant to think that a trained receiver with a table of random numbers and a list of code terminology could soon read it. While Shiroki was employed making these messages, all somehow reminiscent of the secret-agent games he had played as a child, the *Zuikaku* arrived at Eterofu in the Kurile Islands, on the afternoon of the twenty-second, and anchored in Hitokappu Bay.

The sky seen through the porthole was dull and heavy, with lowering clouds. The sea was lead-colored and had a somber gleam. Right ahead was a bleak waste with snow-covered mountain peaks. The harsh interplay of white snow and bare, black earth with not a blade of grass or sign of human habitation created a scene of total desolation. The waters of the North Pacific swung into the bay, breaking against the long line of the single landing stage, and nearby he glimpsed what seemed to be three fishermen's huts with a wireless mast standing coldly above them. As he was watching, a mist descended and the wireless mast faded from sight. There seemed to be a number of ships floating on the leaden waters of the bay, but he did not have time to work out how many.

Next morning all personnel assembled on deck and, after the raising of the ship's ensign, the harvest thanksgiving ceremony was held, for it was the 23rd of November. Small flakes of snow were falling, drifting and swirling in the cold wind, and the chorus of the national anthem was blown away like these scattered flakes, drowning in the cold roar and breaking of the waves. But the spectacle that presented itself to Shiroki made his body go tense with excitement, for this narrow bay encircled by snow-covered mountains was filled with so many ships one could only stare in wonder. The sea seemed to be completely buried under them: armed shapes of hard steel, packed together in these waste northern waters.

What could have happened last night? Or, rather, what was going to happen now? There were four aircraft carriers (the number would increase to six by that evening). He could see the *Akagi* and the *Kaga*, where classmates from his naval medical course would be on board, and also, close at hand, their sister ship, the *Shokaku*, which had accompanied them here from Oita. Then the battleships *Hiei* and *Kirishima* were here, with the heavy cruisers *Tone* and *Chikuma* and a flotilla of small but ferocious-looking destroyers, all ironclad men-of-war built to do battle. Shiroki could only wonder again what was going to happen. As a boy he had often played with toy warships, and in his imagination warships had always been associated with a make-believe world. Even when he had looked at an actual warship this feeling had persisted somewhere in his mind. But the men-of-war before his eyes were most certainly not toys. They had a disturbing sense of

502

naked, raw reality about them. They were real, and their life seemed to deprive nature of its own, for the cold wastes of Eterofu were dead in comparison. The ships looked alive. They were breathing and trembling, straining to be unleashed. But why should this armada of ships have assembled here in these lonely waters, and at what target were they aimed?

Although he had only been on board for six days, Shiroki was well aware that something quite out of the ordinary was happening. He could feel his body trembling, but it was not with the cold. Something really serious was going to occur, and what it was to be he heard early that evening. All officers were assembled in the mess and the captain announced the plan of strategic action that was to be taken. It was not one that any of them had been able to foretell.

Shiroki was made to drink hard that night, not something he was used to, and it was late when he staggered back to his cabin. The paymaster lieutenant was still nowhere to be seen. His head was confused, his brain sluggishly ticking over, but there was also a sense of awakening, of clear-eyed understanding which would not let him go. He sat at his desk and opened his diary.

> I am genuinely thrilled by the idea of attacking Hawaii. I feel deeply that Japan is doing only what can't help being done. The main thing is to make a success of it, for if we don't the Empire will be in danger. But when I think of the tremendous risk being taken I must admit I feel really anxious inside, even though it never seems to cross my mind that I might myself die. I don't believe that I shall die, but there's still this vague anxiety there. I can't escape the idea that everyone I see is thinking about death, earnestly thinking about it, really feeling it. People smile and say if you're going to write your will do it now while there's time, write down some words for those you leave behind while you can, but I don't feel like writing anything. There's nothing that I feel I really have to write, that I must write. I don't give a second's thought to death as something that could happen to me, but I also feel that, if I have to die, then I should do it without fuss and perfectly calmly. It's a strange feeling, thinking like that. A really funny, strange funny feeling. . .

It struck him that he was repeating himself as he scribbled this down in a crude, illegible script, and he decided he was drunker than he thought. He closed his diary, took off his clothes, then climbed unsteadily up the ladder and tumbled into his berth.

The weather in the North Pacific continued wintry and wild when they left Hitokappu Bay. The sky only cleared on one or two days; otherwise gray clouds covered it, so low at times they seemed indistinguishable from the sea, a sea that lacked any kind of warmth and roared as if it still held back its proper power, gray as the clouds yet darker than they, constantly broken wherever one looked by the clash and churn of the waves. Sometimes the waters had the apparent consistency of plasticine, at others they boiled and seethed like iron in a blast furnace, or rolled in long undulations like flowing lava. But after such comparative calms the sea would swing back into howling, shuddering life, its appearance constantly changing, the waves dancing and running and then crumbling with a roar. They came on endlessly, their clear white manes stretching up and up until the fierce wind caught them, beat them down and tore them apart, scattering them in countless drops and fumes of spray across the mad surface of the water, clouding in white foam the tall crest of the following wave.

Thus the strike force moved on through the tyranny of the northern seas with the aircraft carriers at its center, the *Soryu, Hiryu, Akagi, Kaga, Shokaku* and *Zuikaku,* advancing in two groups of three in line-abreast formation. Ahead could be seen the distant, neat shapes of the cruisers *Chikuma* and *Tone,* and astern two floating fortresses with tangles of masts and complex superstructures standing high above the water, the battleships *Hiei* and *Kirishima*. The flotilla of destroyers stayed close to the carriers. All the boats sank and rose, then yawed violently at times, and the *Shokaku,* which was stationed over a thousand yards away to the side, seemed horribly large and close, its flat hull rocking up and down and its bows plunging head on into enormous waves, then righting itself like an unsinkable toy bobbing to the surface. The great storms of spray could be seen reaching as high as the bridge.

The supply tankers accompanying them were having even more trouble. They sent up long plumes of smoke from their funnels, puffing and blowing with the effort as they were tossed by the waves. One day they would seem to have vanished somewhere over the horizon, but the next day they could be seen struggling painfully along and yet overtaking the *Zuikaku* to refuel one of the ships ahead.

One day a thick fog covered the sea, a clammy, viscous gloom that made the outline of the ship immediately in front fade away into vagueness. The other ships were only glimpsed through openings in the general haze. But the sea itself had grown quiet, and the ship, which had been rocking so wildly, scarcely seemed to sway now. The whole world became dreamlike, spectral, as if it were hardly possible they were advancing to attack Hawaii.

Shiroki could not understand why he felt no tension or strain. Admittedly, he had been severely shaken when he had heard about their mission, as had they all, since everybody got abnormally drunk at the party on the eve of their departure, either under the table or slumped over it after a long session of boisterous songs, glasses and plates scattered about the place. Still in a drunken stupor, he had managed to get himself into bed and had lain there awhile between sleeping and waking, when the loudspeaker had ordered everyone to their duty stations. Shiroki's was at the emergency medical station on the gun deck. He had been in such a state that he was sure he would never be able to get up, but if the order was changed to action stations all the hatches would be closed and he could well be shut inside his own cabin. So he heaved himself desperately out of his bunk and was just about able to find his way to his post, feeling much like a schoolboy who has just, but only just, managed to get to school before the bell.

He had felt bad for the rest of that day. There was a sick weight in his chest and the vomit threatened to rise in his throat every time the ship lurched. At first he assumed this was simply a hangover, but he finally realized he was actually suffering from seasickness. He was unable to smoke; he had only to bring a cigarette near his lips to feel the bile starting to rise. Still, he had no desire to show anyone else how he felt, so he forced himself to eat and, after his meal, he casually lit a cigarette, but the very feel of the thing on his lips and the first whiff of smoke aroused feelings of nausea. He could do nothing but allow the lighted cigarette to smolder in his hand, the ash growing longer and longer to no purpose. He was not well up on the family history of his friend Shun'ichi, otherwise he might have been aware that he was reproducing the smoking technique of the founder of the House of Nire.

Other than the morning clinic and checking the equipment and supplies of the emergency medical stations he had no work to do that day, so from time to time he went up on deck and breathed in the damp, salty air that the sea wind blew into his face. The sea was the color of thinly diluted India ink, and there was enough of a swell to create white breakers and gusts of spray here and there. He could see a supply tanker far off to aft being tossed about by the swell. He breathed in deeply a number of times. The bad weather which made him seasick was perfect for hiding the whereabouts of the fleet, and he knew it. He thought of the people at home and how they could never possibly know that, at this moment, he was here, bang in the middle of the North Pacific on a ship that was part of a strike force aimed at Hawaii.

Today duty schedule put forward another hour. Up at 0400 hours. All personnel to duty stations, after that surgery began at 0545. Lunch at ten, dinner at three; feels all wrong. The odd thing is when you look at the time you don't feel like eating, but if you ignore the clock you find you're hungry enough. Telegraphic message dated 26th re Japan-America talks. America suddenly taken tougher line demanding complete Japanese withdrawal from China and Indochina and determined to force through four major principles, and future of talks looks just about hopeless. All officers on board are just hoping the talks can be kept going until we attack Hawaii. Since leaving Hitokappu Bay blackout regulations, with lights dimmed even in living quarters and gangways, which only adds to special feeling of tension.

During his spare time Shiroki played *shogi* in the mess with another young doctor. Shiroki felt dull and stupid, unable to raise enough enthusiasm for the game to make any average opponent think, but this man spent ages pondering each move, muttering to himself as he did so. Shiroki found this muttering and protracted concentration unspeakably irritating, and as soon as it was his own turn he would move a piece straight away. Consequently he was unable to win even one game against this not very powerful opponent.

He often slept after lunch. No matter how long he slept he never seemed to have had a proper sleep, and his mind and body felt lethargic all the time. He found himself thinking vaguely about his family. Sometimes he remembered Aiko's face when she was saying good-bye to him in the crowds in front of Shibuya Station. The listless state of his mind seemed to make her peculiarly grown-up, and she wore the expression of a girl who felt very well disposed toward him.

Daily schedule put forward another hour on 2nd. Up at 0300. As duty officer, slept in sick bay so didn't need to go to station this morning at practice call. Already crossed Date Line so date today should be December 1st same as yesterday, but no change because only have to change back again, or so it seems. So humid on board you feel damp all over. At 1300 we had navy songs but

506

slept till then, yet still feel tired. It must be this irregular way of life. 1300 hours is what used to be 4 P.M. Went up on flight deck. Sky cloudy with long trailing lines of cloud looking as if painted on with thick brush. Ugly color, like the sky before or after a storm. Nasty to look at. Ahead of us the *Akagi* and *Kaga* had the supply tankers in tow. Once the refueling was done the tankers disappeared one after the other. I can only see two ships now, two plumes of black smoke, nothing else. . .

X Day will be December 8th. Report from spy says eight battleships, two carriers, ten cruisers and even a submarine in Pearl Harbor. Our flying crews in great spirits, although it seems their objective will be the island's air bases. Mechanics seem to spend all day occupied with their planes, busily swarming about them. Late afternoon a patient with a high temperature complaining of stomach pains. Obvious case of appendicitis. Suggested operating to principal medical officer, but he said to continue with internal treatment. Just medicine. I don't feel at all happy about it.

Tremendous gale and heavy rain with high seas. Ship starts rocking badly again. Rolling more than twenty degrees. Bump from one wall to the other walking down gangway. Sounds of things falling down in various places. Occasionally a huge wave crashes against the side of the ship and the whole thing shudders as if it's been struck by a torpedo. Went up on the bridge. The rain is like spray, wind strong enough to blow you over, waves washing right over flight deck.

From today internal patrols during the day plus a second call to stations then a third stand-to at dusk. Sky quite clouded over, so the weather remains on our side. Breakfast taken at duty stations so we get the regulation three balls of rice just like the ordinary sailors. At surgery a sailor with a whitlow. Paronychia, I thought, seeing something like *Eiter* in the region of the *Nagelbett,* so used transmission anesthetic and jerked out the nail, but found almost no trace of *Eiter* and realized I had gone too far. Had to blush inside, I must say. . .

Only two days to X. Second call to stations just like yesterday. Beautiful sunrise, sky cloudy but blue far ahead, great long bars of cloud looking dangerously as if weather would be fine. But just as they say about red sky in morning weather turned bad, soon clouding over and wind getting up with rain falling again when dark fell. Will be on first station call tomorrow so had cabin door left open during third stand-to and moved personal belongings to emergency medical station and will sleep there from tonight. . .

The next day, at 1:00 A.M. on the 7th of December Japan Time, all hands stood to. They were already at a latitude as far south as Okinawa, and since last night any trace of chilliness had vanished from the air. When they got up the sky had still been overcast, but bright sunlight was beginning to filter through the clouds. As they watched, the clouds pulled apart and an amazing, limpid blue appeared. For the first time in days they looked up into the full height of a sky unobstructed by clouds. The deep blue seemed unreal, dancing with myriad brilliant points of light. All around, the horizon still lay hidden by cloud; only the dome of the sky was brilliant, bright and clear, miraculously so. And the surface of the ocean, that somber, sad expanse, had been transformed as well: the waves swayed in the sunlight a garish green with bluish black shadows. The white of the foam breaking past the bows was now so dazzling that it hurt the eyes. Shiroki noticed a black seabird skim over the water and finally settle on it. Of course, they were near land now.

The supply tankers had already parted from the fleet and disappeared below the horizon. It was now point D of the operation. The whole strike force took a compass direction due south and increased speed to twenty-four knots. The shuddering of the ship was clearly transmitted to the body, and if you stood at the bows the wind blew with enough force to bowl you over. The water near the hull raced by as if the ship had become a living thing, trembling as it sped forward to the attack. The aircraft carriers had spread out with intervals of 7,700 yards between them, white foam at their bows and an even larger white wake behind as they sped straight for the south. They had now entered waters that the enemy patrolled, and the order was to prepare for action and carry gas masks.

Shiroki again felt worried and guilty at the realization that he did not seem as tense as he had thought he would. He asked himself if he felt afraid and found that he genuinely did not, not a bit. Was he anxious? Yes, he did feel anxious, but not about anything specific. What he mostly felt was a numbness, a sensation of nothing in particular.

His most constant thought was that he would get by somehow. It would turn out all right somehow or other. He couldn't see any marked signs of emotion in the faces of other people either.

He had nothing to do that afternoon so he took a nap, for he still felt sleepy although not understanding why. After dinner he read a story in a magazine someone had lent him. He didn't find the story itself of any particular interest, but he was interested to discover he retained his normal reading habits. The loudspeaker relayed a message from the Strike Force Commander, Admiral Nagumo:

"There are now eight battleships, ten heavy cruisers, and a number of light cruisers and destroyers at anchor in Pearl Harbor. All aircraft carriers are away on mission, and none are berthed there now. Providing no marked change is indicated by any further reports, our attacks will be concentrated on Pearl Harbor. There are no signs at the moment that the enemy is observing any special vigilance."

That night Shiroki lay on his side in the tiny berth in the cramped emergency medical station, and tried to write down his thoughts and feelings as precisely and vividly as he could.

> This evening everything flooded in bright moonlight, waves gold and silver, radiant, and piercing stars in the sky. No indication that the enemy has spotted us. I feel that tomorrow will be a complete success.

He could sense the shuddering of the ship as it lunged forward, and he seemed to feel the spray raining on his skin, but he went off to sleep surprisingly quickly, helped by a dose of sleeping pills which he had been keeping especially for this occasion.

Time passed, restless and confused, with a new sense of urgency about it. But though each moment seemed somehow precise and defined, all Shiroki could experience at the center of his mind was this opaque lethargy which would not go away. He thought the sleeping pills might be to blame. Maybe he had taken a slight overdose.

For some time now the aircraft engines had been turning over on the flight deck, a cacophony of roars and howls and reverberations that filled everything and pressed down on the eardrums so that it seemed they might soon break. He glanced at the flight deck, where the aircraft were like things newly awakened, packed together, wings jostling each other, bodies shuddering heroically as bursts of bluish white flame flared and scattered in the thin half-light. The machines were taking over as the carrier plowed forward at full speed, aircraft alive and waiting on its back. Intelligent life was theirs alone; they dominated the mechanics swarming on the dark deck about them, as if men were being transformed into mere clusters of organic matter.

The sky was still not light. The waning moon, now in its nineteenth day, was hidden behind patches of cloud for a while, then floated forth to show its face again. The sea was so black and wide it seemed to have receded, only the occasional white of a breaking wave indicating it was there. There was still a heavy swell and the *Zuikaku* rocked with it, sometimes making great sideways lurches as well. Somewhere beyond the yet unraised curtain of the dark one could just make out the shapes of other vessels racing through the hidden waters. But now one could also see spirals of cloud at the horizon's edge, for a faint light had come into the sky overhead, like the whitening of frosted glass. Against the background of dark sea and a sky growing gradually lighter, the shapes of the aircraft carriers traveling aft and on both sides had all the desolating horror of wild beasts with their prey immediately in reach.

The roar of engines on the deck had been stilled a short while before. The emergency medical station was a mere eight square yards in size, a steel room at the side of the deck jutting out from just below it, just to the rear of the area between the flight deck and the bridge. Shiroki shared this cramped space with three medical orderlies. The sterilizer was already boiling away, and those instruments which had already been sterilized—scalpels, forceps, suture thread, hypodermic syringes—were laid out on antiseptic gauze. But there was no chance of doing any real surgery here, only first-aid jobs; the serious cases would be carried below. Perhaps nothing would happen, however, and all these preparations would turn out to be so much wasted time and energy. Then again the room might become soaked in sticky blood. Shiroki found he could imagine that prospect, even if only vaguely, with a feeling of cool objectivity despite the fact that his head was working more sluggishly than usual. He shook his head two or three times to try and clear it.

They had two visitors after duty stations had been called. The first was from one of the bomber crews, a youth with a particularly childish face who asked in very apologetic tones for an aspirin. When Shiroki asked him why he wanted one he replied in clipped, formal terms that he was perfectly all right only his head felt a little heavy and he thought he could do with one. The second was a flight mechanic who said he

510

had a piece of grit in his eye. Shiroki raised the man's upper eyelid and finally managed to find a small black speck which he removed with a piece of gauze. It took a surprising amount of time to perform this simple operation, which he was obliged to do himself and not entrust to one of his men, because the ship was swaying so much. He asked the mechanic if the planes would be able to take off, and the man replied with the same kind of military formality as the other that it would be all right and the ship had been rocking much worse last night. He gave the impression it was almost ideal weather for it, real navy weather.

After that there was nothing else to do. The roar of engines started up on the flight deck again, drowning the bubbling sound of the sterilizer, growing higher and louder with each moment. The reverberation was such that it seemed to reach into one's guts. A quite large bottle of Novocain on the shelf was swaying with the motion of the ship. Shiroki began to worry if he might have forgotten something. He began to think he must have forgotten something of grave importance, like leaving a wad of gauze inside a patient after an abdominal operation, but he could not think what it might be. A cold shudder of something like panic, a tense spasm of fear, traveled along his spine. He looked all around the tiny room. The shining scalpels were there, the white gauze, the familiar shapes of the syringes. . . But surely there was something he had forgotten?

It was 1:30 A.M. Japan Time and suddenly one of the medical orderlies who had gone outside was shouting:

"They're taking off! They're taking off, sir."

Shiroki ran outside too. Just in front of the door, slightly below the flight deck, was a pocket for the flight mechanics to retire into, and in front of it was an emplacement for a triple 25-millimeter machine gun. Shiroki stood there and looked at the flight deck stretched out in the faint light.

Just then a Zero fighter raced past right in front of him with an appalling metallic scream that seemed to rip the air apart. Caps were being waved everywhere; on the bridge, on both sides of the deck, men were standing making huge, excited circlings of their arms; and at that moment Shiroki's brain simply suspended all its complex functioning. The exploding roars that troubled the outside world now seemed to burst right inside him, surging through his mind and blowing all his small self-awareness, all his tiny ideas and conceptions away. All that possessed him now was a purely primitive emotion, simple, overwhelming, naked and raw, rising in one swift surge.

The blue signal light winked out again through the thin light on the deck. The chocks were pulled away from the wheels of the second plane by a mechanic who immediately threw himself flat. The Zero fighter roared off down the deck, followed by another, then another, then two more, auxiliary fuel tanks bulging out, navigation lights blinking, up into the subtle half-darkness of the sky.

After six fighters had taken off, it was the turn of the black Type 99 bombers, each with its 550-pound bomb. The pilots at the controls in front stared rigidly ahead of them, with their teeth clenched and their expressions stern and occupied. The extra load their planes were carrying would make takeoff difficult, and the carrier was rolling badly. The navigators at the back looked sideways and waved their hands, some even grinning and showing white teeth as they clenched their hands together in salute. The planes began flashing past, seeming to drop down slightly as they left the deck, but only for a moment, for soon they rose unerringly into the sky which was now turning bright with the dawn.

The carrier rocked up and down in the wind, for it was racing full speed ahead, faster than it had done at any time up to now. The wind cut painfully into Shiroki's left cheek and he felt his face had gone stiff, but not only with the wind. It was a different tension hardening the muscles there, for the sailors in the gun emplacement nearby were waving their caps for all they were worth, and the ones standing over next to the bridge were cheering and cheering, though he could hear no sound from their open mouths as their voices were drowned in the roar of the engines.

The bombers kept taking off, throttles wide open, a constant procession of them passing before him. And the roar, the roar, the roar of the engines filled the brightening air which the violent wind swept through and through. Aware of the strain on his face, Shiroki waved his cap and kept on waving it, his arm held up as high as he could, turning great circles in the living air.

Tetsukichi spent every day in a lethargic, dull, gloomy and fretful frame of mind. He would be sixty next year and lately he had really started to feel old. He felt physical fatigue in every joint in his body. Curiously, this lethargy, this sense of having withdrawn from the fray, gave him a gloomy kind of pleasure, even though he was probably putting more effort into his work as Director of the hospital than he had done before. When he had first completed his *History of Psychiatric Medicine*, that labor of so many years, he had found himself immediately thinking, almost in a kind of panic, about starting work on something else. He had, indeed, done so, going through the old medical record cards at the Matsubara hospital each time he went there, and ordering a filing cabinet and other things. But he soon put a stop to this. Not that he had given up the idea completely; it was simply that he found he could not push this project forward with anything like the energy he had shown in the previous one. He could feel something like a spiritual cramp remaining from that work, an intellectual tiredness and also a physical one, a fatigue accumulated over ten years spent day in and day out on it, years when he had even regretted the hours he spent sleeping.

He knew that he really ought to treat himself to a proper rest. But once he had permitted this indolence to take up temporary abode within him, it seemed to be there to stay, producing additional symptoms of weariness, of loss of energy, of self-neglect, a feeling of just giving in and letting himself go downhill. It was rather like when one oversleeps and finds the mind not refreshed but staler than before. One part of him took a sly, even if slightly guilty delight in this, but another part was critical, and set up a constant, niggling anxiety as to whether he was doing the right thing or not. He would force himself to open a book, but it was like gazing on some scene of arid desolation, and Tetsukichi would eventually push it away from him. He started to feel he had become a stranger to himself, and he marveled at the dull decrepitude that had overtaken him at a not very advanced stage of life. Was fatigue, exhaustion, depression all he could expect from now on? Was it all over; would that fine rapture never return? So he gave himself over to an idleness induced by unsolved questions, and felt a discontent he could never properly name.

This decline was also reflected in his daily life. He had no wife; Nanny Shimoda who had organized the maids and done any amount of minor tasks for him each day was now no more; and naturally the way he lived became a bleak, degenerate mess. His appearance became not so much plain and simple as indicative of a bigoted refusal to accept the possibility that things might be otherwise. He nearly always wore the same suit and tie, partly because he was used to them and preferred them to others, but mainly because he just couldn't be bothered. In spite of this he showed a peculiar scrupulousness in some things, at certain seasons taking great care of his best suit, putting it neatly on a hanger and giving it a good brush. He had odd sleeping habits now, and the maid was never quite sure how to make up his bed. He slept on an iron bedstead which he had put up in his book-filled study a year or so ago, but he had a strong dislike of thick winter quilts, preferring sheets made out of toweling. He used three or four of these. They all looked more or less the same but were in fact different, and he was very punctilious about the order in which they should be laid on one another. On top of these he would have a number of blankets. If the maid got the order of this complex arrangement wrong he would tut in disapproval and give her a good talking-to.

He was unable to avoid the feeling that both his habits and personality were getting worse and he was turning into something objectionable. He seemed unable to view anything in a warm, generous light any more. There were his children, for example. He began to doubt whether he felt any love for them at all. He recalled how depressing he had found it in the past when he had seen Kiichiro pick up Shun'ichi, his baby grandson, and produce a perfunctory compliment about how heavy he was, but he was starting to wonder if he himself might not be worse. Lately, whenever his children went off to visit their mother without telling him, he was forced to admit that he felt something very much like hatred for them.

He had no particular hopes for the girl, even though other people often praised his daughter Aiko as being very attractive. The important ones were the boys, and yet both of them, Shun'ichi and Shuji, achieved results at school that were not only below average but distinctly inferior, and this caused a bitterness in Tetsukichi that was far from being a cool intellectual appraisal of their abilities but was more like rage. He himself had been a prodigy at his local primary school, and after coming to Tokyo, although there had been a period when he'd had language problems, he had always been considered an excellent, even a brilliant student. The thing he found most difficult to understand was the gutlessness of the two boys. It wasn't a question of not being all that bright; they just didn't seem to want to try.

Still, Shun'ichi had at least managed to graduate from medical school and get himself taken on at the Department of Psychiatry at Keio. As his son had gradually come to learn how to handle the terminology of psychiatric thought, Tetsukichi had felt again, after a long interval of time, something like a father's pride in him. Then, of all unexpected misfortunes, Shun'ichi had been drafted into the army, and he had felt similarly fatherly feelings, but this time they were despairing. He was by no means inferior to others in his loyalty to the Emperor and love for his country, but it drove him almost mad to think how the army had taken his son from the path of learning when he had only just set out on it. What made things worse was hearing that Ryuko had not been in the least upset by this. Apparently she had obtained a sword from her mother's family home in Chichibu and handed it over to Shun'ichi, no doubt in the belief that eventually he would become a commissioned officer in the medical corps. Hearing this only made Tetsukichi think how typically presumptious it was of her to do something like that, and his old hatred for this wife he had not seen for so long came back, an irritated loathing whose object was far away and about which he could do nothing.

The results Shuji obtained during his first term at his new school, and then in the special examination held during the second, were more than adequate for fatherly umbrage, although what really distressed both parents was learning that he had been absent from class a significant number of times. Tetsukichi gave his son a powerful telling-off, and his anger was intensified by the attitude Shuji adopted in response to this, merely drooping his head in gloomy fashion and showing little indication of being spurred on to higher things by his father's admonitions.

Anxiety over the protracted negotiations between Japan and America also added to this aging man's burden, and at directors' meetings his mood was only aggravated by matters that would normally have been given an immediate stamp of approval. The major problems for mental institutions at present were an insufficiency of nursing staff, a lack of medicines, and the food shortage imposed on them by rationing whereby the amount of staple rice was restricted to one half-pint per day per person. The Nire Hospital had always been in a lucky position so far as rice was concerned through the fortunate accident that they could obtain supplies from Yamagata, and just before rationing had been introduced they had bought up a whole wagonload of unpolished rice. But when the head of a small private mental hospital approached Tetsukichi, pointing out in extremely formal language that his own hospital could not keep pigs and he had no idea where they got the extra rice to feed theirs, since there were no rice leftovers at his hospital, but then, of course, the Nire Hospital was a very grand affair with plenty of land, and perhaps he might be able to help them out with a little that they didn't want, Tetsukichi felt slightly guilty at having to say no. It was true that at Matsubara they still kept pigs, and were second only to the Matsuzawa Hospital in the splendor of their pig collection, but these belonged to Yonekuni, who was becoming more and more difficult as he grew older, and the Deputy had been heard to say that it would take something like a riot to get even one pig out of him.

Hidekichi Katsumata, known for his excessive admiration of the former Director and his slighting of the present one, and for the many remarkable labors he had performed on behalf of the hospital, now had all the signs of old age: his hair was noticeably thinning, and a decrepitude had crept into his distinctive crane-like gait. He also had been out of temper for some time now, for the question of next year's fifty-fifth anniversary celebrations was quite overshadowed by the much more pressing duty of maintaining a sufficient reserve of coal and charcoal to see them through the winter. On top of that he was in a constant state of nervous dread that the red draft card might come for his only son, who was at present helping him in the hospital office. Katsumata had suffered no falling off in his loyalty to the Emperor and love of his country either, but it was natural that a man like him, who had clearly felt the coming of old age, should hope that they might be able to fight and win the war without needing to call on the services of his son.

He had a longish discussion with Kumagoro, a person he had tended to have little to do with in the past, about the current situation. Kumagoro had raised his thick eyebrows in a proud, confident manner, and said:

"Haven't I been saying all along since back in the twenties that we should let these arrogant Americans have it, strike while we can. . ."

This warlike attitude clearly perturbed the Deputy, for he could only mumble in reply:

"Well, there may be something in that, and maybe not. It's all right for you to say that sort of thing, but perhaps it's not quite so simple. . ."

His eyes moved unconsciously to the portrait of Kiichiro hanging there on the wall, seeking perhaps some advice in his dilemma. Recently, though, there had even been a moment of accord with the present Director. After consultation with Oshu and Tetsukichi, it had been decided to contribute one of the hospital's automobiles to the army. Given the scarcity of gasoline, it was as much as they could do to run even one hospital car. On this matter the Deputy and the Director had been in immediate and rare agreement. . .

516

One morning, the Director woke up around seven o'clock. It was not a pleasant awakening. The night before he had looked over some of the old medical record cards, but had eventually done nothing with them and crawled into bed. On top of that, something had been wrong with the arrangement of his toweling sheets and he had slept badly, so that when he did wake he had the feeling that a part of him had been awake for some time already. His first thought after this unfortunate night and the gloomy return to reality was that he must scold the maid. The unheated room was painfully cold and he could feel the chill air on his cheeks and ears. He particularly felt the cold in the lower half of his legs, which were now skin and bones. Perhaps he really ought to have another blanket, or maybe even a warming pan.

He remembered he had used one in Munich. There was also a friend of his, now a professor of anatomy but a gay dog in his time, who claimed that even in the Yoshiwara red-light district in the old days people had come around selling warming pans. It was certainly a useful thing to have. The only trouble was that sometimes patients at the hospital burned themselves with the things, and since it led to perceptional paralysis in that area there had been some really nasty cases of gangrene. One had to make sure the top of the warming pan was screwed on tight so that it couldn't come loose.

He hesitated a while, then got himself out of bed in one movement. He quickly put on the two undershirts that lay in a messy heap on the floor where he had dropped them last night. Their coldness made him shiver all over for a minute, but he had never been in the habit of putting on underwear after it had been warmed. He then dragged on his long underpants. After that it was the turn of his kimono and a quilted one on top of that, all tied crudely about his waist with a thin sash. This sash was one of very good quality that Ryuko had chosen for him years ago, so it was particularly stiff and tricky to handle, giving him something else to tut about as he tied it.

He then half stooped and turned on the radio next to his cluttered desk. Finally it began to produce the light burr of the warming-up sound. He had got into the habit recently of listening to the radio as soon as he rose in the morning. There was a buzzing and crackling of static, and then a startlingly sudden voice saying:

"Here is a special news announcement. Here is a special news announcement."

Tetsukichi was sufficiently taken aback to stop putting on his *tabi* socks. It was his custom to put them on after he had switched on the

517

radio, but now he stopped in a motionless, slightly apprehensive pose. This was soon transformed into shocked rigidity as he swallowed hard, for what the announcer had said at considerable speed, and what had sounded from the radio distorted by only a slight amount of static, was:

"Imperial Military Headquarters issued the following announcement at 6 A.M. today, the 8th of December. With effect from the early hours of this morning the Imperial Forces have entered into a state of war with the armed forces of America and England in the Western Pacific."

He felt a dull shudder pass over him, and a feeling that the inside of his head was gradually going blank—he could almost see the process as it took place. The whole world about him seemed to go blank as well, and time in his immediate surroundings appeared to have come to a halt. His brain found it impossible even to begin to grasp what the huge consequences of this might be, and his body seemed to be making a similar refusal to comprehend.

For a while he was stupefied, standing there barefoot on the *tatami* matting, his body stiff and his two fists clenched painfully tight at his sides. Then an image passed through the back of his mind, a scene in Vienna on a drab street corner. A sickly, tired-looking housewife, one of those who had been crushed by the harshness of daily life, was watching a horse-drawn cart carrying coal pass by her on the road; she looked as if she were just about to collapse. This scene had always symbolized for him what social chaos meant, with constant inflation and total poverty.

Tetsukichi bit his lower lip and whispered passionately to himself: "We can't lose. We daren't lose. . ."

And then, as trembling excitement took control of his body, he behaved in a way that recalled another scene from his stay in Europe, in the auditorium in Munich, where, filled with humiliation and rage, he had stood and stared at the retreating figure of a white-skinned old scholar. The same words came from his lips now as they had then, spat out with mindless intensity:

"Hairy foreign swine! Hairy damn foreign swine!"

The announcer repeated the news. Tetsukichi started to pull on his *tabi* energetically, lost his balance, staggered, and just about managed to get the fastener above the ankle in place; after which he stood up straight again. But it was difficult to keep still. What he meant to do he did not know, but he felt impelled to leave his room and go quickly down the ill-lit stairs.

At the bottom of the stairs was a small room three mats in size. Next to it was the seven-and-a-half-mat room for the children, and just as he got to the bottom step Shuji appeared, passing through the small room on his way to the toilet. He was wearing his school uniform trousers and an undershirt, and his shoulders were hunched with the cold.

"Shuji. It's started. It's started with the Americans."

Tetsukichi had probably never spoken to a child of his in such a friendly and emotional way before. Shuji stopped and turned his sleepy face in his direction, with at first only a slightly distrustful hesitancy written on it. Then understanding seemed to dawn gradually, growing to a real, astounded awakening:

"Has it? Has it really?"

There was a natural, simple, childlike ring to his voice his father had never heard before. Tetsukichi suddenly saw a liveliness in his son's usually gloomy features; his face seemed to light up in a way it never did on normal days. Shuji then dashed away and disappeared from sight, apparently to listen to the radio.

Tetsukichi remained standing at the bottom of the stairs in a sudden confusion of new emotions. There was the excited movement in his blood he had been feeling for the past few moments, combined now with a restlessness and anxiety, and also a feeling of something like happiness, unreal though it may have been, for that rigid wall there had always been between himself and his son seemed suddenly, at last, removed. It was a state of intoxication that would soon leave him, but for a while he went on standing there, silent and motionless.

III

WELL DONE

Chapter

1

One day at the beginning of the summer of 1942, in the early afternoon when just being still was enough to make the sweat ooze out through the skin, two men were sitting on a pile of timber in the pear orchard that formed one corner of the Matsubara hospital farm. These were those two who spent so much of the time together as to be each other's shadows, Yonekuni Nire and Kumagoro Sakuma. They gave less the impression, even to a casual bystander, of a master and servant linked by bonds of affection as of two members of a shady organization unrelated to the actual functioning of the hospital.

Kumagoro was wearing shabby workman's fatigues and smoking the butt of a cigarette which had grown so short it was about to burn his fingers, so he transferred it to his other hand, pursing his lips in order to extract more puffs from where they no longer were. Yonekuni, who had on slightly cleaner trousers than Kumagoro, gazed vaguely at the worm-eaten bark of the pear tree at his side, or looked with some attention at the unripe fruit that had fallen and was rotting on the ground. From the trees all about them the scorching cries of the summer cicadas descended, and the pale, parched earth was swarming with columns of tiny ants.

Within the enclosure a still considerable number of chickens were stretching their necks and pecking briskly at their feed. There were no longer any turkeys, but two ducks had been added to the flock, and for some reason or other commotions often occurred between them and the chicken majority, although they soon died down. But it was clear that there had been a decline in the quantity of chickens of late, and this was also true of the inhabitants of the pigsty just beyond the henhouse, for although the pigs still snorted through their squat snouts (in a manner not in the least absurd but genuinely impressive) their numbers too had recently been reduced by half.

There was a variety of reasons for this decline, although the principal one was that there was no longer anyone left to look after them. At one time, Yonekuni and Kumagoro had employed three men, but two of them no longer worked here since they had been conscripted, one into the army and the other for some kind of civilian labor, and the only one who remained was a thin, aging man who did not look very dependable. This would surely have been a fine opportunity for the two members of the High Command to lend a helping hand, but congenital inertia and the habits acquired over the years made even the demands of an era such as this incapable of lifting them from their posteriors.

They had now been sitting down for a considerable length of time, but they did not appear to be engaged in any profitable debate over the future of the farm. Although Yonekuni was sitting in the shade, he had not removed his ancient straw hat. There was, of course, his history of lung disease, and he also had an obstinate belief that one should avoid at all costs the direct rays of the sun on the head and face.

Yonekuni spoke Sakuma's name in a strangely hesitant manner. It seemed to imply that Kumagoro was his master's equal or even slightly his superior, which might account for the fact that he had served him for so long. If, for example, Yonekuni had called him more familiarly by a name related in some way to his nickname of "the Bear," pockmarked or otherwise, Kumagoro would probably not have been amused, though it must be admitted that there was another form of address which would have pleased him: that of Kumagoro Nire, which he had bestowed on himself briefly in a fit of drunken euphoria at the end of the party to celebrate the hospital's fiftieth anniversary.

"Doesn't look as if Shinta will ever need to go for a soldier, does it?"

"Shinta?" Kumagoro hesitated a little, but then snorted with contempt. "Ah, the Deputy's boy? Of course, if he got better it's hard to say, but seeing that pleurisy is undoubtedly a form of consumption, well, is he likely to get better? Naturally the Deputy himself will be pleased if he doesn't."

"Not pleurisy; pleuropneumonia."

"About the same thing, isn't it? Kind of consumption."

"Well, I suppose you can say that. . ."

Each time Kumagoro bellowed the word "consumption" in his vulgar voice Yonekuni's eyelids gave a nervous flicker. Deep inside (indeed palpably on the outside as well) he envied the Deputy's only son, Shinta Katsumata, who had been called up a few days before only to be rejected after his medical exam. Yonekuni had a pathological fear that his draft papers might arrive any day now. Although he had heard that the important members of the hospital or municipal office staff would be exempted, he was very worried it might look as if he were merely idling his days away, and, on top of that, he feared that his unfortunate name (with its meaning of "America" if read as "Beikoku") could prove a positive disadvantage in present circumstances. This had become a source of genuine distress, for it was a fact that up to now more people had tended to call him by the present enemy's name than by the correct reading of "Yonekuni."

Suddenly Yonekuni seemed to prick up his ears as if he was listening for something, or about to investigate something as yet unspecified. He allowed his eyes to play over the henhouse and pigsty for a while with an expression of suspicion on his face. Finally he muttered as if to himself:

"Sakuma. Ever had this kind of experience? Suddenly there's this . . . what shall I call it? It's like a curtain, a transparent curtain, a kind of veil between yourself and the world, cutting you off from it. You can see everything perfectly well, you can hear just as before, but everything's quite different to what it was. . ."

"Can't say as I have." Kumagoro showed not the least interest in what his companion had said, and his reply sounded brusque and unfriendly. Yonekuni had the habit of saying things sometimes that roused genuine doubts in most people about his sanity, but when it was an audience like Kumagoro his remarkable statements were as water off a duck's back, for the latter showed no reaction to them whatsoever. This insensitivity may have been another reason why the unlikely partnership had lasted so long.

"You see," Yonekuni continued, "I can hear the chickens. I can hear the pigs. But it's as if they're not really living things. They move. They make noises as they move, and yet I can't feel they're actually living. Can't feel it at all. It's hard to explain, but, you know, it's extraordinarily frightening and yet very interesting at the same time. You know, it makes you wonder what the concept of 'a world,' what the reality of it can. . ."

He then stopped as abruptly as he had started and lapsed into silence. The chickens fluttered and flapped their wings, the pigs produced intermittent and resonant grunts, and the cicadas went on with their persistent, tireless shrieking.

"Pigs may all be the same," reflected Kumagoro, scratching with grubby fingernails his round blob of a nose. "But our pigs seem particularly tough. Maybe it's a mistake to eat them as soon as they're killed."

From somewhere below them came the distant, dull sound of a ball being struck; probably someone on the staff was playing one of the patients. Recently, however, it had become impossible to get hold of new tennis balls, and all one could use was worn-out, deflated balls that winced flatulently each time they were struck. This perhaps accounted for the fact that Kumagoro showed little enthusiasm for the game nowadays.

"There's this patient who steals the balls," said Kumagoro, toying with a packet of Kinshi as he did so. Kinshi ("Golden Kite") was the revised version of the old Golden Bat cigarettes, part of the vogue for replacing English names with authentic Japanese ones. The device on the packet had originally shown a golden kite alighting on a bow (as it was claimed to have done in legend for the first Japanese emperor), but lately the bow seemed to have disappeared. "He was pretty wide-awake; understood things. Good at tennis, too. Then he suddenly got hold of these tennis balls and hid them away; five or six of them. Well, it all ended with him bursting into tears when they were taken off him. . ."

"Healthy people, of course . . . no matter what you might say. . ." Yonekuni's few, obscure words disappeared as quickly as they came, suddenly broken off in mid-passage. Physically he was a fairly tough and athletic-looking specimen, and, combined with a good suntan, which had no doubt been only reluctantly achieved, this gave him the most respectably healthy appearance of the whole Nire family. But these positive aspects were offset, if not canceled out, by his rather hollow eyes which had a dark anxiety about them, a look of something close to chronic suspicion. His mouth was still open, as if he was debating whether he should continue or not, but Kumagoro broke in with his coarse bellow:

"Just over there in that ward on the other side of the tennis courts there's a very interesting woman. Nice-looking, in her own way, and says some pretty funny things, too. Says she's a senior mental patient and we ought to let her go because a senior patient shouldn't be put in with a lot of newcomers. Said it was an affront and she wouldn't put up with it. That's the way she goes on. Still, speaking myself as a senior in the Nire Hospital I will say that what we're getting here nowadays, be it nursing staff or anything else, is pretty low-grade and getting worse. Don't you agree, Mr. Yonekuni? Not sure if I ought to say this, but I can't work out what's happening to this hospital. They're mixing up the seniors and the juniors, and you can't tell the difference. Maybe that mad woman's got some sense after all.''

"Well, I suppose people are. . . ,'' Yonekuni muttered, and again broke off in mid-sentence, but soon took up the thread again. "People are all keeping track of others. Obsessed with watching them. Psychotics often claim that someone is after them, don't they? From that point of view I've always felt I had something in common with them, and the fact is there's not all that much difference between them and us. There's this boundary line, and it's just a question of whether you're this side or that, and I don't like either myself. Like that asparagus over there, look, see how it's coming out through that black earth, full of life, luxuriant . . . you know, the things I feel a real empathy with have somehow gone beyond the mere animal or vegetable distinction, as if my emotions had somehow transcended that; like that asparagus, for example, which, in my eyes, has a true nobility, which can be grasped by imperceptible degrees, as it were, in opposition to, in unawareness of, any shame one might be induced to feel in the voluptuous, almost obscene configuration that it. . .''

"The Deputy said we ought to stop growing asparagus,'' said Kumagoro, interrupting the flow of words with flat abruptness. "Says we ought to have cornfields instead.''

"Corn,'' Yonekuni muttered. "Just over the fence there's nothing but cornfields. Not that I don't like corn. I do, very much. Corn is a plant that shares a particular intimacy with man. Still, I don't want to grow it myself.''

"The Deputy says it's for when we'll have to become self-sufficient.''

"But we're supposed to be quite safe as regards rice. We bought masses of it just before they introduced rationing, didn't we?''

"We're all right for the time being, maybe. But since this war could last a hundred years. . .''

"A hundred years. . . ,'' Yonekuni muttered contemptuously, although it was clear that the thought had raised considerable inner perturbation. "Look here, Sakuma, you can't get fresh asparagus in any restaurant now. I'm growing asparagus *because* we are living through times like these and not in spite of them. People say it can only be grown up north in Hokkaido or Nagano, but I've succeeded here, as anyone can see. There's something in asparagus, some hidden life force. For example, at a moment like this, when that veil has descended, that transparent curtain, and those chickens which were lively up to now become suddenly slow and mechanical and clumsy, like some kind of ambiguous shadow of. . ."

"But asparagus doesn't taste too good, it really doesn't," put in Kumagoro.

They had harvested a lot of asparagus that summer, but it was all fibrous and had an unusual resilience. When the Deputy had first seen it being dished up at the cookhouse he had exclaimed joyfully that the only mental institution that provided asparagus with its meals must be our own, but the cheerful smile was soon wiped off his face when one of the patients complained that they wanted real vegetables, not bits of grass.

"To be quite frank with you it was inedible," said Kumagoro, refusing to mince words as usual.

"It was just a little too large. Anyway, you're only supposed to eat the tips of asparagus, not the whole lot."

"In that case it's uneconomical."

"Uneconomical doesn't have to be a dirty word, you know. Life itself—and by life I'm indicating something that preserves its own self even when the transparent curtain descends—life can all be seen, depending on your viewpoint, as uneconomical in the extreme. . ."

"Well, if you like asparagus that much, then I'm prepared to help you all I can to grow it. Although I still reckon that asparagus isn't suited to wartime conditions."

"Now, don't get me wrong," said Yonekuni, speaking as if he were vexed at this need to defend his own viewpoint. "It's not that I like the taste of asparagus. I'm not concerned like Oshu with eating things that tickle my palate. After all, the human palate is a quite relative thing. I have, for certain reasons, trained myself in the past to put up with the poorest of foods. Quite honestly I'm perfectly happy with plain barley and rice, providing I can sprinkle a little something on it. I can say I have some confidence in myself about this. It's based on beliefs that are firmly rooted in me."

"Well, I call that pretty stupid," said Kumagoro in a tart manner. "No one's saying there's any need for you to eat plain barley and rice. Just so long as you don't eat the kind of rich food Mr. Oshu indulges in.''

"You see, if I was only physically and psychologically normal," said Yonekuni in a bitter, slightly spiteful tone of voice. "That's the real point. What I've always got to bear in mind is that I'm not long for this world. What I need to find out first of all is just what this debility of mine is, exactly to what extent. . ."

"Now, now," said Kumagoro, as unmoved as if he were discussing tomorrow's weather. He sounded as if he were trying to calm down an awkward child with impossible promises as he went on indifferently, "You take my word for it, Yonekuni, you're healthy; you're strong, I can assure you.''

"Healthy?" Yonekuni repeated the word in a tone of dull vacancy suggesting he had encountered a term he had not expected to hear. The expression on his face was a peculiar mixture of amused incredulity and serious concern, while his voice took on a weird tone halfway between restrained laughter and a stifled sob, a complexity of expression that would have given the most practiced of psychiatrists reason to pause. Was it self-contempt, based on a deep moral questioning of his own life, or was it an outburst of rage at the humiliation to which his perfectly reasonable pride in himself had just been subjected?

But Kumagoro remained, as usual, totally unaware of the complex fluctuations in the emotional life of his partner:

"Come to think of it, you were always getting ill when you were a little boy. There was that Spanish influenza. Still, you don't need to worry about your lungs. It's people like you who live longest. Look at my father, now. Never had a day's illness in his life, and then just pops off like that at the age of forty-nine. It's a very mysterious thing all round.''

Yonekuni remained silent, staring at the rotting pears on the ground at his feet. One could see from the droop of his shoulders that he felt they always ganged up on him to say things like that: nasty, unpleasant things, the lot of them, no matter what he did. He just happened to look healthy and nobody understood him, that was the trouble. The depression this thought gave rise to also contained feelings of petulance, and Yonekuni began to look as if he were in a sulk. The cicadas went on shrieking in the heat, and occasionally, probably owing to some variation in the slight breeze, the stench from the henhouse and the pigsty became peculiarly offensive. Yonekuni remained silent for some time, but then seemed to make up his mind and spoke in a different tone of voice.

"All right, Sakuma, just have a look at this, then, will you?"

He rolled up his shirt at the back, and also the undergarment, exposing his back, which was somewhat whiter than his face and arms.

"What is it, now? Do you mean your back?"

"Round about the shoulder blades. Can't you see the peculiar way the muscles are retracted just below that point?"

"Whereabouts?"

"Just here," said Yonekuni, in a serious tone of voice in which a strong undertone of real suffering could be heard, for he had been obliged to contort his arm in order to point his finger at the spot in question. "The muscles here. Compared with the others, you can see they're drawn right in, can't you?"

"Don't seem any different to me," Kumagoro replied, not only without any sign of sympathy but in a tone that implied he was not giving any real attention to the matter.

"That's not possible! Look. Right here. Can't you see?"

"No. Nothing there at all. Can't see a thing. Anyway, what's that supposed to mean?"

Yonekuni made no attempt to explain, but merely abandoned his ungainly posture, slowly and wearily rolling his shirt down with uncertain hands.

"Have you got something wrong there?" asked Kumagoro in bolder tones, as if only remarkable forbearance on his part had enabled him to continue with this subject, in which he could have no possible interest.

"No. It's all right. It doesn't matter," Yonekuni replied, apparently gazing at some distant point. But he seemed to change his mind again, for he added: "I wonder how long this war is really going to last."

"A hundred years," Kumagoro replied cheerfully with a bluntness that he obviously enjoyed, and with an expression on his face that said there was no need to ask a question whose answer was obvious.

"But look here, after the thrashing we've given them in the Coral Sea and at Midway, and combined with the damage they sustained at Pearl Harbor, the enemy can hardly have any aircraft carriers or battleships left now."

"Even so, America itself still remains untouched. This war won't end till we've occupied Washington."

"You can't surely mean they'll go on fighting till then?"

"Now, see here," Kumagoro said deliberately as though threatening the other. "I'm sorry, but I've got to say that you know nothing about these matters. This war's nothing like as simple as you seem to think. Just let me remind you that I've never been wrong. I've prophesied what was going to happen and I've always been right. When you were a little boy I told you all about the eight-eight fleet. Well, we had a chance then. We should have let the Americans have it then, and we could have beaten them within a year. And we could have arranged a peace as well, with Japan in Japan and controlling the Orient and the Americans withdrawing back into America. But it's too late for that now. It's a fight to the finish. Exist or be annihilated; eat or be eaten."

Yonekuni looked away from him in confusion, only managing to utter feebly:

"Of course, I realize all that but. . ."

Kumagoro gazed at him smugly as if viewing him from on high, licked his thick lips, and continued in a tone that now had something of the hectoring style he had used in his diatribes in the past:

"I'll admit that Dr. Kiichiro, your father, was good to me, but, well, let's face it, the fact is I stayed around mainly to please him; help him out, if you like. I had meant to become a politician, but politicians nowadays . . . well, I mean, look at them, just a bunch of cheap amateurs. I don't want to say this, but I don't really think your father was much of a politician, neither. Only third-rate, you see. So that's why I've always stayed in the shadows like this, as it were. Never sought office. Well, I say this who perhaps shouldn't, but my judgment's never been wrong. You can be quite confident in anything I say."

Just as Yonekuni sometimes had weird things to say, so Kumagoro often indulged in perorations of this nature, but Yonekuni was quite different from other people in that he usually listened quietly, sometimes even nodding his head in apparent agreement. The truth is these two could say anything they liked to each other. It was as if they had some unspoken agreement whereby each would listen to what the other had to say, whether out of feelings of generosity or total indifference it was hard to tell.

"Still, those were the good old days, all right," Kumagoro went on, warming to his subject and speaking louder as he did so. "Dr. Kiichiro may have been a washout as a politician but in an age like

531

this he'd be somebody, I can tell you. People in the past, particularly the young people like us, interns as we were then, they all had plenty of spirit, individuality. We used to discuss the future of the country. Even Oshu did. Well, I expected great things of him. I thought he'd become somebody, but I was wrong. Once he started simpering like a girl and talking to me as if he were some kind of pansy, then that was the end of him. Of course, it was marriage that finished him off. Now, I've got an old woman, too, but that doesn't make the slightest bit of difference to me. Don't give a damn about that sort of thing, I don't. Basically I'm a bit of a socialist. Still, considering the fate that awaited the country, the first job was to get the state firmly established. That's the position I took, because I believe in taking the long view. Still, once the war's over I intend to play my part as a real socialist this time. Look at this hospital, for instance. I'll admit you're a bit different from the rest but, frankly, the people here are a dead loss. They're such small people, so lacking in scope. They can't see beyond their own small world. The Director is the Director, the Deputy is the Deputy, and the staff is the staff, and that's all they are and more than that they dare not be. There they all stay in their little rut like a swarm of lice. All they know about is the hospital. Well, it's pretty hard for someone like me to associate with people like that. Have to wear a mask, I can tell you, a mask like my present one of Chief Air Warden Kumagoro Sakuma. Then that fool of a Deputy tells me to build enough air-raid shelters to house all the staff and even the patients. The man's got no grasp, no grasp of anything. He's put into a complete panic by that fiddling little air raid we had this spring, whereas I went off to scrutinize the actual damage. Which was absolutely nothing, just one tiny house knocked down by a single bomb. If this country ever reaches the stage when we're likely to get really big air raids, then we'll have lost already. Pretty hopeless idea trying to get the patients all inside air-raid shelters anyway, since you've no idea where they might take it into their heads to try to run away to."

Yonekuni didn't appear to have been listening to this lengthy speech, for he had more immediate troubles of his own to worry about.

"Well, you're too old to be conscripted. . ." he started mumbling in an obsessed but curiously absentminded way.

"Me? Your humble servant is but forty-seven years of age. In this hundred years' war I don't doubt that I shall be obliged to play some small part, though modesty might forbid me saying that I'm really cut out for command rather than service in the ranks. The role of a mere private soldier is not one that would give proper scope for my talents. Still, I would like a chance to have a go at the Americans. If it were the Chinese . . . well, being an Oriental myself I don't want to kill Chinese, naturally enough. There's Yamaguchi who's just back from China—you know, the one who used to be a nurse here—and he told me the Japanese Army seems to have been doing some pretty terrible things over there. So when they occupy anywhere the people just come and suck up to them now. Before, they used to call Japanese soldiers *Li pen pin*, which seems to have been a pretty objectionable kind of word, but now our Chinese friends call them the Imperial Army. With things like that I can't help feeling the Chinese soldiery now wouldn't be much of an opponent, so there wouldn't be much to be said for fighting them. Pretty unpleasant business, I should think. Whereas the Americans—now there's an opponent on the grand scale. More like a war that would be. After all, there's something sublime in fighting for the Greater East Asia Co-prosperity Sphere. That kind of noble conflict would provide a suitable arena for me to make my appearance in. If I was put in a position of command then I reckon I could reduce that hundred years to something around thirty."

"That's it," said Yonekuni, in a frail, stuttering voice. "You're a brave kind of person, and you've got that sort of strength. In my case, though, I'm grade B but they're starting to draft lots of Bs nowadays, and I'm ill really. I don't want to be specific about this at the moment, but I've a clear understanding of just how long I've got to live. It's that kind of illness, terminal, and one for which there's no known cure. And that's the trouble, since no military doctor is going to be able to understand an illness like mine. Even a proper specialist at Tokyo University could only shake his head over it. No, it's simply impossible for someone like me. I've always meant to be fully responsible for myself, no matter what the state of society might be. I want to be true to myself at all times. So if I were to say that I'm scared at the idea of being called up and becoming a soldier, would you think I was being, say, cowardly? Would it be an un-Japanese attitude, do you think?"

"Now, just you see here, Mr. Yonekuni," said Kumagoro, staring straight at him with wide, sincere eyes. "I'm not one of your small-minded, tight-assed creeps always bothered by finicky details.

The fact is I'm of the caliber of a master politician, and I make no bones about it. The truth of the matter is that if you joined the army you'd be of no use anyway. You'd be much better off growing asparagus. You just leave the business of war to me.''

"But look at Shun'ichi. They called him up just like that.''

"Shun'ichi? Went to Indochina, I believe. Still, he's much better made for it than you. I took his education in hand when he was a boy. It wouldn't surprise me if he performed some pretty remarkable exploits.''

"Indochina? That's right; Indochina," Yonekuni murmured gloomily to himself as if he found the idea wholly depressing. "Will the war really last all that long?''

"A hundred years I've said, and I'm not joking.''

"Sakuma, you're a very different type from me. You're tough; you're bold. When a man knows there's a limit set to his days, and when it's no common symptoms he has, not that I want to talk about that, not at all; but when the life that heaven allows, when there're only a few years left . . . you know, it's the thought that people would consider me un-Japanese that's really hard to bear.''

"Sure. Sure,'' said Kumagoro, waving his hand and showing not the slightest interest in hearing any more of that. "Still, the pigs have got to be fed. A man who could lead armies and direct governments must spend his days like this, retired from the world, biding his time until the call comes.''

"But there's no need for you to do anything!'' said Yonekuni, looking very excited and serious in his attempts to restrain him. "Shimura will feed the pigs.''

"I suppose so. All men have their determined portions in this life,'' said Kumagoro, who had gone through the motions of getting up, but now sank down slowly again onto his seat on the woodpile with a lordly, if grubby, demeanor.

"The figs don't look too good, do they?''

"Well, you can blame that on those long-horned beetles,'' said Yonekuni, looking relieved at this new turn in the conversation. "It's the cerambycid, which lives on fig trees, and the larvae do all the damage.''

"You mean that speckled long-horned beetle?''

"No, no, not at all,'' said Yonekuni fiercely, all traces of weakness vanishing from his face as a sudden energy brought it back to life. "The true cerambycid has a dull, withdrawn appearance. The speckled variety is a commonplace, vulgar insect, of no concern to anyone. It's as I said before, when that transparent veil descends, and I have this feeling that I'm suddenly cut off from the world. Well, it's at times like that when I see the true longicorn, waving its long horns about and walking all over the fig leaves. He's a weird thing, a mysterious form of existence. There seems to be a sort of light playing about him just where he is and his shadow stands out so clearly; a brilliant shadow it is, so alive, so living, such complete proof that he at least really does exist, you know. And then I look all about me and that veil surrounding me is starting to dissolve. Now, the long-horned beetle is at the center of that process, this slow, almost imperceptible, yet definite vanishing away. I start to breathe again, I get this great sense of relief as the air flows soothingly down my throat again. Then it reaches my lungs. I get this very precise awareness of the exact moment when the air is distributed quite evenly throughout my lungs.''

Yonekuni was now firmly engrossed in himself as he went on with this account, apparently addressed to Kumagoro who sat by his side. But Kumagoro stroked his chin with so obvious a show of no emotion that he might have been listening or he might not. A sudden stench gusted from the direction of the henhouse and pigsty. The chorus still descended from the branches of the trees around them.

The wild plants were just beginning to wither and had small berries on their stems. They seemed to fill the whole expanse of the plain and they must have had some amazing will to live, for no matter how much they were trodden down they would spring up again. There were occasional patches of bare earth marked with hoofprints or the ruts left by cartwheels. The plain was a series of gentle undulations, and if you lay down in the grass it was impossible to see the horizon. A low evening mist was beginning to rise, and night was already casting a shadow over the whole area.

Shuji had been lying quite still in the grass for some time now. He lay with a rifle clasped in his hands, but there was no danger for the time being of the instructor giving any fresh orders since he had just gone off to inspect another squad under his command, and Shuji could rest in an easy, comfortable posture. A bittersweet feeling of self-sufficiency seemed to permeate his whole being.

The school had been at Narashino, about twenty miles east of

Tokyo, for two days now. They were doing field training, and for someone as physically incompetent as Shuji this was a constant series of hardships. Only half a day was needed to convince him of the appalling weight of his rifle, even though it was the same 38 he had so much wanted to take in his hands when he had first entered the school, and crawling forward on the ground with it only made matters worse. But the training was only to be of three days' duration, and for students in their third year at middle school this at least meant three days released from schoolwork and could be considered a special kind of holiday, so it was something he was supposed to feel pleased about. There was another reason for rejoicing, too, for they had all been issued with blanks, even if only one clip of five rounds, and allowed to fire them for the very first time.

Although they were blanks, the rifle had given Shuji's shoulder an unexpectedly heavy kick when he had fired it on the first day, but he had welcomed the sensation almost greedily. A pleasant crack rang in his ear and a whiff of cordite drifted across his nostrils. But as soon as he had fired once, he had to advance again. He jerked back the bolt to open the breech, and the spent cartridge energetically popped out and fell into a clump of grass. He started to search desperately for it, but his fingers touched only roots and earth. All the people about him were already running forward and he began running automatically after them, then hesitated, then set off again in despair. By the time he had thrown himself down for the second shot he knew it was too late to do anything about that lost cartridge case; he would never be able to find the right clump of grass again. Well, that was it, then. Nothing to be done about it. He had been running like a mechanical puppet and had thrown himself down like one, but when he fired this time he was careful to pick up the spent cartridge and put it in his ammunition pouch. Anxiety and apprehension were gradually deepening in him, taking on tangible shape, an image of himself alone in a vast plain with night falling and being made to tramp around peering and searching among all the tufts of grass to find that cartridge case. For a brief moment he was totally engrossed by images of the punishment that would inevitably follow, his bodily motions becoming purely mechanical as he lost all notion of what he was doing. But he needn't have worried. When they went back to barracks that evening the empty cartridge cases were collected but nobody made any attempt to count them. He had been lucky.

Now, as he lay sniffing the scent of the grass, he moved his ammunition pouch slightly to one side and recalled the trepidation he had experienced two days ago. It was also a rare piece of good fortune to be allowed to spend more than ten minutes lying in the grass like this. Here and there crickets were noisily chirping, and one large one appeared right in front of him, leisurely dragging itself along as if not quite sure what to do with its hind legs, but then giving a short, sharp jump and disappearing into a tuft of grass. Shuji had followed this brief episode of insect activity with unwavering attention, unconsciously lowering his jaw and resting it on the ground as he did so. He then laid his cheek on the earth. It felt cool, but somehow resistant as well, a prickly, rough sensation that seemed also to promise some kind of richness into which he could be absorbed. It was extremely pleasant, for it invited him far away, into a region where there were no classes and no training, where nothing at all existed that had anything to do with school, where all humiliation could be avoided, and where he could just lie quite still as he was now and do nothing. If he could only go on doing this for a while, with nothing required of him and requiring nothing of others, released from all his cares and trials. If only he could just lie here, thinking and only experiencing this vague sense of simply existing forever. Such retrogressive, escapist desires had become an integral part of his life since entering middle school, and grew more powerful with each new day.

It is true that he had often endeavored to extricate himself from the mean swamp of maudlin incompetence into which he had fallen, and arrive at some more pleasant place where he could be a cheerful and active soul, someone accepted by his peers as one of them, one of the boys. But each attempt had proved to be only a panic-stricken half measure, a clumsy reaction against the predicament into which the weak-spirited always find themselves eventually forced, as with that sudden and ill-considered suggestion he had once made to visit the fruit parlor, likewise leaving only an aftertaste of self-hatred, contempt and, finally, despair.

For example, there was the attitude aroused in him by the unforgettable events of the 8th of December last year, the first anniversary of which would shortly come around, and the humiliation this had led to. Shuji had perhaps been even more moved than most of the other students by what had happened then. He had felt a peculiar tension as he listened to the announcement on the radio that morning; he seemed to have lost control of his legs and could do nothing but tremble on the spot. But no doubt they had all been shaken in some way, for as they arrived at school they formed groups in the playground and whispered to each other in strangely hushed and serious voices. The teachers were all gathered in conclave in the staff room and not one of them appeared in class. Then, just before noon, the Imperial Rescript declaring war was announced. At the same time the students had what must in all truth be called a great disappointment, for it was also proclaimed that the normal curriculum would be resumed that afternoon. A number of them had rejoiced prematurely in the assumption that this unprecedented war would lead to the cancellation of the end-of-term exams, which were close at hand.

Then more announcements concerning the war were made in quick succession: the invasion of Hong Kong, the lightning landing on the Malay Peninsula, and then, at 1 P.M., the statement that "in the early hours of this morning the Imperial Navy launched a death-defying, large-scale air attack on the American fleet and air installations in the Hawaii area." One of the teachers excitedly proclaimed that history was being made anew, and Shuji was strongly affected by the words. It seemed to him that even the leafless cherry trees in the schoolyard looked completely different. Everything seemed renewed, and somehow full of splendor. Surely this was also an opportunity for him to deny his former pathetic, incompetent self, to cut himself free from the past and begin a new life. This was the day of grace on which he would begin.

The second period of that afternoon was devoted to the martial arts, and a test was carried out which took the form of one class competing against another. Shuji had on occasions in the past had hopes (only very transitory ones) about his performance in Judo, the martial art he had chosen to specialize in. He was, as one might have expected, quite hopeless at it and the more he practiced the worse his sense of inferiority in the sport became. But on this day of all days he felt things would be different. Usually in a contest of this kind he would be not so much preoccupied with the idea of winning as of losing in the least awful and undignified fashion possible, and as he prepared to meet the challenge of his opponent before the fight it was normally this negative attitude that dominated him. But today his somehow antiquated, unhealthy-looking face seemed to have grown hard with resolve; in fact, it was contorted with what must have been some extreme elation of the soul. This was to be no mere Judo contest, he promised himself as he prepared for action. He must think of his opponent as an American. His opponent must become an enemy.

This was no mere struggle but open war. It was not a question of throwing his opponent or forcing him down. He must smash him, crush him, beat him to a pulp, strangle the life out of him! He knelt down in the correct posture before the contest began, his eyes riveted on the enemy and trying to see him as an American of roughly the same height as himself, though unfortunately the other boy didn't look like that at all. Then he bowed to him and rushed in to battle, taking a powerful hold on the other's collar. At this point, his wild excess of fighting spirit should have assumed the appropriate form of a slow forcing of his opponent down, a smart pulling from the right and a twisting from the left and then one sudden tripping movement with the leg . . . but nothing of that sort took place, for all he did was kick wildly at his opponent's legs with such force that he threw himself completely off balance and only just managed to stay on his own feet.

Naturally enough, the enemy was not going to remain passive in the face of this onslaught. He tried to jerk Shuji over his hip, but Shuji, who was now doubtless controlled by some supernatural power, managed to evade this ploy by a swift swerving of his own hips. He then made another attempt to leap to the attack and pound the enemy to smithereens, but suddenly something occurred that he was quite unable to comprehend. He felt he had been struck a terrible blow somewhere, and despite the energetic overflow of his fighting spirit he found that all his actual strength seemed to have evaporated. An inexplicable deflation of his powers permeated his entire body in no time, and he realized that his rare manifestation of spirit had been of no avail. It had become impossible for him to continue to fight. He let go of his opponent and allowed himself to collapse slowly onto the floor, crouching there finally in a groveling, doubled-up posture, his hands pressed against the lower part of his abdomen. His opponent was taken aback by this and merely stood there, but the Judo teacher soon realized what had happened. He picked up the cowering Shuji by grasping him from the back about his waist, and then threw him violently onto the floor. He repeated this a number of times.

Once events had reached this stage the other pupils were able to work out what had happened as well: Shuji had been struck in the testicles, with the result that he was temporarily half-ruptured. This caused a snigger to pass around the Judo hall, which eventually became a great wave of laughter filling the far corners. So Shuji's desire for some revolutionary act of self-regeneration ended amid gleeful and unrestrained mirth.

But now Shuji was hidden in the grass, indulging for a few brief moments in sweet reminiscences of periods spent in the fields when a very small boy in the mountains of Hakone. A chorus of whispered warnings from the people scattered about him announced the return of their instructor, a cadet-corps officer who was normally in charge of boys senior to themselves and of whom they had little knowledge or experience. However, it was said that he was much more approachable than the other antiquated NCOs who were attached to the school corps. He barked out his orders sharply enough, but he showed no inclination to cause the students any miseries in addition to those they were obliged to suffer, nor did he appear desperate to expose every blunder they made. What gave particular comfort was that he did not know the individual names and faces of these juniors and so, despite the fact that Shuji was the person most likely to be singled out during training as a shining example to them all of how it should not be done, for the moment he was simply one unremarked and unremarkable face in the crowd.

Shuji started to crawl clumsily forward again, confident that his tardy progress would remain unnoticed among the grass and amid the group. He stole a glance at the instructor and was confirmed in this belief. The instructor didn't know that he was Shuji Nire, the well-known incompetent in military matters. He didn't even think of him as an individual, but merely as a number in a class, in a squad. So Shuji was much more at ease now than he had ever been during class or doing P.T. in the playground. He was aware that his normal tension had started to dissolve away. The training session ended with a bayonet charge, and Shuji fixed his bayonet, jumped up, and bounded across the uneven grass, howling for all he was worth.

"On the whole not too bad," the instructor nodded, whether because he was genuinely satisfied with their performance, or because it had brought back emotional memories of the battlefield, it would be hard to say; but he had them stack their rifles and assemble about him, and then told them old-soldier stories about actual fighting which stirred the interest and admiration of these pimply fifteen-year-olds.

"The fact is," he finally said, "the bayonet charge is perhaps the principal strength of the Japanese military tradition. Now, does anyone know why Stalingrad won't fall? Because the German Army won't resort to the bayonet charge. Their tactics are to avoid the sacrifice of human lives and first of all to break down the enemy resistance by bombardment, advancing when, and only when, resistance has collapsed. . ."

Far away in Soviet Russia the siege of Stalingrad had been going on since the end of summer. The German Army had forced its way into the city during the first fortnight of September and it had seemed only a question of time before the whole city was in German hands, but things did not turn out that way. During October the newspapers were full of headlines like: *"Whole City Reduced to Ashes,"* *"German Army Occupies Central Station,"* *"Red Octobrist Factory Remains,"* *"Only Two Blocks Left in Stalingrad Now."* This interest lasted until the end of that month, when such announcements abruptly came to an end. The attention of the Japanese people then turned to events in the Pacific: the sea engagements at night off Guadalcanal such as the Battle of Savo Island and Cape Esperance, and various sea clashes around the Solomon Islands such as the Battle of Santa Cruz.

"It's started snowing over there. The Russian Army's been waiting for the snow," the instructor went on. "It's at times like that a suicide assault can have a real effect. . ."

One of the listening pupils called out "Sir!" He was a bulky youth who was hopeless at his studies, but he stood out during military training and knew exactly what he ought to do and say in order to get on the right side of instructors:

"If we'd been there at Stalingrad, just our third-year squad, I bet it would have been occupied by now!" This bold remark caused certain stirrings among his fellows, so he grinned foolishly as if he had only meant it as a joke, and added, "or maybe not."

"Well, maybe so," said the instructor, smiling generously in obvious good spirits, much to the relief of them all. They immediately started chattering away to one another as they realized that their intuitions of some terrible reply had been unfounded.

It would soon be night. The wide plain was already growing dark, and people's faces had begun to look small and faintly white. Shuji could hear the sounds of the crickets all about them. But the instructor was clearly in a very good mood. He made no move to return to barracks but decided instead to sing for them in a low voice. He had a surprisingly deep and beautiful voice, and it seemed to penetrate the encroaching darkness to become an intimate, integral part of the fading light.

"Fair weather on the first two days;

>The third and fourth brought wind and rain.
>Our horses stumble on the way,
>The bad road over hill and plain.''

The song itself was not short, and the surprisingly sweet tones of the man's voice seemed to make it longer. Shuji felt he could almost sense the sadness in the boys sitting around him, hear it as an actual sound in the pit of their stomachs.

Shuji himself began to think about things. It was not a bad feeling at all like this, dissolving into the dusk where all individual distinctions vanished, where even one's own consciousness seemed to grow less and less precise and more and more distant, merging with the group. There had been something enjoyable about that charge just now, even though it had made him so painfully breathless. It had seemed to make the blood course fast through the body. He was physically very weak so he got bad marks in military training, but perhaps he would be surprisingly well suited to real action, be it in some smoke-filled Stalingrad or in the Solomon Islands. They would charge forward. Half of them, the majority of them, would fall. If he were hit by a bullet, then death would solve all problems. If he wasn't hit, then he would get through to the enemy lines and thrust deep with his bayonet. Whatever happened, it would all be over in an instant. He felt not in the least afraid of death. If he were to live a long time, he knew there would be little of that joy in store for him which others seemed to obtain with such ease, but much, much more of that suffering engendered by his own wretched and small-minded anxieties, the lukewarm self-obsession that made him an object of distaste to himself. In a bayonet charge a ninety-percent casualty rate could be expected, but he would be among the others as he went, a fellow with them. Thus, on the empty plain in the chill air with the scent of grass and the sweaty smell of training boots and the oily odor of leather equipment, Shuji lost himself in these simpleminded thoughts of the born victim. It was an easy solution to a complex problem and even made him forget his empty stomach; so that when the command to take up their rifles again was given, Shuji was carried away and created such a crash and clatter as he took up his that the others looked critically at him.

When they got back to the huts it was quite dark, and after the duty privates had finished their tussle over the buckets of rice and gravy and all had settled down to eat, squabbles and complaints began to fill the dining hall, a dissolute chorus of dissatisfaction.

"What do you call this muck, then?"

"It's timber, I tell you. Can't get your teeth into it. Hard as a board."

"It's dried herring," someone explained.

"Herring? This isn't herring. Herring's nothing like this. This is straight timber. No one can eat that."

While this hubbub was going on, Shuji, who had been feeling so valiant for a while, could feel himself wincing and crawling back into his shell of nervous anticipation. All the others sat about the bleak, long tables, forgetting their own identity in the grumbling chorus. All were far stronger than he was, overflowing with energy, a race of people whose ability to live at one with the world he could only envy. In fact there were other boys in the class who were weaker than him, and even less talkative and competent, but Shuji's gloomy reflections remained unaffected by that. He pressed his teeth gingerly into the hard, black fish. He was hungry and didn't think the food anything like as bad as the others said it was. The so-called rice that filled his bowl was full of barley and kept sticking in his throat as he tried to gulp it down, but that didn't make him unhappy. What made him miserable was that he was unable to say like the others that the rice was really lousy, nor did he possess the courage to say it was all right. All he could do was bend his head over his bowl and eat in silence this fish which was so elastic it was often difficult to withdraw one's teeth from it after a tentative bite. He ate up his food with much more mannered care than anyone else, leaving his bowl quite clean, and as he did so he remembered their cottage in Hakone and his uncle Yonekuni who alone had eaten rice mixed with barley with just a sprinkling of salt on it. It was that faraway, esoteric look on his uncle's face as he chewed slowly on each mouthful that came back to Shuji so clearly now.

Once the meal was over it was time to sleep. The concrete floor of the hut had been covered on each side with wooden planks, and on these some rough *tatami* matting had been laid. The boys lay down there wrapped in blankets shoulder to shoulder. But after the majority of them had stretched out, there was a small group in one corner of the room who kept on giggling over something. They were all crowded about a small book which they were taking it in turns to read in low whispers. Suddenly one of them read a few phrases in a high-pitched, hysterical screech. The words were so obscene that they completely lacked the power to titillate; they sounded more as if they were from an outspoken textbook on the subject than from a work of true pornography. Even so, they produced some lewd and ill-restrained sniggers which continued for a while.

Since Shuji was on first guard duty that night, he was standing awkwardly with his rifle in the middle of the concrete floor, and he could hear disconnected snatches of the reading from time to time. He didn't know what any of the phrases really meant, but he knew they were about women and so it must have been a pornographic book. The thought made him blush and, so that no one should notice this, he began walking hurriedly about. The sudden flush on his face was his response to the presence of evil—yet there was nothing he would have liked more than casually to join that group gathered around the dirty book. It wasn't that he wanted to see the filth for himself, he just wanted to be with them, to sit there and produce bold, natural, obscene (and thus healthy) laughter, something he knew he could never do.

Eventually this group went off to sleep as well, apparently all dropping off in almost the same brief moment. The rows of schoolboys lay there like tuna fish lined up on a quayside, all breathing or grunting in various ways which nevertheless expressed for Shuji a proud confidence in themselves. The sense of alienation he experienced was much like that which Nanny Shimoda had aroused in him years ago when he had slept with her at night, her outlandish snores producing a similarly cowardly sense of being all alone in the world. Ever since those days, Shuji had suffered from insomnia, and there was an added reason for it here at training camp, which was the incredible number of rampant fleas. So savagely did the fleas attack that on the first night everyone had cried out in the same cheerful way that you would never be able to sleep if you couldn't put up with the fleas. To Shuji their voices had sounded amused by this state of affairs, and their faces had looked full of that healthy energy which demanded restful sleep and soon found it. But he had spent a miserable first night, and was afterward not sure if he had actually slept at all.

A naked light bulb dangled from one of the bare rafters, throwing a dull light on the faces of tired schoolboys, who seemed sucked deep down in layers of mud-like sleep. There was nothing unusual about that, nor anything exceptional in the sight of one of them sitting up abruptly with a confused expression on his face and beginning automatically to scratch himself viciously in various places. This particular youth was well known for the delicacy of his features, but these were now screwed up and twisted as he sought here and there, from his legs to his back, just like a monkey. Shuji had always been attracted to this youth, although he was much too withdrawn even to hope that he might become his friend. Despite the girlish cast of his face and his physique, the boy was extremely good at sports and also at academic work. He was the kind of person who seemed to have been favored by the heavens in a way that Shuji found impossible to grasp or imagine; he could only admire and envy from a distance. But there he was suffering from fleabites just as Shuji did, his face looking as if he were about to burst into tears at any moment, and Shuji felt a sense of relief as he witnessed this, a sense that they were in some way equal. This comradely feeling, however, did not really shorten the distance between them, for even if Shuji had assured the youth that he suffered even more from fleabites, it would hardly have been a reason for establishing immediate ties of friendship.

Shuji's period of guard duty came to an end. He untied his puttees, took off his jacket and trousers, and crawled between the blankets. Then, his body curled up and tense, he waited. The places where he had been bitten last night immediately began to itch, but he lay there resisting the temptation to scratch. Finally (within less than a minute, in fact) he felt some object crawling along his calf, and then another. He knew very well from last night's experiences that there were simply too many fleas to allow one to put up any planned resistance to them, and that it was a waste of time trying to catch them. All one could do, thought the blear-eyed Shuji, was accept the fact that they were there, give up all hope of stopping them, and just hope they would bite as soon as possible, drink their fill, and get it over with. But this stoic thought did not stop his hand from moving in the direction of his thigh, and once he had done that he gave himself up to a profitless search over the rest of his body, scratching in an almost hysterical way. He would have been quite prepared to take his place in the most desperate of *banzai* bayonet charges, but he could not put up with a place where they had fleas. Perhaps he was not cut out for military life after all.

He got up a number of times and rearranged himself, pulling off his blanket and scrutinizing it, then lying down once more in despair, angry at himself for his lack of resolution. This was not a battlefield. His life was in no danger. It was a mere three days of training camp in a hut in Narashino. Suppose he were in the same situation as his brother, what would he do? Shun'ichi was now at the front, exposed constantly to real dangers. Had he forgotten that?

But Shuji could not help feeling that his brother was probably having a good time and passing his days in great good humor. After all, Shun'ichi had prophesied war between Japan and America, and had made preparations for it. Probably at this very moment swarms of those American and Japanese airplanes he was so crazy about were putting on a genuine display of aerial combat right before his eyes; and there was Shun'ichi, at some outpost on the front line, grinning all over his long, thin face, enjoying a grandstand view of the proceedings. . . So Shuji lay beneath his filthy evil-smelling blanket, tormented by fleas in the hut in Narashino, full of childish yet perfectly serious imaginings which the grown-ups of the Nire family would have found it impossible to believe he really had.

Shun'ichi had become a second lieutenant in the Medical Corps, and since that summer he had been attached to the field hospital unit of a joint brigade in Indochina. However, he was due to be posted somewhere else in the near future, and this destination became the subject of conjecture on the part of his father Tetsukichi and the other members of his family, for a few days before Shuji had gone off to his training camp in Narashino a large military envelope labeled "On Public Service" had arrived at Aoyama. Tetsukichi hastily opened it and found a mimeographed message on one large sheet of coarse paper which ran as follows:

Respectful greetings. As the cold season approaches I trust you are in the best of health. My own enthusiastic appreciation of the sacrifice you have made in sparing your son for the major task of protecting our homeland is only enhanced by my knowledge of the great sufferings and privations that you of the home front are now being obliged to endure.

Your son Shun'ichi [the name alone had been written in with a pencil] you may rest assured is in excellent health and playing an energetic role in the major task of protecting our country. I, as his commander, must here record that it is precisely one year since I took up this position. Looking back over that period of time I can hardly forbear from expressions of mutual congratulation at the progress of the military engagements put into effect

546

by the Imperial Rescript of the 8th of December of last year, viewing as I do the enormous victories won in the creation of a Greater Asia by the armed forces under the direction of the august virtue of His Imperial Majesty. Even so, much yet remains to be done; many difficulties still lie in our paths in the prosecution of this Holy War of Reconstruction.

The division has up to now been employed in ensuring a continuing control over Anglo-American interests in North Indochina and in the blockade of China itself, within and without the city of Hanoi. We are now, however, playing a more vital role at BLANK in the middle of the Pacific Ocean.

Your dear son is only one of many sons entrusted to my command, and we shall, in cooperation with the navy, be guarding a key position in the Pacific front line in the defense of our homeland against the American foe. Naturally I am only too painfully aware of the heaviness of my responsibility and the vital nature of our task, and can assure you that I shall spare no efforts that all may be done; yet knowing as I do the poverty of my own abilities and the feebleness of my powers I can only call upon you all for your heartfelt support and sincere encouragement in this undertaking.

Our present situation of BLANK is surrounded on all sides by expanses of blue ocean. Above us extends the endless blue sky. The white clouds, the white waves, come and go. The night sky is full of stars. At times there is a brilliant full moon. Truly this is a place in which to enjoy the beauties of nature. Despite the fact that this is the month when frost first falls, out here the light is still dazzling, we are all in summer uniform, and your son and his comrades are all the possessors of suntanned faces. At this moment, thanks to the blessings bestowed upon him by his country, I can assure you that your son lacks for nothing, although it may well be that he will ask you to send this, or he may ask you to send that, whatever may be of additional service to him, even though it is my own opinion that nothing is required from persons stationed on the home front. However, the occasional letter of encouragement, the occasional tidings of the rivers and mountains of home, would be a most welcome attention.

Commanding Officer Suzuki
November 1942

There was a postscript written in pencil saying "This is to inform you that Shun'ichi has been transferred to this command," but it was clear from the crudeness of the hand in which it was written that this had been appended by no commanding officer but by some private soldier.

A day later a postcard written by Shun'ichi himself arrived:

I'm sorry not to have written for so long but there have been reasons for my silence. Three of Father's letters arrived all at the same time, together with a joint letter from the family at Matsubara. We have left Indochina and come to a really extraordinary place, as you can tell by the address. Perhaps we have been blessed at last by the fortunes of war, for the perfection of the climate and the rich blue of the sea are sometimes very close to what one might call paradise. I am in perfect health—indeed I have not yet once been ill—and I fill my lungs with ozone and bathe myself in ultraviolet rays, using all my energy in my morning tasks while waiting for the day when I shall be of service to my country, and not betray the expectations of people on the home front. I can only write one postcard, so would you please give my best regards to everyone at Matsubara. P.S. If possible could you send me a small English-Japanese dictionary.

The address he had referred to was given as "c/o The Yokosuka Office, No. U103U100 (Su. One)." Yokosuka was the naval base south of Tokyo.

Tetsukichi showed this to Shuji and Aiko, but there was no one at Aoyama he could discuss it with, so he went to Matsubara and showed it to the family there. Oshu's opinion was that it might be an island in some group in the South Pacific and that Shun'ichi must be a member of the garrison defending it. Since both the army and the navy were involved, it couldn't be all that small an island. Still, the main thing was that these South Pacific islands were the wall of steel in the Japanese defense, and to be in one of those stations meant there was no question of his life being in danger. Tetsukichi was completely ignorant about such matters so he nodded in agreement and felt no small relief on hearing this opinion.

"This commanding officer seems the kind of person one could talk to, judging by his letter," added Oshu, in a further attempt to allay his brother-in-law's anxieties.

"He really does," echoed Chiyoko. "That piece about the white waves and the clouds is really rather poetic. He sounds very considerate, too."

Once Tetsukichi had left, however, she revealed a slightly unpleasant interest in analyzing various parts of what Shun'ichi (who was, after all, the eldest son of the largest thorn in Chiyoko's side, namely Ryuko) had written.

"It wasn't the kind of thing one would have expected Shun'ichi to write. 'Blessed at last by the fortunes of war . . . not betray the expectations of people on the home front. . .' Well, he must have had the censor in mind when he wrote that. I imagine him as being really very thin and dejected. I mean, I remember the expression on his face when he joined the army. I've never seen anyone look so miserable about anything. I imagine him on the kind of desert island where there's simply nothing at all. That's why the commanding officer goes out of his way to say they don't need anything. You can also see it in the way he wants an English-Japanese dictionary sent out to him."

"Well, for heaven's sake, you're not likely to find a bookshop on a Pacific island, are you?" said Oshu who seemed thoroughly bored.

"Seems quite worn out from what he writes, too. Right inside, you know. 'Very close to paradise'—there you can see his real feelings coming out and taking that desperate, bitter form. 'I am in perfect health—indeed I have not yet once been ill. . .' Now, don't you think that's a peculiar way of writing? Normally people would say something like 'Just to let you know I'm fit and well. . .' And those remarks about 'using all my energy in my morning tasks' are positively eccentric, surely? 'Indeed I have not yet once been ill . . . sometimes very close to what one might call paradise.' "

"You've certainly got a remarkable memory," said Oshu with a look of astonishment on his face. "I've already forgotten it all."

The person who received the news that Shun'ichi had gone off to some unknown island with the most composure was his mother, Ryuko. Naturally she had stayed away from the living room while Tetsukichi was there, so she did not receive the news until supper that evening. Hisa was having trouble nowadays with her false teeth and could eat nothing but glutinous rice and the most tender boiled fish. Each night a special portion of real, fresh, white fish had to be prepared for her; but at some time or other, unbeknown to Chiyoko, this had become two portions on Ryuko's instructions, which were given directly to the kitchen and entirely on her own initiative.

Ryuko's view of things was that Hisa and herself held a special position in the Matsubara household, and what she had done had been only proper. And just as she could ignore with the greatest ease the existence of others when disposing of delicacies prepared only for herself, so she could remain quite unmoved when asked about the fate of her eldest son.

"The South Pacific," she would say. "That's a place I've always wanted to visit. And a man should experience his fair share of hardships while he's still young."

That was about all she had to say on the subject, and she showed not the least indication that she was anxious about her son as most mothers would be; although this is not to imply that Ryuko did not feel any love for Shun'ichi. She had heard that he wanted an English-Japanese dictionary. She realized that Tetsukichi would probably send him a concise edition since he had asked for a small one. This realization aroused competitive feelings toward the husband from whom she was separated, and she immediately sent off a thick, bulky volume by parcel post, addressed to that obscure island known as "c/o The Yokosuka Office, No. U103U100 (Su. One)."

Nothing but the everlasting ultramarine, the wide expanses of blue ocean, the rise and scattering fall of the waves, and the dauntless task force speeding through those waters. At night the great shapes of the ships loomed larger, black shadows with all their lights dimmed out, like living things possessed of independent wills, plowing through the ocean leaving white wakes of foam behind them.

The carrier *Zuikaku* was still waging war. When Shiroki had first joined the ship it had been jokingly said that he had boarded an unlucky vessel, but in reality things were quite otherwise, for the ship was blessed with such good fortune in battle that her name, "Auspicious Crane"—the crane being a bird of good omen and a symbol of long life—seemed particularly fitting.

Ever since the beginning of the war, Admiral Nagumo's task force (of which the *Zuikaku* was one of six carriers) had been constantly employed on strike missions, launching attacks in all corners of the ocean with lightning speed and recording one remarkable success after the other. Especially during the first few months of the war this high-speed task force had been the spearhead of that amazing advance which had driven the people back home wild with enthusiasm. It seized one strategic point after another, apparently invincible, almost totally unscathed as it laid waste the opposition in the Pacific and even the Indian Ocean. "Laid waste" is hardly an elegant term, but war is rather more destructive than those two words imply, and though the sight of the fleet plowing through the blue water trailing long white ribands behind it may have been aesthetically pleasing, its aims were only bloody ones. The aircrews, the majority of whom were unselfish, generous, friendly people in normal life, became quite violent when they drank. The night after a raid, or before they were due to make one, the storm of violence they released into the world extended as far as Shiroki's cabin:

"What the hell are you sleeping for, Lieutenant? Come on, boys, let's get the idle slob up."

In these incoherent howls, and deep within their bloodshot eyes, Shiroki felt he caught a glimpse at times of that most primitive of human emotions, the fear of death; which was not surprising since there could hardly have been men who had a closer relationship with death than they. These drunkards who smashed things up were the fighter pilots and the bomber crews on whom the task force relied most, and these same men would set out on their missions as if on a picnic, with calm, cheerful faces, the thought of death not even having crossed their minds.

These few months had expanded to an enormous tract of time in Shiroki's memory, a tangled complexity that seemed to leave no room for other thoughts. Normally time became foreshortened when recalled, the events that had passed becoming disappointingly simple and dull, but now it had become ten times as long as it had really been. For example, after the attack on Pearl Harbor they had immediately returned home, but the events of those days now seemed like something from a childhood dream whenever he brought them back to mind. On the day before they saw Japan the airmen had flown off to a land base, creating a terrible sense of depression in Shiroki, a mixture of envy and doubt as to whether Japan could possibly be as close as it was said to be, for it was stiflingly humid and hot in the carrier. But the ship was indeed heading north; by that evening one could feel a definite drop in the temperature, and next morning, in brilliant clear weather, the wind blowing over the wide emptiness of the flight deck was already quite cold. Then, on the horizon, at first far off and dimly blue but gradually becoming clear so that the heart beat wildly, could be seen the two main shapes of the mountains of Shikoku. This was his homeland, where he had been born and grown up, the land that had sent him off to fight in a war quite unrelated to his own will and desires, and yet the land for which he felt he could offer his life with no reservations or regret. As he looked at the island, which had nothing remarkable about it, he felt as though he had completed a long sea voyage, one lasting for at least six months. So they passed the outer island, eating at action stations since there was the danger of submarine attack in this area, then running close to land to avoid the minefields, passing the headland of Satamisaki and entering the Inland Sea. The water here was as smooth and untroubled as a mirror, a sea of peace surrounded by peaceful islands to which he was linked by intimate bonds. It would soon be the third stand-to, and he could feel the joy of a child bubbling within him. He had come home; he had come home at last. He had returned to his homeland after delivering (although he had played no real part in it) a shattering blow to the American Pacific Fleet.

However, the demands of war required reckless haste, and this homecoming was no more than the brief time needed to take on supplies. The day for departure was soon upon them, and as they steamed out to sea again the aircraft returned and were taken on board. So at the next meal all the aircrews were present, and with them the lively atmosphere of the officers' mess returned.

The *Zuikaku* made the long voyage to take part in the attack of the task force on Rabaul, also providing support for the landings on Papua and New Guinea, before eventually returning to the naval base at Truk, where so much fuel was taken on that the supply tanker leaned sideways showing its red keel. On the following day a report came in that the base at nearby Ponape was being attacked, so the carrier made a hurried departure from port. Such visits from enemy ships, to which the *Zuikaku* was obliged to respond, occurred quite frequently after that, and at the end of March, when she had just entered the harbor at Kure, south of Hiroshima, a report came through that Marcus Island, at the southern tip of the Bonins, had been attacked from the air and an enemy fleet was headed for the main Japanese islands, so the order was immediately given to prepare to leave port again. But no matter how actively they pursued the enemy carriers they did not meet up with them.

The *Zuikaku* was next involved in C Operation, which took place in the Indian Ocean. The aim was to attack Ceylon, to sink the British Far Eastern Fleet, and to cut the enemy's shipping lanes and lines of communication. The Nagumo task force had assembled at Starling Bay, and the greatest trial after they had set out was the appalling heat inside the ship. Since all portholes had to be kept permanently closed because of the constant possibility of an attack, it was like living in a cellar. The sick bay was like a steam bath, and even if one didn't actually move one seemed to be boiling inside the heat-resistant clothing, and beads of sweat would stand out on the forehead and hands. To make matters worse there was a continual stream of patients, all of them suffering from nothing more interesting than a cold, and on one morning Shiroki had forty of them. The exhaustion from the heat and overwork was getting him down, and he found himself becoming obsessed with the idea of throwing the porthole open even if only for a second. He just managed to restrain his desire to shout out meaningless oaths.

It was clear that everybody was affected by an abnormal touchiness and awkwardness of temper. When a directive arrived from the executive officer addressed to the medical lieutenant who was Shiroki's superior and demanding an inquiry into the reasons why so many personnel were coming down with colds and asking for countermeasures, the lieutenant's reply aroused considerable displeasure. The executive officer complained in a rough, angry voice that what he said was so abstract and generalized that any layman could have worked that out for himself. The result was the medical staff were obliged to spend hours wandering about the ship studying the sleeping conditions of the men, and coming up with the recommendation that as many men as possible should sleep on deck and the remainder should be permitted to sleep naked; which just about allowed them back into the executive officer's good books, despite the fact that any layman could have arrived at similar conclusions too.

There was also the incident of the nameless warrior. Lieutenant Sasaki, a bomber pilot, had just completed a tour of inspection and was telephoning somewhere from the mess, when suddenly the blood rose to his face and he began bellowing at someone on the other end of the line:

"Look, this is Lieutenant Sasaki and no one messes me around. What's your name, sailor? Come on, let's have it!"

The incident had developed in the following way. As the telephone conversation proceeded, there had been, at the other end, loud snatches of a popular song being sung with deliberate flippancy in the background. This had aroused the lieutenant's wrath and he had demanded to speak to the offender. When this person took the telephone, he turned out to be very intoxicated and could only make stumbling responses to whatever he was asked. Finally, when ordered to give his unit, rank, name and number, he used a phrase from the song he had been singing and replied that he was the nameless warrior.

"What the hell are you saying? Give me your name! I'm asking you to give me your name!"

"That's what it is, sir. I am the nameless warrior, sir."

As Shiroki watched, Sasaki dashed wildly out of the room, return-ing after a while with the man who must have been the culprit, an astigmatic electrician whom Shiroki had previously treated for gonor-rhea. Not only gonorrhea, in fact, for when they had returned to Ja-pan, he had arranged for him to have the lenses in his glasses changed. Shiroki felt friendly toward this man who had been to the sick bay on more than one occasion, simply because he was someone he knew. But now the area around his lips was swollen and bruised. As he pro-ceeded with his interrogation, Sasaki gave a few more sharp double slaps in addition to those that had obviously been administered already. They made a good deal of noise and the electrician reeled under them, crying out in a way that sounded like a mixture of laughter and weeping and was probably no more than a simple reflex, although he seemed to be smiling in a manner that was clear-ly, if only slightly, contemptuous. This further aroused the lieu-tenant's rage, and he went on hitting him, so that the electrician's face began to twitch and a trickle of blood appeared at the corner of his mouth.

Shiroki found the whole scene disgusting and turned his face away, but finally Sasaki decided to release his victim, with the parting threat that when they got back home he would ensure he received no shore leave.

The war continued, however, heedless of these minor personal prob-lems, a struggle of ships against ships, carriers against carriers, and countries against countries. Shiroki and the others only heard about the attack on Colombo the day before it was due to take place. Just after supper that day, as the shadows of evening were falling over the ocean, an enemy flying boat made unexpected contact with them. The *Abukuma*, which was at the head of the task force, opened fire on it, but soon the Zero fighters which provided aerial cover for the ships took over. They provided a spectacle worth watching. The Zeros went into the attack at great speed, looking rather like sparrows mob-bing a crow, and for some time the enemy plane refused to go down. Despite the sluggish way it flew, it managed a few irritating maneuvers, disappearing inside a small cloud or dropping right down to the surface of the ocean and then climbing up again. Finally a plume of smoke began flowing from its fuselage, and it gradually lost altitude until it could be seen to make contact with the water, leaving a thick column of black smoke in the air. All the members of the fleet who had been watching raised delighted cheers. But, while being attacked, the plane must have been able to send off a wireless message announcing that it had discovered the Japanese task force, and the next day's attack on Colombo would have to be made in strength, since the enemy had now been alerted to it.

The feverish excitement surrounding the takeoff of the bombers was something to which they were all now accustomed, but the return this time, showing the telltale marks of flak and with five of them unaccounted for, was a completely new experience. Five planes missing meant ten aviators dead, and one of them was Lieutenant Sasaki. The fact that somebody who had lived among them, who had laughed and cursed, should have suddenly disappeared in this way and would not appear again seemed indescribably mysterious. The mind found it almost impossible to grasp or accept the truth of what had happened.

"We let all the battleships and carriers escape. It wasn't worth it. It wasn't worth the cost," Lieutenant Tsukamoto kept on muttering to himself in the mess, for Sasaki had been a friend of his. "Still, if we hit Trincomalee they'll have to come out this time. Just wait and see, wait and see."

The next morning, before it was light, Shiroki was woken by a medical orderly beating on his cabin door. One of the engine-room staff had been carried up to the sick bay.

"He looks really knocked out," the orderly said in an ominous way.

Shiroki raced off to the sick bay and realized the man was a little more than knocked out. One glance was enough to reveal that his wide-open eyeballs had rolled upward and the pupils were completely dilated. When he felt for his pulse he found he had none, nor could he hear his heart beating. His breathing had also stopped. Shiroki gave him a lobeline injection to stimulate the heart, and then tried artificial respiration, even though it had been obvious from the start that there was nothing he could do. The artificial respiration was kept up for an hour before the man was officially pronounced dead.

Shiroki heard that this petty officer third class had gone on duty the previous afternoon, then suddenly felt sick and vomited, probably from heat prostration since the temperature in the engine room was around 120 degrees Fahrenheit. He was allowed to rest in a cabin where the temperature was only 100 degrees. He was prone to stomach trouble, and since the people around him were at action stations it was simply assumed that he was having another bout of this, so he was not sent to be medically examined. Then, just around dawn, he had had a convulsive fit and it was discovered that he had lost consciousness. Only then was he taken to the sick bay.

An injection of formalin was made into the abdominal cavity and the body was given a sea burial that afternoon. There was a short blast on the bugle; those who were on duty on deck saluted; and the coffin was swallowed up by the deep blue sea with an ease that astounded. On those perpetual dark waters there was no swell, only the occasional rippling wave. The waves breaking at the bow were of a brilliant white, dazzling the eyes, and the wake that spread out along the sides of the ship slid over the finely wrinkled surface of the blue ocean and disappeared to be followed by the next foaming wave.

This was the same ocean that Tetsukichi and Ryuko had voyaged over in the past, the Indian Ocean. Kiichiro himself had crossed it many more years before them. The ship's passengers had slumbered in their deck chairs, yawning in the tedium from which they might be awakened for a moment by the cry that there were flying fish; and at evening, when the colors of the towering cumulus clouds changed and faded, they would think of home.

This was the same ocean, but Shiroki was living in a far different world. Yet as he looked at the expressionless mask of the ocean, drinking in the glowing light of the sun, he too was moved, if only momentarily. The jettisoning of the coffin just now had become unreal, illusory. A man who need not have died had died. An unnecessary death. And that was the meaning of war.

For a while after first joining the ship Shiroki had made detailed entries each day in his diary. Presently these became much briefer and scrappier, and days would pass when he wrote nothing at all. However, on days when they were involved in action and he was in the emergency medical station, he would listen to announcements over the loudspeaker address system and take hurried notes on the state of the battle. Three days after the attack on Colombo the strike force launched an assault on the port of Trincomalee:

April 9th: 0830: Action stations.
  0900: Assault force takes off. Still just daybreak.
  1007: Enemy flying boat spotted 80 degrees starboard.
  1010: Soon shot down 70 degrees starboard.

1100: Report from leader Flight 41 "Bombed enemy anti-aircraft gun emplacements inflicting heavy damage." *Shokaku* squadron says battleships in port.

1105: Enemy carrier and 3 destroyers reported at distance 155 nautical miles direction 18 degrees.

1120: Leader Flight 43 announces "Now bombing 9 light cruisers."

1135: Bombers take off to attack enemy carrier.

1150: Another 15 bombers take off.

1200: Enemy planes approaching. Battle stations.

1253: 2 enemy light cruisers sunk.

1353: 9 enemy bombers launch attack on *Akagi*. Dogfights.

1358: Enemy carrier sunk!

1445: Leader *Shokaku* Flight 24 radios 9 enemy bombers sighted and in pursuit.

1500: 7 enemy bombers shot down. 2 escape in cloud cover.

1613: Our bombers all safely returned.

1900: Air attack stand-by.

2025: Stand down.

There was great uproar in the mess that night since they had at last been able to sink the British aircraft carrier *Hermes*. None of her planes had been on board and she had radioed desperately to land for Hurricane fighter cover. It had taken a mere fifteen minutes to sink her, together with the escort destroyers and a merchant ship that had been in the vicinity.

"It was like twisting a baby's arm," said one of the bomber crew members, his face flushed with beer; and that brash statement seemed to represent the way everybody felt, for the task force had indeed sailed about the Indian Ocean just as it pleased, laying waste wherever it went, its own ships remaining totally undamaged, so naturally they thought they were invincible.

The *Zuikaku* and her sister ship, the *Shokaku*, separated from the main force and set sail for a port in Taiwan, holding the funeral rites for their dead heroes on the way. All hands assembled in the No. 1 upper aircraft hangar, and the ceremony was conducted with a solemn reading of the Buddhist scriptures by a priest. On closer inspection, this priest was seen to be wearing his robes over heat-resistant clothing, and he turned out to be the officer in charge of the maintenance workshop; the person next to him, moreover, who was also chanting with great seriousness, was a mechanic who seemed to suffer from perpetual beriberi and was one of Shiroki's most frequent patients. For a moment Shiroki was seized with a feeling of absurd amusement which was very much out of place, and then immediately afterward by a violent yet empty shudder of fear. People would be lost again from the ship, inevitably. It would go on happening because that was the meaning of war.

Two days later they entered port and he was able to enjoy the sight, a new one to him, of a town mainly in the Chinese style. He even squandered the large sum of a thousand yen, at the principal medical officer's instigation, on a rare inkstone which he thought would make a good souvenir. He had plenty of money since they almost never went ashore and there was no opportunity to spend his pay, which merely accumulated. They were due to stay in port a number of days and the town was going to give them a big welcome party, but news arrived that an enemy task force had appeared, followed that same evening after supper by a cable announcing that the Japanese home islands had suffered an air attack, and they were obliged to put to sea in immediate pursuit the next day. Shiroki felt a weary sense of acceptance at this unpleasant news, but then you had to expect to be busy because there was a war on. Even so, like everyone else on the ship, he still had only a naive idea of what this "war" involved, and assumed that battle and conflict meant the easy path they had trodden so far, and that things would continue as they had. But things did not.

The *Zuikaku* and *Shokaku* became the kingpins of the MO Task Force, and on the 5th of May, with all hands at first stand-by, for they were expecting to make enemy contact, they steamed around the south side of the Solomon Islands and entered the Coral Sea. On the previous day, Japanese troops had landed on Tulagi and had been attacked two or three times by the enemy task force. Japanese transports had also set out from Rabaul to launch an assault on Port Moresby and were now on course for the southeast tip of New Guinea. It seemed that the Japanese and American fleets were fated to fight an engagement within the next couple of days, and it also appeared that this would be the greatest aircraft-carrier battle in history so far. The only thing the flying officers regretted was that they were two days later arriving than expected, for it had taken a surprising amount of time to transport the Zero fighters to a land base at Rabaul. If it had not been for that, they would have been in a position at sea where they could have caught the enemy ships that had attacked the soldiers at Tulagi.

May 6th: Morning. Second stand-to. Finished surgery and hanging around in mess before lunch when order given enemy task force sighted and aircraft to be made ready and aircrews prepared to take off. Everyone suddenly tremendously busy and took hasty meal and then to action stations. But position at first given as 300 nautical miles away, then changed to 400, so the planes couldn't take off and everyone became pessimistic about day's outcome. The fleet was refueling at the time, but this was discontinued and just the 2 destroyers that had already finished taking on fuel set off with *Zuikaku* and *Shokaku* heading south at speed of 26 knots. At night this speed was cut to 10 knots and we headed north again. Couldn't work out what we were trying to do, but Lieutenant Tsukamoto explained that we intended to hold back after making contact and wait until the enemy was drawn out by *Shoho* and others. Hope the plan works as it's meant to.

May 7th: This has been a really bad day, really unlucky. Things still not clear when got up, but around 0600 report from *Shokaku* spotter plane that yesterday's target had been found again, and immediately 12 planes armed with torpedoes took off, and then another 60 planes (including those from *Shokaku*). This turned out to be a mistake by spotter plane, however, since all they found was some tankers and 2 or 3 destroyers. Carrier immediately sent off radio messages ordering them back at once, but messages didn't seem to get through and they took a long time, during which we heard that *Shoho* had been hit by enemy bombers, set ablaze, and sunk almost instantly, and all the time she was calling for support from us and we couldn't give any.

The enemy was still 320 nautical miles away, 5 battleships approaching at speed of 35 knots, so despite sun going down 15 assault planes and bombers took off plus some from *Shokaku*, and the fighters came back but couldn't land on deck because dark, so we had to travel without their protection knowing we were leaving ourselves wide open and for the first time on the ship there was the feeling of gambling, of playing for all or nothing. However one of our pilots told me our torpedo assault planes had been unable to find enemy carriers and while searching were caught by enemy fighters and all except squadron leader shot down. With no fighter support nothing they could do about it. Similarly the bombers had been unable to find any enemy ships, and since they had to make carrier landing at night had jettisoned their bombs and then had terribly bad luck to sight enemy carrier only 10 minutes later.

After day like this of no success and a lot of planes missing, the southern night dark with rain and no stars, pitch-blackness broken by occasional searchlight from escort ship indicating position, atmosphere of tragic intensity as wait for assault planes to return. Already known in mess that Tsukamoto and Muraki lost in action. Lieutenant Muraki only recently married and seemed blessed with happiness and good fortune, and had always seemed pleased with life whenever he spoke, and although all living things doomed to die it's hard to see why he was chosen at this moment of his life. Tomorrow will be their funerals and another day of action, and we can only grit our teeth and get on with both jobs.

In fact the next day, the 8th of May, did see an almost literal head-on clash between the Japanese and American carriers. The spotter planes of each side reported sightings at almost exactly the same time, and both sets of assault planes took off and flew toward their targets. The *Zuikaku* and *Shokaku* had sent off a combined attack force of sixty-nine planes, but as those left on the carrier were watching the last one fade out of sight and receiving the first radio communications from them, a swarm of enemy planes suddenly descended. This made the encounters with flying boats in the Indian Ocean look like mere practice or child's play. Now there were planes screaming overhead, and men shivered with the fear of death.

The sky was full of drifting flocks of broken cloud. Straight ahead was a low-lying cloud trailing the darkish curtain of a rain squall, but the blue sky between them and the cloud was brilliant with dazzling light. The loudspeaker had immediately roared out the command to battle stations against aerial attack, but when Shiroki glanced out through the doorway of the emergency medical station for a moment, nothing in particular seemed to be going on. The *Shokaku* was some nine thousand yards away across a wide expanse of water, but then he noticed what seemed to be a swarm of speckled black stains in the air above her, which increased in size and number as he watched, holding together for a moment and then drifting slowly apart and expanding into thin cloudlets. It was the flak from her anti-aircraft guns. At the same time he observed things like little pebbles falling from the sky in which those black, drifting petals were scattered, descending at a terrifying speed toward the *Shokaku*. What he saw in that brief moment were enemy dive bombers, but beyond that he saw nothing. He saw none of our planes, and indeed he hadn't the leisure to look for them, for at that moment the *Zuikaku* passed through the curtain of the squall and pelting torrents of rain completely obliterated his field of vision. Despite this, all the anti-aircraft guns on the *Zuikaku* opened fire, no doubt as a diversionary tactic. It seemed to Shiroki to be blind shooting in the dark. Not only the high-altitude guns but the machine guns as well were blazing away at the dark clouds, shooting crazily into the rain. The din was enough to burst one's eardrums and the whole ship shook with an electric kind of trembling. The insane noise, the deafening roar and rattle, the random shooting back at nothing gave Shiroki his first real experience of naked physical fear, as if his whole body had been laid open—something he hadn't felt when he first saw those diving planes. Just in front of the emergency medical station was a 25-millimeter machine-gun emplacement, and Shiroki noticed how the expression on the gunner's face was transformed as he sprayed bullets all over the place.

"Reckon that's frightening them off," the machine gunner said when he had stopped firing and had regained some of his composure. "They'll be scared to come now."

But if they were scared, so was Shiroki. He was so scared the pores of his skin had started to widen and his hair was standing on end. During the six months since the war had started he had thought he understood what it was about, even thought he had grown used to it, but he had never started to imagine it could be as terrible as this.

"Stay inside the squall," he whispered inside his own head. "Don't go outside. Stay in."

But the carrier soon passed through it, and the light blue of the sky and sea appeared again, as also did the sight of the *Shokaku* steering a zigzag course in her attempts to avoid the brunt of the enemy attack now being aimed at her. The huge carrier, sister ship to the *Zuikaku*, with whom she had acted in concert ever since the Pacific War had begun, had now almost disappeared behind the spray raised by falling bombs. Black smoke seemed for a moment to be rising from her stern, but once more great columns of spray hid her from sight. It was obvious that she was being subjected to a concerted attack by a number of planes, although one could not see how many planes there were nor calculate if the bombs were hitting their target because of the spray that veiled the whole ship. The *Zuikaku* herself now began to take extreme evasive action, zigzagging at such violent angles that the ship keeled right over at each turn with a great lurch, and then managed once more to hide inside a squall. During this entire engagement the *Zuikaku* had seemed to lead a charmed life, but on leaving the squall for the second time the people on deck saw a sight that made their blood run cold: one of the Japanese cruisers which had been taking a similar blind course of evasive action was so close that they only just avoided ramming her.

As soon as the first wave of the enemy attack had withdrawn, the defensive cover of Zero fighters was taken back on board. One of the pilots had had his fuel tank shot through and oil had splashed into his eyes, so he came to Shiroki to have them bathed.

"The enemy planes are pretty good," he said. "Some of ours had to make suicide runs at them."

Shiroki looked toward the *Shokaku* again and could just make her out far off on the horizon, the hull barely visible but her superstructure and masts apparently unimpaired. But black smoke was pouring from her stern, making her look like an aircraft that had been shot down and was now floating in the water. Then the second wave of enemy planes attacked and he saw a clear column of flame leap from the carrier and the plume of black smoke grow higher. At that moment he decided the *Shokaku* was done for.

His fear had left him some time ago, although he seemed to have lost his sense of time. Anti-aircraft firing was still going on, but at long last the enemy planes withdrew, and they heard the news that the *Saratoga* (it later turned out to have been the *Lexington*) had been sunk, and cheering broke out all over the ship. Even one normally morose medical orderly, a person always absorbed in apparently meaningful silence, was now astonishingly all smiles, a sight such as Shiroki had never hoped to see.

Since the *Zuikaku* had been able to shelter in rain squalls she was undamaged, but once the emergency rations had been eaten as a late lunch and the assault planes started to return, there was terrible and tragic activity on deck.

563

Shiroki ran over to a plane on being told that one of the crew seemed to be dead. The man was slumped forward in the rear cockpit of a Type 99 bomber and was not moving. When Shiroki lifted up the head, he saw it was Chief Petty Officer Arai who had expressed such bitter regret yesterday at the fact that they should have jettisoned their bombs just before sighting the enemy carrier. From the color of his face he seemed to be already dead and Shiroki did not feel his pulse. As the body was lifted out of the cockpit the blood that had accumulated inside the flying suit was scattered about by the sea wind, and great quantities of brilliant liquid spilled out, soaking Shiroki and the mechanic who was carrying the body. They managed to get him into the emergency medical station and found that a machine-gun bullet had entered his right side, making a hole the size of an egg, before emerging just below his left shoulder blade, tearing open a hole large enough for a child's fist to enter and leaving a great area of exposed flesh. Since massive perforation of the lung had introduced air into the pleural cavity there was no question of trying to stimulate the heart. There was absolutely nothing to be done for him, and Shiroki withdrew his bloodstained hands from the body, his head full of black thoughts.

Meanwhile planes had gone on landing on the flight deck. Since the *Shokaku* was now incapable of handling aircraft, all the planes from that carrier made for the *Zuikaku*. In the resultant noise and confusion, which was on a scale Shiroki had never experienced, some of the planes were unable to make the deck and simply crash-landed into the water. Aircraft that had been severely damaged or had something wrong with their engines were now being pushed unceremoniously over the side to make more room. The *Shokaku* herself had clearly withdrawn from the engagement, trailing a great cloud of black smoke behind her, and disappeared over the horizon some time ago. Shiroki had grown accustomed only to battles that went well, so the tense, hectic atmosphere about him and those desperate scenes made the situation appear much worse than in fact it was.

In purely objective terms the Battle of the Coral Sea could be seen as a Japanese victory, and when Shiroki heard the news that the fires on the *Shokaku* had been brought under control and repair work was being carried out he finally managed to feel that they had actually won. The Japanese had lost only the *Shoho*, a warship converted into a carrier with a mere twenty-seven aircraft, whereas the American ship that had been sunk, the *Lexington*, was a genuine carrier, the largest in the U.S. Navy with a ninety-plane capacity, and the *Yorktown* had been seriously damaged as well. In tactical terms, however, Japan had suffered a defeat in that the landing at Port Moresby had to be called off; in addition, a considerable number of irreplaceable aircrews had been lost.

> May 9th: Imperial Headquarters made following announcement about battle today, saying: "Our Imperial Navy commenced an engagement with an apparently joint Anglo-American task force in the Coral Sea on the 6th, on the 7th sinking an American battleship and severely damaging or sinking a British Warspite-class warship. On the 8th the *Saratoga* was sunk and the *Yorktown* was left sinking. Major damage was also inflicted on a California-class battleship, an oil tanker was severely damaged, and a battle cruiser set on fire. This engagement will be named the Battle of the Coral Sea." Despite the ship strength we still have today, the 9th, as far as planes concerned we only have 9 assault planes operational and same number of bombers, so idea of launching attack had to be discarded. Our ship herself has lost, in addition to one crewman dead on arrival and one mechanic lost overboard, 21 aircrew missing in action presumed dead. The loss of aircrew from *Shokaku* is three times ours and reports refer to losses from enemy bombing as 100 dead, 95 seriously injured, 30 lightly injured. Of the seriously injured a considerable number in critical condition. I can imagine what hell they must be going through in the medical stations in that ship. She received bombs on forward flight deck, aft flight deck portside, and starboard gun deck near bridge where defense guns were blown to pieces and blast from explosion hurled most of deck maintenance and flight control personnel into sea. Anchor mechanism also damaged and so deep-sea mooring now impossible and seems to be on way to Kure or Yokosuka to go into dock.

Two days later the entire crew assembled on deck to pay a tribute of one minute's silence to the dead. As the carrier turned her bows back briefly toward the sunset waters of the Coral Sea which they were now leaving, one long, magnificent range of cumulus clouds lay motionless on the horizon. They were deep purple and velvety gray, tinged here and there with scarlet and gold and sometimes green. For a moment the dying sun showed its quietly burning face through the clouds, level with the horizon, and poured its crimson light across the still waters. It was visibly sinking, disappearing beneath the waves. Three bands of mysteriously faint colored light—pink, yellow and blue—shot across the sky and vanished as the surface of the ocean was suddenly covered in shadow. Then came the dark, in which the wake of the ship appeared abnormally long and purposeless. That night it shone superbly white, indicating a massive concentration of phosphorescence in the water. Low down in the sky the Southern Cross began to flicker, but only faintly yet. Shiroki found this natural beauty cruel. It seemed so magnificent and pure it aroused misgivings in him. Was this the painful beauty with which the world would appear to a man at the instant of his death?

But human beings possess an almost innocent egotism that allows them to think mainly of themselves and their immediate situation most of the time. The next day they had left those dangerous waters and were heading for the naval base at Truk, and Shiroki even felt a drowsy kind of elation. As the ships slid over the ultramarine ocean —the *Zuikaku* with her two cruisers and two destroyers, a small force detached now from the MO Task Force—everything seemed pleasantly cheerful, peaceful and at ease.

The sick bay was visited by a man with a moustache called Lieutenant Yamaguchi, a fighter pilot from the *Shokaku* who had been taken on board the *Zuikaku*. He had suffered from gonorrhea for a long time but believed it was all right now, and since he was going to be married quite soon he wanted to be given a clean bill of health. But his hopes were probably premature, for when Shiroki put a urine sample under the microscope he noted a large number of epithelial cells with some dubious-looking bacterial bodies between them.

"Doesn't look too good, I'm afraid. You'll need another checkup."

On hearing this the man looked extraordinarily despondent, like a child on the point of bursting into tears.

"Doctor, do you think it will get better? I mean, do you think it will ever get really better?"

Shiroki undertook to cure him without fail before they got back home, although he then went on to ask him quite frankly why a person in his trade, which had the highest death rate of all, should be thinking in terms of taking a wife. This made Lieutenant Yamaguchi, who was so timid when it came to the question of gonorrhea, turn his moustached face to the ceiling and roar with laughter:

"People don't die all that readily, you know. Even aircraft carriers don't sink so easily. Look what a huge carrier battle that was, and yet the only one we actually lost was the *Shoho*. People may be close to death all the time but they don't die all that much; the closest ones least of all, maybe. Besides, I've no intention of making my wife a widow."

Yamaguchi spoke with such confidence that Shiroki inwardly agreed with what he had heard. But he was mistaken, for each new day the war took an increasing number of victims.

The *Zuikaku* followed the *Shokaku*, which had to go into dry dock, and arrived back in Kure after what had been a longish absence. While the officers were enjoying themselves with those brief relaxations which a port has to offer in the way of *geisha*, some disastrous news arrived.

> June 6th: Terrible communiqué arrived. The carriers taking part in the MI Operation have all been destroyed: *Akagi*, *Kaga*, *Soryu*, *Hiryu*, all bought it apparently. The landing on Midway has been abandoned for the time being, as has the AL Operation. Depressed all day. Overnight the *Zuikaku* had become the only real, serviceable aircraft carrier the country has.

Thus Shiroki became one of those few who were aware of what had really happened in the Battle of Midway, a truth far removed from the great victory that was greeted with such wild public rejoicing; and from that time he would be a man with a secret shadow over him. But he continued to play his part in the war, as did his ship.

Early that summer the *Zuikaku* joined the Northern Fleet and drifted about for some time in the gloomy waters near the fog-bound island of Kiska in the Aleutians, going round and round the same expanse of sea searching for the enemy. As Shiroki gazed at the damp, clinging fog, the soaking wet flight deck, and the gray sea under a dark, lowering sky that seemed to press down on one's head, he remembered the heat of the south as if it were some distant dream. But this did not last for long. In mid-August, the *Zuikaku* set off again for the sea surrounding the Solomon Islands. A short while before, American forces had suddenly landed on Guadalcanal, and the fighting on and about this island, the engagements at sea and in the air and the battering at both supply lines, became more intense with each day, gradually growing into an enormous and long-drawn-out war of attrition. While this was going on, the Battle of the Eastern

Solomons and the Battle of Santa Cruz took place, and the *Zuikaku*, together with the newly repaired *Shokaku*, played a leading role in both. Again the *Zuikaku* was blessed with good fortune, the punishment always being taken by the *Shokaku* and other carriers. Although she kept on losing aircrews, the ship herself remained unscarred, apparently unsinkable.

The crew of the *Zuikaku* came to believe that their ship could never be sunk. Despite, or perhaps because of, the fact that no one knew what might happen tomorrow and their lives were separated from death each day by only the thinnest of divisions, they clung to the superstition of their ship's invincibility as one certainty in an uncertain world. Also, it was so stiflingly hot shut up inside the carrier that one felt little inclination to brood over matters of life and death. Shiroki had finally worked out why the patients in the sick bay always seemed to have a slight temperature: it was because the room itself was way above body temperature, and no matter how much one shook the thermometer it would only go down for a second before climbing above ninety-eight degrees again.

In these conditions Shiroki could only entrust his physical being to the attractions of inertia and the working of fate. Repeated experience of combat had dulled his sensibilities. It was mysterious, but he no longer experienced that naked tension now, and he had ceased to feel afraid. Naturally he felt a tremor of nervous excitement when the order to prepare for attack was given, but it was now much like the frisson a sexually experienced man has with a woman; real enough, but nothing like what it had been the first time. Another doctor had joined the medical team, and Shiroki was no longer attached to the emergency station but to the main sick bay inside the ship. During enemy attacks one knew nothing of what was going on outside except for the loudspeaker announcements. This should have been more terrifying than being on deck, but Shiroki only experienced it as something vaguely unpleasant. He had now reached a state of mind where he seemed indifferent to whether he lived or died. He occasionally thought he might be going a bit queer in the head, something that life in the South Seas was traditionally said to do to people from the north; and, no doubt, it was the insensibility that war brought on as well. He found the amount of beer he consumed after making his rounds had increased appreciably, and, except when he played bridge or *shogi* with other officers, often until late at night, he spent each day in a state of mental and emotional nullity.

A mere ship's doctor was not really in a position to gain an objective grasp of the way the war was going, but Shiroki certainly understood that the setbacks the Japanese Army had met with in Guadalcanal were unprecedented. These were not merely local, temporary reverses, but indications that the troops had cracked under a pressure that was slowly but surely forcing them back. And this applied not only to the engagements there, but everywhere. Shiroki could feel it on the *Zuikaku* herself, where one had to admit that the quality of the aircrews was declining. When hostilities had begun, the fliers on the *Zuikaku* had been said to be technically still inferior to those on the *Akagi*, *Kaga* and the other carriers. But by the time of the Battle of the Coral Sea they had become battle-hardened veterans who were inferior to none. It was these veterans, however, who were lost in that battle and then in increasing numbers during the dogfights that went on for weeks during the struggle for Guadalcanal. Now, hardly one of the original faces remained. And the almost complete turnover in personnel was a change in the direction, not of greater technical efficiency, but of inexperience and immaturity.

Shiroki kept on with his diary, but it had become a mere scribble dashed off in spare moments compared with what it had been when he first joined the ship.

August 24th: 0430: Spotter plane takes off.

0930: Action stations. Seem to have made contact with enemy flying boat. No sighting reported of enemy ships this morning.

1305: Immediate battle stations. Few minutes later order prepare for aerial attack. Petty Officer Nishiki comes with scared look on face tells me *Shokaku* ahead of us being bombed and two or three near misses. First Assault takes off. Large enemy force of 2 carriers, 2 battleships, 6 cruisers, 10 destroyers spotted 250 nautical miles distant. Aerial attack starts. Our ack-ack and machine guns start banging away, and keep feeling all the time going to be hit any moment. Feel better if had something to do or could go outside to see what's going on just to take mind off things. Still, hear later been firing at own fighter cover and gun-deck controllers responsible got terrible dressing down.

1400: Second Assault takes off but no report from them all afternoon. Just as got dark finally came back but despite our hopes whole lot returned without having seen a thing, really depressing result, hardly believe possible. Present fliers do seem pretty hopeless bunch compared with what we had before. Those may have been rough slapdash crowd but certainly got things done.

Not one plane of First Assault Squadron back by 2000 hours, but seems inconceivable all shot down. Probably ran out of gas and had to force land, but in that case should at least been able to radio position, so maybe have been shot down.

With constant strain and tension stomach, which not too good since yesterday, became really bad and went early to bed with no supper. Heard one of our support ships, the *Ryujo*, on fire from enemy bombing and just hope doesn't sink.

August 26th: 0400: Stand-by. Just got through second stand-by and surgery when at 0800 hours ordered to action stations because enemy flying boat around which it took an awful long time to shoot down. Our fighter pilots are really hopeless now, as if it were first time been up in combat, and apparently all very depressing.

During bombing day before yesterday when *Shokaku* taking evasive action one of her bombers fell into sea and 6 people died. Certainly an unlucky ship.

August 28th: 10 bombers dispatched to Buka Island right at the top of Solomons group to assist in attack on Guadalcanal. Been number of attempts since 24th to make landing near enemy positions, but each time called off. This time marines will be landed by destroyer at night. Only hope they can manage to bring it off at last.

August 31st: Been sailing in circles all day. Landings being made on Guadalcanal, but 9 of our fighters made crash landing because of bad weather, and all complete write-offs. What a performance! In afternoon physical checkups for engine-room staff. Nearly all some form of heat rash, and many pale and sickly. Did the paymasters at same time, and even most of them look ill. Really ought to keep a lot of them under surveillance.

September 4th: 0400: Call to stand to. So drowsy I dozed off when I heard second call and got in a panic looking for uniform, but yesterday's duty orderly seemed to have tidied it away somewhere and while I was searching about for it all hatches were closed. I started thinking what it would be like if suddenly torpedoed or bombed, being shut in here like this, and felt could easily go crazy with worry although nothing I could do about it. Don't mind idea of dying itself but to be shut away like this in bottom of ship did not appeal to me at all. Eventually hatches opened but truly horrible experience.

October 15th: 0515: During breakfast announcement of large enemy force seen and thought it strange no sign of our planes taking off, although it turned out what had been seen was small supply convoy and were trying to see if task force behind or not.

0930: Decided to attack this convoy, and torpedo and bomber planes set off close formation.

1200 hours: Second Assault Squadron took off, although now seemed such large attacking force for so inadequate a target that whole engagement must be over in few minutes, when at 1400 hours first attack wave came back with 4 people injured (one seriously); but all treatment given at emergency station on deck so couldn't be sure about any of this. We claimed to have sunk one carrier escort vessel, a Cairo-class cruiser, and badly damaged one destroyer, a pretty hopeless record considering how many planes were sent out, and could only compare with what happened in Indian Ocean or Coral Sea. Those were the good old days all right. We lost one torpedo plane and one bomber.

Second Assault Squadron returned after sunset. Went up onto bridge to watch night landing which we haven't done for some time. First plane made flight deck but drifted so far right it caught rope of signal mast and a wing banged right into entrance to bridge making whole plane swerve right knocking over a dozen people and plunging into sea. Everyone rushed to side to peer anxiously at water, and there it lay upside down with no sign of any survivors and causing panic on deck. Went to emergency station to help out. In all more than 10 people killed or wounded in this incident, and of wounded one seriously injured in chest, bleeding from lungs, condition critical.

This second wave had split up into two groups, of which first group unable to locate any enemy ships, so grand total was 4 hits on cruiser and 2 on cargo ship (which did actually succeed in sinking her). Really pathetic. Everyone gloomily wondering what will happen with fliers like this if get into another situation like the Coral Sea.

October 22nd: Not feeling too good some days now. Not defecating regularly, so either constipated or fits of diarrhea. Seem to have no appetite either, although ought to. Lost pounds in weight, too. Face thin, drawn and gloomy. Cut speed to 12 knots today while other ships refueled. Drifting around in circles again.

Planned attack on Guadalcanal by our forces put off again till tomorrow. Radio message claims we have advantage on land and stating confidence in victory. Headquarters staff have also landed and have around 20,000 troops with more being landed apparently, so doesn't seem they can possibly lose when they attack. Let's hope they do win and then we can go back home to the cool. Had diarrhea five times today. Can't do a thing about it.

October 25th: Bad headache so didn't stand by this morning. Felt much better after hearing over loudspeaker that airfield in Guadalcanal been taken.

Then this afternoon hear that news was mistake; instead fierce fighting going on around airfield perimeter. This really gets us all down because just what happened before. If they haven't captured the airfield why do they say they have? On top of that hear forward troops taken hammering from B-17s, one regiment suffering heavy casualties, only adding to prevailing gloom. Army to attack again this evening at 7 P.M. Am seriously thinking of praying to gods for their success.

October 26th: 0100: Woken by very peculiar noise. Still half dozing when ordered to action stations and struggle like mad to put on uniform. Later hear that B-17 just missed us with bomb and sound I heard was explosion in water. Living dangerously.

Report of sighting of 2 enemy carriers. First and Second Assault Squadrons take off. Soon after, aerial attack. Being on duty in sick bay no idea what going on outside, but hear around 30 planes, one direct hit on *Zuiho*, then attack concentrated on *Shokaku*, 2 direct hits and fires blazing.

0900: Go on deck. Fires on *Zuiho* already out but *Shokaku* sending out great billows of white smoke and fires not yet under control; people saying she really is an unlucky ship.

1000: First Assault Squadron returns, but practically all ours have bought it, only 4 or 5 making it back. Since *Zuiho* and *Shokaku* can't land planes theirs land on us.

1300: Third assault wave takes off. Same time report comes in saying enemy carrier and battleship sunk and one carrier ablaze, which cheers everyone a lot. Third wave sent off to give coup de grâce to burning carrier which still afloat.

Evening: Seems we have had considerable successes, but just as clear have suffered major losses too. Dozens of planes failed to return. We have lost 8 senior officers, and losses among junior and petty officers have been considerable, and there's no getting away from it. Apparently enemy fleet had taken up two brilliant defensive positions with carriers at center and cruisers and destroyers circling around them, and the anti-aircraft firepower they were able to put up was tremendous.

Newspaper accounts arrive by cable. They say Imperial Headquarters announced on 27th results that seem not much in keeping with those here, stating 4 enemy carriers sunk along with other ships. Today an investigatory committee studying this, but unable to reach much agreement on what occurred although seems we sunk 2 carriers and not 4. Fliers from *Junyo* expected here tomorrow and no doubt same disagreements will occur as today, making one realize problems in working out what really happens in a sea battle.

1300: Funeral of Lieutenant Fujita takes place on *Junyo*. He was forced to land there instead of here and found dead in cockpit. We all assemble on starboard side to pay last respects.

At the beginning of November a gray aircraft carrier appeared at dawn just off the Bungo Channel escorted by a number of destroyers. This was the *Zuikaku* returning home after three months' absence, looking dirty and exhausted, as also did her planes and crew. Just before dawn Shiroki had been woken by a kind of explosion he had never experienced before; he had no idea what it was, though it was so powerful he thought at first they must have been hit by a torpedo. There was a succession of loud yet muffled thuds, then more of them again, and more. It couldn't be an enemy attack or the bugle would have gone for battle stations, but he certainly did not feel like turning over and ignoring the noise and going back to sleep again. In fact it was the sound of depth charges dropped by the escort destroyers, a threatening gesture aimed at any enemy submarine that might be prowling around, for they were just about to enter the narrow waters of the Bungo Channel. Shiroki was going home, back to the place he had longed for and dreamed of, where the leaves would be falling in the woods, and it was as if he could already feel the touch of *tatami* again—he seemed to have almost forgotten it—and hear the water boiling peacefully in the iron kettle that steamed on the *hibachi*; back also to the crowded streets of the city, streets that would be full of children and women still dressed in traditional ways. Yet even this homecoming, this return to the peace, relaxation and quietness of mind he had yearned for, was caught up in the toils of war right to the very end.

After only a brief interval for rest and maintenance, the *Zuikaku* spent a number of days off Tokuyama to the west of Hiroshima so that the new aircrews could practice takeoff and landing procedures. During this period a practice flight of the new Type 14 carrier-based assault plane took place, and seeing it land with marvelous ease on the flight deck—probably because it was being flown by a test pilot— only confirmed the importance of having properly experienced aviators; even a layman like Shiroki was painfully reminded of the absence of all those reliable, fully trained pilots they had lost during the past year. Then, as the year drew toward its close, the *Zuikaku* docked at Yokohama, and Shiroki received a furlough of three days and two nights.

He had not been home for a year. The *miso* soup at breakfast was hot and sweet, the onion melting on the tongue, and the white rice had that indefinable taste which it only seems to have when eaten at home. The *sukiyaki* for dinner that evening tasted good as well, although when he asked for some more meat his mother told him apologetically that he had just eaten the whole ration.

The evening before he was due to return to his ship he met Aiko Nire. He had telephoned her, assuring himself that it was principally to hear the latest news about his friend Shun'ichi; but the fact was he really wanted to meet Aiko, although it needn't specifically have been her. Before going back to the war he felt less the desire for the mechanical pleasures that a professional woman could give than the wish simply to look at an innocent young girl. The remembrance he had of Aiko was that she was pretty enough to fill that sentimental role, and he looked forward to the gossipy, light conversation he could have with her, and the superficial, sweet, transitory nature the meeting would have.

The brief encounter, however, did not turn out at all as he had expected, although it was perhaps not surprising that Aiko should have suggested they go out that evening, seeing that she was living apart from her mother, and her father paid no attention to anything she did.

They were in a corner of the Outer Gardens of the Meiji Shrine, near Shinanomachi Station, an area surrounded by lawns and trees. The winter mist had suddenly thickened, and the lights in the street across the way were blurred. The headlights of passing cars lit up the gray particles of fog momentarily, creating a fairy-tale atmosphere about them, then the almost painfully cold darkness would flow back.

Shiroki felt a drunken sensation overtake him, something like a reminiscence of various former intoxications. They were shut off from their surroundings by the darkness and the walls of mist; and the cold on his ears, the profound stillness and silence created a special, muted, toneless world, a rare world apart. It seemed so frail and vulnerable to one who was aware that only a few more hours remained to him.

They were sitting together on a stone bench and had stopped talking a little while before. As he breathed the dark in and the mist and the chill air, the girl beside him became suddenly insubstantial too, an imaginary being made out of thin air.

"Aren't you cold?" he asked her as he had already asked a number of times. Then, as he stood up saying he would see her home, he heard her speak in a tense, low voice, as if this cry from the heart were being forced out of her, words far from anything he had expected to hear.

"You mustn't die. I don't want you to die."

The words were so sudden he had the feeling they were being addressed to the wrong person, for she went on sitting there, staring ahead of her with a hard, rapt expression on her face like a young priestess in a trance. He was unable to reply at first, and before he could do so Aiko repeated the same words, her body tense as before, speaking in a low, broken voice, rather like a mechanical toy producing a recorded message. And then this schoolgirl, wrapped in a staid,

575

navy blue coat, seemed to lose herself in some flood tide of emotion, and swayed toward him, leaning her body against his.

In the cold darkness, in the faint light, Shiroki looked down on this frail, soft creature. The girl's face was raised and she was shuddering slightly as if she were drowning. Since her face was in the shadow cast by his own he could only see its vague outline. No doubt it was pale, no doubt its skin would be cold with the freezing night air, but all he could see was her dark eyes, which were staring blackly at him, full, it seemed, of pain. Her lips were open slightly, curved, swollen and helpless, apparently pleading for something.

Shiroki found himself setting his own mouth on her small one. At first her lips felt cold, although her cheeks were strangely flushed and hot, but soon her fitful spurts of warm breath transformed their kissing into something quite separate from the cold air which further shut them off from the outside world. Shiroki felt her lips open and he could sense the unconscious workings of her nervous, trembling tongue against his own as she swallowed and gulped for breath. The overcoats they were both wearing made this unforeseen embrace clumsy, but beneath the bulky material he could feel how hard her slim body had grown. It seemed to be charged with some extraordinary terror, so tense she might well faint at any moment.

He moved his head away suddenly to look seriously at her face, which had become mysteriously dear to him, but she nestled against his chest and murmured something in a voice very different from the way she had spoken just now. She spoke like a child, but in a sweet voice that sounded, despite the passion in it, or perhaps because of it, artificially assumed, as she still clung frankly yet innocently to him.

"I'm glad that's happened. I feel safe now, easy at last. I wonder why that is? I wonder why?"

The question seemed purely rhetorical. Then she laid her cheek on his shoulder, now completely at ease with herself. She stroked his naval greatcoat with one hand in a manner that suggested they had been lovers for some time, and started speaking at a great pace. Her words, however, were so innocently rambling and beside the point as to be almost infantile.

"I've been thinking for a long, long time that I had another elder brother somewhere and someday he was bound to come home. After all, Shun'ichi may be my real brother but he never ever took me anywhere nice, never anywhere I wanted to go, always going off by himself somewhere, like those airfields. . . So I just used to think about this other brother and the kind of present I would give him when he came back, and that's why I collected lots and lots of erasers. . .''

"Erasers," Shiroki repeated pointlessly.

"That's right; pencil erasers. There are all sorts of different kinds, with different shapes and colors. There's a shop called the Seiundo and we could get things there for nothing. Even so, if I saw a very unusual eraser in a different shop I'd buy it with my own money. Then I put dozens of them all nicely in a box to keep for when my brother came home so I could give them to him, because when I did that I knew he would be pleased and say thank you and stroke me gently. I went on buying them even after I'd started going to girls' school, and I've still got the box. I suppose you must think I'm silly. I'm a fool, aren't I?''

This was another question that seemed to need no answer, so in response he embraced her again, embraced her for speaking of things that were separated by so huge a gap from the life he had been leading for the past year. This time she was quite sure of herself and him so her lips greedily sought his, and for a while their two forms remained motionless in the freezing dark. This sudden drawing together, unthinkable in normal times, was probably imposed by the small amount of time at their disposal. It was, in a way, an accidental embrace, a mere contingency of war.

But Aiko's body, that almost skinny body of a girl due to graduate from high school next year, began to tremble again beneath her overcoat, shaking in little hard shivers, as if there was some terrible fear she could not endure. So she clung tightly to him, squeezing herself two or three times hard against the chest of the man she had decided was to be her husband, holding him desperately tight for no good reason, or for no reason of which she dared to think.

3

While Japan was calling up all its reserves of strength to fight the enemy, the unfortunate possessor of a name that indicated the enemy country, Yonekuni, who might well have wondered by what freak of fate his father had bestowed the name on him, was becoming more and more peculiar, as his mental health seemed to have taken a solid turn for the worse. His odd characteristics, the eccentric words and actions that had aroused considerable suspicion in Chiyoko when she had first met him, had been encouraged by the process of time until they were much more odd and eccentric than they had been then; but it was ten years since Chiyoko had married into the Nire family, so she took very little notice of these things now and merely accepted her brother-in-law as someone who was weird. In fact, since she had a great many grievances pent up inside her concerning the goings-on of Hisa and Ryuko, who still held the real power in the household, she tended to use Yonekuni as an outlet for feelings she could not express to anyone else, and at times derived a kind of perfectly respectable consolation from doing this. Yonekuni also found he could tell his sister-in-law things, now that she had grown to confide in him. His relationship with her was different from the complex one he had with Kumagoro Sakuma, who was not solely a loyal retainer but also at times a crony, and even occasionally a superior officer.

"You know, Chiyoko," he said one day when the two of them remained in the living room after the others had left. He fiddled meaningfully with his teacup to emphasize that he was about to make some major confession, assuming a serious expression which Chiyoko felt simply did not suit him, and then spoke in the low tones of soliloquy: "It's a funny thing. Now that the New Year is over . . . we don't get any more visitors. True, the visitors who came here were all people one had no real wish to see. But now they've stopped coming there's an empty feeling, this sense of vacancy. Don't you feel it? And it's in moments when he has that feeling that a man looks closely at himself, looks at something like his arm, for example, looks very closely and starts to wonder what it really is. Usually there's nothing mysterious about an arm. We forget about it almost as if it wasn't there. Still, you take a good look at it, and what do you see? Something covered with loose skin and with hair growing out of it. It starts to look like something that's got nothing to do with yourself at all, something quite separate. Then you start to wonder just how many hairs there actually are. You feel you've really got to know."

"Don't be so stupid," said Chiyoko. Although she was quite used to the way he talked, its silliness sometimes made her cross. "How many hairs are there, for goodness' sake? Just three more than a monkey has, if you must know."

"No, that's not what I'm saying," said Yonekuni, slightly taken aback and speaking a little hesitantly, although he still looked intently at his arm with gloomy eyes as if he were carrying out an experiment on it. His attitude was not merely out of the ordinary, but indicated an absurd self-assurance which went beyond being merely ludicrous. "It's not the actual number of hairs that matters, but the fact that you get this desire to know that number. I'm talking about the form of consciousness involved. Just looking at it like this gives you a strange sense of the mysterious. Not just the hairs, of course, but all the other holes in the skin, like the sudoriferous and the sebaceous glands, innumerable as they are. Then if you just stroke it gently like this the veins gradually start to stand out. Look; look at that. Look; just feel it."

"No, I certainly won't. It's not very nice, after all. It's unpleasant."

"You're quite right. It isn't very nice. It's unpleasant. It's very unpleasant. You're the only one in this household who seems to understand that, because nobody else does. My own opinion is that it's because this is a medical family. People are too accustomed to the human body. They are accustomed to it as a mere object, and this produces a sort of insensitivity, a frigidity."

"Would you like some more tea, Yonekuni?"

"No, no thank you. No tea. Not a time for tea. You said it was unpleasant, did you not? Not very nice, you said, did you not? A person's own arm becomes not very nice? Very well, but just be a little more patient, keep looking at it, and this strange, rather unpleasant object, your arm, suddenly becomes an object of affection, something

579

dear to you, because of the consciousness that it is indeed your arm. That's the truly mysterious thing, but you have to gaze quite fixedly at your arm for a long time to experience this. And after that comes another experience, another feeling, a different emotion; and what do you think that is? What on earth do you think that is?''

"Well, what on earth would that be, I wonder?" Chiyoko replied with some degree of cold sarcasm, but it was completely lost on Yonekuni, who was not prepared to be laughed at in this matter and was obviously so totally absorbed as to be incapable of misgivings of that kind.

"Emptiness," he pronounced with an impressive air, straightening his back firmly as he did so. "Nothingness. A terrible nothingness. The void. The New Year's just over, the food all eaten up, decorations just taken down, the lousy visitors who only came because they wanted a free drink have stopped coming, and then everywhere about you in all directions is only this wide vacancy; this emptiness is all that remains. You feel something just like the situation we are in now."

"So we've got right back to where we started, our punch line being just how we began." Chiyoko found the uniquely serious expression of her brother-in-law amusing, and poured the tea he showed no inclination to drink into her own cup. "Still, I must say I don't feel any kind of nothingness because we no longer have any visitors. I just feel relieved, that's all. Why do you feel everything is empty just because the New Year is over?"

"You mean that you don't?" said Yonekuni, as if genuinely astounded by this confession. "I'm not really talking about visitors, though. It's New Year itself that I'm concerned with. The real problem is the way the New Year is celebrated in this household. In a normal home the whole family gets together on the morning of New Year's Day and they say 'Happy New Year' to each other and drink the New Year *sake* and eat the New Year food and all that. What you could call a happy family circle exists, doesn't it? But in our house what happens? Everyone just does what they personally feel like doing. No care or concern for anyone else. Look at what it was like in Aoyama in the old days. The children weren't even allowed to go 'within' at all. We children had to go off to the cookhouse and celebrate New Year with the interns and servants. When this house was built here I was secretly hoping that at last we'd have a proper little home, snug and warm and comfortable. But all that happened was the family went even more to pieces. For a start, the whole family never gets together even for a meal. Well, Mother's very old, of course, and there's nothing wrong, I suppose, in her wanting to be in her room and have people come to her. But what about the rest of us just all doing as we please? Bit too egotistical, I'd say. I mean, I've been watching what goes on here on New Year's Day. Mistress Ryu,'' (Yonekuni preserved the traditional form of address for Tetsukichi's estranged bride) ''turns up smartly enough, picks up a *sake* cup, the biggest one at the bottom of the pile, fills it with New Year *sake*, sips a little, and then tells me she doesn't like the taste of it at all and pushes off straight away.''

''Well, that's because she always tends to be in a hurry, I suppose,'' Chiyoko explained in an indifferent but heavily sarcastic tone of voice.

''The next to turn up is Oshu,'' Yonekuni went on, determined not to be led astray from the main point. ''And what does your respected husband do? He seems to notice that it's New Year's Day today, has a look at the paper, pours himself some *sake*, drinks it back by himself, and then goes off somewhere, too. Nobody, but nobody, bothers to say 'Happy New Year' to me. They don't seem, any of them, to have the least inclination to wait for anyone else and celebrate New Year properly with all the others.''

''Because they're all busy. There're the formal celebrations in the hospital they have to get ready for.''

''That's it. Exactly. We've all got to take part in that. Still, it's a mere formality. A mere shell. You know, I don't know if that Deputy's getting senile or not, but don't you think he's becoming a bit fanatical about all that? Do you know how many times he said it was the fifty-fifth anniversary of the founding of the Nire Hospital of Mental Pathology? Five times, I tell you. Gives you the impression he thinks he himself is the Director and Founder of the place. And speaking in that awful way through his nose as well. . .''

''Still, he really has done a great deal for the hospital. Oshu always says so.''

''Of course he has. Of course. I wasn't talking about that. Now, what was I talking about? Ah, yes. I'm saying that the Deputy is only interested in ceremonials, formalities relating to the hospital, and that's typical of this whole place. The home we have is a mere appendage of the hospital. This hospital isn't just a hospital but something that has an influence on all of us as people.''

581

"What do you mean by that?" said Chiyoko as though determined to allow no importance to what he had said. "Are you implying that we're all being infected by mental diseases?"

"Not so much infected," said Yonekuni, looking now as if he were listening attentively to his own words. "Still, I do believe that to a certain extent we are rendered insensitive to most things. For example, among mental patients there are those who are affected by all sorts of delusions. I'm no doctor, of course, but I've been brought up in a mental hospital milieu, you see. There are people who believe that the world is just about to be destroyed. The sky has turned a funny color; the shape of the sun has changed. Strange new miasmas are flowing over the earth. That's how these people actually see it, anyway. Naturally, the doctors themselves are quite unaffected by all this, totally indifferent. If they were to get really involved in these delusions then they'd soon break down themselves. That would be preposterous, of course. Couldn't expect that. So they can laugh at unbelievable terrors, they can grin at the appalling suggestion that the world is about to be destroyed because they've been trained to do so, trained in insensitivity and obtuseness, so they become obtuse and insensitive. Don't you see the egotism in the way we behave on New Year's Day, this indifference as to whether the *sake* is drunk or not, as another expression of some overall tendency?"

"Really, Yonekuni, I've never heard such a farfetched argument," said Chiyoko, laughing out loud in unrestrained amusement. "I admit that in my parents' house the whole family used to get together on New Year's Day, but that was only a custom. I can't see that it has any connection with the imminent destruction of the world. I'll also admit that this is a strange household, but all that indicates is there are a few odd people here, individualists we should call them perhaps. After all, you yourself are a little unusual as a person, don't you think? You won't get married when you have the chance, and though you talk about the house and everyone drinking together, I don't think there's anyone else here who seems so completely unconcerned about the house itself as you do."

"That's only natural. I've always been an outsider, an onlooker. And the reason is very simple. I was born into the House of Nire and yet I never became a doctor."

"Oh, not that again. What's so wonderful about being a doctor? Who ever said that was the best thing to be? I come from a family of tradesmen, and, to be quite honest, I never seem able to feel any affection for doctors and hospitals."

"I know what you're trying to tell me, but it's no good," said Yonekuni, shifting and sitting up straight with a critical expression on his face. "You've been living here for ten years now and, unbeknown to you, all that time you've been gradually infected by what goes on here. But listen to this, then. I've been living in the Nire Hospital much, much longer than you, and yet I've remained quite immune to the poison. Now, why do you think that is?"

Yonekuni allowed a slight pause to let the question sink in, but he answered it himself: "It's because I am ill, and it's a terminal illness, but nobody knows about it. Do you follow me? I shall tell no one until I receive the final, definitive statement on the matter, which will be my death warrant. I've been suffering with this for a number of years now, thinking about nothing but this. Sometimes I've let slip certain hints about my condition, but no one has ever taken me seriously. Oshu simply treats me like a fool, telling me there's nothing wrong with my lungs, nothing wrong at all, old fellow. What does he take me for? It's no joke, believe you me. I'm not making any great fuss about having consumption, although we have a history of it in the family. I can tell you this because it's your family now, but Mother had it some time back. Then my sister, who was some years older than me, died of it. Then there's Satoru who's in hospital with it now. Just think how healthy and lively he used to be; a bit too lively in fact. I mean, it's a clear case of physical heredity. It's clearly being passed on. Frankly I don't think much of Satoru's prospects. Either he'll have a sudden turn for the worse like Mistress Sei, or he'll spend his whole life as an invalid. You just can't say. And finally there's me. I mean, I shouldn't be alive now, today. Should have gone ages ago. I'm not joking. It could have put an end to my respiration and metabolism way back for all I know. But I fought against my consumption; I conquered it. And how do you think I managed that? Because I understand my own physical constitution, and I treat it with the greatest of care, almost killing myself in the effort to stay alive. So I conquered, very painfully, one illness that ought to have buried me, and then what happens? Here I am confronted with a terminal illness, one for which there is absolutely no cure. Now, how do you think I feel about that? Can you possibly imagine my state of mind?"

"I don't particularly want to imagine your state of mind," Chiyoko replied with brisk indifference, for she was determined not to be astonished by anything Yonekuni might say. "Still, I'd like to know why you only think about terminal illnesses and inevitable death and your metabolism stopping and things like that. You don't look all that ill to me. Quite honestly, I've no doubt you'll live to a ripe old age. You'll go on moaning and complaining and outlive us all."

"Ripe old age?" Yonekuni retorted, leaning back slightly in despair or annoyance, his deep, glaring eyes blinking two or three times with the impact of the considerable humiliation he had just received. "Outlive you all?" he repeated, as if struck rigid with amazement. "Well, that takes it. That really does. That is remarkable. I've heard some weird things in my time, but that. . . I don't look all that ill? Now, I would just like to know on what grounds, on what basis, you're able to make irresponsible statements of that kind. But no, don't answer me. There's no need. I'm perfectly aware why. It is simply living proof that you too have been infected by the natural Nire obtuseness and insensitivity. Let me tell you this, though. All you healthy people may be proud of your health, that rude, crude health of which you think so highly; but I'd like to know why you think you have the right to sneer at people who are genuinely ill, people who are incurable and know it. That's what I want to know. It's just like this New Year we were talking about a moment ago. All the New Year means to you is that you've got one year older. But it's a bit different for me. It means I've lost another year; one more year has been taken off the limited amount remaining. For me the New Year is simply a symbolic statement of the approach of annihilation and destruction."

Chiyoko really enjoyed the annihilation and destruction part, and she was well aware that the existence of this weird brother-in-law provided her with a cheerful form of relaxation for which she felt something close to gratitude, although she showed nothing of this in her face when she replied:

"I'm not particularly proud of my health. Look how thin I've got. I'm sure my constitution's much weaker than yours."

"Don't be absurd," said Yonekuni, waving a hand about energetically. "That's pure pretense; absolute deception. If you were afflicted with an illness like mine you wouldn't be able to talk about it calmly like that, let me assure you."

"But, Yonekuni, you talk about your terminal illness just as calmly as that. I suppose I oughtn't to say this, but you sometimes sound as if you're rather proud of being ill and having only a few years to live."

"Proud? How can you say a thing like that? Is a man who's facing death likely to be proud? People who can sit like that looking all confident and saying that sort of thing are just living proof that they have no awareness of death at all. It's all got nothing to do with them. My own opinion is that they're being a bit too presumptuous, too smug in their opinions, and that they're irresponsible and ill-mannered into the bargain."

"Very well, then. I shall ask you quite plainly to tell me what this illness is from which you're suffering. You're always very obscure on that point, aren't you? If you're a man, come on out with it and get it off your chest."

Yonekuni knit his brows together as he stared unwaveringly at his questioner, then hurriedly looked away as if he had seen something unpleasantly distressing there. Now he looked at his fingernails. After a while he turned his hand over and pressed the skin at the base of his thumb with the fingertips of his other hand. He then let out a deep sigh, a sigh that bore a certain resemblance to the discharge of breath a criminal lets out when he is about to begin to confess his misdeeds.

"You mean you really don't know?" he finally murmured. The tremendous sincerity and gravity of his expression had the unavoidable effect of making him look more ludicrous than usual.

"Of course I don't know. I'm hardly likely to know, am I?"

"Really," said Yonekuni, sighing once more; and now some weird rage actually appeared on his face. "Oshu has never taken me seriously. Not that I mind. So I'll tell you instead, although there's not the slightest chance that you'll know what I'm talking about. Anyway, it's called Progressive Spinal Muscular Atrophy."

"Progressive what atrophy?" asked Chiyoko, impressed in spite of herself.

"Progressive Spinal Muscular Atrophy," Yonekuni repeated with peculiar dignity, like a university professor pronouncing an authoritative judgment. It was one of those rare, if transitory, occasions on which he held himself up straight and looked almost impressive. "The Latin name is *Atrophia Musculorum Progressivia Spinalis*."

"It doesn't matter about the Latin name. What I should like to know is just what kind of illness it is."

"There are various kinds," said Yonekuni, starting his explanation with a grave passion that bordered on genuine joy. "There's the kind that principally involves mutations occurring in the dendrites of the neurons of the spinal cord and in the synapses. . ."

"I'm not going to understand a word of that. Can't you tell me simply and concisely what it is?"

"Well, it means the spinal cord is no good and so the muscles become atrophied, sort of shrink. Not infrequently it shows itself just below the shoulder blade. The muscles in that area tend to fall right in, producing a cavity effect there, and you go on getting thinner and thinner."

"But you're not thin at all, are you?"

"That takes place right at the final phase," said Yonekuni with a dismissive wave of the hand. "It starts to show around the shoulder blades mostly in middle age, and then progresses very slowly from then on. Well, all I can say is simply this: just wait and see."

Yonekuni stood up with inappropriate suddenness, pushed open the sliding door with a rough clatter, and left the room. Chiyoko had already become bored by her brother-in-law's complaints, but there might possibly be a grain of truth in what he said, so she couldn't flatly refuse to listen to his various anxieties and obsessions now that he had started to talk to her about them. So she was prepared for his eventual return with a fat, hardcover book which was obviously some specialist volume.

"Here we are. Take a look at this. It's all written down here. Progressive Spinal Muscular Atrophy. Look at the passage about the progress of the illness and its prognosis. . . 'Progresses slowly but can make sudden advances at times and local paralysis can occur, or the diaphragm or other respiratory organs can be contaminated and breathing become impossible. . .' Now read this bit, just here."

Although Chiyoko had been living in the house for years now she still found it ill-mannered and insensitive of Yonekuni to come right around to her side of the table and almost force himself against her as he pointed out the passage in the book.

"It says the prognosis is absolutely negative. So what about treatment? Well, look right here. . . 'Treatment: None. Electrotherapy is purely a solace for the patient. . .' How about that, then? The implications of that? Can you grasp what that really means? . . . Of course this writer is a very remarkable man, an authority on neuropathology, and that kind of writing is just what one expects from a genuine authority. There's no deception here, no attempt to cheer people up or gloss over the truth. It's this calm, almost cruelly unemotional approach that's so scientific. 'Treatment: None.' The purity of expression there is priceless. It gets right to the heart of what Progressive Spinal Muscular Atrophy essentially is.''

Yonekuni had said most of this in what seemed a single breath, and now he suddenly broke off, staring out of the corners of his eyes at some object to one side of him. There was a deep furrow between his eyebrows, and when he frowned, as he did now, all sorts of wretched-looking wrinkles extended to the top of his nose, which was slightly hooked.

"Well, it certainly sounds like . . . a very grave illness," Chiyoko said rather hesitantly, for she was not sure what she ought to say in the circumstances. Despite some minor interest in what he had said she showed not the slightest inclination to be worried about him. She did not really believe one word of the story from beginning to end. "Still, I suppose you are quite sure you really have that illness? There are plenty of doctors in this hospital who could tell you.''

"The disease is extremely difficult to diagnose. After all, no one notices it until their muscles start to retract, and then they go to the doctor. Even the doctors don't really know until it reaches that stage. In my case, whether luckily or unluckily I can't say, I was able to appreciate my condition some years ago. I began to suspect a tendency on the part of the muscles beneath my shoulder blades to retract in that way. It was only very slight, so slight it wasn't certain whether it was tending to happen or not, but I noticed it. That only shows just how carefully I was scrutinizing the workings of my own body. After that I started reading up on the subject and gained a good acquaintance with various kinds of illnesses. Still, there's not much point in telling you my feelings at the time. It's absolutely impossible for a healthy person to understand something like that.''

"But do you mean to say, Yonekuni, that you just left things like that? Didn't you go to see a doctor?''

"Of course I did. I went to see a specialist, probably the most distinguished physician in the field, a professor at Tokyo University; but all he could do was shake his head. Looked very serious, very grave, just like this. And shook his head. It is an extremely difficult illness to diagnose, and it seems that mine is very much in the first stages."

"Still, what did he say to you?"

"He said he just couldn't tell. The disease only develops very, very slowly. There's not one specialist who could make any confident diagnosis of it in the early stage. I went to Keio for a second opinion, but the conclusion was the same. The suspicion exists but no definite statement can be made. Well, that's bound to be the case. Can't say I blame them. In fact I think I know exactly how these specialists must feel. After all, it's a terminal illness, with no known cure for it, no way to treat it. They can hardly tell a patient straight out he's. . ."

"But just a moment, Yonekuni. Surely it's conceivable, it's possible, that you haven't got this spinal whatever it is at all? I'd have thought that fairly likely. . ."

"Believe me, Chiyoko, when it's a question of life and death like this, I'm not going to mess about now, am I? I'm bound to be deadly serious, and I can tell you I've been scrutinizing myself seriously for years. I observed those muscles beneath my shoulder blades; I observed them with incredible application, with the sheer power of my will, with painful endurance and suffering. And the conclusion I had to come to was that those muscles were more retracted than they had been when I first noticed them. I couldn't avoid noticing that."

"In that case why don't you talk this over with Tetsukichi, or with Dr. Nirasawa or Dr. Kanazawa?"

"And suppose I did, what would that lead to? It's an illness for which there is simply no treatment, so all they would try to do is say nice things to cheer me up, I know that. What else could they do? They'd just conspire together in order to cheer me up. However, I want to know exactly what I'm dying of. That's why I went to another hospital and not here. Can you understand that kind of feeling? Hardly, I suppose. Healthy people don't appreciate that sort of thing. Still, I suppose I should let you know that I have told Oshu all this. And, again, if I'm to tell the truth, the naked truth, the whole truth, then I've got to admit that all he did was laugh at me. 'Sneer' might be more like the word. Just not prepared to take it seriously at all. I never realized that my own brother was so callous. Still, what does it matter? I'm perfectly well aware what kind of position I'm in as far as the Nire Hospital is concerned."

"Now, Yonekuni, you shouldn't start talking like that. But there's one thing I should like to know, although of course I can't understand questions of this kind, and that is, since the illness does progress, or get worse I suppose, there must come a point when it can be diagnosed. I don't mean specifically in your case, but just in general.''

"Round about forty, I should think. At that age you can see quite easily that the muscles are becoming atrophied. . . Still, it doesn't do any good diagnosing it because there's simply no way of treating it at all.''

"Yes, but Yonekuni, you're thirty-four now, so in your case the illness has been discovered some years before it would be in a normal person. And any illness can develop in a way that confounds the experts, so when you reach forty it could be that the muscles on your shoulders might even. . .''

"All right, all right," said Yonekuni in a loud, clipped voice, squinting nervously toward one side of the room again. "I know what's going on. You're just laughing at me, making fun of me. You've decided inside that I haven't got Progressive Spinal Muscular Atrophy. No one easier to laugh at than me. But just think of it this way. If after a few years I start to show all the really vile, really horrible symptoms of this disease, how are you going to feel, and how is Oshu going to respond then? Well, you'll find out sometime. Not that I'm intending to blame anybody. My illness is a very rare one, I admit. Only one in ten thousand, one in a hundred thousand maybe, suffers from it. I'm not asking people to sympathize with me, or even understand me. Even so, the way I just get treated openly as a joke, a laughingstock; well, it seems to me a bit beyond what we have the right to expect of other human beings. . . I mean, it's the sort of thing that makes a person feel he really wants to put a great distance between himself and the world at large. Even if I don't go that far, there's still this constant incongruity I feel, the sensation that I'm somehow shut off from the world about me, just me on my own. You'll never know how dull and heavy the pain is, and yet how sharp it is as well. Still, when I get to thinking properly about it, humanity is something that's essentially caught up in this kind of suffering. Call it original sin or whatever, it's just there. That's how I see it, and perhaps the human race needs people who are aware of it, scapegoats perhaps. Take this Nire family, for example, where everyone's so busy and selfishly thinking about themselves and so insensitive to others, and then there's someone like me occasionally, blessed or cursed with a finer sensibility, a representative of the unfortunates of the world, and my role is to feel all this, to be aware of it. Everyone spends their days thinking about nothing . . . empty-headed . . . the unexamined life—I apologize if I've said the wrong thing. There's Tetsukichi who struggled away and produced that great, fat book, but if he'd been a man of feeling like me I don't imagine he could ever have done it. Then look at Oshu, inviting guests and cooking fine meals for them. And that's how it should be, I admit. Nothing wrong with that. Or having a leisurely time hunting, or just like the other day when he collected all those rabbit skins from the Setagaya Hunters Association and donated them to the army and won a citation for it. And a very good thing too and why shouldn't he indeed? I mean, I really think so. I'm not trying to be sarcastic or anything. Still, my work is different. I have a different function. Mine is to feel, to suffer, to stand and wait. This is the role that fate has bestowed on me, and, indeed, it matters not how a man may live, for death is waiting for us all, and we shall all die equally, although in my case I am nearer to death than the rest of you and so limitations have been imposed upon my way of life. It is for that reason I have tried to grasp the nature of my fate, to comprehend it, and it is that accomplishment alone in which I feel a sense of pride, a calm feeling of work well done. If I had not become aware of my illness but only suddenly realized what it was when I reached the final stage, what a state I would be in then! But now I shall at least be able to avoid that kind of panic when the time comes. But which is best? Is it good fortune to die in ignorance, or better to be aware of all? Whichever it is, I know what it must be for me, namely to spend the remaining time left to me, short as it may be, in the cold, objective study of myself and others. What will happen to any being is something we have to leave to that moment when it happens, for no one can know beforehand.''

Yonekuni had poured out this lengthy peroration with a terrible sincerity of expression and a constant flickering of his eyelids. While he was talking, his emotions seemed to undergo a number of minor variations at different levels; at first rather violent, then speaking in a tiresome, nagging tone which finally became a gentle melancholy, indicating something close to a weariness of the world. But he maintained his nervous, bewildered gaze on one wall, and Chiyoko began to feel worried, sensing something ominously unpleasant in the whole business. Yet suddenly he behaved as if transformed into a different person, speaking to her in tones of impeccable politeness and restrained gloom, apologizing for having troubled her peace of mind with this confused talk of his and wishing her good-night. He then stood up abruptly and moved with surprising speed (to Chiyoko's eyes with an almost spectral fleetness) across the room and left, closing the door behind him with one backward extended hand, and vanishing smoothly and noiselessly from her sight. . . And yet, that evening, thoughts of the things Yonekuni had said to her, the way he had spoken and the very out-of-the-ordinary impression he had given, aroused a sense of solicitude in her and doubts as to whether she might not have misjudged him.

So one day she confessed her doubts to her husband and suggested that perhaps Yonekuni might really be suffering from some serious illness. She spoke in a casual manner to see if he would indulge in those callous, irresponsible remarks to which her brother-in-law had referred.

Oshu replied frankly to her queries, not mincing his words, but with no show of annoyance:

"Don't be so foolish. Surely you're not taking what he says seriously?"

Chiyoko felt relieved at this, and once she had managed to get the subject of Yonekuni onto its former comic-relief level and extracted a wry smile from her husband, he obliged by giving an account of his troublesome brother's symptoms:

"Naturally when I heard about it from him I didn't let the matter rest there. But he never once suggested that I take a look at him. Well, I'm no great shakes as a doctor so I can't complain, yet I did what I could: I got in touch with the doctors who had examined him at some time or other. Their replies were identical and just what I'd expected. He didn't have a trace of that kind of illness. He's just running about frightened by his own shadow. I suppose that in itself could be considered a kind of illness, but it's the only kind he's got."

"Well, in that case I shan't worry about it any more. Just listening to him—and heaven knows he talked away enthusiastically enough, spluttering all over the place and over me—was enough to make me quite irritable and tired. Satoru being in hospital like this has worn me out enough already. I only wish I knew where Momoko was and what she's doing—oh, I *am* sorry, I forgot you don't like to hear her name mentioned. But to get back to Yonekuni, he has this expression like a schizophrenic philosopher and talks as if he were the only sane person in the hospital."

"He has a great attachment to illness; any illness," said Oshu, gently stroking his jaw, which had grown even plumper and more flabbily double-chinned recently. "To be quite honest he's frightened of having to join the army, so he wants some certificate that will prove he's seriously ill, something from a university hospital with real authority. Naturally I can't say if he's fully aware himself of this motive, which may or may not be unconscious; but at least in his subconscious that's what he's after."

"Well, now that you say that," put in Chiyoko, nodding with an agreement that was not innocent of spiteful motives, "he's always had this pathological fear of war. And then he's quite excessively bothered about his name. For example, you remember my sister came a little while ago? Well, I just so happened to refer to Yonekuni as Beikoku in front of her. It was only meant as a joke, of course, but he went quite pale and said that the characters with which he wrote his name did not refer to America, but were *yone* and *kuni*, 'rice country,' and this meant the land of reed plains and the auspicious ears of rice of fifteen hundred autumns and was a very patriotic name indeed. He looked so serious as he said that to her. He *is* strange; you're just wondering if he's just made a very odd sort of joke, and then you realize there are times when he can't understand the most obvious kind of joke in the world. Of course, with a war going on, it's quite natural he should feel pretty small and awkward with a name like that. Even so, there's something quite sick about him; all those twisted, bitter ideas he has about things."

"To be brutally honest with you," Oshu mumbled rather painfully, "if Yonekuni goes on like this much longer he'll be a suitable candidate for our kind of hospital. The best cure for him would be to join the army. That's my opinion, anyway."

"Well, I don't think you ought to say that. Poor Yonekuni. He may be strange but I don't think he's a bad person. It's just that he will insist on talking about his incurable illness, and right from the word go one is half making fun of him and eventually one starts to feel very peculiar. I feel that if he really was to die young for some reason—not that I believe any of that stuff about spinal trouble—I should wake up feeling bad every morning, and have this constant sense that it had somehow been my fault."

"Don't worry about that," Oshu butted in, now quite bored by the whole business. "He'll live to a ripe old age. That's just the way things go. I'm quite sure he'll outlive the lot of us."

"That's exactly what I told him," Chiyoko said, and then got up to go and see to her aged mother-in-law.

While Yonekuni Nire was passing his days worrying over his abstruse illness, a care quite unrelated to the war situation which each day was becoming increasingly critical, Tatsunori Shiroki crossed the equator and arrived at the strategic strongpoint of Rabaul on the island of New Britain, toward the end of January 1943, and there he remained. The *Zuikaku*'s aircraft were to be used in a supporting role at the base in Rabaul, and Shiroki was a member of the advance party sent on ahead from Truk by destroyer.

For some time the situation in Guadalcanal had been critical, and now it was reaching breaking point. The Japanese forces had completely lost control of the air and supplies could not be got through, so that the abbreviated way people had of referring to the island as "Ga"-island (the unpronounceable "Guadalcanal" being reduced to the simple "Ga") began to take on the sense of "Starvation Island" (*"ga"* written with the ideogram "starvation") for those in the base at Rabaul. The terrifying, losing struggle the garrison there was putting up began to assume almost legendary proportions, and they talked about little else. People back home could have no idea how energetic and intense the American counteroffensive had been; but those in Rabaul, only a few islands away, certainly could, and were also aware that total disaster was more than a possibility for the isolated garrison.

Piled high near the jetty of Rabaul harbor were great stores of gasoline drums and various goods and materials packed into great, thick, rubber containers. The containers were filled mostly with rice, but also held dried bonito, candles and matches, and the drums were lined with kapok and contained loose rounds of ammunition. These were all to be taken to Guadalcanal on one of the secret night sorties that were the only way of getting supplies to the troops there now. Fast destroyers were used, which would unload the drums and rubber containers into the sea near the beach, and then withdraw. The supplies were supposed to be picked up by the soldiers on Guadalcanal from small dinghies, but it was difficult to work out just what percentage of them got through; and lately even this method of transportation had become too risky, so the soldiers were having to rely on the meager provisions that could be sent by submarine.

Despite the fact that B-17s, the Flying Fortresses, were in regular use now, Rabaul had undergone few really big bombing raids. The troops in the front line were living through hell, but here the officers enjoyed a style of life suitable to a large rearguard base, drinking beer in huts where the lampshades were made tastefully out of palm leaves, while for the lower ranks there were even women, mostly brought in from Korea and Okinawa. They formed long queues outside a wretched, bleak building, the "rest and recreation center" where these women were available, like people waiting to use a public toilet.

But the main thing was the natural surroundings, scenery that was, to Japanese eyes unused to these sharp, clear shapes and colors, very beautiful under the rich, mellow, tropical light. The impression was nothing like as harsh as Shiroki had expected, for everything appeared simply and abundantly bright, so that all was in harmony with the light and even had a soothing quietness about it. Sea, sky and vegetation were all in deep primary colors, but the various brilliant shades seemed to cancel one another out, and the whole panorama did not seem gaudy or vulgar at all. In fact the view from the east airfield toward a conical volcano, which looked like an overturned pot and was called Blossoming Mountain, was, despite the weird, whitish brown earth, oddly reminiscent of Japan, perhaps because of the smooth lines of the skirts of the volcano. But all around were coconut groves, which seemed quite unreal, and the tall trees, the brilliant light turning the luxuriant green foliage almost white, and the burning heat which seemed to slice into one's skin, all confirmed the fact that this was a tropical island far away from home. Places that were shaded from the rays of the sun looked almost black, and it was pleasant to sit there in the coolness brought by the breeze from off the sea.

Shiroki had little time to spend in leisurely appreciation of the scenery. As soon as he landed he went straight to the garrison hospital, where the military director put the wind up him by saying that practically everyone there had dengue fever. There were not enough beds to go around, and coconut leaves had been spread over the concrete floor. After a quick glance at the squalid sight of patients with tropical ulcers and various feverish ailments lying there, he hurried off again, for there were various problems about accommodation for the ground crews and medics from the *Zuikaku* that had be to straightened out. There was also no surgery of any kind, so he went to the nearby HQ of the Yanagihara Regiment and after some negotiations with the unit commander it was arranged that they should make joint use of the medical hut there. Tents were put up for some of the men, and the remainder were found places in huts borrowed from the Kobayashi Regiment, which were disinfected and ready to use that evening, while the medics were to sleep in a ward of the Yanagihara Hospital.

Shiroki was exhausted by the time he got back to the officers' quarters well after dark. The only thing that had given him any consolation during this wearisome day was the resourcefulness of the sergeant he had sent off to the inpatient ward, who had managed to appropriate some quinine, salicylic soda, thermometers, cover glasses and other things. It was more than a year since Shiroki had first boarded his ship, so he had learned how to live within the military system.

Occasional heavy showers beat down on the leaves of the banana trees outside, but they soon passed over. He discussed with one or two other officers whether the rainy season had arrived, and then crawled under his mosquito net, stretching out on the unfamiliar, primitive bed. But just as he was dropping off to sleep the air-raid warning sounded, and he was obliged to get up again. Since he didn't know where the air-raid shelter was, he jumped out of the hut and tried crawling under the raised floor, but was greeted by such a swarm of mosquitoes he was obliged to get out fast; the fact that he was more concerned about mosquitoes than enemy planes indicated he did not yet take air raids on land all that seriously. The B-17s flew at high altitude where they were picked out by the beams of the searchlights, and it was frustrating to watch the flak of the anti-aircraft guns bursting some distance away from them. The guns made a tremendously impressive sound, all the artillery in Rabaul being apparently concentrated on the three enemy planes, but with no effect whatsoever. The planes dropped their flares in an unhurried way, then their bombs, then flew off. The bombs seemed to have caused little damage, so the whole thing had been merely a display of bravado, calculated to irritate and annoy.

Two days later the *Zuikaku*'s aircraft arrived, and as the flights of bombers, assault planes and fighters appeared, dominating the sky and landing in a great roar of engines and clouds of dust, Shiroki found he still felt a tightening of the heart, a surge of expectation for no reason he could explain to himself. One of the base mechanics was standing next to him at the time and said excitedly:

"Now that we have the carrier planes we'll be properly up to strength again. Those carrier pilots know how to fly. You can tell that just by the way they landed. They know how to handle their planes."

Even Shiroki's unprofessional eye could see that these pilots were nothing like as good as those lost in the Battle of the Coral Sea, yet they were apparently much better than the ones here at the base. Still, he felt pleasure at having the unit he was attached to praised, and made a friendly reply that elicited an unrestrained response:

"We'll be able to make a real attack this time, now we've got all these carrier planes in support. We can't go on being pushed back all the time, can we? Stands to reason."

But this mechanic was unaware of the truth of the situation, as naturally was Shiroki: the higher powers had deemed that Guadalcanal could not be held, and the crack carrier planes had been sent in to help in what would be a very difficult evacuation of the island.

Since the other doctor on the *Zuikaku* was ill in bed, Shiroki's days in Rabaul were occupied entirely with constant work, a burden made heavier by lack of sleep caused by the regular bombing raids. He was also waiting for his expected transfer order to come through. If he was taken off ship duty and given a post back in Japan he was seriously thinking of getting married to Aiko Nire. The chance happening that night, enclosed in the fog and the darkness, meant for him the exchange of a definite promise between them. When he recalled it now, it was as if it had happened in a dream long ago, though only a month had elapsed; the whole experience had taken on such a vague and unreal quality perhaps it had never happened at all. Certainly he had doubts about the wisdom of what he had done, for he was quite aware of how rash he had been, but when he remembered Aiko's childish lips pressed on his own he felt promptings that quite contradicted any reservations he might have had. What had taken place had become a support for him, something to cling to amid the deadly inertia of war where he felt he might lose all hold on himself, as he knew he had quite definitely been doing. It had enabled him to think seriously about his own life again, as if one rash act had given him back a sense of living that he had lost. The conclusion he had come to was that, if he were spared, if there seemed a possibility of his living for a reasonably long time, he seriously wanted to make Aiko his wife. His thoughts on the subject had the simpleminded purity of the plans of a small boy, for he had no idea how he was going to put this vague resolution into effect, and the quite uncomplex nature of this resolve somehow reflected the uninvolved, almost mindless daily routine he followed here in Rabaul.

Around 0300 hours another air raid. Enemy planes caught in searchlights but our ack-ack guns pose no kind of threat. Watched it all from under floor with mosquitoes stinging all the time making me all the more angry, while the guns banged away futilely just making one awful racket.

This morning assault planes set off to attack Buin on Bougain-ville Island, but had to return because of clouds. Lieutenant Miyajima has temperature of 104. Sometimes he sweats heavily and seems to feel better, but temperature goes up again, and this evening with temperature of 102 complains of pains in waist, joints, head and eyes, which means it looks like dengue fever, so will do a blood test tomorrow.

Tonight drank beer with Lieutenant Imazu and during conversa-tion found out that Major Kobayashi who'd been in same surgery department as me in Tokyo was here with the Ota Regi-ment but due to leave for Munda Point in New Guinea tomor-row. Dashed off to see him and luckily he was in their officers' mess so I was able to apologize for not having got in touch before and we talked for about half an hour. He looked very different with a shaven head and grown very thin after a bout of dengue fever, but sounded cheerful enough. We talked about how things were at university now and medical situation at home. Since he was leaving early tomorrow we had to say good-bye soon. Hope he'll be all right.

Large enemy fleet (4 battleships, 4 cruisers, some destroyers) reported. 75 planes sent out in pursuit. Radio report says due to arrive combat area around dusk, but no detailed statement since then.

Air raid at 0300 hours. Flying much lower than usual this time. Planes looked very beautiful glittering in searchlights. Ack-ack records no hits, as usual.

Assault crews arrive at airport by truck but takeoff postponed because of bad weather. Flight commanders as powerless as medical officers. Patient who spat blood yesterday has some form of TB. Will send him to hospital tomorrow.

Hospital ship *Takasago Maru* arrived in port today, took patients on board, and left immediately.

0200: Tonight's bombing raid destroyed a dozen or so of our carrier planes. 6 assault planes went up in flames, and 2 fighters and 2 bombers are beyond repair. Sky above airfield turned bright red. Raid has had bad effect on all our nerves.

Morning: 22 Zero fighters set off for Buin. Remaining assault planes return to Kavieng on New Ireland. If only we had twice the number of aircraft.

Had certain amount of leisure so made sketch of the three peaks of the volcanoes and coconut groves etc. I mean to color it when I get back on board. It was quiet drawing and so I suddenly started thinking about life and whatever lies in store. Some natives, thick eyebrows, goggling eyes, brilliant white teeth, passed by, and kept saying in pidgin English that "Japanese boy number one, American boy number ten." When offered a cigarette one of them grinned with huge pleasure and began his version of our "Patriotic March."

Lieutenant Yoshimura, who made a forced landing in the sea yesterday evening, managed to stay afloat all night and was discovered and picked up by a flying boat this morning. Considering he'd been in the water 18 hours he seems very well. He even joked about it. Still, for a man who has been as close to death as that for so long, the division between life and death must have become a very thin, indistinct one.

The air raid tonight was over in less than an hour. From today our regular air-raid shelters are to be ones a little way from our huts. Lieutenant Miyajima's temperature has returned to normal, which is a great relief. Still, more than 30 of our section are down with some illness or other.

During the morning had rare daylight attack by Boeings. Lieutenant Yoshida's flight tried to engage them but it was no good.

The garrison on Guadalcanal appears to have been evacuated. It is depressing to realize we have been involved in a withdrawal action and not a counterattack.

Lieutenant Araki and the others got back from Buin after dinner. All the planes returned safely, which has not happened for some time now. Tremendous rainstorm during night.

A little while after Shiroki made this entry the transfer telegram he had been expecting arrived. He was being posted to a ship called the *Shinko Maru*, a steamer that had been converted into a gunboat. Her base was Ominato, right at the northern tip of Honshu, on Mutsu Bay. He was not very pleased at the idea of patrolling the northern seas in a tramp steamer of that kind, but at least it would be nothing like as dangerous as being on an aircraft carrier, and he was now obsessed with the idea that he should be as careful of his one and only life as possible. More important than the posting itself was the fact that he would most likely get a few days leave in Tokyo on the way. He would then be able to meet Aiko and they could talk things over in a calmer and more leisurely way this time.

This was followed by an order for *Zuikaku* personnel to pull out from the base. The planes were to depart on the tenth, and the remaining personnel would leave for Truk by destroyer on the twelfth. But on the 9th of February another change was made and they were to leave on two ships of the Seventeenth Fleet which were due to arrive in port on the eleventh. While they were desperately involved in preparations, the withdrawal from Guadalcanal was announced over the radio at 7 P.M. Japan Time, although the official communiqué did not use the word "withdrawal."

"The troops engaged in a tactical mission on the island of Guadalcanal, having restricted the numerically superior enemy forces, which have been landing since August, to one sector of the island, inflicting crippling damage on them in a series of heroic engagements and thereby fulfilling their mission, have left the island with effect from the first week of February and have been redeployed elsewhere."

"If they lost they ought to say so quite clearly," said the principal MO, who was greatly annoyed by the announcement. "That kind of deception makes the people back home ignorant of what's going on out here, and they assume everything's all right when it's not."

That night, when they were in bed, the air-raid warning sounded again after a silence of three days during which bad weather had allowed them to sleep in peace. Everyone trundled out of the hut grumbling and muttering that they hoped this would be their last farewell to the Rabaul air raids. Few people actually went inside the shelters; most stood at the entrances, still extremely annoyed but quite prepared to watch something much more spectacular than any fireworks display.

"Getting in the shelter?"

"No. Can't stand the mosquitoes."

"You're more scared of them than of those?"

"I'm scared all right. There's one thing I don't want and that's dengue."

The enemy planes were flying low this evening. The bluish white fuselages would be caught in the crisscross of searchlights, and the anti-aircraft guns would bang noisily but pointlessly away, producing bursts of flack either in front of them or behind. The machine guns sent lines of tracer wavering mysteriously across the night sky. The enemy planes seemed to be firing back and the occasional cross-hatching of red and blue tracer made transitory patterns of great beauty in the sky.

"Damn it. Never hit anything."

"Not likely to hit anything firing like that. What the hell do they think they're up to?"

The planes began to bomb the east airfield, then the town of Rabaul itself. Great shuddering explosions which could be felt in the pit of the stomach came from that direction, and all the time there was the fierce sound of our guns answering back. Three Flying Fortresses flew over, then another three could be seen coming in at low altitude, this time heading straight toward them. There seemed to be more following them. Shiroki was standing by the entrance to the dugout and was thinking of crawling inside since somebody behind him had shouted out they should get down and take cover. But another voice told them not to worry since they were going to miss them. So those who were about to enter the shelter stopped by the entrance and looked up at the airplanes, whose angle of flight was indeed taking them slightly to one side of where they were standing.

Shiroki was standing with this group, and since they were bunched together he was in a much more upright and conspicuous position than he would naturally have chosen for himself. As he gazed up at a white plane picked out in the searchlight beams he felt a sudden sense of danger. The enemy's machine guns were raking the ground with fire, and in a flash he saw red and blue tracer shells like balls of flame coming in his direction. The next moment something brilliant burst open and shattered before his eyes. There was a blinding light and a roar.

A shell from the enemy plane had exploded just in front of him. Shiroki was struck on the head and chest as if by a club, and his consciousness faded and went out.

After Tetsukichi had completed his massive tour de force in 1939 he had planned another project, a psychiatric *Lehrbuch* which would be based on information gathered from cases that had occurred in Japan; but for a long time he had been unable to get down to work on it. Of course there had been the accumulated exhaustion of many years, and the prostration he had felt on the completion of his great labor had persisted, in some form or other, for a remarkably long period. Then there had been the sudden outbreak of war against the British and the Americans, and the constant news of various military successes had plunged this aging doctor, this scholar, this Director of a mental hospital, into a delirious whirlpool of rejoicing just like any small child. But, unlike a small child, he was aware that wars could be lost as well as won, and his feelings remained much as they had been at the very outset of this war when the news had created in him a passionate realization that they must never lose.

He had, at first, been astounded by the speed and decisiveness of the Japanese advance, amazed at the power that the country appeared to have, and every time he heard the "Warship March" or "Tens of Thousands of the Enemy" (those preludes to some piece of cheerful news) he would become hot inside and walk excitedly about his room, behavior unbecoming at his venerable age although perhaps occasioned by it. He was continually going to the cinema to see the newsreels, and as he watched the small but intrepid Japanese soldiers, either storming ashore on a beachhead in the teeth of the enemy or dropping in swarms by parachute to destroy the forces of the white men and set up the Greater East Asia Co-prosperity Sphere, he would be so excited that tears would come to his eyes and he would sit right through the program to see it all over again. Thus, while this state of affairs continued he was obviously unable to find the repose needed to begin the new work he contemplated.

Once the front line had been extended far to the south he at last began, at first only gradually but with increasing zeal, to collect examples of those psychiatric cases which were still matter for speculation. He went through all the medical cards of the Nire Hospital since the time of the great fire, and also paid occasional visits to Tokyo University and Keio University, taking notes of any cases that were interesting enough to be made the subject of a clinical lecture. Since he came across a number of examples of hysteria, he decided to concentrate his attention first on that illness, and he collected records of as many cases as he could. According to the foreign textbooks, the classic symptoms of this illness consisted in the patient straining his or her body backward like a bow and having convulsions much like those associated with epilepsy. However, on collecting a considerable number of Japanese cases, he found there were strikingly few examples of this kind of behavior, and such examples became even fewer as this century progressed.

It would obviously be meaningful to look at one of these cases in detail, thought Tetsukichi, taking a scholarly attitude such as had played little part in his mental and emotional life over the past few months. This attitude did not seem particularly deep-rooted, however, since he immediately began considering the causes of this difference between patients in Japan and the West in the manner of any amateur "thinker," although the scholar in him should at least have suggested that he was still at a stage where such "thoughts" should not have been allowed even casual entrance to his mind. The trouble was these damned white women were allowed to get away with almost anything, so their behavior was always exaggerated and the ways they expressed emotion were inevitably excessive. Compared with Japanese women, who knew how to put up with things, these spoiled Western women were disgracefully feeble, slovenly crybabies simply unable to cope with any personal or emotional crisis, and certainly not with an event like war. There were other similar reflections. . .

Ironically, Tetsukichi's ant-like labor began to get going smoothly again just as the Axis armies started to run out of steam and their overpowering advances had ground to a halt. Now the initiative had passed to the enemy, who was gradually edging forward in a series of counteroffensives. Tetsukichi took a more than usual interest in the war situation of our ally Germany, and would scan the newspapers for indications of what might be going on in that sector.

At the beginning of February 1943, the year in which he was sixty-one, Tetsukichi saw a small news item in the paper that filled him with gloom. It took up very little space compared with related stories which had appeared during the autumn of the previous year under banner headlines when the fall of Stalingrad had seemed imminent. Now the situation had been reversed: the massive German divisions had in turn been encircled and totally cut off, and huge losses had finally forced their surrender, a tragedy recorded in such inconspicuous, small type in Japanese newspapers that it was easy to overlook entirely. Beneath the headlines *"End of Hostilities in Stalingrad"* . . . *"Communiqué from Führer's General Headquarters"* . . . *"Heroes Mourned"* . . . *"Resolve of Whole German People,"* it announced:

> *Special cable from Berlin. Following the special announcement from Berlin Radio of the cessation of hostilities in the Stalingrad area, the "Horst Wessel March" was played to mourn fallen comrades, followed by a performance of Beethoven's Fifth Symphony. The German government has proclaimed four days of national mourning from today until the sixth. During this period all theaters, concert halls and cabarets will be closed, and all other forms of entertainment suspended. Confronted as they are by the harshness of the present situation, the German people are resolved to brace themselves for one final effort.*

This item appeared a month and a half after an article that told of the Führer's concern over the state of the Russian front, describing how Hitler had paid a flying visit to the front line in person and then returned to Berlin. *"The Führer gave an address in which he maintained that all was now quiet on the eastern front and offered the nation's thanks to the shades of its 542,000 departed heroes."*

But this was not a time solely for concern over the German tragedy. The Imperial Military Headquarters announcement of the "redeployment from Guadalcanal" came only five days after the news of the defeat at Stalingrad. Tetsukichi was acutely anxious now about the future of his own country and its ally Germany. In his zealous prayers for military fortune and his heartfelt hopes for the morale and fighting spirit of the troops at the front (among whom his own eldest son Shun'ichi was numbered) he was no less passionate than those strikingly numerous embodiments of insane patriotism at the time, the leaders of the small neighborhood organizations. Still, there had been a period when, by mere chance, Tetsukichi had done something that a section of these patriots would certainly have considered unpardonably anti-Japanese, for it must be confessed that he had been guilty of hoarding a considerable quantity of canned food acquired on the black market.

On one of his visits to the main hospital at Matsubara, various small matters had kept him there later than usual, and he had dinner at Oshu's house, an occurrence that had almost never happened before. From Tetsukichi's point of view the meal prepared here was, in contrast with what was on offer at Aoyama, a genuine feast, and no doubt this was true of dinner every night. He could not help feeling certain pangs of jealousy at the thought. In fact that night's meal was not all that remarkable, the vegetables being few and of poor quality, but since his brother-in-law visited so seldom, Oshu apologized for what was offered and said he would get out some canned food which he hoped might serve as some kind of compensation. He bustled off to the kitchen himself to get it, nimbly opening the cans and loading up a few plates with their contents. Fiddling about with food was, of course, one of his greatest pleasures.

He brought back king crab, corned beef and asparagus, all of which had become rarities at the time. This was particularly true of the corned beef and asparagus, for they were products of Japan's present enemy, the United States. The asparagus was thick and tender and seemed to dissolve on Tetsukichi's tongue, and his palate was more than satisfied by the king crab and corned beef.

"Very nice, very nice indeed," he said, moving his chopsticks briskly about and constantly praising the food (which in normal times would only have been acceptable at picnics) with a rare enthusiasm in his voice—it was very much as if he had discovered some exceptional psychiatric case history.

At Aoyama, lacking, as he did, a wife and even someone who could genuinely be said to be in charge of the kitchen, the cuisine was so inadequate that it failed to satisfy even Tetsukichi's modest demands. He had never been a connoisseur in such matters, very much the opposite in fact, but he had a greedy liking for food and this tendency had increased with his years. After Nanny Shimoda died, the kitchen had been more or less run by an old servant called Shige, who had been one of the maids "within" in former days although she was now only a small, shriveled and bigoted example of crabbed old age. The way she spoke was not what it should have been, indeed she was often quite vulgar, and if she saw the children standing about in the kitchen she would say:

"I'm not going to have you lot hanging about my kitchen all day making a nuisance of yourselves. Just be off with you. Come on, out you go, get out!"

All this might have been acceptable if she had been an accomplished cook, but the food she prepared was much the same as the cookhouse fare, being sensible, practical, boring and tasteless, and the most abject flatterer would have found it hard to use even a noncommittal word like "nice" in reference to it.

"This asparagus tastes really marvelous," Tetsukichi mumbled for the umpteenth time like some starving orphan child.

"It's a bit different from the kind Yonekuni grows," said Oshu, although the wit of the statement (Yonekuni=Beikoku=America) was lost on the literal-minded Tetsukichi.

"It's a foreign product, is it? Surprised you can lay your hands on this sort of thing at a time like this," said Tetsukichi, looking patently envious.

"All through the black market," Oshu said bluntly. "I have a connection. Done through the family of one of my patients at Matsuzawa. Of course, it costs a bit. Still, in times like these when everything seems to be gradually disappearing, I thought I'd better lay up a decent supply. If you really like it, I'll let you have some."

"Would you really? I'd be extremely grateful."

Hisa was not present at table for she was having one of her now only very occasional nights out. If Ryuko was at home, she had, of course, gone out of her way to avoid her husband and was probably concealed in her own room. The only woman present was Oshu's wife Chiyoko.

"The fact is we have to hide the canned food in our own living room," she said. "Nowadays Mother's old habit has got much worse, and she'll shut almost anything away in her own cupboard: dry goods, candy, canned food. . . Then when she remembers about it she'll sometimes give it to people in the hospital and we hardly see any of it."

"Well, it is rather pathological," said Oshu, with a wry smile. "She puts everything she gets in there, and that's the last we see of it. If she does produce a piece of candy or a cake or something it's always got mildew all over it."

"I must say she had a great deal of cloth and material in there. The whole top half of that cupboard is jammed tight with it. It would be a real help if she'd let some of it into circulation so it could be used in some way.''

"That's right; and there's a great deal of Asahi Candy," said Oshu, grinning and rubbing his double chin. "Anyway, her hoarding obsession is very remarkable. I sometimes think we'd be well advised to follow her example to some extent.''

"But she appropriates everything that's offered to the hospital, so we don't ever have anything to hoard anyway.''

Chiyoko kept up her grumbling for a while after this. She would dearly have loved to get going on "the honorable middle," Ryuko, but realized it was hardly the thing to do in front of Tetsukichi. So the two men talked hospital gossip for a while.

"Isuke still in good health at your place?"

"Well, yes. He's very old, of course. Completely bent over now. Finds it a great strain to walk. Hobbles about with a stick. His wife has recently taken over the rice cooking in his stead.''

"Oishi must be pretty old, too. The truth is the Nire Hospital could do with an infusion of fresh blood, yet all the healthy young people have been taken away by the army. I don't know if you realize quite how many people we've lost here, both clerical and nursing. Even someone like Shigematsu, who's forty-five," (this was Shigematsu Shimoda, the driver who had attempted to bring Momoko back into the fold outside Mitsukoshi Department Store some years ago) "has been drafted. If things go on like this the running of the hospital could become very tricky indeed, even impossible. The day may come when we find ourselves with no young nursing staff and will simply have to turn away any violent, or even unruly, patients. Only the other day a very powerfully built schizoid smashed down a door in a protective cell. He's said to be third grade in Judo and he suffers from the delusion that everyone in the hospital is an American spy. 'I'll smash you to pieces, you American swine,' he says, and nobody feels much like going near him. It just so happened that I had to go to that particular ward and was there while that kind of rumpus was going on, so I found myself obliged to indulge in a spot of Judo after a very long layoff. I couldn't have managed him on my own, of course, since he was full of that old fight-to-the-last-round-of-ammunition spirit, unlike me. So as I tackled him three others joined in and we managed to hold him down till we were able to get the electric treatment working. You only need one like that to reduce the whole ward to a battlefield, everyone nervous as if they're under fire. At Matsuzawa they still have people who've been specially trained to manage such patients."

"Well, I hope at least you'll be able to avoid any serious accident," said Tetsukichi, who had stopped chewing for a moment in order to put in this observation. "The trouble is we're a private institution. In the past it only needed one patient to escape for the whole police force to be at our throats. Private and public hospitals ought to be dealt with in the same way. I can't see the need to force ourselves to accept more people in this hospital when we already have more patients than we can cope with. If you have any more like that, you ought to pass them on to Matsuzawa. Of course it's not really your decision, but you might still pass the idea on to Nirasawa."

"Yes. That's the policy I've been thinking of following, although the Deputy keeps complaining nowadays about the way the number of patients goes on falling. He seems a bit under the weather lately. Did you see him today?"

"Yes. As you say, he doesn't seem to have the energy he used to have. Perhaps he's becoming senile."

"Not at all; he's still hale and hearty," Chiyoko butted in. "At least that's how it looks to me. Admittedly he doesn't hop about in the way he used to, but mentally he seems to be becoming more vigorous—he has what look like large-scale delusions of grandeur. Just recently he said he hoped to see a branch of the Nire Hospital set up in Singapore while he was still alive and kicking. . . Well, really, even as a joke it's. . . And then, you remember, he had that shrine put up. Right next to the tennis courts. It's dedicated to the fox deity in its protective aspect or something. He picked up the idea from one of the ancient inhabitants hereabouts. It has a proper shrine gateway, and a little stall selling fried bean curd—for superstitious purposes only, of course. The patients doing occupational therapy keep going there one by one to pray. . . I was really astonished to see it, I can tell you. Of course they've been ordered to do that by the Deputy."

"Well, it does no harm," said Oshu, who seemed much more amused by this state of affairs than shocked or offended by it. "The Deputy is a remarkable man, a man of distinction. . . Don't see why he shouldn't put up the odd shrine. I'm sure my father would have done the same if he had still been alive."

Tetsukichi seemed to be in complete agreement with this last opinion. What particularly impressed him, however, was the change that had come over Chiyoko. When she had first arrived as Oshu's bride she had sat looking modestly downward and never uttered a word, and now at some stage she had turned into this talkative person who showed no compunction about airing a stream of complaints and critical remarks. The speed with which she spoke was a bit irritating, and also vaguely reminiscent of Ryuko's eloquent tongue—at least it was not totally dissimilar. No doubt any woman who lived in the Nire Hospital for some length of time would be influenced in that direction. Or perhaps it was because all women were essentially like that?

Tetsukichi was not inclined to push these reflections any further, for he was more concerned with polishing off the few pieces of asparagus that remained on the table, even though his host and hostess had already arrived at the tea stage.

"Oshu," he said, speaking with a deeper seriousness than when he had discussed hospital affairs. "This is really delicious, you know. Of course I should be very glad to receive the odd can or two, but still, I've been thinking—I suppose it wouldn't be possible to have this connection of yours sell me some of this?"

"I don't see why something shouldn't be arranged. I'll have a word with him about it."

"If you would. . . You know, I don't need all that much. Just a bit would do. Only a small amount. Still, all things considered, it might be better to get quite a lot, this time anyway."

So it was in this way that Tetsukichi had bought a dozen cans each of American corned beef and asparagus, and of superior-quality king crab. He was quite ignorant about purchases of this kind and could not resist the feeling that such a transaction was a more sinful luxury than acquiring expensive foreign books; and this feeling that he was doing something wrong was an additional attraction. When he assembled the thirty-six cans, some square, some round, in little piles on the *tatami* in his room, he experienced an excited sense of guilt, and for a while he gazed at the labels or solemnly weighed the cans in his hand. This food was not something to be eaten frivolously. The war was bound to go on for a very long time yet, no matter what. Hard times were coming, and then these provisions would be worth their weight in gold. Aoyama did not provide the kind of food that was available at Matsubara, but Shuji and Aiko still got enough to eat so there was no particular need to share any of this with them.

Tetsukichi then thought about his work. He could not say he had really started yet on his next assignment, but he was getting material for it together bit by bit, and he assumed he would have it done in two or three years. Just thinking about it made his body go tense with a premonition of the hopes and anxieties the task would entail. He would experience those long hours of solitude again, hours of entrancement and bleak boredom too, caught up in the scholar's task to which he was now so well accustomed and yet which also gave him the sensation of doing something clumsily that he would never really get used to. Those hours would seem endless, hopeless, but it was this alone that gave any sense of purpose to his life—for this was indeed the sole meaning it had. Then while he was working away, during those small intervals of rest he would revive his flagging spirits by eating some of his canned food, and what could possibly be wrong about that? Nothing at all, and now he began to think about the matter in some detail. Beside his desk, on a small tray, he would have a bottle of mayonnaise and a thermos flask full of hot tea. On nights when his pen was running smoothly he would open a can of crab or asparagus. It would provide some light relish for his tongue, and slide pleasantly down his throat. On nights when he was having trouble with his work he would open a can of corned beef, and that white fat clinging to the inside of the lid would no doubt conjure up some new life in him. But before then, before those most important and least frivolous of moments, it was imperative that he should not touch any of the canned food.

So he went and fetched a trunk of his that happened to be empty, one he had used when a student abroad and which was covered with the labels of various hotels, and he packed the cans inside. But the cans of asparagus were too bulky and he saw it was going to be impossible to get them all in. So he emptied the contents out of a much larger trunk with two great straps, more like a chest than a trunk, which he had also used when a student overseas, and put his newly acquired treasure in this. This time the trunk was much too big, and the cans nestling at the bottom looked insignificantly few. Tetsukichi was overtaken by a sense of insufficiency, of inadequacy and regret. The old medical scholar, blear-eyed, shortsighted, bespectacled, slightly bowed with a head of mostly white hair, muttered to himself like a child dissatisfied with a toy it has just received:

"It's not enough. I'll have to get some more."

So he traipsed downstairs to the gloomy, damp, smelly kitchen, and began to question the gloomy, small, sulky Shige about what canned goods they had in store, though this new zeal for housekeeping hardly suited him. He was relieved to find that they had quite a supply of their own hidden away out of sight. None of it was of superior quality, though he had not expected it would be. There was salmon, beef, scallops and bamboo shoots, all Japanese products. Tetsukichi got Shige's permission to take some of these away to his room.

Cans of fish and meat were subject to rationing at the time, but it was still possible to get hold of them occasionally in town. Tetsukichi, with a passion close to that with which formerly he had sought out works on the history of psychopathology, managed to acquire various kinds of canned goods after that. He made no attempt to eat any of them, but merely collected them as if they were rare specimens relating to some mysterious branch of knowledge, and as they began to pile up higher in his large trunk he experienced an indescribable satisfaction. Once, when he got hold of a dozen cans of broiled eels, he was sorely urged to find out what the contents were actually like, but by a massive exertion of the will he managed to resist the temptation.

Although he merely stored his cans, neither consuming any of them himself nor even considering the idea of giving them to Aiko or Shuji, he did think of trying to send some of them to his eldest son, Shun'ichi, who was now fighting for his country on a remote island somewhere in the South Pacific. Communications occasionally came from that quarter, acknowledging the various letters and parcels sent to him and stating that he was still avoiding illness and spending each day in good spirits. But, in contradiction to the mimeographed remarks they had received from his commanding officer, Shun'ichi always ended his letters with requests for things, such as a lighter and spare flints, claiming there was nothing on this island at all and he was short of just about everything. All he had, he said, was time and money. Then a letter had arrived at Matsubara recently which contained the odd and contradictory statements that he was "healthier and happier all the time. Water stale or non-existent; no fruit either. Money grows but nothing here to buy with it," which sounded as if he were trying his hand at satirical verses.

So Tetsukichi chose two cans each of crab, salmon and eels and put them in a parcel, sending them off "c/o The Yokosuka Office, No. U103U100 (Su. One)." He had wanted to send some corned beef, but had decided it would not be the thing to do, seeing it was a product of the country they were fighting. He had also considered sending rather more than what he finally sent, but decided against it since he assumed that army food could not be all that bad. So he closed the lid of his trunk firmly on his remaining hoard, nodding to himself with the expression of a miser who knows he is still self-sufficient.

Naturally this was only one small aspect of his life at the time. The war was not going well, and each day it went worse. One event that cast a shadow over Tetsukichi's features was the powerful attack launched by the Allies in North Africa and the steady retreat of the Italian Army. Then toward the end of May came evil tidings that caused him acute distress. The death in action of Admiral Isoroku Yamamoto, the commander of the Combined Fleet which bore all the hopes of the Japanese people, was announced on the 21st of May. Shortly afterward, on the thirtieth, Imperial Military Headquarters announced the heroic annihilation of the garrison on Attu, one of the Aleutian Islands. Tetsukichi heard of this on the seven o'clock news while he was having dinner with Aiko and Shuji. Ever since Midway the military had glossed over reverses by such subterfuges as referring to retreats as redeployments, and this was the first time a defeat had been clearly announced as such:

"Since the 12th of May, the severely outnumbered garrison on Attu has been involved in a succession of bloody engagements with a numerically far superior force under battle conditions of extreme difficulty. On the twenty-ninth the decision was taken to deliver a final hammerblow against the main enemy forces, so demonstrating the essential spirit of the Imperial Army, and an all-out assault of great heroism was performed. Since then all lines of communication have been lost, and it is judged that the whole unit has sacrificed itself in this magnificent way. The wounded who were unable to take part in the final charge destroyed themselves without exception beforehand. The garrison consisted of more than two thousand men led by Colonel Yasuyo Yamazaki. The enemy force consisted of some twenty thousand specially equipped men whose losses until the 28th of May had been not less than six thousand."

Tetsukichi laid down his chopsticks, aghast at the news. At his side he could hear Shuji swallowing hard. But even allowing for the horror of this kind of heroic mass suicide, announcements of which were eventually to become what might with some exaggeration be called a normal part of everyday life, Aiko's response to the news was so different to the lip-biting silence of her father and brother that it astonished both of them.

Aiko had graduated from the Toyo Eiwa Girls' School (with the outbreak of hostilities a change in one of the characters with which the name was written had transformed it from the Oriental Anglo-Japanese Girls' School to the Oriental Eternal Japanese Girls' School) in the spring of that year, and become a pupil at Seishin Women's Academy. All of a sudden she had grown taller, lost the last traces of the childishness of a schoolgirl and, despite the fact that she was still excessively slim, she showed all the signs of approaching womanhood. Her face had also become strikingly thin, and she had shadows under her eyes which gave the impression of actual emaciation.

When Aiko heard the news of the illustrious massacre she began quite openly to sob, her head lowered and shoulders shaking; at first they were low sobs but they gradually mounted in volume and violence, culminating in a scream that was almost hysterical:

"How horrible!" she cried. "How horrible!"

As her father and brother looked on in consternation, her tear-stained face became hideously contorted and took on the pallor almost of advanced anemia. The next moment she stood up abruptly and dashed out, escaping to the shelter of her own room. She staggered shamelessly as she went, covering her face with both hands. . .

There was good reason for this outburst of emotion, which arose from anxiety for the safety of the person she had decided some time ago was to be her future husband. She was also sleeping badly at night. Ever since she had exchanged those unexpected kisses with Tatsunori Shiroki at the end of last year her character had become remarkably changeable, showing the trembling instability of the nineteen-year-old as her feelings swung from extremes of ecstasy to depths of despair. At times she had experienced a pure joy in which her own personality seemed to be forgotten. Her friends at the Toyo Eiwa Girls' School, many of whom were her fervent admirers, had never seen her eyes shining with such brilliance or looking so alive.

"Aiko, why do you have such beautiful, sad eyes?" asked one girl, who had become sentimental because the day when they would part was finally approaching.

"Really? Are my eyes pretty? Really pretty? Well, I *am* glad; I'm so glad, and you're my friend for life," Aiko replied in a mocking way that exemplified the erratic and high-strung manner in which she tended to speak at times now. She squeezed her friend until it hurt and then turned her eyes away toward nothing in particular as if she were preoccupied with thoughts all her own.

As graduation day grew closer, they were taken up with writing farewell messages and signing their signatures in one another's notebooks, or with various group photographs or with reminiscences of Miss Hamilton, headmistress until the war broke out and then no longer so; a constant round of nervous activity, strangely sad and happy at the same time. But Aiko, always the leader in most things, was now incomprehensibly changed, becoming each day more and more silent and withdrawn.

She had received just one letter from Shiroki, written while he was still at the base on Truk (although she, of course, had no idea where he was); this had arrived at the end of January. It was a very hastily written letter containing few specific references to a future life together, but Aiko felt from it that she was truly loved. The letter had ended with a promise that he would write again sometime, but the long-awaited letter never came. Even if he was engaged in some major operation it should, going by past experience, have been over inside three months, and he should have been back within four. That was what Shiroki himself had said just before they parted, although as they normally docked at Kure he didn't know if they would be able to meet next time; but he was due for a transfer, and though it wasn't yet clear where it would be there was a good chance he might be stationed somewhere in Japan. With the slow passage of time, Aiko's original feeling of intoxicated happiness gradually gave way to anxiety and emptiness. One month passed, then two, and finally three, and still there was no word from him.

She began to listen to the news bulletins each day, tense with the effort of paying deliberately casual attention. She would hear the list of enemy ships sunk in battles like that fought off Rennell Island, hoping against hope that no news of damage sustained by one of our carriers would follow. So day followed day of painful tension, made worse because she had no one to confide in. She said nothing about Shiroki—not to her mother, on Aiko's increasingly rare visits to the house at Matsubara, nor even to her closest friends; for she was proud, believing she could decide all matters of importance in her life herself. This pride was a somewhat modified version of the obstinate dignity so pronounced in her mother, but in someone as young as Aiko there was still a certain charm about it.

When she started going to Seishin, her new environment only brought out the fretful, suspicious qualities that seemed to have become dominant in her character. She had been allowed to do what she liked since she was a child and was too spoiled to be able to adapt to a passive role in life, or to put up with things and simply wait in silence. Again, the war situation, although not perhaps yet approaching those "harshest of extremities" of which the newspaper editorials so earnestly spoke, permitted no optimism, and this made the anxiety she felt even more intense. For some time now she had tended to wake from the same nightmare: black swarms of enemy planes filled the sky and a rain of bombs descended, tearing the sea below into a fury of leaping water, and there an aircraft carrier, seemingly the *Zuikaku*, was sinking, lying aslant, wrapped in black smoke and flames, clearly in her death throes. The morning after such a nightmare she would have dark rings around her eyes, and her reputation at her new school was the exact opposite of what it had been at her last. She had been transformed into a gloomy, depressed young woman who spoke little and was generally inaccessible.

It was while she was going through this period that the news of the heroic massacre on Attu Island came through. Although there could be no connection between this disaster in the Aleutians and the personal fate of Tatsunori Shiroki, it had a very deep and powerful effect on her. A whole four months had passed since his last letter had arrived. Something must be wrong. Something must have happened. Some misfortune, something she did not want to think about but had to think about, must have taken place. This intuition of hers, this premonition, could perhaps be put down to the pressure that the war news brought to bear on her, although since she was soon to know it was true maybe it was more than that. Whichever the case, Aiko found the burden insupportable, although she did manage to bear with it for a while. She hesitated, not knowing what to do, but then suddenly made up her mind. She decided to go to Shiroki's parents' house and ask about him.

Despite the fact that Shun'ichi Nire and Tatsunori Shiroki had been close friends for so long, there had never been any intercourse between the two families. So when, one Sunday afternoon, Aiko went to look for his house, which was somewhere in the Kamiuma district of Setagaya, all she had to rely on was an address she had found in a memorandum book in Shun'ichi's room.

It was a very quiet neighborhood, a residential area full of fairly similar houses of no great distinction. It took her a long time to find the house; she had to ask people two or three times, but finally she came across a wooden gate with the name Shiroki on it. The blue sky of early summer had a faint shadow over it, making the air seem hazy. Aiko hesitated again before the gate. Just then, something flew quickly past overhead, and when she looked up she saw the white underbelly of a swallow as it rolled over and soared amazingly into the upper air.

"Oh, it's a swallow," she said to herself, watching the neat shape for a moment as it sped far away from her. Swallows were supposed to come in the spring, but she could not recall having yet seen one this year. She felt it must be lucky to have seen her first swallow just as she was about to enter Shiroki's house; the bird could be a bearer of good fortune, a sign that the oppressive doubts that clung to her were now being wiped away. She had finally managed to find the house, and then the swallow had come; and with new courage she slid open the gate.

She found herself immediately before the doorway into the house itself, with a trellis door leading to an entrance hall. It was a one-storied, Japanese-style house of considerable age. To one side was a garden, but it was shut off by a bamboo fence with a wicket gate, so the main room of the house remained hidden. She pushed the bell and waited. It was quite a long time before she heard the sound of footsteps. In response to the voice from inside she laid her hand on the trellis door, which slid open much more easily than she had expected. The interior of the house was dark. The lady standing there must be Tatsunori's mother, although it was difficult to tell from her face.

The lady asked her who she was. Aiko remained silent for quite a while so she repeated the formal question. The voice was stiff and unfriendly, and Aiko finally responded all in one breath:

"I'm Shun'ichi Nire's younger sister. My brother. . ." but at this point she broke off.

"Ah . . . I see. . . You're Miss Nire, are you? Well, this is most kind. . ."

The lady's voice had relaxed a little, but to Aiko it still sounded cold and hard. She raised her slightly lowered face and asked, again in one breath, the only question she could think of:

"I was wondering how Tatsunori was. Have you had any news from him lately?"

There was a short silence, although it felt to Aiko as if it would go on forever; but then she clearly heard the terrible words, clear and dreadful as in a nightmare:

"Tatsunori was killed in action."

Shiroki's mother spoke in a low voice, but distinctly enough; then the next moment she jumped down from the raised *tatami* of the entrance hall into the stone area by the door, still in her stockinged feet, for she was obliged to hold up this young girl she had never seen before who looked as if she were about to faint by her front door. The girl, who said she was the sister of a close friend of her dead son, had suddenly gone limp and then started to collapse.

It had not required Oshu's words to make it clear that more than a few of the people connected with the hospital had been drafted into the armed forces. The hospital at Matsubara had always been crawling with unneeded people who had nothing to do, but gradually their numbers decreased until there was an actual shortage of personnel, both of administrative staff and of nurses. Nineteen forty-three was the fifty-fifth anniversary of the founding of the hospital, but in these difficult times the Deputy had been obliged to abandon the idea of any grand celebration, and only a simple ceremony and a modest prize giving were held. Also the Deputy himself had grown old and no longer experienced the spiritual exaltation of five years ago. Then in June the man who held the unofficial record for never working and yet living off the hospital, Kumagoro Sakuma, now forty-eight years old, had received his red call-up papers.

This fact filled Yonekuni with great trepidation, and he grasped the hand of his valued servant, crony and even overseer fearfully, as if he felt he was going off to the war himself. But the man in question was quite unconcerned. Whether this was due to the high level of his morale, the plucky nature of his character, or because his sensibilities were too crude to allow him to know any better, it was hard to say, but with a calm look on his face he declared:

"It's all right, Mr. Yonekuni," raising his bushy eyebrows a little.

"I'll do your share of the fighting as well as mine. It's perfectly in order for you to be at peace with yourself and grow asparagus. And look after those long-horned beetles, too."

He made even bolder pronouncements before the hospital staff as a whole:

"Kumagoro is off to the wars!" he said, striking a fine attitude. "The time has come at last when I, in the autumn of my years, must take up arms. Well, it's the old story of setting off majestically in the direction of BLANK BLANK BLANK on schedule to arrive at BLANK BLANK. Gentlemen, you may expect great things of me. I shall fulfill my obligations to His Imperial Majesty and to the Nire Hospital. . ."

Kumagoro now had a wife, who was still a nurse in the hospital, and a small son, and how he behaved in front of them we do not know, but in public he was bold and fearless, a slight smile playing about his lips as if he were indeed to take up some post of command, and when he departed from Tokyo Station he was seen off by considerable numbers of people from the Nire Hospital, led by Yonekuni. Since his birthplace was in Yamaguchi in the far west, he joined the 233rd Regiment, the Yamaguchi Infantry.

Up to now he had spent his life in perfect idleness, cleverly managing to do very much as he pleased. Because of his long years of experience and his natural impudence, he assumed all too readily he would be able to get along in much the same manner in the army and in actual fighting as well. But when he joined his unit, which consisted of a motley collection of B2-grade reservists who ranged from a youthful twenty-two to old men of fifty, and where Kumagoro was no commander in chief and never likely to be one but merely a lowly private soldier, he was quickly and totally disabused. Once his military training had begun he found that a great deal of face slapping went on each day, much more than had been rumored even, and he seemed to receive much more than his share, perhaps due to that haughty look he had in his eye. The havoc wrought on his face was supplemented by the assault innumerable bedbugs launched on the nape of his neck, which became red and swollen. Then, on the very first day, he had been offered a sandbag, which, moreover, was full of sand. His future role in the army depended on this, for those who could lift it five or six times would be on light machine guns or grenade throwers, those who managed seven or eight times on heavy machine guns, and those who could do no better than two or three times would be mere riflemen. Kumagoro only managed to lift his sandbag twice, not because he was aware of the dubious rewards that awaited achievement in this field and was deliberately performing badly, but because it was all he could do. But the thickset, bull-necked Kumagoro did look, superficially at least, quite strong.

"Come on, damn you, you're not even trying. You can do better than that."

But he could not do better than that, no matter how much he sweated and grappled with the thing. The special existence he had enjoyed at the Nire Hospital for many years had dulled him not only mentally but even more so physically.

He was only with the Yamaguchi Infantry for a short period. After a week, he and the rest of his draft had been crammed into a train which was shipped by ferry from Shimonoseki, the port on the very western tip of Honshu, to Pusan in Korea. Because of enemy submarine warnings the ship zigzagged all the way there, arriving at night. Kumagoro found he was being sent by way of Manchuria far off into the Chinese hinterland, so his stated conviction that it was more honorable and glorious to fight against the Americans had come to nothing. Once they had crossed the Manchurian frontier they were transferred to freight wagons. They traveled in these non-stop for two, three, then four days. His body became stiff as a board, and the worst thing was having to urinate from a moving wagon that was jam-packed with soldiers. Once, they passed a train going the other way. This also consisted of freight cars crammed with soldiers, but these were going back home. They had dreadful, staring eyes from which one naturally turned one's own away, and their skin was dry and harsh, the very color of the earth of this continent. Their faces had in common something so remote from the fresh, inexperienced faces of the new troops arriving from home that they looked like creatures of a different species.

After a journey across the endless cornfields of North China they got off the train at Pukow, on the other side of the river from Nanking. It was murderously hot, the sun burning down. On the way to their barracks there was not one drop of water to drink, and Kumagoro experienced a thirst that made it seem as if his throat were about to crack open, and also made it impossible to produce any sound from that region. They arrived in Nanking by boat. Now they were plagued by bad water, and stomach pains and diarrhea began. They moved on again, by boat upriver to Hankow. During those three days Kumagoro had such severe diarrhea he was able to eat nothing, and simply lay gasping feebly on deck, looking as if he were sulking rather than ill. Everyone about him had diarrhea all the time as well, and one or two were judged to have dysentery and were taken off the boat. Kumagoro, however, remained on board, with the result that when they reached Hankow he was totally unable to move, and alone received special permission to be transported by truck.

They spent about a fortnight in Hankow. They were housed in brick barracks, their diarrhea gradually got better, and they were apportioned the dull task of picking bits of dirt out of heaps of rice. They were also able to go outside the barracks and could sell cigarettes and buy cakes. Kumagoro had now recovered from his initial shock and was planning how to utilize the skills with which he had controlled things at the Nire Hospital so as to enable him to exist more easily in this military setup, but there was no diminution in the number of slaps he received on the face. Japanese bombers flew overhead each day toward Chungking, and they would all gaze up at them as they passed.

From Hankow they went to Shayangchen by truck. They drove through appalling clouds of dust and even their messtins became encrusted with a layer of dry, yellowish sand. From there they marched for twenty days to Dongshih, which was the battalion headquarters, and here they were given six months of basic training. In the burning heat of the height of summer two soldiers died during route marches, but Kumagoro managed to avoid any really tough training for a while since he had to have an operation for piles, an operation that also deprived him of the leisure or inclination to deplore and condemn the Italian surrender when it was announced. He had always tended to suffer from piles, but since they had now started to protrude alarmingly he was sent to regimental HQ to have an operation, and then again to divisional headquarters at Tangyang to have the operation done again. He was given just one injection of anesthetic in his spine, his legs were suspended by a pulley from the ceiling, and the operation consisted in merely snipping off the offending matter. It was simple to the point of crudity. The doctor told the night-duty orderly that since Kumagoro had been so definitively cut about it would be in order for him to groan that night; which he did, spending the whole night moaning loudly with teeth tightly clenched and thick beads of sweat standing out on his skin. They might at least have given him one more injection, and then possibly he might have borne up under the strain, but as it was it was too much for him. Here lay a man who at his departure for the front had spoken in large phrases, as if the whole conduct of the war had been entrusted to his hands, but what a wretched and undignified position he found himself in now. Luckily no one blamed him for it, although he could hardly have cared if they had, for the unbearable pain tormented him all night long, and he moaned and groaned, then moaned and groaned again.

In December he was sent with some others to join his company at Choujiacheng, and from there his platoon marched another seven miles to an outpost at a place called Banyuehshan, or Half-Moon Mountain. Thus a way of life began of boredom and meaningless repetition, in which no changes occurred despite the constant threat of danger from guerrilla forces.

The land around Half-Moon Mountain was a succession of low, bare hills. The place itself was a refugee settlement of some fifty or sixty buildings. The outpost was a mile or so from the settlement, on a small rise among paddy fields and the occasional isolated farmhouse. It consisted of some dugouts surrounded by coils of barbed wire, with a platoon hut in the middle where the soldiers slept. Each day was either spent on guard or on fatigues such as wood chopping, charcoal burning, or going to buy things in the refugee settlement. That was their way of life. Since the company was more than seven miles away, there was no point in setting up a field telephone, for it would inevitably be cut the next night. Thus headquarters was informed of an enemy attack by the sound of guns being fired, and it was the job of the seventeen or eighteen men in the outpost to hang on until reinforcements arrived.

These enemy attacks were always on a minor scale, guerrilla sorties that took place on average twice a month. A dog would start barking in one of the farmhouses in the paddy fields and they would be aware that they were in for trouble that night. If they weren't careful a hand grenade might be thrown among them, as it was occasionally. And for this reason guard duty, from the watchtower during the day or patrolling inside the perimeter at night, was of major importance. Sometimes the soldiers might make a "punitive" excursion during the hours of daylight, but once the enemy caught sight of a Japanese patrol they would melt away without firing a shot, fleeing from them in such a manner as to give Kumagoro a pleasing sense of his own importance, and also making him easier in his mind.

In January of the new year Kumagoro underwent some kind of test at Dongshih, which he passed, and was promoted to private first class. But that was as far as he was ever to be promoted, for he managed to perform no outstanding exploits. On the contrary, he was idle enough to allow a prisoner to escape, for which misdemeanor he was punished by having to do extra guard duty for a month.

The only events that provided anything like pleasure were the visits to the refugee settlement, and the arrival of letters and gift parcels sent to company HQ every ten days, which three soldiers with loaded, cocked rifles went to collect. Letters from home normally took two months to arrive. Kumagoro would read those from his wife and Yonekuni, and the group efforts from employees at the hospital, with great attention, lost in melancholy reveries. The elation he had expressed so glibly before he joined the army, and the bold spirit that had presumably occasioned it, had grown less with each day and were now quite gone.

However, on those rare evenings when he had been able to drink, this square-faced, bull-necked, squat, stubby individual would display an occasional glimpse of that fire he had shown when addressing cookhouse circles in the Nire Hospital, edifying his fellow privates first class with some of his ancient bluster. One habit of his was to revile the slovenly behavior of the Italians.

"That damn Badoglio is a disgrace to his country! Filthy traitor! Bet the Germans were only too glad to get them off their backs. Even so, that Badoglio is an insult to the military; contemptible swine not worthy of his uniform!"

If it was not international politics, then it would be the exercise of his genius on the complexities of the present military situation.

"We shouldn't hang about guarding places like this, but make a bold attack on Chungking. If I were commander in chief I would give that order. Your humble servant Sakuma has various ideas on the execution of this campaign of no mean order, I can assure you."

Right in the middle of the Pacific, at latitude 166 degrees east and longitude 19 degrees north, almost exactly midway between Japan and Hawaii, is the island of Wake, a small, low-lying island floating on the waves, which had been renamed Otorishima ("Big Bird Island") since the Japanese occupation. Its total area was less than two square miles, but it had a circumference of eighteen miles or so.

The whole island was formed of coral, with a number of coral boulders, and then mostly pebbles also formed by the polyps, plus stone fragments and sand. That was all, and all this glittered murderously white under a violently burning sun. There was not a single coconut tree, the only vegetation being a coarse, round-leafed scrub and a certain amount of wild grass. The natural inhabitants were flocks of innumerable seabirds and swarms of field mice. It was a wretched waste of an island, a piece of land whose long boomerang shape seemed about to vanish beneath the waves with each high tide.

Plainly it was not an island for human beings to live on, but, because of its strategic importance, four thousand American soldiers had been stationed here when the war began, and the Japanese had occupied it with a combined army and navy garrison of some five thousand men. Then, in September of 1942, a regiment of the joint brigade in Indochina had been dispatched here. Among them was a medical officer called Shun'ichi Nire.

Yet the rhythm of daily life here was relaxed and easy. All there was to see was a level expanse of sand and rock whitely reflecting the blinding light of the sun, and the only things to hear were the endless sounds of the waves and the hoarse cries of the seabirds. There was all the leisure one needed, for there was practically nothing to do. They were incarcerated on this island, it seemed, in a perpetual summer; cut off from the real world like ghosts.

In the beginning, life on the island, so far as accommodation and food were concerned, had been extremely comfortable, for they had been able to use the well-built huts and the plentiful provisions (pickles, olives, even ice cream) the American garrison had left. Their own supply ship came at regular intervals. They were protected by their own air squadrons, for there were three runways in the south of the island, and at times there would be as many as eighty land-based assault planes and fighters on the airfield. One of the pleasant things about having so much spare time was that Shun'ichi was able to go to the airfield and watch the cigar-shaped assault planes take off on patrol, and then wander over to where the Zero fighters were all lined up and talk to the mechanics or touch and stroke the duralumin fuselages in fond fascination. He had been given an early sight of these machines, standing on the beach at Hayama in the year before the war had started, much in the way a youth might catch a glimpse of the long-imagined girl of his dreams, and now these marvelously attractive, intrepid fighter planes were here before his

623

eyes, scores of them, lined up wing tip to wing tip. Every time he visited the airfield, his face was wreathed in foolish, slack smiles, expressing a pure joy quite unrelated to war, a benevolent innocence that one might find hard to imagine in a man who had spent two years involved in military life.

"Is this engine a Sakae? It sounds a bit different to the Kotobuki," he would say to a mechanic in the confident tones of an expert. "I suppose you know what the Zero was like in its first stages? Filleting was longer, looked smarter than this one, I seem to remember. Of course, it looks more powerful now."

But Wake Island was not always a haven of peace and quiet. Once, what had seemed to be the eternal silence of the island was disturbed by a bombardment from enemy ships, including battleships, as carrier-based enemy planes launched a lightning bombing raid. The attack came as a total surprise, so that nearly all the Japanese planes were caught on the ground where they were bombed to pieces. But even this disaster was not accompanied by any deaths, nor were any of the land installations seriously damaged, so Shun'ichi, who was no hero, was relieved to find that war meant only that sort of thing.

But the changes taking place in the war situation were not to leave the island untouched and peaceful forever. Once the American forces had gained complete control of Guadalcanal they began to put their island-hopping policy into operation, landing on Rendova Island on the 30th of June and Vella Lavella on the 15th of August, so that it was obvious they were aiming at the strategic strongpoint of Bougainville Island, which in turn would lead to an attack on Rabaul. These setbacks in the Solomon Islands made their repercussions clearly felt on lonely, distant Wake, for aircraft began to be transferred away from there, the fighters on which the defense of the island mainly depended, until only ten of them remained; and the whole situation changed with dramatic abruptness during the first week of October 1943, when Wake Island suffered an intense bombing raid of a kind they had never experienced before from a large enemy task force.

It was still not yet dawn when the waves of the carrier-based planes began flying over and started bombing. Shun'ichi, at his post in the combat medical dugout, stood listening for a long time to the uninterrupted series of explosions, but this endless waiting, to which he was quite unused, became vexing, then painful, and finally unbearable. Not a single wounded person had been brought in yet, so he poked his head outside to have a look at what was going on. He particularly wanted to see the enemy planes, for even in a situation of this dangerous kind his curiosity remained unabated, although this misplaced curiosity and ignorant coolness immediately vanished at what he saw outside. The whitening dawn sky was completely covered with a thin, black haze of smoke, and the whole appearance of the island seemed to have been transformed by the flashing and banging of guns and the stench of cordite. Across that murky sky, ominous black shapes swooped at alarming speed, a massive swarm of enemy Grummans, so many they seemed to be genuinely innumerable. Just in one glance he observed about thirty planes coming in from the north and another forty from the airfield to the south, all heading in his direction. He saw a great cloud of sand, like a violent squall, blow up into the air some distance away, and that was enough for him, for it seemed as if all the enemy planes were making a beeline for the red cross on top of the medical station. As he turned around to take further stock of the situation something seemed to push him up from behind with a jerk, and he was hurled bodily back inside the dugout by the blast of a bomb. He was conscious that all the blood had drained from his face, and he also realized why not one casualty had been brought here yet. The stretcher-bearers would be unable to move while this storm of bullets and cannon and bombs continued.

Then, just as a squall passes by, the first wave of enemy planes disappeared, and the wounded began to be carried in. Since Shun'ichi was no surgeon he could only assist at the operations, but he was lucky to have that amount of work to do to occupy his mind. Outside, a bombardment from enemy ships seemed to have begun. The nerve-racking scream of shells falling went on endlessly, and the only thing that allowed him to preserve his presence of mind was his being too busy to have the leisure to listen to them. At times, however, he had to leave the operating table, since he was on the point of fainting. He had only become a doctor for the inadequate reason that he had been born into a medical family, and the principal reason for his choosing psychiatric medicine was that he would be spared the sight of blood. When he was a student he had swooned when watching something as trivial as the lancing of a boil, and now his arms and coat were soaked in blood and the floor was wet and slippery with it too.

At noon the enemy bombardment halted for a while. Shun'ichi and Lieutenant Sato, a graduate of the Medical School of Tokyo

University, whom he had been with right from the period in Indochina, went outside together and so gained their first sight of the enemy warships. One quick glance all around revealed a dozen or more of the gray hulls dotted here and there in the ocean, surprisingly close at hand. One could only conclude that the small island was completely surrounded by the enemy.

"It looks as if they mean to land," muttered Lieutenant Sato, looking at the cratered confusion of the sandhills about them. Shun'ichi had no reply to this, although he also believed this was going to happen, for he was praying fervently if silently to the Combined Fleet, begging it to come now and attack the enemy in the rear. There was supposed to be a pretty large fleet at Truk, and it really must try and get here as fast as possible. The huge enemy task force was just out there, right in front of their eyes, a perfect target, floating calmly on the deep in a most irritating way, and it was only a matter of time before the bastards would smash Shun'ichi and the rest of them to smithereens. The Combined Fleet had been formed for just such an occasion as this, so Shun'ichi pleaded with it, begged it, to come.

Lieutenant Sato's assumption could hardly have been described as leaping to conclusions, nor was there anything comic about Shun'ichi's impassioned appeal, for it came to seem more and more likely that the enemy did intend to land. The ships surrounding the island made no sign of leaving, and the enemy planes kept on attacking. That night, all night, the bombardment from the ships continued, and at dawn the planes came swarming back again. The defending force of ten Zeros had taken off yesterday to intercept the enemy, and naturally not one of them had returned, so the sky was filled with enemy planes which could flit about just as they pleased. When the order to burn and destroy all important documents was given, it was obvious that headquarters was expecting a landing as well. Anti-aircraft fire had ceased from that morning, and the heavy-gun emplacements and machine-gun nests had been reduced to silence. All one could do was wait with nerves torn to pieces; wait for the enemy landing.

There were intermittent lulls in the bombing raids, and Shun'ichi went outside hoping for the virtually impossible best. But the enemy fleet was still there, looking as if it meant to remain until Wake Island had been obliterated. What looked like destroyers were changing position slowly, and the large stationary ships beyond them must have been battleships. There was no sign of any aircraft carriers, but presumably they were stationed well back over the horizon so that they could dispatch their aircraft in this direction.

Shun'ichi had slept badly the previous night. His normally long, peaceful face was now undeniably haggard. The strain imposed on him since dawn yesterday had all accumulated to form this present exhaustion, and he sat down wearily on the shingle as if he hardly cared what happened any more. This transitory, unbelievable, oppressive quiet with no sign of any enemy planes and no shelling from the ships gave him the irresistible sense that all was finished now, all was lost. There was nothing that could be done. He no longer really expected the Combined Fleet, for which he had prayed so fervently yesterday, to come to their rescue—a rare piece of objective thinking on his part. The fleet would arrive sometime, he was sure, but it would probably be too late to save them. If the enemy were to land tomorrow morning, as seemed likely, it would not take long for that huge force to wipe them out.

The thought made him shake his head unconsciously, and he was overwhelmed by a terrible wave of regret. He was twenty-eight years old, and it looked as if his life was due to end in this pointless fashion on a little flat island miles from anywhere. It seemed all too short a life to come to an end now. Although death was normal in war he was still ruled by the feeling that to die like this was unacceptable. If only he could be allowed to return home once more, to breathe the air there again and see the light, then he felt he would be able to die without the regrets that plagued him now. They were so far away here it seemed doubtful that what remained of him would be shipped back for burial, and the emptiness of the prospect was too much for him. An image of his country floated before him, the same simple red shape that appeared on the map they had used at primary school. This image then gave way immediately to the photographs of three girls, which had been shown to him as those of possible brides. His mother had produced them when he had still been working in the medical faculty at Keio and had been on a visit to Matsubara. Ryuko had said quite openly that these were photographs she had been asked to show him, and that if there was a young lady among them whom he liked the look of he should say so without any reservation. He had replied straight off that he had no intention of getting married before he was thirty, although he had still studied the photographs and additional information about the girls with absorbed interest. One of them was rather good-looking, though there was something about her eyes that was a bit too sharp, too forward. Another one . . . but what would it have been like to have married that girl? To have had, say, just a month of married life with her? The only experience he'd had of women was with one skinny Annamese girl he'd slept with in Indochina.

A noise like distant thunder spread from one far corner of the sky, announcing one more of those raids, as the planes assembled like persistent vultures above a dead carcass. If they went on like this the island itself would vanish before they could land on it. Shun'ichi broke off his brief thoughts and crawled back into the dugout that served as the combat medical station.

On the second night, once the bombing raids had ended, the shelling from the ships was even worse than it had been the night before. It seemed clear now that an enemy landing was unavoidable; everything pointed in that direction. So that night, though Shun'ichi did not hear it, a series of machine-gun bursts came from the direction of the marines who were defending the north of the island. They were executing, as a swift, preliminary measure, all the Americans who were still on the island, the hundred or so technicians who remained from an original number of four thousand prisoners.

But next morning, contrary to all expectations, the enemy fleet had gone. There was not even a trace of smoke on the horizon from which the blue ocean flowed unobstructed to break here on the blackened rock and shingle. The island still remained. Here and there were huge craters, but the coral island itself looked, surprisingly, little different, though all the man-built installations had been totally destroyed. Once more the burning, dreary light of the sun shone only on the scrub and fine particles of glittering sand.

Shun'ichi, worn out by two sleepless nights which had left him hollow-eyed, and also by his conviction that he was certainly going to die, could only look at the light curve of the horizon with its backcloth of cumulus clouds, feeling a sense of total letdown, of lethargy so complete that the strength seemed to ebb from his legs, and they almost gave way beneath him.

Chapter

5

Here in the mountains of Hakone the swarms of cicadas still kept up their pure, vibrating song. The slopes and hills about Myojogatake retained their gentle elegance and the breeze that filtered through the cedar woods was cool. As Tetsukichi listened to the chorus of cicadas the war seemed very far away, and he felt an unreasoning sense of guilt.

Gora was certainly quiet, this summer of 1944. Many of the summer cottages remained closed and one saw fewer children with butterfly nets compared with former years. There were more foreigners, however, Germans whom one came across quite frequently as they walked briskly about. Tetsukichi had learned from a woman who ran a shop in front of the station that a lot of them had been given places to live hereabouts. In June the Allied forces had landed in Normandy, and despite the use of their new weapon, the V-1, our ally Germany was obviously struggling to withstand pressure from both east and west. When Tetsukichi met these Germans on his walks, they usually took no notice of him but merely walked by, though very rarely one might greet him with a mechanical "good day," to which Tetsukichi would respond in the same manner. This brief exchange of greetings over, both would continue on their equally solitary ways.

He had brought a maid with him to Gora, but he had now sent her back and was living alone, doing his own cooking and generally looking after his own needs. It was his custom to come to Hakone each summer, but his main reason for coming this summer was that he had assembled a good deal of material for his second major opus, and was hoping to be able to start on this work, which would probably be his last. In the old days he had normally managed to get half the year's labor done during his three months in the mountains.

This year was also marked by the absence of the children, whose voices had always disturbed him each year, but there were no games

629

to be played now. With the mobilization of students for industrial work, which had begun that April and continued ever since, Aiko and Shuji were spending the summer working in two different factories. They had both been removed completely from school and classwork, commuting each day to a munitions plant, for the war situation had become critical enough to require this. Just a short while ago the tragic news of the slaughter of the Saipan garrison had come through, and it seemed that the Japanese civilian population there had chosen the same fate as the soldiers.

"*The sublime end of our comrades on Saipan, the calm suicides of women and children too—this glorious example of consummate patriotism has astounded the world,*" wrote an overseas correspondent in an article dispatched from Stockholm.

Saipan was the main strategic stronghold in the South Pacific. Its defensive positions were known to be extremely solid, and the ability of the enemy task force to overrun it apparently at will not only filled Tetsukichi with regret but with a vexation that made him clench his fists and grit his teeth. What, he wondered, was our invincible Combined Fleet doing?

He thought of his eldest son, Shun'ichi, who must be somewhere in the South Pacific. For more than six months he had received no tidings from him and, given the way the situation was developing, the chances of his being alive and well were probably very slight. Even so, he felt no inclination to succumb to these forebodings, but told himself that he must not brood over personal matters, for the plight of the country was too grave to permit such luxuries. Hadn't everybody offered their sons and husbands in the service of His Imperial Majesty?

Tetsukichi's mind had been well indoctrinated, despite or rather because of his venerable age, with the simpleminded sentiment of "Drive Out the American Devils" that informed the newspaper editorials; yet when he considered how he spent his days he was obliged to feel that not only was he remote from the ideals of self-denial and serving the country, but that his activity was merely selfish and quite unrelated to the war effort. So, as he lived alone, secluded in his summer cottage, it was not surprising that he should have felt guilt clinging, as it were, to his back.

Presumably he would not have felt this so strongly if he had been making real progress in his work, no matter how personal that work might be judged to be; but the result of his constant fiddling with his piles of material was merely to put off setting out on his main task, and he came to feel even more frustrated about the negative role he seemed doomed to play in life. While he was idling his time away like this Shun'ichi was fighting and exposing himself to danger. Even his brother-in-law, Yonekuni, had been drafted at the beginning of that summer. Then Aiko and Shuji, who were still children (or so they seemed to Tetsukichi), were helping to make weapons to be sent to the front. Surely he ought to be ashamed of himself, leaving the hospital in the hands of the Assistant Director, Seisaku Kanazawa, and coming to this mountain resort to escape the summer heat? Even though his plan to write a psychiatric textbook based on Japanese and not Western case histories was perhaps some kind of meaningful contribution to the new society, he still felt this sense of shame and disgrace.

The truth is that he was being obliged to recognize, as yet only dimly perhaps, that the ambition, the constant mental vitality that had made him strain every nerve and recklessly expend every ounce of energy on his work in the past, had gradually declined until it was near the point of vanishing completely. His hair was now mostly white, his myopic eyes bleared and lifeless behind the thick lenses of his spectacles, and as he gazed—as he was prone to do these days—on the contours of the distant circle of mountains, it was only matters relating to the past that came vaguely back to him.

As evening approached he bent over a very simplified version of a kitchen range, an empty oil drum with a hole in it, and pushed some dry cedar leaves inside. His posture only emphasized how round his shoulders had become. When lit, the leaves smoldered, giving off smoke that made his eyes sting. He added twigs and firewood, finally placing a thick iron pot containing today's small ration of rice on the fire. He then squatted down on the stone floor of the kitchen in the twilight, and waited. At last the familiar smell of boiling rice and thick, clammy steam began to filter from beneath the wooden lid. He next took some glowing embers from the drum and transferred them to a smaller range, much like a gas ring although usually heated by charcoal, and on this he warmed up some *miso* soup with eggplant. He hadn't done his own cooking like this since his student days abroad, in Munich at the house of the "Japanese granny," where he had occasionally boiled up some Italian rice. In spring he had once gone to a wood on the outskirts of the city and gathered young bracken, which, though common enough in Japanese cooking, was something that nobody there ever picked; and, beneath the old lady's quizzical gaze, for she was greatly concerned as to the propriety of anyone eating such things, he had boiled it up into an egg soup and wolfed it down. At that time in his life, although he was advanced in years when compared with the other Japanese students there, he had been full of ardor and enthusiasm. It seemed far off in the past now, a distant memory among the many of that period that came back vividly at times as if to announce his own life was finally drawing to its close.

In contrast to this decline in enthusiasm for his work, his appetite for food showed no sign of falling off; and although he was glad this was so, it was another thing of which he felt obliged to be ashamed. He opened a can of salmon. For a while he concentrated his entire attention on the resistance the lid of the can showed to the key that was slowly opening it, and then on the beautiful cross sections of meat it finally revealed. He had brought some of the higher-quality canned foods he had so laboriously collected here with him. But each time he was about to open one of them he felt a mysterious hesitation. It seemed so wasteful; he really ought to save them longer, wait until the last possible moment, when they would be absolutely vital. He marveled at how parsimonious he had become lately, although he had, in fact, always been like that, and he had no real intention of being critical of this aspect of his behavior.

There was something satisfying about this meal of hot rice, salmon sprinkled with soy sauce, *miso* soup with eggplant, eaten in the deserted summer cottage beneath the dull glow of the electric light with its grubby lampshade, and he ate it up noisily and with relish, slapping his tongue and licking his lips. It wasn't a bad way of life. People ought to be satisfied, content with small pleasures like these, for he himself now obtained sufficient satisfaction from them. If he could only get started on his work, and if the war situation would only look up a little, and if he could only lose this feeling of guilt he had concerning the labors and sufferings of his sons and daughter. . .

Sitting by a window, against which a number of moths were beating and fluttering their wings, he began picking unconsciously at his teeth with a fingernail as he poured some more of the over-stewed tea into his cup.

The lives of Shuji and Aiko as munition workers were nothing like as full of hardships, adversities, or pathos as their father, alone in his summer cottage, supposed. Shuji had been posted to a factory in Omori which mostly made bombing units and machine guns for aircraft. Certainly he had been given some heavy physical work to do at first, being attached to the warehouse and having to pile thick bars of steel and long bits of square timber onto the transport trucks. The heavy bars took the skin off his shoulders when he carried them, and if one wasn't very careful there was always the chance of crushing one's fingers beneath them. He felt envious of those who had been set to work on the factory floor and were handling lathes and other tools; he had watched them working with these machines, to which they were still unaccustomed, and thought how interesting it must be to make real screws out of metal bars as they were doing. They certainly seemed to be enjoying themselves more than they did at school, for here there was no teaching or exams to vex them, and all they had to do was wield their roughing tools and send sprays of cutting oil all over the place.

Shuji found that there was something to be said for being in the warehouse once he had grown used to it. When there was no work to do one was free to do nothing, and on most days work came to an end during the morning, so that Shuji and his companions could monopolize the ping-pong table before lunchtime and tirelessly enjoy a version of table tennis with rules of their own making. Since it was necessary to give as many people a chance as possible, the game was decided by the first person to reach seven or even five points. There was also the no-touch rule whereby even if one player was ahead on points he could still lose if he failed to make contact with a ferocious smash from his opponent, and the match would immediately be decided in that person's favor. They also worked out a method of getting away from the factory before clocking-off time. They drew lots to decide who would be the unlucky one to remain behind and get all their cards stamped at the correct time by the time clock. The ones who had escaped would go and see an afternoon movie, or spend the time playing baseball and other games in the grounds of the Hongan-ji temple, which was not far away. As they occupied half the day absorbed in the kind of games they had played at primary school, it was as if they had gone back years in time. The war and the compulsory factory labor were little more than a long holiday which seemed as if it would never end.

"There's this woman in the office in Number One workshop,

keeps staring every time she goes by. Reckon she must fancy me.''

"Do you know that creep Tanaka always has a dirty book under his arm when he gets on the streetcar? He wants the schoolgirls to get a good look at the picture on the cover.''

That was the sort of thing they talked about.

Shuji found life in the factory much more relaxed and pleasant than doing classwork at school, free from those gloomy feelings of inferiority which had filled his schooldays. However, with the fall of Saipan and the American landings on Tinian things changed, for Shuji and his friends were given clerical work to do. In Shuji's case, this consisted in investigating productivity in Number Two workshop. Although extremely easy work in itself, it also happened to be in some respects an unpleasant, even nerve-racking task. Four times a day they had to go around the workshop checking which of the noisily clattering lathes, milling cutters and shaping machines were not functioning properly because of some mechanical failure, and thus how many people were not actually working. This information was recorded on a sheet of paper and was meant to show the working capacity of the factory at particular moments, a form of productivity research that was not aimed at finding out if the workers were being idle or not, but merely how the efficiency in the use of the workshop varied from hour to hour. Not that the workers saw it in that light: they took it as a measure directed at themselves. As Shuji patrolled the shop floor with his clipboard, taking down the number of any defective machine, the occasional worker, idling away his time in the vicinity of his neighbor's machine, would shout at Shuji in a flustered, threatening voice:

"Careful there, schoolboy. That machine's working all right, you know. We wouldn't want any mistake about that, would we?''

It was perfectly clear that the workers looked on Shuji and his companion as spies set to keep watch over them, and Shuji found himself growing more and more reluctant to make these rounds of the shop floor. Each circuit took fifteen minutes, and another fifteen minutes was required to work out and fill in the efficiency data sheet. This was repeated four times a day, and after that there was nothing else to do. In addition, Shuji and the other person who worked with him had been given a room to themselves on the upper floor of the factory, where they were able to read or simply mess about exactly as they pleased. However, for the fainthearted Shuji these working conditions were simply too good, and he was unable to accept his good fortune but lived in a constant state of anxiety. The principal cause of this anxiety was the teacher who worked as their overseer, a little old man nicknamed "the Fright," who had the remarkable ability to appear always when he was least expected, inevitably at those moments when the two of them were doing absolutely nothing.

Ever since the school had been mobilized, the Fright had enthusiastically performed his self-appointed task of touring the factory to see how his boys were getting on. As he watched them working away, soaked in sweat, a great lump would come into his throat and he would say with tears in his eyes:

"Don't overdo it, lads. Don't injure yourselves. Sure you're all right?"

But if he found any of his boys merely chattering to some other slacker, he would lose his temper:

"Haven't you got anything to do? I hope you're not being idle, because you certainly look as if you are."

During his round, the Fright would always drop in once on Shuji and friend, although somehow or other he never managed to come when Shuji was doing his rounds or making up the productivity sheet, but always when he was having a rest after his brief labors. This happened so consistently it seemed almost deliberate.

"Haven't we got any work to do? We seem to have adequate leisure, don't we?"

"We've just finished making out the sheet, sir."

"Which means we've nothing else to do, does it? We're always sitting around like that doing damn all, are we?"

Eventually the two of them worked out a plan. They decided they would not make out the productivity sheet as soon as they had completed their circuit of the shop floor. Instead one of them would keep a constant watch from a chair by the window, waiting for the Fright to emerge from the dark interior of the warehouse. Then, when the small podgy figure finally started to turn his wandering, uncertain footsteps in their direction, the lookout would shout "Enemy attack!" and both would immediately get down to work, busily writing complex series of numbers on their sheets of paper. The zealous teacher would heave himself slowly up the staircase, enter, stare over their shoulders at the tables of figures he could make neither head nor tail of, and then breathe out in apparent satisfaction:

"You lads seem to be pretty busy these days. Don't overdo it now, all right?"

Meanwhile, Shuji's sister Aiko was working in an electronics factory near Hiroobashi in Azabu, along with the other girls from her school. They all wore khaki overalls and a scarf with the Japanese flag on it about their foreheads, and sat in lines at a long table making electric coils. The girls had been given a special room quite apart from the other women workers. The almost total silence that reigned over the room was an indication of how well these girls had been brought up; they worked away earnestly at their task with hardly a word of unnecessary conversation the whole time. Aiko Nire herself seemed twice as fastidious in this respect as the others, bending lower over her work than was necessary, only her fingers moving. The aggressively plain khaki overalls emphasized how thin she had become. Her face was strikingly haggard compared with what it had been. There was little color in her cheeks, and so dark and melancholy was the impression she gave that she appeared to be suffering from some kind of illness. As far as the girls in her class were concerned, her character was identical with her appearance. The only impression they had been able to form of her was of a silent, frigid person who kept very much to herself. There were two other girls who had been at the Toyo Eiwa Girls' School with her and were aware of what she had been like before, but they found it almost impossible to understand why she should suddenly have changed in this way as soon as she entered Seishin. How could it be that Ako, the genius of nicknames, the organizer of practical jokes that went beyond being a joke, the girl with the amazing facility for telling the most preposterous of stories with the most convincing of poker faces, that cheerful ball of energy, that arrogant Aiko Nire, should have changed beyond recognition into a gloomy, silent being, always withdrawn into herself?

"Ten minutes more," whispered one girl to her neighbor, who looked up at the electric clock on the wall and giggled.

"I wonder how high he'll bounce today?"

The girls' supervisor was a man of little more than thirty with excessively projecting cheekbones and eyes that also stuck out in a manner well beyond the human norm. He was unquestionably of a very serious disposition and obviously finding it a constant source of embarrassment to be in charge of these young girls of eminently marriageable age. It had turned him into something like a clockwork toy in his behavior, particularly when the girls paid their respects to him on the completion of the day's work, for then he would leap to his feet very much in the manner of a mechanical, bouncing toy. Because of this unusual hopping, bounding or bouncing, the nickname of "the Frog" was conferred on him behind his back. Each time he would bounce up from his chair, body quivering with nervous strain as he stood rigidly to attention and gave the girls a brisk salute. Being so tense, his arm would be bent at a very clumsy angle, his fingers all aflutter with the effort he was putting into this performance; and while assuming this unreal posture, he would repeat in the same mechanical tones the same wooden response:

"Well done; and carry on."

The thing the girls most enjoyed since being mobilized was this jumping up and down, the unique salute, and his military manner of address. Merely because they wanted to see him bounce some more they had adopted the same sort of formalities at lunchtime as well. The head girl, their representative, would say:

"May we go to lunch now, sir?"

Whereupon he would bounce up frenziedly into the air, an energetic leap combining the characteristics of both frog and grasshopper, flash out his tremendous salute, and gasp out his wooden refrain:

"Well done; and carry on."

The girls would control their smiles, assuming solemn expressions and holding their breath until they had filed outside, where they let it all out in laughs and grins and giggles and shoulder slapping.

"Today's bounce wasn't up to much."

"Yes, he seems a bit feeble these days. It's a very sad thing to see the Frog so tired. He must stop leaping about for a while."

At such moments Aiko hardly smiled at all.

The girls from Seishin ate the packed lunches they brought with them each day in the dining hall, though at the very beginning of their mobilization, lunch was provided by the factory. The manager had explained that if they brought their own rice, which could be much less than the ration they received, he could assure them that his kitchen staff would prepare a nutritious meal. On the first day, they tried this out and received a form of meat hash and rice that was very satisfactory. But this only happened once, for the next day something the very opposite of satisfactory was provided, a wretched meal consisting basically of *hijiki* (a kind of brown, tasteless algae) mixed with dried potato, and a mere smattering of actual rice. Although they had all eaten the factory food at first, people gradually started bringing their own lunchboxes until finally practically everyone did. This was a time when hardly anyone ate plain, unadulterated rice, normally boiling it up with something else, yet most of these girls ate pure rice at lunchtime which they had brought with them from home.

Naturally there were a few exceptions. One of these was a small, bespectacled girl called Chieko Arai who still persisted in eating the *hijiki* meal the factory dished out, even though she came from a family that lived in a house of almost breathtaking magnificence. People began to whisper that perhaps she was not all there in the head. Once she had stuffed down the factory meal, she would open a lunchbox, which contained enough food for a normal lunch, and start on that.

"I'm surprised you can eat all that. Wherever do you put it?"

"I have to eat a lot because I'm thin. You people aren't eating enough, I'm afraid," said Chieko Arai in all seriousness.

"In that case why don't you bring a bigger lunch from home? The stuff the factory doles out is disgusting, surely?"

"Not at all. It's very nice. The sliced potato is a bit tough, I'll admit. You know, it was all black today. Still, *hijiki* is really nice, much nicer than I thought it could be as a main food. After all, it's just a kind of seaweed. By the way, have you ever had any of that rice porridge they sell in those special shops? Our maid bought a bucketful of it recently. It's lovely if you eat it nice and hot. All thick and gooey. I could go on slurping it down forever."

Chieko certainly had an enormous appetite considering her size, which was very small, and she ate everything with indiscriminate joy. There was, for example, dried banana. This was black and hard and often distributed at the time, though most people tended to have no idea what to do with it. But Chieko had an endless craving for it and would dispatch any amount of it into the apparently bottomless pit of her bowels.

This day, as always, her voracity was a topic of discussion and laughter among the girls, though Chieko herself was not in the least ashamed of her superior appetite. She saw it as something on which she could openly pride herself.

"What would happen to you if you just had rations to live on, Chieko?"

"I'd be all right because I don't pick and choose like you. Look at the way you turn up your nose at that lovely banana. You're just not qualified to be a wartime woman at all."

"When the time comes when we've got to eat it, then I will. Still, when it gets like that and there's only a third of everything we have now, you'll be the first to starve to death, believe me."

"No I won't," said Chieko, who always remained serious during these discussions. "I've been thinking about that, don't you worry, and lately I've started on a diet."

This made everyone squeal with laughter, till the tears ran down their cheeks, although there was one person sitting in the corner who never laughed; she merely showed her teeth a little and then closed her lips again. In an attempt to cheer Aiko up one of the girls who had known her at her previous school said:

"None of you know this, but Aiko Nire used to be a tremendous eater. She would have beaten Chieko any day. She always used to go up for seconds three times at school meals."

They all expressed surprise, and looked in Aiko's direction. She, however, said nothing, smiling slightly in an embarrassed way. It was only the trace of a smile, causing but slight disturbance to her features; a sad smile, a lonely, melancholy smile, a smile she seemed to be putting on out of politeness only.

The mobilization of Aiko and Shuji had caused little real change in their lives, and certainly nothing on the scale that grown-ups might have imagined. By comparison, the drafting of Yonekuni was an event of magnitude, something that had every nerve in his body trembling. Here was the onset of something nightmarishly monstrous, the grim, menacing jaws of Destiny. Outwardly he gave the appearance of having stood up to the shock, and maintained a mysterious silence on the matter as if it meant nothing to him. Oshu advised him to apply immediately for officer training school, and even Chiyoko felt the need to express some words of genuine concern about her brother-in-law's health; but in response to all this Yonekuni simply allowed the same mysterious, slight smile to play about his lips and merely nodded and said nothing. He was posted rather eccentrically to the Chiba First Railway Regiment, since the draft system was extremely disorganized at the time, leaving almost immediately after he had paid his respects and said farewell to the people at Aoyama.

What Yonekuni had placed all his trust in, what he had secretly hoped would succor him in his hour of need, had turned out to be of no avail at all, and the fine thread of faith had snapped on his very first day. They were lined up on the parade square, and when the command "All sick men one pace forward" had rung out, Yonekuni had been one of those who edged furtively out of the ranks, even if a little behind the others. Standing before the medical officer, he had opened his mouth with firm resolution, first giving his illness as amyloid degeneration of the lungs, and then producing his desperate trump card of Progressive Spinal Muscular Atrophy.

"What? What did you say?"

"I was told at the university hospital I had Progressive Spinal Muscular Atrophy."

"Muscular atrophy? Where? Show me!"

Despite all his prayers and pleas to the powers of light and darkness, Yonekuni could only conclude that this doctor didn't even know the name of this most grave of diseases. After a nominal medical inspection the man had only revealed further depths of ignorance by howling at him in an unpleasantly uncouth voice:

"Not a damned sign of it. Nothing. No atrophy of your muscles, my man."

Thus in one fell moment the fate of Yonekuni Nire, who had lived in such terrible fear of his uncommon disease and of military service, was settled.

More misfortunes followed thick and fast. He failed to pass the officer cadet test, a rare achievement in those days, and was sent off to the continent of China that August, together with another six hundred comrades-in-arms, all privates second class like himself. They were going to Hengyang, which had only recently been occupied by the Eleventh Army.

The send-off from the station was an extremely unimpressive one. The bottom of the barrel had been scraped to find these reservists, and since they had neither rifles, helmets, nor even military boots but only crude leather-soled *tabi* socks, their only piece of equipment being the bamboo canteens hanging from their shoulders, they looked more like stragglers from a defeated army than bold heroes setting off for the front.

More small units were added all the way along the line on their railway journey west, until they made a grand total of about one thousand men. They traveled on through Korea, Manchuria and North China, taking the same route as Kumagoro had before them, swaying in the same kind of freight wagon. Over the endless cornfields of North China swarms of locusts flew, myriads of them forming weird, dark clouds in the sky. These were moving in the opposite direction to the train, which made their speed seem much greater than it was. They grew into one great swarm that literally darkened the sun, too enormous for the mind to grasp, and taking thirty minutes to pass. Yonekuni had read a translation of Pearl Buck's *The Good Earth* and also seen the film, and this swarm of locusts was just as awe-inspiring as the one described there. The sight symbolized the hugeness of the continent, its unknowable variety and complexity. His eyes half-closed, Yonekuni gazed up at the various strata of the thick cloud of insects as they flew endlessly past, his exhausted body swaying in the freight car, convinced that now he was done for, really done for.

At Hankow they were issued with helmets, rifles and leather boots for the first time and began to look a little more like soldiers at last. Then, properly accoutered and hoping to get their first decent night's sleep in their new barracks, they were woken in the middle of the night by a large-scale air attack by B-24s which seemed to have been deliberately waiting for their arrival. The ammunition dump was hit and a succession of thundering explosions continued from it until morning. A wild rumor also went around that gas bombs had exploded in the blaze, which had a disastrous effect on this rabble of mainly middle-aged reservists, who could only turn pale and tremble. Yonekuni crouched down among them, trying to stay still and small, and thinking desperately to himself:

"It's no good. I've had it. I'm going to catch it now. It's bound to happen. If I were back home I'd still have a few more years. But it's all over now." He had already muttered these words to himself on dozens of occasions since setting off from Chiba.

They went as far as Yuehchow by freight train, and from there they started to march. It was from this area that the crack troops of the Eleventh Army had begun their advance upon Changsha, Hengyang, Kweilin and Liuchow in May of that year. The main objectives of this operation were to occupy airfields that were being prepared for use by B-29s, and to open a land route between the South and Japan by attacking along the railway line, since sea transportation had become so difficult. But the real motive behind the mounting of this bold, large-scale campaign, despite all the odds against it working out, was probably the desire to produce news of a great victory at least here on the Chinese continent, since the story elsewhere was of defeat on all sides. Despite American control of the skies, the Eleventh Army pushed on through Changsha and Hengyang and kept on moving west. Since the prime task was the reopening of the railway, the Chiba First Railway Regiment set up headquarters at Hengyang, and it was there that Yonekuni's unit was headed.

As the army was still pushing ahead with its offensive, this was in theory a triumphal moving forward of reserves, but in practice, since the supply lines were overextended, it turned out to be a march of terrifying difficulty. The road forward from Yuehchow was one newly made by the military, and ran up and down along a ridge of hills where there were few trees and only a sparse covering of bushes and coarse grass. With rain falling every day the bare, yellowish earth was transformed into a morass. It was all one could do to avoid slipping, and even at the slow pace they went people kept losing their footing. Sometimes the mud came up to one's knees, a thick, clinging slime that held on to one's feet as if it were malevolently intent on not letting go. Vehicles found the going particularly hard, and Yonekuni and the others on foot overtook trucks and horse-drawn field guns stranded in the mud.

At first they marched only at night to avoid enemy air attacks, resting during the day in the shadows of the hills or in farmhouses and peasant huts, and setting out after dark. All about them was pitch-darkness and one could only blunder along half groping with one's hands, a whole night's march covering only four or five miles. These certainly far from robust soldiers, most of whom were in advanced middle age, soon began to look a little more than merely tired but patently exhausted, staggering half-asleep and soaked in the rain, uphill and downhill, step by slippery step, simply endeavoring not to lose sight of the person in front. Occasionally the stupefied Yonekuni would think he had seen something suspicious, and a terrible start would go through him at the thought that it must be the enemy, the guerrillas. But it always turned out to be a clump of trees.

The night marches were given up after a number of people had been left behind. During the march there would be short rest intervals, and in the darkness some would drop off to sleep; when the order to move on would be whispered back from the head of the column to the rear there would be those who did not hear it and were left sleeping there. Also it had been heavily overcast, when not actually raining, for the past few days, and though the sound of aircraft could be heard above the low cloud cover not one enemy plane had been seen, so it was decided to march by day. As they did so, they passed ample evidence of how much the Americans now controlled the skies, for piles of burned-out trucks lay overturned by the wayside.

Despite the fact that they were marching in daylight, they did not seem to make much more progress than they had at night. The constant mud clinging to their feet and the physical attrition through never having enough to eat meant that they moved only at the snail's pace of half a mile an hour. The food had been inadequate since the very first day they had set out. On leaving Hankow they had been given one dried codfish each, which was to constitute their whole ration of animal protein. They were ordered to eat it gradually, the head today, the breast tomorrow, and so on; but the soldiers were starving and most of them had eaten it all in one go. All that remained was dried *miso* and soy, and some rock salt which they had been sternly ordered to carry with them since it could be bartered for food on the way, the column only carrying a few days' supplies. After this was eaten up they would have to forage for themselves.

When they came across paddy fields, the exhausted soldiers would press forward with shouts of joy, indiscriminately tearing off the ears of rice with both hands, and the entire night was spent hulling rice into their steel helmets. The same thing happened if they passed a field of soybeans. They had one piece of rare good fortune when they discovered a great vat of rice wine fermenting in a farmhouse, and all of them managed to get drunk. But after a fortnight of this they were all obviously debilitated, and the number of soldiers who could not get up in the morning when the order to march was given gradually increased.

On the road to Hengyang was the town of Changsha, which they had all been looking forward to reaching. Changsha was a real town and they had all heard of it; there had to be something there. When they arrived, however, they found that U.S. planes had pounded it into a heap of rubble in which a few soldiers were drifting about in ungaitered boots. These were patients from the Changsha Field Hospital and they were wandering among the ruins looking for food.

"I've had it. I'm done for. I can't make it. I'll collapse before we get to Hengyang, I know I will. I'm bound to collapse," Yonekuni assured himself. The fact is that after they had passed Changsha his face had started to swell, though the problem was by no means restricted to him. One soldier, for example, during a rest day in a pleasant spot by a stream where they had stopped to recuperate, had been using the water to do his washing in since morning. Late that afternoon, however, one of his squad thought there was something funny about the way he was lying and tried to rouse him, only to see his head sink loosely back again. He was dead. No one knew when it had happened, but it was whispered that he had died from malnutrition. They all had the same swollen faces.

The only thing that maintained discipline under these conditions was the authority of a few NCOs, or rather the fear in which they were held. The officers themselves were not the real leaders, for the lieutenant in charge of transport was a product of higher education and he would never shout at the men; neither would the trainee medical officer. This was left to the four sergeants, who already had plenty of experience of combat on the continent and were typically seasoned regulars. They certainly had energy enough to beat up the exhausted old men under their command. The traditional strength of the Imperial Army had always depended on the fear induced by sergeants of this kind. It was they who had the fullest knowledge of war and it was undeniable that in all practical matters the inexperienced officers had to bow their heads to them. The reason their energy seemed inexhaustible was probably that they were attended by a small number of strong, cunning soldiers who managed to conjure up things like alcohol from somewhere on night camps, when provisions of any kind were supposed to be unobtainable, or even a chicken which they boiled up in their messtins. These sergeants had an almost religious conviction that defeat was unthinkable and that the Land of the Gods was indestructible; and in this spirit they goaded on their hungry, weary squads with howls and cries.

"Pull your stomachs in when you march! How do you expect to get anywhere in a state like that?"

This urging onward, however, had a contrary effect on Yonekuni; he felt that his already worn-out limbs were being further pounded to pieces by this verbal assault.

"It's no good. I've had it. Never make it. Fall down soon. Fall down any moment."

Yet he didn't fall down, but went on with his rifle digging deep into his shoulder, solely concerned with keeping up with the man in front of him. If you fell out you were bound to die. The Japanese Army had a few forts here and there, but the surrounding land was all enemy territory, although Yonekuni had not seen a single enemy soldier all the way along this road, nor, in fact, a single Chinese living here. The only exception was a peasant with a straw basket on his back, seen far off on the other side of a field and running away from them.

That night he was lucky enough to find a peasant hut to sleep in. He boiled up some green soybeans in his messtin, ate them, and then sucked a piece of dried *miso*. He had always had a liking for green soybeans, but the amount was so small that he felt doubtful they had actually entered his stomach, for he could feel them nowhere. In the past he had supped on rice mixed with barley and just a little something sprinkled on top to satisfy a certain belief of his, confident that he was thus developing the ability to survive under no matter what circumstances. But now he would have given anything for a bowl of the stuff.

In the past few days he had quite forgotten about something that had always been uppermost in his mind, the Progressive Spinal Muscular Atrophy from which he suffered, although it might be truer to say that rather than having been forgotten it had come to seem of no importance compared with the various other problems that now engaged his attention. Tonight, however, feeling safe under a genuine roof, he began to think about that illness of his again. He wondered what was happening to his back. With malnutrition and the weight of his rifle it seemed more than likely that the muscles would have really caved in.

"It's no good. I've had it. It's hopeless," he grumbled to himself, slowly taking off his boots. The soles were starting to peel right off. He shouldn't have put his feet out like that with his wet boots on to dry in front of the fire he'd made of straw. How could he possibly march a long way in boots like that?

He winced again as he took off his socks. From beneath each sock a soiled bandage appeared. He had discovered some large sores on his feet a few days ago, but the medical orderly wouldn't change the bandages for a minor injury of that kind. He might at least have let him have a bit of cotton wool to put in there. For a moment he recalled the surgery at home in Matsubara. He must have received treatment there on a number of occasions for slight injuries that most people would have ignored. First it was carefully washed in oxydol, then mercurochrome was spread on it and a little iodoform powder sprinkled over that, and finally a piece of gauze, so white your eyes would open wide. . . He looked pathetically at the mud-soaked sock he had just taken off. It was supposed to be made of thick, white, pure cotton, but now it was worn so thin that, although there were no holes in it yet, the beginnings of holes could be seen. Clearly he would not be able to rely on these socks much longer.

"Socks starting to fall to pieces. Be nothing left of them soon. Ah, it's hopeless. It's all over."

Next he had a look at the knees of his trousers. A hole had opened in each leg at the point where the top of his puttees rubbed against them, and his underwear was showing through.

"Trousers starting to fall to pieces as well. Can't possibly make it all the way to Hengyang like this. Never make it. Hopeless. I'm finished."

That night he dreamed fondly of the hospital at Matsubara, of the chicken coop that occupied a corner of the farm he had ruled over. Dozens of chickens were clucking peacefully, pecking at their feed. The turkeys were swelling out their feathers. Kumagoro was there, and then his face came nearer, a face heavily pockmarked just as it had been in the days at Aoyama, and he asked him very kindly which of the birds he would like to have. Yonekuni pointed to a fat, round hen and said that one would do. He would have that one, roasted to a turn. Kumagoro asked him if he would like a turkey. A turkey approached. It was inordinately plump, and it looked more like a pig. I'll have the pig, the pig, he was saying in a terrible hurry when he woke up to find himself lying on his bed of damp straw.

That morning one of the dreaded sergeants came around to wake up those who just would not get up. They included Yonekuni. The sergeant cast his eye swiftly over them and bawled:

"You load of crap! You've not even started fighting yet and look at the shape you're in!"

Immediately, however, his voice became gentle and low. This veteran also knew the advantages of the psychological approach:

"Look, men, just make it to Chuchow and there'll be a train. There'll be a train, get me? A train. Just one last effort, that's all."

Certainly there was a railroad of sorts at Chuchow, or at least bits of one in patches, though it was doubtful if it deserved this title at all. There was also something called a light engine, which was in fact little more than a jumped-up version of a handcar, and parts of the track were made of wood. Still, they did get packed into a train drawn by this contraption and were carried quite a distance in it. Then they came to a break in the line and had to get out and walk the rest of the way. For days they had not seen the sun, but only dull, black, lowering clouds from which a thin, cold rain fell ceaselessly. The dull roaring of engines above the clouds had become more frequent. They would all be enemy planes. Distant bursts of machine-gun fire could be heard, which gave a weird feeling in the pit of the stomach. The firing seemed to come from some way ahead, behind the mist of rain. Some railway station must have caught it.

Yonekuni walked on, soaked by the rain, staggering sometimes, treading on one railway sleeper after another.

"If there're another thousand sleepers, say. . . But can I last that long? No, it's hopeless. I'm finished. I'll never make it."

He constantly felt the same way and thought the same thoughts, always telling himself what he felt and thought, yet showing no real sign of collapsing, staring persistently with deep, sunken, glaring eyes at the back of the man ahead of him, the obsession of many years, his terrible illness, now totally forgotten as he trudged and staggered on, step by step, lifting heavy, dull, dead feet.

When a short halt was called and he sank down on the earth the drizzling rain felt cold on his skin. It had grown cold at night and in the early morning, too. He could clearly feel the change of season now beginning all over the great continent.

In the middle of October of that year, 1944, a great victory was announced, which gave the Japanese people a rare opportunity to exult after months of silence. According to Imperial Military Headquarters, the enemy task force that had been insolently making repeated landings on the Philippines, Okinawa, Amami Oshima and various places in Taiwan, had been caught by our own air force off the east coast of Taiwan and there subjected to an "annihilating attack." Of its aircraft carriers alone, thirteen had been sunk, and now the whole fleet was in flight. It was a "debacle" and a "rout," to use the vocabulary of the communiqué.

There was an old-fashioned radio in the main office of the Matsubara hospital next door to the Deputy's private office. The Deputy was aware that it was time for the news, and when he heard the

"Warship March" and "Tens of Thousands of the Enemy" he propelled his minute frame, now grown even more frail and thin, at great speed into the main office in that peculiarly stilted and jerky manner which had become more noticeable of late.

When he had finished listening to the announcement of this enormous air victory over the enemy fleet, he remained silent for a while, then turned to one of the office workers and said in tones of unprecedented solemnity:

"You see there, my boy, the fate of the Mongolian invaders."

"The what?"

"The Mongolian invaders. Back in the thirteenth century. The fate that awaits all those who attempt to defile our shores. Every single one of their ships sank beneath the waves, and there was not one soldier who returned to his native land. Do you think the Americans will still refuse to surrender now?"

"Well, I mean. . . ," the man mumbled, although he had certainly not been stinting in gleeful applause at the news of the famous victory. "I don't think they're quite on the point of surrender, not just yet. . ."

"But look here. They've lost thirteen carriers, which must surely mean their fleet has been annihilated, mustn't it? They're hardly in a position to attack now, are they? After all, if he doesn't have planes to look after him your American soldier is a pretty cowardly specimen. There should be little problem in getting Saipan and the other islands back. . . I'm an old man now, but I refuse to die until I've seen the day of victory. On victory day I shall put on an enormous celebration in the hospital. It will be a bit more of a show than the fiftieth anniversary, believe you me. You know, the important thing in life is the ability to see two or three years ahead. With this blow the American counterattack has been stopped in its tracks. Now you'll see, our Combined Fleet will set out on the attack again."

But the mysterious thing was that the American fleet, which was supposed to have been completely annihilated under these hammer-blows, made a foray into Leyte Gulf in the Philippines almost immediately afterward, and proceeded to force through landings on the islands of Suluan and Leyte. At the same time, of course, our fleet also went on the attack and, according to the newspapers, achieved "repeated glorious successes." This took the form of another fifteen aircraft carriers definitely sunk.

"You know, I must say the enemy seems to have an awful lot of carriers. This makes twenty-eight of them sunk if you include those destroyed off Taiwan. They must have just about run out of them, though, by now.''

''Well, I wouldn't be too sure about that. They do say it's a country with rich material resources.''

''No matter how rich in material resources it may be, after all it's twenty-eight carriers, you know. Twenty-eight. They can hardly have an endless supply of them. But still, all right, let's say they have a few more. Even so, eight-tenths of their navy at least must have been destroyed. And yet they still insist on making fresh landings, and that's where we'll have them because they won't be able to withdraw. We're seeing them at their last gasp. We can surround them both on land and from the sea and wipe them all out. They won't get away with it this time; we'll drive them into the sea. Just you wait and see. Now is the time for the entire Combined Fleet to set forth. It's the obvious tactic to use. Dr. Kiichiro would most certainly have given such an order.''

Unfortunately the Deputy was quite unaware (not surprisingly, since so were almost all his fellow citizens) that this very Combined Fleet had suffered such losses in the Sibuyan Sea in October that no hope of its being reformed existed. During this battle the super battleship *Musashi* had been sunk, as also had the one aircraft carrier that still remained of those that had taken part in the raid on Pearl Harbor, the *Zuikaku*, on which Tatsunori Shiroki had once served.

What the Deputy could never understand was why the Combined Fleet would not come out and sink all the enemy's convoys, and why the American Army was being allowed to consolidate more and more fresh landings. In place of the Combined Fleet the *kamikaze* special attack force was used, and it was announced that these planes had sunk nine enemy carriers; but still there was no end to the American offensives, and great numbers of their aircraft still seemed to flit about the skies much as they pleased. The Deputy began to find the question of how many carriers the enemy possessed an unpleasantly unnerving one, and ceased to produce the cheerful Kiichiro-type remarks he had formerly used. With reference to the *kamikaze* pilots, he said that they were ''incomparably loyal and courageous'' but did not proffer this time his customary advice to ''wait and see.''

In due course, the B-29 Superfortresses based on Saipan began to invade the airspace over Tokyo. At first they performed only high-altitude reconnaissance flights and dropped no bombs, but the sight of the glittering, silver-white machines flying high up in splendid formation and at high speed, though seemingly only drifting casually across the sky of the Imperial Capital, became available to onlookers on more and more days.

It would soon be winter, and the weather had changed. The sky was now so clear that one seemed to be able to see with absolute clarity far up to where the B-29s were gliding across, and it was easy to make out each large fuselage, the long, pointed wings and the four engines. Thin white vapor trailed behind the wings, and this soon congealed into brilliant lines of cloud.

The Deputy stood at the entrance to the air-raid shelter, half in curiosity and half in fear, and his eyes followed the progress of a flight of Superfortresses. His head was covered in a protective hood with a steel helmet perched on top, which made him look like a child with an oversized skull, wretched and yet also ludicrous. Flak from the anti-aircraft guns burst sporadically on all sides of the planes, but most of it was well wide of the mark, only creating a thin mist of black cloud, and the enemy aircraft continued to glide peacefully further and further away.

"Those are B-29s, are they?" murmured Hidekichi Katsumata, still in his original posture of scared astonishment. After a short pause he repeated the same remark for lack of anything else to say. This was, indeed, all he said, and he added no strikingly critical remarks concerning the Superfortresses. He stood watching the planes as they receded into the distant sky, and it was possible to see in his wrinkled face, which still retained, along with its glittering rimless spectacles, the condescending expression unchanged, considerable excitement, considerable, if imprecise, anxiety, and signs of something very close to admiration.

Chapter

6

The town of Matsumoto is some hundred and fifty miles west of Tokyo in the mountains of Nagano Prefecture. A very small streetcar used to run back and forth from the main railway station to the nearby hot spring of Asama. Along the route was a stop called Yokota, a place well known since days gone by as a post town plentifully provided with brothels, with a number of ordinary houses as well. If one went slightly south from this quarter, however, one arrived at Motomachi, the original town center. Here houses lined the road only, and once one turned off it there was nothing but an expanse of cultivated fields with the odd farm cottage here and there.

It was freezing cold and the occasional lights from the windows of the houses were blurred, seemingly absorbed into the chill, frosty night air. The snow that had fallen some days ago still lay frozen hard along the paths between the rice fields, and to the east the tall peaks of mountains were dressed in midwinter white. On the edge of a paddy field overlooked by these mountains, which were visible even at night from here, one house alone seemed to have fallen deep into slumber, with no light shining through the darkness. On approaching closer, however, a dim glow could be seen in the porch before the trellis front door, and by this light it was possible to make out the name "Miyazaki."

Someone approached the door from the side and called out into the darkness within, into which he seemed to be peering:

"Evening!"

"Who is it?" a voice immediately replied from inside. "Oh, Mr. Shinoda. Evening to you. How nice of you to come. Such a cold evening as it is. It's really very kind. How are you?"

There was something about that fairly high and rather slovenly voice that seemed familiar. It would certainly have been easily recognized by anyone of the Nire household, as would the face of the

651

plump woman who swiftly jerked the door open; the face had narrow eyes and slightly puffed eyelids, round, dimpled cheeks, and a youthful, cheerful charm about it that seemed to have been unaffected by the passage of the years. For this was, astonishingly, Momoko Nire, who had left Japan in 1938 and since then had not been in touch with a soul, not even the old couple at the Seiundo, so that nobody knew if she was alive or dead.

She had, unknown to anybody, returned to Japan late in 1943. Her husband had been running a textile factory in Shanghai with a friend of his, and the venture had been a great success, employing quite a few people. His decision to return with wife and child to Japan had not been inspired by any grasp of the deteriorating military situation, nor even by Momoko's longing for her home country, but because his parents were now very old and his one and only child, his daughter Sachie, was due to go to primary school in the coming year and he wanted her educated at a Japanese one. Having returned and set up home with his parents, he had started a workshop in Matsumoto which made oval briquettes for the military. This meant that he occasionally had to go up to Tokyo on business, but Momoko had never once accompanied him. She had no desire at all to go to Tokyo, home of the Nire family. There had been a period after she had been cut so openly by her mother outside the Mitsukoshi Department Store when her hatred for the House of Nire and all its works had been of an extraordinary intensity, so that she had something insulting to say about it every time she opened her mouth. But with the passage of time this also changed, and although she would never mention any of the members of the family, she would talk over and over again about people like Nanny Shimoda, the pockmarked Kumagoro, Billiken the newspaper reciter, the neurotic Senaga, and Toyobei the porter, even though her husband had heard all about them on many, many occasions before. For this reason Inosuke Miyazaki had always assumed she would make a beeline for the Seiundo as soon as they got back to Japan; but far from it, and now that they had settled in what was then still known as the Shinshu region she seemed to have made some stern resolve to repress that part of her emotional life. She seemed to feel that the Momoko of the past was dead, and that she had started a new life as a different woman. It was all very well to talk with affection about the past when it was far away, but now she was back in Japan she had no intention of letting it become entangled with the present again.

Despite the simplicity of this resolve, it was clearly based on a confused and contradictory state of mind. Take the case of Mr. Shinoda who was now present in the house: he was a man who lived in town and had been of some service to Miyazaki when he had been starting up his workshop in Matsumoto, but around the time of the First World War he had been living in Aoyama, not all that far from the Nire Hospital. When Momoko learned of this, she showed an extraordinary excitement and surprised her husband by announcing in a tone of voice full of something close to pride that she was a daughter of that very hospital. Of course this might have been from mere impulse, reflecting little of what was going on in her mind, perhaps even the very opposite.

"Now, do come in, Mr. Shinoda. I'm afraid my husband is having his bath at the moment but he'll soon be out. . . Yes, the old people have already gone to bed . . . Sachie as well. Ever since she got into the habit of sleeping with them, well, she's started going to bed early at night, almost as soon as she's finished her supper."

Momoko cheerfully invited Shinoda to sit down at the *kotatsu*, and he tucked his legs inside to make them nice and warm. She then brought the tea things and a plate piled high with various dried pickles.

"Do try some of these pickles. It's the first time I've tried my hand at making this local kind and people say they're really not too bad."

Shinoda speared a piece with an orange stick and transferred it to his mouth, and when Momoko had followed suit and her plump cheeks were bulging with the delicacy, he produced the appropriate compliment:

"Well, very nice indeed. Just can't believe this is your first try at it; can't believe it, that I can't."

He then turned his attention to the thick black curtain draped across the window, totally concealing it.

"I'll say this, Missus, you've got your air-raid precautions done just about perfect, that you have."

"Everyone teases me about it. Still, once I get a thing into my head I'm such a worrier I have to do it. There's a crack in those wooden shutters, you see. That's why I've done it like that. Bit exaggerated, I admit. . ."

"Well, they're having a bad time of it with the air raids in Tokyo, but I reckon we should be all right here in Matsumoto."

"Still, they do say those B-29s have a tremendous range, don't they? It really makes my husband mad. He keeps on sitting there wondering when the siren's going to go and wanting to get it over with. They're bound to come sometime, I tell him, and that they certainly are. I get very worried about it. Must be my age, I suppose— worrying like that.''

"Now then, now then, you're still young, Missus, still young.''

Momoko seemed not at all displeased by crude compliment-paying of this kind. Her skin was still lustrous, and although there were a number of small wrinkles about her eyes she certainly looked four, perhaps even five, and at bad times at least three years younger than her age. Momoko was very proud of this, which was why she liked to refer to her advanced years on almost any occasion.

She now produced some *yokan*, a very sweet kind of thick jelly made out of beans, which was a great luxury at the time although her husband was able to get hold of it because of the military connection he had through his work. She cut the long object into generously thick slivers and urged it on her guest, beginning a conversation that led by way of gradual steps and progressions to talk about the Aoyama neighborhood. It began some distance away at the Meiji Shrine, moved slowly over the bridge at Ondenbashi, and eventually ended up at the main road near her old home.

"Do you remember the noodle shop that used to be on the corner there, the Masudaya?''

"Now, was there a noodle shop there? It's all a pretty long time ago. . .''

"Well, if you walked along the narrow street from there you passed a stationer's called the Seiundo. . .''

"Can't say I do. Of course, it's all. . .''

"You know. There was a ricksha company next door at that time.''

This was the stage the conversation had reached when her husband turned up at the table fresh from his bath to join them, but Momoko wouldn't let things drop until she had finally talked Shinoda into praising the former glories of the Nire Hospital.

"Of course we used to walk pretty quick past the mental hospital, I can tell you that. You looked at it from the cemetery and you saw this brick building with iron bars all over the windows, and there was this pale-faced woman beckoning at you from behind the bars, telling you to come in. Come on in, come on, she'd say. One of the wards it would have been. Used to really put the wind up us, I can tell you.''

Momoko in turn began talking about the woman locked up in a cell who spent all her time making bank notes of five, ten and even a hundred yen in value, all done by hand with a writing brush, the work of Satsuki Shimada who guaranteed their validity in all the countries of the world; and of Momoko's own frustration on finding that one couldn't buy anything with them even at the night stalls in the temple grounds. She trotted all this out at a breathless pace, often folding up like a jackknife with mirth and giggling like a little girl.

Despite this vivaciousness, after Shinoda had talked to her husband for a while about the small matter of business on which he had come and then gone home, Momoko sat gloomily silent and vacant, huddled up in the *kotatsu* for a long time, not even bothering to clear away the tea things.

It was not unusual for Inosuke Miyazaki to be given glimpses of what appeared to be some mental suffering on the part of his wife, so as he sat there, sweating in front from the heat of the *kotatsu* and feeling the night air chill on his back, he said to her:

"Why don't you make up your mind to go to Tokyo? There's Morita at Shakujii who'd be only too glad to put you up. If you don't want to do that, then you could at least write a letter to the Seiundo. You spend all this time brooding here by yourself, and yet just think how pleased they'd be to get a letter from you. I've got no right to say this perhaps, but the fact is that Nanny Shimoda and the old couple at the Seiundo can't be all that. . ."

Momoko shook her whole body energetically in a gesture of dissent. This was enough to put an abrupt end to her husband's flow of words. She bit her lip and stared fixedly ahead. In the past those large, fake-looking tears would have begun to roll out of her small eyes and down her cheeks at this stage, but this time she did not cry. Perhaps one of the results of living six years abroad was that she had learned how to control her tear ducts. However, her friendly face was now distorted with emotion, and she fully looked her nearly forty years. She burst out:

"I'm a bad woman. I'm no good. I'm evil. And yet as long as I keep away from the Nire Hospital then I can manage to get by as someone quite normal, someone who's accepted. I do my best for you and Sachie, don't I? I'm a good wife, I'm a good mother, aren't I? I like to remember about the Nire Hospital because it's got nothing to do with my real life now. It's a world that disappeared years ago, just like a fairy story. There's a girl in that story called Momoko Nire who used to love going shopping and to the cinema and. . . But now I'm Momoko Miyazaki and I've got nothing to do with the Nire family because they just threw me away like a pair of old sandals. All right, I know I wasn't blameless. I know I did wrong. It's because I keep myself shut away here that I can still go on living like a human being. Anyway, as far as the old couple at the Seiundo are concerned I'm just someone who died years ago.''

"Come on, there's no need to think like that. All right, you've got nothing to do with the Nire Hospital, but I can't see how that stops you seeing the Seiundo couple."

"But it's been such years since then. Nanny Shimoda will have grown really old, and those two at the Seiundo will be pretty old, too. And then . . . leaving Japan like that as if I were running away. . . I'd be like Taro Urashima coming back from the sea after hundreds of years with everything changed. I'd go visiting them like a ghost. And then suppose I found that none of them were alive any more, what would I do? I'd go mad, I tell you, go raving mad."

"Don't be stupid. All you can think about is the worst, like you're trying to punish yourself or something, lying there alone in bed worrying and tormenting yourself. They'll be all right. Nanny Shimoda will be very old, so there's always that possibility, I admit, but the old pair at the Seiundo are bound to be alive and well, don't you worry. You're always telling me how they've never had a day's illness in their lives."

"But suppose I do go to the Seiundo," she said, raising her face so that the dim light from the lamp fell full on it, showing dark circles about her eyes. She spoke in a high-pitched squeak like a fretful child. "What am I supposed to talk to them about? We're hardly going to talk about the good old days all the time, are we? They'll talk about all that's happened since I've been away, and it will just release all this poison that's been building up inside me over the years. I'm a hapless, unlucky woman. Always have been since the day I was born. Because of you and Sachie I'm able to live as if I wasn't, looking as if perhaps I was made to be happy. But how can someone like you hope to understand the feelings of a woman who's abandoned her own child? When I think how much Satoru must hate me—bound to hate me, I know it. That's what people will talk about . . . how he was brought up and that sort of thing. And I won't listen to it. I can't. I'm not that sort of person. I've got no right to listen to it, anyway. And I just couldn't put up with it. Couldn't stand it. I know I couldn't.''

Her eyes at last began to glisten and tears started to seep out, suggesting there might well be an overflow, but she strained her eyes to stop this happening, gave her nose a good blow, and just about managed to hold back the powerful emotions that had seemed on the point of overwhelming her.

''I wonder how they're all getting on, though, with those air raids every day. I really hate what the House of Nire stands for, but I don't have only bad feelings toward the people in it. Mistress Ai will be a big girl now. Then there's little Shuji. . . Still, there're plenty of trees in Aoyama and Matsubara's well in the suburbs, so it must be relatively safe. . . Mistress Ai was such a nice girl, really kind and gentle. Very rare thing, very special really. She's just about reaching an age when they'll be thinking of her getting married. But I don't want to see her. It would only make me miserable. After all, she's the same age as Satoru.''

In January the night air in Shinshu is inordinately cold. The whole room, except for the space inside the *kotatsu*, was full of still, cold air, and the lintel and ceiling seemed to be creaking and groaning with the pressure of it, for they were made of very ancient wood.

''Well, better start thinking of getting to bed, I suppose,'' said her husband in a tired voice.

Momoko nodded gloomily, but before she rose listlessly from the *kotatsu* she indulged in the following tragic soliloquy:

''So I'll go on living here quietly, and no one will know. And I'll grow old and die, and no one will know. If by some chance I should ever meet Mistress Ai or little Shuji, although it couldn't possibly happen, I'm sure it would send me into a dreadful quiver all over and I'd faint there and then, I'm sure I would. All I can do is pray that they're still all right at the Seiundo; just sit here praying. That is the fate I was born for, after all.''

What Momoko did not even begin to imagine was that her child by her former husband, Satoru, was no longer alive. In the summer of the previous year he had died in hospital of miliary tuberculosis. Another thing that would not have occurred to her was that at that very moment Shuji, whom she had just been talking about, should

657

have been staying on his own in a room at the Asama hot spring, only a fifteen-minute streetcar ride from where she was.

Exams for entry into higher schools that year had been brought forward to the end of January. The first stage of this exam depended on confidential school reports, but the second stage was to consist of a written test and an essay, although since the examinees had all been mobilized and had no school tuition it was officially stated that the questions would be such that "even those who have performed no studies should be capable of answering them." Obviously this was a logical impossibility, so Shuji had been sent away to Shinshu, for the first time in his life, in order to cram for the written part, and now he was huddled over a *kotatsu* in a hotel room in Asama with a volume of mathematical formulas in front of him that aroused little but feelings of alienation.

Toward the end of last year, the life of the mobilized students had gradually become one of almost dissolute idleness, with constant interruptions imposed by the dull blare of sirens announcing air raids. The production machines began to be evacuated outside Tokyo, and the majority of the students became no more than surplus personnel. Just a short while before that air battle off Taiwan which had so roused Hidekichi Katsumata, Shuji had been set to work on a lathe, and just like the old Deputy his breast had been powerfully stirred by the news announced over the loudspeaker that huge numbers of enemy aircraft carriers had been sunk, and he had handled the bite of his machine in a dazed reverie of pride. Now, however, there were three students to each lathe, and, to make matters worse, the supply of parts and raw material appeared to have virtually dried up. Occasionally they were sent out to bring in material, and that would mean clinging desperately to metal bars piled on a truck as it drove through the icy wind, but when the task was over there was nothing to do but loaf about in some corner of the factory.

Shuji still sometimes joined the group that pushed off from the factory at lunchtime and went to the cinema and other entertainments. Occasionally they would go to areas where the buildings had been evacuated to make fire lanes, and helped pull them down, although no one had invited them to do so. As one two-storied building crashed down with a solid roar the air-raid warden, on whose rope they had been helpfully pulling, wiped the sweat from his forehead and asked them pleasantly which factory they were working at.

"Omori, sir."

"Power cut today, is there?"

"Yes, sir. We're bored with nothing to do so we thought we'd come along here and give a hand."

"Did you, now," he replied, nodding in obvious satisfaction and clapping the nearest student on the shoulder. "I'll tell you what. As long as we've got young fellows like you, Japan's not going to lose. What about it then, eh?"

The people who had been evacuated from these houses were selling the household items they couldn't take with them at the side of the road. The boys acquired a number of empty *sake* bottles and enjoyed themselves for a while throwing stones at them from a distance. It was the act of destruction that they particularly enjoyed, whether it involved the dull crash of houses being torn down or the clear, dry, splintering sound of glass breaking. Pointless activities like this enabled Shuji to lose himself among the other members of the group, and at such times he was released from his normal gloom, feeling a quite uncharacteristic ability to breathe freely and easily. To what extent this was actual freedom is, of course, doubtful, but there could be no doubt they were leading a life far removed from that order and regularity, those rules and laws, which in normal times would have governed the lives of these fifth-grade schoolboys.

Whenever they heard that some part of Tokyo had been particularly badly bombed, they would go off to see the sights, which were nearly always remarkably similar. There would be piles of ashes and cinders and a trickle of water from broken pipes. Telegraph poles would be charred and fallen, the wires lying tangled all over the ground like spider's webs. It was the same uniformity the insides of human beings have when exposed, no matter how different people may all look on the surface.

Shuji would feel a powerful hatred for the enemy planes that had done this, yet he also experienced an incomprehensible sense of pleasure as he gazed at the spacious landscape the bombs had revealed. He was thinking how everything looked the same when it had been burned up like that, and how death made all creatures equal no matter how they might have lived. He could sense the approach of his own death, smell it in the world about him. It was something quite close at hand, advancing to claim him. He kicked the scorched earth with the toe of his shoe and became aware that the expression on his face had become cheerful now; that the shadows had lifted from it in a way they had not done for years, not since the days in his childhood when he had played at will in the mountains of Hakone with his sister and cousin.

At the end of the afternoon, Shuji and his companions would return to the factory to clock off and then start out on their homeward journey, looking like true warriors of the industrial front. A few of them changed back into their school uniforms, but the majority still wore the khaki jackets they had been given as working overalls, and it was fashionable to have more oil splattered over them than could possibly have been necessary in order to look properly squalid. Among them were some with a large *A* or *O* done in paint on their chests, which identified their blood group. When they swarmed onto the crowded train the other passengers drew back to avoid these oily, smelly objects, and this gave them a pleasant thrill as well. They talked to one another in loud voices, insolently ignoring everyone about them.

"We really bought it after you slobs cleared out. Got stuck with all the work. Piles of it."

"Sorry, lads. No hard feelings. We'll do yours for you tomorrow."

"Had to change the position of three of the damn lathes."

"Those four-foot cutting lathes, too. Falling to bits they are. Can't do a damn thing with them."

"Some of those bastards in Number One gave Kusama and a couple of the boys a bit of a shove around and are talking real big. Reckon we ought to get them to a nice quiet place and work them over a bit."

These loud-mouthed topics would then give place to a quieter discussion of the entrance exams that would soon be upon them. Going on to a higher school only meant a change of factory, as they well knew, but the passionate yearning they had long experienced for those marvelous grubby caps with the white line in them was still a real part of their lives, and in that sense, in that sense only perhaps, they could still be considered schoolboys.

Shuji left his friends at Shibuya and took the subway to Jingu-mae, and walked home from there. The road home was a dark one through trees, and night was coming on. The rare passerby would be imposingly dressed for emergencies with a protective hood over the head. Occasionally a dog could be heard barking far away, but no answering bark came back. Most pet dogs had been abandoned or killed. The night now fast descending over the capital, already sorely scarred in places, seemed peculiarly thick and deep. It was how the night must have been in ancient days, in really primitive times. Shuji listened to the unpleasantly loud sound made by his shoes as he walked in a strangely hushed and reverential frame of mind that accorded with the atmosphere about him. He passed the large house that had achieved a certain fame all those years ago when the old lady living there had provided tea for the soldiers of the Third Regiment on their return from training. That had still been an easy time, when the "home front" had meant being well away from the actual fighting. Everything he had experienced then had been quite innocent, like a game: the contribution of his beloved tops to the war effort, the donations of money, and even the air-raid practices. But perhaps the situation now, with the landing of American forces at Lingayen in the Philippines, the increasing severity of the bombing raids on the Japanese mainland, and his days spent going back and forth to the factory, might take on a similar aspect in his memory later on and seem to have been a time of childish indolence and ease.

Shuji started breathing deeply through his nose, breathing the cold night air of January 1945. He felt he'd had a premonition of some scent in the air, the odor of death no doubt, though death to him was merely an idea, a pure fantasy which seemed to him a glorious yet simple way of solving everything. There was, of course, no chance of his grasping the nature of his illusion, because it was a physical misapprehension only, the only way a weak, cowardly person of few years and less experience could respond to the fact that finally war was being brought home to him. Some form of war had been going on continuously ever since he was a small child, yet he lacked the ability to think what war might be and in what way he was affected by it, or to imagine that something called peace might actually exist in the world.

Shuji had never once considered the possibility that Japan could be defeated, even though the war situation made it quite clear that this was more than a possibility. Nor did he think in terms of an eventual victory over the United States either. All he imagined was that the Americans would attempt to land in Japan and he would have to fight against them, and the outcome of this "last decisive battle" (although it hadn't yet come to be referred to in this way) was one that did not personally concern him, for what it would mean would be destruction on the grandest possible scale, a wild, confused holocaust making no distinction between friend or foe, a huge celebration of death, a festival in which he would be one of the slain. When Shuji thought like this, believing what he thought, he found that his mind became free of any sort of anxiety or despair, because he was not going to die alone but would be taking part in a larger death, a holy death that would descend equally on all things.

All his thoughts and actions had come to be ruled by this point of view. When, for example, he slipped out of the factory and went to the cinema (one aspect of the city in the grip of air-raid terror was the surprising number of people wandering about with time to spare and nowhere to go), he acted with a bold confidence and casual indifference that the former Shuji could never have attained.

One day he inspected the cinema ads in the newspaper and set out that morning for what used to be a flourishing part of the entertainment district of Shibuya, although there was no trace of any such atmosphere remaining. The cinema he had noted in the newspaper was in a particularly bad state of disrepair, and it was difficult to believe it was actually open for business. However, it had a battered billboard outside, and there was a girl sitting alone in the tiny ticket office. The walls inside were cracked and crumbling, the plaster showing through, and the aisles were filled with empty cans. He went upstairs to the circle seats and found there was nobody there but himself, though there was still some time to go before the show began. The seats were worn and frayed and in most cases the springs and stuffing had broken through. He began to have doubts whether there really would be a film show in a place like this, so he looked over the rail into the auditorium below and noticed that there were in fact a few people sitting here and there. Still, this desolation seemed to please him rather than otherwise, and as he gazed up at the one light that was on in the ceiling he lost himself in a fantasy more real than the world around him. He was thinking how well this ruin of a building with its strangely fictive character would serve for the final scenes of bloody carnage in a ferocious piece of street fighting; rifle barrels poking out of the windows, the echoing whine of ricocheting bullets, and dry flakes of plaster falling from the ceiling. The stench of cordite fumes would fill the hall, suppurating blood would form dull pools, and bodies, suddenly reduced to mere dead flesh, would crumple and fall with heavy, reverberating thuds. . .

He remained absorbed in this fantasy until at last the sluggish performance bell rang to usher in a very old period movie.

Shuji hunched his shoulders in the cold and whispered to himself that he had to stay alive until that time came. He was certainly not going to throw his life away in any pointless death.

At night he used to sleep with his puttees, steel helmet, and canvas satchel with emergency rations and first-aid kit inside next to his pillow, and this gave him the kind of satisfaction he'd had at infants' school when he was looking forward to a picnic on the following day. He had begun to feel slightly disappointed when the air-raid siren didn't sound at night, although since the final weeks of the previous year the Superfortresses tended to come over every night, not just once but on a number of occasions, a single plane each time, as if they were merely trying to make a nuisance of themselves. At first Shuji used to get up when the siren went and dress, wind on his puttees, and wait in readiness, but when the massive, spectacular raid he had imagined did not occur, he would lose interest and change back into his night clothes. When the sound of anti-aircraft fire came closer he would lean out of the window and look up at the night sky. The thin shafts of the searchlights wandered nervously about the sky looking for the solitary plane, and he felt he was hardly likely to die in a trivial air raid of that kind.

So he would crawl back into bed again, for once untroubled by the insomnia that had plagued him since he was a small boy right up until this eighteenth year of his life. Now he would fall strangely and swiftly into a deep sleep, a sleep of such sweetness, of such blessed profundity, as he had never experienced before.

That was more or less what daily life had been in Tokyo, until he was obliged to go to Matsumoto and stay there a few days to take the local entrance exam. Shuji had never been taken on any kind of journey by his parents or his elder brother, and a trip of this distance was the first piece of real travel he had performed in his life. He looked out of the train window at the gentle slopes of Mt. Yatsugatake and the frozen, leaden waters of Lake Suwa with a mixture of slight interest and vague indifference, but once they had passed Shiojiri and the train had slowed down he could see, far off to the left, the mountainous vanguard of the Japan Alps lightly covered with snow. Through the reddish branches of feather columbine, the hazy, bluish white range looked very beautiful. And yet, rising clearly beyond, could be glimpsed a great palace of rock and snow, solid and majestic in a manner that beggared description, and that was Mt. Hotaka. Another peak was quite covered with snow, Mt. Norikuradake, a rather feminine shape that glittered with a strong white purity. The train creaked and rattled, giving off puffs of black smoke as it traveled over the wide valley where snow remained here and there in patches. From the right-hand window gentler slopes could be seen, until finally a ragged, rocky shape appeared, known locally as "the King's Nose," and the train had arrived at Matsumoto, which looked like the small, secluded country town it was.

A streetcar line ran straight as a die from in front of the station, past the backs of houses that looked as if they had been stained with soot, and an almost ludicrously small streetcar arrived, bound for the Asama hot spring. Tetsukichi had gone to the trouble of reserving his son a room there, yet the only parting advice he gave the boy about his exams was the platitudinous remark that he'd be able to answer all the questions so long as he didn't panic.

When Shuji got off the streetcar the air was bitterly cold, so cold it seemed to pierce the lobes of his ears. And yet it was limpid and still, as remote as possible from the factory noise and air-raid alarms of Tokyo. In the already fading light the linked peaks of the Alps were solid and harsh, all ranged there in the early dusk like a huge folding screen. But as he looked at them they changed, for the light withdrew across the sky and the now purplish mountains were suddenly deprived of solidity and depth, taking on instead the two-dimensional quality of a painting.

On arriving at his inn he noticed a number of small children milling up and down the corridor. They were evacuees from Tokyo, as he soon discovered. The day's journey to an unknown part of the world, a quite new experience for him, had made Shuji feel sentimental, so when supper was over he took a packet of biscuits out of his case and went to visit the primary-school children. They were sitting in twos and threes in a cramped room, not making the kind of rumpus one would expect from children of that age, but listless and apathetic, some clumsily darning socks, others lying on their stomachs absorbed in letters that must have been from home, or merely sitting there with mouths slightly open watching what the other children were doing. They showed not a trace of life or energy. It looked much like a concentration camp. There was one child who appeared to be messing about in a corner, but he turned out to be searching with great seriousness in the seams of his shirt. Perhaps he had lice. When Shuji produced his packet of biscuits, the children seemed unwilling at first to put out their hands for them, but once one of them had done so the packet was soon empty.

In the middle of the room was a *shogi* board, made by hand out of a sheet of cardboard. The pieces—thin, handmade ones as well—were scattered about on it.

"Anyone want a game?" asked Shuji, but nobody showed much enthusiasm, each child suggesting someone else might want to, until after a few minutes of indecision the one who was supposed to be best at the game was picked on. Thus a sickly-looking child sat down facing the board as Shuji's opponent.

Shuji had learned how to play *shogi* soon after entering primary school, taught in a rough-and-ready fashion by the same intern who had instructed him in the art of writing the character "*kotobuki*," and when Nanny Shimoda has seen him at the board she had beamed all over her face, rejoicing in one more instance of his being a chip off the old block, for, as she had pointed out, the great doctor himself had reached second grade at *shogi* and was famous for his ability to defeat the expert who came to teach him. Unlike his famous grandfather, Shuji did not employ the master ruse of moving two pieces at the same time, but when he played the game in a corner of the factory he had won the reputation among the students and workers of being reasonably good.

This sickly-looking evacuee, however, turned out to be amazingly good at *shogi*, and both the games Shuji played he lost. The other children had gathered round and watched with passionate interest, and for the very first time he saw them laugh and smile as if they were happy. These simple children could have had very few pleasures living apart from their parents like this. During the time he spent with them Shuji was conscious of how grown-up he was himself, almost a real adult; yet he also felt an embarrassment at being there, a vague yet tangible sense of shame. He reflected that if he was lucky enough to pass his entrance exams, a new, quite different world might be waiting for him, though perhaps it would only mean leading the same kind of life at a different factory.

The written exam was held in the Matsumoto Higher School, an old-fashioned building surrounded by Himalayan cedars. During the break he went out into the school playground and watched three or four pupils playing football in a corner of the playing field. The sky was blue but it was bitterly cold. One of these pupils, the goalkeeper, was properly dressed in soccer kit and was dripping with sweat as he kept hurling himself at the ball. The other players were taking it in turns to shoot at the goal, although one of them still had his cape on, which made him look like a large crow flapping about, and was shod in *geta* instead of football boots, with long hair that came down to his shoulders. It was in many ways an extraordinary sight, on this almost deserted playing field, with the buildings of the Commercial College in the background all painted over with an uneven, jet-black camouflage design. It became even more extraordinary if one reflected that most of the Matsumoto students would have been mobilized for industrial work, so the presence of this small, eccentric-looking group was symbolic of an ease and leisure in life that had become impossible now, a scene that belonged to some other age and seemed a hallucination in this present one. To one side of the playing field was a student dormitory, but most of the windows were closed and shuttered. At two or three of the windows, however, bedding had been put on the sills to air in the sun, which indicated that some students were still there, even if only a very few.

The following day it snowed from morning without any intermission, and since Shuji had no exams that day he stayed in his room, dreaming vaguely over the *kotatsu*, although his physical sensations seemed very acute. He watched the snowflakes fall ceaselessly from the gray sky. All about was quiet and he felt he had been shut away from reality, the war being something that was going on in a distant country. In the evening the snow stopped, which made the silence seem only greater as the Matsumoto Plain lay enclosed in a deep, white sleep, all movement stilled. Yet this silence had a depth and weight that made it curiously real, or else it seemed like an illusion with more truth to it than reality itself had.

There was only an oral examination and a physical inspection the next day, so Shuji's exams had come to an end. But he decided to put off his return to Tokyo for twenty-four hours. Ever since his first sight of the Japan Alps he had felt an unusual attraction, and although they could obviously not be climbed at this time of year he still wanted to get a little closer to the heart of them, and he thought he could do that by having a look at the old post station of Shimashima, the gateway to the higher mountains.

He took the electric railway from Matsumoto and got off at the terminus. He then walked to the old post station up along a rural road covered with the snow of two days ago, with the sound of the water of the Azusa River in his ears. There were fields of mulberry trees with their branches bound up, farmhouses with thatched roofs, and he met villagers walking slowly along with firewood on their backs.

When he stopped to look behind him he saw that the eastern mountains beyond the Utsukushigahara Plateau were silver as they reflected the winter sun. The feeling that he was in the depths of the natural world untouched by the faintest shadow of the war, the sensation that though his footsteps on the snow-covered road were muffled they were in some way meaningful—all this was a new experience for Shuji and he was surprised by the vivid sense of reality it seemed to give him.

He reached the quiet, deserted post station and then went further up, following the river. After he had passed a small village called Inakoki, the blue sky started to cloud over, and the landscape around him became increasingly severe. He had now left the Azusa River— he could see its dark water flowing below—and the mountains on both sides seemed to lean over him. The road was frozen in patches now, and he slipped at times.

Then specks of white started to fall. It was snowing. The snowflakes fell slantingly, driven onward by the wind that swept along the river, blowing full into Shuji's face. He hesitated to go any further up. The main thing now was to find somewhere to shelter from the snow. There was a path leading off from the road where it crossed a bridge, which passed below the overhanging edge of a cliff dense with trees. That seemed a likely place, so Shuji set off toward it. He was lucky enough to find a small cave in the side of the cliff which seemed to have been made just for him. A number of thin icicles hung from the roof near the entrance, and on the damp surface of the rock were bands of some kind of ore jutting out. Shuji crouched inside and waited for the snow to stop. It was being blown sideways now by the wind, sometimes even swirling up again to the sky, yet always falling silently in the end. There was the danger of its turning into a genuine snowstorm, but he remembered how clear the sky had been that morning and decided to wait a little and see how things turned out. He had brought a lunchbox with him and he opened it, but when he took off his glove to use his chopsticks his fingers were immediately numbed by the cold, and he had to keep blowing on them as he ate.

Despite the apparent darkness inside the cave he came to realize that it did have a special light of its own, perhaps caused by the reflections from the snow outside. The icicles of differing lengths at the entrance gave off a special shining as well, a brilliant green or bluish light, each one different. But the main thing was the cold, the terrible

667

cold that pierced his cheeks and the backs of his hands, a cruel yet clean cold. Once he had quickly disposed of his lunch he could only sit still and cower, and he began to feel genuine fear, something close to awe. It was a fear he had never experienced in Tokyo despite the fact that his life was threatened daily in a much more obvious way by the air raids. In the thin, bluish light inside the cave, in the cold which almost hurt, the snow swirling outside, there came a strange rebirth of instinctive feelings within him. In that moment at least, his own life had become precious to him again.

Before long the snow ended as suddenly as it had begun; blue patches of sky appeared, and he walked back over the thin covering of freshly fallen snow to the station at Shimashima. Thus his brief stay at Matsumoto came to an end.

Once he got on the train the next day he was inevitably drawn back into the reality of war from which he had been so far away for those few days. The train kept stopping and starting in the area of the Fujimi Plateau to avoid enemy aircraft, and far up in the sky the glittering shapes of a flight of B-29s could be seen heading in the direction of Tokyo. The passengers watched them in stony silence.

They arrived at Shinjuku at night, more than two hours late. The station was in near uproar, with swarms of people pushing and jostling each other. The central area around Nihonbashi and Ginza had been hit and the railway line had become impassable in a number of places, creating this huge crowd in which it was virtually impossible to move. Among them were people weighed down with baggage who were obviously victims of the air raids. There was one middle-aged man with a grubby face who was still wearing his steel helmet, but in his hollow eyes glittered a vitality that seemed very close to joy.

"I've lost everything," he shouted, staring around at the people about him. "Everything's gone up in flames, the whole lot. Nothing to worry about now, though. I can fight and not need to bother myself about anything. And so can we all, now, can't we?"

He caught hold of a working man who was just squeezing past him:

"Shake hands, friend. I've never felt so relieved in all my life."

A crowded train entered the station, and as the swarms of people suddenly started to move the cries of the man were lost, although he was still shouting about something.

As he was mauled about in the ruck of people, Shuji called to mind, with a sentimentality appropriate to his years, the grand peaks of the Alps, the rarefied purity of the air, and that small cave full of pale, bluish light. The images suggested another way of life, a new style of existence, a different form of thought such as he had never considered up to this moment. If only he could manage to pass the exam, and then spend some time in that schoolhouse surrounded by Himalayan cedars. . . He found himself actually hoping to pass the exam, a natural enough sentiment but one he had never felt before, not when he had set off for Matsumoto nor at any time during the exams. It had all been a matter of indifference to him, as if it concerned someone else. But now he was genuinely praying for success.

A week passed, however, and the hoped-for news did not arrive. Once he understood he had failed he experienced a normal sense of disappointment and depression, but he recovered with a speed that would have been inconceivable for any student in normal times. He told himself it didn't matter whether one passed or not, because the fate awaiting him was fixed and certain and would remain the same. He thought of this unchangeable fate, these fantastic images of destruction, with solemnity, even with pleasure. It was inevitable and it would end everything; and certainly events at the time appeared to be underwriting his belief, for in the Philippines the American forces had struck across the Luzon Plain and entered Manila, and in Europe the Red Army was pouring into Berlin. Every day the warning sirens sounded, and the alarm bells rang on the radio with sullen regularity.

"Here is an announcement for the Eastern Military Zone. A number of enemy planes have been sighted over the southern ocean and are now approaching the mainland."

"Kanto area. Kanto area. Warning of aerial attack. Eastern Military Zone Headquarters announces air-raid warning in operation for Kanto area with effect 1030 hours. That is the end of the warning."

"At this moment the main force of the enemy attack is over the Central Military Zone, but the rearguard is continuing north and precautions are necessary. . ."

"The rearguard of enemy planes is still flying north and is now over the Ito Peninsula."

"The enemy force invading the Tokyo-Yokohama area consists of three aircraft, repeat three aircraft. The main force still remains over the Shizuoka area."

The intermittent ringing of bells on the radio and the sirens echoing through the already scarred streets were wild enough to make Shuji's premonition of a holocaust seem to be turning gradually into reality, an experience almost of aesthetic pleasure. Every few days there was a large-scale raid and a town somewhere would be set on fire. There was now a scurry to remove industrial machinery to the countryside, and Shuji and his friends spent more time sweating to load trucks than working on their lathes. But one doubts how much of this machinery found its way into the mountains, for the stations were jammed tight with freight and one or two stations would be set alight each time there was an raid.

It was bitterly cold each day; not the pleasant severity of the clear, cold air of Shinshu, but only the irritating, sour cold of the city which seemed to epitomize the war. Breaking the thick ice that formed on the fire buckets was part of each household's daily routine. When there was a night raid people would rush to pour hot water on the ice, but one kettleful was not enough to melt it. Shuji had never known Tokyo to be so cold as it was that winter. Almost every day the sky was clear and blue, with thin trails of cloud left behind by the aircraft that flew across it, clouds with which the sky itself seemed pleased.

Sometimes Shuji wondered what death might be. He only thought about it in the vaguest of terms; naturally, since he was a member of the Nire family whose brains were traditionally unattuned to intellectual problems, but also because his mind had been further stunted by long years of militaristic education and the time he had been forced to devote to the industrial war effort. Still, he thought about death, and was surprised to find how little knowledge he actually had of it. The one experience he had of observing the process of dying had been the death of Nanny Shimoda. In her case death had been waiting at the end of a long, painful journey during which her face became hollow and thin, her skin grew disgustingly discolored, her breath came in agonizing gasps, and she screamed with the pain she had grown unable to endure. He hadn't seen the way his cousin Satoru had died, but he imagined it must have been a similar kind of death.

Since he knew so little about death, he felt it must be something rare, belonging to the order of the exceptional. When a person died, many people gathered to lament his passing, arrange flowers, and read the funeral service. It was because death was something extraordinary, arousing surprise and wonder, that it could threaten people and fill them with horror.

But things were different today, for death had become an everyday thing. So numerous were the dead and dying they were like pebbles on the shore. The basic assumption that death existed on the periphery of life had to be seen as a mistake, or as a deliberate deception. Surely the truth was that it was death that should be placed in the center of things, life a mere afterthought appended to it. But there was another deception: that death, for example, was caused by bombs as they exploded. That might seem to be the case, but in fact the explosion merely provided an opportunity to die and did not create death. A piece of shrapnel merely acted as a catalyst whereby death was set free from its underground kingdom and brought into existence. Life was merely an appearance, a borrowed form, whereas death was the original shape from which it all began and to which all returned. It was only occasionally, with the accident of war, for instance, that the curtain which had been idly lowered for so long was raised and death stepped forth from the dark shadows of its dominions and showed itself openly beneath the heavens, striding about the world in broad daylight.

Shuji's thoughts on the subject were confused, but his own experience seemed to accord with this prejudiced view of things, and the incoherent illogicality of the ideas ensured they would find a way to his heart and be welcomed there.

Death would eventually dominate the earth, a death of such preposterous and sublime splendor as to beggar the imagination, the most precise fulfillment of the idea of nothing, of the void. Before it all living things would be reduced to transient, insignificant shadows. Shuji thought how unsatisfactory his life had been up to now, how wretched and fearful. He had been almost afraid to breathe, so powerful had been his sense of his own endless inferiority. But when this resplendent death strode boldly forward, all such pathetic self-consciousness could be laughed to scorn. As he thought like this, Shuji felt that for the very first time in his life he was able to breathe freely, to take large, generous gulps of air.

This "death" he thought about with such passion was never more than a conceptualized illusion, for the real point was how he was actually going to die, and Shuji found himself dominated by an image of his own end. Tokyo would eventually be turned into a battlefield (Shuji believed this so firmly it almost seemed something he was praying for), and on that final day the air would fill with the smoke of guns. Only a landscape of burned-out, russet rubble would remain, with Shuji crouching in his foxhole, clasping a land mine to his breast, straining his ears for the sound of the caterpillar tracks of an approaching tank. There would be a tremendous explosion, the enemy tank would burst into flames, with he himself blown limb from limb, scattered into tiny fragments, leaving no trace. He assumed he could do this quite calmly and casually, with no increase in his heartbeat and without batting an eyelid. He simply had to make sure he didn't die before that time came. . .

Sometimes he woke up when it wasn't yet light and spent the time before going to the factory walking in the Tateyama Cemetery near his home. In the silence of the graveyard, a silence unrelated to the rhythms of this war, he felt free to indulge in all his wild images and dreams of "death." At that hour in winter, in the dull half-light, the frost crunched sweetly underfoot and his breath was white. He walked in no direction along the paths, passing the graves inside their small enclosures of hedgerow or railings. Sometimes a winter haze blurred the surrounding landscape, producing an unreal fairy-tale effect, and a distant memory would revive of his beloved nanny singing in her toneless chant about the three white ghosts and the three red ghosts of Aoyama Cemetery. But the old memory would annoy him, and he thrust it away with something like rage. What a stupid, pointless memory it was. Even the graves, the black gravestones covered with moss, seemed pointless and irrelevant to him, for all they recorded was ordinary, boring deaths, and when set before that great "death" which was to come these stones were worthless, ludicrous bits of nonsense. . . As he nodded over these thoughts of his, he imagined his expression must have taken on an exceptional dignity.

One morning Shuji crossed the small valley and went to the Aoyama Cemetery. This was much larger than the cemetery he had been spending his time in, but it was also too well cared for, too orderly, and he felt it was an actual hindrance to the growth of his fantasies. Just as he was about to leave, however, the air-raid siren

672

suddenly began to sound. This was an unusual time for a raid, surely. He looked at his watch and saw that it was still not seven o'clock. The siren at first had been the slow wail of the air-raid warning, but now it changed abruptly to the low staccato burst that indicated an immediate attack.

Since our fighter planes were already in the air, this might well be a large-scale raid, and public transport would have been brought to a standstill, so it seemed wiser to stay here and see what happened rather than try to rush off to the factory. He walked slowly back along the road through the cemetery, and as he did so he could hear the roar of engines somewhere in the sky. But there was a layer of thin cloud and no aircraft were visible. And then far off he heard a noise like gunfire, but it was hard to tell if it was bombs exploding or anti-aircraft fire. This was followed by a succession of pulsating explosions and then a Type 3 army fighter flew past, skimming just above the trees of the cemetery, making Shuji grimace and mutter at the noise.

He had come to a part of the cemetery where he could look down from a cliff over the huddle of low-lying houses below. Just beyond this valley was the field he had often played in as a child; to the left of that was the smaller cemetery, and to the right the rear of the Nire Hospital could be seen. He decided he would go home and find out what was happening from the radio, but just as he had made up his mind to do this he heard someone shouting out from somewhere down among the houses below. It was a great bellowing voice that reached his ears and appeared to belong to the air-raid warden, saying they were small aircraft so everybody should watch out. But how could small planes ever make it here all the way from Saipan, thought Shuji. Maybe they were carrier planes? Perhaps an enemy task force had at last come to launch an attack on the Japanese mainland.

But there was no time to examine these possibilities for there were now shouts to take cover, and at the same time Shuji saw what they were shouting about. In the sky just above the field beyond the valley a swarm of a dozen or so jet-black fighters of an unfamiliar type were heading straight in his direction, and as he watched them the tight formation broke apart and climbed away at tremendous speed. They were American carrier-based fighters, Corsair F-4Us, there could be no doubt about that, and they had dispersed in that way because a number of Japanese fighters had intercepted from the direction of the

Tateyama Cemetery to the left. An indescribable, spine-chilling, groaning roar had filled the sky as they abruptly opened their throttles and soared upward.

He had no time to watch the behavior of any individual machine, and the swirling dogfights he had hoped to see did not take place. After both groups of planes had broken formation they swooped into head-on attack and then separated again, most of them disappearing behind the thin cloud cover, and within a very short space of time all of them had vanished from his field of vision; all except for one plane that was drifting falteringly across the overcast sky, losing speed, turning round and round limply like a kite when its string has broken, and falling with absurd slowness, not even sending out a trail of smoke in its sluggish descent. Shuji strained his eyes and ascertained that it was a Japanese Type 3. He found himself swearing violently inside with frustration.

Once the falling aircraft had disappeared, the sky was quite empty, and the battle that had just taken place became completely unreal. It was as if it had never happened, a phantom attack, all over in a second. Shuji realized that he had been standing completed exposed, not bothering to take cover. He had paid no attention to the possibility of being struck by a bullet from the bursts of machine-gun fire that had been exchanged during this skirmish. He felt he must have been extraordinarily brave and was inordinately proud of himself, although the fact was he had merely been standing agape and had lost all awareness of what he was doing.

The sky was calm now. Although the noise of engines could be heard far away, no new emergency seemed likely to occur for the time being, so Shuji trotted down the slope and went swiftly home. When he got there the house was empty—they must all have been in the shelter behind it. The radio had been left on, making announcements to the accompaniment of constant warning bells. The enemy planes were launching attacks on airfields, trains and shipping over the whole Kanto area. The radio gave their numbers as several hundred, although the newspapers next day changed this figure to a thousand. What was abundantly clear from the announcements was that a great many planes, which had flown off from aircraft carriers, had attacked the Japanese mainland, flying arrogantly about the sky. Shuji sat in front of the radio in the deserted room, but went outside sometimes to look at the sky, where only a handful of Japanese planes could be seen. During the afternoon he saw a squadron of what seemed to be Grummans flying at high altitude and at great speed. The enemy carrier-based attacks continued until that evening.

The next day the attacks began soon after dawn. Anti-aircraft guns fired here and there, and from where the Third Regiment was stationed machine guns blazed away. Small clouds from exploding shells could be seen scattered and drifting about the sky, while tight formations of Grummans and Corsairs flew across it like black, ominous shadows. Today there were strikingly fewer Japanese planes, and the aircraft that continued to appear on the scene were always enemy ones. Shuji recognized these from photos in those aeronautical handbooks of his brother's, and the aircraft thus seemed to have suddenly sprung from the pages of fiction to flaunt themselves in the real world, zooming past each other at high speed and flitting insolently about. The impression they made on him was strangely lacking in reality. They were more like the images in a dream on a night of troubled sleep, though this only associated them all the more with his concept of "death," and as he looked up intently at the sky he felt a strong sense of satisfaction, for surely "that time" was now close at hand. As if to guarantee this assumption the American Army chose the same day to land on the beaches of Iwojima.

A few days later the snow came, a heavy fall of snow of a kind only rarely experienced in Tokyo. The snow fell all day, and Shuji became completely covered in it as he walked the road homeward that evening. Nobody was about in the Aoyama area, and Shuji had sometimes almost to burrow his way through the occasional drifts, which were two feet high in places. The snow had absorbed all casual sounds, creating silence and a dull half-light in the darkened streets.

The journey to work next day was particularly hard. The snow had turned into ice on the edges of the platforms and it was all he could do to keep from being pushed onto the line by the crowds shoving behind. The train was a long time coming, and when it finally did arrive it was jam-packed, and there was such a commotion he had no hope of getting on. He did eventually manage to struggle aboard a train after watching several pass by, but it refused to go except in fits and starts, making virtually no progress. It was impossible to move in the crowded compartment, and the close, fusty smell of human bodies plus the bone-breaking pressure from them proved too much for some people, and cries of complaint and wrath began to be heard. It took Shuji more than three hours to get to work, only to find that half the usual number of students and apprentice workers had turned up, and they had lit a fire in a corner of the factory and were boiling up some rice. Since the parts to work on had been delayed there was nothing to do, so they ate their rice and talked about the rumor that there was going to be a huge assault by the special attack force, the *kamikaze*.

"The sea around Iwojima is swarming with enemy ships. There couldn't be a better target."

"Well, I don't know," said one in slightly pessimistic tones. "Our bases have taken a bit of a beating."

"Sure, but the specials have always gone in groups of a dozen or half a dozen up to now, right? This time they're going to send in three or four hundred. Get that whole lot attacking and something pretty big's bound to come of it."

"They say they're short of bomb releases," put in another, normally quiet student. "I heard that they're only building the special type now at Number Two."

"Bit late in the day for bomb releases, friend. Don't need them any more. Just tie the thing on with a bit of string and off they go."

They all laughed in a loose, sloppy way. Shuji laughed with them. His voice sounded a bit like a maniac's.

There had not been a fall of snow like this for years and, before it had time to melt, two days later snow fell again. That day a huge combined force of B-29s and carrier planes attacked, and in a number of places not far from the Nire Hospital fires could be seen burning through the falling, drifting snow, large tongues of flame licking out as if the half-paralyzed city were breathing frantically in pain. Great columns of black smoke ascended to the sky and the fires went on persistently burning, as persistent as the snow that went on falling as if it would never end.

At night all became quiet, and the wounded city settled down to sleep, wrapped in thick snow. In this massive accumulation of snow with its faint, white light, Shuji sensed something meaningful, a symbol of some great change to come, as it shone through the night. He slept now in the room that had belonged to his brother who, it was now assumed, was probably dead, and as he was putting his air-raid satchel by his pillow and neatly folding his clothes and puttees, he was visited by the fantasy that this abnormal snowfall would continue for days, would indeed never stop, but shroud the whole city and the conflict and the fighting in a thick layer of white until the whole globe was covered with ice as well, for this could only be the beginning of the next ice age. It was one more fantasy of how his final days would be, one more dream of an ending, although that night his sleep was exceptionally peaceful.

Obviously, as the war went on great changes were to be seen in the running and management of the Nire Hospital of Mental Pathology. At the time of the fall of Saipan the number of employees at both the Matsubara and Aoyama hospitals had fallen to half what it had been when the war began, and that of the patients had been reduced to about one-third. Once the air raids had started there was an immediate decline in the number of patients in all mental hospitals, since the policy was to take in no more as there was nothing one could do for mentally disturbed people now. They were simply forgotten.

Despite the problem's being often discussed at meetings of the directors of mental institutions, there was, in fact, nothing hospitals could do in the event of a direct air raid. At the Nire Hospital the idea of creating one shelter to house all the patients was out of the question, and since individual supervision was needed for each patient who was liable to escape while being directed to some safe place, it seemed more than likely that a number of them must go missing. In order to prepare for the probable worst they held a practice exercise in taking cover, but this was restricted to only the mild cases among the patients, a tacit recognition of the fact that there was nothing to be done about the serious cases at all. So far as therapy and treatment were concerned, the lack of doctors, nurses and medicine was beyond solution, and it was considered a major achievement simply to house the patients and avoid any real accidents.

The same was happening in all medical establishments at the time. For example, the psychiatric department at Keio (which had provided part-time staff for the Nire Hospital for years) found itself, owing to the numbers of people who had been drafted, reduced to a medical staff of only two (discounting the academic staff who were permanent members of the university). In the old days, a professor at Keio Hospital whom Tetsukichi knew well used to hold consultations in a manner that Tetsukichi had admired because it seemed so traditional and fitted his image of what the psychiatric profession should be. He would sit in an easy chair, placing his large pipe in his mouth as if he had only just remembered its existence, and listen carefully to what the patient and the patient's family had to say. He himself spoke little, being precise and relevant as he indicated to his secretary the main points of the patient's condition. For this reason only an experienced member of the staff could function well as a secretary, for he had to record on the patient's medical card far more than what the professor actually said. Normally there would also be a young assistant in attendance, which meant that a consultation for outpatients held by one professor required a staff of two if it was to retain the dignity proper to it. But now the entire medical staff had shrunk to only two, with the result that one of them had to be allocated to the morning outpatients surgery while the other was on duty in the wards.

The latter, however, was still in attendance whenever the professor gave his consultations, although only until 11 A.M., for at that time he had to give dextrose injections to those patients who were on insulin treatment in order to wake them up. So at 11 A.M. the assistant would stand up, beg leave of the professor to be excused, and then dash off to the wards. Thus the professor found that he was left all alone and had to fill in the medical cards painstakingly on the side while interviewing the patients. He had even stopped smoking his pipe. He now took one rationed cigarette, cut it into three equal portions, and then smoked each portion in a *kiseru*, the old-fashioned Japanese pipe which can only hold about that much tobacco, with the inelegant haste that such a pipe imposes. One can only say that the traditional dignity and authority of the professorial consultation was much impaired by all this.

When Tetsukichi visited Keio, which he did on occasion, and saw the conditions to which it had been reduced, he could only groan inwardly at the thought that even universities had come to this pass. It was clear that a point had been reached where it was foolish to think in terms of proper treatment, for it was all one could do merely to keep the hospital going. People had died during the fire in the mid-1920s, and one couldn't start to calculate what might happen if the hospital were bombed. For that reason he had wanted to close the place down for the duration, and had been reducing the number of patients there for some time; but the hospital nevertheless stayed open.

During the first fortnight of February that year, however, the whole problem was solved by a directive from the authorities. An organization called the Japan Medical Association was set up, and all large medical institutions were placed under national control. The main hospital at Matsubara came under the large institution category and was bought up by the Tokyo City Council and turned into a branch of the Matsuzawa Hospital. At the same time the Aoyama hospital received a police order to transfer its patients, and to close down as soon as this relocation had been completed.

It was no time to be sentimental, and Oshu himself had neither the time nor the inclination to be so. He accepted the proposals immediately, although he was not on paper responsible for the hospital at Matsubara, and seemed very pleased to pass on the burden to the City Council. Even the ancient Hisa, who had stoutly refused Oshu's suggestion that she be evacuated to Chichibu by declaring that she would never live away from the hospital, was silent for a while on hearing this suggestion, and then mumbled that if it was a directive from the powers on high there was nothing one could do but acquiesce. She added that she supposed she would be going to Chichibu now, since she didn't want to cause the two of them any more trouble.

She certainly had been causing more and more trouble recently. She found it difficult to walk now and every time there was an air raid she had to be trundled to the shelter in a handcart.

Hisa's indifferent and almost unintelligible comment was felt to embody the feeling shared by all the Nire household, that the directive had inevitably to be accepted. Even the Deputy, who was still considered by some as the true leader of the Nire clan, made no particular objection.

"It has to be done if the Empire is to carry the day," he said, standing with Oshu at the gate of the hospital and looking behind him, his eyes even narrower than usual behind his spectacles. He had become very old and looked it, his small frame having apparently shrunk even further. There was no sign of that energy which had called for an American surrender on the occasion of the alleged victory after the battle off Taiwan. He kept sniffing all the while, presumably because he had a cold.

"I suppose we'll have to lower the flag," he said in a slightly petulant tone of voice, still sniffing, looking up at what had once been a blue flag dangling from the iron pole on the roof. It had faded during the seven years it had been hanging there, ever since that day when, to celebrate the fiftieth anniversary of the founding of the hospital, Hidekichi Katsumata had brought this flag into being with such feverish zeal.

Oshu looked up at the flag as if he couldn't have cared less what happened to it and said:

"Katsumata, haven't you caught a cold? Sure you don't have a temperature?"

"Oh, it's only a little cold in the nose. Still, Dr. Oshu, this Matsubara hospital will never burn, air raids or no air raids. Because this land was chosen by Dr. Kiichiro. There's still plenty of woodland and cornfields round about."

"Well, no one knows what's going to happen, do they?" Oshu replied bluntly.

"No. But this place will be absolutely safe. Even Aoyama should probably be all right. No great need to worry about it since it's already been visited by one calamity. It can only be visited by good fortune next time. If the good old doctor had still been with us I don't think the hospital there would have been closed down. I don't doubt he would have said that it was particularly in times like these that the hospital's duty was to put a brave face on things."

Oshu said nothing in reply.

"Still, what it means is that the name will change. We'll be called the Matsuzawa Branch Hospital, and the Nire Hospital of Mental Pathology will disappear. . . To be quite honest I never dreamed that such a thing could happen. It all feels so strange, and I can't believe it's really happening. Well, well, these are hard, grave times we live in."

Standing beside the stolid-looking Oshu, the Deputy seemed particularly small and fragile as he went on sniffing and snuffling, muttering finally to himself:

"Yet everything's being done to carry the day, I suppose. Even so, these are grave times we live in. Most certainly so. Hard, grave times."

Shun'ichi awoke from a restless noonday nap. He was lying down in his dugout, which was made of wooden planks with coral rocks placed on top. It was cramped, dark, badly ventilated and stifling hot, and he opened his eyes in deep gloom. A heavy lethargy filled his body, his tongue felt so swollen it seemed stiff with cramp, and there was a dull, burning pain in his stomach which was a continuation of something he had felt in his noonday dream, a dream from which he had not wished to wake.

Shun'ichi Nire, whose life had been despaired of by his family, with his thin, drawn face and thin, bony chest over which rivulets of sweat were running, had been dreaming of home. While he had been sleeping a part of his consciousness had stayed awake, whispering to him all the time that he should not be deceived, and yet though he had told himself that it was indeed just a dream, could only be a dream, he had gained some momentary satisfaction from pursuing its insubstantial images; so when he awoke he felt the deep-rooted disillusion and despair he always experienced on waking these days.

In his dreams the crowds on Ginza would appear. Sometimes he saw his classroom at middle school and some of his friends. But what he saw most frequently were the Nire hospitals at Aoyama and Matsubara and many of the people who lived there; although it should also be said that his dreams always had some connection with food. He would, for example, be standing outside the restaurant in a department store, looking at the display case packed tight with all the various meals available, and then this image would fade to one of the dark kitchen at Aoyama, with Nanny Shimoda standing in one corner in front of a huge mortar preparing yam soup. She kept grinding away with the wooden pestle, making a constant, soporific sound, and her work seemed never-ending. Shun'ichi opened the steaming pot of rice that was just there by his side and piled great heaps of it into the mortar. Then he jammed handfuls of the same rice greedily into his mouth, pushing it right down his throat. It had a very transparent taste, and no matter how much he ate his stomach was never full. . .

Just now he had been dreaming of a large reception room in what seemed to be a Japanese-style restaurant. The room was full of low, individual tray-tables, and seated in the place of honor was his granny, Hisa, her face expressionless as a Nō mask. He could see his father's face, too, and also, surprisingly, his mother's. The Deputy raised his small, thin frame to its full extent and spoke a few words of address. They must have been holding a dinner party to celebrate something. But when he cast his eyes over the tables he saw no food or crockery on them, only piles of round, metal cans. They seemed to be cans of Asahi Candy, made in the home of his uncle Oshu's wife.

Now, lying on his bed of straw matting, Shun'ichi's consciousness had finally returned clearly to him. Any physical movement produced a sense of total weariness, but for some unknown reason he found himself opening his mouth and muttering:

"Rice for the empty stomach. Asahi Candy for coughs."

The words had so direct and obvious a connection with his simple, basic desires that he couldn't even smile wryly at them, but felt a dull melancholy occupy his soul. Perhaps the mere thought of the candy had been a bad stimulus, and was responsible for this stinging pain in his stomach. He was so tired and listless and had so little inclination to do anything that he found it irksome even to remain quietly lying down like this. The unbearable demands that persistently thrust against the inner wall of his stomach were causing him such distress he found it impossible to remain still.

He got up sluggishly and put his mouth to the canteen hanging on the wall. There had been little rain recently and water too had become precious. Ever since the big raid in which all the ground installations, food storehouses and water tanks had been destroyed, the two or three springs and wells had suddenly become of major importance, although, on a low-lying coral island like this, the water they provided was always brackish and clouded. When there was an insufficiency of rainwater this salty water had to be used both for cooking and drinking.

Shun'ichi took a few swigs of the lukewarm liquid. Experience had taught him, however, that no amount of water could assuage the pangs of starvation.

"Bush gruel would be better. Don't see how I can last out to suppertime like this."

To their ration of a mere handful of rice the soldiers would add great quantities of round leaves that grew on the scrub and make a kind of gruel. This gave the sensation that to some extent one's stomach was full, but the problem was that the leaves tended to cause diarrhea, although on some people it had the reverse effect of acute constipation, and the momentary relief the gruel gave was illusory; its ultimate effect was debilitating. The soldiers also made use of something they called "octopus grass," a plant with fat, broad leaves from which string-like tendrils hung, preparing it in the same way with similar results. For this reason a ban was enforced on the eating of all wild vegetation, and all Shun'ichi had been able to put in the recesses of his stomach that day was a meager cupful of rice and a bowl of watery *miso* soup with a scattering of dried vegetable in it, just enough to cling to the tips of one's chopsticks, which the orderly had brought that morning. The rice transported here by submarine was unmixed with barley or anything else, being so pure, soft and swollen when cooked, so white and precious in appearance, that it was inevitably a disappointment to eat, providing only a peculiarly rarefied taste as it went down. Shun'ichi would hold it in his mouth to savor it, but he lacked the restraint to chew it slowly, and soon swallowed it all in three large gulps. He would then wonder what he had just eaten since it seemed to have done nothing for his stomach, and his unbearable hunger pangs were stronger than they had been before. Each time he finished a meal the almost insane idea crossed his mind that if this was the result he might be better off eating nothing at all. There would, in fact, be nothing to eat until evening, since for a while now they had been forced to reduce the number of meals a day to only two.

Shun'ichi's face had always been too long, and now that his cheeks had become extremely hollow and his complexion an unpleasantly livid color despite his suntan, it seemed even more lacking in firmness and character than ever. His rib cage showed clearly through the skin on his chest, and his shins, exposed by the short pants he wore, were almost ludicrous sticks of bone. Even so, Shun'ichi was in better shape than most people on the island, and could be thought of as belonging to the ranks of the healthy. In every camp there were textbook examples of malnutrition, soldiers who were mere skin and bones but with stomachs grotesquely swollen, who lacked the ability to move of their own accord but lay about with hollow, vacant eyes. These were people upon whom sentence of death had clearly been passed, for the only hope of recovery they had was to be given enough to eat. But it had been stipulated that people who could not work were to have their rations cut.

Death approached them slowly but surely, step by step. When they finally died it was like dying of old age, or as a candle gutters and expires, an imperceptible relinquishing of life which occurred at no particular time. Somebody who had been breathing normally just now, either waking or in sleep, someone who had been groaning, would be found to have become strangely quiet. His heart had stopped beating and his sunken eyelids would open no more, the color of his lips quite changed, the dry, coarse skin having lost its warmth, with rigor mortis soon to occupy those limbs. This kind of death, a death which made no noise, against which the dying did not struggle, which caused no disturbance to the people round about, had become something quite normal on the island. It happened every day. It was a part of life, just like the rising of the sun when night had ended, the burning, white-hot rays spreading across the sand and grit and pebbles.

Already as many as twenty or thirty people had been lost in this way. On one occasion there had been a meal consisting only of a piece of dried bonito, nothing else, and a number of people swiftly succumbed after that. It was clear that the garrison on Wake Island had reached the limits of its endurance.

How long was it now since they had seen the dear old supply ship (although on her last appearance she had been nothing but a wretched little boat of some fifty tons with an old-fashioned 50-millimeter gun in her bows)? Since the fall of Kwajalein and Roi-Namur (both garrisons heroically fought to the last man), Wake had been completely isolated, left behind as the war progressed. And since that time the real adversary had not been enemy aircraft but slowly advancing hunger and starvation.

Yet when food restrictions had first been put into effect, things had not been all that bad. There might not be one coconut tree on the island, but there were reasonable supplies of food to be had if one looked for them. There was a plentiful supply of fish in the sea. Some time before, they had made nets by taking parachutes to pieces and started fishing mainly for pleasure. Although the nets were difficult to cast the fish were attracted by the leftover scraps of rice used as bait, and there seemed to be as many fish, of one or two feet in length, as one could want. Whenever there was a bombing raid an enormous number of dead fish would float to the surface. Again, there was an abundance of seabirds, sea gulls, gooneys and particularly petrels which came seasonally in huge flocks, the airfield turning black with their numbers, to lay their eggs. The speckled white eggs, like small chicken's eggs, lay all over the ground, so many there was scarcely room to tread, and the orderly could be made to cook a more than adequate omelette, using a tin washing bowl to mix the eggs in.

But all these things started to disappear once they began to be used as serious sources of food. Each company sent out soldiers who had formerly been fishermen to work the water systematically; they even used dynamite, though this was supposed to be forbidden. The result was that the fish, which had been so abundant one could almost catch them in one's hand, began to disappear, with now practically none at all to be had. The seabirds' eggs had vanished too, for the birds had become wary of the bombings and the efforts of hungry men to catch them, and they kept clear of the island.

And the bombings continued, for enemy planes attacked the island at frequent and regular intervals. Four-engined Consolidateds and Catalina flying boats came every day, patrolled around the island, and dropped the odd bomb as a parting gift. Occasionally there would be an attack by carrier-based planes—the Consolidateds and Catalinas were land-based, presumably at Midway. Shun'ichi assumed that the enemy task forces that passed near Wake regarded it as a sort of firing range, and would send off their planes to perform practice attacks on it on their way to and from their main objectives. On more than a few occasions, peering from the entrance to his dugout, he has caught glimpses of the Douglas Dauntless dive bomber and the Grumman Hellcat fighter, not singly but in great black swarms, filling the air with their spine-chilling roar as they swooped and soared pretentiously above the island. This was the same Shun'ichi who had once spent most of the day at Haneda or Tachikawa or Oppama gaping up tirelessly into the sky, his heart beating with excitement and his long face flushed with enthusiasm as he watched the various aircraft flying overhead. But now he was sick to death of the things. From the bottom of his heart he felt he could stand no more of them. They were creations of the devil, monstrous creatures that shook his nerves to pieces, threatened his life, and had driven all the fish and birds away from the island.

After the fish and the birds, the next things that could be eaten were the mice. When Shun'ichi had first been posted here the mice had been so numerous that a truck driven along the road would always leave a number of squashed bodies behind it. But, not surprisingly, the soldiers had made no move to catch these creatures at first, since they were afraid of the infections associated with rats, of which these were an obvious relation. This wasn't for long, however, for word got about that the MO ate mice, and immediately everyone was after them. The way to catch them was to make a trap out of a box with bait inside. Unfortunately, this device proved so successful that before long the mice had also completely disappeared, despite their previously huge numbers and apparently limitless ability to propagate. After that, anything edible—lizards, sea urchins, sea slugs —was eaten, but there was too little to make any real difference. The situation with regard to vegetation was worse, for what plants there were, bush grass, octopus grass and thorn apple, were much more harmful than nutritious.

So the shadow of starvation gradually settled on the island. The only reason why they had not all yet starved to death was that supplies had been brought in on several occasions by submarine. These supply runs were mostly made at night to avoid enemy planes, the submarine surfacing in the dark and off-loading rubber containers full of provisions into the sea, where they would be collected by soldiers in small boats; but Shun'ichi heard that even this method of supply had been discontinued. It was common knowledge that the war was heading toward defeat, for enemy forces had landed on Okinawa, and in addition the Japanese mainland was being bombed day after day. It was obvious that they were surrounded on all sides, with no way out, and no matter how optimistically one looked at the situation, the chances of anyone getting home alive looked absolutely negligible. Not that Shun'ichi worried himself with such somber thoughts. Nor did he feel any kind of despair. He was not leading the kind of life that allowed luxuries of that kind. All he was truly concerned about was finding a mouthful to eat. That was the first problem, the main thing to be borne in mind.

Shun'ichi was well aware that once malnutrition had reached the stage of advanced dystrophy there was nothing to be done about it and the patient invariably died. In fact, one part of the combat medical station was a ward for incurables, and the medical orderly would only call in a doctor when the patient had reached a point where his pulse had begun to skip beats. If a cardiac or dextrose injection were given, the almost non-existent pulse might struggle back to life, but only for a while, and the treatment itself was a pure formality. Real dystrophy is not cured by any amount of vitamins or dextrose, as Shun'ichi and the others had come to learn by bitter experience, and they knew there was no hope for such a patient. People who could not walk could not catch fish or hermit crabs, and because they couldn't do that they were finished. The food ration did not provide enough calories even to do something like lie on a bed all day.

All activity on the island was now centered on the quest for food, and whenever food became an issue military order and discipline broke down. The army had one cookhouse, and orderlies were sent from each detachment to collect the food. It happened more than once that these orderlies would hide behind a bush on their return with the rice, and stuff it into their own mouths. Again, when the rice was being handed out to individuals at their units it was weighed on homemade scales, and as the amounts were measured out a number of soldiers would gather round and oversee the proceedings with expressions of profound suspicion on their faces. The truth was that you simply couldn't be too careful. If you were boiling up a piece of mouse flesh in a messtin and left it momentarily, it would be stolen by somebody. If you had a good catch of fish, dried some of them, and hid them somewhere, somebody would smell the treasure out and it would disappear. The combat medical station had once had a supply of green beans for patients with beriberi, and these too were frequently stolen. This so annoyed the MO, Lieutenant Sato, that he undertook to take charge of them himself, loosening one of the planks beneath his bed and hiding the box in there. Even so, the beans kept disappearing. The reason, no doubt, was that Sato used to spend long hours fishing and any would-be thief had plenty of time to sneak in and steal the beans; but the scandal-mongering medical orderlies whispered that the lieutenant might say the beans were being stolen, but maybe he was eating them himself. On hearing this, Sato became even more annoyed and determined to catch the criminal, and he placed a slide of polished glass on top of the bean box. The idea was to get a record of the criminal's fingerprints this way, but the man who was willing to risk his life to steal green beans managed to go on performing his crimes with an ability to remain undetected superior to any famous thief in fiction.

Lieutenant Sato had been a very valuable companion for Shun'-ichi and the other members of the medical unit. Each company had formed its own fishing squad, and the two MPs, the only ones on the island who had nothing to do, had even made a trawl net which they dragged energetically about all day; but there were no former fishermen in the medical unit. Luckily the enterprising Sato had twisted out some wire, worked on it with a file, and produced a fishhook, making a line for it out of a piece of camouflage netting. He even fashioned a pair of underwater goggles for himself by cutting two round pieces of glass and using rubber from an old tire. Thus equipped, he managed to catch a number of fish—at this time there were still a few left in the sea—which added an element of luxury to mealtimes. Even Shun'ichi had learned how to fish, and found himself spending much more of each day as a fisherman rather than a doctor.

It hadn't been so bad then, when he had been attached to the combat medical station. But some while ago he had been transferred to a different post as MO to a combat battalion, and he had his own private dugout now. Admittedly, he had been kept pretty busy looking after patients back then, but at least after giving a round of dextrose injections he had been able to break open one of the ampoules and drink the contents down himself. When he had served them diluted glucose he had managed to have a lick of glucose too. Here he had almost no work to do, but neither did he have all the perks that went with being a doctor. His former orderly had been a nice person too. Certainly Shun'ichi had treated him well, but there had been that time, for example, when the man had been attempting to grow cucumbers in empty cans filled with earth, and he had brought one of them to Shun'ichi as if he had won some prize in a show, and said:

"Managed to grow one at last, sir. Perhaps you would like to try it?"

Shun'ichi gratefully accepted the gift, which was the size of his little finger, broke it in half, handed half back to the orderly, and tasted the other with great care. Fresh vegetables were worth their weight in gold.

With his present orderly any such human interchange was out of the question. He was a morose person who gave the impression that he found the act of speech itself irksome. This may in fact have had nothing to do with his character, being more a vice that could be laid at the door of the food situation, which had now reached crisis point. In the past, when Shun'ichi had enjoyed a good day's fishing, he would generously hand the whole catch over to his orderly.

Nowadays he was having difficulty obtaining even enough for himself, and if he did manage a good catch he would stash it away somewhere like a careful miser, quite unlike the Shun'ichi of old, always the first to fork out the ten sen at school for baked potatoes. Clearly it was unreasonable for him to expect anything more from the man than that minimum which duty required. Again, this orderly was unlucky enough to belong to a tank squadron which had been sent to reinforce Wake Island just after that major attack by the enemy task force. At the time, when everyone had thought a landing was imminent, they had all welcomed the arrival of these strong, dependable tanks. Now, however, the men of the tank squadron were merely an extra burden, more useless mouths to feed, people who had made the food situation even worse, and the tanks themselves had been hidden in dugouts near the airfield to avoid air attack, where they remained unused, immobile, without meaning. That was part of the reason—and Shun'ichi himself thought that he was being illogically and childishly prejudiced—why he found he was unable to feel well disposed toward this man. He also could not free himself of the suspicion that the man was appropriating a hundred, perhaps even two hundred, grains of his rice while bringing it to his dugout. This was an unworthy thought, he admitted, and he disliked himself each time it came into his mind, but stronger than the emotion of self-contempt was the pressure of the hunger that lay inside his stomach like an immovable rock.

In the past, when they had been living the good life with lots of American provisions, the complete lack of women on the island had made him think about them a good deal. Now, however, women were simply beneath one's notice, an irrelevance. It was a long time since he had woken up in the morning with an erection, and women never once appeared in his dreams as objects of physical desire. What one thought about all the time was food, and food was the sole object of one's imagination. First, images of meals that had been particularly succulent or filling rose up in the mind. Golden fried *tempura*, for example, a Suehiro beefsteak perhaps, or three large portions of Olympic lobster deep-fried (with parsley and white sauce, so delicious you could even eat the tails). The steak needed to be specially big, and you slapped some mustard on the fatty bit and ate that first. *Sukiyaki* was probably the best way to have meat, though—a great plate piled high with lovely thin slices of dazzling red beef, put in the iron pan to sizzle, and just before it was quite done you put three eggs, nice and raw, into your bowl and then wolfed the lot down. Then a little *sushi* would not come amiss, say forty little rice balls made savory with tuna, octopus, clam. Your stomach might be getting a bit tight by now, but you could always manage some tea and rice with a pickle or two, like those slivers of purple eggplant or some cucumber pips just lightly dipped in soy sauce to help it all down. Fried mushrooms, of course, were always a delight, and you ought to have a few of them, too. If that still wasn't quite enough, well, anything would do, but perhaps a nice pork cutlet, deep-fried, didn't matter whether it was much of a restaurant or not, so long as the meat was good and thick, plenty of Bulldog sauce poured over it, pouring the sauce over a big, overflowing bowl of rice at the same time and eating both together, using a fork instead of chopsticks, opening your mouth wide and just piling it in. . .

These gluttonous dreams were pathetic in their childish crudity, but they were becoming plainer with the passage of time, now that starvation was a genuine threat to life. Gone were the elaborate feasts he had once imagined, for now he dreamed of big, plump rice cakes swollen with bean jam, a great pyramid of them rising before him, and with both hands he would start from the side of the pile and cram them continuously into his ever-unsated mouth. This image appeared not only when he slept but hovered before him in his waking moments, too. Finally, the last remaining thing, he dreamed about plain rice. He wanted to eat enough rice to fill his stomach; plain, boiled rice. He wanted to fill his mouth until his gullet was jammed with it and he could put in no more. But no, he didn't want all that much. Once, just once, once only, he would like to be able to eat until he felt full and satisfied.

So now, as he lay on his mattress in the murky light of his dugout, Shun'ichi pursued these vain shadows that perpetually eluded him. Now he was in Aoyama, in the cookhouse of the old Nire Hospital before it burned down. The fires under the great cauldrons had been raked out, water splashed on the embers, and blackened cinders of firewood lay scattered, smoldering on the concrete floor. Old Isuke with his humped back was taking the lid off one of the great vats that contained as much as a bushel of rice, and the steam billowed forth, thick clouds with that clammy, familiar odor. Tiny Isuke stood on a wooden stool and stirred with his large paddle of a spoon the hot, swollen, beautifully cooked rice. Finally he uttered the hoarse syllables that served as a signal, an unnaturally long shout of the word "R-E-A-D-Y," and many hands set instantly to work transferring the rice into the aluminum bowls for the patients. How Shun'ichi would have loved to dig his hands into that vast mound of rice! How rich and rounded an odor it gave off! How wonderfully satisfying it would be merely to touch it!

But it was all illusion, profitless fantasy. All that remained after it had gone was a feeling of emptiness in the stomach and a more generalized sense of emptiness that irritated him and wouldn't let him rest.

He let his head droop and whispered pathetically to himself:

"Rice for the empty stomach. Asahi Candy for coughs."

How was his grandmother, his old granny, getting on? Was she still alive? Was that mask-like face still in this world? Was she still hoarding all those piles of Asahi Candy in her cupboard?

He had another drink from his canteen, pulled on his handmade straw sandals, and wearing only short pants went out through the tortuous entrance to his dugout. The reflections of sheer, white, blinding light struck at his eyes. The slightly undulating landscape of rocks and pebbles glittered, and waves of heat rose from it. Behind him, toward the center of the island, some soldiers were attempting to create a kind of green belt, using a bush with a very hard stem, a type of stunted sandalwood found on beaches, and also that round-leafed bush which had inevitably become a source of food again; and perhaps both kinds of shrub were being planted for that purpose. But in terms of natural beauty there was little to be said for the idea, for these plants were hardly any joy to look upon, having, despite the fatty gloss on their leaves, an air of desolation that positively repelled any warm human feeling.

Just a little ahead of him was the sea, a genial, calm sea that caught the rays of the afternoon sun, a shining, bright deep blue; a gorgeous, dazzling ocean with the fascinating, all-absorbing ultramarine of the South Seas. Shun'ichi tended to avoid looking at it, for the sea disturbed him, making him feel frustrated and annoyed, the cruel being that kept him pent up on this pointless little island.

Once outside, he walked around the small mound that was his dugout. In the shade of that mound he had his farm, less than eight square yards of it. When seeds had been distributed from among the provisions brought by submarine, everybody had been ordered to farm the same area of land. The island, which naturally consisted only of stones and sand, did in fact have some soil on it near the airfield. Apparently the Americans had transported some earth here years ago to construct a vegetable garden, and the Japanese troops made their own little allotments here. Greens grew rather well, as did tobacco. However, the sweet potatoes, of which much had been expected, came to nothing. The eggplants were also unsuccessful, for the stalks grew very large to almost bush-like proportions but hardly fruited at all, although they would flower over and over again if given water.

Shun'ichi had humped his own ration of earth all the way over to his dugout and made his own tiny allotment there. A certain amount of edible green leaves appeared, which made a very slight contribution to his intake of vitamins, but provided no satisfaction to his stomach. In one corner of his plot was the unattractive creeper of a sweet potato plant. This grew rapidly for a number of days, then stopped altogether and refused to grow another inch. He dug carefully about near the roots to see how the tubers were getting on, but there weren't any, no sign at all of the all-important potatoes.

Shun'ichi squatted down in that area and lowered his pants. He had been constipated for some days now. This was another source of discomfort in addition to his hunger pains. He bent forward and took up a posture like someone in motionless prayer, his hands clasped listlessly in front of him. The backs of those hands were withered like an old man's. The rays of the sun beat tediously down on his back. His skin had been blackened by exposure year in, year out to the direct rays of the sun, but it was no healthy-looking tan, more of a sickly discoloration just beneath the skin.

From where he was squatting he could see the line of the seashore, and two or three figures slowly moving there. They were soldiers clothed in tattered uniforms and they were fishing. Out on the reef, which was now being exposed by the receding tide, someone naked except for a loincloth could be seen making slow and probably painful progress.

It was time he himself got moving, thought Shun'ichi. He really ought to try somehow or other to land some fish today. Whenever he managed to acquire an extra supply of food, he would spend most of the time it lasted trying to conserve energy by sleeping as much as or more than was possible. Once he had eaten it up, however, he would be assaulted by a feeling of crisis, by the thought that he must soon get hold of something from somewhere, and it would nag at his nerves all the time. Sometimes nearly a whole day of effort would be rewarded by one tiny fish. This was certainly no recompense for the outlay of energy put into catching it, but if one relied solely on the regulation handout it was pretty obvious one would just waste away. He had to get some extra food; this was the anxiety that plagued him, and even if it was merely some poor little minnow, it was still crucial, if only for psychological reasons, that he be able to put something in his mouth over and above the official rations.

"Three or four of those horse mackerel wouldn't go amiss," he thought with painful intensity, still crouched in his strained posture.

After thirty minutes of this undignified display he finally gave up. The fruit of his labor was one turd, painfully achieved and as hard as a stone. With great care he buried this object, in shape like a slug of dog shit, in a small hole he dug in the earth next to the sweet potato plant. That was one thing done to his satisfaction, anyway. Now all that remained was to catch some fish.

Being the medical officer of a combat battalion meant that he had scarcely any role to play in its affairs, and it would be small exaggeration to say that he usually had nothing to do. There was nothing one could do about people suffering from malnutrition; indeed it would be more accurate to say that they were all suffering from it, including himself. There was little point in having regular medical inspections and choosing the most serious cases for hospitalization, for the hospital could not take any more patients. The daily deaths did not require procedures that involved Shun'ichi. The death certificates were all the same mimeographed form and all that was needed was the dead man's name, which could safely be left to a medical orderly. Shun'ichi's proper role was the giving of emergency medical treatment to those injured in combat, meaning bombing raids, although seriously injured cases were sent on to the combat medical station, which functioned as a field hospital. So he had nothing on his hands at all. Previously, when there had been an attack by enemy aircraft, the anti-aircraft guns and machine-gun posts had responded with a hail of fire, but since this had very little effect on the enemy and merely resulted in more casualties on the island, the practice nowadays, no matter how intense the attack, was to offer little in the way of retaliation, and people usually took cover and remained quietly in their dugouts until it was all over. The odd thing was that Shun'ichi received not a single casualty to attend to. Occasionally some emplacement or dugout would be unlucky and receive a direct hit and everyone inside would be killed outright. But there were no half measures where casualties were concerned.

Soldiers who broke into the storehouse and were caught doing so were put in a field punishment cell. Since they were given practically nothing to eat they soon died. If one of them began to find blood in his stool the doctor would be called in; but this also was a pure formality since there were no measures to be taken. The man had received his death sentence, and would be allowed to die. Shun'ichi realized it was virtually a form of murder, and he became aware that what would be, by ordinary standards, a terrifying idea had taken root deep inside him, namely that the more people died the longer their food supplies would last. If someone died, then you yourself had been given a few more days' lease of life. Four thousand soldiers were incarcerated on this island, with a limited supply of food which was not going to be replenished from outside. Shun'ichi had once heard a medical orderly say that the only thing that would save them would be if lots of people went on dying, and the words were rather more than the joke they were apparently intended to be.

When he had first joined the medical staff at Keio, one of his patients became critically ill. Obviously the man was dying, yet, together with a more experienced doctor, Shun'ichi stayed in attendance on him around the clock, giving him cardiac injections and shots of Ringer's solution. The patient held out a surprisingly long time, and didn't finally stop breathing until just before dawn on the third night. The idea that had naturally arisen then was of the importance of each human life and the gravity of a single death. But on this island death had become a matter of indifference, something simple which suddenly happened and was over in a moment, making less and less impact as the days went by. Whereas the dead had once been cremated and buried in a hill known as the Army Cemetery, now only a finger was cut off for burning and the body was cast into a bomb crater or a corner of a tank shelter and there covered over with a casual layer of stones and grit. The island had, in many respects, reached a point at which human life was ceasing to be possible on it. Suicides had begun to take place. One captain shot himself with a pistol, and although this was judged to have been a momentary aberration, in a sense the sudden increase in the number of people who died of blowfish poisoning could also be considered as suicide, for blowfish was, after all, notoriously poisonous, and orders forbidding its consumption had been issued on several occasions.

Shun'ichi tended to keep his eyes firmly averted from these

frightful aspects of the situation, since it only made one feel desperate if one thought about them, the more desperate the more one thought. It was a natural characteristic of his to ignore anything that required thought anyway, but a more important reason was that anyone who spends day and night with his head empty or vaguely dreaming about things finds it difficult to concentrate his mind on any single subject. So once Shun'ichi had finished his ablutions and gone back inside his dugout, all that he had on his mind was those ever-encroaching hunger pains and the thought of one horse mackerel, nothing else, a nice, shiny blue, fragrant horse mackerel, firm to the touch like the one he had caught three days ago. He picked up an empty can that he kept by his bed, and armed with his homemade fishing tackle, service cap on head and still half-naked, he went outside again.

The usual enemy planes had been over that morning, but the afternoon was pleasantly peaceful, for the moment at least. He walked slowly, picking his way across the shingle. What he particularly noticed nowadays was how lethargic and tired he felt all over and how soon he seemed to get out of breath. When he bent down to pass through the entrance to his dugout he often staggered slightly and had to steady himself by placing a hand against the stone threshold. He often failed to make it when casually leaping across a hole or puddle that looked no size at all. His body seemed to be functioning very differently from the way it used to in the past. He couldn't rely on himself physically any more, and he wondered if things could be as bad as this for a seventy-year-old man.

On the beach to the right was the hulk of the *Suwa Maru*, which had run aground there with her stern stuck in the water. When the war had still been going well, this ship, their regular supply ship, had been torpedoed right in front of their eyes by an enemy submarine just a little way offshore. The crew had managed to keep the ship afloat and deliberately beached her here, the wreck still remaining pathetically half in and half out of the water. He had done most of his fishing here when working in the combat medical station. There was a hole low down in the bows of the ship, out of the water and large enough to get through, and from there you could make your way through the hold and up on deck. At low tide the sea withdrew just far enough to reveal the middle of the ship, and from the slanting deck you could dangle your fishing line in the sea and catch wrasse, mullet and horse mackerel.

The *Suwa Maru* was too far away for him now, and he turned left instead and walked toward the reef, which extended way out into the sea. The pebbles kept giving way, making it difficult to walk in his straw sandals. These pebbles were, naturally, only bits of coral made round by the sea, yet often with interesting porous shapes, tinged with yellow and occasionally pale red stripes. When the island had still been peaceful, Shun'ichi had often walked here looking for interesting stones and had made quite a collection of them. Now the shore was merely a waste expanse of futile things that made it difficult to walk, objects of no interest reflecting the glare of the sun.

There was a tank shelter with a growth of bushes over it, which he deliberately avoided as he walked toward the water. The bushes were surrounded by parched, shriveled grass with prickly burrs which stung one's feet and legs and got stuck in the seams of one's pants. There had been a time when they reminded him of a kind of amaranthus back home, and he had been quite sentimental about them. Now, however, he would frown and pick the filthy burrs off him, flinging them down on the ground in annoyance. He had begun reluctantly to recognize that what little nature there was on the island, even the dreary vegetation, held some collective enmity toward man: the awful pebbles, which were always dazzling and hurting one's eyes; the constant thunder of the waves, which had gone on for so many years.

He slowly clambered up the wet rocks onto the reef, taking great care not to slip and fall. Even a small graze could ulcerate here, forming a festering sore that would not readily heal. Two or three figures could be seen a long way off, right at the very tip of the reef. There were also soldiers fishing in the sea nearby, a few here and there, some with the water almost up to their shoulders or even with only the head showing. In the great, glittering expanse of ocean these heads seemed very small and solitary, out of touch with each other. Shun'ichi was well accustomed to this kind of scene, but it still filled him with a desolate sense of the human condition. They would never join forces, they would always stay apart like that, solitary, alone, searching for fish; and he, too, was part of that general isolation. But he had soon forgotten even this vague reflection as, totally involved in his own emotions of expectation and anxiety, he became preoccupied with fish. Round about the middle of the reef, at a point where the sea just below foamed into a shallows, he made his careful preparations. He extracted one hermit crab from the bottom of his can, pulled it out of its shell, and tore it into small pieces.

Before, there used to be quite large crabs nestling in their turbo shells, and those could be used as food, but now only tiny ones remained, which merely served as bait.

He attached the bait to a small hook and let it dangle in the sea. His fishing rod was very thin, made out of the bamboo sections of a practice sword all insecurely fastened together. The fishing line was made of cotton. The water was remarkably transparent, even unpleasantly so, and the shadows forming on the surface of the sea were reflected in movements of light and shade on the rocks below and on the sand. Though these waters had been virtually fished out, there were still quite a lot of gobies in the shallows where Shun'ichi was fishing; the soldiers referred to them as tiddlers, and they were roughly the size of one's little finger. Not all that long ago the sea around this reef had been full of shoals of beautifully colored, eccentrically shaped tropical fish.

The thing with tiddler fishing was that you had to jerk them out as soon as they made contact, and Shun'ichi had been straining his nerves, staring unblinkingly at his patch of the sea. Then he felt a nibble at the end of his line much sooner than he had expected. The fish he pulled up turned out to be, on inspection, an unremarkable little gray specimen, although the first sight of it, with its glistening scales and its energetic thrashing about, had been marvelous. It gave a wonderful feeling of vitality.

"Not doing too badly today. Looks like I'm in luck," thought Shun'ichi, and in a very short time he had caught three fish, all of them tiddlers. This was only the first stage, however, and now he prepared to start on the next, that real fishing which would, he hoped, provide him with something to satisfy his empty stomach and put some strength back into his limbs. He took one of the tiddlers he had just caught and attached it to a larger hook. This was part of a different set of fishing tackle, consisting of a crude wooden rod, a line made out of camouflage netting, a weight made of a piece of steel, and then finally the thick hook with the tiddler on it. With this equipment he had caught countless fish in the past.

Yet that day's fishing, which had seemed to promise so well, produced absolutely nothing. The sun poured down its piercing rays, the waves crashed against the rocks leaving delicate trails of foam, and a little farther off the surface of the ocean dazzled and shone; but the line he dangled into the sea remained motionless. There was not even a twitch.

On the surface of the sea to the side of him, a small head entered his field of vision. The man kept lowering his face into the water and raising it again. That was the best way to fish, the way you could be most certain of catching something. As you swam along, preferably with goggles on, you peered down into the water for fish swimming near the bottom which you caught by hand. At first Shun'ichi himself had fished that way, but he didn't have the stamina for it any more.

A long, weary, melancholy time passed. Shun'ichi clumsily shifted his sitting position and altered his grasp on the rod. He started to wonder what he thought he was doing. Why did he have to sit here in this miserable way waiting hopefully for one wretched fish? The sun was slowly scorching his back. He could feel what little physical and mental energy he had steadily draining out of him. There was no doubt that the sun did you no good. Maybe he ought to give up and just cook the tiddlers. No, that was out of the question. Those stupid little fish were practically all bone, and would be no recompense for the effort he had already put into this. Need a lot more than that, somehow or other. He had to eat the kind of fish that would put flesh on his bones and get the blood going inside him again.

Yet he still felt no kind of movement in his hands.

After some time he noticed there was no sign of anyone on the reef or in the water. It must be around suppertime. The tide had started to flow back again and the sound of the waves breaking against the coral reef had become louder.

So he made up his mind to give up, telling himself that at least mealtime had come around again, and made his way back to his dugout at a faster pace than when he had left it.

When he had finished the meal, which consisted of the usual cupful of rice with a little dried vegetable cooked with it and a fragment of canned fish, he felt, as he always did, that this hunger had reached a point where the mere act of lying still and trying to contain it was no longer endurable. He had done his best to chew the food as slowly as possible and to keep putting off the moment when he would swallow it. Yet the grains of rice seemed to have disappeared in the twinkling of an eye, leaving him with the hysterical feeling that he simply couldn't bear any more, just couldn't go on.

Perhaps a miracle would occur. Perhaps a supply ship or a hospital ship would turn up one day. But with the Japanese mainland in imminent danger such hopes were quite baseless. They were said to be going through terrible air raids in Japan. It was all just as he had imagined and prophesied it would be when he was at school. Ah, if only the Japanese had shared just one iota of his concern with aircraft they need never have got themselves into this mess. He had been right, he had seen what the future held in store, so surely he deserved at least another cupful of rice. If only the enemy would make up its mind to land, then at least an emergency ration of rice balls would be handed out. One big ball of steaming hot rice and he'd be ready to stand on the beachhead, brandishing that ancient sword his mother had given him, right in the jaws of an enemy landing craft. There was nothing to it. It was dead easy. But he must have that rice ball, that rice ball, that feeling of fulfillment as he held it in his mouth and let it slide down his throat. . . He didn't want a lot. Just one would do. Just one. That was all he asked. One great big rice ball, a rice ball, a rice ball. . . Finally Shun'ichi was saying this refrain out loud.

Holding his head in his hands, he collapsed onto his mattress. He had to calm down. He had to keep a hold on himself. He mustn't get hysterical. If he was to keep himself alive on this island he had to stay cool and collected. He mustn't let hunger push him into eating those tiny tiddlers. No, he ought to try his luck again. What about tonight, while the tiddlers were still fresh? He'd been going to bed as soon as it got dark for some time now. In the big dugouts they had their own electric generators, but in his there were only candles. Hadn't he once caught fish like red sea bream at night? Still, right now, he really ought to lie down and not move. He ought to calm his breathing and get some rest.

So that night, while the half-moon cast a dull light over the island and the sea, Shun'ichi was on the sloping deck of the *Suwa Maru*. The sea had come up as far as the bottom of the bridge, dashing against it in heavy waves that receded with a melancholy boom. The ship had become a heap of functionless scrap long ago, and it gave one a weird, gloomy feeling to be here alone with the smell of rusty iron all around. The view of the island from here, under the pale half-moon, spreading out flat and far away, was one of complete desolation. You could see dugouts and bunkers standing out in the paleness, but there was no sign of anyone moving at all.

Still, the landscape aroused no emotions in him, since he was concerned with other things. He had already spent an hour or more with his line dangling over the rail into the water, waiting with all his nerves tensed up for a bite. What a day it had been today. Not one real bite, not even a nibble. Incredible not to get even a . . . although he found it difficult to repress the doubt that arose in him whether this was all that rare a day. All the other days had been the same. Things were not going to get better. It would probably be a good idea to fish only for tiddlers and catch enough of them to make a meal.

Shun'ichi drew in his line for the umpteenth time, checked that the bait was fixed on the hook all right, and then twisted his body for a good swing that would take the line well away from the ship. As he did so, his feet in their straw sandals slipped, and he was immediately over on his back and sliding down the sloping deck, to be pulled into the waiting whirlpool of waves.

For an instant he felt himself being whisked down underwater. His lungs hurt, he struggled and swallowed some water, then just managed to get his head up through the surface and take wild drafts of air. His confused brain tried to make sense of the situation and he found to his surprise that he was quite a distance away from the half-submerged hull of the *Suwa Maru*. He ought to have come up at least somewhere near the stern. But he didn't panic: the shore was still near, and he was a competent swimmer even if he was in poor physical shape. A few strokes would soon have him back in his own depth. It was then he noticed he still had the end of the fishing line in his hand. He tried to pull the whole line in but it snapped halfway. Now he had lost the hook he had taken such trouble to make, but he went on swimming with the broken line in his hand.

The beach came no nearer at all. The *Suwa Maru* was to one side now, and he was gradually drifting away from her black shape. He then realized with horror that he was being carried out by the tide. He was being carried backward at an angle from the shore, further and further out to sea.

He dashed his face into the water and broke into a crawl, swimming wildly and recklessly. He beat and kicked at the water, hardly able to believe he had as much strength as this left in his body. Then he raised his face. The shore was still no nearer. So he repeated his frantic efforts, but his arms grew exhausted and his legs went numb, particularly his left leg, which he must have banged against something a little while before because it wasn't moving very well. The beach was patently further away now. The tide was flowing faster than he could swim. So he shouted. He shouted three or four times, but he soon realized that it was futile. The sound of the waves would easily drown his voice.

A sudden weary despair overtook him and his arms and legs quite failed to act, so he just let himself be carried by the waves, trying to be sure he swallowed no water and making slight, lethargic movements with his heavy hands. While doing this, he felt the coldness of the sea penetrating his body. Even at night the water near the shore was still warm, as he knew from experience, but the flowing waters of the tide about him were quite cold. They continued to drag him along at considerable speed.

Even now he did not feel all that desperate, perhaps because the fluctuating thoughts and emotions passing through his mind had brought about some kind of mental failure, a partial numbness that saw all this almost as if it were happening to someone else. What was going to happen to that person? Would he really drown like this?

He tried hard to swim again, but realized it was just as ineffective as before; and then he felt a true fear of the water seize hold of his heart. Was he, Shun'ichi, going to die; die in this simple, pointless, miserable way? A wave covered him and he struggled for breath. The line of the shore was moving further and further away. He could see the half-moon in the sky, and the stars. A wave covered his face again, but he kept on moving his arms although they were growing heavy and tired, keeping up his hopeless efforts merely to stay afloat. Was he going to die, then? Really going to die? He was beginning to resign himself to the idea.

An image of his mother appeared in a corner of his mind. Ryuko was giving him a sword and telling him to fight bravely. Then his own room at home appeared before him. In that cupboard in the recess there should still be more than a hundred of those pictures of airplanes he'd drawn with such laborious care. He had stored his emergency rations in there, too: hard tack. He saw before his eyes what had happened to that hard tack, a few crumbs remaining and the weevils crawling about inside the bag. The image was in very clear detail. Then he saw that deluxe yo-yo he had played with many years before. Shuji had cried because he wanted the yo-yo so much. He saw Shuji sitting there with a wistful, longing expression on his face, looking unwaveringly in this direction. He'd had this big bowl of jelly with strawberries in it and was deliberately eating it very slowly in front of his little brother, flaunting each spoonful as he put it in his mouth.

So all these fragmentary images of the past and the people in it filed swiftly across his mind, and he decided he was done for. He was floating on his back with his mouth just barely above the water, and although he still struggled he realized he must die. When you remembered your past like that it meant you were at last on the point of dying.

An eternity seemed to pass, and, only semi-conscious, he raised his head a little again to avoid drinking the seawater. He could see the shore right in front of him. At first he thought it must be a mirage, but there was a long white line of breakers and beyond it he could see quite clearly the shape of the island with the shingle white under the moonlight and the black forms of the shrubs. The tide had turned and brought him back near the island again without his even knowing it.

As he splashed desperately with hands that could hardly move he found his legs had touched the bottom. He staggered and stumbled his way up to the beach, collapsing face downward on it. He was in the last extremes of fatigue and had no energy to move a pace further, but tears were running down his cheeks. A corner of his mind registered these as tears because they were warmer than the drops of seawater with which they mingled on his face.

Chapter

8

The months of March and April, dark months which saw the fall of Iwojima, the American landings on Okinawa, the resignation of the Koiso cabinet, and in Europe the entry of the Red Army into Berlin, were a busy time of sudden changes in the Nire Hospital.

The sign at the main hospital in Matsubara was taken down, and in its place a new one went up, saying "Umegaoka Hospital: Tokyo Matsuzawa Municipal Branch Hospital." There was little real change now that the hospital was being run by the City Council, the patients and most of the nursing staff staying just as they were; but the head doctors now came from the main Matsuzawa Hospital, replacing people like Katsujiro Nirasawa, who in fact went with his family to an obscure rural area in the Izu Peninsula to escape the bombing and open a practice there. On top of that the Deputy, Hidekichi Katsumata, had no choice but to resign. Despite the profundity of his feelings in this matter there was no way whereby he might continue in the traditional and honored post of Deputy in a municipal hospital. Since, also, the hospital at Aoyama was permanently closed, there was no question of his being transferred there either. So he went into unavoidable retirement, renting a house near Gotokuji Station, not far from the hospital, for the time being, and saying he meant to move out into the country in the near future, to the Kai district west of Tokyo. Hisa gave one of her extremely rare displays of emotion on this occasion, her face showing actual feeling as she grasped the hands of the tiny, skinny old man who had sustained the pillars of the great edifice since her husband's death, and offered cordial words of thanks. She also nagged Oshu into giving the Deputy a specially generous retirement grant. She herself, in her seventy-seventh year, finally took everybody's advice and allowed herself to be evacuated to her family home in Chichibu.

The actual owner of the place, Oshu, having sold a very large hospital to the City Council, should have received a very large sum of money. Indeed, the cookhouse circles found time, despite the severity of the war situation, to gossip and speculate about this, maintaining that he must have made an absolute pile, become a millionaire, selling a hospital the size of this one; even if the Council had made a compulsory purchase order they must have forked out a fair amount, you could bet your life. So Oshu took this opportunity to divide up the Nire estate between himself and Tetsukichi, after the two had talked things over, with the result that Aoyama became a separate branch of the Nire family. As Oshu said to his wife Chiyoko afterward:

"This means my job is over. I expect Dad's weeping in his grave but there really was nothing I could do about it. The fact is these aren't the right times for a man to run a hospital on his own."

He then went on:

"Psychiatrists don't look as if they're going to be much use to anyone, so I mean to become a farmer. Food's going to be the big problem in the future."

Chiyoko was not at all sure what she should make of this, whether she should see it as one of his idle jokes or not. But Oshu was already making arrangements to buy some land way up north in Hokkaido. If the worst came to the worst he was planning to give up the medical profession, for which he had never had much enthusiasm anyway, and run his own farm. He expected that worst to happen, since he had felt for some time now that the war outlook was simply hopeless. It was strange that he, a person who had probably failed more exams than anyone else and who had lived an uncommonly quiet life, should have managed to retain something that was in very short supply at the time, namely common sense. In the whole Nire family he was the only one who thought Japan could be defeated. When the Americans advanced into the central Pacific islands, the Hunters Association he belonged to was ordered by the military to round up all its shotguns. The obsolete single-shot infantry rifles that Japanese soldiers were using in the jungles of the south were proving ineffective against the enemy's automatic rifles, and one idea was to give them shotguns to provide a wider range of effect. Oshu was not so much depressed at having to hand over his favorite guns as immediately convinced, when he heard of this desperate, last-ditch idea, that the war was already lost. So this eldest son of the House of Nire, who had always left the care of his hospital to other people and had never had one positive contribution to make to the running of it, made up his own mind and actually thought something out for the first time in his life. The hospitals in Matsubara and Aoyama, he decided, indeed the Matsuzawa Hospital where he was employed as well, would, at some time, all go up in flames and be burned to the ground. He would therefore become the owner of some of the new territory in Hokkaido and start life afresh on a farm, a way of life that would continue a sight longer than the Nire Hospital. His first step in that direction was to dispose of the house he had been living in ever since he married, and move into cramped married quarters belonging to the Matsuzawa Hospital.

The person who was most put out and plunged into confusion by all this was Ryuko, for she now had nowhere to live. She had imagined that Oshu would retain the house even if the hospital itself became municipal property; and if he did let it go, she had assumed he would only buy a new one. There was no question of her going with Hisa into the safe retreat of Chichibu, nor of joining Oshu and his wife in their new quarters, which consisted of only three rooms. So she had a good, long think about the problem, allowing her ideas to mature and then rethinking them, thinking them out in fine detail and then brooding on that detail, with the final result that she decided to go and apologize to the husband from whom she had been separated for more than a decade and on whom she had not once laid eyes during that period. Once she had made up her mind to do this, she proceeded to do it boldly and unflinchingly. Tetsukichi, of course, was hardly thrilled at the prospect of having her back, but felt that he would have to accept the inevitable. One reason for his acquiescence was that the only remaining maid in the house at Aoyama wanted to go back to her home village, and old Shige, who had in theory taken charge of the kitchen after Nanny Shimoda's death, was due to escape to her niece's home in Chiba Prefecture almost any day now. The chances of finding another maid at this stage of the war were negligible. And, with this in mind, Tetsukichi provisionally and sullenly agreed to the idea of Ryuko's return. The two children, Aiko and Shuji, were naturally delighted.

Shige and the other maid eventually left the house in Aoyama, and with the children working at their factories during the day, Tetsukichi and Ryuko were left to face each other over a gloomy meal in the horribly deserted house.

"What's this rice supposed to be?" said Tetsukichi. "It's only half-cooked. Isn't it about about time you learned how to boil rice?"

"I would have you know," Ryuko replied calmly, the nape of her neck held straight and firm, and in a tone that suggested this was a matter of self-congratulation rather than reproach, "I have never once cooked rice, or anything else, in the whole of my reasonably long life."

The hospital at Aoyama had been gradually emptying each day and was now practically deserted. The patients either went home or were transferred to other hospitals, and the staff left with them. The rice cooks, Isuke and his wife, had left long ago. The chauffeur Katagiri, when the car had to be sold because there was no gasoline to run it on, went with the car to its new owner, a government minister, and was now employed in that ministry. The Chief Accountant, Oishi, had remained to the end, but once the transfer of the patients was completed he also left for a village in Ibaraki Prefecture, northeast of Tokyo.

Just three people remained in the deserted, run-down hospital: Yasusaburo Sugano, Chief Nurse Watanabe who had been there for donkey's years, and a young nurse who was her niece. There was also another mysterious person whom nobody wanted there, but he had somehow taken possession of a room and seemed determined to stay put. This character had the suspect name of Norose, ominous not only because of its oddity but its overtones of slowness, stupidity and malediction, and the man himself seemed to go well with his name. He had originally been a resident patient at the Matsubara hospital, but when discharged he had not, at the request of his family, gone home but had been given a job at the Aoyama hospital as there was a staff shortage at the time. Clearly, however, it would have been far better if he had remained a patient, since that was about all he was fit for. His appearance was very peculiar for a start. His head was twice the size of a normal person's, but his physique tapered off from the shoulders downward, ending in legs and feet that were those of a primary-school child; it was as if they had ceased to develop since early childhood. Still, he could move surprisingly quickly on those minute feet, appearing in odd places clearly in quest of something, occasionally even hanging around the back of the house. Ryuko did not realize for quite a while that he was actually attached to the hospital staff.

Then one day Norose suddenly appeared in the front entrance hall, and when Ryuko came out to see who it was he asked her:

"Here, Missus, don't want any cakes, do you?"

He held a plate in his hand on which were a dozen or so of the un-baked variety, topped with arrowroot or bean curd, the very sweet kind that are eaten with green tea.

Ryuko lost her temper at his "Here, Missus," form of address and drove him imperiously from the house. Later she asked the Chief Nurse about him.

"Who is that person, the man with the preposterously big head?"

"Oh, madam, that man is a dreadful person," Watanabe replied, and she proceeded to give a general outline of the situation. "He came here just a little while before our hospital closed down. All he does every day is just sort of wander and hang about various places, although he always comes back for his meals, puts his own down in a flash, and other people's too if they're not careful. . ."

"What might be his illness? Is he an idiot?"

"I don't know, madam, because he was at Matsubara. Still, he does seem to be intelligent enough. They say he graduated from the Tokyo First High School."

"Why is it necessary to have a person of that kind remaining in the hospital?"

"Well, we have written to his family a number of times to come and take him back, but we've never had a word in reply. Of course, he does spend all his time in town, except for meals. He manages to find those cakes somewhere. Cakes, at a time like this. . . I suppose it might be some kind of cleverness left over from his high-school days. Then it seems he goes around the big houses in the neighborhood sell-ing them. But that's not all, not by any means. The other day I saw him going out the back way with a bundle under his arm, so I caught hold of him to see what he'd got, and what should I find but it was full of rice. He's been stealing the hospital rice. Probably been ex-changing the rice for those cakes."

"Well, really! Please tell Yasusaburo to chase the man out im-mediately."

"Of course, madam. What really makes me sad is that he's on the books as an employee. When I think how long I've been working here, and all the funny patients I've had to deal with, and yet I never thought I'd see the day when I'd be living with a colleague of that kind. I know I never. . ."

Despite the firm stand Ryuko had apparently taken on this matter, remarkably the man remained, looking as if he had achieved permanent status, wandering about from place to place and at surprising speed on those tiny feet. And all the while, the Director of this hospital, now no more than a number of buildings, was away in the mountains of Yamagata, staying in the town of Kaminoyama.

Once the decision to close the hospital had been made, Tetsukichi had begun to think about evacuating from Tokyo. The records of special psychiatric case histories, his notebooks, his card index, all the things relevant to his research that he'd assembled over the years, now made up a considerable collection. Everything he needed to get started on his new work was in order and ready to go, but there were also those piles of medical records accumulated since the fire at Aoyama, priceless and irreplaceable treasures for the hospital and for Tetsukichi in his present research, and they too must certainly be preserved. There were also a number of invaluable books which he would not like to see go up in flames.

What confirmed Tetsukichi in his resolve to move out into the country was the first great night fire raid on Tokyo on the 10th of March. Up to then he had, basically, been taking a casual view of the situation, or rather he had tended to accept his own wishful thinking that while other places might burn down, his own house would be safe. However, the 10th of March saw a change in bombing tactics as, from midnight onward, 130 B-29s approached in waves, either singly or in groups, from the Boso Peninsula to the southeast, scattering huge numbers of incendiary bombs over a wide area. All night long the sky was a weird, amazing red and people's faces could be seen quite clearly in the garish light. When day dawned the extent of the disaster was much greater than imagined, and it was said that the destruction had been on an even larger scale than that of the Great Kanto Earthquake. A friend of Aiko's who lived in Honjo on the east bank of the Sumida River was known to have died in the flames. Shuji said that three of his friends at the factory had not come to work that morning, which meant of course they must have died. He gave this information with an odd trance-like look on his face.

Tetsukichi kept having visions of flames licking forward and devouring all his books with feral tongues, for he still bore the scars caused by that fire in the 1920s, and since then the idea of fire had never ceased to arouse terror in him. All the hospital business was now taken care of and Ryuko could look after the children, who had to remain in Tokyo to work at their factories, so he made up his mind to get away as soon as possible, a decision he realized might look somewhat selfish. His brother Shirokichi was running that inn in Kaminoyama, and if he went there something could be arranged. Once he was settled there he could get started on the final labor he had to complete before he died.

Deciding what was to be taken with him to the safety of the country turned out to be much more troublesome than he had thought. He was one of those indecisive people who find it hard to make judgments about anything, a trait that had grown much worse lately, so he found it hard to determine which of his books he should take and which should be left behind. He would decide to leave a certain book, then have second thoughts about it, and find he had spent most of the day leafing through his volumes and coming to no conclusions. Finally he decided to try to save at least some of the books he must leave behind, so he had Yasusaburo Sugano and Shuji (made to take time off work for this purpose) move them into the empty garage, offering words of encouragement as they did so, and then changing his mind and having them move them all into a brick-built storehouse at the back of the house.

"Not much good putting them in a place like that," said Shuji, who had become depressingly frank and outspoken recently. "The window's not shuttered and the door's made of wood."

"No, no, that's not so," said Tetsukichi, but with no confidence. "Anyway, no one knows what's going to happen. After all, they'll certainly be safer here than they would be in the house."

There was another treasure he wanted to take with him at all costs, and that was the large trunk he had filled with quality canned food all those years ago: cans of crab, asparagus, corned beef, eel and so on, which, like the most niggardly of skinflints, he had hardly even touched yet. Eventually a huge amount of baggage, consisting, from Tetsukichi's point of view, of a mere fraction of his books and medical cards, was sent off, and he himself traveled alone to Yamagata, leaving his wife and children behind.

The Takamatsuya, which Shirokichi Mihira managed, was on the outskirts of Kaminoyama. The garden was nicely cared for and the sign on the gate was of a respectable antiquity, but, as Japanese inns go, this one was second-class and half of its guests were local farmers who were taking the waters as a health cure.

Shirokichi bade him welcome in the inner room, where the two men sat around the sunken hearth in the center. As he bowed, his bald head was visibly flushed, and he reached out his hand for another jar of warm *sake*.

"Now you're here you just have a good rest. Reckon you might be the boss down there in Tokyo, but up here I'm the one who's going to look after you. I'll make sure everything's all right, don't you worry. Still, the trouble is I've just been told they're going to turn this place into an army hospital. First I'd heard of it. Very sudden decision. Anyway, I won't be able to let you stay, and that's why I went to talk it over with Iku."

Iku was Tetsukichi's younger sister, who lived in the village of Hotta just outside Kaminoyama, next door to the village in which Tetsukichi had been born. She had married a man from that village called Jiemon Suzuki, and it seemed the Suzuki family would put Tetsukichi up there if he had nowhere else to go. In the year before war broke out with America, Tetsukichi had stayed a while at the Takamatsuya, paid visits to his parents' graves, and seen his relations, but this was the first time he had been back since then.

"Reckon tomorrow you might drop in at Jiemon's and have a few words after you've been to the cemetery. Well, it must be pretty bad in Tokyo but we're gradually getting caught up in the excitement here. Don't know if we can manage. If you count on staying some time we'll have to work a lot of things out."

"That we will," said Tetsukichi, dropping back into the dialect he hadn't used since he was a boy, naturally and without realizing it.

He didn't know where he was going to stay yet, but, wherever it was, he had to have space for all that baggage he was bringing. Still, he thought, as his cup was refilled with *sake*, when the time came all that canned food he had been hoarding with such obsessive miserliness would come in handy. There could be no more welcome gift for a potential evacuee to offer than those high-class canned foods worth their weight in gold. The possibility never crossed his mind, flushed and cheerful as he now was with *sake* and the reunion with his brother after all these years, that his precious provisions and all his other irreplaceable possessions—books, medical cards, research material—might never reach him but perhaps be destroyed in some burning station awaiting forwarding.

The fall of Berlin and Hitler's suicide were announced. The unconditional surrender of Germany, Japan's ally over all these years, took place on the 7th of May. The battle for Okinawa had now reached the point of desperation, and from Kyushu in the south to Tohoku in the north the skies of Japan were violated each day by enemy aircraft. Already P-51 fighters had joined in the raids from bases in Iwojima, and all forms of transportation and even ordinary people on foot were being subjected to a hail of machine-gun bullets.

The factory at Omori where Shuji was working was destroyed in a fire raid in the middle of April. Once the burned-out ruins had been tidied up, all the mobilized students were dismissed, given a fortnight's leave, and then ordered to report to a pioneer battalion in Chiba Prefecture. But before setting off for Chiba, where they were to build fortifications to repel the enemy's expected landings on the mainland, they were made to dig underground bunkers for three days at the battalion headquarters near Tokyo and given some more leave.

Students who had passed their exams into a higher school were obliged to remain in their present employment until August, although term started in April. Exceptions, however, would be made if a letter were produced from the new school stating that one would be enlisted in the work force related to that school. So the students broke up into two groups, those who were leaving and those who would be mobilized from middle school and sent off to the pioneer battalion. Since Shuji had failed yet another entrance examination, he was naturally in the latter group.

These students, who had studied nothing for more than a year, spent their last few days of leisure holding a series of farewell parties with their closest friends. They would all bring the *sake* ration and some food from their homes and get together in a friend's house. Perhaps they grew to understand the meaning of the word "parting" during these days, since it was now actually happening. They all wrote their addresses in each other's notebooks, their home address and that of the school dormitory they would be going to. Then they got drunk on the unfamiliar *sake* and sang songs, all sorts of songs: popular songs of days gone by, bits of Chinese poetry in Japanese-style recitation, songs that the rebellious young officers were said to have sung during the heroic days of the February mutiny in 1936, all in their high, lusty voices. Finally they all linked arms and sang "Farewell, Rabaul," the song of the Rabaul air force which was the great hit song of that moment.

"All the best. Stay alive."

"Not likely to die in any air raid."

So those who were going on to higher schools in the country said good-bye and departed.

One night this kind of party took place in Shuji's house. When they had finally dispersed very late at night, Ryuko, who had not been best pleased with her maid's role, raised her eyebrows in disgust and said:

"What kind of friends do you think you have? All they can do is talk the most appalling and irresponsible drivel. I have never heard anything like it."

"You see," said Shuji quietly, looking away, "it's because they're all going to die anyway."

Only two days before, in fact, as many as two hundred and fifty B-29s had launched another night raid, and the area around the Keio Hospital had been set ablaze. Shuji, who had gone outside the shelter, suddenly heard directly above him the steam-whistle sound of incendiaries falling. Great pillars of flame were rising from the rows of houses in the valley between the Nire Hospital and the Aoyama Cemetery. His immediate and automatic response on seeing this was to take all the bedding and bundle it into a hole they had dug for that purpose, covering everything over with earth; but by some miracle the fires in those houses were put out, and the next morning he had to retrieve the various *futon* he had fouled with such labor and spread them out in the sun to dry.

"The great thing in life is to stay calm," said Ryuko, grimacing as she brushed the dirt off the bedding in an irritated way. She was now dressed in a no-nonsense duster jacket with the sleeves rolled up, and baggy work pants gathered at the ankles.

"It was just a bit of luck those fires got put out," Shuji replied with a sulky, angry look on his face. Aiko, who had taken time off from her factory, went on silently working with her shovel.

After a large-scale air raid the enemy no doubt needed time to service its planes, so normally there was a lull of a few days between attacks, but this time there was a pause of only one day, and just after 10 P.M. on the night of the twenty-fifth the air-raid sirens sounded again. From the radio announcements it seemed as if it was going to be another massive raid.

Ryuko and Aiko went almost immediately into the dugout shelter at the back. Shuji alone remained outside, wearing his protective

712

hood with a steel helmet on top, holding the object used for beating out flames as though armed with a bayonet, standing in stern readiness and sometimes running back into the house to listen to more radio broadcasts. He noticed a light shining from their dugout and, when he went to investigate, he saw his mother crouched calmly in one corner with a volume of No texts open on her knees which she was reading by the glow of a small flashlight. Still, there was no point in reproaching her for that faint light, as the whole night sky was beginning to glow red.

This was a replay of the fire raid on the 10th of March, even bigger perhaps, for the raiding aircraft kept on coming and coming, flying in low singly from the east toward the west. The wandering searchlights picked out their bluish white duralumin shapes, and down rained the incendiaries, falling like the scattered drops of a huge fountain. Red globes of trembling fire kept rising with a terrible slowness into the night sky, then suddenly vanished while others took their place.

The sky behind the cemetery across the valley, just to the right-hand side, had turned a bright red which grew deeper each moment, so bright it dimmed the radiance of the searchlight beams. Up above, the shape of one B-29 and then another could be seen as they scattered more incendiaries which burst in the air, showers of incandescent fire falling continuously on the already burning earth. It was a matter of wonder that all these bombs seemed necessary, and yet as one B-29 disappeared enveloped in clouds of smoke from the anti-aircraft flak another would appear.

Shuji was shouting inside himself, calling out encouragement to the people in areas on fire to carry on with the struggle, not to give in, but when he ran back to the deserted house the radio, which had been left on, went on announcing the imminent arrival of more enemy planes.

A strong wind had risen. The thick red on the horizon was quite different from anything he had seen before, with columns of flame shooting up in places; in their trembling light the black shapes of the houses in front of him stood out with vivid clarity. There seemed no sign of any letup in the aerial onslaught. The arcs of tracer bullets converging on each plane continued, but there seemed to have been some slackening in their intensity. He saw a small red light apparently pursuing an enemy plane, and assumed it must be one of our fighters. Right at the outset of the raid, when two or three of the

B-29s had caught fire there had been shouts of applause from the neighboring darkness, but people must have been exhausted by the never-ending attacks and now nothing of that kind could be heard.

Sometimes Shuji opened the air-raid shelter and passed on the latest news to his mother, who had, unsurprisingly, closed her volume of No texts, and to his sister, who was simply crouching in silence.

"That's five of them we've got. Still, they seem to have plenty more."

"Settle down. Come on, come inside," Ryuko scolded him.

"I'm invulnerable. They can't kill me." After this wild parting shot, he went back to stare at the night sky, driven by his obscure compulsion to look upon this splendid, monstrous sign that the final destruction of the city was now at hand.

Suddenly he heard a great roar immediately overhead and there, through the branches of the nearby ginkgo tree, was the huge shape of a B-29 looming so close it seemed he could reach out and touch it. Although he could see it all clearly, even the fact that its bomb doors were open, it was no mere object in the real world—streamlined, metallic, the ultimate in industrial art—but rather the metamorphosis of some mythical bird. The wings and fuselage gave off dull reflections of the light, a pale, strange beauty that made his skin creep. Shuji forgot for a moment the danger he was in and stood rooted to the spot, gazing into the sky entranced.

"The enemy's giving it a go, too," he muttered meaninglessly to himself once his trance had left him, but the B-29 was now even nearer and, in a sudden flash, something glittered open in the sky and countless star-like fragments began to fall, sparkling in their uneven descent. Shuji hurled himself into the dugout shelter, automatically curling his body up tight and waiting for the explosion. But no explosion came, or at least he heard nothing. He went outside again to look, and saw a great blaze of fire rising near the Aoyama main road. He also heard something metallic fall on the roof of the house, probably shrapnel from one of the anti-aircraft guns. So he ducked down into the shelter again, intending to wait there a short while, but when he got up to go outside his mother suddenly grasped his two hands in her own. She held on to him surprisingly tightly.

"Can't you keep still a moment? Keep still! You're not to keep on trotting in and out all the time!" She spoke in the angry tones of a mother scolding an infant, and kept an even firmer grip on his hands.

At that very moment the Matsubara hospital, on whose soil the former head of the Nire household, Kiichiro, had collapsed while measuring it, and which was now the Umegaoka Hospital, a branch of the Matsuzawa Hospital, was a blazing inferno. Since the surroundings were still mostly woods and fields, few of its employees had dreamed that events could catch up with them as swiftly as this. The Director's report described the circumstances as follows:

11:05 P.M. Air-raid warning. 11:23: Imminent enemy air attack announced. All employees deployed to action stations. Measures to evacuate all patients set in readiness. Enemy force of 250 B-29s approaching from both southeast and southwest. First outbreak of fire to east gradually spreading north, then closing in from all directions. Wind from southwest gradually increasing in strength.

Around 1:30 A.M. first incendiaries dropped on hospital buildings, inside and out, all of which extinguished by hospital fire wardens with preliminary fire precaution techniques. Surrounding area on all sides fiercely aflame with thick smoke and air full of flying sparks, so obliged to begin evacuation of women's wards, losing some six or seven patients in confusion. In men's wards all patients assembled in concrete corridor and roll call held, with no absentees to report. Loss of patients due to breakin by ordinary citizens into hospital grounds through hole made in fence in northwest area and patients mingling with them.

First outbreak of fire successfully extinguished without major mishap, general feeling raid over and just ordered first-aid attention to wounded member of staff, Shunji Nojima, when around 2:30 A.M. rain of incendiaries from enemy plane (unidentified owing to thick smoke) on main building, cookhouse, all ward buildings and environs, estimated at more than two hundred. Patient Kobayashi (due to highly excitable state) and patient Fujimoto (due to direct hit from incendiary; died 3:00) on stretchers. Otherwise all evacuated, although four patients escaped during this operation, and it was found impossible to rescue patient Kihara.

At this point majority of wards and greater part of main

building on fire, with cookhouse and other outbuildings. Realized no measures could be taken. Evacuation of patients from all buildings completed, general assembly and roll call held in tennis courts. Missing patients now amounted to thirteen (13) with three (3) members of staff injured.

Shuji remained in the shelter for a fairly long time, occasionally taking a quick glance outside to make sure that the house and the hospital buildings beyond it were still all right.

This strange period of tension eventually passed and he realized the air raid was over; but the sky was now an extraordinary color, not the red glow on the horizon he had seen at the beginning but more like a constant flame arising from all corners, reaching up into the high dome of the night. It was a violent, purplish, turbid red that made him shudder, a confusion of thick colors, tints and shades that seemed unreal, unearthly.

A strong wind was blowing from the south. When had the wind suddenly got up like this? It had the force almost of a typhoon, making it difficult to stand, and it roared and stormed under the weird red sky bearing hosts of blinding, glittering sparks of fire.

Shuji ran to the front door of the house. There was a fire bucket in a corner of the entrance hall. He filled it with water and stood there pointlessly holding it in his hand.

Just then a crowd of refugees began pouring along the pathway leading from the Seinan Primary School. Some seemed to be carrying some kind of equipment on their shoulders, running past the Nire Hospital with a clatter of military boots as they went. They must have been the crew of the anti-aircraft gun stationed on top of the primary school.

"So the soldiers are running away now, are they?" thought Shuji, full of bitterness and rage. "Well, I'm not going to run."

Mixed with the roar of the blustering gale was a dreadful rumbling noise, a booming reverberation that seemed to issue from the earth itself; but Shuji was in too great a state of excitement to be properly conscious of it, for he was running along in the pale light of the road trying to find out what was happening in their area. There was no sign of anybody in the row of houses facing the hospital. As he ran, the gate used by the employees at the hospital opened and he saw a small figure dart out and make off in the direction of the Tateyama Cemetery. It was a man with a very large head and he was carrying a bundle in each hand. There could be no doubt it was Norose, who was still living in the hospital. Shuji called out to him, but the small figure with the tiny legs simply vanished into the gale and the driving sparks as he watched.

Shuji went in through the same gate, but Yasusaburo Sugano and Chief Nurse Watanabe were nowhere to be seen. Circling around the back of the wards he noticed small tongues of flame licking out from a spot under the upstairs eaves. Some of the sparks must have lodged there. It was on a corner hidden from the wind, but as the flames climbed the wind caught them and fanned them viciously, making them even stronger. Shuji looked at his bucket, but there was almost no water left in it. He looked around and saw there was a supply of water not far off.

The first bucketful of water he threw never reached the flames but was blown away by the wind. He took more care the second time, controlling his breath, adjusting his swing and waiting for a lull in the wind. This was a complete success, putting the flames out immediately. He could hardly believe it. He threw another two bucketfuls just to make sure, deciding it was a great thing he had done, the action of a potential hero. However, having completed a circuit of the hospital in this glorious frame of mind, he returned to the house to find his mother had left the dugout and was standing by the front door. She was furious.

"Where do you think you've been? There's no time to waste. We must get away from here."

He saw she was right, for a sea of flame was rolling in their direction from Minami Aoyama, and the sparks were blowing as far as the area immediately in front of the house.

"Where are we going to escape to?"

Two ideas crossed Shuji's mind. One was to take the road leading from Omote Sando to the Meiji Shrine; the other was to go via the field next door across to the cemetery. The cemetery would be exposed to the flames, but it would be impossible to get to Omote Sando now, so he decided they should escape across the field, which would be all right until the hospital itself caught fire. He then suddenly realized that none of the family possessions had been brought out of the house. Even the bedding that he'd hastily buried in a hole the day

717

before yesterday was still hanging out to dry. Still, there was the radio. He ought to get that at least. So, ignoring his mother's protests, he dashed into the house.

It was pitch-dark inside. The electricity had been cut off some time before and he didn't have a flashlight with him. He felt his way across the living room, picked up the radio, and began to back out again, finding himself bumping against a soft body, Aiko's presumably, in the darkness.

"Shuji?" It was definitely her voice, sounding as if she was on the verge of tears. "It's so dark. Don't the lights work?"

"Don't worry about that. We've got to get out of here quick."

Aiko seemed to have come inside to fetch something too, but she followed Shuji outside. When they got out, their mother was waiting for them and shouted in a state of almost unbelievable rage:

"Don't take anything. Nothing. Nothing at all. Only what you stand up in."

"Only what you stand up in?" thought Shuji, and suddenly he found the words excruciatingly funny and his face was momentarily contorted with suppressed laughter. Then immediately he was aware of the crisis again, the fact that what he did now would determine if he were to live or die. He listened to the sound of the wind as it gathered its strength and howled, his body trembling with unbearable tension.

Shuji leaped at the fire bucket and poured its contents over his head, steel helmet, protective hood and all. He did this three times, successfully soaking himself.

"Oh, stop that!" said Ryuko harshly. "It'd be much wiser to bring the water in the bucket."

So all three of them took a bucket and went from the back of the house toward the rear of the hospital. On the way, Shuji tossed the radio he was holding deep inside the dugout shelter.

The field was separated from the hospital by an inadequate fence, at the bottom of which the wire had been pulled away in a number of places, so there was no problem in finding a hole big enough to squeeze through. Once through that, however, Shuji saw something that made his blood run cold.

When he had walked around the hospital only a while ago, the field had still been a genuine field, dark and wide, a good safe place that might be threatened by flames on all sides but would not catch fire. When he looked at it now, however, great shafts of flame were leaping across it, transforming the whole field into a sea of fire, a scene straight out of hell. He looked at it then a little more calmly and realized that these weren't flames but billions and billions of flying sparks, driven onward by the wind, swirling about like a tornado.

The three of them began to cross the field, ducking down and covering their faces with their free arms. The sky was howling and raging; the earth roared. The wind felt as if it would blow them over, and before their eyes flew these mad myriads of red dots. The burning wind caught the bucket Aiko was carrying, now almost empty of water since it had spilled out while she was running, and blew it from her hand.

Before long they arrived at the cemetery, where the trees protected them from the flying sparks. A great crowd had taken refuge here.

When they looked back to where they had come from, they were just in time to see the hospital catch fire. It was almost hidden behind a curtain of leaping, spinning, whirling sparks, so it was difficult to tell which were genuine flames and which were not, but finally the whole hospital, so much a part of their landscape for so many years, was engulfed in fire in a matter of seconds. It made one great blaze, retaining the original outline of the buildings, as, fanned by the raging, storming wind, the fire formed a giant, slender, torch-like flame.

They were all three in a state of near collapse but managed to make it to the middle of the cemetery. Numerous people were here, crouching behind gravestones and trees. Ryuko and her children squatted down by the side of a wide, gravel path. To one side they heard a woman ask if the cemetery was safe, and a man replied that it should be all right and the flames would have passed by soon.

Shuji found he couldn't open one of his eyes. A spark seemed to have flown into it as they were crossing the field. It was starting to really hurt now, tears flowing from it, and he was shaking terribly with the cold. Those three bucketfuls of water he had thrown over himself before starting out had been more than effective, for his clothes had not dried out at all even with all those sparks, and now he was drenched from head to foot, feeling wretched and knowing he looked it. He took off his helmet and hood, and this youngest scion of the House of Nire, who had felt he had been behaving so heroically until only a few minutes ago, found he had no more courage left. He sat there trembling with the cold and the unbearable pain in his eye, his close-shaven, childish skull bared for all to see.

So Shuji unashamedly put both arms around his mother and pulled her toward him. She, in turn, laid the head of her son, who seemed suddenly to have lost control of himself, on her lap, stroking his back with her hand, and looking defiantly through the trees to where the clouds of sparks still spun and dipped and flowed. At her side Aiko was cowering in a spiritless way, her head drooping like an idiot. She hadn't said a word for some time now.

Two days later, in the afternoon, Aiko and Shuji were walking among the ruins of their home. The piles of ashes had not yet cooled, and when they trod on them the layers beneath were still hot and crumbled underfoot.

Even though the hospital had been only a much smaller version of the one erected during the Kiichiro era, the land it occupied had always seemed quite considerable in size. But now that the whole edifice had been destroyed in the fire, they were struck by how little space there really was, wondering that so large a building could possibly have been built on so limited an area.

The two pillars at the main entrance remained, as also did the empty garage. The brick-built storehouse round the back had only half caved in, but in one corner was a fat pile of ashes, clearly the remains of Tetsukichi's books. Everything else had vanished in the fire, leaving only the stone foundations and desolate heaps of cinders, so deep one's feet sunk into them.

Shuji had soon regained his spirits. Indeed, he was now in a state of meaningless elation as he stomped about through the charred wreckage and kicked aside the odd twisted iron bar from the ward windows.

After the night spent in the cemetery, they had gone to stay in the house of the Assistant Director, Seisaku Kanazawa, which had somehow survived intact. The house was in the small valley between the hospital and Aoyama Cemetery, and by some miracle all the houses packed into that confined space had escaped the flames. Apparently the wind had been so strong the sea of fire had leaped right across the valley, leaving it unharmed.

Shuji was as yet unable to know precisely how terrible and on how great a scale the destruction caused by the raid had been, but he could certainly grasp it impressionistically and intuitively. The day before, he had borrowed a bicycle and cycled about the whole area from Minami Aoyama to the Meiji Shrine. Tangled skeins of telegraph wires lay all over the road, and in places the ruins were still smoldering, giving off clouds of smoke and a very peculiar stench. Seinan Primary School was still there, but only a scorched and blackened shell with all its windows smashed. Shuji had meant to visit the house of a friend of his in Shibuya to see if he and his family were all right, but he soon realized how pointless this would be. The occasional stone building still remained, but otherwise the whole area had been laid bare and one's view round about was so unimpeded it seemed quite unreal. The earth had rid itself of the shadows cast by all those irrelevant buildings that had weighed it down, and its scorched flesh was now exposed for all to see. A reddish brown desert stretched far away, an unbelievable expanse of dead emptiness.

But there were worse sights to see. In the Aoyama main road a group of men were at work digging open a line of dugout shelters along the sidewalk and dragging out lumps fused together that must once have been bodies. When he arrived at Omote Sando, Shuji saw something that forced even him to look away: a great pile of corpses forming a pyramid over six feet high. Some of the bodies were still wrapped in clothes, some naked, some indistinguishable from bits of charred timber. There was another of these piles a little further on.

Shuji cycled down Omote Sando a short distance. The avenue of zelkova trees had disappeared, and it felt strange to find that where there had been houses before nothing now existed. The asphalt of the road was pitted with hexagonal scars caused by thousands of incendiary bombs falling on this area. They must have rained down on people as they tried to escape into the precincts of the Meiji Shrine.

The bitterly detached feeling that filled his whole being as he pedaled along and looked with strangely cool eyes at this monstrous carnage found only one thought to speak for it, the thought that it had come at last. "That time" was fast approaching; and this was all he could now imagine as he walked among the ruins of his own home. There had been a vegetable garden, just a small one, here, and green things had been growing in it, but now it was completely gone. The same was true of the trees; only the roots of the great ginkgo tree remained, weirdly charred and twisted. The dugout near the tree had been burned inside too, and the radio he had taken the trouble to throw inside had been destroyed, only the metal interior remaining.

Shuji picked up three scorched steel helmets out of the ashes. They might come in useful. He also picked up a charred stick and wrote in large letters on the cream-colored steel door of the garage: "NIRE. ALL SAFE. NOW c/o KANAZAWA."

Aiko, on the other hand, had been standing in the same place all the time. Although it was impossible to be quite sure where the rooms had been, her room must have been around here. When the house had been threatened by the fire storm and flight was inevitable, and when Shuji had gone back inside to get the radio, she too had run into the dark house for a specific reason. She had gone to get her diary, which was in the drawer of her desk, or rather not the diary itself but what was folded up inside it, a remembrance of something about which she could speak to nobody. It was the one and only letter she had received from Tatsunori Shiroki, the one thing she had to remember him by. But she hadn't been able to retrieve it, and the letter must have burned with everything else, so she crouched down and searched with her fingers among the ashes, scooping them up. There may have been fragments of that letter among the gray cinders she held in the palm of her hand, but it was all so futile, and after a while she let them fall. She did not weep.

"Let's get going. What are you messing about there for?" Shuji said roughly. He had piled the three helmets together and held them under his arm. He was too occupied with his own thoughts to have any time for worrying about his silent, brooding sister.

Ryuko and Aiko had talked things over last night and decided they would shortly join Tetsukichi in Yamagata. Shuji, however, still had his job to do as a mobilized student. On the 1st of June all the students were due to assemble at Azabu Middle School and then go off to the pioneer battalion in Chiba. Shuji himself seemed quite untroubled by the prospect, for the place was an appropriate setting for the kind of "death" he had long imagined. The long beaches there had featured years ago in the most famous of those futuristic fantasies about the coming war as the likeliest spot for the Americans to land.

"Come on, hurry up," he urged her again, and when he saw her rising slowly to her feet he set off without bothering to wait.

He crossed the small expanse of hospital ground, passed the remains of the bathhouse which was now full of bricks, and arrived at the field, where most of the grass had been burned or scorched. After walking a little way across it, he turned around to look for his sister. She was some ten paces behind him, just at the boundary between the field and the hospital. She was looking down, the usual sad, absorbed expression on her face, prodding at some dark object with the toe of her shoe in an absentminded way. The object was a rectangular kind of stick of a dark green color, and was half-buried in ash.

Shuji thought it looked like an incendiary bomb. Must have dropped here. Might be a good idea to take the spent case home to show people.

He had taken two or three paces in her direction when it suddenly happened, without any kind of warning or premonition on his part. The incendiary exploded. He saw a thick red-orange flame burst diagonally into the air and a momentary cloud of black smoke. He shouted out something, and at the same time heard a piercing scream from Aiko who was staggering out of the smoke.

Her hair was on fire. He saw it quite plainly burning. He threw himself on her and knocked her to the ground, forcing her desperately into the earth, and he beat at her hair with his hands. It was hard to do because she kept rolling about in pain and terror.

When he finally raised her to her feet again he could smell the peculiar stench of scorched hair and flesh. Her hair had only been burned on the surface, but down the side of her face, from the temple to the upper left cheek, the skin had peeled off, exposing inflamed flesh in a manner that made him turn his eyes away.

Chapter

9

The earth in the field was parched and white. Fine weather had lasted for a number of days, and the leaves of the cucumbers and kidney beans drooped limply. The insects on the backs of the eggplant leaves moved slowly around to the front, opened their wings listlessly, and flew off, although they would immediately return to the same leaf.

Tetsukichi was walking slowly past this field as if he was not quite sure where to go. He wore an old straw hat on his head, an ancient *yukata* covering his now ancient body, and leather-soled *tabi* on his feet, in appearance no different from the villagers. His face, compared with what it had looked like when he first came to live here, was suddenly years older, an indication of the mental suffering he had gone through. As he walked along, rather bowed forward now, there was hardly a trace of black hair to be seen even at the back of his head.

After his brother's inn had been commandeered as an army hospital, Tetsukichi had been taken in by Jiemon Suzuki, his younger sister's husband, who lived in the village of Horita. Jiemon's farmhouse was a large one by village standards. His eldest son had been drafted into the army and had gone to the front, leaving a two-year-old daughter behind, and his second daughter, who had married into a family in Tokyo, had come back to escape the air raids, bringing her three children with her. So Tetsukichi was found room in the storehouse, and the various psychological tensions the very kindness of their treatment of him imposed were certainly not made easier by the succession of ill tidings that reached him.

The first thing he heard was that all his baggage had been lost. It had been burned to cinders, and the shock was greater because the news came just as he was looking forward to its immediate safe arrival. For a number of days he lived in a trance, since all that remained was a few books and notebooks he had brought with him separately as personal luggage. He found it impossible to believe that such a huge mass of research material could have vanished into thin air. True, he had been less passionate about this work than when engaged on his history of psychiatric medicine; but the years he had spent getting all those cards together . . . all that effort, all that writing, so how could it all have vanished like this? Then there were the medical cards of the hospital since 1927; the whole lot of them. They were simply irreplaceable. Yes, they were irreplaceable, and they too were gone. Every single document, every note, every piece of research had been reduced to ashes and lost forever. All he had left was himself, and what sort of man was he? An ancient, dying animal that had lost all its teeth could present no more wretched and futile a spectacle than himself.

He had sat in the half-light in his room, quite still, holding his head in his hands. He had made no reply to his sister who came to his door to say that dinner was ready. So she called him again, telling him he would be late, which brought him slowly to his feet.

"If you go on worrying yourself like that you'll make yourself ill and that's for sure." Iku normally treated her brother with circumspection, and the fact that she should have spoken like this made it clear how striking his emaciation had become.

When he heard the hospital had burned down and everything with it he was not so profoundly shaken. Something like that was bound to happen. Even so, when he read the telegram "BURNED DOWN. ALL SAFE. RYUKO," he found himself simply gazing blankly at it a number of times, not really taking it in. In order to steady his mind he went down to the nearby river and sat in the shade of the bushes and grass to read it again. "Burned down" was so direct, blunt and unfeeling. Surely she could have expressed herself better than that? He couldn't believe she was trying to economize on the expense of the telegram, and a feeling of real anger rose against this wife whose ideas about matters like this would never accord with his own.

The following day a slightly longer telegram arrived from an acquaintance living in Aoyama, and this was couched in much politer terms but still gave only the same information. In a fire raid of that kind it was quite out of the question that the brick-built storeroom with his books in it should have been spared.

He tried to convince himself that it was inevitable the hospital should have been destroyed, and that the great thing was that everybody was safe, but when he thought about all those books he felt a heavy pain about the heart. It was now more than twenty years since the great fire when he had dug out the scorched remains of his books from the ashes of the others that had gone up in flames. He remembered swearing never to collect them in his life again, but somehow they had accumulated in his room like dust, until finally the room had been buried in those intimates of his that were as dear to him as a wife might have been. Among them he had passed his cheerless days, days with so little pleasure in them, and now again his books had been taken away from him by fire. Even so, he could bear that. He could endure that. The main thing now was his country, at this point in history, when its very survival hung in the balance.

The news of Aiko's disfigurement, however, following hard on the heels of the other, provided such torment that existence itself seemed intolerable. He thought of how little he had troubled himself over his own daughter. Ryuko's detailed letter took a further week to arrive. In it she said that Aiko was at a small surgery in the Umegaoka area (luckily the doctor in charge was on very good terms with Oshu) and she had managed to get her a bed there.

Aiko had to stay in hospital for a whole month. Owing to the shortage of proper medicines at the time, it had not been possible to prevent the wound from ulcerating. Although it was now more or less healed, a dreadful scar remained, an ugly, uneven network of cicatrices on her left upper cheek, red and shiny in a repulsive way. There was no possibility of additional treatment. And now, just ten days ago, Ryuko had brought Aiko here to Yamagata, as the Suzukis had been urging for so long. In fact right at this moment, as Tetsukichi walked the road between the fields, he could look over his shoulder and see his daughter.

She was wearing a straw hat and dressed in baggy trousers tied at the ankle—in typical peasant style—and was bending down in a field, weeding. Tetsukichi had hoped she would do things like this so as to be of some assistance to the Suzukis, but she hadn't needed any telling. Tetsukichi himself was not without the depressing guilt feelings of a person who had not done a stroke of work since coming here and was a mere extra mouth to feed. He had tried to be useful, following his sister Iku, whose back was starting to bend as those of peasants do, into the fields, saying he would help with the weeding. But he soon found he was not made for the task. He immediately started to get pains in his shoulders, then his back, and his fingers

726

didn't seem to do what was expected of them.

Iku, whose nimble fingers pulled up the weeds at great speed, turned around to tell him that he really needn't bother, and found that he had already stopped and was simply standing there gaping at her in astonishment. He complimented her on her skill and praised this sister from whom he had been separated since early childhood. He had also once said he would lend a hand with the potato digging, although the result was exactly the same, as he ended up just standing to one side and watching.

Since his wife and child were also being looked after by the Suzukis, he said to Ryuko at the very beginning:

"Now, look, don't just sit about doing nothing but give them a hand with the weeding."

Ryuko remained silent for a while, finally replying with an ambiguous affirmative. That was the only ambiguity she showed, however, for she never once made a move to do any work in the fields. Not only that, she always remained in their room in the storehouse, making no attempt even to get to know the people to whom she was under such an obligation. At mealtimes she would get through her own food with her usual haste. She never tried to join the family circle which formed after each meal, but would immediately stand up by herself and leave the table. Tetsukichi criticized her for her behavior, but she remained obdurate, absolutely refusing to participate in anything like weeding.

The one who most suffered from this was Aiko, caught up in the quarrel between her parents. She had never once voiced any grievance or complaint about the dreadful accident she had suffered, the injury that would probably ruin her life. Her heart was full of a much greater despair, and she had decided that life had nothing to offer any more. This total resignation, this desperate acceptance of her situation, allowed her to take what seemed, on the surface, a positive attitude toward each day's activities, for she would look after the little children and always volunteered to work with the others weeding the fields. Not that she really thought about the matter: she did it all quite automatically.

Beneath her straw hat, her head was wrapped in a hand towel. Her hair had all been shaved off and had hardly started to grow back. The towel did not cover the scar on her cheek, however, and from a distance it looked like some disfiguring birthmark as she crouched beside her aunt, whom she hardly knew, and worked as hard as she could at her weeding. During occasional periods of rest she would look up at the blazing summer sky with a dejected expression on her face.

Yet she had once been a cheerful, pert little miss, always determined to lord it over her playmates and nearly always managing to. This was the same person who had told the other children at Gora that her grandfather had donated these swings in the park, and that if they didn't believe her they could go and ask at the Hakone Land Company; and who had swung triumphantly high into the air, so high that the wind blew up her skirt to reveal her thighs. This was the little girl who had exposed herself bravely above the top of her mattress dugout and told those "mufti corps" cowards to come on if they dared. She was the one who had explained to the other girls at school about the unlucky year in which their formidable teacher had been born, and the superstition that had scared off every man in her life, afraid that they would be eaten by that monstrous mouth; who had laughed mischievously with all the girls and maintained that this unhappy teacher was truly a tragic heroine, someone with whom they should enthusiastically sympathize, in words of a splendidly bogus poetic nature. But as Aiko moved awkwardly in her crouching position from one patch of ground to the next, one could hardly believe in what she had been, and she herself must have forgotten all such memories long ago.

Tetsukichi did not, in fact, turn back to look at his daughter. On a bamboo pole put there to support a cucumber plant, a red dragonfly spread its glittering wings, looked as if it would stay, then hovered in the air again.

To the east the mountain range around Mt. Zao could be seen, gently sloping at the foot but wrinkled with sharp, heavily shadowed lines further up, the highest peak covered in cloud, unseen. The farmers of the region considered the mountain sacred and worshiped it. The mountain meant a great deal to Tetsukichi, too; he felt it was a part of his life, of himself, for he had lived in its shadow when he was a boy, observing it morning and evening and knowing he was constantly in its presence. The mountains here were totally unaltered since that time, yet he himself was old, standing here with a bitterness of heart that he could barely overcome. He found it a great mystery that he should be like this. He was astonished at the creature he had become, and found his very existence a mystery, something almost inconceivable.

Toward the west the land was lower and a river, the Sukawa, flowed there. There was an embankment on the other side, along which the railway passed. Just then a goods train was crawling along it, sending out puffs of thick smoke across the river, and the sound it made had a lingering reverberation that he seemed to feel within his body, pulsing with his blood.

All around, single figures could be seen working in the fields, one here, one there. The sun blazed down and the loud, persistent summer cicadas could be heard singing from a pear orchard just below.

It all looked so peaceful, yet the ramifications of war had reached even as far as this remote village in the northeast. Since the beginning of July air-raid warnings had become frequent, and each time the fire bell would clatter out on the village watchtower. Only a few days before, an air-raid alert for the whole northeast had been announced, and around one o'clock on the same day the industrial port of Kamaishi had been subjected to a naval bombardment. Even as far as the village of Hotta glass doors and windows had cracked, and the dull boom of the guns could be dimly heard all those miles away. The following day the radio had reported air raids over the whole length and breadth of the island of Hokkaido, and that the port of Muroran on the south coast of the island had been bombarded from the sea. If Japan could be attacked from the sea like that it must mean the enemy was free to do as it liked.

Tetsukichi could only wonder gloomily about what was to come, and then the thought of his eldest son crossed his mind, the son who must have been killed long ago. He whispered to himself that the boy had given his life for his country, and tried to straighten his back at the thought. Then, standing by the field of cucumbers, he felt a rush of excitement, a sudden tension throughout his body, and he clenched his fists firmly and swore in his heart that the war must not be lost. It was still not too late. There was still time. Something could be done because they must not lose.

On the 6th of August the "new bomb" was dropped on Hiroshima. On the ninth a second fell on Nagasaki. On the same day the Russians declared war on Japan and invaded Manchuria and Sakhalin, while more than sixteen hundred carrier-based planes attacked towns in Tohoku. Kamaishi was again bombarded from the sea.

So a few more days passed, which Tetsukichi occupied with dark and dismal thoughts.

On the 15th of August the weather had been fair since morning. There was a cloudless blue sky, and indoors it was so hot one sweated even sitting still. The earth in the garden was baked whitish brown, and Jiemon was watering his trees and bushes. Even quite unpretentious farmhouses in this region had beautiful gardens, and the farmers seemed to devote more energy to them than they did to their fields.

Tetsukichi was feeling very unsettled. He had already quarreled three times with Ryuko that morning. Also he had known since yesterday that His Imperial Majesty was to address the nation over the radio at noon. At eleven o'clock he rinsed out his mouth and washed his hands. The day before yesterday he had found mawworms had somehow worked their way up into his mouth on two occasions, and the thought of something like that creeping through his lips while he was listening to the imperial broadcast was causing him acute anxiety. He then changed into traditional dress of *haori* and *hakama*. He rinsed out his mouth and washed his hands again.

"You'd better dress yourself a bit smarter than that," he said to Ryuko.

"How am I expected to do that?" she replied angrily. "You know I don't have a single kimono left."

At 11:30 Iku and the others came back from the fields. When they saw the formal way in which Tetsukichi was dressed they all went and changed, and there was a certain bustle of excitement.

"It's real hot today."

"What's His Majesty going to talk about? What for?"

"Well, we're at war with the Soviets, aren't we? So I expect we'll be told we've all got to do our best and not give in."

This was Jiemon's daughter telling her children what was going to happen.

"I reckon it'll be the one-hundred-million sacrifice at last," Jiemon said morosely, and Tetsukichi nodded deeply in agreement.

"When we hear His Majesty's voice then I'm sure we'll all be ready to die any time," said Iku.

Aiko's colorless face showed signs of some kind of resolve, and she slowly unwound the towel from her head. The ugly, shaven skull was revealed, making it difficult to tell if she was a girl or a boy.

Then they all knelt formally about the hearth with the radio on the shelf in front of them.

The noonday tone sounded, and the announcer's voice said:

"His Imperial Majesty has graciously agreed to broadcast to us. Let us listen with reverence. Would you all please stand."

On this command everybody stood to attention in front of the radio, even the little children.

The national anthem was played. At his back Tetsukichi could hear Iku constantly clearing her throat with the tension. . .

People listened to this broadcast in any number of far-flung places. Down in Chiba, during a break from working on the sea defenses, Shuji listened to it standing on the earthen floor of the farmhouse in which he was lodging. The Emperor's voice was peculiarly high and difficult to follow, and this was made worse by the constant buzz and crackle of static. It was not until he noticed the shoulders of a student in front of him shaking with stifled sobs that Shuji grasped what was happening. The Emperor was not delivering a final call to the hundred million to arise, but was making the wholly unexpected announcement of the ending of hostilities, of defeat, in fact. The news left him dumbfounded more than anything else. What was he supposed to think about this? It had never once crossed his mind that any human agency could simply call a halt to the war like this when there were so many Japanese people still alive. He had assumed the war was a natural phenomenon beyond the power of man to change, and it would continue until the whole race had been exterminated. But now what had happened? The Allied declaration had been accepted! We had surrendered! How was it possible? He stumbled out of the house into the yard. The white rays of the sun burned down above his head. The sky was clear and blue as porcelain; and yet the emptiness of that blue! The blank pointlessness of it all! He felt a slight spell of giddiness, caused either by his state of mind or by the dry heat of the sun, and he shook his head two or three times. . .

In Matsumoto in Shinshu, Momoko was bowed forward in front of the radio, weeping those large tears she had not shed for a long time now. The last few days had been spent in a state of indefinable terror. A wide and unfounded rumor had gone around that the new bomb which had apparently caused such appalling damage in Hiroshima and Nagasaki (some whispered that it was called an atomic bomb)

731

was going to be dropped on Matsumoto next. A great many people had loaded their household possessions onto carts and escaped into nearby villages. Momoko herself had only returned the day before from a village near the mountains where she had decided to leave Sachie, the first step in a planned evacuation. Now her husband was at the factory, and his old parents had been unable to grasp the contents of the broadcast, so they could only look at the weeping Momoko in stupefaction. With her face soaked in tears she raised her head and told her old father-in-law that Japan had lost. She blurted out the words, feeling all the hopelessness, the bitterness, the anxiety about what was going to happen next; and yet there was also a slight sense of relief, a relief that at least they weren't going to be killed by the new bomb. The half-unreal sense of reprieve hesitated within her and then seemed to surge throughout her body.

There were also people who knew nothing whatsoever about this broadcast. One of these was Kumagoro Sakuma, who had on occasions referred to himself as Kumagoro Nire. In April of 1945 the division he belonged to was transferred to Manchuria, since the possibility of Soviet intervention was already anticipated at that stage. After marching to Hankow, they got back onto the freight train again and were carried across North China, though since Japan had completely lost control of the skies the train was able to move only at night. All the steel bridges across the Yellow River had been destroyed, so that when they eventually reached a place called Ssu'ping in Manchuria it was already July, and the Soviet declaration of war on Japan occurred almost immediately after their arrival.

It appeared that the Kwantung Army had totally collapsed before the Russian onslaught, and on the 15th and 16th of August the men of Kumagoro's company were on a hill some five miles from Ssu'-ping, all busily digging their own foxholes. This was to be the final line of defense, and the order had been given to hold it to the last man. By the afternoon of the second day Kumagoro's dugout was almost complete. When he looked to either side it seemed that the nearest foxholes were a long way off and all he could see of his comrades were their small heads. He knew that a flimsy defense position like theirs could never hold off any full-scale attack. So it seemed at last his end had come, and he thought about his wife and child. He also thought he would shout out ''Long live the Emperor'' when he died. He then thought he would dig a hollow in the wall of his newly made foxhole to serve as a shelf where he could line up his cartridges. . . This operation caused a certain amount of earth to accumulate at his feet, and while he was getting rid of this outside his hole, he saw a soldier on a horse coming toward them from the rear. He was a messenger, and the message he brought was that the war was over. They returned to Ssu'ping that night. They wept as they filed the imperial chrysanthemum crests off their rifles.

After another three days the Russian Army arrived. The common people threw a hail of stones at the unarmed troops as they were marched away. They were kept in a temporary warehouse for a month and a half. Then, as the weather was starting to turn cold, they were loaded onto a train. So Kumagoro was transported into Russia, Siberian Russia, to a camp on the shores of Lake Baikal. Of the 700 prisoners in that camp 560 died. The survivors were repatriated after two years, but the well-known face of Kumagoro Sakuma was not among them.

Tetsukichi trudged slowly along the roads between the fields of Hotta village, over the pebbles by the side of the river, up the paths through the hills, head forward and feeling downcast. This was the vacant way he spent these empty days. His feet dragged, he leaned on a stick, his back was bent as he walked on in a doddering, tottering way. He knew that he must look like an old man who had reached the end of his days.

The country to which his life belonged had been defeated; his hospital had burned down; there was no news of his eldest son; his daughter had been cruelly injured; he had lost all the material for the work he had planned as his last. All that seemed to remain was the mountains and rivers, the natural world where he had spent his childhood days, and they had not altered in the least.

There was a clump of eulalia by the side of the field and he stopped in its shade, sitting there in silence, although he was thinking of nothing, full only of the awareness of exhaustion, resignation, and the fact that his life was over. The light of late summer was still strong. There was the harsh scent of moldering grass and the odor of the earth.

In the afternoon he came to the shade of a cherry tree by the river's side, and sat down there in solitary silence again. He held his breath as he sat. The endless sound of the water seemed to be enticing him back into the past, into the distant past.

Most of the stones on this dry part of the riverbed were whitish, with no bog moss or green fur on them, for though the water looked pure and clear it was very acidic, and no fish could live here nor insects breed. If the water was used in the paddy fields it would damage the crops, and so at some time it had been given the name Sukawa, or "Vinegar River." In the past, when the Sukawa overflowed its banks, at one point it would spill into the neighboring river and great shoals of fish would float to the surface. So a dike had been built between the two rivers where they almost met, but when Tetsukichi was a boy somebody had made a deliberate breach in the dike and the vinegary waters flowed into the other river. So many dead fish floated downstream that the surface was black with them. They caught as many in their traps as they could, and the rest they just left to drift away. This incident was referred to by the villagers as "Vinegar River overflow," and when there was any sign of it happening again laborers were sent by the village authorities to shore up the dike. The villagers themselves would descend on the river before the vinegar pollution was too bad and catch scores of fish that had only been enfeebled as yet. This was one of the extra perquisites of life and provided the villagers with the pleasure of getting around the laws about fishing rights. It was almost as if it were one of the regular festivals or celebrations of the year. As soon as Tetsukichi heard about the overflow he would run off so fast it seemed his lungs would burst, with eyes only for the small struggling fish he scooped up with both hands.

"You've got a good catch today, Tetsukichi," his mother would say cheerfully to him.

"Still plenty more where they came from."

The Sukawa remained the same, as did the sound its water made. By the side of the faintly shining waters he walked on alone, bending forward as he sought out which stones to tread on. It seemed a very long time since then, since he had been a boy, and yet what had happened in between seemed to have passed in a flash, a moment. All that he really understood now was that he was old and tired and empty, as if his life had been squeezed dry.

As he continued these aimless strolls the season changed. The evening primroses, of which there had been so many by the riverside, had gone; late summer plants had spread luxuriantly here, but now they too had become faded, torn and ragged.

Ryuko went back to Tokyo to look for a house. Aiko and Shuji, who had been released from his pioneer battalion, were staying at the inn, the Takamatsuya. Tetsukichi had at first been against Ryuko's going to Tokyo. It was hardly likely one would find a house to live in on the burned-out plain that Tokyo had become. Even if she did, they would find it difficult to get food. But Ryuko was as obstinate as ever, and put her plan into effect right away. So far as she was concerned, she would rather be without enough food than live away from the city and suffer this unbearable country life. Ryuko also had an ability to live in the present that Tetsukichi did not appreciate. In a relatively short space of time she found a small house of only four rooms in the western suburbs, near Nishi Ogikubo Station, and now that she had a home for them she soon made Aiko and Shuji return. In addition to their various bits of personal baggage they secretly carried back two bushels of rice.

So Tetsukichi found himself alone again, still living in the storehouse at Jiemon's house, meaning to spend at least the winter here. Public life had become confused and noisy, with great changes taking place. The arrest of war criminals began. The Emperor paid a visit to General MacArthur. GHQ announced in quick succession the repeal of the Maintenance of Public Order Act, the immediate release of former political prisoners, and the freedom to criticize the imperial system. Swarms of tramps and war orphans gathered at the main stations, and the radio said that of those who spent the night in the underpasses some were often found dead the next morning. A great many people were obviously going to starve to death this winter.

Tetsukichi found the idea of the city terrifying. At least here in the country there would be adequate supplies of well-cooked, unadulterated rice, *miso* soup and fresh vegetables. The rumor which had spread immediately after the war among the villagers that the occupying army would plunder and rape had at least been shown to be untrue. From a rational point of view, he hadn't imagined the American forces would do anything of the sort, but when he considered what kind of war it had been he had found it impossible to oppose the villagers' fears with any form of confidence. The other day he had seen members of the occupation army for the first time; a jeep was parked at the entrance to the village and three young GIs, who could hardly have been more than twenty years old, were talking and laughing cheerfully with each other. Tetsukichi walked past them in fear and trembling as if he had never seen a foreigner in his life before.

At night he would sometimes open one of his few remaining books, such as Kraepelin's handbook, but he soon found it tedious and closed it. He also had a certain number of his own notebooks left, and although these would not allow him to write anything comprehensive, there was still certainly enough material for a short article. But when he had taken them out and glanced over them he found the idea and the notebooks themselves displeasing, even offensive, and he stuffed them back into the suitcase. The fact was he had already lost the will and energy to do anything, nor did he have the physical capacity to sustain any kind of real work. He had nothing, nothing at all. At least, that was how it seemed to him. He knew, of course, of cases of Western scholars who had produced voluminous works of great intellectual vitality after they had retired, but he didn't find such examples in the least inspiring; they were only another reason for feeling depressed.

The physical aspects of old age, which seemed to have come on him earlier than usual, also encouraged feelings of resignation. He only had to walk a little and he found himself out of breath. The inside of his head always felt oppressive and dull, and he had to urinate more and more frequently. As in most of the houses in the region there was only an outdoor toilet here, and there were more than one or two occasions when he was guilty of incontinence at night.

The rice harvest was over, and you could no longer see the figures of children gleaning in the rice fields. It was noticeably cold at night. Sleeping alone in the storehouse, he could hear the sound of dead persimmon leaves tapping gently against the eaves as they fell. He was finding it difficult to get to sleep now, and he would think about his family in Tokyo and how they were getting on in their new life. According to Ryuko's letters, sealed only in cellophane because of the occupation censorship, life in Tokyo was expensive in a way that people in the provinces could not even start to imagine. Well, it was hardly surprising since they had lost everything in the fire except the clothes they stood up in. However, the sums of money she required began to make him uneasy, and finally to frighten him, although the truth was that, as a considerable beneficiary from the sale of the Matsubara hospital, he was still a fairly rich man.

He wrote to her telling her to try not to be wasteful, and she replied by return of post pointing out she was not being wasteful in the least. They slept at night wrapped in the issue blankets handed out to fire victims, and did not have one proper quilt between them. They were just about managing to get by because she had been all the way to the cottage in Hakone for things, and then begged the rest from acquaintances. Yesterday she had spent the whole day running from place to place at the demobilization offices trying to find out where Shun'ichi was, subsisting the whole day on just one slice of stale bread. The result of all her labor was that she hadn't been able to find out a single thing about it. It really was a bit too much when someone who was having a nice lazy time in the country should start to decide that she was being wasteful.

Tetsukichi blinked his eyes on reading this like a small child being roundly scolded. He folded up the letter again and listened to the persimmon leaves dropping softly onto the eaves.

One afternoon of incomparably clear, bright weather, Tetsukichi set off on a routine walk. He was wearing a worn, black, Western-style suit, but with leather-soled *tabi* instead of shoes, and leaning on his walking stick.

Just a little way along the village road he met a jeep driving along at tremendous speed. They must have been GIs stationed at Yamagata City. The vehicle was sending up a massive cloud of dust and he moved hurriedly to the side of the road to avoid it, managing to stagger out of the way but almost falling into the ditch as a result. He didn't in fact fall in, but at that moment he really loathed those soldiers. Had his country beaten the Chinese and the Russians at the turn of the century just to be defeated in the end by these scoundrels? This was the first sign of spirit he had shown for a long time.

He readjusted his hold on his stick and walked along the road some more, turning to the right up a gentle slope. It was the lane that led to Takayu ("High Water"), one of the hot-spring outlets of Mt. Zao.

It was autumn, late autumn, but there was still a pleasant, generous warmth in the sunlight as it filtered through the variously colored leaves of the mountain woods. Insects were singing in the withered grass beneath the trees. Enfeebled grasshoppers crawled out on the road, and then crawled off again. Some of the trees had turned beautifully and had brilliant crimson leaves. Others had yellow leaves that glittered in the sun. And some leaves were just beginning to turn a delicate light brown or a more solid, somber shade. Among all this, the dark green of the evergreens made a dull, somehow dejected contrast.

One sumac tree was a great blaze of red. Tetsukichi stopped beside it, got his breath back, and looked intently at the crimson leaves he had known so well as a boy. And then a memory of the distant past came back, a flood of images in which he nearly drowned.

It was when he had been going to primary school. There was an older boy who bossed all the small children around, sometimes luring them away from school to spend a whole day playing about in the hills. One spring day he had led Tetsukichi and the others to a sumac tree. Small buds were appearing on the ends of the branches and he picked off some of them and ordered all the children to stand in a row and roll up their sleeves. Then, using the white sap that oozed out of the buds when pressed, he drew on the inside of each of their forearms a crude, childish representation of a vagina and a penis. The children all seemed pleased to have this drawing made, and laughed out loud. Tetsukichi laughed as well. The Japanese sumac is the tree from which *urushi*, the raw form of lacquer, is taken, so when the children compared their forearms with each other on the following day they found that all the originally white outlines had dried into a black pattern; all except Tetsukichi's arm, that is, on which the drawing had become red and slightly inflamed. With the passage of time it started to itch, then to exude a thin liquid. Tetsukichi was unable to tell his parents about this since he now had an unshakable sense of guilt about the whole episode. Someone said if you smashed a river crab and smeared the insides on the sore it would cure it, so he caught a little crab in the swamp and rubbed its viscera against his wound, which was now starting to ulcerate, but it didn't seem to make it any better at all. A scab did form over it, but just when he thought it was starting to heal he saw that the ulceration of the wound beneath had grown deeper and much worse. So after more than a month of suffering and worry he at last showed it to his mother and confessed how it happened. She took him to his father. Tetsukichi had expected a good scolding, but he simply roared with laughter and put some thick, muddy ointment on it. The sore cleared up very quickly, and the boy felt an even more profound respect for his father, something very close to awe.

It left a scar behind that must have lasted till about the time he entered high school. The aged Tetsukichi impulsively pushed up the sleeve of his jacket and carefully scrutinized his inner forearm. Naturally, there wasn't the slightest trace of such a scar. He felt a confused sense of shame at his action and unconsciously looked about him to see if anyone had been watching. But there were only the leaves reflecting the light of the afternoon sun.

He set off again. There were sometimes pieces of charcoal on the road. There was a charcoal burner's hut further up and bits fell off when the charcoal was being carried away.

The road became steep; he had to stop several times to regain his breath, and eventually he sat down on the root of a pine tree by the wayside. A number of black crickets shot out from around his feet. He was sweating a bit because of the walking he had done and the strong rays of the sun.

He was on a small rise. Looking down, half the view was blocked by trees, but the other half showed a prospect of village land, now deserted since the rice harvest had ended. It was an ordinary enough scene: the occasional small farmhouse with its thatched roof, the village temple surrounded by pines, somber fields, the single glittering line of the river, the toy-like railway line; and, beyond, the rolling hills were already turning from russet to tawny. All the dullness of his home village was there, but for him this was the one landscape that could still genuinely move him.

This was the land he had left for far-off Tokyo, for his adoptive father's hospital, in order to study and better himself. Still, it was all so long ago it seemed unreal, just ancient history. Now he remembered, though: his father had taken him across the mountain pass when he had left for Tokyo. It had been a hard journey. He had dreamed about it once when he was in Munich, lying in bed in his lodgings. That's right: just before they had reached the Sakunami hot spring they had seen cavalrymen on a training exercise. The ordinary soldiers had worn uniforms with yellow braid on the front of their tunics and a yellow stripe down their trousers, but the officers had black braid and a red stripe. A detachment had deployed on the bank of the Hirose River and fired their rifles. Then they fixed bayonets and charged across the bridge. It was the first time he had seen anything like it, and he had forgotten for a while the soreness of his feet.

Then he recalled that time in Tokyo, in the grounds of the Kannon Temple at Asakusa, where there had been a panorama of the battle for Pyongyang during the Sino-Japanese War, and how excited he had been when he went to see it. Beyond where the officers of divisional command were standing, pillars of smoke rose skyward, and that smoke seemed to be really moving in great billows. There was also an old lady in the temple grounds who used to make pictures with sand. She had a bag with five or six differently colored sands, and as she told ancient tales of priests and princesses and spirit visitations she would cleverly illustrate them with pictures. She would make a silver fox, for example, starting with a tail in white sand and ending with a red tongue lolling lightly from its mouth, and solid black eyes. . . Of course, it was all such a long time ago; all vague, as if he had dreamed it. Not surprising, really: horse-drawn streetcars were just appearing at the time. But even with these horsecars, it was the pictures of them he had seen in the village that were clearest now in his mind, rather than the actual ones he had seen in Tokyo. How miserable his village had seemed compared with the capital! It had been the poverty-stricken back of beyond.

Then, how they had all laughed at him at school in Tokyo and mimicked him every time he opened his mouth. Yet he was determined not to let them beat him. It was with that childish aim he had studied so hard.

> I regret to have to inform you that the results I obtained in the April examinations have been uniformly bad. I apologize profoundly and offer no excuses. Out of some two hundred examinees I have been placed eleventh. At first I was second, then fourth, now eleventh. It is, perhaps, at times like these that people begin to make idle complaints or blame all on the heavens or fate, but I know that to do so would only weaken my resolve, and I shall therefore abstain from so doing.

He had sent this letter to his brother, who had died in the Russo-Japanese War. Of course, it hadn't only been the desire to beat those other boys that had made him devote his life to his medical studies. There had also been the attraction of the art of healing itself.

> "You see, this is a special device of my own invention. The only one of its kind in Japan. I suppose I should not be saying this myself, but I am a first-class doctor, as perhaps you may not have known. And a well-known authority on these things. It was lucky for you you brought him here."

It was strange how the way his adoptive father used to boast of his skills had not seemed peculiar, but perfectly right and sensible. Then Kiichiro had always made the same promise whenever Tetsukichi succeeded in something, when he passed his entrance exams for the First

High School and the Imperial University, for example. "Tetsukichi, you've done well. I'm proud of you, my boy. I shall give you a gold watch."

As he sat on the tree root, the old man Tetsukichi had become felt he could hear Kiichiro's voice as if he were actually standing beside him.

Tetsukichi now took a gold watch out of his waistcoat pocket—a Kiichiro watch, but received after Kiichiro had died, for his adoptive father had never actually given him one while he was alive. He pulled the pocket watch out by its chain, snapped open the lid, and saw that it was some time after four o'clock. He stared at the long second hand for a while as it jerked around the face of the watch. Seconds turned into minutes, those minutes into hours, and finally into one full day, yet if one just looked at it like this, time seemed as if it ought not to pass all that quickly. But somehow it did, so very, very quickly, and all that had happened drifted away into nothingness.

He was suddenly invaded by a sense that his life had run its course. He bowed his head until it was almost touching his chest. The country had been totally defeated in war. So little remained; only the natural world. Perhaps it was as well now that his own decrepit self, his worn-out life, should soon end as well.

Where had all that youthful ambition and effort, that absolute devotion to study, brought him? What had happened to the man who stood with trembling fists in the auditorium and glared at Emil Kraepelin as he walked away from him? What of the man who spent those thousands and thousands of nights working like an ant building a nest to produce the stately edifice of the *History of Psychiatric Medicine*?

The position of the sun had changed, and where he was sitting was now in shadow. He felt a slight touch of cold, but made no attempt to move.

His history—the book was his child, born of his own flesh and blood. He could feel some satisfaction in that achievement. And yet he felt no pride. He had made such sacrifices to bring it into existence and he loved it, but he could feel no pride. Was it really his own child? No, it was the product of many people, other scholars; he had merely looked after it and brought it up. If he hadn't done it somebody else would have sometime. Still, at least in purely sentimental terms it could be considered a child of his.

He thought then of his actual children: Shuji, Aiko, Shun'ichi. He

741

had not been a good father to them, never gone to any trouble for them; perhaps he had even been a source of unhappiness for them. Did they understand that it was not because he didn't love them? It was, well, just the way he had been, his character, lots of things, some sort of destiny that had made everything as it was. Not that he was trying to excuse himself. He had been a cold, seemingly unloving father. He had certainly not been what society would consider a good father. It was just that there had always been something that seemed to make him behave the way he did. It would do so for the rest of his life.

He had been a fool. His whole life had been a sequence of stupidities; all of it an empty foolishness, perhaps. All that energy, all that study, and all to no purpose. It had given him no real understanding, no critical grasp of things. He had simply spent his by no means brief life like a dray horse of scholarship, dragging along an unseen burden it could not understand. Still, he was not the only fool. The people he knew, certainly all those living in the Nire Hospital, had all, quite frankly, been fools. But there were degrees of foolishness, and even a fool could have lived more wisely. Why had he not been able to manage his life differently? If he could perhaps have been easier with his wife, gentler to his children; or at least learned to think the way he did now much earlier in his life. But how tired he felt now, right to the depths of his being, weak in both body and mind.

He wondered if there was anyone who would say that he had done his best according to his lights. After all, he had rebuilt the hospital, struggling with all those problems of which he'd had no experience at all. Then, while working full time at his profession, he had got all that research material together, gone without sleep and read all night, organized it, shaped it. The hospital might be burned down now and all the material for his final work destroyed by fire, but that had been beyond his individual control, or anyone else's. He had done his best; he had tried; he had worked. What need was there to regret his life, to condemn it as a mere absurdity? None, perhaps, but he wanted someone else to tell him so. Even the irresponsible Kiichiro would do. Let him step forth from the shadows and say:

"Tetsukichi, you've done well. I'm proud of you, my boy. I shall give you a gold watch."

Nobody would, of course. The sun was going down; the temperature had suddenly fallen. The leaves on the trees still glittered as their branches received the last warmth of that day's sun.

How sad and quiet the last days of autumn were here in the mountains; and yet why do we feel so intimate with fall, with the yellow and red leaves that never lose their power to move us, never weary us? But only here, he thought; only in Japan. There were no autumn leaves like this in Europe. Strange that he should have gone all the way to Europe to study. Unreal now, Germany after the First World War, after defeat. While the other Japanese students had lived in luxury he had drunk soup like salt water with the laborers, eaten meat like leather, saving his money to buy books. He had stood for long periods alone watching the jackdaws about the ancient, dark gray cathedral, or the Danube, freezing in winter, the harsh sound as the ice moved, like coarse cloth rubbing over the expanse of water. Dreams; all dreams. The one real thing was that he was here, in his own village, as his life came to a close, and sitting now on the root of this pine tree.

Beautiful autumn woods, their reddening leaves: how much he loved them now. But it would be winter soon. One morning he would see a white covering of snow on the summit of Mt. Zao. That whiteness would come nearer every day. One day it would fall on the village. The whole expanse of these woods would be blanketed in snow, deep snow. The long winter would come; the long, cruel winter when even the children suffered.

Snow. That white glittering, that cold, inanimate object over the earth. As a child he had felt an awe approaching terror as gradually the whole landscape turned to a vast plain of snow. Often it had been difficult to get to school on snowy mornings, sinking right up to the waist in it. Then in spring there had been the joy of seeing patches of dry earth along the road, which children called the ''*zori* path,'' because you could walk along it just in slip-on sandals and not need boots.

A leaf fell slowly from a tree, although there was no wind. He felt the cold. He must have been feeling the cold for some time. It was time to be thinking of going home.

When he tried to stand up the dry leaves scuffled loudly beneath his feet. He soon understood why. His left leg wasn't moving properly; not moving, in fact, at all. He tried his left arm as well, and it just hung limply. It, too, was gone. It didn't move. He tried to make hurried use of his medical knowledge. The first thing was to move as little as possible, to lie down and keep still. He lay down. The fallen

743

leaves pricked his face, but that was nothing to be concerned about. His mind was quite orderly and clear.

It must be paralysis; partial paralysis of the left side. No extravasation probably. Minor thrombosis, perhaps; a blood clot. He felt strangely objective about his condition. Rest like this a while and probably get over it. Should settle down all right. All right so long as there's no real stroke. Hope so, anyway.

So he lay quite still on his side and looked at the withered grass and the earth under the tree. Then suddenly he felt an unmistakable shudder of fear run down his spine, contradicting his belief that he no longer clung to life. The tremor seemed to spread all over his body, yet his body was cold and motionless, particularly the left side of it. He did not want to die. He knew that now. Finally he did not want to die.

Then his mind, which had been so terrifyingly lucid about his condition, began to cloud over, turning imprecise and vague. His eyes seemed to be gradually clouding over as well. He could see the leaves: brown, yellow, black; and yet they were all slowly turning white. Now everything to the side of his vision seemed white.

Was it snow? No, it was only an illusion. Yet still the world was growing whiter. He closed his eyes and opened them again. Now everything was white, a world of whiteness, a pure, soft, glittering white, a total covering, incomparably clean, unsullied, flooding his whole field of vision, a world of whiteness spreading everywhere. He heard his heart beating in the amazing silence.

Yet even now his memory was at work, providing one more image of the past. It was midwinter. His elder brother was fifteen; one of the young men of the village now. He had got a fox. He had put an explosive charge in a salmon head and got the fox that way. Now he was walking with his brother through the deep snow. The fox they were after had shed spots of blood behind it. The brilliant red stains led off through the trees, going further and further off. In his confused consciousness Tetsukichi was wondering how far he would have to follow that trail of blood. . .

Then a greater haziness, a heavier, sluggish wave, surged over him, washing away even that minimal awareness. . .

Half an hour later a passing villager found him, still lying at the foot of the pine tree. When the man raised him up Tetsukichi could speak slightly and his pulse was apparently still steady.

On a chill, overcast day, nearly three months after the war had ended, Momoko stood among the gutted ruins of the Nire Hospital in Aoyama. She was wearing an old-fashioned velvet traveling coat, the kind that would have been thought much too luxurious a garment during the puritanical war years. This was her first visit to Tokyo since she had returned from Shanghai and shut herself away in Shinshu. It had been some time ago, not long after her declaration to her husband that she would never go near anyone connected with the House of Nire again, that her resolution had faltered and she had sent a letter to the lady of the Seiundo. No very frequent exchange of letters had followed, since the war had not really permitted it, but Momoko knew before coming that the child she had left behind had died of consumption, that Nanny Shimoda had been dead some time, that Yonekuni and Shun'ichi were at the front, and that both the hospitals at Matsubara and Aoyama had burned down during the fire raid on the 25th of May. Naturally the Seiundo had also been destroyed, and for the time being the couple seemed to have moved in somewhere near Seisaku Kanazawa, in the low-lying district by the Aoyama Cemetery that had miraculously escaped intact. A letter from the master of the shop had arrived just before the war ended saying that his wife O-ume's eyesight was poor and she was going to the doctor about it. That was the last news she had received.

The decision to come to Tokyo had been taken on the spur of the moment. Her husband was about to leave on a business trip and suggested she might come up with him, and she had been obliged to make her mind up quickly. Her main reason had been to pay a visit to her son's grave in the cemetery of the Nichirinji temple in Asakusa, but before she did that she wanted to see the lady of the Seiundo and talk about all the things that had happened during the long interval of years. At the same time, she also wanted to see whatever remained of the hospital at Aoyama; this was, after all, the place where she had grown up, and she still recalled much of her life there with affection. But when she walked along the Aoyama main road there was nothing to stir any emotional reminiscence of days gone by. Everything had been swept away. There were not even the stalls of black marketeers, only depressing, barrack-like hovels made out of tin. There were very few people about either. Not a single landmark remained, and even the pattern of the streets was almost impossible to make out, and certainly not one that she remembered, so at first she couldn't find the narrow lane that had led down to the Seiundo. The noodle shop on the corner had disappeared. There was only a flat expanse of rubble where it had been, and when she did finally discover the alley she found it hard to believe it had really been as narrow as this.

The one building standing was the concrete Seinan Primary School, completely blackened and burned with all its glass windows still shattered, although boards had been nailed across some of them. That house over there, this large residence here, all the houses whose names she had known, had vanished, leaving only the occasional garden wall behind. In all this wasteland only one storehouse had survived the flames, and there it stood, quite alone.

She stood at the corner of the hospital land and surveyed the ruins. Here, too, the brick wall remained, although the sight of it only filled her with pain, for it was blackened and derelict and surely shouldn't have been as low as that. She remembered it as quite impressive.

Inside the wall was like everywhere else, nothing at all remaining. Then she noticed some of the main entrance hall still seemed to be standing and was not merely a pile of rubble; but as she approached she saw it was only the garage, still much as it had been. On the cream-painted steel door was written in large letters: "NIRE. ALL SAFE. NOW c/o KANAZAWA," which she finally managed to make out. There was an address written beside it.

Someone must have written it after the disaster. She was wondering whose handwriting it might be when she heard something moving about in the garage. The door was half-open, and suddenly the grubby face of a man poked out. He was a squalid-looking person of around fifty with tangled, matted hair and beard, and wearing what looked like the ragged remnants of a people's uniform. He looked at her with a terrible glance suggesting profound suspicion and mistrust.

Momoko unconsciously took a step backward. She then assumed

that perhaps this was someone connected with the hospital in some way who was still living on the premises. Even so, surely he was much too filthy and dubious a character for that?

"Want something, do you?"

The man spoke as if he were demanding an explanation of her presence, and this annoyed Momoko so much she explained, stuttering slightly, that she was . . . well, a relation. The man grunted, looked her up and down awhile, and then said:

"One of the family, eh? Right, then you can tell them this from me. Tell them I'm not going. I'm staying put, right here. I've been living here all the time and I've got a right. Get me?"

"I haven't come to . . . I mean I've just come to look at the damage, that's all. Who might you be, anyway?"

"Don't matter who I might be. I just so happen to be living here, that's all. Get me? This is where I'm living."

He glanced suspiciously at her again and then went back inside the garage. Momoko felt extremely insulted. The place might have nothing to do with her now, of course, but the attitude of this mysterious man and the vulgar way he spoke had annoyed her. What most annoyed her was the callous way in which this creature had ruined all those sentimental feelings she had just begun to experience on revisiting the home of so many memories. She set off rapidly away from the hospital ruins, trying to put some distance between them and herself as soon as possible, but after about twenty paces taken in this overwrought state she began to hesitate, then finally stopped and started to retrace her steps. After all, she would never come here again. This was to be the last time.

Still, what a very rude man that was. They really oughtn't to allow someone like that to throw his weight around. She felt as angry as if someone had forced his way into her own home, but then she reflected that Tokyo was probably like that now. It was hard to understand when you were in the country, because the pace of life was still quite slow and orderly, but living in Tokyo must be dreadful. Still, what a very rude man, completely indifferent to other people's feelings. . .

Taking care to keep away from the garage, she walked around the back of the hospital. It was strange that none of the new hospital came back to her, but only images of the old one, with its seven towers and its columns, all burned down more than twenty years ago. This was where the old cookhouse had been. This was where old humped Isuke had walked about. Just over there was where the radium bath and the tenement houses had been. All she had ever done then was play ball. She had been so proud because she felt no one could possibly beat her at ball bouncing. A fragment of one of those ball-bouncing songs passed across her mind:

Go to the shrine across the road,
Penny in the box and say your prayers.
Then to the little shop next door,
Sit you down, and drink your tea.
Drink it slowly, drink it dry,
While you spy. . .

But the rest of it just wouldn't come. She wondered why that should be, since the song had once been as natural to her as breathing. She had always had such a good memory, too. Perhaps she really was getting old.

The sky was now clouded over as if it might snow, the air had become much more chill, and there seemed no point in standing here where only the stone foundations remained among charred ruins. She completed her circuit of the land, then left by the spot that had once been the gate outside her home and was now only a gap between two portions of brick wall, and went out into the deserted road.

So she had done it, passed through the gateway she had never expected to enter again for the rest of her life. She had been in through it and come out through it. But she had only been able to do this because there was nobody there, because the house was not there. She would not have been welcomed by anybody if they had been there, and so it was meaningless. After all, none of them even thought she might still be alive.

So she left the ruins of her family home behind her, adjusting the bundle of Shinshu noodles she had brought from the country as a present for the old Seiundo couple. She took the path across the field of Moto-no-hara and noticed the remains of what must have been a fairly large building. Some of the field had been built on while she was away.

This was where she had met that young man, Red Pants, on a number of occasions. He had been a nice, agreeable young man. Really nice. But how silly and inexperienced she had been. All she had talked about was the movies.

The sky was becoming more and more gloomy and dark, so she

hurried. After ten minutes she arrived at what seemed to be the one area in Aoyama that had not burned down, the small valley full of tiny, higgledy-piggledy houses. She looked for the number and immediately found one that must be somewhere nearby. It was a longish, ancient, dilapidated, tenement-like building. There was a dirty pool of stagnant water in the open ditch outside.

Momoko raised her voice and asked for the Takada house and was told, by an unfriendly-looking housewife who seemed annoyed at having to poke her head out and give this information, that it was next door. The building had been partitioned at some time or other, and there was another sliding door next to this one. It had Takada written on it, and also the name of the people she was looking for.

As Momoko laid her hand on the door she felt a quickening of her pulse. There were only two people connected with her family who could be relied on to welcome her, and she had not seen them for seven years. She hoped they would be in.

At first, indeed, she thought perhaps they were out, for the door appeared to be locked, but that was only because it was badly made and would not slide open properly.

Once she was able to work that out, she managed to get it open wide enough to squeeze in. Just as she was preparing to announce her presence she heard a low, hoarse voice from inside asking who it was.

There was little space to stand in the narrow hallway. Immediately in front of her was a small, four-and-a-half-mat room. To the left was what seemed to be a small kitchen. The voice came from beyond a thin paper sliding door, which led into another room.

Momoko made no reply, waiting for the old lady to open the door, recognize her, and come running to welcome her. During the moment she was waiting for this to happen she suddenly recalled something from long ago. She had picked up a pencil sharpener from the shop front as if she meant to make off with it; also a dozen or so erasers shaped like rabbits. She could visualize them all quite clearly.

The paper door slid open and a little old lady appeared. It was undoubtedly O-ume, the lady who had run the Seiundo, but her eyelids were almost totally closed and just a fraction of the whites of her eyes could be seen.

"Who is it? My husband is away at the moment. . ."

She was looking upward slightly, and she moved a little toward Momoko with her arms extended. Momoko was rendered speechless by this sight. O-ume was blind. Momoko had heard she was having trouble with her eyes, and during that period when Momoko had put off writing a reply she had gone completely blind.

When the old lady asked again who it was, Momoko called out her name and told her it was Momoko. The old lady repeated the name twice and moved toward her as if she were swimming. Momoko kicked off her *geta* and went up into the room. She supported the frail, small body with both hands. The present she had brought clattered to the floor.

The old lady, her unseeing eyes upturned, felt with her hands to be sure. With small, dry, shriveled hands she felt Momoko's hair, her forehead, her cheeks, her nose, her mouth.

"It really is Momoko; it really is. I can't see any more. . . I went blind all of a sudden and can't make out anything any more. Still, I know it's you. I couldn't forget. It's you."

All Momoko could do was say the old lady's name. Then for some time after that she could say nothing.

Quite by accident, at almost the same time, or, more precisely, on the evening of the same day, another totally unexpected visitor arrived, but at the house in Nishi Ogikubo where Ryuko and her children were living.

A fortnight before, Ryuko had left for Yamagata immediately after hearing the news of Tetsukichi's stroke, and she had just returned five days previously. As one might have expected, she was looking not in the least happy about this new turn of events. Her husband's life had been spared, but he was obviously paralyzed down the whole of his left side and she had been told he must have absolute peace and quiet. Consequently she had been obliged to ask the Suzukis to continue to look after him. With considerable effort she had managed to get a nurse to come from Yamagata City and remain in attendance on him, and then she lost no time in returning to Tokyo. It was a period when traveling presented chronic difficulties. You had to queue all day to acquire a train ticket, and the trains were so crowded it was only possible to get on by crawling in through a window, after which the whole journey was spent standing in a crush of people. On returning to Tokyo, Ryuko had taken to her bed, something she almost never did during the day, and had called Aiko to her side, complaining in an exaggerated way that she felt she herself was perhaps not much longer for this world. But it was only accumulated fatigue and there was nothing in fact wrong with her. So she soon recovered, got up, and the very same day went off quite cheerfully to visit Oshu and Chiyoko in their Matsuzawa Hospital quarters. The object of her visit was a third person who was now living with them again, her mother Hisa, returned from Chichibu, and Ryuko used her powers of persuasion to extract three bedsheets from her.

The unexpected visitor arrived after ten that evening. Ryuko had already gone to bed, after taking Shuji to task for not working harder at his entrance exams, adding various complaints about other matters. Shuji was not prepared to take this lying down and had made a number of rebellious remarks, so Ryuko had pointed out that his father was ill and she herself would not be with them much longer, retiring to bed in a huff. Since Aiko had nothing to do she was just thinking of locking up and going to bed herself, when she heard the front door slide open and realized she had forgotten about it. Mother was always saying that we lived in dangerous times and the front door should be locked as soon as it got dark.

Who could it possibly be at this time of night? She went into the tiny entrance hall to see. In the shadow of the dim light from the porch she saw a very fat man in military uniform dumping a large trunk on the floor. She switched on the hall light and turned around again to look at the man. His ragged uniform appeared to be splitting at the seams from the corpulence within, and his face was fat and flabby, with narrow sleepy-looking eyes beneath puffed lids. The man called out her name, and she heard herself murmuring his, in an amazed whisper, before she went weak all over and flopped down on the *tatami* with her back against the wall.

It was, in fact, Shun'ichi, although he was now very different from the thin, lanky object she had said good-bye to, for his face, hands and body were swollen in a most unusual way. What cruel trick had the lord of creation played to transform him thus? Here was no healthy plumpness but a dropsical, slack face, both ludicrous and somehow tragic as well.

The garrison on Wake Island, when just on the point of starving to death, had formally surrendered on the 16th of August. On the 2nd of September the American Army had landed and their Japanese prisoners were given the luxurious U.S. Army rations. Since Shun'ichi was not only an officer but an MO, he was able to eat particularly well. Within two months, the skinny Shun'ichi, whom malnutrition had reduced to new extremes of thinness, had been transformed by some freakish physiological process into this monstrous, inflated, unhealthy body topped by an unsightly and absurd face.

That day he had been demobilized at the port of Uraga and had immediately set off for home, bearing his large trunk on his shoulders. He had arrived at the ruins in Aoyama. From there he had gone to Kanazawa's house, learned this address, and once more set out without pausing for rest. And now, despite his exhausted state, he had finally made it. This amazingly plump brother seemed to have reached the limits of his physical and mental endurance. He was gasping hugely for breath, and he slumped down heavily onto the wooden step. He bent down with his back to her as if attempting to untie his bootlaces, but straightened up again, struggling for breath, and turned around to look at her.

"Everyone all right? . . . Aiko, what's happened to your face? Have you hurt yourself?"

This question, delivered by a brother she had never expected to see, who was supposed to be dead and had suddenly appeared like a ghost, was too much for Aiko, who had been holding back her grief for so long now. When she had received this dreadful burn she had cried out in pain and despair, but she had not wept since, certainly not in front of other people, over the hideous network of scars she would carry for life.

But with her brother's return from the dead something in her heart had broken. Her face, with such classical features on one side despite the dismal expression, and so disfigured on the other, became wretchedly contorted, and she threw herself against the ample back of this fat brother, letting loose the long, trembling sobs she could no longer restrain.

At the same time Shuji appeared from the doorway on the left. He, too, could not work out at first that this eccentrically swollen man was his brother, being equally dumbfounded when he realized it must be.

"Shun'ichi? Are you still alive?"

With the ending of the war, Shuji had regained his former spiritless expression, accentuated now by what seemed an even greater indifference to life. But on this gloomy, depressed face a flash of something close to joy appeared, and this extended all over it, causing a great contraction of the facial muscles.

"I must say you're pretty fat, anyway . . . I mean, for heaven's sake . . . how did you manage to get all podgy and plump like that?"

When he said this he laughed. He didn't collapse with mirth, however, but stood up straight and gave a neurotic, unpleasant, hysterical burst of laughter. For a little while the tiny hall was filled with the mingled sound of Shuji's far from normal laughter and Aiko's long, hiccuping sobs.

The year came to an end; a new year began: one exhausting, wearying year turning into another. One month passed and then one more. Many days passed; many exhausting, wearying days.

Yet time passed with the days, and the season turned and changed. Out of the sky a soft sunlight fell, so soft and warm there seemed to be something almost furtive about it. A train, still with some of its windows boarded up, had just stopped in Nishi Ogikubo Station, but there above it a small butterfly, a cabbage white, was flying. In its cheerful lightness the butterfly seemed quite unrelated to this world, where shabby hordes of dirty people spewed out of crowded trains.

There still seemed to be so many people. At the end of last year, Finance Minister Shibusawa had calculated ten million people would die of starvation by the spring, and GHQ had issued a paper saying that the Japanese economy was in a state of crisis, with a shortage of three million tons of food; yet it was so crowded here one could only marvel that so many people should still be alive.

There was another reason for the crowded confusion in and about the station: spraying with DDT was being carried out to prevent the spread of typhus. Officials were placed at the entrance and exits to the platforms, and the passengers were obliged to endure a heavy shower of the stuff whether they liked it or not. The powder was sprayed into the apertures of clothes, at the collar, sleeves and breast (ladies in kimono notwithstanding), and great scatterings of it clung to people's already filthy clothes. This was being overseen by two American MPs who showed only a perfunctory interest in the proceedings. Their white-helmeted heads stood out well above the swarming throng of Japanese below them, symbols of absolute authority.

This area had escaped the fires, but there had been large-scale compulsory evacuations to create a wide fire lane in front of the station sometime during the final year of the war, and it was here that the black-market stalls had been set up. The words "market" and "stalls" give the wrong impression since there was not one structure that even vaguely resembled a shop. Most consisted of sheets of paper spread out on the road, or perhaps a wooden crate or even sometimes a low wooden table, on which various foodstuffs and other objects were set out for the purpose of trade. There were slivers of sweet potato, steamed or dried; small piles of mandarin oranges, various kinds of dried fish, dried cuttlefish, little heaps of groundnuts. There were even things that looked like *imagawayaki* (a form of muffin with hot bean jam inside), but the bean jam had been made out of dried sweet potato and was an odd green color. One man who seemed to be a demobilized soldier had unfolded a sheet of newspaper with some balls of cooked rice on it and they were all soon bought up. There were hand-rolled cigarettes and handy cigarette rollers, cast-iron pots and pans, messtins and aluminum lunchboxes, and some metallic objects which looked as if they were meant to be meat-mincing machines. There were bundles of brand-new white work gloves, belts made from processed canvas; needles and thread here, a dully glinting array of knives and cutting devices over there. The people who did the selling, most of whom had presumably been transformed into traders overnight, kept cardboard boxes crudely stuffed with ten-yen bank notes beside them. These were either the old notes that had been in circulation until mid-February, the sort known as the "wild boar" which now had a certificate stamp in one corner showing they were still legal tender, or else they were the new greenish note that was replacing the other and was commonly known as the American ten yen.

These tradesmen made no attempt to attract customers, by any cheerful crying of their wares, but mostly stood or sat silently by their goods. The same silence extended to their potential customers, great droves of whom swarmed about looking enviously at the goods on display. Occasionally one of them would hurriedly produce some money and go off with a bag of dried potato. Even so, there was something in the atmosphere of the market, a feeling of desperate life, of straitened energy, that gave a kind of vigor to the shabby gloom of the place.

It was already late afternoon. From the direction of the level crossing a fat man wearing an army uniform with threadbare sleeves was approaching, a slightly pained expression on his face as if he was finding it difficult to make up his mind about something. His swollen features at first seemed almost cheerfully relaxed, but there was also a hint of idiocy about them, or perhaps a melancholy pathos. But this originally long, thin face could give little indication of any inner life, for it lacked any capacity for sensitive expression. Shun'ichi Nire was on his way back from the public bathhouse, wearing on his feet a pair of brand-new wooden *geta* which were, unhappily, too small for him.

Shun'ichi's first few days after demobilization had been spent lazily in bed in a form of physical prostration. This had seemed only natural to his family, since he had been incarcerated on that island in the midst of the ocean for so long and had only barely managed to escape with his life. Regrettably, these first few days turned into more than a few, and the period of natural prostration seemed much too prolonged. True, he had been back to the psychiatric department at Keio, but only once merely to pay his respects, and he showed no desire to get back to work there right away. Early in the new year he went to Yamagata to see his father for the first time since his return. Tetsukichi had moved from the Suzukis' to a room in his brother's inn in Kaminoyama as it was easier to nurse him there. After a few days, Shun'ichi had returned home laden with a haversack of rice, and his first words on entering were childish cries of jubilation at having been able to eat his fill of rice cakes. He then reported on his father's condition, telling Ryuko that his case was hopeless since even if he lived he would be a cripple for life. Ryuko nodded heavily in acceptance of these words, although she was also very relieved to hear them, for at least they sounded like the kind of statement a doctor might be expected to make. For some time she had been seriously worried that Shun'ichi's wartime experiences had transformed him into a genuine imbecile.

From February he did in fact start going to work at Keio each day. The actual Keio Hospital had been destroyed by fire, but some of the older buildings on the campus at Senri, including the auditorium, were still intact, and the psychiatric department had been set up there. An outpatients surgery was quickly established, and the old members of staff came back from the army, so there was no shortage of people working there. Since almost none of the staff who had been taken on during wartime remained, Shun'ichi found he was the most junior member. Naturally he received no salary. He also showed little zeal for his work. He was often very late in the mornings, and sometimes took the whole day off without reason or excuse. Usually he would merely loaf around on his frequent days off, though sometimes, if the mood took him, he would lend Shuji a hand with the small vegetable patch they had out back, then set off for the station to buy one of the many cheap pulp magazines that were being published at the time, come home again, and lie on his back on the *tatami* and read. When bored with that he would croon to himself, in a stupefied, weary voice, the first song he had learned on returning to Japan, that great hit of the immediate postwar era, the "Apple Song":

"Touch the apple with your lips and the-hen silently
Look up at the blue, blue sky; like the apple quietly.
The re-hed apple says no word, and yet I feel that I. . ."

He had returned rather too early from work again today, visited the public bath, and was on his way home. He always wore the old Western-style suit his uncle Oshu had given him when he went to "work," but for the bathhouse he would change into his ragged soldier's uniform, for he knew that clothes occasionally disappeared there. The bath was unbelievably crowded, the large tub jammed with wretched-looking naked bodies with hardly an inch of space between them, and it was difficult to work your way in unless you waited a considerable length of time for an opening. And Shun'ichi's body certainly took up much more space than it formerly had, which made matters worse. But he had slimmed down quite a bit, if slim is the word, during his months back home, and his flabby, swollen body was now in some sort of shape, though hardly the kind of physique one could feel anything other than shame at exposing in public. It was still obviously unhealthy, with a sick corpulence close enough to dropsy to look pathological.

However, he managed to get into the bath, which was his first for a week. Despite the crush it was pleasant in the hot water, though the mild joy he experienced was not something his podgy features were able to give any precise expression to, any more than they could reflect the thoughts passing through his mind—recollections of the radium bath they used to have at home when he was a boy and of how spacious it had been, and yet how there was still nothing like a good hot bath any day.

As he walked along now he heard a dull roar in the darkening twilight sky. It was the sound of a liquid-cooled engine, and as he looked up he saw a flight of three small planes pass overhead. "Must be P-51s—Mustangs—," he murmured to himself. There was something in his attitude reminiscent of an old man, a libertine in youth but now reduced to senile impotence, gazing with complex and confused emotions at exotic young women in foreign parts.

He went by way of the black-market area, for he thought he would just drop in there for a while. He stood and stared at the dried fish for a time, standing quite motionless and gaping at their blue sheen. He stood even longer before some glossy red apples. He stared fixedly at a middle-aged housewife who was buying some rice cakes full of "bean jam" (the potato variety), and then at the bundles of ten-yen notes the man selling them had in front of him.

Before the change had been made to the new yen, Shun'ichi had been able to buy most of the things available in the black market, but now with the freezing of all bank accounts the total amount of savings the head of a family was able to withdraw each month was limited to a mere 300 yen, with an extra 100 yen for each member of the family. This small sum, plus the rent they received from letting the cottage at Hakone, was all the income they had, since they had no possessions they could sell to buy other things. So there was no pocket money for Shun'ichi, and all he had when leaving the house was the money for the bath, and not even the change over to buy himself an apple. Even so, he liked walking around the black market just looking at things. Immediately before the war ended on Wake Island, when starving soldiers had been dying like flies, you could search the whole length and breadth of the island and there was truly nothing. But now there were things, real goods, here in front of his eyes, and it was a source of quiet pleasure just to be able to look at them. The main thing was that the restrictions should be taken off bank accounts, he reflected enviously as he moved away from a mound of mandarin oranges. Things would be fine if only they did that, since the family should still have plenty of money in the bank.

Even this vague cheerfulness soon disappeared after he had returned home, for there was no pleasure or comfort to be had there. The six-mat living room, twelve feet by nine, lacked any real piece of furniture, not even a chest of drawers. It was a bleak place with only a radio (received from Oshu, who had two of them) on an upturned orange box. The house itself was badly built and falling to pieces into the bargain. Although there were recesses in the outer wall to hold wooden rain shutters, the shutters themselves no longer existed, the only possible explanation being that the former occupant had chopped them up for firewood. There was no piped water, although there was a well just outside the back door, but with no proper bucket, only a tin can with a hammer attached as a weight, which one pulled up hand over hand on a rope. The water obtained in this way was stored in an empty oil drum. There was gas, but it was constantly being cut off and one could never be sure when it would come on. The trick was to turn the gas faucet full on and wait. After a long delay, usually quite late in the evening, the gas would start to hiss and was lit in haste. Despite all efforts to make the utmost use of the time when the gas was available, it would often be cut off again before the food had been cooked, and this would then be hurriedly transferred to a portable heater which used a fuel that, although reliable, was expensive and hard to obtain anyway.

The living room did have a low dining table of a decent size, and Shun'ichi saw that preparations for supper were almost complete. But his response on seeing what was in store that evening was only to mutter, "Potato bread again," and slump down on the *tatami*, his weary back supported by the wall. Each meal, day in, day out, seemed to consist of little else. There was a device known as a portable bread baker, a rectangular box with both ends made of metal, in which one could put things like powdered vermicelli or cornmeal with a little salt, switch it on, and make bread of a kind quite easily. Since the basic ingredients of this "bread" were potatoes and cornmeal, not even the most avidly cheerful of people could have praised its appearance, and the dry, crumbly food itself tasted pleasant to no one.

There was to be something else besides the staple bread this evening. Aiko was seated on the *tatami*, her face lowered, crouching over a can trying to open it. The can was dark green, one of those distributed by the U.S. Forces, and, naturally, when these were given out there was a compensating reduction in other rations. Only opened on very rare occasions since it seemed wasteful to do so, they were of various kinds, from powdered egg to cheese and butter and occasionally canned soup. The cans had something stamped on them in English, but this remained quite cryptic to these people, who had no idea of the contents until the lid was off and they could see inside. Once, a really enormous can had come into their possession, so large both hands were needed to hold it. When opened it was found to be full of turkey and gelatine, and they had been able to stuff themselves to the ears with this treat. Unfortunately the food they had already prepared to go with this mystery was steamed potatoes Japanese-style, and the combination was not a success.

Aiko gave a little gasp of surprise and disappointment on completing her task this time.

"It's a powder of some kind. I wonder what it is?"

Ryuko came out of the kitchen, bent down, and licked the stuff.

"Tastes like peas. That's what it is. Pea powder."

"Oh no, not powder for dinner again," muttered Shun'ichi; so instead they each had two slices of bread with some black-market jam, and that was supper. Shun'ichi grumbled about the quality of the bread. There was another machine fixed to the edge of the dining table, made of metal with a clumsy-looking handle, much like a meat mincer in appearance, but it did not mince so much as reduce anything and everything to powder. Ryuko would grind soy beans with this to mix in with the bread, and recently she had taken to putting dry, used tea leaves through the machine and adding that to the bread as well.

"Those tea leaves are ruining the bread," Shun'ichi mumbled listlessly. "Got no nutritious value at all, either."

"It is perfectly nutritious, I can assure you. After all, during the war, didn't we all save our old tea leaves to feed the army horses? A horse would be quite pleased to eat it, and it would make him a healthy, sprightly horse as well."

Shun'ichi merely sighed pathetically. Despite his gloom, he also seemed to be suffering from some kind of nervous disability which obliged him to talk on and on all the time. This sigh was only a prelude to another display of the endless, futile garrulity.

"If I'd known it was going to be like this I'd have brought that chocolate and candy back with me. Only wish I had. What a fool I was, only bringing a lot of rubbish home. Could really do with some of that chocolate now. God, I wish I had that chocolate. . ."

Once he had become a prisoner of the Americans on Wake Island he had got into the habit of saving the chocolate and candy they distributed with the other rations; but when the repatriation ship arrived he left it all behind. It had been rumored that the towns back home had been burned to the ground and it was more important to have daily necessities other than food. After all, Japan was occupied by the same army that was handing out this abundance of rations on Wake, so it was hard for them to imagine any critical shortage of food. Thus the contents of the large trunk Shun'ichi had struggled all that way with consisted of tattered socks and underwear, some yellowing paper he had acquired while still in Indochina, tooth powder, toothbrushes and things of that nature. There was even some soft soap solution in a rubber container. He brought home practically all his possessions except papers and diaries, and his only regret was that he had been fool enough not to acquire one of the microscopes from the combat medical station, because something could have been made out of that. Unhappily his brain had been so dulled by island fatigue and malnutrition he had lacked the wit to do so.

He had finished his bread some time ago, and was now leaning wearily against the wall, maintaining his persistent, plaintive monologue:

"You know, Aiko, I had these really huge bars of chocolate. Why didn't I bring them back with me? Can't think why I didn't. . ."

He sighed in pain and wonder again, and then unexpectedly started crooning in his weary voice:

"Touch the apple with your lips and the-hen silently. . ."

"Shun'ichi!" rang out the voice of Ryuko in severe rebuke. She appeared to have been seized by a sudden access of rage. No doubt the wretched spectacle the Nire family at table now afforded had become intolerable when given such emphasis by the decadent behavior of her eldest son. She repeated his name with additional fervor and continued:

"You are the eldest son. Do you understand that? You are the eldest son of the House of Nire. In particular, now that your father has been reduced to his present state, you have a duty to perform. That duty is to rebuild the hospital, the Nire Hospital. You must never forget that. The year after the Great Earthquake we had that terrible fire. Our condition was desperate. There was no insurance money. And yet the hospital rose again from the ashes. In your case I am obliged to say. . ."

"All right, I know," mumbled Shun'ichi, looking slightly embarrassed, but this produced no halt in his mother's verbal flow.

"Don't you dare to imagine that our family is rich. The property tax has deprived us of most of our capital. What little remains we are not allowed to use. Nor can Oshu be relied on to help us any more. They've become virtual beggars themselves. . ."

Although the Matsubara hospital had been burned down, the married quarters in the Matsuzawa Hospital which Oshu and his wife had moved into had emerged unscathed and they still lived there. He had also managed to send a considerable number of his possessions to Chichibu, and these were unharmed as well. This being the case, one would have expected Oshu to be living a life of some comfort despite the inevitable restrictions, but with the ending of the war he had been dealt an enormous blow, greater in material terms than those suffered by the Aoyama family. Soon after he had sold the Matsubara hospital he had bought land in Hokkaido, planning to start a new life as a farmer when the time came. When the hospital burned down, people were envious of his good fortune and his foresight, but in the winter of 1945 the new Land Reforms started to come into effect. As an absentee landlord Oshu had all his land in Hokkaido confiscated, and the new property tax meant the virtual disappearance of any other assets he had. So this man who had always lived in luxury was reduced to managing on his salary from the Matsuzawa Hospital and whatever income could be raised by selling his possessions.

Another source of misery to Oshu and his wife was the senile decay of his mother. Hisa still insisted on only soft, glutinous rice as her staple diet, and although she ate very little it definitely had to be that kind of rice or she would be very upset indeed. She had also recently acquired a great enthusiasm for grated radish (the large, white kind), apparently because someone had told her it was a favorite dish of His Imperial Majesty. She liked grated radish with just a dash of sliced onion mixed in with it, done very carefully with a wooden spoon, and then pounded into the glutinous rice. It was not very appetizing to look at.

Chiyoko took great pains to get hold of this special rice and the onion and radish, although she received small thanks from Hisa, who maintained that no matter what food shortages there might be she was quite sure there would always be enough for her, considering how little she ate.

Hisa filled up the empty cupboard in her room in these cramped quarters until it was packed tight with her own things. She still had plenty of cloth and dress material, and a lot of other things as well, but she absolutely refused to hand any of these over to Chiyoko. Sometimes Ryuko would set out on a "shopping expedition," which simply meant currying favor with her mother. On these occasions Hisa would produce from inside the *kotatsu*, which she still used even in spring, a potful of sweet potatoes supposedly preserved by steaming, and hand one to Ryuko with the brusque injunction to eat it. The potato seemed to be pretty old, and when broken open usually streaked with black. After hearing a long, dramatic account of all the woes and bitterness of her present way of life, Ryuko would be rewarded with the sight of Hisa rising slowly and waveringly to her feet and taking just one hand towel out of her store, which she then passed over with the mumbled information that Ryuko could have it.

Once, when Oshu had a guest, Chiyoko returned to the living room after seeing him off to find Hisa, who was supposedly unable to get about any more, busily drinking up whatever of the dulcin-sweetened tea the guest had left, with obsessed, oblivious, slurping sounds. The image she presented was not so much one of human senility as of some disgusting existence that had lost all sense of restraint or judgment, animal life at its furthest limit, its last gasp. This creature then seemed suddenly to remember something and asked:

"Hasn't Yonekuni come back yet?"

He had not. All they had been able to find out was that his unit had apparently been demobilized some time ago, and although he was not on the official death list there was now no hope of his returning alive. It was impossible even to begin to imagine what his fate might have been in the chaos that had existed in the hinterlands of China immediately after the end of the war. So while Hisa mumbled her inquiry after the lost son she seemed suddenly to have remembered, Chiyoko got her sitting straight at the table, and Hisa picked up her spoon with a trembling hand and started to eat her food. The slack, squalid way in which she ate made a sight it was only too natural to turn away from. . .

Having reflected on Oshu's condition, Ryuko was even more angrily fervent in her insistence that Shun'ichi could not rely on his uncle. She went on:

"Why can't you set up a practice? It doesn't matter how small it is, just so long as you put the Nire Hospital sign up again. Can't you do even that? If you had the inclination to do so, I could find you a certain amount of capital. We could sell the land at Aoyama and the cottage in Hakone. I could go around all my Gakushuin friends, no matter what it might cost me. I am quite prepared to humiliate myself. Of course they're not rich like they used to be. Poor like us, in fact. What with the new currency and. . ."

"Look, Mother, that's simply impossible. It can't be done," Shun'ichi broke in, still leaning against the wall. "For a start I've only just begun as a psychiatrist. I'd only just got into the department when I was drafted into the army. I've still got everything to learn."

"Learn? Of course you have, and there's nothing wrong with that. But do you have the will or the ability to learn? You don't show much zeal or application about going to your department. You're hardly going to learn much like that, are you? Now, let me remind you that your appointed task is to rebuild the Nire Hospital. Heaven knows you need reminding, since you seem to have so little awareness of where your duty lies!"

Her high-handed manner certainly had its effect on Shun'ichi, who went so far as to move his clumsy corpulence away from the wall and sit up straight before beginning on the following hasty, sulky diatribe:

"Look, Mother, you've got it all wrong. Do you think I'm physically all right now? Do you? Then let me tell you I most certainly am not. This isn't a normal, healthy physique. I tire easily. Only have to walk fast a bit and I get palpitations. Get dizzy spells while I'm standing. I tell you it's a miracle I got back alive. I still don't know how I managed it. I still can't believe sometimes that I really am alive like this. And nobody understands. Nobody even wants to understand."

Shun'ichi was now being carried away by the power of his own words:

"That island's not a place for anyone to live. Foul damn place . . . just a heap of stones and sand . . . sun beating down on it. . . It's not possible I should have been able to live through that. Ought to have died twice, once when I just about drowned in the sea, another time when a shell exploded bang next to my dugout. I was knocked out and half buried alive. And that's not all, fighting every day to find something to eat, not knowing if you were going to live or die. Just to get hold of some rotten little fish. Honestly it doesn't bear thinking about now. The only thing that saved us was the hospital ship turning up in July and taking a thousand people off. If that hadn't come we'd all have died, starved to death before the war ended. Oh, for God's sake, I don't want to remember it. It was hell out there, pure hell. I still keep dreaming about it. Wake up at night and I'm in a cold sweat. . ."

Having delivered this outburst in what seemed like one breath, spurred on by some passionate rage, he now slumped back exhausted against the wall. An awkward gloom had inevitably descended over the dinner table. Aiko was sitting with her head lowered drinking her tea. Shuji was sitting frowning slightly, deliberately turned away

763

from the table as if to show this was all no concern of his, and flicking through the pages of a pulp magazine. Ryuko herself felt a certain sympathy with what Shun'ichi had said, but she had a much greater rage within her than any he felt. It was a rage that had elements of hopelessness, disgust, even slight resignation in it; a complex of psychic states that had accumulated to form a great passion at that moment. It was no mere annoyance with her eldest son for not living up to her expectations, but more a confused feeling directed comprehensively at the times in which they were living.

She sat for a while looking critically at the plump, flaccid features of her silent, sulking son. She then looked away and her eyes rested on Shuji with his magazine. Well, she couldn't expect anything of that one. That one was hopeless.

Shuji had failed his entrance exams again this year, for high school and now for pre-medical college. The main trouble was he did not appear to have the slightest desire to learn anything. When told to go to a school that would prepare him for the next set of exams, he simply said it didn't matter and he didn't want to. He always tended to look peeved about something and said very little, merely stating as an afterthought that he was off to the library when he left the house. In fact he did go to the library, not to work but only to read cheap detective thrillers, and even then he showed little desire to expend even the minimal intellectual effort such trash demanded. Around him others would be engrossed in their books, but this atmosphere of serious diligence only aroused the depressing reflection that he himself had nothing he really wanted to do. He had certainly looked lively enough when his home had burned down and when he had been building underground bunkers at Chiba to prevent the enemy landing, but all that had vanished from his face, now always gloomy, indifferent and dull, the look of someone who thought he had put off dying until it was now too late, and he could never forget or forgive himself the blunder. That splendid image he had once possessed of "death" with all its illusory magnificence had crumbled into ashes long ago, so he had forced himself deliberately into a quite different world, that of inferior printed trash. At least it was a world apart; corrupt, foolish, sometimes lascivious, but a world into which death also entered, the easy death of the inevitable murder. For a while he would follow the plot of the story, but at some point he would look away from the book and ask himself how much it really mattered if one life was lost or not. Obviously it didn't; it was stupid, ridiculous, meaning nothing in the kind of world they lived in now.

The Shuji Ryuko observed was merely flipping through the pages of his cheap magazine with a bored, peevish, solitary look on his face, so she turned away from him and gazed finally at her daughter Aiko who was sitting with her head bowed sipping tea. She was seated so that Ryuko saw only the melancholy profile of the right side of her face. Her hair had grown back at last, and the delicate lines of her slim nose and the slightly pouting lips showed a perfect harmony, so complete that Ryuko was startled by the remarkable resemblance to Seiko, as if she had come back to life again.

Her deceased father Kiichiro, she reflected, had always believed in having talented doctors marry his daughters so he could bring them into his family as his adopted sons. In this manner he had ensured the continued prosperity of the hospital. It was a splendid method, one of the Nire Hospital traditions.

But Aiko put down her cup and looked in Ryuko's direction, and that terrible scar from her left temple down the side of her face, that painful, purplish mark which went so deep, was all too horribly apparent. Ryuko was thinking in terms of another operation when better times came, but no kind of operation could more than half cure that disfigurement. Even though Aiko had been very well brought up, there was no hope of her marrying into a good family.

So Ryuko was forced to the bitter, humiliating conclusion she could expect as little from her children as from her useless husband. She was filled by a sense of the hopelessness of it all, of the terrible pathos of her own situation, although to feel in this way was something so humiliating she soon rejected it. She would not give in. She, and she alone perhaps, would not flinch or be downhearted as she faced this crisis. She would never surrender, no matter how hopeless other people were or how disgracefully they behaved. She was seized with another spasm of irrational anger. She could not sit still but must do something, so she stood up briskly and marched into the kitchen. She then stomped back noisily carrying some dry, used tea leaves. She put these in the machine at the side of the table which transformed all things into powder. Then she knelt before it, back straight, head back, neck firm, biting her lips as if she were daring somebody, anybody, to oppose her; and she began to turn the handle, round and round, busily, relentlessly, with all her might. . .